THE PLAYS OF OSCAR WILDE

THE PLAYS OF OSCAR WILDE

Introduction and Notes by
ANNE VARTY
Royal Holloway

WORDSWORTH CLASSICS

For my husband

ANTHONY JOHN RANSON

with love from your wife, the publisher.
Eternally grateful for your unconditional love.

Readers who are interested in other titles from Wordsworth Editions are invited to visit our website at www.wordsworth-editions.com

For our latest list and a full mail-order service, contact Bibliophile Books, 5 Datapoint, South Crescent, London E16 4TL
TEL: +44 (0)20 7474 2474 FAX: +44 (0)20 7474 8589
ORDERS: orders@bibliophilebooks.com
WEBSITE: www.bibliophilebooks.com

This edition published 2000 by Wordsworth Editions Limited
8B East Street, Ware, Hertfordshire SG12 9ET

ISBN 978 1 84022 418 4

Wordsworth Editions
is the company founded in 1987 by

MICHAEL TRAYLER

Typeset in Great Britain by Antony Gray
Printed and bound by Clays Ltd, St Ives plc

INTRODUCTION

Oscar Wilde was a remarkable playwright. His work was hailed as unique by the influential theatre critic William Archer:

> The one essential fact about Mr Oscar Wilde's dramatic work is that it must be taken on the very highest plane of modern English drama, and, furthermore, that it stands alone on that plane. In intellectual calibre, artistic competence – and in dramatic instinct – Mr Wilde has no rival among his fellow workers for the stage.[1]

Wilde was writing for the stage at a time when critics and fellow playwrights were campaigning for new theatre writing to be 'literary', offering intellectual and political challenges to its audiences. Continental playwrights such as Zola, Ibsen and Strindberg had already demonstrated that the stage could air radical social ideas. These innovators, and their British counterparts, were rebelling against the commercial interests which dominated theatre practice at the time. They rejected the traditions of spectacular melodrama, music hall, long-running revivals of Shakespeare's plays and, in Britain, translations of French well-made plays, all of which made up the standard fare of theatrical entertainment in the latter half of the nineteenth century. In this context Wilde was revolutionary because he delivered plays which were politically engaged, artistically innovative and commercially successful.

Wilde's prominence on the London stage lasted for only three years, from the opening of *Lady Windermere's Fan* in 1892 to that of *The Importance of Being Earnest* in 1895. Superficially it may seem that Wilde was a born playwright who simply stepped into dazzling success and whose career was then cut short by the tragic events of his arrest, trial and imprisonment in 1895. But in fact the learning process by which Wilde arrived at his major achievements had been

1 William Archer, review of *A Woman of No Importance* in *World*, 26 April 1893

slow and painstaking, and had involved experiments, false starts and frustrations.

Wilde's professional involvement with theatre began in 1879 when he moved from Oxford to London. He began to work as a journalist and theatre critic, contributing to *The Dramatic Review* and *Theatre*. In 1879 he saw the French actress Sarah Bernhardt star in *Phèdre* when the Comédie Française visited London. It is said that he greeted Bernhardt with a bouquet of white lilies when she stepped on to English soil; it is certain that from this point on Wilde became a personal friend and great admirer of Bernhardt as a performer. He composed two parts for her in his own work, Vera in his first play *Vera; or, The Nihilists* (1881), and the title role in *Salomé* (1892). The English premières of both of these plays were censored and closed down during rehearsal. During the 1880s Wilde made friends with many influential performers including Ellen Terry, Elizabeth Robins and Henry Irving. These friendships signal his involvement with every level of theatre, and they had a practical impact on his work. He claimed that he took the advice of every actor he knew to help shape his first play, and the result was a fluent and thrilling piece of dramatic writing with well-defined parts for even the most minor of roles.

During the 1880s Wilde developed the view that theatre was a supremely collaborative art form, involving the participation of designers, scene painters, actors, playwrights and, in charge of it all, the figure whom Wilde called the 'cultured despot', the director. Wilde even went so far as to state that 'theatrical audiences are far more impressed by what they look at than by what they listen to'. He wrote this in an article for *The Dramatic Review* called 'Shakespeare on Scenery' (14 March 1885) which begins as an analysis of Shakespeare's plays and turns into a radical critique of contemporary British theatre practice. Wilde's sensitivity to theatre as a visual art was heightened by his friendship with the innovative designer and architect Edward William Godwin (1833–1886). Godwin founded 'The Costume Society' in 1882 to promote awareness amongst theatre practitioners of a need for historical accuracy in the design of costumes and sets in order to create both authentic and aesthetically harmonious productions. Godwin put his theories into practice by contributing designs for a number of experimental productions, including a Greek revivalist play, *Helena of Troas*, by John Todhunter in 1886. Constance Wilde, pregnant with Wilde's second son, acted in this production, as a chiton-wearing handmaiden to Helena, and Wilde himself reviewed it for *The Dramatic Review*.

Wilde was scrupulous about all the aspects of production that went into any performance of his own work, and he was fortunate that the directors, or actor-managers, who accepted his plays shared his production values. The actor-manager at the St James's Theatre in London, George Alexander, who produced *Lady Windermere's Fan*, was not just an expert editor of Wilde's dramatic structure and dialogue, but he was renowned for detailed attention to the requirements of set and costume. After the play had finished its first London season it began to tour the provinces. A reviewer in Leeds commended the show because:

> Mr Alexander toured the play with all the London props, scenery and costume. And the trouble is well worth taking; for half the effect of a play like *Lady Windermere's Fan* lies in its 'society' atmosphere. The exquisite taste and suitability of the dresses, the care with which the minor parts are performed, are essential to the success of the production.[2]

This review itself testifies to the validity of Wilde's view of theatre as a collaborative art. But Wilde found it hard in practice to relinquish control of his own work into the hands of the 'cultured despot'. He attended all rehearsals of his plays and interfered regularly with the business on stage. Beerbohm Tree, who produced *A Woman of No Importance* at the London Haymarket, even went so far as to ban Wilde from rehearsals for the final week.

Early Plays

Wilde made his debut as a playwright with two apprentice plays, *Vera; or, The Nihilists* (1881) and *The Duchess of Padua* (1883), both composed during his mid twenties, and both dogged by unsuccessful performance history. At the centre of each of these historical tragedies is a strong woman whose intellectual insights and ambitions are overwhelmed by passionate and destructive love. In style and content there is little to link them with the mature plays of the 1890s. Yet there are features in their composition which make sense retrospectively, pointing forwards to the comedy of manners which became the hallmark of Wilde's most popular dramas. They also provided Wilde with an opportunity to gain experience in the practicalities of stagecraft which he would later deploy with such confidence and panache.

Vera; or, The Nihilists is a tragedy set in Russia between 1795 and

2 unsigned review, *The Era*, 22 October 1892

1800. Despite the ostensible historical setting, this first play does not display the scrupulosity about historical accuracy that Wilde later espoused. It is riddled with anachronisms, such as references to trains, liberated serfs (serfs were not freed until the reign of Alexander II, who was Czar when Wilde wrote the play) and the term 'nihilism' itself, which was coined by Turgenev in *Fathers and Sons* (1861). The character of the heroine Vera also brings the subject matter of the play into the contemporary period because it is modelled on the widely reported story of the twenty-two-year-old Vera Zassoulich who attempted to assassinate the chief of police in St Petersburg in January 1878. Although Wilde claimed that the play was more about passion than politics, its political agenda, in so far as it has one, is that of a campaign for republicanism and democracy. Wilde presents his own sympathies for Irish Home Rule through the mask of Russian history. The contemporaneous nature of the subject matter did not go unnoticed. Czar Alexander II was assassinated by Nihilists on 1 March 1881. The Prince of Wales, married to the Russian Princess Alexandra, found himself brother-in-law to the murdered Czar's daughter, and may have felt particularly exposed by the prospective stage representation of assassination and anti-monarchist feeling. In November 1881, just as *Vera* was about to go into rehearsal with Mrs Bernard Beere in the title role and Don Boucicault directing, the licence for performance was withdrawn and the production closed down. The play was eventually staged in New York in 1883, but received unfavourably.

There is one character in this play whose actions and dialogue look forward to that of the dandies in Wilde's mature plays. It is Prince Paul Maraloffski, prime minister of Russia, an aristocrat in the Wildean mode, personally disengaged from the succession of crises, yet controlling them all and commenting upon them with epigrams that would fit comfortably in the mature plays. For example, challenged about the iniquities of his government, he pronounces 'experience, the name men give to their mistakes' (p. 21), or when asked to swear allegiance to the Nihilists' oath he states, 'Yes, president, I agree completely with Article Five. A family is a terrible incumbrance, especially when one is not married' (p. 35).

Commissioned as a star vehicle by the American actress Mary Anderson, who was to perform the tragic role of the duchess, *The Duchess of Padua* has fewer redeeming features. As its title suggests, it is written in a pseudo-Jacobean style, attempting to rival the verse and complex plotting of Webster's dramas (for example, *The Duchess of Malfi*). Although both verse and plotting are competent, there are many echoes of Shakespeare and his contemporaries, and the action is melodramatic. It is unsurprising that Mary Anderson rejected the play on completion. It was not staged until 1891, when it had a New York première under the title *Guido Ferranti*, but this shift of emphasis was not enough to rescue it from hostile criticism.

The Duchess of Padua, with its setting in Renaissance Italy and its blank verse form, looks forward to *A Florentine Tragedy* which Wilde wrote during 1894 but which was never staged. This 'fragment' stands as a virtually complete play. It casts into dramatic form the kind of surprising fable which Wilde published as 'Poems in Prose' in 1894. A Florentine cloth merchant arrives home to find his wife entertaining the heir to the city state of Florence. He pretends to believe that the prince's visit is an innocent business call but gradually manipulates him into a duel and kills him. Having watched the prince die, the merchant says, 'Now for the other' (p. 442). We expect him to turn the sword on his adulterous wife. But the play ends with an unexpected twist:

SIMONE *rises and looks at* BIANCA. *She comes towards him as one dazed with wonder and with outstretched arms.*

BIANCA: Why
Did you not tell me you were so strong?
SIMONE: Why
Did you not tell me you were beautiful?
(*he kisses her on the mouth*)

The estranged partners are reunited by this crisis and their newly discovered love lifts them out of the conventions of morality and time. The curtain falls on their embrace so that their emotional encounter is held in a powerful tableau. It signals their defiant victory over the expected ethical consequences of their actions.

Symbolist Drama

Following *The Duchess of Padua*, Wilde composed *Salomé* in French while he was living in Paris in the winter of 1891, and put it into production in London in June 1892 with the forty-seven-year-old Sarah Bernhardt in the title role. The play was censored on the grounds that it depicted biblical personages, a prohibition that had been introduced in the sixteenth century (the irrelevance of which incensed Wilde), and the production was aborted. It seems much more likely that censorship was imposed because of the monstrous sexual desires explored in the play. The subject matter is taken from the Gospel account of the beheading of John the Baptist by King Herod (e.g., Matthew 14:8). In the Bible this event marks a watershed between the Old and New Testaments. It is a pivotal moment in which the last prophet before Christ is killed to make way for the new Saviour and his new law. Salomé, a key agent in this story, became the most notorious *femme fatale* of the *fin de siècle*. For the culture of the 1890s the figure of the beautiful but vengeful and patriarchally destructive girl who ushered out the old and heralded the new held a particularly resonant power. Many artists chose to represent Salomé during this period, and Wilde was joining in with writers and painters such as Gautier, Maeterlinck, Anatole France, Marcel Schwob, Flaubert, Heine, Mallarmé, Laforgue, Huysmans and Moreau.

Wilde chose to present his version of the legend as a piece of symbolist theatre. The primary exponent of this style of drama was the Belgian playwright Maeterlinck, for whom the dramatist was a kind of priest. In symbolist theatre the audience is introduced to a higher plane of spiritual awareness, encouraged to meditate on the mysteries of life, the inevitability of fate, and to cultivate a profoundly inward vision. Wilde achieves these ends in *Salomé* by two means in particular: the use of language, which is archaic, portentious and mesmerising, and the use of the setting, which is that of a moonlit night where reason is banished and the submerged forces of desire and fear within the subconscious are unleashed.

The action of the play is tightly structured and is built around three major duologues. The first is between Salomé and the prophet Jokanaan, the second between Herod and Salomé, and the third between Salomé and the severed head. The play opens with minor characters discussing the appearance of the Princess Salomé at Herod's feast, and commenting on the heady atmosphere of the evening. The voice of the prophet erupts into their talk, like a disruptive Dionysian power from his cistern-prison beneath the earth. The Page and Soldiers cannot protect Herod's court from anything so insubstantial as a voice. Conflict becomes immediately apparent between the sectarian, pagan world of imperial Rome and the apprehended values of the Christianity which Jokanaan foretells. Salomé rushes on stage, escaping from the oppressive atmosphere of Herod's banquet, and her duologue with the prophet begins to take shape. Salomé stands for the ravishing beauty of the visible world, while Jokannaan announces the presence of an invisible new order. Their contest culminates in Salomé's inspection of the prophet, as she commands him out of his cistern. She usurps his verbal medium by talking as eloquently as he does, and forces him metaphorically to change places

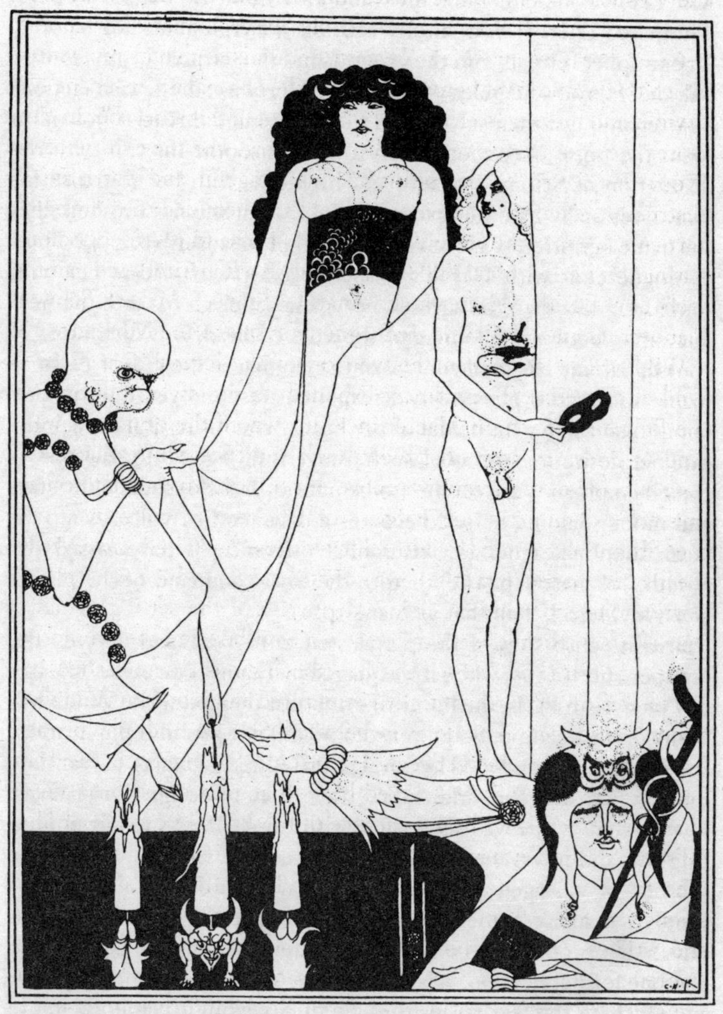

Aubrey Beardsley's illustration 'Enter Herodias' from the original published version of *Salomé*. The figure in the lower-right-hand corner, holding a copy of the play and gesturing towards the stage, is a caricature of Oscar Wilde.

with her by compelling him into moonlit visibility so that he occupies her space. Then Herod enters, with his court, looking for Salomé. The prophet retreats into the ground, and the tetrarch begins to woo Salomé. Herod squabbles with his wife Herodias, the Jewish factions quarrel amongst themselves until the frightening threats of Jokanaan focus the noise once more. Herod tries to soothe his fear with the distraction of Salomé's beauty and he pleads with her to dance for him. Eventually Salomé agrees but only when she has finished does she name her price, 'I ask of you the head of Jokanaan' (p. 155). Their duologue ends with Herod's desperate efforts to placate her with something less than the severed head. His failure leads into the final duologue, between Salomé and the severed head, in which now, of course, Salomé has total control of the language. She gives free voice to her monstrous physical and sexual desires, and revenges herself upon Jokanaan for his denial of her beauty and his refusal to reciprocate her desire for him. At last the stage is plunged into darkness as Herod commands the torches to be put out and clouds hide the stars and moon. Salomé herself becomes a disembodied voice. A moonbeam illuminates her last triumphal utterance, 'I have kissed thy mouth, Jokanaan' (p. 161), before the final command of the play is given by Herod, 'Kill that woman!' (p. 161).

British censorship of the play lasted until 1931 and delayed the première until 1896, when it was staged by Lugné-Poë at the Théâtre de l'Oeuvre in Paris, the home of symbolist theatre, while Wilde was in prison in Reading. Stage censorship did not prohibit publication, and Wilde commissioned his lover, Lord Alfred Douglas, to translate the play into English, and Aubrey Beardsley to design illustrations. In the event Wilde was dissatisfied with Lord Alfred's rendition into English, and intervened himself to correct the English text. In the absence of a staged version of the play, Beardsley's illustrations supply a visual commentary for the dialogue. These too ran into censorship problems, as three of his original plates were deemed too obscene for publication. His illustrations are witty and meretricious, embellishing the text rather than literally seeking to embody it. He emphasises in particular the disturbing sexualities expressed by the drama, teases with physical display and concealment, and confuses the genders of Salomé and Jokanaan by depicting them as mirror images of one another, their faces identical. *Salomé* was published in French in 1893 and in English in 1894. After Wilde's death in 1900, *Salomé* enjoyed huge popularity in Europe, and was set as an opera by Strauss in 1905.

In 1894 Wilde made one further excursion into symbolist theatre,

Aubrey Beardsley's illustration 'The dancer's reward' from the original published version of *Salomé*

with the fragment *La Sainte Courtisane or The Woman Covered with Jewels*. This is another Salomé story, and draws heavily on Anatole France's *Thaïs* (1890). The Baptist figure, a hermit prophet, is called Honorius 'who will not look on the face of woman' (p. 421). The woman he particularly refuses to look at is Myrrhina, La Sainte Courtisane, but she desires his gaze. Eventually Honorius and Myrrhina do look at one another and the result is that they wish to exchange roles: 'Myrrhina, the scales have fallen from my eyes and I see now clearly what I did not see before. Take me to Alexandria and let me taste of the seven sins' (p. 426). In the prophet's haste towards the transfiguration of sensuous self-destruction, that will be simultaneously purging and annihilative, Wilde exposes the death wish of the *fin de siècle* that partly accounts for the compulsive attention to the Salomé legend.

Society Comedies

Wilde is most popularly remembered for his society comedies, great artistic and commercial successes from the moment of their first productions through to the present day. Three of them are well-made plays, while the fourth, *The Importance of Being Earnest*, is his only farce. There are structural, stylistic and thematic resemblances between these plays which mark them as belonging to a particular era but which also brand them as uniquely Wilde's. The deployment of the well-made play structure, with its four dramatic movements comprising exposition, complication, crisis and resolution, is typical of nineteenth-century drama following the development of this successful formula by the French playwrights Scribe and Sardou. Also characteristic of drama of the period was the theme of 'the woman with a past'. She is typically a social outsider and her presence threatens to destabilise the existing social harmony and hierarchy. Wilde's characters Mrs Erlynne, Mrs Arbuthnot and Mrs Cheveley are all examples of this type and they take their places in theatre history beside heroines created, amongst others, by Pinero, Henry Arthur Jones and Shaw. Wilde uses this theme in all four of these plays, but for *The Importance of Being Earnest* he deploys one of his many reversals of perspective which cleverly alters the formula. In this final play he presents a plot which is resolved, not by hounding out the socially unacceptable woman or by allowing her to break free of the circumstances which threaten to overwhelm her, but in which the denoument is complete when a man, rather than a woman, rushes to embrace the concealed past and discovers that he is not Jack Worthing but really Ernest Moncrieff.

One distinguishing feature of Wilde's social comedies is the style of the dialogue, with its firework display of aphorisms. Epigrams, paradoxes and aphorisms are particularly characteristic of the dandy, a stock figure in Wilde's plays. Witty, astonishing, shocking, but always authoritative, this linguistic style constitutes the dandy's main weapon against the complacent or rigidly codified morality of late Victorian society. As Ernest Newman, one of Wilde's early critics, argues, the paradox serves to deliver wisdom, and the seer is the dandy.[3] Wilde's deployment of this character on stage allows him to demonstrate fundamental principles in the philosophy of dandyism, as it developed from George Brummell (1778–1840), Jules Barbey d'Aurevilly (1808-1889) and Charles Baudelaire (1821–67), namely, that art and life are inseparable, and that perfection lies in the cultivation of artifice. 'The first duty in life is to be as artificial as possible,' Wilde states in *Phrases and Philosophies for the Use of the Young* (1894). Wilde's dandies are literally able to act this out, with their discourse, as elegant as their clothes, distinguished by the delivery of aesthetic comment where ethical judgement is expected. Mrs Erlynne illustrates the provocation of their pose, in *Lady Windermere's Fan*, when she announces her departure to Lord Windermere:

> . . . what consoles one nowadays is not repentance, but pleasure. Repentance is quite out of date. And besides, if a woman really repents, she has to go to a bad dressmaker, otherwise no one believes in her. And nothing in the world would induce me to do that. [p. 212]

Far from exemplifying the popular view of dandy as shallow fop, Wilde's deployment of this figure challenges received wisdom and forces revaluation of accepted *mores*.

In order to afford such commentary, the dandy has to remain detached from the action. Wilde demonstrates the importance of intellectual and emotional distance by showing how this figure loses authority, poise and linguistic precision once embroiled in the plot. Lord Darlington in *Lady Windermere's Fan* acts as a dandy commentator until he becomes Lady Windermere's lover; in courting her he loses his self-possession, surrenders his special status, and his role is passed on to Cecil Graham. Lord Illingworth in *A Woman of No Importance* is conspicuous for his cynical wit until the last act when his villainy is exposed and he attempts to marry the protagonist. He

3 Ernest Newman, 'Oscar Wilde: A Literary Appreciation', *Free Review*, 1 June 1895

becomes an object of contempt and there is nothing left for him to do but to announce his own redundancy: 'There is not much then for me to do here, Rachel?' (p. 277). Lord Goring in *An Ideal Husband* is proud of his position on the margins of society, but he falls from dandy to fiancé when he is finally ushered into the fold as a husband-to-be. Wilde experiments with the gender of authority by allowing female characters such as Mrs Erlynne, Mrs Allonby and Mabel Chiltern to adopt the aphoristic idiom of the dandy. *The Importance of Being Earnest* is again unique in Wilde's negotiation of convention because in that play all the characters speak in epigrams, display the same debonair mood in response to the absurd complexities of the plot, and celebrate the triumph of artifice. As Gwendolen states, 'in matters of grave importance, style, not sincerity, is the vital thing' (p. 405).

Lady Windermere's Fan

The exposition of this play sets the society scene at the Windermeres' London home and introduces the occasion of Lady Windermere's twenty-first birthday ball. All of the major characters are brought on, either in person or in discussion. The entry of Mrs Erlynne is delayed until Act II. The threat posed by this mysterious woman both to the public order and to the private harmony of the Windermeres' marriage is a constant theme throughout the exposition. The complication of the plot, which corresponds with Act II, concerns Mrs Erlynne's arrival at Lady Windermere's birthday celebration, and the latter's unfulfilled threat to strike Mrs Erlynne with her fan, a birthday present from her husband, should she come uninvited to the ball. The complication peaks with Lady Windermere's decision to run away with Lord Darlington. Mrs Erlynne reveals her identity as Lady Windermere's mother in soliloquy towards the end of this act. Wilde himself had wanted to delay this revelation until the very end of the play, so that Mrs Erlynne's act of self sacrifice in the crisis scene at Lord Darlington's rooms, where she steps forward to give Lady Windermere opportunity to escape unnoticed by the men, would seem mysterious and generous rather than the conventional gesture of a mother to protect her daughter. He was persuaded to alter the structure of revelations by the director George Alexander.

The crisis takes place in Lord Darlington's rooms, where Lady Windermere goes after leaving her birthday ball. She believes her husband is conducting an affair with Mrs Erlynne and she wishes to revenge herself by running off with a lover. Mrs Erlynne discovers her daughter's intention and pursues her in order to prevent a repetition of the mistake which she herself had made in her youth and which caused her to be ostracised by the society into which she now seeks re-entry. When the men arrive, the women hide behind a curtain, but revelation is forced upon them when Lady Windermere's fan is noticed lying on the sofa. Mrs Erlynne, having persuaded Lady Windermere that a return to her husband and baby son would be in her best interests, compromises herself to allow Lady Windermere to get away in secret. Wilde notoriously borrowed the structure of this scene from Sheridan's *School for Scandal* which was revived in London during the 1880s.

For the resolution of the plot, which occupies Act IV, the action returns to the Windermeres' home on the following morning. Mrs Erlynne visits ostensibly to return the birthday fan. Traditionally, a well-made play about a fallen woman would end with the ejection of that woman from society by a respectable and reactionary male figure. Instead Mrs Erlynne becomes the artificer of her own salvation: she finds a new husband, reunites herself with her daughter while maintaining the secret of her identity, and she announces her own departure for the Continent because, she says, the climate in London does not suit her. Her discourse throughout the play is as authoritative as her actions are radical and decisive. She is an unusual character for the period not just because her behaviour threatens gender norms, but also because she represents two paradoxes. She is a virtuous adventuress and a defiantly unmotherly mother.

This play celebrates paradox. Dialogue, situation and conclusion revel in the coherence of surprising conflict and ambiguity. Rather than end conventionally with the exposure of all concealments, Wilde manipulates his audience into colluding with his heroine, Mrs Erlynne, the fallen woman seeking her way back into society, to keep three major secrets of the plot, on which her paradoxical status rests. Lady Windermere never discovers that Mrs Erlynne is her mother; Lord Windermere never hears about his wife's attempted elopement with Lord Darlington; Lord Augustus is tricked by Mrs Erlynne about her behaviour in Lord Darlington's rooms. Wilde's adaptation of the conventions of the well-made play is matched by his revision of the reactionary social values the form traditionally contains. The play ends with Lady Windermere's description of Mrs Erlynne as 'a very good woman' (p. 217). The audience, and even Lord Windermere to whom it is partially addressed, know that this is not straightforwardly true. Lady Windermere believes herself to be passing a moral judgement. The audience, however, knows that her assessment is based on appearances and that she has been misled about the pragmatic realities underlying them. Her use of the term 'good' is therefore an aesthetic evaluation rather than the ethical one she believes it to be. By allowing the two conflicting value systems of aesthetics and ethics to cohere, however ambiguously, in the final words of the play, Wilde subtly alters the idiomatic currency of 'good' and the moral codes from which it stems.

Lady Windermere's Fan opened at the St James's Theatre on 20 February 1892 where it ran to packed houses until 29 July. It then toured the provinces for two months and returned to London for a last month at the St James's. The play was effectively in continuous performance from February to November during its first year. It was a huge critical and commercial success and earned Wilde £7000, in the currency of the day, as his percentage of box office receipts during its first year alone. His wealth and status seemed assured.

A Woman of No Importance

A Woman of No Importance was commissioned by the actor-manager Herbert Beerbohm Tree, for the Haymarket Theatre, as a direct result of the success of *Lady Windermere's Fan*. Wilde composed it during the summer of 1892 and it opened in April 1893.

It too concerns the fate of a fallen woman, Mrs Arbuthnot, and her illegitimate son Gerald, and depicts their re-entry to respectable society. It has a country-house setting where the decadent society of leisured aristocrats is disturbed by two factors: the revelation that the father of Mrs Arbuthnot's son is the powerful and witty star of this house party, Lord Illingworth, and the blistering, puritanical morality of the young American guest, Hester. Her ethical position is set in conflict with that of the complacent aristocrats, much as Jokanaan and Salomé had been locked into struggle. Again, Wilde deploys the structure of the well-made play only to defy its conventionally reactionary politics. By the end of the play, Lord Illingworth is humiliated, Hester is engaged to Gerald, and Mrs Arbuthnot, whose virtue is confirmed rather than compromised by the revelation of her past, leaves with Hester and Gerald for a new life in America.

The play is much more uneven in tone than its predecessor *Lady Windermere's Fan*. The first act, which Wilde himself particularly admired, contains no action whatsoever, as the drama is constituted by a magnificent display of aphoristic wit which constructs an image of a corrupt but seductive society. Much of the dialogue of this play is lifted from *The Picture of Dorian Gray* (1890), and Lord Illingworth is a reworking of Dorian's mephistophelian tempter Lord Henry Wotton. Languor at the start of the play is set against an excessive display of melodrama at the end of Act III when the crisis reaches its climax and Gerald becomes aware of the identity of his father. Wilde paints a picture of emotional extremes:

> MRS ARBUTHNOT: Stop, Gerald, stop! He is your own father!
>
> GERALD *clutches his mother's hands and looks into her face. She sinks slowly on the ground in shame.* HESTER *steals towards the door.* LORD ILLINGWORTH *frowns and bites his lip. After a time,* GERALD *raises his mother up, puts his arm round her, and leads her from the room*
>
> [p. 265]

Contemporary critics were hostile to this feature of the play. Yet in its juxtaposition with the superficial calm of educated conversation which dominates the play, this moment of melodrama parodies the extreme and absolute judgements made by society on the subjects of illegitimacy and the fallen woman. Just as in *Lady Windermere's Fan* Wilde can be seen to be adjusting the conventional meaning of moral terms such as 'good' and 'bad', so in this play he argues for an amelioration of absolute but hypocritical judgements meted out by society and religious orthodoxy.

Furthermore, the display of emotional and ethical extremes in this tableau shows the paradox on which the whole drama hinges. The only character with conscience, moral vision and ethical depth in this play is the so-called fallen woman. Only Mrs Arbuthnot, the woman of no importance, the woman with a past, the woman who has no legitimate place in society, has sufficient moral understanding to experience shame, and is good enough to teach others the humility which she herself has learned.

In this play, as in its predecessor, Wilde's deployment of paradox extends well beyond the level of dialogue and his use of comic form contains subversive politics.

An Ideal Husband

An Ideal Husband is Wilde's most conventional play. Yet, even while deploying the structure of the well-made play at its most formulaic, Wilde achieves a resolution that depends on an evolution of the central characters' moral understanding rather than a restoration of the inflexible Victorian *mores* which governed at the outset of the play. The witty women in *A Woman of No Importance* had toyed with the idea of 'an Ideal Husband' and dismissed the notion as an absurd paradox, preferring instead the idea of an 'Ideal Man' (p. 238). Wilde was highly critical of the Victorian institution of marriage. In *The Soul of Man under Socialism* (1891) he had argued that marriage was founded on corrupt ethics of ownership, possession and property in which it was impossible for individuals to flourish. In *An Ideal Husband* Wilde explores the folly of a husband and wife who initially believe in marriage as an ideal state but exhibit a relationship founded conspicuously on the possession of property and high social status. At the beginning of the play the 'ideal husband' seems to be Sir Robert Chiltern, an ambitious and successful politician in the Conservative Party. By the end of the play, it is evident that the role of ideal husband is taken over by the dandy, Lord Goring, whose ethics are founded in a version of Christian Socialism.

Lord Goring is Wilde's most radical revision of the dandy figure; he uses wit and apparent detachment to mask his real participation in the moral crisis of the play. His words and actions interpret the significance of the Boucher tapestry, *The Triumph of Love*, which hangs as a backdrop to the glamorous party in the Chilterns' home with which the play begins. He speaks not for the decadent eroticism associated with Boucher's work and with the popular conception of dandyism, but for rigorous self-sacrifice and generous forgiveness in relation to others. At the resolution of the play, when Sir Robert intervenes to prevent Lord Goring's marriage to Mabel because he believes, wrongly, that Lord Goring is conducting an affair with Mrs Cheveley, the dandy prefers to suffer false dishonour rather than clear his name in a manner which would inevitably, though equally falsely, indict Lady Chiltern. She, however, steps in to explain Lord Goring's innocence. The dandy had been ready to sacrifice his own needs rather than to upset the harmony he had worked so hard to restore between the Chilterns. Not only does he speak with the aphoristic authority characteristic of the dandy, but his appearance, modelled on Wilde's own self-fashioning, invests him with an authorial presence. At the start of Act III he enters dressed as Wilde himself:

> *in evening dress with a buttonhole. He is wearing a silk hat and Inverness cape. White-gloved, he carries a Louis-Seize cane . . . One sees that he stands in immediate relation to modern life, makes it indeed, and so masters it. He is the first well-dressed philosopher in the history of thought.* [p. 327]

Wilde added these stage directions for publication of the play in 1899, after his release from prison, and is citing his own self-description in his major prison work *De Profundis*, where he claimed that he stood in symbolic relation to the art and culture of his age.

The threat to Sir Robert's marriage and his career is posed by the blackmailing adventuress Mrs Cheveley who proposes to reveal to the press the corrupt insider dealing in which he engaged, buying shares in the Argentine Canal Scheme eighteen years previously, to launch his career. Wilde based the portrait of a politician vulnerable to blackmail on two contemporary models. One is Sir Charles Dilke (1843–1911), Wilde's friend, who was the under-secretary for foreign affairs in the Liberal Party from 1880 to 1882 before becoming president of the Local Government Board of Trade until 1885. His career ended abruptly when he appeared as the co-respondent in a divorce case. The other model is Charles Stuart Parnell (1846–91), who was the leader of the Irish campaign for Home Rule. In 1889 Parnell found himself embroiled in a high-profile controversy in which he was accused of having condoned politically motivated murder. His 'guilt' was demonstrated in *The Times* by the publication of his correspondence relating to the murder. Parnell's actions were the subject of a public inquiry in which he was acquitted when it emerged that the letters had all been forged. However, shortly after his acquittal, Parnell was cited as the co-respondent in a divorce case brought by the husband of his mistress, Kitty O'Shea. His career was instantly over. The real vulnerability of those in public office and the power of the press to influence public opinion are demonstrated by Mrs Cheveley's ruthless and powerful threats to mobilise the press against Sir Robert.

An Ideal Husband was commissioned by John Hare for the Garrick Theatre but he turned it down before Wilde had finished it. Wilde then took the play to the Haymarket Theatre where it was directed by Lewis Waller (who played Sir Robert), opening to a good reception on 3 January 1895.

The Importance of Being Earnest

Wilde's ultimate dramatic triumph, *The Importance of Being Earnest*, was directed by George Alexander at the St James's Theatre, where it opened on 14 February 1895. Thanks to Alexander's astute editing, and delicate negotiations with Wilde, it has a tight three-act structure, typical for farce of the period, rather than the looser four-act structure which Wilde first presented to him. Like exponents of farce in the twentieth century, such as Dario Fo and Joe Orton, Wilde deploys comedy and the effects of laughter to make a subversive critique of the dominant culture and customs of his day. In an interview before the play opened, Wilde announced that the play was:

> exquisitely trivial, a delicate bubble of fancy, and it has its philosophy . . . that we should treat all the trivial things of life very seriously, and all the serious things with sincere and studied triviality.[4]

The numerous political targets, or 'serious things', at which this play aims centre on the exposure of the moral bankruptcy of the codes governing society. Wilde uses farce to ridicule social etiquette by depicting characters so harnessed by the inflexibility of the social system that their attempts to accommodate their own individuality within it result in deception (Bunburying), self-deception (Cecily and her diary), tyranny (Lady Bracknell's prohibitions) and aggression (Cecily and Gwendolen at tea).

The driving motive of the plot, marriage, has a political edge because society itself could only be properly perpetuated by appropriate intermarriages amongst leading families. The overarching trajectory of the narrative is simple. Two men fall in love with two women and, after various impediments to the happy conclusion are overcome, their marriages are announced. Wilde throws in a third marriage, between Miss Prism and Canon Chasuble. Only Lady Bracknell, the outsider and major source of impediment, remains unchanged though overwhelmed by events, signalling the outmoded customs of the older generation. This simple story is told by means of a highly complicated plot which concerns the difficulties that must be overcome before the matches can be made. Both men, Jack and Algernon, have invented *alter egos* to facilitate their social mobility. Jack Worthing, whose home is in the country, goes under the name of Ernest in town and has informed his household that he has a notorious 'brother' who requires his frequent assistance. Algernon Moncrieff has invented an ailing relative, Bunbury, whose invalidity requires frequent attention, and so he ensures his unquestioned departure to the country. When Jack, known as Ernest, proposes to Algernon's cousin Gwendolen, Algernon takes advantage of Jack's alias to visit Jack's ward, Cecily. Suddenly there are two men masquerading as Ernest Worthing and two women determined to marry a man called Ernest. The proliferation of 'Ernests' coincides with Jack's decision to kill off his fictitious brother. It then emerges that Cecily had been conducting an imaginary affair with 'Ernest Worthing' in her diary. Algernon's appearance under this name

4 Wilde interviewed by Robert Ross in the *St James's Gazette*, 18 January 1895

seems simply to consummate her fiction and bring it to life. Finally, both men find themselves encumbered with their own fictions, the brother they thought they never had, in the shape of each other, as it is revealed that Jack – not Worthing but Moncrieff – really was christened 'Ernest' before Miss Prism lost him in her handbag. Wilde succeeds in airing subversive social views while shaping them within an aspect of his own aesthetic philosophy outlined in 'The Decay of Lying' (1891). The aestheticism announced in this critical dialogue, indebted to Whistler's notorious 'Ten O'Clock Lecture' (1885), argues that life imitates art. When 'the art of lying' decays, the imagination is atrophied and takes to a 'morbid and unhealthy faculty of truth-telling'. Wilde suggests that lies, or fictions, are vital for progress because they initiate change, and he contends that our conceptual framework is conditioned by art. 'Things are because we see them, and what we see, and how we see it, depends on the Arts that have influenced us.' The significance of these arguments is clear for *The Importance of Being Earnest*, in which the young men really encounter their duplicitously conceived doubles and the projections of Cecily's diary are fulfilled.

The climax of the comic complications arises when the multiple fictions of the individual players come into collision. This occurs in Act II when Jack enters, dressed in mourning, to announce the death of his brother Ernest. Jack is ignorant of what the audience knows, namely that Algernon masquerading as Ernest, has recently arrived and is being entertained in the house by Cecily. Jack makes a spectacular and hilarious entrance:

> *Enter* JACK *slowly from the back of the garden. He is dressed in the deepest mourning, with crape hatband and black gloves*

. . .

CHASUBLE: Dear Mr Worthing, I trust this garb of woe does not betoken some terrible calamity?
JACK: My brother.
MISS PRISM: More shameful debts and extravagance?
CHASUBLE: Still leading his life of pleasure?
JACK (*shaking his head*): Dead!
CHASUBLE: Your brother Ernest dead?
JACK: Quite dead.
MISS PRISM: What a lesson for him! I trust he will profit by it.

[p. 387]

The dramatic irony in this scene generates a marvellous comic tension as the audience contemplates the exposure of both Jack and Algernon. But equally significant as sources of humour are the stock responses of Prism, Chasuble and Jack. Each character is locked into a social role that conditions words and actions, and each is exposed as insincere. They live by the prescriptive rules of Victorian etiquette which govern every aspect of social life, from visiting friends, to drinking tea or expressing the grief of bereavement. In trying to live up to these standards by copying them mechanically, the characters reveal the ultimate hollowness of the codes that control their lives.

In this beautifully crafted play, marriage is not only the driving motive of the plot but also a leitmotif of the dialogue, introduced in the expository exchange between Algernon and his butler Lane:

> ALGERNON: Why is it that at a bachelor's establishment the servants invariably drink the champagne? I ask merely for information.
>
> LANE: I attribute it to the superior quality of the wine, sir. I have often observed that in married households the champagne is rarely of a first-rate brand.
>
> ALGERNON: Good heavens! Is marriage so demoralising as that?
>
> LANE: I believe it *is* a very pleasant state, sir . . . [p. 363]

Lane's final surprise rejoinder states in comic form the premise put forward in *The Soul of Man under Socialism*, that 'with the abolition of private property, marriage in its present form must disappear'. Marriage as a subject continues to resonate until the final tableau of the play. As all the characters gather for revelations to make sense of mysteries, Jack returns the handbag in which he was mislaid as a baby to Miss Prism. In discovering that the handbag is hers, he assumes that she must be his mother and rushes to embrace her:

> JACK: Unmarried! I do not deny that is a serious blow. But after all, who has the right to cast a stone against one who has suffered? Cannot repentance wipe out an act of folly? Why should there be one law for men, and another for women? Mother, I forgive you. (*tries to embrace her again*) [p. 415]

The sententiousness of Jack's speech is undercut by the irony of his mistake about his mother's identity. The comic absurdity of the situation makes the message palatable and, because it is already detached from the context of its utterance, affords it a broader significance.

This contrasts with the way in which exactly the same line is received by the audience of *A Woman of No Importance*. There the puritan Hester had stormed, 'Don't have one law for men and another for women' (p. 242). Because her statement is sincere in a context where everyone else is insincere, its significance is dwarfed and she is made to look ridiculous. Wilde's later context for one of his cherished principles of equality illustrates precisely the philosophy of treating 'serious things with sincere and studied triviality' which underlies *The Importance of Being Ernest*. His ingenious manipulation of the conventions of farce to deliver serious critiques of marriage and gender sets this work apart from solemn treatments of these themes by his Naturalist predecessors. His last play is as devastating in its political comment as the tormented drama of Strindberg (*The Father*, 1887) and the moral ferocity of Ibsen (*A Doll's House*, 1879). But where they construct complex, three-dimensional characters, Wilde paints two-dimensional figures; where the deaths or departures of their characters are plotted as final and real, in Wilde's work they are transient figments; where they use tragedy, Wilde, deliberately and perversely, uses farce.

Four days after the opening of *The Importance of Being Earnest*, on 18 February 1895, the Marquess of Queensberry left his calling card for Wilde at the Albemarle Club. On the back of the card he had scribbled the notorious message, 'To Oscar Wilde posing as a Somdomite', which began the disastrous chain of events that led Wilde to prison. When Wilde lost his libel suit against Queensberry, on 5 April 1895, he was immediately arrested and tried for 'gross indecency' under the terms of the Criminal Law Amendment Act of 1885. Two of his plays, *An Ideal Husband* and *The Importance of Being Earnest*, were being performed to full houses in London at that time. Overnight both theatres removed Wilde's name from their hoardings and soon both productions were withdrawn as the real drama of Wilde's disgrace and humiliation captivated London and the Western world. George Alexander, who had directed the first productions of *Lady Windermere's Fan* and *The Importance of Being Earnest*, bought the production rights to these two plays at the bankruptcy sale of Wilde's possessions later in April 1895. They were beginning to be performed again after Wilde's release from prison in 1897, and Alexander offered Wilde, who was poverty stricken, some payments from the income they generated in the last years of the nineteenth century. Alexander himself revived *The Importance of Being Earnest* in 1901, a year after Wilde's death, and the play has continued to draw audiences ever since.

On first opening, this play did not meet with the widespread acclaim and admiration which it commands today. Although generally well received, there were voices of dissent. G. B. Shaw, for instance, found that he was overwhelmed by what he termed 'miserable mechanical laughter',[5] while William Archer, usually one of Wilde's most perceptive critics, asked rhetorically:

> What can a poor critic do with a play which raises no principle, whether of art or morals, creates its own canons and conventions, and is nothing but an absolutely wilful expression of an irrepressibly witty personality?[6]

Today the play is prized for its ability to provoke hilarity coupled with serious reflection, and it stands for the epitome of Wilde's style.

His literary reputation and the significance of his life and trials have only recently been reassessed. The publication of Richard Ellmann's extraordinary biographical study *Oscar Wilde* in 1987 marked the beginning of the most intense interest his life and work have received since his lifetime. Wilde is now championed as one of the most radical and progressive writers of the 1890s, challenging conventions, whether aesthetic, social or political, from within. Feminists now see beyond Wilde's commodifications of womanhood (in *Lady Windermere's Fan*, for example), conventional with Aestheticism, to a more profound questioning of social and sexual inequality. Queer theorists and historians of sexuality explore the representation of masculinity in his plays and point to Wilde's conviction in 1895 as the moment which defined the visibility of male homosexuality in Western society. Postmodernists emphasise Wilde's collusion with the media in the construction of his public *persona* (for instance, Lord Goring in *An Ideal Husband*), and his exploitation of himself as a marketable brand name. Psychoanalysts explore the dark and distorted expressions of desire in his works, such as that evident in *Salomé*. Theatre historians examine the debt of Wilde's plays to popular culture, and his deployments of dramatic form. It is certain that Wilde has now a reputation and stature of major significance in Anglo-Irish literature, and that his work, as his friend Ada Leverson remarked, continues to 'amuse the mob, frighten the burgess, and fascinate the aristocrat' just as it did before his disgrace in 1895.

ANNE VARTY
Royal Holloway

5 G. B. Shaw, review of *The Importance of Being Earnest*, *The Saturday Review*, 23 February 1895

6 William Archer, review of *The Importance of Being Earnest*, *World*, 20 February 1895

FURTHER READING

Harold Bloom (ed.), *The Importance of Being Earnest*, Modern Critical Interpretations, Chelsea House Publishers, New York 1988

Richard Ellmann, *Oscar Wilde*, Hamish Hamilton, London 1987

Sos Eltis, *Revising Wilde: Society and Subversion in the Plays of Oscar Wilde*, Clarendon Press, Oxford 1996

Jessica R. Feldman, *Gender on the Divide: The Dandy in Modernist Literature*, Cornell University Press, Ithaca, London 1993

Regenia Gagnier, *Idylls of the Marketplace: Oscar Wilde and the Victorian Public*, Scolar, London 1987

Josephine Guy and Ian Small, *Oscar Wilde's Profession: Writing and the Culture Industry in the Late Nineteenth Century*, Oxford University Press, Oxford 2000

Joel Kaplan (ed.), *Modern Drama*, Volume 37.1 (1994) – a volume of this periodical dedicated to research essays on Wilde's plays

Joel H. Kaplan and Shiela Stowell, *Theatre and Fashion: Oscar Wilde to the Suffragettes*, Cambridge University Press, Cambridge 1994

Margery Morgan, *File on Wilde*, Methuen, London 1990

Kerry Powell, *Oscar Wilde and the Theatre of the 1890s*, Cambridge University Press, Cambridge 1990

Peter Raby, *Oscar Wilde*, Cambridge University Press, Cambridge 1988

Peter Raby (ed.), *The Cambridge Companion to Oscar Wilde*, Cambridge University Press, Cambridge 1997

Neil Sammells, *Wilde Style: The Plays and Prose of Oscar Wilde*, Pearson Education Ltd, Harlow 2000

William Tydeman and Stephen Price, *Wilde: 'Salomé'*, Plays in Production, Cambridge University Press, Cambridge 1996

William Tydeman (ed.), *Wilde: Comedies*, Casebook Series, Macmillan, London 1982

Anne Varty, *A Preface to Oscar Wilde*, Longman, Harlow 1998

Katharine Worth, *Oscar Wilde*, Macmillan, London 1983

Websites

There are many websites devoted to the discussion of Wilde's life and work, and they are constantly being updated. A simple web search for 'Oscar Wilde' will yield many entries, some of them more scholarly and reliable than others.

For general information about Wilde, including societies, journals, works, collections, exhibitions, bibliographies and links to other sites, the website for the 1890s Society is recommended: www.1890s.org. The World-Wide Wilde Web is at: www.showgate.com. An overview of his life, works and times is at: http://landow.stg.brown.edu/victorian/victov.html.

CONTENTS

VERA

A DRAMA IN A PROLOGUE AND FOUR ACTS

PERSONS IN THE PROLOGUE

PETER SABOUROFF, *an innkeeper*
VERA SABOUROFF, *his daughter*
MICHAEL, *a peasant*
COLONEL KOTEMKIN

SCENE: Russia
TIME: 1795

PERSONS IN THE PLAY

IVAN THE CZAR
PRINCE PAUL MARALOFFSKI, *Prime Minister of Russia*
PRINCE PETROVITCH
COUNT ROUVALOFF
MARQUIS DE POIVRARD
BARON RAFF
GENERAL KOTEMKIN
COUNT PETOUCHOF
COLONEL OF THE GUARD
PAGE

Nihilists
PETER TCHERNAVITCH, *president of the Nihilists*
MICHAEL
ALEXIS IVANACIEVITCH, *known as student of medicine*
PROFESSOR MARFA
VERA SABOUROFF

Soldiers, conspirators, etc.

SCENE: Moscow
TIME: 1800

VERA

PROLOGUE

A Russian inn. Large door opening on snowy landscape at back of stage. PETER SABOUROFF AND MICHAEL

PETER (*warming his hands at a stove*): Has Vera not come back yet, Michael?

MICHAEL: No, father Peter, not yet; 'tis a good three miles to the post office, and she has to milk the cows besides, and that dun one is a rare plaguey creature for a wench to handle.

PETER: Why didn't you go with her, you young fool? she'll never love you unless you are always at her heels; women like to be bothered.

MICHAEL: She says I bother her too much already, father Peter, and I fear she'll never love me after all.

PETER: Tut, tut, boy, why shouldn't she? you're young and wouldn't be ill-favoured either, had God or thy mother given thee another face. Aren't you one of Prince Maraloffski's gamekeepers; and haven't you got a good grass farm, and the best cow in the village? What more does a girl want?

MICHAEL: But Vera, father Peter –

PETER: Vera, my lad, has got too many ideas; I don't think much of ideas myself; I've got on well enough in life without 'em; why shouldn't my children? There's Dmitri! could have stayed here and kept the inn; many a young lad would have jumped at the offer in these hard times: but he, scatterbrained featherhead of a boy, must needs go off to Moscow to study the law! What does he want knowing about the law! let a man do his duty, say I, and no one will trouble him.

MICHAEL: Ay! but, father Peter, they say a good lawyer can break the law as often as he likes, and no one can say him nay.

PETER: That is about all they are good for; and there he stays, and has not written a line to us for four months now – a good son that, eh?

MICHAEL: Come, come, father Peter, Dmitri's letters must have gone astray – perhaps the new postman can't read; he looks stupid enough, and Dmitri, why, he was the best fellow in the village. Do you remember how he shot the bear at the barn in the great winter?

PETER: Ay, it was a good shot; I never did a better myself.

MICHAEL: And as for dancing, he tired out three fiddlers Christmas come two years.

PETER: Ay, ay, he was a merry lad. It is the girl that has the seriousness – she goes about as solemn as a priest for days at a time.

MICHAEL: Vera is always thinking of others.

PETER: There is her mistake, boy. Let God and our little father look to the world. It is none of my work to mend my neighbour's thatch. Why, last winter old Michael was frozen to death in his sleigh in the snowstorm, and his wife and children starved afterwards when the hard times came; but what business was it of mine? I didn't make the world. Let God and the Czar look to it. And then the blight came, and the black plague with it, and the priests couldn't bury the people fast enough, and they lay dead on the roads – men and women both. But what business was it of mine? I didn't make the world. Let God and the Czar look to it. Or two autumns ago, when the river overflowed on a sudden, and the children's school was carried away and drowned every girl and boy in it. I didn't make the world – let God and the Czar look to it.

MICHAEL: But, father Peter –

PETER: No, no, boy; no man could live if he took his neighbour's pack on his shoulders. (*Enter* VERA *in peasant's dress*) Well, my girl, you've been long enough away – where is the letter?

VERA: There is none today, father.

PETER: I knew it.

VERA: But there will be one tomorrow, father.

PETER: Curse him, for an ungrateful son.

VERA: Oh, father, don't say that; he must be sick

PETER: Ay! sick of profligacy, perhaps.

VERA: How dare you say that of him, father? You know that is not true.

PETER: Where does the money go, then? Michael, listen. I gave Dmitri half his mother's fortune to bring with him to pay the lawyer folk of Moscow. He has only written three times, and every time for more money. He got it, not at my wish, but at hers (*pointing to* VERA), and now for five months, close on six almost, we have heard nothing from him.

VERA: Father, he will come back.

PETER: Ay! the prodigals always return; but let him never darken my doors again.

VERA (*sitting down pensive*): Some evil has come on him; he must be dead! Oh! Michael, I am so wretched about Dmitri.

MICHAEL: Will you never love anyone but him, Vera?

VERA (*smiling*) I don't know; there is so much else to do in the world but love.

MICHAEL: Nothing else worth doing, Vera.

PETER: What noise is that, Vera? (*a metallic clink is heard*)

VERA (*rising and going to the door*): I don't know, father, it is not like the cattle bells, or I would think Nicholas had come from the fair. Oh! father! it is soldiers! – coming down the hill – there is one of them on horseback. How pretty they look! But there are some men with them with chains on! They must be robbers. Oh! don't let them in, father; I couldn't look at them.

PETER: Men in chains! Why, we are in luck, my child! I heard this was to be the new road to Siberia, to bring the prisoners to the mines; but I didn't believe it. My fortune is made! Bustle, Vera, bustle! I'll die a rich man after all. There will be no lack of good customers now. An honest man should have the chance of making his living out of rascals now and then.

VERA: Are these men rascals, father? What have they done?

PETER: I reckon they're some of those Nihilists the priest warns us against. Don't stand there idle, my girl.

VERA: I suppose, then, they are all wicked men.

Sound of soldiers outside; cry of 'Halt!' Enter Russian officer with a body of soldiers and eight men in chains, raggedly dressed; one of them on entering hurriedly puts his coat above his ears and hides his face; some soldiers guard the door, others sit down; the prisoners stand

COLONEL: Innkeeper!

PETER: Yes, colonel.

COLONEL (*pointing to Nihilists*): Give these men some bread and water.

PETER (*to himself*): I shan't make much out of that order.

COLONEL: As for myself, what have you got fit to eat?

PETER: Some good dried venison, your excellency – and some rye whisky.

COLONEL: Nothing else?

PETER: Why, more whisky, your excellency.

COLONEL: What clods these peasants are! You have a better room than this?

PETER: Yes, sir.

COLONEL: Bring me there. Sergeant, post your picket outside, and see that these scoundrels do not communicate with anyone. No letter writing, you dogs, or you'll be flogged for it. Now for the venison. (*To* PETER *bowing before him*) Get out of the way, you fool! Who is that girl? (*sees* VERA)

PETER: My daughter, your highness.

COLONEL: Can she read and write?

PETER: Ay, that she can, sir.

COLONEL: Then she is a dangerous woman. No peasant should be allowed to do anything of the kind. Till your fields, store your harvest, pay your taxes, and obey your masters – that is your duty.

VERA: Who are our masters?

COLONEL: Young woman, these men are going to the mines for life for asking the same foolish question.

VERA: Then they have been unjustly condemned.

PETER: Vera, keep your tongue quiet. She is a foolish girl, sir, who talks too much.

COLONEL: Every woman does talk too much. Come, where is this venison? Count, I am waiting for you. How can you see anything in a girl with coarse hands? (*he passes with* PETER *and his* AIDE-DE-CAMP *into an inner room*)

VERA (*to one of the Nihilists*): Won't you sit down? you must be tired.

SERGEANT: Come now, young woman, no talking to my prisoners.

VERA: I shall speak to them. How much do you want?

SERGEANT: How much have you?

VERA: Will you let these men sit down if I give you this? (*takes off her peasant's necklace*) It is all I have; it was my mother's.

SERGEANT: Well, it looks pretty enough, and it is heavy too. What do you want with these men?

VERA: They are hungry and tired. Let me go to them.

ONE OF THE SOLDIERS: Let the wench be, if she pays us.

SERGEANT: Well, have your way. If the colonel sees you, you may have to come with us, my pretty one.

VERA (*advances to the Nihilists*) Sit down; you must be tired. (*serves them food*) What are you?

PRISONER: Nihilists.

VERA: Who put you in chains?

PRISONER: Our father, the Czar.

VERA: Why?

PRISONER: For loving liberty too well.

VERA (*to prisoner, who hides his face*): What did you want to do?

DMITRI: To give liberty to thirty millions of people enslaved to one man

VERA (*startled at the voice*): What is your name?

DMITRI: I have no name.

VERA: Where are your friends?

DMITRI: I have no friends.

VERA: Let me see your face.

DMITRI: You will see nothing but suffering in it. They have tortured me.

VERA (*tears the cloak from his face*): Oh, God! Dmitri! my brother!

DMITRI: Hush! Vera; be calm. You must not let my father know; it would kill him. I thought I could free Russia. I heard men talk of liberty one night in a café. I had never heard the word before. It seemed to be a new god they spoke of. I joined them. It was there all the money went. Five months ago they seized us. They found me printing the paper. I am going to the mines for life. I could not write. I thought it would be better to let you think I was dead; for they are bringing me to a living tomb.

VERA (*looking round*): You must escape, Dmitri. I will take your place.

DMITRI: Impossible! You can only revenge us.

VERA: I shall revenge you.

DMITRI: Listen! there is a house in Moscow –

SERGEANT: Prisoners, attention! – the colonel is coming – young woman, your time is up.

Enter COLONEL, AIDE-DE-CAMP *and* PETER

PETER: I hope your highness is pleased with the venison. I shot it myself.

COLONEL: It had been better had you talked less about it. Sergeant, get ready. (*gives purse to* PETER) Here, you cheating rascal!

PETER: My fortune is made! Long live your highness. I hope your highness will come often this way.

COLONEL: By St Nicholas, I hope not. It is too cold here for me. (*To* VERA. Young girl, don't ask questions again about what does not concern you. I will not forget your face.

VERA: Nor I yours, or what you are doing.

COLONEL: You peasants are getting too saucy since you ceased to be serfs, and the knout is the best school for you to learn politics in. Sergeant, proceed.

The COLONEL *turns and goes to top of stage. The prisoners pass out in double file; as* DMITRI *passes* VERA *he lets a piece of paper fall on the ground; she puts her foot on it and remains immobile.*

PETER (*who has been counting the money the* COLONEL *gave him*): Long life to your highness. I will hope to see another batch soon. (*Suddenly catches sight of* DMITRI *as he is going out of the door, and screams and rushes up*) Dmitri! Dmitri! my God! what brings you here? he is innocent, I tell you. I'll pay for him. Take your money (*flings money on the ground*), take all I have, give me my son. Villains! Villains! where are you bringing him?

COLONEL: To Siberia, old man.

PETER: No, no; take me instead.

COLONEL: He is a Nihilist.

PETER: You lie! you lie! He is innocent. (*The soldiers force him back with their guns and shut the door against him. He beats with his fists against it*) Dmitri! Dmitri! a Nihilist! (*Falls down on floor*)

VERA (*who has remained motionless, picks up paper now from under her foot and reads*): 'Number 99, Rue Tchernavaya, Moscow. To strangle whatever nature is in me; neither to love nor to be loved; neither to pity nor to be pitied; neither to marry nor to be given in marriage, till the end is come.' My brother, I shall keep the oath. (*kisses the paper*) You shall be revenged!

VERA *stands immobile, holding paper in her lifted hand.* PETER *is lying on the floor.* MICHAEL, *who has just come in, is bending over him*

END OF PROLOGUE

ACT ONE

Number 99, Rue Tchernavaya, Moscow. A large garret lit by oil lamps hung from ceiling. Some masked men standing silent and apart from one another. A man in a scarlet mask is writing at a table. Door at back. Man in yellow with drawn sword at it. Knocks heard. Figures in cloaks and masks enter.

VOICE: *Per crucem ad lucem.*

ANSWER: *Per sanguinem ad libertatem.*

Clock strikes; conspirators form a semicircle in the middle of the stage

PRESIDENT: What is the word?

FIRST CONSPIRATOR: Nabat.

PRESIDENT: The answer?

SECOND CONSPIRATOR: Kalit.

PRESIDENT: What hour is it?

THIRD CONSPIRATOR: The hour to suffer.

PRESIDENT: What day?

FOURTH CONSPIRATOR: The day of oppression.

PRESIDENT: What year?

FIFTH CONSPIRATOR: Since the Revolution of France, the ninth year.

PRESIDENT: How many are we in number?

SIXTH CONSPIRATOR: Ten, nine, and three.

PRESIDENT: The Galilæan had less to conquer the world; but what is our mission?

SEVENTH CONSPIRATOR: To give freedom.

PRESIDENT: Our creed?

EIGHTH CONSPIRATOR: To annihilate.

PRESIDENT: Our duty?

NINTH CONSPIRATOR: To obey.

PRESIDENT: Brothers, the questions have been answered well. There are none but Nihilists present. Let us see each other's faces! (*the conspirators unmask*) Michael, recite the oath.

MICHAEL: To strangle whatever nature is in us; neither to love nor to be loved, neither to pity nor to be pitied, neither to marry nor to be given in marriage, till the end is come; to stab secretly by night;

to drop poison in the glass; to set father against son, and husband against wife; without fear, without hope, without future, to suffer, to annihilate, to revenge.

PRESIDENT: Are we all agreed?

CONSPIRATORS: We are all agreed. (*they disperse in various directions about the stage*)

PRESIDENT: 'Tis after the hour, Michael, and she is not yet here.

MICHAEL: Would that she were! We can do little without her.

ALEXIS: She cannot have been seized, president? but the police are on her track, I know.

MICHAEL: You always seem to know a good deal about the movements of the police in Moscow – too much for an honest conspirator.

PRESIDENT: If those dogs have caught her, the red flag of the people will float on a barricade in every street till we find her! It was foolish of her to go to the Grand Duke's ball. I told her so, but she said she wanted to see the Czar and all his cursed brood face to face.

ALEXIS: Gone to the state ball?

MICHAEL: I have no fear. She is as hard to capture as a she-wolf is, and twice as dangerous; besides, she is well disguised. But is there any news from the palace tonight, president? What is that bloody despot doing now besides torturing his only son? Have any of you seen him? One hears strange stories about him. They say he loves the people; but a king's son never does that. You cannot breed them like that.

PRESIDENT: Since he came back from abroad a year ago his father has kept him in close prison in his palace.

MICHAEL: An excellent training to make him a tyrant in his turn, but is there any news, I say?

PRESIDENT: A council is to be held tomorrow, at four o'clock, on some secret business the spies cannot find out.

MICHAEL: A council in a king's palace is sure to be about some bloody work or other. But in what room is this council to be held?

PRESIDENT (*reading from letter*) In the yellow tapestry room called after the Empress Catherine.

MICHAEL: I care not for such long-sounding names. I would know where it is.

PRESIDENT: I cannot tell, Michael. I know more about the insides of prisons than of palaces.

MICHAEL (*speaking suddenly to* ALEXIS): Where is this room, Alexis?

ALEXIS: It is on the first floor, looking out on to the inner courtyard. But why do you ask, Michael?

MICHAEL: Nothing, nothing, boy! I merely take a great interest in the Czar's life and movements and I knew you could tell me all about the palace. Every poor student of medicine in Moscow knows all about king's houses. It is their duty is it not?

ALEXIS (*aside*): Can Michael suspect me? There is something strange in his manner tonight. Why doesn't she come? The whole fire of revolution seems fallen into dull ashes when she is not here.

MICHAEL: Have you cured many patients lately, at your hospital, boy?

ALEXIS: There is one who lies sick to death I would fain cure, but cannot.

MICHAEL: Ay, and who is that?

ALEXIS: Russia, our mother.

MICHAEL: The curing of Russia is surgeon's business, and must be done by the knife. I like not your method of medicine.

PRESIDENT: Professor, we have read the proofs of your last article; it is very good indeed.

MICHAEL: What is it about, professor?

PROFESSOR: The subject, my good brother, is assassination considered as a method of political reform.

MICHAEL: I think little of pen and ink in revolutions. One dagger will do more than a hundred epigrams. Still, let us read this scholar's last production. Give it to me. I will read it myself.

PROFESSOR: Brother, you never mind your stops; let Alexis read it.

MICHAEL: Ay! he is as tripping of speech as if he were some young aristocrat; but for my own part I care not for the stops so that the sense be plain.

ALEXIS (*reading*): 'The past has belonged to the tyrant, and he has defiled it; ours is the future, and we shall make it holy.' Ay! let us make the future holy; let there be one revolution at least which is not bred in crime, nurtured in murder!

MICHAEL: They have spoken to us by the sword, and by the sword we shall answer! You are too delicate for us, Alexis. There should be none here but men whose hands are rough with labour or red with blood.

PRESIDENT: Peace, Michael, peace! He is the bravest heart among us.

MICHAEL (*aside*): He will need be brave tonight.

The sound of the sleigh bells is heard outside

VOICE (*outside*): *Per crucem ad lucem.*

MAN ON GUARD: *Per sanguinem ad libertatem.*

MICHAEL: Who is that?

VERA: God save the people!

PRESIDENT: Welcome, Vera, welcome! We have been sick at heart till we saw you; but now methinks the star of freedom has come to wake us from the night.

VERA: It is night, indeed, brother! Night without moon or star! Russia is smitten to the heart! The man Ivan whom men call the Czar strikes now at our mother with a dagger deadlier than ever forged by tyranny against a people's life!

MICHAEL: What has the tyrant done now?

VERA: Tomorrow martial law is to be proclaimed in Russia.

ALL: Martial law! We are lost! We are lost.

ALEXIS: Martial law! Impossible!

MICHAEL: Fool, nothing is impossible in Russia but reform.

VERA: Ay, martial law. The last right to which the people clung has been taken from them. Without trial, without appeal, without accuser even, our brothers will be taken from their houses, shot in the streets like dogs, sent away to die in the snow, to starve in the dungeon, to rot in the mine. Do you know what martial law means? It means the strangling of a whole nation. The streets will be filled with soldiers night and day; there will be sentinels at every door. No man dare walk abroad now but the spy or the traitor. Cooped up in the dens we hide in, meeting by stealth, speaking with bated breath; what good can we do now for Russia?

PRESIDENT: We can suffer at least.

VERA: We have done that too much already. The hour is now come to annihilate and to revenge.

PRESIDENT: Up to this the people have borne everything.

VERA: Because they have understood nothing. But now we, the Nihilists, have given them the tree of knowledge to eat of, and the day of silent suffering is over for Russia.

MICHAEL: Martial law, Vera! This is fearful tidings you bring.

PRESIDENT: It is the death warrant of liberty in Russia.

VERA: Or the tocsin of revolution.

MICHAEL: Are you sure it is true?

VERA: Here is the proclamation. I stole it myself at the ball tonight from a young fool, one of Prince Paul's secretaries, who had been given it to copy. It was that which made me so late.(VERA *hands proclamation to* MICHAEL, *who reads it*)

MICHAEL: 'To ensure the public safety – martial law. By order of the Czar, father of his people.' The father of his people!

VERA: Ay! a father whose name shall not be hallowed, whose kingdom shall change to a republic, whose trespasses shall not be forgiven him, because he has robbed us of our daily bread; with whom is neither might, nor right, nor glory, now or for ever.

PRESIDENT: It must be about this that the council meet tomorrow. It has not yet been signed.

ALEXIS: It shall not be while I have a tongue to plead with.

MICHAEL: Or while I have hands to smite with.

VERA: Martial law! O God, how easy it is for a king to kill his people by thousands, but we cannot rid ourselves of one crowned man in Europe! What is there of awful majesty in these men which makes the hand unsteady, the dagger treacherous, the pistol-shot harmless? Are they not men of like passions with ourselves, vulnerable to the same diseases, of flesh and blood not different from our own? What made Olgiati tremble at the supreme crisis of that Roman life, and Guido's nerve fail him when he should have been of iron and of steel? A plague, I say, on these fools of Naples, Berlin, and Spain! Methinks that if I stood face to face with one of the crowned men my eye would see more clearly, my aim be more sure, my whole body gain a strength and power that was not my own! Oh, to think what stands between us and freedom in Europe! a few old men, wrinkled, feeble, tottering dotards whom a boy could strangle for a ducat, or a woman stab in a night-time. And these are the things that keep us from democracy, that keep us from liberty. But now methinks the brood of men is dead and the dull earth grown sick of child-bearing, else would no crowned dog pollute God's air by living.

ALL: Try us! Try us! Try us!

MICHAEL: We shall try thee, too, some day, Vera.

VERA: I pray God thou mayest! Have I not strangled whatever nature is in me, and shall I not keep my oath?

MICHAEL (*to* PRESIDENT): Martial law, president! Come, there is no time to be lost. We have twelve hours yet before us till the council meet. Twelve hours! One can overthrow a dynasty in less time than that.

PRESIDENT: Ay! or lose one's own head.

MICHAEL *and the* PRESIDENT *retire to one corner of the stage and sit whispering.* VERA *takes up the proclamation, and reads it to herself,* ALEXIS *watches and suddenly rushes up to her.*

ALEXIS: Vera!

VERA: Alexis, you here! Foolish boy, have I not prayed you to stay away? All of us here are doomed to die before our time, fated to expiate by suffering whatever good we do; but you, with your bright boyish face, you are too young to die yet.

ALEXIS: One is never to young to die for one's country!

VERA: Why do you come here night after night?

ALEXIS: Because I love the people.

VERA: But your fellow-students must miss you. Are there no traitors among them? You know what spies there are in the university here. Oh, Alexis, you must go! You see how desperate suffering has made us. There is no room here for a nature like yours. You must not come again.

ALEXIS: Why do you think so poorly of me? Why should I live while my brothers suffer?

VERA: You spake to me of your mother once. You said you loved her. Oh, think of her!

ALEXIS: I have no mother now but Russia, my life is hers to take or give away; but tonight I am here to see you. They tell me you are leaving for Novgorod tomorrow.

VERA: I must. They are getting faint-hearted there, and I would fan the flame of this revolution into such a blaze that the eyes of all kings in Europe shall be blinded. If martial law is passed they will need me all the more there. There is no limit, it seems, to the tyranny of one man; but there shall be a limit to the suffering of a whole people.

ALEXIS: God knows it, I am with you. But you must not go. The police are watching every train for you. When you are seized they have orders to place you without trial in the lowest dungeon of the palace. I know it – no matter how. Oh, think how without you the sun goes from our life, how the people will lose their leader and liberty her priestess. Vera, you must not go!

VERA: If you wish it, I will stay. I would live a little longer for freedom, a little longer for Russia.

ALEXIS: When you die then Russia is smitten indeed; when you die then I shall lose all hope – all . . . Vera, this is fearful news you bring – martial law – it is too terrible. I knew it not, by my soul, I knew it not!

VERA: How could you have known it? It is too well laid a plot for that. This great White Czar, whose hands are red with the blood of the people he has murdered, whose soul is black with his iniquity, is the cleverest conspirator of us all. Oh, how could Russia bear two hearts like yours and his!

ALEXIS: Vera, the Emperor was not always like this. There was a time when he loved the people. It is that devil, whom God curse, Prince Paul Maraloffski who has brought him to this. Tomorrow, I swear it, I shall plead for the people to the Emperor.

VERA: Plead to the Czar! Foolish boy, it is only those who are sentenced to death that ever see our Czar. Besides, what should he care for a voice that pleads for mercy? The cry of a strong nation in its agony has not moved that heart of stone.

ALEXIS (*Aside*): Yet I shall plead to him. They can but kill me.

PROFESSOR: Here are the proclamations, Vera. Do you think they will do?

VERA: I shall read them. How fair he looks! Methinks he never seemed so noble as tonight. Liberty is blessed in having such a lover.

ALEXIS: Well, president, what are you deep in?

MICHAEL: We are thinking of the best way of killing bears. (*whispers to* PRESIDENT *and leads him aside*)

PROFESSOR (*to* VERA): And the letters from our brothers at Paris and Berlin. What answer shall we send to them?

VERA (*takes them mechanically*): Had I not strangled nature, sworn neither to love nor to be loved, methinks I might have loved him. Oh, I am a fool, a traitor myself, a traitor myself! But why did he come amongst us with his bright young face, his heart aflame for liberty, his pure white soul? Why does he make me feel at times as if I would have him as my king, Republican though I be? Oh, fool, fool, fool! False to your oath! weak as water! Have done! Remember what you are – a Nihilist, a Nihilist!

PRESIDENT (*to* MICHAEL): But you will be seized, Michael.

MICHAEL: I think not. I will wear the uniform of the Imperial Guard, and the colonel on duty is one of us. It is on the first floor, you remember; so I can take a long shot.

PRESIDENT: Shall I tell the brethren?

MICHAEL: Not a word, not a word! There is a traitor amongst us.

VERA: Come, are these the proclamations? Yes, they will do; yes, they will do. Send five hundred to Kiev and Odessa and Novgorod, five hundred to Warsaw, and have twice the number distributed among the Southern Provinces, though these dull Russian peasants care little for our proclamations, and less for our martyrdoms. When the blow is struck it must be from the town, not from the country.

MICHAEL: Ay, and by the sword, not by the goose-quill.

VERA: Where are the letters from Poland?

PROFESSOR: Here.

VERA: Unhappy Poland! The eagles of Russia have fed on her heart. We must not forget our brothers there.

PRESIDENT: Is this true, Michael?

MICHAEL: Ay, I stake my life on it.

PRESIDENT: Let the doors be locked, then. Alexis Ivanacievitch, entered on our roll of the brothers as a student of the School of Medicine at Moscow. Why did you not tell us of this bloody scheme of martial law?

ALEXIS: I, president?

MICHAEL: Ay, you! You knew it, none better. Such weapons as these are not forged in a day. Why did you not tell us of it? A week ago there had been time to lay the mine, to raise the barricade, to strike one blow at least for liberty. But now the hour is past! It is too late, it is too late! Why did you keep it a secret from us, I say?

ALEXIS: Now by the hand of freedom, Michael, my brother, you wrong me. I knew nothing of this hideous law. By my soul, my brothers, I knew not of it! How should I know?

MICHAEL: Because you are a traitor! Where did you go when you left us the night of our last meeting here?

ALEXIS: To mine own house, Michael.

MICHAEL: Liar! I was on your track. You left here an hour after midnight. Wrapped in a large cloak, you crossed the river in a boat a mile below the second bridge, and gave the ferryman a gold piece, you, the poor student of medicine! You doubled back twice, and hid in an archway so long that I had almost made up my mind to stab you at once, only that I am fond of hunting. So! you thought that you had baffled all pursuit, did you? Fool! I am a bloodhound that never loses the scent. I followed you from street to street. At last I saw you pass swiftly across the Place St Isaac, whisper to the guards the secret password, enter the palace by a private door with your own key.

CONSPIRATORS: The palace!

VERA: Alexis!

MICHAEL: I waited. All through the dreary watches of our long Russian night I waited, that I might kill you with your Judas hire still hot in your hand. But you never came out; you never left that palace at all. I saw the blood-red sun rise through the yellow fog over the murky town; I saw a new day of oppression dawn on Russia; but you never came out. So you pass nights in the palace, do you? You know the password for the guards! you have a key to a secret door. Oh, you are a spy – you are a spy! I never trusted you, with your soft white hands, your curled hair, your pretty graces. You have no mark of suffering about you; you cannot be of the people. You are a spy – a spy – traitor.

ALL: Kill him! Kill him! (*draw their knives*)

VERA (*rushing in front of* ALEXIS): Stand back, I say, Michael! Stand back all! Do not dare lay a hand upon him! He is the noblest heart amongst us.

ALL: Kill him! Kill him! He is a spy!

VERA: Dare to lay a finger on him and I leave you all to yourselves.

PRESIDENT: Vera, did you not hear what Michael said of him? He stayed all night in the Czar's palace. He has a password and a private key. What else should he be but a spy?

VERA: Bah! I do not believe Michael. It is a lie! It is a lie! Alexis, say it is a lie!

ALEXIS: It is true. Michael has told what he saw. I did pass that night in the Czar's palace. Michael has spoken the truth.

VERA: Stand back, I say; stand back! Alexis, I do not care. I trust you; you would not betray us; you would not sell the people for money. You are honest, true! Oh, say you are no spy!

ALEXIS: Spy? You know I am not. I am with you, my brothers, to the death.

MICHAEL: Ay, to your own death.

ALEXIS: Vera, you know I am true.

VERA: I know it well.

PRESIDENT: Why are you here, traitor?

ALEXIS: Because I love the people.

MICHAEL: Then you can be a martyr for them?

VERA: You must kill me first, Michael, before you lay a finger on him.

PRESIDENT: Michael, we dare not lose Vera. It is her whim to let this boy live. We can keep him here tonight. Up to this he has not betrayed us.

Tramp of soldiers outside, knocking at door

VOICE: Open in the name of the Emperor!

MICHAEL: He *has* betrayed us. This is your doing, spy!

PRESIDENT: Come, Michael, come. We have no time to cut one another's throats while we have our own heads to save.

VOICE: Open in the name of the Emperor!

PRESIDENT: Brothers, be masked all of you. Michael, open the door. It is our only chance.

Enter GENERAL KOTEMKIN *and soldiers*

GENERAL: All honest citizens should be in their own houses at an hour before midnight, and not more than five people have a right to meet privately. Have you not noticed the proclamation, fellow?

MICHAEL: Ay, you have spoiled every honest wall in Moscow with it.

VERA: Peace, Michael, peace. Nay, sir, we knew it not. We are a company of strolling players travelling from Samara to Moscow to amuse his imperial majesty the Czar.

GENERAL: But I heard loud voices before I entered. What was that?

VERA: We were rehearsing a new tragedy.

GENERAL: Your answers are too *honest* to be true. Come, let me see who you are. Take off those players' masks. By St Nicholas, my beauty, if your face matches your figure, you must be a choice morsel! Come, I say, pretty one; I would sooner see your face than those of all the others.

PRESIDENT: O God! if he sees it is Vera, we are all lost!

GENERAL: No coquetting, my girl. Come, unmask, I say, or I shall tell my guards to do it for you.

ALEXIS: Stand back, I say, General Kotemkin!

GENERAL: Who are you, fellow, that talks with such a tripping tongue to your betters? (ALEXIS *takes his mask off*) His imperial highness the Czarevitch!

ALL: The Czarevitch! It is all over!

PRESIDENT: He will give us up to the soldiers.

MICHAEL (*to* VERA): Why did you not let me kill him? Come, we must fight to the death for it.

VERA: Peace! he will not betray us.

ALEXIS: A whim of mine, general! You know how my father keeps me from the world and imprisons me in the palace. I should really be bored to death if I could not get out at night in disguise sometimes, and have some romantic adventure in town. I fell in with these honest folks a few hours ago.

GENERAL: But, your highness –

ALEXIS: Oh, they are excellent actors, I assure you. If you had come in ten minutes ago, you would have witnessed a most interesting scene.

GENERAL: Actors, are they, prince?

ALEXIS: Ay, and very ambitious actors, too. They only care to play before kings.

GENERAL: I' faith, your highness, I was in hopes I had made a good haul of Nihilists.

ALEXIS: Nihilists in Moscow, general! with you as head of the police? Impossible!

GENERAL: So I always tell your imperial father. But I heard at the council today that that woman Vera Sabouroff, the head of them, had been seen in this very city. The Emperor's face turned as white as the snow outside. I think I never saw such terror in any man before.

ALEXIS: She is a dangerous woman, then, this Vera Sabouroff?

GENERAL: The most dangerous in all Europe

ALEXIS: Did you ever see her, general?

GENERAL: Why, five years ago, when I was a plain colonel, I remember her, your highness, a common waiting girl in an inn. If I had known then what she was going to turn out to be, I would have flogged her to death on the roadside. She is not a woman at all; she is a sort of devil! For the last eighteen months I have been hunting her, and I caught sight of her once, last September, outside Odessa.

ALEXIS: How did you let her go, general?

GENERAL: I was by myself, and she shot one of my horses just as I was gaining on her. If I see her again I shan't miss my chance. The Emperor has put twenty thousand roubles on her head.

ALEXIS: I hope you will get it, general; but meanwhile you are frightening these honest people out of their wits, and disturbing the tragedy. Good-night, general.

GENERAL: Yes; but I should like to see their faces, your highness.

ALEXIS: No, general; you must not ask that; you know how these gypsies hate to be stared at.

GENERAL: Yes. But, your highness –

ALEXIS (*haughtily*): General, they are my friends, that is enough. And, general, not a word of this little adventure here, you understand. I shall rely on you.

GENERAL: I shall not forget, prince. But shall we not see you back to the palace? The state ball is almost over and you are expected.

ALEXIS: I shall be there; but I shall return alone. Remember, not a word about my strolling players.

GENERAL: Or your pretty gypsy, eh, prince? your pretty gypsy! I' faith, I should like to see her before I go; she has such fine eyes through her mask. Well, good-night, your highness; good-night.

ALEXIS: Good-night, general.

(*Exit* GENERAL *and the soldiers*)

VERA (*throwing off her mask*): Saved! and by you!

ALEXIS (*clasping her hand*): Brothers, you trust me now?

END OF ACT ONE

ACT TWO

Council chamber in the Emperor's palace, hung with heavy tapestry. Table, with chair of state, set for the Czar; window behind, opening on to a balcony. As the scene progresses the light outside gets darker. Present – PRINCE PAUL MARALOFFSKI, PRINCE PETROVITCH, COUNT ROUVALOFF, BARON RAFF, COUNT PETOUCHOF.

PRINCE PETROVITCH: So our young scatterbrained Czarevitch has been forgiven at last, and is to take his seat here again.

PRINCE PAUL: Yes, if that is not meant as an extra punishment. For my own part, at least, I find these cabinet councils extremely exhausting.

PRINCE PETROVITCH: Naturally; you are always speaking.

PRINCE PAUL: No; I think it must be that I have to listen sometimes.

COUNT ROUVALOFF: Still, anything is better than being kept in a sort of prison, like he was – never allowed to go out into the world.

PRINCE PAUL: My dear count, for romantic young people like he is, the world always looks best at a distance; and a prison where one's allowed to order one's own dinner is not at all a bad place.

Enter the CZAREVITCH; *the courtiers rise*

Ah! good afternoon, prince. Your highness is looking a little pale today.

CZAREVITCH (*slowly, after a pause*): I want a change of air.

PRINCE PAUL (*smiling*): A most revolutionary sentiment! Your imperial father would highly disapprove of any reforms with the thermometer in Russia.

CZAREVITCH (*bitterly*): My imperial father had kept me for six months in this dungeon of a palace This morning he had me suddenly woke up to see some wretched Nihilists hung; it sickened me, the bloody butchery, though it was a noble thing to see how well these men can die.

PRINCE PAUL: When you are as old as I am, prince, you will understand that there are few things easier than to live badly and to die well.

CZAREVITCH: Easy to die well! A lesson experience cannot have taught you, whatever you may know of a bad life.

PRINCE PAUL (*shrugging his shoulders*): Experience, the name men give to their mistakes. I never commit any.

CZAREVITCH (*bitterly*): No; crimes are more in your line.

PRINCE PETROVITCH (*to the* CZAREVITCH): The Emperor was a good deal agitated about your late appearance at the ball last night, prince.

COUNT ROUVALOFF (*laughing*): I believe he thought the Nihilists had broken into the palace and carried you off.

BARON RAFF: If they had you would have missed a charming dance.

PRINCE PAUL: And an excellent supper. Gringoire really excelled himself in his salad. Ah! you may laugh, baron; but to make a good salad is a much more difficult thing than cooking accounts. To make a good salad is to be a brilliant diplomatist – the problem is so entirely the same in both cases. To know exactly how much oil one must put with one's vinegar.

BARON RAFF: A cook and a diplomatist! an excellent parallel. If I had a son who was a fool I'd make him one or the other.

PRINCE PAUL: I see your father did not hold the same opinion, baron. But, believe me, you are wrong to run down cookery. For myself, the only immortality I desire is to invent a new sauce. I have never had time enough to think seriously about it, but I feel it is in me, I feel it is in me.

CZAREVITCH: You have certainly missed your *métier*, Prince Paul; the *cordon bleu* would have suited you much better than the Grand Cross of Honour. But you know you could never have worn your white apron well; you would have soiled it too soon, your hands are not clean enough.

PRINCE PAUL (*bowing*): Que voulez vous? I manage your father's business.

CZAREVITCH (*bitterly*): You mismanage my father's business, you mean! Evil genius of his life that you are! before you came there was some love left in him. It is you who have embittered his nature, poured into his ear the poison of treacherous counsel, made him hated by the whole people, made him what he is – a tyrant!

The courtiers look significantly at each other

PRINCE PAUL (*calmly*): I see your highness does want change of air. But I have been an eldest son myself. (*lights a cigarette*) I know what it is when a father won't die to please one.

The CZAREVITCH *goes to the top of the stage and leans against the window, looking out*

PRINCE PETROVITCH (*to* BARON RAFF): Foolish boy! He will be sent into exile, or worse, if he is not careful.

BARON RAFF: Yes. What a mistake it is to be sincere!

PRINCE PETROVITCH: The only folly you have never committed, baron.

BARON RAFF: One has only one head, you know, prince.

PRINCE PAUL: My dear baron, your head is the last thing anyone would wish to take from you. (*Pulls out snuffbox and offers it to* PRINCE PETROVITCH)

PRINCE PETROVITCH: Thanks, prince! Thanks!

PRINCE PAUL: Very delicate, isn't it? I get it direct from Paris. But under this vulgar Republic everything has degenerated over there. 'Cotelettes à l'impériale' vanished, of course, with the Bourbon, and omelettes went out with the Orleanists. La belle France is entirely ruined, prince, through bad morals and worse cookery.

Enter the MARQUIS DE POIVRARD

Ah! marquis. I trust Madame la Marquise is quite well.

MARQUIS DE POIVARD: You ought to know better than I do, Prince Paul; you see more *of* her.

PRINCE PAUL (*bowing*): Perhaps I see more in her, marquis. Your wife is really a charming woman, so full of *esprit*, and so satirical too; she talks continually of you when we are together.

PRINCE PETROVITCH (*looking at the clock*): His majesty is a little late today, is he not?

PRINCE PAUL: What has happened to you, my dear Petrovitch? you seem quite out of sorts. You haven't quarrelled with your cook, I hope? What a tragedy that would be for you; you would lose all your friends.

PRINCE PETROVITCH: I fear I wouldn't be so fortunate as that. You forget I would still have my purse. But you are wrong for once; my chef and I are on excellent terms.

PRINCE PAUL: Then your creditors or Mademoiselle Vera Sabouroff have been writing to you? I find both of them such excellent correspondents. But really you needn't be alarmed. I find the most violent proclamations from the Executive Committee, as they call it, left all over my house. I never read them; they are so badly spelt as a rule.

PRINCE PETROVITCH: Wrong again, prince; the Nihilists leave me alone for some reason or other.

PRINCE PAUL (*aside*): Ah! true. I forgot. Indifference is the revenge the world takes on mediocrities.

PRINCE PETROVITCH: I am bored with life, prince. Since the opera season ended I have been a perpetual martyr to *ennui*.

PRINCE PAUL: The *maladie du siècle*! You want a new excitement, prince. Let me see – you have been married twice already; suppose you try – falling in love, for once.

BARON RAFF: Prince, I have been thinking a good deal lately –

PRINCE PAUL (*interrupting*): You surprise me very much, baron.

BARON RAFF: I cannot understand your nature.

PRINCE PAUL (*smiling*): If my nature had been made to suit your comprehension rather than my own requirements, I am afraid I would have made a very poor figure in the world.

COUNT ROUVALOFF: There seems to be nothing in life about which you would not jest.

PRINCE PAUL: Ah! my dear count, life is much too important a thing ever to talk seriously about it.

CZAREVITCH (*coming back from the window*): I don't think Prince Paul's nature is such a mystery. He would stab his best friend for the sake of writing an epigram on his tombstone, or experiencing a new sensation.

PRINCE PAUL: *Parbleu!* I would sooner lose my best friend than my worst enemy. To have friends, you know, one need only be good-natured; but when a man has no enemy left there must be something mean about him.

CZAREVITCH (*bitterly*): If to have enemies is a measure of greatness, then you must be a colossus, indeed, prince.

PRINCE PAUL: Yes, I know I'm the most hated man in Russia, except your father, except your father, of course, prince. He doesn't seem to like it much, by the way, but I do, I assure you. (*bitterly*) I love to drive through the streets and see how the *canaille* scowl at me from every corner. It makes me feel I am a power in Russia; one man against a hundred millions! Besides, I have no ambition to be a popular hero, to be crowned with laurels one year and pelted with stones the next; I prefer dying peaceably in my own bed.

CZAREVITCH: And after death?

PRINCE PAUL (*shrugging his shoulders*): Heaven is a despotism. I shall be at home there.

CZAREVITCH: Do you never think of the people and their rights?

PRINCE PAUL: The people and their rights bore me. I am sick of both. In these modern days to be vulgar, illiterate, common and vicious, seems to give a man a marvellous infinity of rights that his honest fathers never dreamed of. Believe me, prince, in a good democracy every man should be an aristocrat; but these people in Russia who seek to thrust us out are no better than the animals in one's preserves, and made to be shot at, most of them.

CZAREVITCH (*excitedly*): If they are common, illiterate, vulgar, no better than the beasts of the field, who made them so?

Enter AIDE-DE-CAMP

AIDE-DE-CAMP: His imperial majesty, the Emperor! (PRINCE PAUL *looks at the* CZAREVITCH, *and smiles*)

Enter the CZAR, *surrounded by his guard*

CZAREVITCH (*rushing forward to meet him*): Sire!

CZAR (*nervous and frightened*): Don't come too near me, boy! Don't come too near me, I say! There is always something about an heir to a crown unwholesome to his father. Who is that man over there? I don't know him. What is he doing? Is he a conspirator? Have you searched him? Give him till tomorrow to confess, then hang him! – hang him!

PRINCE PAUL: Sire, you are anticipating history. This is Count Petouchof, your new ambassador to Berlin. He is come to kiss hands on his appointment.

CZAR: To kiss my hand? There is some plot in it. He wants to poison me. There, kiss my son's hand! it will do quite as well.

PRINCE PAUL *signs to* PETOUCHOF *to leave the room. Exit* PETOUCHOF *and the guards.* CZAR *sinks down into his chair. The courtiers remain silent*

PRINCE PAUL (*approaching*): Sire! will your majesty –

CZAR: What do you startle me like that for? No, I won't. (*watches the courtiers nervously*) Why are you clattering your sword, sir? (*To* COUNT ROUVALOFF) Take it off, I shall have no man wear a sword in my presence (*looking at* CZAREVITCH), least of all my son. (*To* PRINCE PAUL) You are not angry with me, prince? You won't desert me, will you? Say you won't desert me. What do you want? You can have anything – anything.

PRINCE PAUL (*bowing very low*): Sire! 'tis enough for me to have your confidence. (*Aside*) I was afraid he was going to revenge himself, and give me another decoration.

CZAR (*returning to his chair*): Well, gentlemen.

MARQUIS DE POIVRARD: Sire, I have the honour to present to you a loyal address from your subjects in the province of Archangel, expressing their horror at the last attempt on your majesty's life.

PRINCE PAUL: The last attempt but two, you ought to have said, marquis. Don't you see it is dated three weeks back?

CZAR: They are good people in the province of Archangel – honest, loyal people. They love me very much – simple, loyal people; give them a new saint, it costs nothing. Well, Alexis (*turning to the* CZAREVITCH) – how many traitors were hung this morning?

CZAREVITCH: There were three men strangled, sire.

CZAR: There should have been three thousand. I would to God that this people had but one neck that I might strangle them with one noose! Did they tell anything? whom did they implicate? what did they confess?

CZAREVITCH: Nothing, sire.

CZAR: They should have been tortured then; why weren't they tortured? Must I always be fighting in the dark? Am I never to know from what root these traitors spring?

CZAREVITCH: What root should there be of discontent among the people but tyranny and injustice amongst their rulers?

CZAR: What did you say, boy? tyranny! tyranny! Am I a tyrant? I am not. I love the people. I'm their father. I'm called so in every official proclamation. Have a care, boy; have a care. You don't seem to be cured yet of your foolish tongue. (*Goes over to* PRINCE PAUL *and puts his hand on his shoulder*) Prince Paul, tell me, were there many people there this morning to see the Nihilists hung?

PRINCE PAUL: Hanging is of course a good deal less of a novelty in Russia now, sire, than it was three or four years ago; and you know how easily the people get tired even of their best amusements. But the square and the tops of the houses were really quite crowded, were they not, prince? (*to the* CZAREVITCH *who takes no notice*)

CZAR: That's right; all loyal citizens should be there. It shows them what to look forward to. Did you arrest anyone in the crowd?

PRINCE PAUL: Yes, sire, a woman for cursing your name. (*The* CZAREVITCH *starts anxiously*) She was the mother of the two criminals.

CZAR (*looking at* CZAREVITCH): She should have blessed me for having rid her of her children. Send her to prison.

CZAREVITCH: The prisons of Russia are too full already, sire. There is no room in them for any more victims.

CZAR: They don't die fast enough, then. You should put more of them into one cell at once. You don't keep them long enough in the mines. If you do they're sure to die; but you're all too merciful. I'm too merciful myself. Send her to Siberia. She is sure to die on the way. (*Enter an* AIDE-DE-CAMP) Who's that? Who's that?

AIDE-DE-CAMP: A letter for his imperial majesty.

CZAR (*to* PRINCE PAUL): I won't open it. There may be something in it.

PRINCE PAUL: It would be a very disappointing letter, sire, if there wasn't. (*takes letter himself, and reads it*)

PRINCE PETROVITCH (*to* COUNT ROUVALOFF): It must be some sad news. I know that smile too well.

PRINCE PAUL: From the Chief of Police at Archangel, sire. 'The Governor of the province was shot this morning by a woman as he was entering the courtyard of his own house. The assassin has been seized.'

CZAR: I never trusted the people of Archangel. It's a nest of Nihilists and conspirators. Take away their saints; they don't deserve them.

PRINCE PAUL: Your Highness would punish them more severely by giving them an extra one. Three governors shot in two months. (*smiles to himself*) Sire, permit me to recommend your loyal subject, the Marquis de Poivrard, as the new governor of your province of Archangel.

MARQUIS DE POIVRARD (*hurriedly*): Sire, I am unfit for this post.

PRINCE PAUL: Marquis, you are too modest. Believe me, there is no man in Russia I would sooner see Governor of Archangel than yourself. (*whispers to* CZAR)

CZAR: Quite right, Prince Paul; you are always right. See that the marquis's letters are made out at once.

PRINCE PAUL: He can start tonight, sire. I shall really miss you very much, marquis. I always liked your tastes in wines and wives extremely.

MARQUIS DE POIVRARD (*to the* CZAR): Start tonight, sire?

PRINCE PAUL *whispers to the* CZAR

CZAR: Yes, marquis, tonight; it is better to go at once.

PRINCE PAUL: I shall see that Madame la Marquise is not too lonely while you are away; so you need not be alarmed for her.

COUNT ROUVALOFF (*to* PRINCE PETROVITCH): I should be more alarmed for myself.

CZAR: The Governor of Archangel shot in his own courtyard by a woman! I'm not safe here. I'm not safe anywhere, with that she-devil of the revolution, Vera Sabouroff, here in Moscow. Prince Paul, is that woman still here?

PRINCE PAUL: They tell me she was at the Grand Duke's ball last night. I can hardly believe that; but she certainly had intended to leave for Novgorod today, sire. The police were watching every train for her; but, for some reason or other, she did not go. Some traitor must have warned her. But I shall catch her yet. A chase after a beautiful woman is always exciting.

CZAR: You must hunt her down with bloodhounds, and when she is taken I shall hew her limb from limb. I shall stretch her on the rack till her pale white body is twisted and curled like paper in the fire.

PRINCE PAUL: Oh, we shall have another hunt immediately for her, sire! Prince Alexis will assist us, I am sure.

CZAREVITCH: You never require any assistance to ruin a woman, Prince Paul.

CZAR: Vera, the Nihilist, in Moscow! O God, were it not better to die at once the dog's death they plot for me than to live as I live now! Never to sleep, or, if I do, to dream such horrid dreams that hell itself were peace when matched with them. To trust none but those I have bought, to buy none worth trusting! To see a traitor in every smile, poison in every dish, a dagger in every hand! To lie awake at night, listening from hour to hour for the stealthy creeping of the murderer, for the laying of the damned mine! You are all spies! you are all spies! You worst of all – you, my own son! Which of you is it who hides these bloody proclamations under my own pillow, or at the table where I sit? Which of ye all is the Judas who betrays me? O God! O God! methinks there was a time once, in our war with England, when nothing could make me afraid. (*This with more calm and pathos*) I have ridden into the crimson heart of war, and borne back an eagle which those wild islanders had taken from us. Men said I was brave then. My father gave me the Iron Cross of valour. Oh, could he see me now with this coward's livery ever in my cheek! (*Sinks into his chair*) I never knew any love when I was a boy. I was ruled by terror myself, how else should I rule now? (*Starts up*) But I will have revenge; I will have revenge. For every hour I have lain awake at night, waiting for the noose or the dagger, they shall pass years in Siberia, centuries in the mines! Ay! I shall have revenge.

CZAREVITCH: Father! have mercy on the people. Give them what they ask.

PRINCE PAUL: And begin, sire, with your own head; they have a particular liking for that.

CZAR: The people! the people! A tiger which I have let loose upon myself; but I will fight with it to the death. I am done with half measures. I shall crush these Nihilists at a blow. There shall not be a man of them, ay, or a woman either, left alive in Russia. Am I emperor for nothing, that a woman should hold me at bay? Vera Sabouroff shall be in my power, I swear it, before a week is ended, though I burn my whole city to find her. She shall be flogged by the knout, stifled in the fortress, strangled in the square!

CZAREVITCH: O God!

CZAR: For two years her hands have been clutching at my throat; for two years she has made my life a hell; but I shall have revenge. Martial law, prince, martial law over the whole empire; that will give me revenge. A good measure, prince, eh? a good measure.

PRINCE PAUL: And an economical one too, sire. It would carry off your surplus population in six months; and save you many expenses in courts of justice; they will not be needed now.

CZAR: Quite right. There are too many people in Russia, too much money spent on them, too much money in courts of justice. I'll shut them up.

CZAREVITCH: Sire, reflect before –

CZAR: When can you have the proclamations ready, Prince Paul?

PRINCE PAUL: They have been printed for the last six months, sire. I knew you would need them.

CZAR: That's good! That's very good! Let us begin at once. Ah, prince, if every king in Europe had a minister like you –

CZAREVITCH: There would be fewer kings in Europe than there are.

CZAR (*in frightened whisper, to* PRINCE PAUL): What does he mean? Do you trust him? His prison hasn't cured him yet? Shall I banish him? Shall I (*whispers*) . . . ? The Emperor Paul did it. The Empress Catherine there (*points to picture on the wall*) did it. Why shouldn't I?

PRINCE PAUL: Your majesty, there is no need for alarm. The prince is a very ingenuous young man. He pretends to be devoted to the people, and lives in a palace; preaches socialism, and draws a salary that would support a province. He'll find out one day that the best cure for republicanism is the imperial crown, and will cut up the 'bonnet rouge' of democracy to make decorations for his prime minister.

CZAR: You are right. If he really loved the people, he could not be my son.

PRINCE PAUL: If he lived with the people for a fortnight, their bad dinners would soon cure him of his democracy. Shall we begin, sire!

CZAR: At once. Read the proclamation. Gentlemen, be seated. Alexis, Alexis, I say, come and hear it! It will be good practice for you; you will be doing it yourself some day.

CZAREVITCH: I have heard too much of it already. (*Takes his seat at the table.* COUNT ROUVALOFF *whispers to him*)

CZAR: What are you whispering about there, Count Rouvaloff?

COUNT ROUVALOFF: I was giving his royal highness some good advice, your majesty.

PRINCE PAUL: Count Rouvaloff is the typical spendthrift, sire; he is always giving away what he needs most. (*Lays papers before the* CZAR) I think, sire, you will approve of this – 'love of the people', 'father of his people', 'martial law', and the usual allusions to Providence in the last line. All it requires now is your imperial majesty's signature.

CZAREVITCH: Sire!

PRINCE PAUL (*hurriedly*): I promise your majesty to crush every Nihilist in Russia in six months if you sign this proclamation; every Nihilist in Russia.

CZAR: Say that again! To crush every Nihilist in Russia; to crush this woman, their leader, who makes war upon me in my own city? Prince Paul Maraloffski, I create you field marshal of the whole Russian Empire to help you to carry out martial law. Give me the proclamation. I will sign it at once.

PRINCE PAUL (*points on paper*): Here, sire.

CZAREVITCH (*starts up and puts his hands on the paper*) Stay! I tell you, stay! The priests have taken heaven from the people, and you would take the earth away too.

PRINCE PAUL: We have no time, prince, now. This boy will ruin everything. The pen, sire.

CZAREVITCH: What! is it so small a thing to strangle a nation, to murder a kingdom, to wreck an empire? Who are we who dare lay this ban of terror on a people? Have we less vices than they have, that we bring them to the bar of judgment before us?

PRINCE PAUL: What a communist the prince is! He would have an equal distribution of sin as well as of property.

CZAREVITCH: Warmed by the same sun, nurtured by the same air, fashioned of flesh and blood like to our own, wherein are they different from us, save that they starve while we surfeit, that they toil while we idle, that they sicken while we poison, that they die while we strangle?

CZAR: How dare – ?

CZAREVITCH: I dare all for the people; but you would rob them of the common rights of common men.

CZAR: The people have no rights.

CZAREVITCH: Then they have great wrongs. Father, they have won your battles for you; from the pine forests of the Baltic to the palms of India they have ridden on victory's mighty wings in search of your glory! Boy as I am in years, I have seen wave after wave of living men sweep up the heights of battle to their death; ay, and snatch perilous conquest from the scales of war when the bloody crescent seemed to shake above our eagles.

CZAR (*somewhat moved*): Those men are dead. What have I to do with them?

CZAREVITCH: Nothing! The dead are safe; you cannot harm them now. They sleep their last long sleep. Some in Turkish waters, others by the windswept heights of Norway and the Dane! But these, the living, our brothers, what have you done for them? They asked you for bread, you gave them a stone. They sought for freedom, you scourged them with scorpions. You have sown the seeds of this revolution yourself!

PRINCE PAUL: And are we not cutting down the harvest?

CZAREVITCH: O my brothers! better far that ye had died in the iron hail and screaming shells of battle than to come back to such a doom as this! The beasts of the forests have their lairs, and the wild beasts their caverns, but the people of Russia, conquerors of the world, have not where to lay their heads.

PRINCE PAUL: They have the headsman's block.

CZAREVITCH: The headsman's block! Ay! you have killed their souls at your pleasure, you would kill their bodies now.

CZAR: Insolent boy! Have you forgotten who is Emperor of Russia?

CZAREVITCH: No! The people reign now, by the grace of God. You should have been their shepherd; you have fled away like the hireling, and let the wolves in upon them.

CZAR: Take him away! Take him away, Prince Paul!

CZAREVITCH: God hath given this people tongues to speak with; you would cut them out that they may be dumb in their agony, silent in their torture! But God hath given them hands to smite with and they shall smite! Ay! from the sick and labouring womb of this unhappy land some revolution, like a bloody child, shall rise up and slay you.

CZAR (*leaping up*): Devil! Assassin! Why do you beard me thus to my face?

CZAREVITCH: Because I am a Nihilist!

The ministers start to their feet; there is a dead silence for a few minutes

CZAR: A Nihilist! a Nihilist! Scorpion whom I have nurtured, traitor whom I have fondled, is this your bloody secret? Prince Paul Maraloffski, Field Marshal of the Russian Empire, arrest the Czarevitch!

MINISTERS: Arrest the Czarevitch!

CZAR: A Nihilist! If you have sown with them, you shall reap with them! If you have talked with them, you shall rot with them! If you have lived with them, with them you shall die!

PRINCE PETROVITCH: Die!

CZAR: A plague on all sons, I say! There should be no more marriages in Russia when one can breed such vipers as you are! Arrest the Czarevitch, I say!

PRINCE PAUL: Czarevitch! by order of the Emperor, I demand your sword. (CZAREVITCH *gives up sword;* PRINCE PAUL *places it on the table*) Foolish boy! you are not made for a conspirator; you have not learned to hold your tongue. Heroics are out of place in a palace.

CZAR (*sinks into his chair with his eyes fixed on the* CZAREVITCH) O God!

CZAREVITCH: If I am to die for the people, I am ready; one Nihilist more or less in Russia, what does that matter?

PRINCE PAUL (*aside*): A good deal, I should say, to the one Nihilist.

CZAREVITCH: The mighty brotherhood to which I belong has a thousand such as I am, ten thousand better still! (*The* CZAR *starts in his seat*) The star of freedom has risen already, and far off I hear the mighty wave democracy break on these cursed shores.

PRINCE PAUL (*to* PRINCE PETROVITCH): In that case you and I had better learn how to swim.

CZAREVITCH: Father, Emperor, imperial master, I plead not for my own life, but for the lives of my brothers, the people.

PRINCE PAUL (*bitterly*): Your brothers, the people, prince, are not content with their own lives, they always want to take their neighbour's too.

CZAR (*standing up*): I am sick of being afraid. I have done with terror now. From this day I proclaim war against the people – war to their annihilation. As they have dealt with me, so shall I deal with them. I shall grind them to powder, and strew their dust upon the air. There shall be a spy in every man's house, a traitor on every hearth, a hangman in every village, a gibbet in every square. Plague, leprosy or fever shall be less deadly than my wrath; I will make every frontier a graveyard, every province a lazar-house, and cure the sick by the sword. I shall have peace in Russia, though it be the peace of the dead. Who said I was a coward? Who said I was afraid? See, thus shall I crush this people beneath my feet! (*takes up sword of* CZAREVITCH *off table and tramples on it*)

CZAREVITCH: Father, beware the sword you tread on may turn and wound you. The people suffer long, but vengeance comes at last, vengeance with red hands and bloody purpose.

PRINCE PAUL: Bah! the people are bad shots; they always miss one.

CZAREVITCH: There are times when the people are instruments of God.

CZAR: Ay! and when kings are God's scourges for the people. Oh, my own son, in my own house! My own flesh and blood against me! Take him away! Take him away! Bring in my guards. (*Enter the Imperial Guard.* CZAR *points to* CZAREVITCH, *who stands alone at the side of the stage*) To the blackest prison in Moscow! Let me never see his face again. (CZAREVITCH *is being led out*) No, no, leave him! I don't trust guards. They are all Nihilists! They would let him escape and he would kill me, kill me! No, I'll bring him to prison myself, you and I (*to* PRINCE PAUL). I trust you, you have no mercy. I shall have no mercy. Oh, my own son against me! How hot it is! The air stifles me! I feel as if I were going to faint, as if something were at my throat. Open the windows I say! Out of my sight! Out of my sight! I can't bear his eyes. Wait, wait for me. (*throws windows open and goes out on balcony*)

PRINCE PAUL (*looking at his watch*): The dinner is sure to be spoiled. How annoying politics are and eldest sons!

VOICE (*outside, in the street*): God save the people! (CZAR *is shot, and staggers back into the room*)

CZAREVITCH (*breaking from the guards and rushing over*): Father!

CZAR: Murderer! Murderer! You did it. Murderer! (*dies*)

END OF ACT TWO

ACT THREE

Same scene and business as Act One. Man in yellow dress, with drawn sword, at the door.

VOICE *(outside)*: *Vae tyrannis.*
ANSWER: *Vae victis (repeated three times).*

Enter conspirators, who form a semicircle, masked and cloaked

PRESIDENT: What hour is it?
FIRST CONSPIRATOR: The hour to strike.
PRESIDENT: What day?
SECOND CONSPIRATOR: The day of Marat.
PRESIDENT: In what month?
THIRD CONSPIRATOR: The month of liberty.
PRESIDENT: What is our duty?
FOURTH CONSPIRATOR: To obey.
PRESIDENT: Our creed?
FIFTH CONSPIRATOR: Parbleu, Monsieur le President, I never knew you had one.
CONSPIRATORS: A spy! A spy! Unmask! Unmask! A spy!
PRESIDENT: Let the doors be shut. There are others but Nihilists present.
CONSPIRATORS: Unmask! Unmask! Kill him! kill him! (*Masked conspirator unmasks*) Prince Paul!
VERA: Devil! Who lured you into the lions' den!
CONSPIRATORS: Kill him! kill him!
PRINCE PAUL: En vérité, messieurs, you are not over-hospitable in your welcome!
VERA: Welcome! What welcome should we give you but the dagger or the noose?
PRINCE PAUL: I had no idea, really, that the Nihilists were so exclusive. Let me assure you that if I had not always had an *entrée* to the very best society, and the very worst conspirators, I could never have been prime minister in Russia.
VERA: The tiger cannot change its nature, nor the snake lose its venom; but are you turned a lover of the people?

PRINCE PAUL: Mon dieu, non, mademoiselle! I would much sooner talk scandal in a drawing-room than treason in a cellar. Besides, I hate the common mob, who smell of garlic, smoke bad tobacco, get up early, and dine off one dish.

PRESIDENT: What have you to gain, then, by a revolution?

PRINCE PAUL: Mon ami, I have nothing left to lose. That scatter-brained boy, this new Czar, has banished me.

VERA: To Siberia?

PRINCE PAUL: No, to Paris. He has confiscated my estates, robbed me of my office and my cook. I have nothing left but my decorations. I am here for revenge.

PRESIDENT: Then you have a right to be one of us. We also meet daily for revenge.

PRINCE PAUL: You want money, of course. No one ever joins a conspiracy who has any. Here. (*Throws money on table*) You have so many spies that I should think you want information. Well, you will find me the best informed man in Russia on the abuses of our government. I made them nearly all myself.

VERA: President, I don't trust this man. He has done us too much harm in Russia to let him go in safety.

PRINCE PAUL: Believe me, mademoiselle, you are wrong; I will be a most valuable addition to your circle; as for you, gentlemen, if I had not thought that you would be useful to me I shouldn't have risked my neck among you, or dined an hour earlier than usual so as to be in time.

PRESIDENT: Ay, if he had wanted to spy on us, Vera, he wouldn't have come himself.

PRINCE PAUL (*aside*): No; I should have sent my best friend.

PRESIDENT: Besides, Vera, he is just the man to give us the information we want about some business we have in hand tonight.

VERA: Be it so if you wish it.

PRESIDENT: Brothers, is it your will that Prince Paul Maraloffski be admitted, and take the oath of the Nihilist?

CONSPIRATORS: It is! it is!

PRESIDENT (*holding out dagger and a paper*): Prince Paul, the dagger or the oath?

PRINCE PAUL (*smiles sardonically*): I would sooner annihilate than be annihilated. (*takes paper*)

PRESIDENT: Remember: Betray us, and as long as the earth holds poison or steel, as long as men can strike or woman betray, you shall not escape vengeance. The Nihilists never forget their friends, nor forgive their enemies.

PRINCE PAUL: Really? I did not think you were so civilised.

VERA (*pacing up and down*): Why is he not here? He will not keep the crown. I know him well.

PRESIDENT: Sign. (PRINCE PAUL *signs*) You said you thought we had no creed. You were wrong. Read it!

VERA: This is a dangerous thing, president. What can we do with this man?

PRESIDENT: We can use him.

VERA: And afterwards?

PRESIDENT (*shrugging his shoulders*): Strangle him.

PRINCE PAUL (*reading*): 'The rights of humanity!' In the old times men carried out their rights for themselves as they lived, but nowadays every baby seems born with a social manifesto in its mouth much bigger than itself. 'Nature is not a temple, but a workshop: we demand the right to labour.' Ah, I shall surrender my own rights in that respect.

VERA (*pacing up and down behind*): Oh, will he never come? will he never come?

PRINCE PAUL: 'The family, as subversive of true socialistic and communal unity, is to be annihilated.' Yes, president, I agree completely with Article Five. A family is a terrible incumbrance, especially when one is not married. (*Three knocks at the door*)

VERA: Alexis at last!

VOICE: *Vae tyrannis!*

ANSWER: *Vae victis!*

Enter MICHAEL STROGANOFF

PRESIDENT: Michael, the regicide! Brothers, let us do honour to a man who has killed a king.

VERA (*aside*): Oh, he will come yet.

PRESIDENT: Michael, you have saved Russia.

MICHAEL: Ay, Russia was free for a moment when the tyrant fell, but the sun of liberty has set again like that false dawn which cheats our eyes in autumn.

PRESIDENT: The dread night of tyranny is not yet past for Russia?

MICHAEL (*clutching his knife*): One more blow, and the end is come indeed.

VERA (*aside*): One more blow! What does he mean? Oh, impossible! but why is he not with us? Alexis! Alexis! why are you not here?

PRESIDENT: But how did you escape, Michael? They said you had been seized.

MICHAEL: I was dressed in the uniform of the Imperial Guard. The colonel on duty was a brother, and gave me the password. I drove through the troops in safety with it, and, thanks to my good horse, reached the walls before the gates were closed.

PRESIDENT: What a chance his coming out on the balcony was!

MICHAEL: A chance? There is no such thing as chance. It was God's finger led him there.

PRESIDENT: And where have you been these three days?

MICHAEL: Hiding in the house of the priest Nicholas at the cross-roads.

PRESIDENT: Nicholas is an honest man.

MICHAEL: Ay, honest enough for a priest. I am here now for vengeance on a traitor.

VERA (*aside*): O God, will he never come? Alexis! why are you not here? You cannot have turned traitor!

MICHAEL (*seeing* PRINCE PAUL): Prince Paul Maraloffski here! By George, a lucky capture! This must have been Vera's doing. She is the only one who could have lured that serpent into the trap.

PRESIDENT: Prince Paul has just taken the oath.

VERA: Alexis, the Czar, has banished him from Russia.

MICHAEL: Bah! A blind to cheat us. We will keep Prince Paul here, and find some office for him in our reign of terror. He is well accustomed by this time to bloody work.

PRINCE PAUL (*approaching* MICHAEL): That was a long shot of yours, mon camarade.

MICHAEL: I have had a good deal of practice shooting, since I was a boy, off your highness's wild boars.

PRINCE PAUL: Are my gamekeepers like moles then, always asleep!

MICHAEL: No, prince. I am one of them, but like you I am fond of robbing what I am put to watch.

PRESIDENT: This must be a new atmosphere for you, Prince Paul. We speak the truth to one another here.

PRINCE PAUL: How misleading you must find it. You have an odd medley here, president – a little rococo, I am afraid.

PRESIDENT: You recognise a good many friends, I dare say?

PRINCE PAUL: Yes, there is always more brass than brains in an aristocracy.

PRESIDENT: But you are here yourself?

PRINCE PAUL: I? As I cannot be prime minister, I must be a Nihilist. There is no alternative.

VERA: O God, will he never come? The hand is on the stroke of the hour. Will he never come?

MICHAEL (*aside*): President, you know what we have to do? 'Tis but a sorry hunter who leaves the wolf cub alive to avenge his father. How are we to get at this boy? It must be tonight. Tomorrow he will be throwing some sop of reform to the people, and it will be too late for a republic.

PRINCE PAUL: You are quite right. Good kings are the enemies of democracy, and when he has begun by banishing me you may be sure he intends to be a patriot.

MICHAEL: I am sick of patriot kings, what Russia needs is a republic.

PRINCE PAUL: Messieurs, I have brought you two documents which I think will interest you – the proclamation which this young Czar intends publishing tomorrow, and a plan of the Winter Palace, where he sleeps tonight. (*hands paper*)

VERA: I dare not ask them what they are plotting about. Oh, why is Alexis not here?

PRESIDENT: Prince, this is most valuable information. Michael, you were right. If it is not tonight it will be too late. Read that.

MICHAEL: Ah! A loaf of bread flung to a starving nation. A lie to cheat the people. (*tears it up*) It must be tonight. I do not believe in him. Would he have kept his crown had he loved the people? But how are we to get at him?

PRINCE PAUL: The key of the private door in the street. (*hands key*)

PRESIDENT: Prince, we are in your debt.

PRINCE PAUL (*smiling*): The normal condition of the Nihilists.

MICHAEL: Ay, but we are paying our debts off with interest now. Two emperors in one week. That will make the balance straight. We would have thrown in a prime minister if you had not come.

PRINCE PAUL: Ah, I am sorry you told me. It robs my visit of all its picturesqueness and adventure. I thought I was perilling my head by coming here, and you tell me I have saved it. One is sure to be disappointed if one tries to get romance out of modern life.

MICHAEL: It is not so romantic a thing to lose one's head, Prince Paul.

PRINCE PAUL: No, but it must often be very dull to keep it. Don't you find that sometimes? (*clock strikes six*)

VERA (*sinking into a seat*): Oh, it is past the hour! It is past the hour!

MICHAEL (*to* PRESIDENT): Remember tomorrow will be too late.

PRESIDENT: Brothers, it is full time. Which of us is absent?

CONSPIRATORS: Alexis! Alexis!

PRESIDENT: Michael, read Rule Seven.

MICHAEL: 'When any brother shall have disobeyed a summons to be present, the president shall enquire if there is anything alleged against him.'

PRESIDENT: Is there anything against our brother Alexis?

CONSPIRATOR: He wears a crown! He wears a crown!

PRESIDENT: Michael, read Article Seven of the Code of Revolution.

MICHAEL: 'Between the Nihilists and all men who wear crowns above their fellows, there is war to the death.'

PRESIDENT: Brothers, what say you? Is Alexis, the Czar, guilty or not?

ALL: He is guilty!

PRESIDENT: What shall the penalty be?

ALL: Death!

PRESIDENT: Let the lots be prepared; it shall be tonight.

PRINCE PAUL: Ah, this is really interesting! I was getting afraid conspiracies were as dull as courts are.

PROFESSOR MARFA: My forte is more in writing pamphlets than in taking shots. Still a regicide has always a place in history.

MICHAEL: If your pistol is as harmless as your pen, this young tyrant will have a long life.

PRINCE PAUL: You ought to remember, too, professor, that if you were seized, as you probably would be, and hung, as you certainly would be, there would be nobody left to read your own articles.

PRESIDENT: Brothers, are you ready?

VERA (*starting up*): Not yet! Not yet! I have a word to say.

MICHAEL (*aside*): Plague take her! I knew it would come to this.

VERA: This boy has been our brother. Night after night he has perilled his own life to come here. Night after night, when every street was filled with spies, every house with traitors. Delicately nurtured like a king's son, he has dwelt among us.

PRESIDENT: Ay! under a false name. He lied to us at the beginning. He lies to us now at the end.

VERA: I swear he is true. There is not a man here who does not owe him his life a thousand times. When the bloodhounds were on us that night, who saved us from arrest, torture, flogging, death, but he ye seek to kill?

MICHAEL: To kill all tyrants is our mission!

VERA: He is no tyrant. I know him well! He loves the people.

PRESIDENT: We know him too; he is a traitor.

VERA: A traitor! Three days ago he could have betrayed every man of you here, and the gibbet would have been your doom. He gave you all your lives once. Give him a little time – a week, a month, a few days; but not now! – O God, not now!

CONSPIRATORS (*brandishing daggers*): Tonight! tonight! tonight!

VERA: Peace, you gorged adders; peace!

MICHAEL: What, are we not here to annihilate? shall we not keep our oath?

VERA: Your oath! your oath! Greedy that you are of gain, every man's hand lusting for his neighbour's pelf, every heart set on pillage and rapine; who, of ye all, if the crown were set on his head, would give an empire up for the mob to scramble for? The people are not ye fit for a republic in Russia.

PRESIDENT: Every nation is fit for a republic.

MICHAEL: The man is a tyrant.

VERA: A tyrant! Hath he not dismissed his evil counsellors? That ill-omened raven of his father's life hath had his wings clipped and his claws pared, and comes to us croaking for revenge. Oh, have mercy on him! Give him a week to live!

PRESIDENT: Vera pleading for a king!

VERA (*proudly*): I plead not for a king, but for a brother.

MICHAEL: For a traitor to his oath, for a coward who should have flung the purple back to the fools that gave it to him. No, Vera, no. The brood of men is not dead yet, nor the dull earth grown sick of child-bearing. No crowned man in Russia shall pollute God's air by living.

PRESIDENT: You bade us try you once; we have tried you, and you are found wanting.

MICHAEL: Vera, I am not blind; I know your secret. You love this boy, this young prince with his pretty face, his curled hair, his soft white hands. Fool that you are, dupe of a lying tongue, do you know what he would have done to you, this boy you think loved you? He would have made you his mistress, used your body at his pleasure, thrown you away when he was wearied of you; you, the priestess of liberty, the flame of revolution, the torch of democracy.

VERA: What he would have done to me matters little. To the people, at least, he will be true. He loves the people – at least, he loves liberty.

PRESIDENT: So he would play the citizen-king, would he, while we starve? Would flatter us with sweet speeches, would cheat us with promises like his father, would lie to us as his whole race have lied?

MICHAEL: And you whose very name made every despot tremble for his life, you, Vera Sabouroff, you would betray liberty for a lover and the people for a paramour!

CONSPIRATORS: Traitress! Draw the lots; draw the lots!

VERA: In thy throat thou liest, Michael! I love him not. He loves me not.

MICHAEL: You love him not? Shall he not die then?

VERA (*with an effort, clenching her hands*): Ay, it is right that he should die. He hath broken his oath. There should be no crowned man in Europe. Have I not sworn it? To be strong our new republic should be drunk with the blood of kings. He hath broken his oath. As the father died so let the son die too. Yet not tonight, not tonight. Russia, that hath borne her centuries of wrong, can wait a week for liberty. Give him a week.

PRESIDENT: We will have none of you! Begone from us to this boy you love.

MICHAEL: Though I find him in your arms I shall kill him.

CONSPIRATORS: Tonight! Tonight! Tonight!

MICHAEL (*holding up his hand*): A moment! I have something to say. (*approaches* VERA; *speaks very slowly*) Vera Sabouroff, have you forgotten your brother? (*pauses to see effect*; VERA *starts*) Have you forgotten that young face, pale with famine; those young limbs, twisted with torture; the iron chains they made him walk in? What week of liberty did they give him? What pity did they show him for a day? (VERA *falls in a chair*) Oh! you could talk glibly enough then of vengeance, glibly enough of liberty. When you said you would come to Moscow, your old father caught you by the knees and begged you not to leave him childless and alone. I seem to hear his cries still ringing in my ears, but you were as deaf to him as the rocks on the roadside; as chill and cold as the snow on the hill. You left your father that night, and three weeks after he died of a broken heart. You wrote to me to follow you here. I did so; first because I loved you; but you soon cured me of that; whatever gentle feeling, whatever pity, whatever humanity, was in my heart you withered up and destroyed, as the canker worm eats the corn, and the plague kills the child. You bade me cast out love from my breast as a vile thing, you turned my hand to iron and my heart to stone; you told me to live for freedom and for revenge. I have done so; but you, what have you done?

VERA: Let the lots be drawn! (*Conspirators applaud*)

PRINCE PAUL (*aside*): Ah, the Grand Duke will come to the throne sooner than he expected. He is sure to make a good king under my guidance. He is so cruel to animals, and never keeps his word.

MICHAEL: Now you are yourself at last, Vera.

VERA (*standing motionless in the middle*): The lots, I say, the lots! I am no woman now. My blood seems turned to gall; my heart is as cold as steel is; my hand shall be more deadly. From the desert and the tomb the voice of my prisoned brother cries aloud, and bids me strike one blow for liberty. The lots, I say, the lots!

PRESIDENT: Are you ready? Michael, you have the right to draw first; you are a regicide.

VERA: O God, into my hands! Into my hands! (*They draw the lots from a bowl surmounted by a skull*)

PRESIDENT: Open your lots.

VERA (*opening her lot*): The lot is mine! see the bloody sign upon it! Dmitri, my brother, you shall have your revenge now.

PRESIDENT: Vera Sabouroff, you are chosen to be a regicide. God has been good to you. The dagger or the poison? (*offers her dagger and vial*)

VERA: I can trust my hand better with the dagger; it never fails. (*takes dagger*) I shall stab him to the heart, as he has stabbed me. Traitor, to leave us for a riband, a gaud, a bauble, to lie to me every day he came here, to forget us in an hour. Michael was right, he loved me not, nor the people either. Methinks that if I was a mother and bore a man-child I would poison my breast to him, lest he might grow to a traitor or to a king. (PRINCE PAUL *whispers to the* PRESIDENT)

PRESIDENT: Ay, Prince Paul, that is the best way. Vera, the Czar sleeps tonight in his own room in the north wing of the palace. Here is the key of the private door in the street. The passwords of the guards will be given to you. His own servants will be drugged. You will find him alone.

VERA: It is well. I shall not fail.

PRESIDENT: We will wait outside in the Place St Isaac, under the window. As the clock strikes twelve from the tower of St Nicholas you will give us the sign that the dog is dead.

VERA: And what shall the sign be?

PRESIDENT: You are to throw us out the bloody dagger.

MICHAEL: Dripping with the traitor's life.

PRESIDENT: Else we shall know that you have been seized, and we will burst our way in, drag you from his guards.

MICHAEL: And kill him in the midst of them.

PRESIDENT: Michael, will you head us?

MICHAEL: Ay, I shall head you. See that your hand fails not, Vera Sabouroff.

VERA: Fool, is it so hard to thing to kill one's enemy?

PRINCE PAUL (*aside*): This is the ninth conspiracy, I have been in in Russia. They always end in a 'voyage en Siberie' for my friends and a new decoration for myself.

MICHAEL: It is your last conspiracy, prince.

PRESIDENT: At twelve o'clock, the bloody dagger.

VERA: Ay, red with the blood of that false heart. I shall not forget it. (*Standing in the middle of the stage*) To strangle whatever nature is in me, neither to love nor to be loved, neither to pity nor to be pitied. Ay! it is an oath, an oath. Methinks the spirit of Charlotte Corday has entered my soul now. I shall carve my name on the world, and be ranked among the great heroines. Ay! the spirit of Charlotte Corday beats in each petty vein, and nerves my woman's hand to strike, as I have nerved my woman's heart to hate. Though he laugh in his dreams, I shall not falter. Though he sleep peacefully, I shall not miss my blow. Be glad, my brother, in your stifled cell; be glad and laugh tonight. Tonight this new-fledged Czar shall post with bloody feet to hell, and greet his father there! This Czar! O traitor, liar, false to his oath, false to me! To play the patriot amongst us, and now to wear a crown; to sell us, like Judas, for thirty silver pieces, to betray us with a kiss! (*With more passion*) O Liberty, O mighty mother of eternal time, thy robe is purple with the blood of those who have died for thee! Thy throne is the Calvary of the people, thy crown the crown of thorns. O crucified mother, the despot has driven a nail through thy right hand, and the tyrant through thy left! Thy feet are pierced with their iron. When thou wert athirst thou callest on the priests for water, and they gave thee bitter drink. They thrust a sword into thy side. They mocked thee in thine agony of age on age. Here, on thy altar, O Liberty, do I dedicate myself to thy service; do with me as thou wilt! (*brandishing dagger*) The end has come now, and by thy sacred wounds, O crucified mother, O Liberty, I swear that Russia shall be saved!

END OF ACT THREE

ACT FOUR

Antechamber of the Czar's private room. Large window at the back, with drawn curtains over it. Present – PRINCE PETROVITCH, BARON RAFF, MARQUIS DE POIVRARD, COUNT ROUVALOFF.

PRINCE PETROVITCH: He is beginning well, this young Czar.

BARON RAFF (*shrugs his shoulders*): All young Czars do begin well.

COUNT ROUVALOFF: And end badly.

MARQUIS DE POIVRARD: Well, I have no right to complain. He has done me one good service, at any rate.

PRINCE PETROVITCH: Cancelled your appointment to Archangel, I suppose?

MARQUIS DE POIVRARD: Yes; my head wouldn't have been safe there for an hour.

Enter GENERAL KOTEMKIN

BARON RAFF: Ah! general, any more news of our romantic Emperor?

GENERAL KOTEMKIN: You are quite right to call him romantic, baron; a week ago I found him amusing himself in a garret with a company of strolling players; today his whim is all the convicts in Siberia are to be recalled, and political prisoners, as he calls them, amnestied.

PRINCE PETROVITCH: Political prisoners! Why, half of them are no better than common murderers!

COUNT ROUVALOFF: And the other half much worse!

BARON RAFF: Oh, you wrong them, surely, count. Wholesale trade has always been more respectable than retail.

COUNT ROUVALOFF: But he is really too romantic. He objected yesterday to my having the monopoly of the salt tax. He said the people had a right to have cheap salt.

MARQUIS DE POIVRARD: Oh, that's nothing; but he actually disapproved of a state banquet every night because there is a famine in the southern provinces.

The young CZAR *enters unobserved, and overhears the rest*

PRINCE PETROVITCH: Quelle bétise! The more starvation there is among the people, the better. It teaches them self-denial, an excellent virtue, baron, an excellent virtue.

BARON RAFF: I have often heard so; I have often heard so.

GENERAL KOTEMKIN: He talked of a parliament, too, in Russia, and said the people should have deputies to represent them.

BARON RAFF: As if there was not enough brawling in the streets already, but we must give the people a room to do it in. But, messieurs, the worst is yet to come. He threatens a complete reform in the public service on the ground that the people are too heavily taxed.

MARQUIS DE POIVRARD: He can't be serious there. What is the use of the people except to get money out of? But talking of taxes, my dear baron, you must really let me have forty thousand roubles tomorrow? my wife says she must have a new diamond bracelet.

COUNT ROUVALOFF: (*aside to* BARON RAFF): Ah, to match the one Prince Paul gave her last week, I suppose.

PRINCE PETROVITCH: I must have sixty thousand roubles at once, baron. My son is overwhelmed with debts of honour which he can't pay.

BARON RAFF: What an excellent son to imitate his father so carefully!

GENERAL KOTEMKIN: You are always getting money. I never get a single kopeck I have not got a right to. It's unbearable; it's ridiculous! My nephew is going to be married. I must get his dowry for him.

PRINCE PETROVITCH: My dear general, your nephew must be a perfect Turk. He seems to get married three times a week regularly.

GENERAL KOTEMKIN: Well, he wants a dowry to console him.

COUNT ROUVALOFF: I am sick of the town. I want a house in the country.

MARQUIS DE POIVRARD: I am sick of the country. I want a house in town.

BARON RAFF: Mes amis, I am extremely sorry for you. It is out of the question.

PRINCE PETROVITCH: But my son, baron?

GENERAL KOTEMKIN: But my nephew?

MARQUIS DE POIVRARD: But my house in town?

COUNT ROUVALOFF: But my house in the country?

MARQUIS DE POIVRARD: But my wife's diamond bracelet?

BARON RAFF: Gentlemen, impossible! The old regime in Russia is dead; the funeral begins today.

COUNT ROUVALOFF: Then I shall wait for the resurrection.

PRINCE PETROVITCH: Yes, but, *en attendant*, what are we to do?

BARON RAFF: What have we always done in Russia when a Czar suggests reform? – nothing. You forget we are diplomatists. Men of thought should have nothing to do with action. Reforms in Russia are very tragic, but they always end in a farce.

COUNT ROUVALOFF: I wish Prince Paul were here. By the by, I think this boy is rather ungrateful to him. If that clever old prince had not proclaimed him Emperor at once without giving him time to think about it, he would have given up his crown, I believe, to the first cobbler he met in the street.

PRINCE PETROVITCH: But do you think, baron, that Prince Paul is really going?

BARON RAFF: He is exiled.

PRINCE PETROVITCH: Yes; but is he going?

BARON RAFF: I am sure of it; at least he told me he had sent two telegrams already to Paris about his dinner.

COUNT ROUVALOFF: Ah! that settles the matter.

CZAR (*coming forward*): Prince Paul better send a third telegram and order (*counting them*) six extra places.

BARON RAFF: The devil!

CZAR: No, baron, the Czar. Traitors! There would be no bad kings in the world if there were no bad ministers like you. It is men such as you who wreck mighty empires on the rock of their own greatness. Our mother, Russia, hath no need of such unnatural sons. You can make no atonement now; it is too late for that. The grave cannot give back your dead, nor the gibbet your martyrs, but I shall be more merciful to you. I give you your lives! That is the curse I would lay on you. But if there is a man of you found in Moscow by tomorrow night your heads will be off your shoulders.

BARON RAFF: You remind us wonderfully, sire, of your imperial father.

CZAR: I banish you all from Russia. Your estates are confiscated to the people. You may carry your titles with you. Reforms in Russia, baron, always end in a farce. You will have a good opportunity Prince Petrovitch, of practising self-denial, that excellent virtue! that excellent virtue! So, baron, you think a parliament in Russia would be merely a place for brawling. Well, I will see that the reports of each session are sent to you regularly.

BARON RAFF: Sire, you are adding another horror to exile.

CZAR: But you will have such time for literature now. You forget you are diplomatists. Men of thought should have nothing to do with action.

PRINCE PETROVITCH: Sire, we did but jest.

CZAR: Then I banish you for your bad jokes. Bon voyage, messieurs. If you value your lives you will catch the first train for Paris. (*Exeunt*

MINISTERS) Russia is well rid of such men as these. They are the jackals that follow in the lion's track. They have no courage themselves, except to pillage and rob. But for these men and for Prince Paul my father would have been a good king, would not have died so horribly as he did die. How strange it is, the most real parts of one's life always seem to be a dream! the council, the fearful law which was to kill the people, the arrest, the cry in the courtyard, the pistol-shot, my father's bloody hands, and then the crown! One can live for years sometimes, without living at all, and then all life comes crowding into a single hour. I had no time to think. Before my father's hideous shriek of death had died in my ears I found this crown on my head, the purple robe around me, and heard myself called a king. I would have given it all up then; it seemed nothing to me then; but now, can I give it up now? Well, colonel, well?

Enter COLONEL OF THE GUARD

COLONEL: What password does your imperial majesty desire should be given tonight?

CZAR: Password?

COLONEL: For the cordon of guards, sire, on night duty around the palace.

CZAR: You can dismiss them. I have no need of them. (*Exit* COLONEL) (*Goes to the crown lying on the table*) What subtle potency lies hidden in this gaudy bauble, the crown, that makes one feel like a god when one wears it? To hold in one's hand this little fiery coloured world, to reach out one's arm to earth's uttermost limit, to girdle the seas with one's hosts; this is to wear a crown! to wear a crown! The meanest serf in Russia who is loved is better crowned than I. How love outweighs the balance! How poor appears the widest empire of this golden world when matched with love! Pent up in this palace, with spies dogging every step, I have heard nothing of her; I have not seen her once since that fearful hour three days ago, when I found myself suddenly the Czar of this wide waste, Russia. Oh, could I see her for a moment; tell her now the secret of my life I have never dared utter before: tell her why I wear this crown, when I have sworn eternal war against all crowned men! There was a meeting tonight. I received my summons by an unknown hand; but how could I go? I who have broken my oath! who have broken my oath!

Enter PAGE

PAGE: It is after eleven, sire. Shall I take the first watch in your room tonight?

CZAR: Why should you watch me, boy? The stars are my best sentinels.

PAGE: It was your imperial father's wish, sire, never to be left alone while he slept.

CZAR: My father was troubled with bad dreams. Go get to your bed, boy; it is nigh on midnight and these late hours will spoil those red cheeks (PAGE *tries to kiss his hand*) Nay, nay; we have played together too often as children for that. Oh, to breathe the same air as her, and not to see her! the light seems to have gone from my life, the sun vanished from my day.

PAGE: Sire – Alexis – let me stay with you tonight! There is some danger over you; I feel there is.

CZAR: What should I fear? I have banished all my enemies from Russia. Set the brazier here, by me; it is very cold, and I would sit by it for a time. Go, boy, go; I have much to think about tonight. (*Goes to back of stage, draws aside curtain. View of Moscow by moonlight*) The snow has fallen heavily since sunset. How white and cold my city looks under this pale moon! And yet, what hot and fiery hearts beat in this icy Russia, for all its frost and snow! Oh, to see her for a moment; to tell her all; to tell her why I am king! But she does not doubt me, she said she would trust in me. Though I have broken my oath, she will have trust. It is very cold. Where is my cloak? I shall sleep for an hour. Then I have ordered my sledge, and, though I die for it, I shall see Vera tonight. Did I not bid thee go, boy? What! must I play the tyrant so soon? Go, go! I cannot live without seeing her. My horses will be here in an hour; one hour between me and love! How heavy this charcoal fire smells. (*Exit the* PAGE. *Lies down on a couch beside brazier*)

Enter VERA *in a black cloak*

VERA: Asleep! God! thou art good! Who shall deliver him from my hands now? This is he! The democrat who would make himself a king, the republican who hath worn a crown, the traitor who hath lied to us. Michael was right. He loved not the people. He loved me not. (*Bends over him*) Oh, why should such deadly poison lie in such sweet lips? Was there not gold enough in his hair before, that he should tarnish it with this crown? But my day has come now; the day of the people, of liberty, has come! Your day, my brother, has come! Though I have strangled whatever nature is in me, I did not think it had been so easy to kill. One blow and it is over, and I can wash my hands in water afterwards, I can wash my hands afterwards. Come, I shall save Russia. I have sworn it. (*raises dagger to strike*)

CZAR (*starting up, seizes her by both hands*): Vera, you here! My dream was no dream at all. Why have you left me three days alone, when I most needed you? O God, you think I am a traitor, a liar, a king? I am, for love of you. Vera, it was for you I broke my oath and wear my father's crown. I would lay at your feet this mighty Russia, which you and I have loved so well; would give you this earth as a footstool! set this crown on your head. The people will love us. We will rule them by love, as a father rules his children. There shall be liberty in Russia for every man to think as his heart bids him; liberty for men to speak as they think. I have banished the wolves that preyed on us; I have brought back your brother from Siberia; I have opened the blackened jaws of the mine. The courier is already on his way; within a week Dmitri and all those with him will be back in their own land. The people shall be free – are free now – and you and I, Emperor and Empress of this mighty realm, will walk among them openly, in love. When they gave me this crown first, I would have flung it back to them, had it not been for you, Vera. O God! It is men's custom in Russia to bring gifts to those they love. I said, I will bring to the woman I love a people, an empire, a world! Vera, it is for you, for you alone, I kept this crown; for you alone I am a king. Oh, I have loved you better than my oath! Why will you not speak to me? You love me not! You love me not! You have come to warn me of some plot against my life. What is life worth to me without you? (*Conspirators murmur outside*)

VERA: Oh, lost! lost! lost!

CZAR: Nay, you are safe here. It wants five hours still of dawn. Tomorrow, I will lead you forth to the whole people –

VERA: Tomorrow!

CZAR: Will crown you with my own hands as Empress in that great cathedral which my fathers built.

VERA (*loosens her hands violently from him, and starts up*): I am a Nihilist! I cannot wear a crown!

CZAR (*falls at her feet*): I am no king now. I am only a boy who has loved you better than his honour, better than his oath. For love of the people I would have been a patriot. For love of you I have been a traitor. Let us go forth together, we will live amongst the common people. I am no king. I will toil for you like the peasant or the serf. Oh, love me a little too! (*Conspirators murmur outside*)

VERA (*clutching dagger*): To strangle whatever nature is in me, neither to love nor to be loved, neither to pity nor – Oh, I am a woman! God help me, I am a woman! O Alexis! I too have broken my oath; I am a traitor. I love. Oh, do not speak, do not speak – (*kisses his lips*) – the first, the last time. (*He clasps her in his arms; they sit on the couch together*)

CZAR: I could die now.

VERA: What does death do in thy lips? Thy life, thy love are enemies of death. Speak not of death. Not yet, not yet.

CZAR: I know not why death came into my heart. Perchance the cup of life is filled too full of pleasure to endure. This is our wedding night.

VERA: Our wedding night!

CZAR: And if death came himself, methinks that I could kiss his pallid mouth, and suck sweet poison from it.

VERA: Our wedding night! Nay, nay. Death should not sit at the feast. There is no such thing as death.

CZAR: There shall not be for us. (*Conspirators murmur outside*)

VERA: What is that? Did you not hear something?

CZAR: Only your voice, that fowler's note which lures my heart away like a poor bird upon the limed twig.

VERA: Methought that someone laughed.

CZAR: It was but the wind and rain; the night is full of storm. (*Conspirators murmur outside*)

VERA: It should be so indeed. Oh, where are your guards? where are your guards?

CZAR: Where should they be but at home? I shall not live pent round by sword and steel. The love of a people is a king's best bodyguard.

VERA: The love of a people!

CZAR: Sweet, you are safe here. Nothing can harm you here. O love, I knew you trusted me! You said you would have trust.

VERA: I have had trust. O love, the past seems but some dull grey dream from which our souls have wakened. This is life at last.

CZAR: Ay, life at last.

VERA: Our wedding night! Oh, let me drink my fill of love tonight! Nay, sweet, not yet, not yet. How still it is, and yet methinks the air is full of music. It is some nightingale, who, wearying of the south, has come to sing in this bleak north to lovers such as we. It is the nightingale. Dost thou not hear it?

CZAR: Oh, sweet, mine ears are clogged to all sweet sounds save thine own voice, and mine eyes blinded to all sights but thee, else had I heard that nightingale, and seen the golden-vestured morning sun itself steal from its sombre east before its time for jealousy that thou art twice as fair.

VERA: Yet would that thou hadst heard the nightingale. Methinks that bird will never sing again.

CZAR: It is no nightingale. 'Tis love himself singing for very ecstasy of joy that thou art changed into his votaress. (*Clock begins striking twelve*) Oh, listen, sweet; it is the lover's hour. Come, let us stand without and hear the midnight answered from tower to tower over the wide white town. Our wedding night! What is that? What is that? (*Loud murmurs of conspirators in the street*)

VERA (*breaks from him and rushes across the stage*): The wedding guests are here already! Ay, you shall have your sign! (*stabs herself*) You shall have your sign! (*rushes to the window*)

CZAR (*intercepts her by rushing between her and window, and snatches dagger out of her hand*): Vera!

VERA (*clinging to him*): Give me back the dagger! Give me back the dagger! There are men in the street who seek your life! Your guards have betrayed you! This bloody dagger is the signal that you are dead. (*Conspirators begin to shout below in the street*) Oh, there is not a moment to be lost! Throw it out! Throw it out! Nothing can save me now; this dagger is poisoned! I feel death already in my heart.

CZAR (*holding dagger out of her reach*): Death is in my heart too; we shall die together.

VERA: Oh, love! love! love! be merciful to me! The wolves are hot upon you! you must live for liberty, for Russia, for me! Oh, you do not love me! You offered me an empire once! Give me this dagger now! Oh, you are cruel! My life for yours! What does it matter! (*Loud shouts in the street, 'Vera! Vera! To the rescue! To the rescue!'*)

CZAR: The bitterness of death is past for me.

VERA: Oh, they are breaking in below! See! The bloody man behind you! (CZAR *turns round for an instant*) Ah! (VERA *snatches dagger and flings it out of window*)

CONSPIRATORS (*below*): Long live the people!

CZAR: What have you done!

VERA: I have saved Russia. (*dies*)

CURTAIN

THE DUCHESS OF PADUA

CHARACTERS IN THE PLAY

SIMONE GESSO, *Duke of Padua*

BEATRICE, *his wife*

ANDREA POLLAJUOLO, *Cardinal of Padua*

MAFFIO PETRUCCI JEPPO VITELLOZZO TADDEO BARDI	} *courtiers of the Duke*

GUIDO FERRANTI, *a young man*

ASCANIO CRISTOFANO, *his friend*

COUNT MORANZONE, *an old man*

BERNARDO CAVALCANTI, *Lord Justice of Padua*

HUGO, *the headsman*

LUCY, *a Tyre woman*

Servants, citizens, soldiers, monks, falconers with their hawks and dogs, etc.

PLACE: *Padua*

TIME: *The latter half of the sixteenth century*

ACT ONE	*The marketplace of Padua*
ACT TWO	*A state room in the Duke's palace*
ACT THREE	*A corridor in the Duke's palace*
ACT FOUR	*The Hall of Justice*
ACT FIVE	*A dungeon*

STYLE OF ARCHITECTURE:
Italian, Gothic and Romanesque

THE DUCHESS OF PADUA

ACT ONE

The marketplace of Padua at noon; in the background is the great cathedral of Padua; the architecture is Romanesque and wrought in black and white marbles; a flight of marble steps leads up to the cathedral door; at the foot of the steps are two large stone lions; the houses on each side of the stage have coloured awnings from their windows and are flanked by stone arcades; on the right of the stage is the public fountain with a triton in green bronze blowing from a conch; around the fountain is a stone seat; the bell of the cathedral is ringing and the citizens – men, women and children – are passing into the cathedral. Enter GUIDO FERRANTI *and* ASCANIO CRISTOFANO

ASCANIO Now by my life, Guido, I will go no farther; for if I walk another step I will have no life left to swear by; this wild-goose errand of yours! (*sits down on the steps of the fountain*)

GUIDO I think it must be here. (*goes up to passer-by and doffs his cap*) Pray, sir, is this the marketplace, and that the church of Santa Croce? (CITIZEN *bows*) I thank you, sir.

ASCANIO Well?

GUIDO Ay! It is here.

ASCANIO I would it were somewhere else, for I see no wine-shop.

GUIDO (*taking a letter from his pocket and reading it*) 'The hour noon; the city, Padua; the place, the market; and the day, Saint Philip's Day.'

ASCANIO And what of the man, how shall we know him?

GUIDO (*reading still*) 'I will wear a violet cloak with a silver falcon broidered on the shoulder.' A brave attire, Ascanio.

ASCANIO I'd sooner have my leathern jerkin. And you think he will tell you of your father?

GUIDO Why, yes! It is a month ago now, you remember; I was in the vineyard, just at the corner nearest the road, where the goats used to get in, when a man rode up and asked me was my name Guido, and gave me this letter, signed 'Your Father's Friend', bidding me be here today if I would know the secret of my birth, and telling me how to recognise the writer! I had always thought old Pedro was my uncle, but he told me that he was not, but that I had been left a child in his charge by someone he had never since seen.

ASCANIO And you don't know who your father is?

GUIDO No.

ASCANIO No recollection of him even?

GUIDO None, Ascanio, none.

ASCANIO (*laughing*) Then he could never have boxed your ears so often as my father did mine.

GUIDO (*smiling*) I am sure you never deserved it.

ASCANIO Never; and that made it worse. I hadn't the consciousness of guilt to buoy me up. What hour did you say he fixed?

GUIDO Noon. (*clock in the cathedral strikes*)

ASCANIO It is that now, and your man has not come. I don't believe in him, Guido. I think it is some wench who has set her eye at you; and, as I have followed you from Perugia to Padua, I swear you shall follow me to the nearest tavern. (*rises*) By the great gods of eating, Guido, I am as hungry as a widow is for a husband, as tired as a young maid is of good advice, and as dry as a monk's sermon. Come, Guido, you stand there looking at nothing, like the fool who tried to look into his own mind; your man will not come.

GUIDO Well, I suppose you are right. Ah! (*Just as he is leaving the stage with* ASCANIO, *enter* LORD MORANZONE *in a violet cloak, with a silver falcon broidered on the shoulder; he passes across to the cathedral, and just as he is going in* GUIDO *runs up and touches him*)

MORANZONE Guido Ferranti, thou hast come in time.

GUIDO What! Does my father live?

MORANZONE Ay! Lives in you.
Thou art the same in mould and lineament,
Carriage and form, and outward semblances;
I trust thou art in noble mind the same.

GUIDO Oh, tell me of my father; I have lived
But for this moment.

MORANZONE We must be alone.

GUIDO This is my dearest friend, who out of love
Has followed me to Padua; as two brothers,
There is no secret which we do not share.

MORANZONE There is one secret which ye shall not share
Bid him go hence.

GUIDO (*to* ASCANIO) Come back within the hour.
He does not know that nothing in this world
Can dim the perfect mirror of our love.
Within the hour come.

ASCANIO Speak not to him,
There is a dreadful terror in his look.

GUIDO (*laughing*) Nay, nay, I doubt not that he has come to tell
That I am some great Lord of Italy,
And we will have long days of joy together.
Within the hour, dear Ascanio. (*exit* ASCANIO)
Now tell me of my father? (*sits down on a stone seat*)
Stood he tall?
I warrant he looked tall upon his horse.
His hair was black? Or perhaps a reddish gold,
Like a red fire of gold? Was his voice low?
The very bravest men have voices sometimes
Full of low music; or a clarion was it
That brake with terror all his enemies?
Did he ride singly? Or with many squires
And valiant gentlemen to serve his state?
For oftentimes methinks I feel my veins
Beat with the blood of kings. Was he a king?

MORANZONE Ay, of all men he was the kingliest.

GUIDO (*proudly*) Then when you saw my noble father last
He was set high above the heads of men?

MORANZONE Ay, he was high above the heads of men,
(*walks over to* GUIDO *and puts his hand upon his shoulder*)
On a red scaffold, with a butcher's block
Set for his neck.

GUIDO (*leaping up*) What dreadful man art thou,
That like a raven, or the midnight owl,
Com'st with this awful message from the grave?

MORANZONE I am known here as the Count Moranzone,
Lord of a barren castle on a rock,
With a few acres of unkindly land
And six not thrifty servants. But I was one
Of Parma's noblest princes; more that that,

I was your father's friend.

GUIDO (*clasping his hand*) Tell me of him.

MORANZONE You are the son of that great Duke Lorenzo,
Whose banner waved on many a well-fought field.
Against the Saracen, and heretic Turk.
He was the Prince of Parma, and the Duke
Of all the fair domains of Lombardy
Down to the gates of Florence; nay, Florence even
Was wont to pay him tribute –

GUIDO Come to his death.

MORANZONE You will hear that soon enough. Being at war –
O noble lion of war, that would not suffer
Injustice done in Italy! – he led
The very flower of chivalry against
That foul adulterous Lord of Rimini,
Giovanni Malatesta – whom God curse!
And was by him in treacherous ambush taken,
And was by him in common fetters bound,
And like a villain, or a low-born knave,
Was by him on the public scaffold murdered.

GUIDO (*clutching his dagger*) Doth Malatesta live?

MORANZONE No, he is dead.

GUIDO Did you say dead? O too swift runner, Death,
Couldst thou not wait for me a little space,
And I had done thy bidding!

MORANZONE (*clutching his wrist*) Thou canst do it!
The man who sold thy father is alive.

GUIDO Sold! was my father sold?

MORANZONE Ay! trafficked for,
Like a vile chattel, for a price betrayed,
Bartered and bargained for in privy market
By one whom he had held his perfect friend,
One he had trusted, one he had well loved,
One whom by ties of kindness he had bound –
Oh! To sow seeds of kindness in this world
Is but to reap ingratitude!

GUIDO And he lives
Who sold my father?

MORANZONE I will bring you to him.

GUIDO So, Judas, thou art living! well, I will make
This world thy field of blood, so buy it straightway,
For thou must hang there.

MORANZONE Judas said you, boy?
Yes, Judas in his treachery, but still
He was more wise than Judas was, and held
Those thirty silver pieces not enough.

GUIDO What got he for my father's blood?

MORANZONE What got he?
Why cities, fiefs, and principalities,
Vineyards, and lands.

GUIDO Of which he shall but keep
Six feet of ground to rot in. Where is he,
This damned villain, this foul devil? Where?
Show me the man, and come he cased in steel,
In complete panoply and pride of war,
Ay, guarded by a thousand men-at-arms,
Yet I shall reach him through their spears, and feel
The last black drop of blood from his black heart
Crawl down my blade. Show me the man, I say,
And I will kill him.

MORANZONE (*coldly*) Fool, what revenge is there?
Death is the common heritage of all,
And death comes best when it comes suddenly.
(*goes up close to* GUIDO) Thy father was betrayed,
there is your cue;
For you shall sell the seller in his turn.
I will make you of his household, you will sit
At the same board with him, eat of his bread –

GUIDO O bitter bread!

MORANZONE Your palate is too nice,
Revenge will make it sweet. Thou shalt o' nights
Pledge him in wine, drink from his cup, and be
His intimate, so he will fawn on thee,
Love thee, and trust thee in all secret things.
If he bids thee be merry thou must laugh,
And if it be his humour to be sad
Thou shalt don sables.
Then when the time is ripe – (GUIDO *clutches his sword*)
Nay, nay, I trust thee not; your hot young blood,
Undisciplined nature, and too violent rage
Will never tarry for this great revenge,
But wreck itself on passion.

GUIDO Thou knowest me not.
Tell me the man, and I in everything

Will do thy bidding.

MORANZONE Well, when the time is ripe,
The victim trusting and the occasion sure,
I will by sudden secret messenger
Send thee a sign.

GUIDO How shall I kill him, tell me?

MORANZONE That night thou shalt creep into his private chamber;
That night remember.

GUIDO I shall not forget.

MORANZONE I do not know if guilty people sleep,
But if he sleeps see that you wake him first,
And hold your hand upon his throat, ay! that way,
Then having told him of what blood you are,
Sprung from what father, and for what revenge,
Bid him to pray for mercy; when he prays,
Bid him to set a price upon his life,
And when he strips himself of all his gold
Tell him thou needest not gold, and hast not mercy,
And do thy business straight away. Swear to me
You will not kill him till I bid you do it,
Or else I go to mine own house, and leave
You ignorant, and your father unavenged.

GUIDO Now by my father's sword –

MORANZONE The common hangman
Brake that in sunder in the public square.

GUIDO Then by my father's grave –

MORANZONE What grave? What grave?
Your noble father lieth in no grave,
I saw his dust strewn on the air, his ashes
Whirled through the windy streets like common straws
To plague a beggar's eyesight, and his head,
That gentle head, set on the prison spike,
Girt with the mockery of a paper crown,
For the vile rabble in their insolence
To shoot their tongues at.

GUIDO Was it so indeed?
Then by my father's spotless memory,
And by the shameful manner of his death,
And by the base betrayal by his friend,
For these at least remain, by these I swear
I will not lay my hand upon his life
Until you bid me, then – God help his soul,

For he shall die as never dog died yet.
And now, the sign, what is it?
MORANZONE This dagger, boy;
It was your father's.
GUIDO Oh, let me look at it!
I do remember now my reputed uncle,
That good old husbandman I left at home,
Told me a cloak wrapped round me when a babe
Bare too much yellow leopards wrought in gold;
I like them best in steel, as they are here,
They suit my purpose better. Tell me, sir,
Have you no message from my father to me?
MORANZONE Poor boy, you never saw that noble father,
For when by his false friend he had been sold,
Alone of all his gentlemen I escaped
To bear the news to Parma to the Duchess.
GUIDO Speak to me of my mother.
MORANZONE When your mother,
Than whom no saint in heaven was more pure,
Heard my black news, she fell into a swoon,
And, being with untimely travail seized –
Indeed, she was but seven months a bride –
Bare thee into the world before thy time,
And then her soul went heavenward, to wait
Thy father, at the gates of Paradise.
GUIDO A mother dead, a father sold and bartered!
I seem to stand on some beleaguered wall,
And messenger comes after messenger
With a new tale of terror; give me breath,
Mine ears are tired.
MORANZONE When thy mother died,
Fearing our enemies, I gave it out
Thou wert dead also, and then privily
Conveyed thee to an ancient servitor,
Who by Perugia lived; the rest thou knowest.
GUIDO Saw you my father afterwards?
MORANZONE Ay! once:
In mean attire, like a vineyard dresser,
I stole to Rimini.
GUIDO (*taking his hand*) O generous heart!
MORANZONE One can buy everything in Rimini,
And so I bought the gaolers! When your father

Heard that a man child had been born to him,
His noble face lit up beneath his helm
Like a great fire seen far out at sea,
And taking my two hands, he bade me, Guido,
To rear you worthy of him; so I have reared you
To revenge his death upon the friend who sold him.

GUIDO Thou hast done well; I for my father thank you.
And now his name?

MORANZONE How you remind me of him,
You have each gesture that your father had.

GUIDO The traitor's name?

MORANZONE Thou wilt hear that anon;
The Duke and other nobles at the court
Are coming hither.

GUIDO What of that? His name?

MORANZONE Do they not seem a valiant company
Of honourable, honest gentlemen?

GUIDO His name, milord?

Enter the DUKE OF PADUA *with* COUNT BARDI, MAFFIO PETRUCCI, *and other gentlemen of his court*

MORANZONE (*quickly*) The man to whom I kneel
Is he who sold your father! mark me well.

GUIDO (*clutches his dagger*) The Duke!

MORANZONE Leave off that fingering of thy knife.
Hast thou so soon forgotten?
(*Kneels to the* DUKE) My noble Lord.

DUKE Welcome, Count Moranzone; 'tis some time
Since we have seen you here in Padua.
We hunted near your castle yesterday –
Call you it castle? That bleak house of yours
Wherein you sit a-mumbling o'er your beads,
Telling your vices like a good old man.
I trust I'll never be a good old man.
God would grow weary if I told my sins.
(*catches sight of* GUIDO *and starts back*)
Who is that?

MORANZONE My sister's son, your grace,
Who being now of age to carry arms,
Would for a season tarry at your court.

DUKE (*still looking at* GUIDO) What is his name?

MORANZONE Guido Ferranti, sir.

DUKE His city?

MORANZONE He is Mantuan by birth.

DUKE (*advancing towards* GUIDO) You have the eyes of one I used to know,
But he died childless. So, sir, you would serve me;
Well, we lack soldiers ; are you honest, boy?
Then be not spendthrift of your honesty,
But keep it to yourself; in Padua
Men think that honesty is ostentatious, so
It is not of the fashion. Look at these lords
Smelling of civet and the pomander box . . .

BARDI (*aside*) Here is some bitter arrow for us, sure.

DUKE Why, every man among them has his price,
Although, to do them justice, some of them
Are quite expensive.

BARDI (*aside*) There it comes indeed.

DUKE So be not honest; eccentricity
Is not a thing should ever be encouraged,
Although, in this dull stupid age of ours,
The most eccentric thing a man can do
Is to have brains, then the mob mocks at him;
And for the mob, despise it as I do,
I hold its bubble praise and windy favours
In such account that popularity
Is the one insult I have never suffered.

MAFFIO (*aside*) He has enough of hate, if he needs that.

DUKE Have prudence; in your dealings with the world
Be not too hasty; act on the second thought,
First impulses are generally not good.

GUIDO (*aside*) Surely a toad sits on his lips, and spills its venom there.

DUKE See thou hast enemies,
Else will the world think very little of thee,
It is its test of power; yet see you show
A smiling mask of friendship to all men,
Until you have them safely in your grip,
Then you can crush them.

GUIDO (*aside*) O wise philosopher!
That for thyself dost dig so deep a grave.

MORANZONE (*to him*) Dost thou mark his words?

GUIDO Oh, be thou sure I do.

DUKE And be not overscrupulous; clean hands

With nothing in them make a sorry show.
If you would have the lion's share of life
You must wear the fox's skin. Oh, it will fit you;
It is a coat which fitteth every man,
The fat, the lean, the tall man, and the short,
Whoever makes that coat, boy, is a tailor
That never lacks a customer.

GUIDO Your grace,
I shall remember.

DUKE That is well, boy, well.
I would not have about me shallow fools,
Who with mean scruples weigh the gold of life,
And faltering, paltering, end by failure; failure,
The only crime which I have not committed:
I would have *men* about me. As for conscience,
Conscience is but the name which cowardice
Fleeing from battle scrawls upon its shield.
You understand me, boy?

GUIDO I do, your grace,
And will in all things carry out the creed
Which you have taught me.

MAFFIO I never heard your grace
So much in the vein for preaching; let the Cardinal
Look to his laurels, sir.

DUKE The Cardinal!
Men follow my creed, and they gabble his.
I do not think much of the Cardinal;
Although he is a holy churchman, and
I quite admit his dullness. Well, sir, from now
We count you of our household.

He holds out his hand for GUIDO *to kiss.* GUIDO *starts back in horror, but at a gesture from* COUNT MORANZONE, *kneels and kisses it*

We will see
That you are furnished with such equipage
As doth befit your honour and our state.

GUIDO I thank your grace most heartily.

DUKE Tell me again
What is your name?

GUIDO Guido Ferranti, sir.

DUKE And you are Mantuan? Look to your wives, my lords,

When such a gallant comes to Padua.
Thou dost well to laugh, Count Bardi; I have noted
How merry is that husband by whose hearth
Sits an uncomely wife.

MAFFIO May it please your grace,
The wives of Padua are above suspicion.

DUKE What, are they so ill-favoured! Let us go,
This Cardinal detains our pious Duchess;
His sermon and his beard want cutting both:
Will you come with us, sir, and hear a text
From holy Jerome?

MORANZONE (*bowing*) My liege, there are some matters –

DUKE (*interrupting*) Thou needst make no excuse
for missing mass.
Come, gentlemen. (*exit with his suite into cathedral*)

GUIDO (*after a pause*) So the Duke sold my father;
I kissed his hand.

MORANZONE Thou shalt do that many times.

GUIDO Must it be so?

MORANZONE Ay! thou hast sworn an oath.

GUIDO That oath shall make me marble.

MORANZONE Farewell, boy,
Thou wilt not see me till the time is ripe.

GUIDO I pray thou comest quickly.

MORANZONE I will come
When it is time; be ready.

GUIDO Fear me not.

MORANZONE Here is your friend; see that you banish *him*
Both from your heart and Padua.

GUIDO From Padua,
Not from my heart.

MORANZONE Nay, from thy heart as well,
I will not leave thee till I see thee do it.

GUIDO Can I have no friend?

MORANZONE Revenge shall be thy friend,
Thou need'st no other.

GUIDO Well, then be it so.

Enter ASCANIO CRISTOFANO

ASCANIO Come, Guido, I have been beforehand with you in everything, for I have drunk a flagon of wine, eaten a pasty, and kissed the maid who served it. Why, you look as melancholy as a schoolboy who cannot buy apples, or a politician who cannot sell his vote. What news, Guido, what news?

GUIDO Why, that we two must part, Ascanio.

ASCANIO That would be news indeed, but it is not true.

GUIDO Too true it is, you must get hence, Ascanio,
And never look upon my face again.

ASCANIO No, no; indeed you do not know me, Guido;
'Tis true I am a common yeoman's son,
Nor versed in fashions of much courtesy;
But, if you are nobly born, cannot I be
Your serving man? I will tend you with more love
Than any hired servant.

GUIDO (*clasping his hand*) Ascanio!
(*sees* MORANZONE *looking at him and drops* ASCANIO'S *hand*)
It cannot be.

ASCANIO What, is it so with you?
I thought the friendship of the antique world
Was not yet dead, but that the Roman type
Might even in this poor and common age
Find counterparts of love; then by this love
Which beats between us like a summer sea,
Whatever lot has fallen to your hand
May I not share it?

GUIDO Share it?

ASCANIO Ay!

GUIDO No, no.

ASCANIO Have you then come to some inheritance
Of lordly castle, or of stored-up gold?

GUIDO (*bitterly*) Ay! I have come to my inheritance.
O bloody legacy! and O murderous dole!
Which, like the thrifty miser, must I hoard,
And to my own self keep; and so, I pray you,
Let us part here.

ASCANIO What, shall we never more
Sit hand in hand, as we were wont to sit,
Over some book of ancient chivalry,
Stealing a truant holiday from school;
Follow the huntsmen through the autumn woods,
And watch the falcons burst their tasselled jesses,
When the hare breaks from covert?

GUIDO Never more.
ASCANIO Must I go hence without a word of love?
GUIDO You must go hence, and may love go with you.
ASCANIO You are unknightly, and ungenerous.
GUIDO Unknightly and ungenerous if you will.
Why should we waste more words about the matter?
Let us part now.
ASCANIO Have you no message, Guido?
GUIDO None; my whole past was but a schoolboy's dream,
Today my life begins. Farewell.
ASCANIO Farewell. (*exit slowly*)
GUIDO Now are you satisfied? Have you not seen
My dearest friend, and my most loved companion,
Thrust from me like a common kitchen knave!
Oh, that I did it! Are you not satisfied?
MORANZONE Ay! I am satisfied. Now I go hence,
Back to my lonely castle on the hill.
Do not forget the sign, your father's dagger,
And do the business when I send it to you.
GUIDO Be sure I shall. (*exit* LORD MORANZONE)
O thou eternal heaven!
If there is aught of nature in my soul,
Of gentle pity, or fond kindliness,
Wither it up, blast it, bring it to nothing,
Or if thou wilt not, then will I myself
Cut pity with a sharp knife from my heart
And strangle mercy in her sleep at night
Lest she speak to me. Vengeance there I have it.
Be thou my comrade and my bedfellow,
Sit by my side, ride to the chase with me,
When I am weary sing me pretty songs,
When I am light o' heart, make jest with me,
And when I dream, whisper into my ear
The dreadful secret of a father's murder –
Did I say murder? (*draws his dagger*)
Listen, thou terrible God!
Thou God that punishest all broken oaths,
And bid some angel write this oath in fire,
That from this hour, till my dear father's murder
In blood I have revenged, I do forswear
The noble ties of honourable friendship,
The noble joys of dear companionship,

Affection's bonds, and loyal gratitude,
Ay, more, from this same hour I do forswear
All love of women, and the barren thing
Which men call beauty –

The organ peals in the cathedral, and under a canopy of cloth of silver tissue, borne by four pages in scarlet, the DUCHESS OF PADUA *comes down the steps; as she passes across their eyes meet for a moment, and as she leaves the stage she looks back at* GUIDO, *and the dagger falls from his hand.*

Oh! Who is that?

A CITIZEN The Duchess of Padua!

END OF ACT ONE

ACT TWO

A state room in the Duke's palace, hung with tapestries representing the Masque of Venus; a large door in the centre opens into a colonnade of red marble, through which one can see a view of Padua; a large canopy is set (right of centre) with three thrones, one a little lower than the others; the ceiling is made of long gilded beams; furniture of the period, chairs covered with gilt leather, buffets set with gold and silver plate and chests painted with mythological scenes. A number of the courtiers are out in the colonnade looking from it down into the street below; from the street comes the roar of a mob and cries of 'Death to the Duke': after a little interval enter the DUKE *very calmly; he is leaning on the arm of* GUIDO FERRANTI; *with him enters also the* LORD CARDINAL; *the mob still shouting.*

DUKE — No, my Lord Cardinal, I weary of her!
Why, she is worse than ugly, she is good.

MAFFIO — (*excitedly*) Your grace, there are two thousand people there
Who every moment grow more clamorous.

DUKE — Tut, man, they waste their strength upon their lungs!
People who shout so loud, my lords, do nothing,
The only men I fear are silent men.
(*a yell from the people*)
You see, Lord Cardinal, how my people love me.
This is their serenade, I like it better
Than the soft murmurs of the amorous lute;
Is it not sweet to listen to? (*another yell*)
I fear
They have become a little out of tune,
So I must tell my men to fire on them.
I cannot bear bad music! Go, Petrucci,
And tell the captain of the guard below
To clear the square. Do you not hear me, sir?
Do what I bid you. (*exit* PETRUCCI)

CARDINAL — I beseech your grace
To listen to their grievances.

DUKE (*sitting on his throne*) Ay! the peaches
Are not so big this year as they were last.
I crave your pardon, my lord Cardinal,
I thought you spake of peaches.
(*A cheer from the people*) What is that?

GUIDO (*rushes to the window*) The Duchess has gone forth into the square,
And stands between the people and the guard,
And will not let them shoot.

DUKE The devil take her!

GUIDO (*still at the window*) And followed by a dozen of the citizens
Has come into the palace.

DUKE (*standing at the window*) By St James,
Our Duchess waxes bold!

BARDI Here comes the Duchess.

DUKE Shut that door there; this morning air is cold.
(*they close the door on the colonnade*)

Enter the DUCHESS *followed by a crowd of meanly dressed citizens*

DUCHESS (*flinging herself upon her knees*) I do beseech your grace to give us audience.

DUKE Am I a tailor, madame, that you come
With such a ragged retinue before us?

DUCHESS I think that their rags speak their grievances
With better eloquence than I can speak.

DUKE What are these grievances?

DUCHESS Alas, my lord,
Such common things as neither you nor I,
Nor any of these noble gentlemen,
Have ever need at all to think about;
They say the bread, the very bread they eat,
Is made of sorry chaff –

I CITIZEN Ay! So it is,
Nothing but chaff.

DUKE And very good food too,
I give it to my horses.

DUCHESS (*restraining herself*) They say the water,
Set in the public cisterns for their use,
Has, through the breaking of the aqueduct,
To stagnant pools and muddy puddles turned.

DUKE They should drink wine; water is quite unwholesome.

2 CITIZEN Alack, your grace, the taxes which the customs
Take at the city gate are grown so high
We cannot buy wine.

DUKE Then you should bless the taxes
Which make you temperate.

DUCHESS Think, while we sit
In gorgeous pomp and state and nothing lack
Of all that wealth and luxury can give,
And many servants have to wait upon us
And tend our meanest need, gaunt poverty
Creeps through their sunless lanes, and with sharp knives
Cuts the warm throats of children stealthily
And no word said.

3 CITIZEN Ay! Marry, that is true,
My little son died yesternight from hunger,
He was but six years old; I am so poor,
I cannot bury him.

DUKE If you are poor,
Are you not blessed in that? Why, poverty
Is one of the Christian virtues (*turns to the* CARDINAL),
Is it not?
I know, Lord Cardinal, you have great revenues,
Rich abbey-lands, and tithes, and large estates
For preaching voluntary poverty.

DUCHESS Nay but, my lord the Duke, be generous
While we sit here within a noble house
With shaded porticoes against the sun,
And walls and roofs to keep the winter out,
There are many citizens of Padua
Who in vile tenements live so full of holes,
That the chill rain, the snow, and the rude blast,
Are tenants also with them; others sleep
Under the arches of the public bridges
All through the autumn nights, till the wet mist
Stiffens their limbs, and fevers come, and so –

DUKE And so they go to Abraham's bosom, madam.
They should thank me for sending them to heaven,
If they are wretched here.
(*To the* CARDINAL) Is it not said
Somewhere in holy writ, that every man
Should be contented with that state of life

God calls him to? Why should I change their state,
Or meddle with an all-wise providence,
Which has apportioned that some men should starve
And others surfeit? I did not make the world.

1 CITIZEN He hath a hard heart.

2 CITIZEN Nay, be silent, neighbour;
I think the Cardinal will speak for us.

CARDINAL True, it is Christian to bear misery,
For out of misery God bringeth good,
Yet it is Christian also to be kind,
To feed the hungry, and to heal the sick,
And there seem many evils in this town,
Which in your wisdom might your grace reform.

1 CITIZEN What is that word reform? What does it mean?

2 CITIZEN Marry, it means leaving things as they are; I like it not.

DUKE Reform, Lord Cardinal, did *you* say reform?
There is a man in Germany called Luther,
Who would reform the Holy Catholic Church.
Have you not made him heretic, and uttered
Anathema, maranatha, against him?

CARDINAL (*rising from his seat*) He would have led the sheep
out of the fold,
We do but ask of you to feed the sheep.

DUKE When I have shorn their fleeces I may feed them.
As for these rebels –
(DUCHESS *entreats him*)

1 CITIZEN That is a kind word,
He means to give us something.

2 CITIZEN Is that so?

DUKE These ragged knaves who come before us here,
With mouths chock-full of treason.

3 CITIZEN Good my lord,
Fill up our mouths with bread; we'll hold our tongues.

DUKE Ye shall hold your tongues, whether you starve or not.
My lords, this age is so familiar grown,
That the low peasant hardly doffs his hat
Unless you beat him; and the raw mechanic
Elbows the noble in the public streets.
As for this rabble here, I am their scourge,
And sent by God to lash them for their sins.

DUCHESS Hast thou the right? Art thou so free from sin?

DUKE When sin is lashed by virtue it is nothing,

But when sin lashes sin then is God glad.
DUCHESS Oh, are you not afraid?
DUKE What have I to fear?
Being man's enemy am I not God's friend?
(*To the* CITIZENS) Well, my good loyal citizens of Padua,
Still as our gentle Duchess has so prayed us,
And to refuse so beautiful a beggar
Were to lack both courtesy and love,
Touching your grievances, I promise this –
1 CITIZEN Marry, he will lighten the taxes!
2 CITIZEN Or a dole of bread, think you, for each man?
DUKE – That, on next Sunday, the Lord Cardinal
Shall, after holy mass, preach you a sermon
Upon the beauty of obedience. (CITIZENS *murmur*)
1 CITIZEN I' faith, that will not fill our stomachs!
2 CITIZEN A sermon is but a sorry sauce, when
You have nothing to eat with it.
DUCHESS Poor people,
You see I have no power with the Duke,
But if you go into the court without,
My almoner shall from my private purse,
Which is not ever too well stuffed with gold,
Divide a hundred ducats 'mongst you all.
ALMONER Your grace has but a hundred ducats left.
DUCHESS Give what I have.
1 CITIZEN God save the Duchess, say I.
2 CITIZEN God save her.
DUCHESS And every Monday morn shall bread be set
For those who lack it. (CITIZENS *applaud and go out*)
1 CITIZEN (*going out*) Why, God save the Duchess again!
DUKE (*calling him back*) Come hither, fellow! What is your name?
1 CITIZEN Dominick, sir.
DUKE A good name! Why were you called Dominick?
1 CITIZEN (*scratching his head*) Marry, because I was born on St George's day.
DUKE A good reason! Here is a ducat for you!
Will you not cry for me God save the Duke?
1 CITIZEN (*feebly*) God save the Duke.
DUKE Nay! Louder, fellow, louder.
1 CITIZEN (*a little louder*) God save the Duke!
DUKE More lustily, fellow, put more heart in it!

Here is another ducat for you.

I CITIZEN (*enthusiastically*) God save the Duke!

DUKE (*mockingly*) Why, gentlemen, this simple fellow's love
Touches me much.
(*To the* CITIZEN, *harshly*) Go! (*exit* CITIZEN, *bowing*)
This is the way, my lords,
You can buy popularity nowadays.
Oh, we are nothing if not democratic!
(*To the* DUCHESS) Well, madam,
You spread rebellion 'midst our citizens,
And by your doles and daily charities,
Have made the common people love you. Well,
I will not have you loved.

DUCHESS (*looking at* GUIDO) Indeed, my lord,
I am not.

DUKE And I will not have you give
Bread to the poor merely because they are hungry.

DUCHESS My lord, the poor have rights you cannot touch,
The right to pity, and the right to mercy.

DUKE So, so, you argue with me? This is she,
The gentle Duchess for whose hand I yielded
Three of the fairest towns in Italy,
Pisa, and Genoa, and Orvieto.

DUCHESS Promised, my Lord, not yielded: in that matter
Brake you your word as ever.

DUKE You wrong us, madam,
There were state reasons.

DUCHESS What state reasons are there
For breaking holy promises to a state?

DUKE There are wild boars at Pisa in a forest
Close to the city: when I promised Pisa
Unto your noble and most trusting father, I had
forgotten there was hunting there.

DUCHESS Those who forget what honour is, forget
All things, my lord.

DUKE At Genoa they say,
Indeed I doubt them not, that the red mullet
Runs larger in the harbour of that town
Than anywhere in Italy.
(*Turning to one of the court*) You, my lord,
Whose gluttonous appetite is your only god,
Could satisfy our Duchess on that point.

DUCHESS And Orvieto?

DUKE (*yawning*) I cannot now recall
Why I did not surrender Orvieto
According to the word of my contract.
Maybe it was because I did not choose.
(*goes over to the* DUCHESS) Why look you, madam,
you are here alone;
'Tis many a dusty league to your grey France,
And even there your father barely keeps
A hundred ragged squires for his court.
What hope have you, I say? Which of these lords
And noble gentlemen of Padua
Stands by thy side.

DUCHESS There is not one.

(GUIDO *starts, but restrains himself*)

DUKE Nor shall be,
While I am Duke in Padua: listen, madam,
I am grown weary of your airs and graces,
Being mine own, you shall do as I will,
And if it be my will you keep the house,
Why then, this palace shall your prison be;
And if it be my will you walk abroad,
Why, you shall take the air from morn to night.

DUCHESS Sir, by what right – ?

DUKE Madam, my second duchess
Asked the same question once: her monument
Lies in the chapel of Bartholomew,
Wrought in red marble; very beautiful.
Guido, your arm. Come, gentlemen, let us go
And spur our falcons for the midday chase.
Bethink you, madam, you are here alone.

(*exit the* DUKE *leaning on* GUIDO, *with his court*)

DUCHESS (*looking after them*) Is it not strange that one
who seems so fair
Should thus affect the Duke, hang on each word
Which falls like poison from those cruel lips,
And never leave his side, as though he loved him?
Well, well, it makes no matter unto me,
I am alone, and out of reach of love.
The Duke said rightly that I was alone;
Deserted, and dishonoured, and defamed,
Stood ever woman so alone indeed?

Men when they woo us call us pretty children,
Tell us we have not wit to make our lives,
And so they mar them for us. Did I say woo?
We are their chattels, and their common slaves,
Less dear than the poor hound that licks their hand,
Less fondled than the hawk upon their wrist.
Woo, did I say? Bought rather, sold and bartered,
Our very bodies being merchandise.
I know it is the general lot of women,
Each miserably mated to some man
Wrecks her own life upon his selfishness.
That it is general makes it not less bitter.
I think I never heard a woman laugh,
Laugh for pure merriment, except one woman;
That was at night time in the public streets.
Poor soul, she walked with painted lips, and wore
The mask of pleasure: I would not laugh like her;
No, death were better.

Enter GUIDO *behind unobserved; the* DUCHESS *flings herself down before a picture of the Madonna*

O Mary mother, with your sweet pale face
Bending between the little angel heads
That hover round you, have you no help for me?
Mother of God, have you no help for me?

GUIDO I can endure no longer.
This is my love, and I will speak to her.
Lady, am I a stranger to your prayers?

DUCHESS (*rising*) None but the wretched need my prayers, my lord.

GUIDO Then must I need them, lady.

DUCHESS How is that?
Does not the Duke show thee sufficient honour,
Or dost thou lack advancement at the court?
Ah, sir, that lies not in my power to give you,
Being, my own self held of no account.

GUIDO Your grace, I lack no favours from the Duke,
Whom my soul loathes as I loathe wickedness,
But come to proffer on my bended knees,
My loyal service to thee unto death.

DUCHESS Alas! I am so fallen in estate
I can but give thee a poor meed of thanks.

GUIDO (*seizing her hand*) Hast thou no love to give me?
(*the* DUCHESS *starts, and* GUIDO *falls at her feet*)
O dear saint,
If I have been too daring, pardon me!
Thy beauty sets my boyish blood aflame,
And, when my reverent lips touch thy white hand,
Each little nerve with such wild passion thrills
That there is nothing which I would not do
To gain thy love. (*leaps up*)
Bid me reach forth and pluck
Perilous honour from the lion's jaws,
And I will wrestle with the Nemean beast
On the bare desert! Fling to the cave of War
A gaud, a ribbon, a dead flower, something
That once has touched thee, and I'll bring it back
Though all the hosts of Christendom were there,
Inviolate again! Ay, more than this,
Set me to scale the pallid white-faced cliffs
Of mighty England, and from that arrogant shield
Will I raze out the lilies of your France
Which England, that sea-lion of the sea,
Hath taken from her!
O dear Beatrice,
Drive me not from thy presence! Without thee
The heavy minutes crawl with feet of lead,
But, while I look upon thy loveliness,
The hours fly like winged Mercuries
And leave existence golden.

DUCHESS I did not think
I would be ever loved: do you indeed
Love me so much as now you say you do?

GUIDO Ask of the sea-bird if it loves the sea,
Ask of the roses if they love the rain,
Ask of the little lark, that will not sing
Till day break, if it loves to see the day –
And yet, these are but empty images,
Mere shadows of my love, which is a fire
So great that all the waters of the main
Cannot avail to quench it. Will you not speak?

DUCHESS I hardly know what I should say to you.

GUIDO Will you not say you love me?

DUCHESS Is that my lesson?

Must I say all at once? 'Twere a good lesson
If I did love you, sir; but, if I do not,
What shall I say then?

GUIDO If you do not love me,
Say, none the less, you do, for on your tongue
Falsehood for very shame would turn to truth.

DUCHESS What if I do not speak at all? They say
Lovers are happiest when they are in doubt.

GUIDO Nay, doubt would kill me, and if I must die,
Why, let me die for joy and not for doubt.
Oh, tell me, may I stay or must I go?

DUCHESS I would not have you either stay or go;
For if you stay you steal my love from me,
And if you go you take my love away.
Guido, though all the morning stars could sing
They could not tell the measure of my love.
I love you, Guido.

GUIDO (*stretching out his hands*) Oh, do not cease at all;
I thought the nightingale sang but at night;
Or if thou needst must cease, then let my lips
Touch the sweet lips that can such music make.

DUCHESS To touch my lips is not to touch my heart.

GUIDO Do you close that against me?

DUCHESS Alas! My lord,
I have it not: the first day that I saw you
I let you take my heart away from me;
Unwilling thief that without meaning it
Didst break into my fenced treasury
And filch my jewel from it! Oh, strange theft,
Which made you richer though you knew it not,
And left me poorer, and yet glad of it!

GUIDO (*clasping her in his arms*) O love, love, love! Nay, sweet, lift up your head,
Let me unlock those little scarlet doors
That shut in music, let me dive for coral
In your red lips, and I'll bear back a prize
Richer than all the gold the Griffin guards
In rude Armenia.

DUCHESS You are my lord,
And what I have is yours, and what I have not
Your fancy lends me, like a prodigal
Spending its wealth on what is nothing worth. (*kisses him*)

GUIDO Methinks I am bold to look upon you thus:
The gentle violet hides beneath its leaf
And is afraid to look at the great sun
For fear of too much splendour, but my eyes,
O daring eyes! Are grown so venturous
That like fixed stars they stand, gazing at you,
And surfeit sense with beauty.

DUCHESS Dear love, I would
You could look upon me ever, for your eyes
Are polished mirrors, and when I peer
Into those mirrors I can see myself,
And so I know my image lives in you.

GUIDO (*taking her in his arms*) Stand still, thou hurrying
orb in the high heavens,
And make this hour immortal! (*a pause*)

DUCHESS Sit down here,
A little lower than me: yes, just so, sweet,
That I may run my fingers through your hair,
And see your face turn upwards like a flower
To meet my kiss.
Have you not sometimes noted,
When we unlock some long-disuséd room
With heavy dust and soiling mildew filled,
Where never foot of man has come for years,
And from the windows take the rusty bar,
And fling the broken shutters to the air,
And let the bright sun in, how the good sun
Turns every grimy particle of dust
Into a little thing of dancing gold?
Guido, my heart is that long-empty room,
But you have let love in, and with its gold
Gilded all life. Do you not think that love
Fills up the sum of life?

GUIDO Ay! without love
Life is no better than the unhewn stone
Which in the quarry lies, before the sculptor
Has set the God within it. Without love
Life is as silent as the common reeds
That through the marshes or by rivers grow,
And have no music in them.

DUCHESS Yet out of these
The singer, who is Love, will make a pipe

And from them he draws music; so I think
Love will bring music out of any life.
Is that not true?

GUIDO Sweet, women make it true.
There are men who paint pictures, and carve statues,
Paul of Verona and the dyer's son,
Or their great rival, who, by the sea at Venice,
Has set God's little maid upon the stair,
White as her own white lily, and as tall,
Or Raphael, whose Madonnas are divine
Because they are mothers merely; yet I think
Women are the best artists of the world,
For they can take the common lives of men,
Soiled with the money-getting of our age,
And with love make them beautiful.

DUCHESS Ah, dear
I wish that you and I were very poor;
The poor, who love each other, are so rich.

GUIDO Tell me again you love me, Beatrice.

DUCHESS (*fingering his collar*) How well this collar lies
about your throat.

LORD MORANZONE *looks through the door from the colonnade outside*

GUIDO Nay, tell me that you love me.

DUCHESS I remember,
That when I was a child in my dear France,
Being at court at Fontainebleau, the King
Wore such a collar.

GUIDO Will you not say you love me?

DUCHESS (*smiling*) He was a very royal man, King Francis,
Yet he was not royal as you are.
Why need I tell you, Guido, that I love you?
(*takes his head in her hands and turns his face up to her*)
Do you not know that I am yours for ever,
Body and soul. (*kisses him, and then suddenly catches sight of* MORANZONE *and leaps up*)
Oh, what is that? (MORANZONE *disappears*)

GUIDO What, love?

DUCHESS Methought I saw a face with eyes of flame
Look at us through the doorway.

GUIDO Nay, 'twas nothing:
The passing shadow of the man on guard.

The DUCHESS *still stands looking at the window*

'Twas nothing, sweet.

DUCHESS Ay! What can harm us now.
Who are in Love's hand? I do not think I'd care
Though the vile world should with its lackey Slander
Trample and tread upon my life; why should I?
They say the common field-flowers of the field
Have sweeter scent when they are trodden on
Than when they bloom alone, and that some herbs
Which have no perfume, on being bruiséd die
With all Arabia round them; so it is
With the young lives this dull world seeks to crush,
It does but bring the sweetness out of them,
And makes them lovelier often. And besides,
While we have love we have the best of life:
Is it not so?

GUIDO Dear, shall we play or sing?
I think that I could sing now.

DUCHESS Do not speak,
For there are times when all existences
Seem narrowed to one single ecstasy,
And Passion sets a seal upon the lips.

GUIDO Oh, with mine own lips let me break that seal!
You love me, Beatrice?

DUCHESS Ay! Is it not strange
I should so love mine enemy?

GUIDO Who is he?

DUCHESS Why, you: that with your shaft didst pierce my heart!
Poor heart, that lived its little lonely life
Until it met your arrow.

GUIDO Ah, dear love,
I am so wounded by that bolt myself
That with untended wounds I lie a-dying,
Unless you cure me, dear physician.

DUCHESS I would not have you cured; for I am sick
With the same malady.

GUIDO Oh how I love you!
See, I must steal the cuckoo's voice, and tell
The one tale over.

DUCHESS Tell no other tale!
For, if that is the little cuckoo's song,

The nightingale is hoarse, and the loud lark
Has lost its music.

GUIDO Kiss me, Beatrice!

(She takes his face in her hands and bends down and kisses him; a loud knocking then comes at the door, and GUIDO *leaps up; enter* A SERVANT*)*

SERVANT A package for you, sir.

GUIDO *(carelessly)* Ah! give it to me.

(Servant hands package wrapped in vermilion silk, and exit; as GUIDO *is about to open it the* DUCHESS *comes up behind and in sport takes it from him)*

DUCHESS *(laughing)* Now I will wager it is from some girl
Who would have you wear her favour; I am so jealous
I will not give up the least part in you,
But like a miser keep you to myself,
And spoil you perhaps in keeping.

GUIDO It is nothing.

DUCHESS Nay, it is from some girl.

GUIDO You know 'tis not.

DUCHESS *(turns her back and opens it)*
Now, traitor, tell me what does this sign mean,
A dagger with two leopards wrought in steel?

GUIDO *(taking it from her)* O God!

DUCHESS I'll from the window look, and try
If I can't see the porter's livery
Who left it at the gate! I will not rest
Till I have learned your secret.

(runs laughing into the colonnade)

GUIDO Oh, horrible!
Had I so soon forgot my father's death,
Did I so soon let love into my heart,
And must I banish love, and let in murder
That beats and clamours at the outer gate?
Ay, that I must! Have I not sworn an oath?
Yet not tonight; nay, it must be tonight.
Farewell then all the joy and light of life,
All dear recorded memories, farewell,
Farewell all love! Could I with bloody hands
Fondle and paddle with her innocent hands?
Could I with lips fresh from this butchery
Play with her lips? Could I with murderous eyes
Look in those violet eyes, whose purity

Would strike mine blind, and make each eyeball reel
In night perpetual? No, murder has set
A barrier between us far too high
For us to kiss across it.

DUCHESS Guido!

GUIDO Beatrice,
You must forget that name, and banish me
Out of your life for ever.

DUCHESS (*going towards him*) O dear love!

GUIDO (*stepping back*) There lies a barrier between us two
We dare not pass.

DUCHESS I dare do anything
So that you are beside me.

GUIDO Ah! There it is,
I cannot be beside you, cannot breathe
The air you breathe; I cannot any more
Stand face to face with beauty, which unnerves
My shaking heart, and makes my desperate hand
Fail of its purpose. Let me go hence, I pray;
Forget you ever looked upon me.

DUCHESS What!
With your hot kisses fresh upon my lips
Forget the vows of love you made to me?

GUIDO I take them back!

DUCHESS Alas, you cannot, Guido,
For they are part of nature now; the air
Is tremulous with their music, and outside
The little birds sing sweeter for those vows.

GUIDO There lies a barrier between us now,
Which then I knew not, or I had forgot.

DUCHESS There is no barrier, Guido; why, I will go
In poor attire, and will follow you
Over the world.

GUIDO (*wildly*) The world's not wide enough
To hold us two! Farewell, farewell for ever.

DUCHESS (*calm, and controlling her passion*)
Why did you come into my life at all, then,
Or in the desolate garden of my heart
Sow that white flower of love –

GUIDO O Beatrice!

DUCHESS – Which now you would dig up, uproot, tear out,
Though each small fibre doth so hold my heart

That if you break one, my heart breaks with it?
Why did you come into my life? Why open
The secret wells of love I had sealed up?
Why did you open them –

GUIDO O God!

DUCHESS (*clenching her hand*) – and let
The floodgates of my passion swell and burst
Till, like the wave when rivers overflow
That sweeps the forest and the farm away,
Love in the splendid avalanche of its might
Swept my life with it? Must I drop by drop
Gather these waters back and seal them up?
Alas! Each drop will be a tear, and so
Will with its saltness make life very bitter.

GUIDO I pray you speak no more, for I must go
Forth from your life and love, and make a way
On which you cannot follow.

DUCHESS I have heard
That sailors dying of thirst upon a raft,
Poor castaways upon a lonely sea,
Dream of green fields and pleasant watercourses,
And then wake up with red thirst in their throats,
And die more miserably because sleep
Has cheated them: so they die cursing sleep
For having sent them dreams: I will not curse you
Though I am cast away upon the sea
Which men call Desolation.

GUIDO O God, God!

DUCHESS But you will stay: listen, I love you, Guido.
(*she waits a little*)
Is echo dead, that when I say I love you
There is no answer?

GUIDO Everything is dead,
Save one thing only, which shall die tonight!

DUCHESS Then I must train my lips to say farewell,
And yet I think they will not learn that lesson,
For when I shape them for such utterance
They do but say I love you: must I chide them?
And if so, can my lips chide one another?
Alas, they both are guilty, and refuse
To say the word.

GUIDO Then I must say it for them,

Farewell, we two can never meet again.

(rushes towards her)

DUCHESS If you are going, touch me not, but go.

(exit GUIDO*)*

Never again, did he say never again?
Well, well, I know my business! I will change
The torch of love into a funeral torch,
And with the flowers of love will strew my bier,
And from love's songs will make a dirge, and so
Die, as the swan dies, singing.
O Misery,
If thou wert so enamoured of my life,
Why couldst thou not some other form have borne?
The mask of pain, and not the mask of love,
The raven's voice, and not the nightingale's,
The blind mole's eyes, and not those agate eyes
Which, like the summer heavens, were so blue
That one could fancy one saw God in them,
So, Misery, I had known thee.
Barrier! Barrier!
Why did he say there was a barrier?
There is no barrier between us two.
He lied to me, and shall I for that reason
Loathe what I love, and what I worshipped, hate?
I think we women do not love like that.
For if I cut his image from my heart,
My heart would, like a bleeding pilgrim, follow
That image through the world, and call it back
With little cries of love.

Enter DUKE *equipped for the chase, with falconers and hounds*

DUKE Madam, you keep us waiting;
You keep my dogs waiting.

DUCHESS I will not ride today.

DUKE How now, what's this?

DUCHESS My lord, I cannot go.

DUKE What, pale face, do you dare to stand against me?
Why, I could set you on a sorry jade
And lead you through the town, till the low rabble
You feed toss up their hats and mock at you.

DUCHESS Have you no word of kindness ever for me?

DUKE Kind words are lime to snare our enemies!

I hold you in the hollow of my hand
And have no need on you to waste kind words.

DUCHESS Well, I will go.

DUKE (*slapping his boot with his whip*)
No, I have changed my mind,
You will stay here, and like a faithful wife
Watch from the window for our coming back.
Were it not dreadful if some accident
By chance should happen to your loving lord?
Come, gentlemen, my hounds begin to chafe,
And I chafe too, having a patient wife.
Where is young Guido?

MAFFIO My liege, I have not seen him
For a full hour past.

DUKE It matters not,
I dare say I shall see him soon enough.
Well, madam, you will sit at home and spin.
I do protest, sirs, the domestic virtues
Are often very beautiful in others.

Exit DUKE *with his court*

DUCHESS The stars have fought against me, that is all,
And thus tonight when my lord lieth asleep,
Will I fall upon my dagger, and so cease.
My heart is such a stone nothing can reach it
Except the dagger's edge: let it go there,
To find what name it carries: ay! Tonight
Death will divorce the Duke; and yet tonight
He may die also, he is very old.
Why should he not die? Yesterday his hand
Shook with a palsy: men have died from palsy,
And why not he? Are there not fevers also,
Agues and chills, and other maladies
Most incident to old age?
No, no, he will not die, he is too sinful;
Honest men die before their proper time.
Good men will die: men by whose side the Duke
In all the sick pollution of his life
Seems like a leper: women and children die,
But the Duke will not die, he is too sinful.
Oh, can it be
There is some immortality in sin,

Which virtue has not? And does the wicked man
Draw life from what to other men were death,
Like poisonous plants that on corruption live?
No, no, I think God would not suffer that:
Yet the Duke will not die: he is too sinful.
But I will die alone, and on this night
Grim Death shall be my bridegroom, and the tomb
My secret house of pleasure: well, what of that?
The world's a graveyard, and we each, like coffins,
Within us bear a skeleton.

Enter LORD MORANZONE *all in black, he passes across the back of the stage looking anxiously about*

MORANZONE Where is Guido?
I cannot find him anywhere.

DUCHESS (*catches sight of him*) O God!
'Twas thou who took my love away from me.

MORANZONE (*with a look of joy*) What, has he left you?

DUCHESS Nay, you know he has.
Oh, give him back to me, give him back, I say,
Or I will tear your body limb from limb,
And to the common gibbet nail your head
Until the carrion crows have stripped it bare.
Better you had crossed a hungry lioness
Before you came between me and my love.
(*With more pathos*)
Nay, give him back, you know not how I love him.
Here by this chair he knelt a half-hour since,
'Twas there he stood, and there he looked at me;
This is the hand he kissed, these are the lips
His lips made havoc of, and these the ears
Into whose open portals he did pour
A tale of love so musical that all
The birds stopped singing! Oh, give him back to me.

MORANZONE He does not love you, madam.

DUCHESS May the plague
Wither the tongue that says so! Give him back.

MORANZONE Madam, I tell you you will never see him,
Neither tonight, nor any other night.

DUCHESS What is your name?

MORANZONE My name? Revenge! (*exit*)

DUCHESS Revenge!

I think I never harmed a little child.
What should Revenge do coming to my door?
It matters not, for death is there already,
Waiting with his dim torch to light my way.
'Tis true men hate thee, Death, and yet I think
Thou wilt be kinder to me than my lover,
And so dispatch the messengers at once,
Hurry the lazy steeds of lingering day,
And let the night, thy sister, come instead,
And drape the world in mourning; let the owl.
Who is thy minister, scream from his tower
And wake the toad with hooting, and the bat,
That is the slave of dim Persephone,
Wheel through the sombre air on wandering wing!
Tear up the shrieking mandrakes from the earth
And bid them make us music, and tell the mole
To dig deep down thy cold and narrow bed,
For I shall lie within thine arms tonight.

END OF ACT TWO

ACT THREE

A large corridor in the Duke's palace: a window, left of centre, looks out on a view of Padua by moonlight; a staircase, right of centre, leads up to a door with a portière of crimson velvet, with the Duke's arms embroidered in gold on it; on the lowest step of the staircase a figure draped in black is sitting; the hall is lit by an iron cresset filled with burning tow; thunder and lightning outside; the time is night. Enter GUIDO *through the window.*

GUIDO The wind is rising: how my ladder shook!
I thought that every gust would break the cords!
(*looks out at the city*)
Christ! What a night:
Great thunder in the heavens, and wild lightnings
Striking from pinnacle to pinnacle
Across the city, till the dim houses seem
To shudder and to shake as each new glare
Dashes adown the street.
(*passes across the stage to foot of staircase*)
Ah! Who art thou
That sittest on the stair, like unto Death
Waiting a guilty soul? (*a pause*)
Canst thou not speak?
Or has this storm laid palsy on your tongue,
And chilled your utterance? Get from my path,
For I have certain business in yon chamber,
Which I must do alone.
(*The figure rises and takes off his mask*)

MORANZONE Guido Ferranti,
Thy murdered father laughs for joy tonight.

GUIDO (*confusedly*) What, art thou here?

MORANZONE Ay, waiting for your coming.

GUIDO (*looking away from him*) I did not think to see you, but am glad,
That thou mayest know the very thing I mean to do.

MORANZONE First, I would have you know my well-laid plans;
Listen: I have set horses at the gate

Which leads to Parma: when thou hast done thy business
We will ride hence, and by tomorrow night,
If our good horses fail not by the way,
Parma will see us coming; I have advised
Many old friends of your great father there,
Who have prepared the citizens for revolt.
With money, and with golden promises,
The which we need not keep, I have bought over
Many that stand by this usurping Duke.
As for the soldiers, they, the Duke being dead,
Will fling allegiance to the winds, so thou
Shalt sit again within thy father's palace,
As Parma's rightful lord.

GUIDO It cannot be.

MORANZONE Nay, but it shall.

GUIDO Listen, Lord Moranzone,
I am resolved not to kill this man.

MORANZONE Surely my ears are traitors, speak again:
It cannot be but age has dulled my powers,
I am an old man now: what did you say?
You said that with that dagger in your belt
You would avenge your father's bloody murder;
Did you not say that?

GUIDO No, my lord, I said
I was resolved not to kill the Duke.

MORANZONE You said not that; it is my senses mock me;
Or else this midnight air o'ercharged with storm
Alters your message in the giving it.

GUIDO Nay, you heard rightly; I'll not kill this man.

MORANZONE What of thine oath, thou traitor, what of thine oath?

GUIDO I am resolved not to keep that oath.

MORANZONE What of thy murdered father?

GUIDO Dost thou think
My father would be glad to see me coming,
This old man's blood still hot upon mine hands?

MORANZONE Ay! He would laugh for joy.

GUIDO I do not think so,
There is better knowledge in the other world;
Vengeance is God's, let God himself revenge.

MORANZONE Thou art God's minister of vengeance.

GUIDO No!
God hath no minister but his own hand.

I will not kill this man.

MORANZONE Why are you here,
If not to kill him, then?

GUIDO Lord Moranzone,
I purpose to ascend to the Duke's chamber,
And as he lies asleep lay on his breast
The dagger and this writing; when he awakes
Then he will know who held him in his power
And slew him not: this is the noblest vengeance
Which I can take.

MORANZONE You will not slay him?

GUIDO No.

MORANZONE Ignoble son of a noble father,
Who sufferest this man who sold that father
To live an hour.

GUIDO 'Twas thou that hindered me;
I would have killed him in the open square,
The day I saw him first.

MORANZONE It was not yet time;
Now it is time, and, like some green-faced girl,
Thou pratest of forgiveness.

GUIDO No! revenge:
The right revenge my father's son should take.

MORANZONE O wretched father, thus again betrayed,
And by thine own son too! You are a coward.
Take out the knife, get to the Duke's chamber,
And bring me back his heart upon the blade.
When he is dead, then you can talk to me
Of noble vengeances.

GUIDO Upon thine honour,
And by the love thou bearest my father's name,
Dost thou think my father, that great gentleman,
That generous soldier, that most chivalrous lord,
Would have crept at night-time, like a common thief,
And stabbed an old man sleeping in his bed,
However he had wronged him: tell me that.

MORANZONE (*after some hesitation*) You have sworn an oath,
see that you keep that oath.
Boy, do you think I do not know your secret,
Your traffic with the Duchess?

GUIDO Silence, liar!
The very moon in heaven is not more chaste,

Nor the white stars so pure.

MORANZONE And yet, you love her;
Weak fool, to let love in upon your life,
Save as a plaything.

GUIDO You do well to talk:
Within your veins, old man, the pulse of youth
Throbs with no ardour. Your eyes full of rheum
Have against Beauty closed their filmy doors,
And your clogged ears, losing their natural sense,
Have shut you from the music of the world.
You talk of love! You know not what it is.

MORANZONE Oh, in my time, boy, have I walked i' the moon,
Swore I would live on kisses and on blisses,
Swore I would die for love, and did not die,
Wrote love bad verses; ay, and sung them badly,
Like all true lovers. Oh, I have done the tricks!
I know the partings and the chamberings;
We are all animals at best, and love
Is merely passion with a holy name.

GUIDO Now then I know you have not loved at all.
Love is the sacrament of life; it sets
Virtue where virtue was not; cleanses men
Of all the vile pollutions of this world;
It is the fire which purges gold from dross,
It is the fan which winnows wheat from chaff,
It is the spring which in some wintry soil
Makes innocence to blossom like a rose.
The days are over when God walked with men,
But Love, which is his image, holds His place.
When a man loves a woman, then he knows
God's secret, and the secret of the world.
There is no house so lowly or so mean
Which, if their hearts be pure who live in it,
Love will not enter; but if bloody murder
Knock at the palace gate and is let in,
Love like a wounded thing creeps out and dies.
This is the punishment God sets on sin.
The wicked cannot love.
(*A groan comes from the* DUKE'S *chamber.*)
Ah! What is that?
Do you not hear? 'Twas nothing.
So I think

That it is women's mission by their love
To save the souls of men: and loving her,
My lady, my white Beatrice, I begin
To see a nobler and a holier vengeance
In letting this man live, than doth reside
In bloody deeds o' night, stabs in the dark,
And young hands clutching at a palsied throat.
It was, I think, for love's sake that Lord Christ,
Who was indeed himself incarnate Love,
Bade every man forgive his enemy.

MORANZONE (*sneeringly*) That was in Palestine, not Padua;
And said for saints: I have to do with men.

GUIDO It was for all time said.

MORANZONE And your white Duchess.
What will she do to thank you? Will she not come.
And put her cheek to yours, and fondle you,
For having left her lord to plague her life?

GUIDO Alas, I will not see her face again.
'Tis but twelve hours since I parted from her,
So suddenly, and with such violent passion,
That she has shut her heart against me now:
No, I will never see her.

MORANZONE What will you do?

GUIDO After that I have laid the dagger there,
Get hence tonight from Padua.

MORANZONE And then?

GUIDO I will take service with the Doge at Venice,
And bid him pack me straightway to the wars,
In Holy Land against the Infidel;
And there I will, being now sick of life,
Throw that poor life against some desperate spear.
(*A groan from the* DUKE'S *chamber again*)
Did you not hear a voice?

MORANZONE I always hear,
From the dim confines of some sepulchre,
A voice that cries for vengeance. We waste time,
It will be morning soon; are you resolved
You will not kill the Duke?

GUIDO I am resolved.

MORANZONE Guido Ferranti, in that chamber yonder
There lies the man who sold your father's life,
And gave him to the hangman's murderous hands.

There does he sleep: you have your father's dagger;
Will you not kill him?

GUIDO No, I will not kill him.

MORANZONE O wretched father, lying unavenged.

GUIDO More wretched were thy son a murderer.

MORANZONE Why, what is life?

GUIDO I do not know, my lord,
I did not give it, and I dare not take it.

MORANZONE I do not thank God often; but I think
I thank him now that I have got no son!
And you, what bastard blood flows in your veins
That when you have your enemy in your grasp
You let him go! I would that I had left you
With the dull hinds that reared you.

GUIDO Better perhaps
That you had done so! May be better still
I'd not been born to this distressful world.

MORANZONE Farewell!

GUIDO Farewell! Some day, Lord Moranzone,
You will understand my vengeance.

MORANZONE Never, boy.

(*gets out of window and exit by rope ladder*)

GUIDO Father, I think thou knowest my resolve,
And with this nobler vengeance are content.
Father, I think in letting this man live
That I am doing what you would have done.
Father, I know not if a human voice
Can pierce the iron gateway of the dead,
Or if the dead are set in ignorance
Of what we do, or do not, for their sakes.
And yet I feel a presence in the air,
There is a shadow standing at my side,
And ghostly kisses seem to touch my lips,
And leave them holier. (*kneels down*)
O father, if 'tis thou,
Canst thou not burst though the decrees of death,
And in corporeal semblance show thyself,
That I may touch thy hand!
No, there is nothing. (*rises*)
'Tis the night that cheats us with its phantoms,
And, like a puppet-master, makes us think
That things are real which are not. It grows late.

Now must I to my business.
(*pulls out a letter from his doublet and reads it*)
When he wakes,
And sees this letter, and the dagger with it,
Will he not have some loathing for his life,
Repent, perchance, and lead a better life,
Or will he mock because a young man spared
His natural enemy? I do not care.
Father, it is your bidding that I do,
Your bidding, and the bidding of my love
Which teaches me to know you as you are.
(*Ascends staircase stealthily, and just as he reaches out his hand to draw back the curtain the* DUCHESS *appears all in white.* GUIDO *starts back*)

DUCHESS Guido! What do you here so late?
GUIDO O white and spotless angel of my life,
Sure thou hast come from heaven with a message
That mercy is more noble than revenge?
DUCHESS Ay! I do pray for mercy earnestly.
GUIDO O father, now I know I do your bidding,
For hand in hand with Mercy, like a God,
Has Love come forth to meet me on the way.
DUCHESS I felt you would come back to me again,
Although you left me very cruelly:
Why did you leave me? Nay, that matters not,
For I can hold you now, and feel your heart
Beat against mine with little throbs of love:
Our hearts are two caged birds, trying to kiss
Across their cages' bars: but the time goes,
It will be morning in an hour or so;
Let us get horses: I must post to Venice,
They will not think of looking for me there.
GUIDO Love, I will follow you across the world.
DUCHESS But are you sure you love me?
GUIDO Is the lark
Sure that it loves the dawn that bids it sing?
DUCHESS Could nothing ever change you?
GUIDO Nothing ever:
The shipman's needle is not set more sure
Than I am to the lodestone of your love.
DUCHESS There is no barrier between us now.

GUIDO None, love, nor shall be.
DUCHESS I have seen to that.
GUIDO Tarry here for me.
DUCHESS No, you are not going?
You will not leave me as you did before?
GUIDO I will return within a moment's space,
But first I must repair to the Duke's chamber,
And leave this letter and this dagger there,
That when he wakes –
DUCHESS When who wakes?
GUIDO Why, the Duke.
DUCHESS He will not wake again.
GUIDO What, is he dead?
DUCHESS Ay! He is dead.
GUIDO O God! How wonderful
Are all thy secret ways! Who would have said
That on this very night, when I had yielded
Into thy hands the vengeance that is Thine,
Thou with thy finger should have touched the man,
And bade him come before thy judgment seat.
DUCHESS I have just killed him.
GUIDO (*in horror*) Oh!
DUCHESS He was asleep;
Come closer, love, and I will tell you all.
Kiss me upon the mouth, and I will tell you.
You will not kiss me now? – well, you will kiss me
When I have told you how I killed the Duke.
After you left me with such bitter words,
Feeling my life went lame without your love,
I had resolved to kill myself tonight.
About an hour ago I waked from sleep,
And took my dagger from beneath my pillow,
Where I had hidden it to serve my need,
And drew it from the sheath, and felt the edge,
And thought of you, and how I loved you, Guido,
And turned to fall upon it, when I marked
The old man sleeping, full of years and sin;
There lay he muttering curses in his sleep,
And as I looked upon his evil face
Suddenly like a flame there flashed across me,
There is the barrier which Guido spoke of:
You said there lay a barrier between us,

What barrier but he? –
I hardly know
What happened, but a steaming mist of blood
Rose up between us two.

GUIDO O horrible!

DUCHESS You would have said so had you seen that mist:
And then the air rained blood and then he groaned,
And then he groaned no more! I only heard
The dripping of the blood upon the floor.

GUIDO Enough, enough.

DUCHESS Will you not kiss me now?
Do you remember saying that women's love
Turns men to angels? Well, the love of man
Turns women into martyrs; for its sake
We do or suffer anything.

GUIDO O God!

DUCHESS Will you not speak?

GUIDO I cannot speak at all.

DUCHESS This is the knife with which I killed the Duke.
I did not think he would have bled so much,
But I can wash my hands in water after;
Can I not wash my hands? Ay, but my soul?
Let us not talk of this! Let us go hence:
Is not the barrier broken down between us?
What would you more? Come, it is almost morning.
(*puts her hand on* GUIDO's)

GUIDO (*breaking from her*) O damned saint! O angel fresh
from hell!
What bloody devil tempted thee to this!
That thou hast killed thy husband, that is nothing –
Hell was already gaping for his soul –
But thou hast murdered Love, and in its place
Hast set a horrible and bloodstained thing,
Whose very breath breeds pestilence and plague,
And strangles Love.

DUCHESS (*in amazed wonder*) I did it all for you.
I would not have you do it, had you willed it,
For I would keep you without blot or stain,
A thing unblemished, unassailed, untarnished.
Men do not know what women do for love.
Have I not wrecked my soul for your dear sake,

Here and hereafter?
Oh be kind to me.
I did it all for you.

GUIDO
No, do not touch me.
Between us lies a thin red stream of blood,
I dare not look across it: when you stabbed him
You stabbed Love with a sharp knife to the heart.
We cannot meet again.

DUCHESS
(*wringing her hands*) For you! For you!
I did it all for you: have you forgotten?
You said there was a barrier between us;
That barrier lies now i' the upper chamber
Upset, overthrown, beaten, and battered down,
And will not part us ever.

GUIDO
No, you mistook:
Sin was the barrier, you have raised it up;
Crime was the barrier, you have set it there.
The barrier was murder, and your hand
Has builded it so high it shuts out heaven,
It shuts out God.

DUCHESS
I did it all for you;
You dare not leave me now: nay, Guido, listen.
Get horses ready, we will fly tonight.
The past is a bad dream, we will forget it:
Before us lies the future: will we not have
Sweet days of love beneath our vines and laugh? –
No, no, we will not laugh, but, when we weep,
Well, we will weep together; I will serve you
Like a poor housewife, like a common slave;
I will be very meek and very gentle:
You do not know me.

GUIDO
Nay, I know you now;
Get hence, I say, out of my sight.

DUCHESS
(*pacing up and down*) O God,
How I have loved this man!

GUIDO
You never loved me.
Had it been so, Love would have stopped your hand,
Nor suffered you to stain his holy shrine,
Where none can enter but the innocent.

DUCHESS
These are but words, words, words.

GUIDO
Get hence, I pray:
How could we sit together at Love's table?

You have poured poison in the sacred wine,
And Murder dips his fingers in the sop.
Rather than this, I had died a thousand deaths.

DUCHESS I having done it, die a thousand deaths.

GUIDO It is not death but life that you should fear.

DUCHESS (*throws herself on her knees*) Then slay me now!
I have spilt blood tonight,
You shall spill more, so we go hand in hand
To heaven or to hell. Draw your sword, Guido,
And traffic quickly for my life with Death,
Who is grown greedy of such merchandise.
Quick, let your soul go chambering in my heart,
It will but find its master's image there.
Nay, if you will not slay me with your sword,
Bid me to fall upon this reeking knife,
And I will do it.

GUIDO (*wresting knife from her*) Give it to me, I say.
O God, your very hands are wet with blood!
This place is hell, I cannot tarry here.

DUCHESS Will you not raise me up before you go,
Or must I like a beggar keep my knees.

GUIDO I pray you let me see your face no more.

DUCHESS Better for me I had not seen your face.
Oh, think it was for you I killed this man.
(GUIDO *recoils; she seizes his hands as she kneels*)
Nay, Guido, listen for a while:
Until you came to Padua I lived
Wretched indeed, but with no murderous thought,
Very submissive to a cruel lord,
Very obedient to unjust commands,
As pure I think as any gentle girl
Who now would turn in horror from my hands –
You came: ah! Guido, the first kindly words
I ever heard since I had come from France
Were from your lips: well, well, that is no matter.
You came, and in the passion of your eyes
I read love's meaning, everything you said
Touched my dumb soul to music, and you seemed
Fair as that young St Michael on the wall
In Santa Croce, where we go and pray.
I wonder will I ever pray again?
Well, you were fair, and in your boyish face

The morning seemed to lighten, so I loved you.
And yet I did not tell you of my love.
'Twas you who sought me out, knelt at my feet
As I kneel now at yours, and with sweet vows (*kneels*),
Whose music seems to linger in my ears,
Swore that you loved me, and I trusted you.
I think there are many women in the world
Who had they been unto this vile Duke mated,
Chained to his side, as the poor galley slave
Is to a leper chained – ay! many women
Who would have tempted you to kill the man.
I did not.
Yet I know that had I done so,
I had not been thus humbled in the dust (*stands up*),
But you had loved me very faithfully.
(*after a pause approaches him timidly*)
I do not think you understand me, Guido:
It was for your sake that I wrought this deed
Whose horror now chills my young blood to ice,
For your sake only. (*stretching out her arm*)
Will you not speak to me?
Love me a little: in my girlish life
I have been starved for love, and kindliness
Has passed me by.

GUIDO I dare not look at you:
You come to me with too pronounced a favour,
Get to your tirewomen.

DUCHESS Ay, there it is!
There speaks the man! Yet had you come to me
With any heavy sin upon your soul,
Some murder done for hire, not for love,
Why, I had sat and watched at your bedside
All through the night-time, lest Remorse might come
And pour his poisons in your ear, and so
Keep you from sleeping! Sure it is the guilty,
Who, being very wretched, need love most.

GUIDO There is no love where there is any guilt.

DUCHESS No love where there is any guilt! O God,
How differently do we love from men!
There is many a woman here in Padua,
Some workman's wife, or ruder artisan's,
Whose husband spends the wages of the week

In a coarse revel, or a tavern brawl,
And reeling home late on the Saturday night,
Finds his wife sitting by a fireless hearth,
Trying to hush the child who cries for hunger,
And then sets to and beats his wife because
The child is hungry, and the fire black.
Yet the wife loves him! And will rise next day
With some red bruise across a careworn face,
And sweep the house, and do the common service,
And try and smile, and only be too glad
If he does not beat her a second time
Before her child! – that is how women love.
(*a pause:* GUIDO *says nothing*) Do you say nothing?
Oh be kind to me
While yet I know the summer of my days.
I think you will not drive me from your side.
Where have I got to go if you reject me? –
You for whose sake this hand has murdered life,
You for whose sake my soul has wrecked itself
Beyond all hope of pardon.

GUIDO Get thee gone:
The dead man is a ghost, and our love too,
Flits like a ghost about its desolate tomb,
And wanders through this charnel house, and weeps
That when you slew your lord you slew it also.
Do you not see?

DUCHESS I see when men love women
They give them but a little of their lives,
But women when they love give everything;
I see that, Guido, now.

GUIDO Away, away,
And come not back till you have waked your dead.

DUCHESS I would to God that I could wake the dead,
Put vision in the glazéd eyes, and give
The tongue its natural utterance, and bid
The heart to beat again: that cannot be:
For what is done, is done: and what is dead
Is dead for ever: the fire cannot warm him:
The winter cannot hurt him with its snows;
Something has gone from him; if you call him now,
He will not answer; if you mock him now,
He will not laugh; and if you stab him now,

He will not bleed.
I would that I could wake him!
O God, put back the sun a little space,
And from the roll of time blot out tonight,
And bid it not have been! put back the sun,
And make me what I was an hour ago!
No, no, time will not stop for anything,
Nor the sun stay its courses, though Repentance
Calling it back grow hoarse; but you, my love,
Have you no word of pity even for me?
O Guido, Guido, will you not kiss me once?
Drive me not to some desperate resolve:
Women grow mad when they are treated thus:
Will you not kiss me once?

GUIDO (*holding up knife*) I will not kiss you
Until the blood grows dry upon this knife,
And not even then.

DUCHESS Dear Christ! How little pity
We women get in this untimely world;
Men lure us to some dreadful precipice,
And, when we fall, they leave us.

GUIDO (*wildly*) Back to your dead!

DUCHESS (*going up the stairs*) Why, then, I will be gone! And may you find
More mercy than you showed to me tonight!

GUIDO Let me find mercy when I go at night
And do foul murder.

DUCHESS (*coming down a few steps*) Murder did you say?
Murder is hungry, and still cries for more,
And Death, his brother, is not satisfied,
But walks the house, and will not go away,
Unless he has a comrade! Tarry, Death,
For I will give thee a most faithful lackey
To travel with thee! Murder, call no more,
For thou shalt eat thy fill.
There is a storm
Will break upon this house before the morning,
So horrible, that the white moon already
Turns grey and sick with terror, the low wind
Goes moaning round the house, and the high stars
Run madly through the vaulted firmament,
As though the night wept tears of liquid fire

For what the day shall look upon. Oh weep,
Thou lamentable heaven! Weep thy fill!
Though sorrow like a cataract drench the fields,
And make the earth one bitter lake of tears,
It would not be enough. (*a peal of thunder*)
Do you not hear,
There is artillery in the heaven tonight.
Vengeance is wakened up, and has unloosed
His dogs upon the world, and in this matter
Which lies between us two, let him who draws
The thunder on his head beware the ruin
Which the forked flame brings after.
(*a flash of lightning followed by a peal of thunder*)

GUIDO Away! Away!

(*Exit the* DUCHESS, *who as she lifts the crimson curtain looks back for a moment at* GUIDO, *but he makes no sign; more thunder*)

Now is life fallen in ashes at my feet
And noble love self-slain; and in its place
Crept murder with its silent bloody feet.
And she who wrought it – Oh! And yet she loved me,
And for my sake did do this dreadful thing.
I have been cruel to her: Beatrice!
Beatrice, I say, come back
(*begins to ascend staircase, when the noise of soldiers is heard*)
Ah! What is that?
Torches ablaze, and noise of hurrying feet.
Pray God they have not seized her. (*noise grows louder*)
Beatrice!
There is yet time to escape. Come down, come out!
(*The voice of the* DUCHESS *outside*)
This way went he, the man who slew my lord.

(*down the staircase come hurrying a confused body of soldiers;* GUIDO *is not seen at first, till the* DUCHESS *surrounded by servants carrying torches appears at the top of the staircase and points to* GUIDO, *who is seized at once, one of the soldiers dragging the knife from his hand and showing it to the captain of the guard in sight of the audience. Tableau.*)

END OF ACT THREE

ACT FOUR

The Hall of Justice: the walls are hung with stamped grey velvet; above the hangings the wall is red, and gilt symbolical figures bear up the roof, which is made of red beams with grey soffits and moulding; a canopy of white satin flowered with gold is set for the Duchess; below it a long bench with red cloth for the judges; below that a table for the clerks of the court. Two SOLDIERS *stand on each side of the canopy, and two* SOLDIERS *guard the door; the* CITIZENS *have some of them collected in the court, others are coming in greeting one another; two* TIPSTAFFS *in violet keep order with long white wands.*

1 CITIZEN Goodmorrow, neighbour Anthony.

2 CITIZEN Goodmorrow, neighbour Dominick.

1 CITIZEN This is a strange day for Padua, is it not? – the Duke being dead.

2 CITIZEN I tell you, neighbour Dominick, I have not known such a day since the last Duke died: and if you believe me not, I am no true man.

1 CITIZEN They will try him first, and sentence him afterwards, will they not, neighbour Anthony?

2 CITIZEN Nay, for he might 'scape his punishment then; but they will condemn him first so that he gets his deserts, and give him trial afterwards so that no injustice is done.

1 CITIZEN Well, well, it will go hard with him I doubt not.

2 CITIZEN Surely it is a grievous thing to shed a duke's blood.

3 CITIZEN They say a duke has blue blood,

2 CITIZEN I think our Duke's blood was black like his soul.

1 CITIZEN Have a watch, neighbour Anthony, the officer is looking at thee.

2 CITIZEN I care not if he does but look at me; he cannot whip me with the lashes of his eye.

3 CITIZEN What think you of this young man who stuck the knife into the Duke?

2 CITIZEN Why, that he is a well-behaved, and a well-meaning, and a well-favoured lad, and yet wicked in that he killed the Duke.

3 CITIZEN 'Twas the first time he did it; may be the law will not be hard on him, as he did not do it before.

2 CITIZEN True.

TIPSTAFF Silence, knave.

2 CITIZEN Am I thy looking-glass, Master Tipstaff, that thou callest me knave?

1 CITIZEN Here be one of the household coming. Well, Dame Lucy, thou art of the court, how does thy poor mistress the Duchess, with her sweet face?

MS LUCY Oh well-a-day! O miserable day! O day! O misery! Why it is just nineteen years last June, at Michaelmas, since I was married to my husband, and it is August now, and here is the Duke murdered; there is a coincidence for you!

2 CITIZEN Why, if it is a coincidence, they may not kill the young man: there is no law against coincidences.

1 CITIZEN But how does the Duchess?

MS LUCY Well, well, I knew some harm would happen to the house: six weeks ago the cakes were all burned on one side, and last St Martin even as ever was, there flew into the candle a big moth that had wings, and a'most scared me.

1 CITIZEN But come to the Duchess, good gossip: what of her?

MS LUCY Marry, it is time you should ask after her, poor lady; she is distraught almost. Why, she has not slept, but paced the chamber all night long. I prayed her to have a posset, or some aqua-vitae, and to get to bed and sleep a little for her health's sake, but she answered me she was afraid she might dream. That was a strange answer, was it not?

2 CITIZEN These great folk have not much sense, so Providence makes it up to them in fine clothes.

MS LUCY Well, well, God keep murder from us, I say, as long as we are alive.

Enter LORD MORANZONE *hurriedly*

MORANZONE Is the Duke dead?

2 CITIZEN He has a knife in his heart, which they say is not healthy for any man.

MORANZONE Who is accused of having killed him?

2 CITIZEN Why, the prisoner, sir

MORANZONE But who is the prisoner?

2 CITIZEN Why, he that is accused of the Duke's murder.

MORANZONE I mean, what is his name?

2 CITIZEN Faith, the same which his godfathers gave him: what else should it be?

TIPSTAFF Guido Ferranti is his name, my lord.

MORANZONE I almost knew thine answer ere you gave it.
(*Aside*) Yet it is strange he should have killed the Duke
Seeing he left me in such different mood.
It is most likely when he saw the man,
This devil who had sold his father's life,
That passion from their seat within his heart
Thrust all his boyish theories of love
And in their place set vengeance; yet I marvel
That he escaped not.
(*Turning again to the crowd*)
How was he taken, tell me

3 CITIZEN Marry, sir, he was taken by the heels.

MORANZONE But who seized him?

3 CITIZEN Why, those that did lay hold of him.

MORANZONE How was the alarm given?

3 CITIZEN That I cannot tell you, sir,

MS LUCY It was the Duchess herself who pointed him out.

MORANZONE (*aside*) The Duchess! There is something strange in this.

MS LUCY Ay! And the dagger was in his hand – the Duchess's own dagger.

MORANZONE What did you say?

MS LUCY Why, marry, that it was with the Duchess's dagger that the Duke was killed.

MORANZONE (*aside*) There is some mystery about this: I cannot understand it.

2 CITIZEN They be very long a-coming.

1 CITIZEN I warrant they will come soon enough for the prisoner.

TIPSTAFF Silence in the court!

1 CITIZEN Thou dost break silence in bidding us keep it, Master Tipstaff.

Enter the LORD JUSTICE *and the other judges*

2 CITIZEN Who is he in scarlet? Is he the headsman?

3 CITIZEN Nay, he is the Lord Justice.

Enter GUIDO *guarded*

2 CITIZEN There be the prisoner surely.

3 CITIZEN He looks honest.

I CITIZEN That be his villainy: knaves nowadays do look so honest that honest folk are forced to look like knaves so as to be different.

Enter the HEADSMAN, *who takes his stand behind* GUIDO

2 CITIZEN Yon be the headsman then! O Lord! Is the axe sharp, think you?

I CITIZEN Ay! Sharper than thy wits are; but the edge is not towards him, mark you.

2 CITIZEN I' faith, I like it not so near.

I CITIZEN Tut, thou need'st not be afraid; they never cut the heads off common folk: they do but hang us. (*trumpets outside*)

3 CITIZEN What are the trumpets for? Is the trial over?

I CITIZEN Nay, 'tis for the Duchess.

Enter the DUCHESS *in black velvet, her train of flowered black velvet is carried by two pages in violet; with her is the* CARDINAL *in scarlet,* and *the* GENTLEMEN OF THE COURT *in black; she takes her seat on the throne above the* JUDGES, *who rise and take their caps off as she enters; the* CARDINAL *sits next to her a little lower; the* COURTIERS *group themselves about the throne*

2 CITIZEN Oh, poor lady, how pale she is! Will she sit there?

I CITIZEN Ay! She is in the Duke's place now.

2 CITIZEN That is a good thing for Padua; the Duchess is a very kind and merciful Duchess; why, she cured my child of the ague once.

3 CITIZEN Ay, and has given us bread: do not forget the bread.

A SOLDIER Stand back, good people.

2 CITIZEN If we be good, why should we stand back?

TIPSTAFF Silence in the court!

LD JUSTICE May it please your grace,
Is it your pleasure we proceed to trial
Of the Duke's murder? (DUCHESS *bows*)
Set the prisoner forth.
What is thy name?

GUIDO It matters not, my lord.

LD JUSTICE Guido Ferranti is thy name in Padua.

GUIDO A man may die as well under that name as any other.

GUIDO Thou art not ignorant
What dreadful charge men lay against thee here,
Namely, the treacherous murder of thy lord,
Simone Gesso, Duke of Padua;

What dost thou say in answer?

GUIDO I say nothing.

LD JUSTICE Dost thou admit this accusation, then?

GUIDO I admit naught, and yet I naught deny.
I pray thee, my Lord Justice, be as brief
As the court's custom and the laws allow.
I will not speak.

LD JUSTICE Why, then, it cannot be
That of this murder thou art innocent,
But rather that thy stony obstinate heart
Hath shut its doors against the voice of justice.
Think not thy silence will avail thee aught,
'Twill rather aggravate thy desperate guilt,
Of which indeed we are most well assured;
Again I bid thee speak.

GUIDO I will say nothing.

LD JUSTICE Then naught remains for me but to pronounce
Upon thy head the sentence of swift death.

GUIDO I pray thee give thy message speedily,
Thou couldst not bring me anything more dear.

LD JUSTICE (*rising*) Guido Ferranti –

MORANZONE Tarry, my Lord Justice.

LD JUSTICE Who art thou that bid'st justice tarry, sir?

MORANZONE So be it justice it can go its way;
But if it be not justice –

LD JUSTICE Who is this?

BARDI A very noble gentleman, and well known
To the late Duke.

LD JUSTICE Sir, thou art come in time
To see the murder of the Duke avenged.
There stands the man who did this heinous thing.

MORANZONE Has merely blind suspicion fixed on him,
Or have ye any proof he did the deed?

LD JUSTICE Thrice has the court entreated him to speak,
But surely guilt weighs heavy on the tongue,
For he says nothing in defence, nor tries
To purge himself of this most dread account,
Which innocence would surely do.

MORANZONE My lord,
I ask again what proof have ye?

LD JUSTICE (*holding up the dagger*) This dagger,
Which from his bloodstained hands, itself all blood,

Last night the soldiers seized: what further proof
Need we indeed?

MORANZONE (*takes the dagger and approaches the* DUCHESS)
Saw I not such a dagger
Hang from your grace's girdle yesterday?
(*The* duchess *shudders and makes no answer*)
Ah! My Lord Justice, may I speak a moment
With this young man, who in such peril stands?

LD JUSTICE Ay, willingly, my lord, and may you turn him
To make a full avowal of his guilt.

(LORD MORANZONE *goes over to* GUIDO, *who stands on stage right, and clutches him by the hand*)

MORANZONE (*in a low voice*) She did it! Nay, I saw it in her eyes.
Boy, dost thou think I'll let thy father's son
Be by this woman butchered to his death?
Her husband sold your father, and the wife
Would sell the son in turn.

GUIDO Lord Moranzone
I alone did this thing: be satisfied,
My father is avenged.

MORANZONE Enough, enough,
I know you did not kill him; had it been you,
Your father's dagger, not this woman's toy,
Had done the business: see how she glares at us!
By heaven, I will tear off that marble mask,
And tax her with this murder before all.

GUIDO You shall not do it.

MORANZONE Nay, be sure I shall.

GUIDO My lord, you must not dare to speak.

MORANZONE Why not?
If she is innocent she can prove it so
If guilty, let her die.

GUIDO What shall I do?

MORANZONE Or thou or I shall tell the truth in court.

GUIDO The truth is that I did it.

MORANZONE Sayest thou so?
Well, I will see what the good Duchess says.

GUIDO No, no, I'll tell the tale.

MORANZONE That is well, Guido.
Her sins be on her head and not on thine.
Did she not give you to the guard?

GUIDO She did.

MORANZONE Then upon her revenge thy father's death:
She was the wife of Judas.

GUIDO Ay, she was.

MORANZONE I think you need no prompting now to do it
Though you were weak and like a boy last night.

GUIDO Weak like a boy was I indeed last night?
Be sure I will not be like that today.

LD JUSTICE Doth he confess?

GUIDO My lord, I do confess
That foul unnatural murder has been done.

I CITIZEN Why, look at that: he has a pitiful heart, and does not like murder; they will let him go for that.

LD JUSTICE Say you no more?

GUIDO My lord, I say this also,
That to spill human blood is deadly sin.

2 CITIZEN Marry, he should tell that to the headsman: 'tis a good sentiment.

GUIDO Lastly, my lord, I do entreat the court
To give me leave to utter openly
The dreadful secret of this mystery,
And to point out the very guilty one
Who with this dagger last night slew the Duke.

LD JUSTICE Thou hast leave to speak.

DUCHESS (*rising*) I say he shall not speak:
What need have we of further evidence?
Was he not taken in the house at night
In Guilt's own bloody livery.

LD JUSTICE (*showing her the statute*) Your grace
Can read the law.

DUCHESS (*waiving, book aside*) Bethink you, my Lord Justice,
Is it not very like that such a one
May, in the presence of the people here,
Utter some slanderous word against my lord,
Against the city, or the city's honour,
Perchance against myself.

LD JUSTICE My liege, the law.

DUCHESS He shall not speak, but, with gags in his mouth,
Shall climb the ladder to the bloody block.

LD JUSTICE The law, my liege.

DUCHESS We are not bound by law,
But with it we bind others.

MORANZONE My Lord Justice,

Thou wilt not suffer this injustice here.

LD JUSTICE The court needs not thy voice, Lord Moranzone.
Madam, it were a precedent most evil
To wrest the law from its appointed course,
For, though the cause be just, yet anarchy
Might on this licence touch these golden scales
And unjust causes unjust victories gain.

BARDI I do not think your grace can stay the law.

DUCHESS Ay, it is well to preach and prate of law:
Methinks, my haughty lords of Padua,
If ye are hurt in pocket or estate,
So much as makes your monstrous revenues
Less by the value of one ferry toll,
Ye do not wait the tedious law's delay
With such sweet patience as ye counsel me.

BARDI Madam, I think you wrong our nobles here.

DUCHESS I think I wrong them not. Which of ye all,
Finding a thief within his house at night,
With some poor chattel thrust into his rags,
Will stop and parley with him? Do ye not
Give him unto the officer and his hook
To be dragged gaolwards straightway?
And so now,
Had ye been men, finding this fellow here,
With my lord's life still hot upon his hands,
Ye would have haled him out into the court,
And struck his head of with an axe.

GUIDO O God!

DUCHESS Speak, my Lord Justice.

LD JUSTICE Your Grace, it cannot be:
The laws of Padua are most certain here:
And by those laws the common murderer even
May with his own lips plead, and make defence.

DUCHESS Tarry a little with thy righteousness.
This is no common murderer, Lord Justice,
But a great outlaw, and a most vile traitor,
Taken in open arms against the state.
For he who slays the man who rules a state,
Slays the state also, widows every wife
And makes each child an orphan, and no less
Is to be held a public enemy,
Than if he came with mighty ordonnance,

And all the spears of Venice at his back,
To beat and batter at our city gates –
Nay, is more dangerous to our commonwealth
Than gleaming spears and thundering ordonnance,
For walls and gates, bastions and forts, and things
Whose common elements are wood and stone
May be raised up, but who can raise again
The ruined body of my murdered lord,
And bid it live and laugh?

MAFFIO Now by St Paul
I do not think that they will let him speak.

JEPPO VITELLOZZO There is much in this, listen.

DUCHESS Wherefore now,
Throw ashes on the head of Padua,
With sable banners hang each silent street,
Let every man be clad in solemn black,
But ere we turn to these sad rites of mourning
Let us bethink us of the desperate hand
Which wrought and brought this ruin on our state,
And straightway pack him to that narrow house,
Where no voice is, but with a little dust
Death fills right up the lying mouths of men.

GUIDO Unhand me, knaves! I tell thee, my Lord Justice,
Thou mightst as well bid the untrammelled ocean,
The winter whirlwind, or the Alpine storm,
Nor roar their will, as bid me hold my peace!
Ay! Though ye put your knives into my throat,
Each grim and gaping wound shall find a tongue,
And cry against you.

LD JUSTICE Sir, this violence
Avails you nothing; for save the tribunal
Give thee a lawful right to open speech,
Naught that thou sayest can be credited.

(*The* DUCHESS *smiles and* GUIDO *falls back with a gesture of despair*)

Madam, myself, and these wise Justices,
Will with your grace's sanction now retire
Into another chamber, to decide
Upon this difficult matter of the law,
And search the statutes and the precedents.

DUCHESS Go, my Lord Justice, search the statutes well,
Nor let this brawling traitor have his way.

MORANZONE Go, my Lord Justice, search thy conscience well,
Nor let a man be sent to death unheard.

Exit the LORD JUSTICE *and the judges*

DUCHESS Silence, thou evil genius of my life!
Thou com'st between us two a second time;
This time, my lord, I think the turn is mine.

GUIDO I shall not die till I have uttered voice.

DUCHESS Thou shalt die silent, and thy secret with thee.

GUIDO Art thou that Beatrice, Duchess of Padua?

DUCHESS I am what thou hast made me; look at me well,
I am thy handiwork.

MAFFIO See, is she not
Like that white tigress which we saw at Venice,
Sent by some Indian soldan to the Doge.

JEPPO Hush! She may hear thy chatter.

HEADSMAN My young fellow,
I do not know why thou shouldst care to speak,
Seeing my axe is close upon thy neck,
And words of thine will never blunt its edge.
But if thou art so bent upon it, why
Thou mightest plead unto the Churchman yonder:
The common people call him kindly here,
Indeed I know he has a kindly soul.

GUIDO This man, whose trade is death, hath courtesies
More than the others.

HEADSMAN Why, God love you, sir,
I'll do you your last service on this earth.

GUIDO My good Lord Cardinal, in a Christian land,
With Lord Christ's face of mercy looking down
From the high seat of Judgment, shall a man
Die unabsolved, unshrived? And if not so
May I not tell this dreadful tale of sin,
If any sin there be upon my soul.

DUCHESS Thou dost but waste thy time.

CARDINAL Alack, my son,
I have no power with the secular arm.
My task begins when justice has been done,
To urge the wavering sinner to repent
And to confess to Holy Church's ear
The dreadful secrets of a sinful mind.

DUCHESS Thou mayest speak to the confessional

Until thy lips grow weary of their tale,
But here thou shalt not speak.

GUIDO My reverend father,
You bring me but cold comfort.

CARDINAL Nay, my son.
For the great power of our mother Church,
Ends not with this poor bubble of a world,
Of which we are but dust, as Jerome saith,
For if the sinner doth repentant die,
Our prayers and holy masses much avail
To bring the guilty soul from purgatory.

DUCHESS And when in purgatory thou seest my lord
With that red star of blood upon his heart,
Tell him I sent thee hither.

GUIDO O dear God!

MORANZONE This is the woman, is it, whom you loved?

CARDINAL Your grace is very cruel to this man.

DUCHESS No more than he was cruel to her grace.

CARDINAL Ay! He did slay your husband.

DUCHESS Ay! He did.

CARDINAL Yet mercy is the sovereign right of princes.

DUCHESS I got no mercy, and I give it not.
He hath changed my heart into a heart of stone,
He hath sown rank nettles in a goodly field,
He hath poisoned the wells of pity in my breast,
He hath withered up all kindness at the root;
My life is as some famine-murdered land,
Whence all good things have perished utterly:
I am what he hath made me. (*the* DUCHESS *weeps*)

JEPPO Is it not strange
That she should so have loved the wicked Duke?

MAFFIO It is most strange when women love their lords,
And when they love them not it is most strange.

JEPPO What a philosopher thou art, Petrucci!

MAFFIO Ay! I can bear the ills of other men,
Which is philosophy.

DUCHESS They tarry long,
These greybeards and their council; bid them come;
Bid them come quickly, else I think my heart
Will beat itself to bursting: not indeed,
That I here care to live; God knows my life
Is not so full of joy; yet, for all that,

I would not die companionless, or go
Lonely to hell.
Look, my Lord Cardinal,
Canst thou not see across my forehead here,
In scarlet letters writ, the word Revenge?
Fetch me some water, I will wash it of:
'Twas branded there last night, but in the daytime
I need not wear it, need I, my Lord Cardinal?
Oh how it sears and burns into my brain:
Give me a knife – not that one, but another –
And I will cut it out.

CARDINAL It is most natural
To be incensed against the murderous hand
That treacherously stabbed your sleeping lord.

DUCHESS I would, old Cardinal, I could burn that hand;
But it will burn hereafter.

CARDINAL Nay, the Church
Ordains us to forgive our enemies.

DUCHESS Forgiveness? What is that? I never got it.
They come at last: well, my Lord Justice, well.

Enter the LORD JUSTICE

LD JUSTICE Most gracious lady, and our sovereign liege,
We have long pondered on the point at issue,
And much considered of your grace's wisdom,
And never wisdom spake from fairer lips –

DUCHESS Proceed, sir, without compliment.

LD JUSTICE We find,
As your own grace did rightly signify,
That any citizen who by force or craft
Conspires against the person of the liege,
Is *ipso facto* outlaw, void of rights
Such as pertain to other citizens,
Is traitor, and a public enemy,
Who may by any casual sword be slain
Without the slayer's danger, nay if brought
Into the presence of the tribunal,
Must with dumb lips and silence reverent
Listen unto his well-deserved doom,
Nor has the privilege of open speech.

DUCHESS I thank thee, my Lord Justice, heartily;
I like your law: and now I pray dispatch
This public outlaw to his righteous doom;

For I am weary, and the headsman weary,
What is there more?

LD JUSTICE Ay, there is more, your grace.
This man being alien born, not Paduan,
Nor by allegiance bound unto the Duke,
Save such as common nature doth lay down,
Hath, though accused of treasons manifold,
Whose slightest penalty is certain death,
Yet still the right of public utterance
Before the people and the open court,
Nay, shall be much entreated by the court,
To make some formal pleading for his life,
Lest his own city, righteously incensed,
Should with an unjust trial tax our state,
And wars spring up against the commonwealth:
So merciful are the laws of Padua
Unto the stranger living in her gates.

DUCHESS Being of my lord's household, is he stranger here?

LD JUSTICE Ay, until seven years of service spent
He cannot be a Paduan citizen.

GUIDO I thank thee, my Lord Justice, heartily;
I like your law.

2 CITIZEN I like no law at all:
Were there no law there'd be no lawbreakers,
So all men would be virtuous.

I CITIZEN So they would;
'Tis a wise saying that, and brings you far.

TIPSTAFF Ay! To the gallows, knave.

DUCHESS Is this the law?

LD JUSTICE It is the law most certainly, my liege.

DUCHESS Show me the book: 'tis written in blood-red.

JEPPO Look at the Duchess.

DUCHESS Thou accursed law,
I would that I could tear thee from the state
As easy as I tear thee from this book. (*tears out the page*)
Come here, Count Bardi: are you honourable?
Get a horse ready for me at my house,
For I must ride to Venice instantly.

BARDI To Venice, madam?

DUCHESS Not a word of this,
Go, go at once. (*exit* COUNT BARDI)
A moment, my Lord Justice.

If, as thou sayest it, this is the law –
Nay, nay, I doubt not that thou sayest right,
Though right be wrong in such a case as this –
May I not by the virtue of mine office
Adjourn this court until another day?

LD JUSTICE Madam, you cannot stay a trial for blood.

DUCHESS I will not tarry then to hear this man
Rail with rude tongue against our sacred person.
I have some business also in my house
Which I must do : Come, gentlemen.

LD JUSTICE My liege,
You cannot leave this court until the prisoner
Be purged or guilty of this dread offence.

DUCHESS Cannot, Lord Justice? By what right do you
Set barriers in my path where I should go?
Am I not Duchess here in Padua,
And the state's regent?

LD JUSTICE For that reason, madam,
Being the fountainhead of life and death
Whence, like a mighty river, justice flows,
Without thy presence justice is dried up
And fails of purpose: thou must tarry here.

DUCHESS What, wilt thou keep me here against my will?

LD JUSTICE We pray thy will be not against the law.

DUCHESS What if I force my way out of the court?

LD JUSTICE Thou canst not force the court to give thee way.

DUCHESS I will not tarry. (*rises from her seat*)

LD JUSTICE Is the usher here?
Let him stand forth. (USHER *comes forward*)
Thou knowest thy business, sir.

(*The* USHER *closes the doors of the court, which are on stage left, and when the* DUCHESS *and her retinue approach, kneels down*)

USHER In all humility I beseech your grace
Turn not my duty to discourtesy,
Nor make my unwelcome office an offence.
The selfsame laws which make your grace the regent
Bid me watch here: my liege, to break those laws
Is but to break thine office and not mine.

DUCHESS Is there no gentleman amongst you all
To prick this prating fellow from our way.

MAFFIO (*drawing his sword*) Ay! That will I.

LD JUSTICE Count Maffio, have a care,
And you, sir. (*to* JEPPO)
The first man who draws his sword
Upon the meanest officer of this court,
Dies before nightfall.

DUCHESS Sirs, put up your swords:
It is most meet that I should hear this man.
(*goes back to throne*)

MORANZONE Now hast thou got thy enemy in thy hand.

LD JUSTICE (*taking the timeglass up*) Guido Ferranti, while the crumbling sand
Falls through this timeglass, thou hast leave to speak.
This and no more.

GUIDO It is enough, my lord.

LD JUSTICE Thou standest on the extreme verge of death;
See that thou speakest nothing but the truth,
Naught else will serve thee.

GUIDO If I speak it not,
Then give my body to the headsman there.

LD JUSTICE (*turns the timeglass*) Let there be silence while the prisoner speaks.

TIPSTAFF Silence in the court there.

GUIDO My Lords Justices,
And reverent judges of this worthy court,
I hardly know where to begin my tale,
So strangely dreadful is this history.
First, let me tell you of what birth I am.
I am the son of that good Duke Lorenzo
Who was with damned treachery done to death
By a most wicked villain, lately Duke
Of this good town of Padua.

LD JUSTICE Have a care,
It will avail thee nought to mock this prince
Who now lies in his coffin.

MAFFIO By St James,
This is the Duke of Parma's rightful heir.

JEPPO I always thought him noble.

GUIDO I confess
That with the purport of a just revenge,
A most just vengeance on a man of blood,
I entered the Duke's household, served his will,
Sat at his board, drank of his wine, and was

His intimate: so much I will confess,
And this too, that I waited till he grew
To give the fondest secrets of his life
Into my keeping, till he fawned on me,
And trusted me in every private matter
Even as my noble father trusted him;
That for this thing I waited.
(*to the* HEADSMAN) Thou man of blood !
Turn not thine axe on me before the time.
Who knows if it be time for me to die?
Is there no other neck in court but mine?

LD JUSTICE The sand within the timeglass flows apace.
Come quickly to the murder of the Duke.

GUIDO I will be brief. Last night at twelve o' the clock,
By a strong rope I scaled the palace wall,
With purport to revenge my father's murder –
Ay! With that purport I confess, my lord.
This much I will acknowledge, and this also,
That as with stealthy feet I climbed the stair
Which led unto the chamber of the Duke,
And reached my hand out for the scarlet cloth
Which shook and shivered in the gusty door,
Lo! the white moon that sailed in the great heaven
Flooded with silver light the darkened room,
Night lit her candles for me, and I saw
The man I hated, cursing in his sleep,
And thinking of a most dear father murdered,
Sold to the scaffold, bartered to the block,
I smote the treacherous villain to the heart
With this same dagger, which by chance I found
Within the chamber

DUCHESS (*rising from her seat*)) Oh!

GUIDO (*hurriedly*) I killed the Duke.
Now, my Lord Justice, if I may crave a boon,
Suffer me not to see another sun
Light up the misery of this loathsome world.

LD JUSTICE Thy boon is granted, thou shalt die tonight.
Lead him away: Come, madam.

(GUIDO *is led off; as he goes the* DUCHESS *stretches out her arms and rushes down the stage*)

DUCHESS Guido! Guido! (*faints*)

TABLEAU AND END OF ACT FOUR

ACT FIVE

A dungeon in the public prison of Padua; GUIDO *lies asleep on a pallet left of centre; a table with a goblet on it is set also left of centre; five* SOLDIERS *are drinking and playing dice in the corner on a stone table; one of them has a lantern hung to his halbert; a torch is set in the wall over Guido's head; two grated windows behind, one on each side of the door, which is at stage centre, look out into a passage; the stage is rather dark.*

1 SOLDIER (*throws dice*) Sixes again! good Pietro.

2 SOLDIER I' faith, lieutenant, I will play with thee no more. I will lose everything.

3 SOLDIER Except thy wits, thou art safe there!

2 SOLDIER Ay, ay, he cannot take them from me.

3 SOLDIER No; for thou hast no wits to give him.

SOLDIERS (*loudly*) Ha! Ha! Ha!

1 SOLDIER Silence! You will wake the prisoner; he is asleep.

2 SOLDIER What matter? He will get sleep enough when he is buried. I warrant he'd be glad if we could wake him when he's in the grave.

3 SOLDIER Nay! For when he wakes there it will be judgment day.

2 SOLDIER Ay, and he has done a grievous thing; for, look you, to murder one of us who are but flesh and blood is a sin, and to kill a Duke goes being near against the law.

1 SOLDIER Well, well, he was a wicked Duke.

2 SOLDIER And so he should not have touched him; if one meddles with wicked people, one is like to be tainted with their wickedness.

3 SOLDIER Ay, that is true. How old is the prisoner?

2 SOLDIER Old enough to do wrong, and not old enough to be wise.

1 SOLDIER Why, then, he might be any age.

2 SOLDIER They say the Duchess wanted to pardon him.

1 SOLDIER Is that so?

2 SOLDIER Ay, and did much entreat the Lord Justice, but he would not.

1 SOLDIER I had thought, Pietro, that the Duchess was omnipotent.

2 SOLDIER True, she is well-favoured, I know none so comely.

SOLDIERS Ha! Ha! Ha!

I SOLDIER I meant I had thought our Duchess could do anything.

2 SOLDIER Nay, for he is now given over to the Justices, and they will see that justice be done; they and stout Hugh the headsman; but when his head is off, why then the Duchess can pardon him if she like; there is no law against that.

I SOLDIER I do not think that stout Hugh, as you call him, will do the business for him after all. This Guido is of gentle birth, and so by the law can drink poison first, if it so be his pleasure.

3 SOLDIER Faith, to drink poison is a poor pleasure.

2 SOLDIER What kind of poison is it?

I SOLDIER Why, of the kind that kills.

2 SOLDIER What sort of a thing is poison?

I SOLDIER It is a drink, like water, only not so healthy: if you would taste it there is some in the cup there.

2 SOLDIER By St James, if it be not healthy, I will have none of it!

3 SOLDIER And if he does not drink it?

I SOLDIER Why, then, they will kill him.

3 SOLDIER And if he does drink it?

I SOLDIER Why, then, he will die.

2 SOLDIER He has a grave choice to make. I trust he will choose wisely. (*knocking comes at the door*)

I SOLDIER See who that is.

(THIRD SOLDIER *goes over and looks through the wicket*)

3 SOLDIER It is a woman, sir.

I SOLDIER Is she pretty?

3 SOLDIER I can't tell. She is masked, lieutenant.

I SOLDIER It is only very ugly or very beautiful women who ever hide their faces. Let her in.

SOLDIER *opens the door, and the* DUCHESS *masked and cloaked enters*

DUCHESS (*to* THIRD SOLDIER) Are you the officer on guard?

I SOLDIER (*coming forward*) I am, madam.

DUCHESS I must see the prisoner alone.

I SOLDIER I am afraid that is impossible. (DUCHESS *hands him a ring; he looks at it and returns it to her with a bow and makes a sign to the* SOLDIERS) Stand without there.

(*exeunt the* SOLDIERS)

DUCHESS Officer, your men are somewhat rough.

I SOLDIER They mean no harm.

DUCHESS I will be going back in few minutes. As I pass through the corridor do not let them try and lift my mask.

I SOLDIER You need not be afraid, madam.

DUCHESS I have a particular reason for wishing my face not to be seen.

I SOLDIER Madam, with this ring you can go in and out as you please; it is the Duchess's own ring.

DUCHESS Leave us. (SOLDIER *turns to go out.*) A moment, sir. For what hour is . . .

I SOLDIER At twelve o'clock, madam, we have orders to lead him out; but I dare say he won't wait for us; he's more like to take a drink out of that poison yonder. Men are afraid of the headsman.

DUCHESS Is that poison?

I SOLDIER Ay, madam, and very sure poison too.

DUCHESS You may go, sir.

I SOLDIER By St James, a pretty hand! I wonder who she is. Some woman who loved him, perhaps. *(exit)*

DUCHESS (*taking her mask off*) At last! He can escape now in
this cloak and vizard,
We are of a height almost: they will not know him;
As for myself what matter?
So that he does not curse me as he goes,
I care but little: I wonder will he curse me,
He has the right. It is eleven now,
They will not come till twelve. What will they say
When they find the bird has flown? (*goes over to the table*)
So this is poison.
Is it not strange that in this liquor here
There lies the key to all philosophies? (*takes the cup up*)
It smells of poppies. I remember well
That, when I was a child in Sicily,
I took the scarlet poppies from the corn,
And made a little wreath, and my grave uncle,
Don John of Naples, laughed: I did not know
That they had power to stay the springs of life,
To make the pulse cease beating, and to chill
The blood in its own vessels, till men come
And with a hook hale the poor body out,
And throw it in a ditch: the body, ay –
What of the soul? that goes to heaven or hell.
Where will mine go?

(*takes the torch from the wall, and goes over to the bed*)
How peacefully here he sleeps,
Like a young schoolboy tired out with play:
I would that I could sleep so peacefully,
But I have dreams. (*bending over him*)
Poor boy: what if I kissed him?
No, no, my lips would burn him like a fire.
He has had enough of love. Still that white neck
Will 'scape the headsman: I have seen to that:
He will get hence from Padua tonight,
And that is well. You are very wise, Lord Justices,
And yet you are not half so wise as I am,
And that is well.
O God! how I have loved you,
And what a bloody flower did Love bear!
(*comes back to the table*)
What if I drank these juices, and so ceased?
Were it not better than to wait till Death
Come to my bed with all his serving men,
Remorse, disease, old age, and misery?
I wonder does one suffer much: I think
That I am very young to die like this,
But so it must be. Why, why should I die?
He will escape tonight, and so his blood
Will not be on my head. No, I must die;
I have been guilty, therefore I must die;
He loves me not, and therefore I must die:
I would die happier if he would kiss me,
But he will not do that. I did not know him,
I thought he meant to sell me to the judge;
That is not strange; we women never know
Our lovers till they leave us.
(*Bell begins to toll*) Thou vile bell,
That like a bloodhound from thy brazen throat
Call'st for this man's life, cease! thou shalt not get it.
He stirs – I must be quick: (*takes up cup*)
O Love, Love, Love,
I did not think that I would pledge thee thus!
(*drinks poison, and sets the cup down on the table behind her: the noise wakens* GUIDO, *who starts up, and does not see what she has done; there is silence for a minute, each looking at the other*)

I do not come to ask your pardon now,
Seeing I know I stand beyond all pardon,
A very guilty, very wicked woman;
Enough of that: I have already, sir,
Confessed my sin to the Lords Justices;
They would not listen to me: and some said
I did invent a tale to save your life,
You having trafficked with me; others said
That women played with pity as with men;
Others that grief for my slain lord and husband
Had robbed me of my wits: they would not hear me,
And, when I swore it on the holy book,
They bade the doctor cure me. They are ten,
Ten against one, and they possess your life.
They call me Duchess here in Padua.
I do not know, sir; if I be the Duchess,
I wrote your pardon, and they would not take it;
They call it treason, say I taught them that;
Maybe I did. Within an hour, Guido,
They will be here, and drag you from the cell,
And bind your hands behind your back, and bid you
Kneel at the block: I am before them there;
Here is the signet ring of Padua,
'Twill bring you safely through the men on guard.
There is my cloak and vizard; they have orders
Not to be curious: when you pass the gate
Turn to the left, and at the second bridge
You will find horses waiting: by tomorrow
You will be at Venice, safe. (*a pause*)
Do you not speak?
Will you not even curse me ere you go?
You have the right. (*a pause*)
You do not understand
There lies between you and the headsman's axe
Hardly so much sand in the hourglass
As a child's palm could carry: here is the ring.
I have washed my hand: there is no blood upon it:
You need not fear. Will you not take the ring?

GUIDO (*takes ring and kisses it*) Ay! gladly, madam.

DUCHESS And leave Padua.

GUIDO Leave Padua.

DUCHESS But it must be tonight.

GUIDO Tonight it shall be.

DUCHESS Oh, thank God for that!

GUIDO So I can live; life never seemed so sweet
As at this moment.

DUCHESS Do not tarry, Guido,
There is my cloak: the horse is at the bridge,
The second bridge below the ferry house:
Why do you tarry? Can your ears not hear
This dreadful bell, whose every ringing stroke
Robs one brief minute from your boyish life.
Go quickly.

GUIDO Ay! He will come soon enough.

DUCHESS Who?

GUIDO (*calmly*) Why, the headsman.

DUCHESS No, no.

GUIDO Only he
Can bring me out of Padua.

DUCHESS You dare not!
You dare not burden my o'erburdened soul
With two dead men! I think one is enough.
For when I stand before God, face to face,
I would not have you, with a scarlet thread
Around your white throat, coming up behind
To say I did it: why, the very devils
Who howl away in hell would pity me;
You will not be more cruel than the devils
Who are shut out from God?

GUIDO Madam, I wait.

DUCHESS No, no, you cannot: you do not understand,
I have less power in Padua tonight
Than any common woman; they will kill you.
I saw the scaffold as I crossed the square;
Already the low rabble throng about it
With fearful jests, and horrid merriment,
As though it were a morris-dancers' platform
And not Death's sable throne. O Guido, Guido,
You must escape!

GUIDO Ay, by the hand of Death,
Not by your hand.

DUCHESS Oh, you are merciless,
Merciless now as ever: no, no, Guido,

You must go hence.

GUIDO Madam, I tarry here.

DUCHESS Guido, you shall not: it would be a thing
So terrible that the amazed stars
Would fall from heaven, and the palsied moon
Be in her sphere eclipsed, and the great sun
Refuse to shine upon the unjust earth
Which saw thee die.

GUIDO Be sure I shall not stir.

DUCHESS (*wringing her hands*) You do not know: once that the judges come
I have no power to keep you from the axe;
You cannot wait: have I not sinned enough?
Is one sin not enough but must it breed
A second sin more horrible again
Than was the one that bare it? O God, God,
Seal up sin's teeming womb, and make it barren,
I will not have more blood upon my hand
Than I have now,

GUIDO (*seizing her hand*) What! Am I fallen so low
That I may not have leave to die for you?

DUCHESS (*tearing her hand away*) Die for me? – No, my life is a vile thing,
Thrown to the miry highways of this world;
You shall not die for me, you shall not, Guido,
I am a guilty woman.

GUIDO Guilty? – let those
Who know not what a thing temptation is,
Let those who have not walked as we have done
In the red fire of passion, those whose lives
Are dull and colourless, in a word let those,
If any such there be, who have not loved
Cast stones against you. As for me –

DUCHESS Alas!

GUIDO (*falling at her feet*) You are my lady, and you are my love!
O hair of gold, O crimson lips, O face
Made for the luring and the love of man!
Incarnate image of pure loveliness!
Worshipping thee I do forget the past,
Worshipping thee my soul comes close to thine,
Worshipping thee I seem to be a god,
And though they give my body to the block,

Yet is my love eternal!

(DUCHESS *puts her hands over her face;*
GUIDO *draws them down*)

Sweet, lift up
The trailing curtains that overhang thine eyes
That I may look into those eyes, and tell you
I love you, never more than now when Death
Thrusts his cold lips between us: Beatrice,
I love you: have you no word left to say?
Oh, I can bear the executioner,
But not this silence: will you not say you love me?
Speak but that word and Death shall lose his sting,
But speak it not, and fifty thousand deaths
Are, in comparison, mercy. Oh, you are cruel,
And do not love me.

DUCHESS Alas! I have no right.
For I have stained the innocent hands of love
With spilt-out blood: there is blood on the ground,
I set it there.

GUIDO Sweet, it was not yourself,
It was some devil tempted you.

DUCHESS (*rising suddenly*) No, no,
We are each our own devil, and we make
This world our hell.

GUIDO Then let high Paradise
Fall into Tartarus! for I shall make
This world my heaven for a little space.
I love you, Beatrice.

DUCHESS I am not worthy,
Being a thing of sin.

GUIDO No, my Lord Christ,
The sin was mine, if any sin there was.
'Twas I who nurtured murder in my heart,
Sweetened my meats, seasoned my wine with it,
And in my fancy slew the accursed Duke
A hundred times a day. Why, had this man
Died half so often as I wished him to,
Death had been stalking ever through the house,
And murder had not slept.

But you, fond heart,
Whose little eyes grew tender over a whipt hound;
You, whom the little children laughed to see

Because you brought the sunlight where you passed;
You, the white angel of God's purity,
This which men call your sin, what was it?

DUCHESS Ay!
What was it? There are times it seems a dream,
An evil dream sent by an evil god,
And then I see the dead face in the coffin
And know it is no dream, but that my hand
Is red with blood, and that my desperate soul,
Striving to find some haven for its love
From the wild tempest of this raging world,
Has wrecked its bark upon the rocks of sin.
What was it, said you? – murder merely? Nothing
But murder, horrible murder.

GUIDO Nay, nay, nay,
'Twas but the passion-flower of your love
That in one moment leapt to terrible life,
And in one moment bore this gory fruit,
Which I had plucked in thought a thousand times.
My soul was murderous, but my hand refused;
Your hand wrought murder, but your soul was pure.
And so I love you, Beatrice, and let him
Who has no mercy for your stricken head,
Lack mercy up in heaven! Kiss me, sweet.
(*tries to kiss her*)

DUCHESS No, no, your lips are pure, and mine are soiled,
For Guilt has been my paramour, and Sin
Lain in my bed: O Guido, if you love me
Get hence, for every moment is a worm
Which gnaws your life away: nay, sweet, get hence,
And if in after time you think of me,
Think of me as of one who loved you more
Than anything on earth; think of me, Guido,
As of a woman merely, one who tried
To make her life a sacrifice to love,
And slew love in the trial. Oh, what is that?
The bell has stopped from ringing, and I hear
The feet of armed men upon the stair.

GUIDO (*aside*) That is the signal for the guard to come,

DUCHESS Why has the bell stopped ringing?

GUIDO If you must know,
That stops my life on this side of the grave,

But on the other we shall meet again.

DUCHESS No, no, 'tis not too late: you must get hence;
The horse is by the bridge, there is still time.
Away, away, you must not tarry here!
(*noise of* SOLDIERS *in the passage*)

VOICE OUTSIDE Room for the Lord Justice of Padua!

The LORD JUSTICE *is seen through the grated window passing down the corridor, preceded by men bearing torches*

DUCHESS It is too late.

VOICE OUTSIDE Room for the headsman.

DUCHESS Oh!

The HEADSMAN *with his axe on his shoulder is seen passing down the corridor, followed by* MONKS *bearing candles*

GUIDO Farewell, dear love, for I must drink this poison.
I do not fear the headsman, but I would die
Not on the lonely scaffold.

DUCHESS Oh!

GUIDO But here,
Here in thine arms, kissing thy mouth: farewell!
(*goes to the table and takes the goblet up*)
What, art thou empty? (*throws it to the ground*)
O thou churlish gaoler,
Even of poisons niggard!

DUCHESS (*faintly*) Blame him not.
O God! You have not drunk it, Beatrice?
Tell me you have not?

DUCHESS Were I to deny it,
There is a fire eating at my heart
Which would find utterance.

GUIDO O treacherous love,
Why have you not left a drop for me?

DUCHESS No, no, it held but death enough for one.

GUIDO Is there no poison still upon your lips,
That I may draw it from them?

DUCHESS Why should you die?
You have not spilt blood, and so need not die:
I have spilt blood, and therefore I must die.
Was it not said blood should be spilt for blood?
Who said that? I forget.

GUIDO Tarry for me,

Our souls will go together.

DUCHESS Nay, you must live.
There are many other women in the world
Who will love you, and not murder for your sake.

GUIDO I love you only.

DUCHESS You need not die for that.

GUIDO Ah, if we die together, love, why then
Can we not lie together in one grave?

DUCHESS A grave is but a narrow wedding-bed.

GUIDO It is enough for us.

DUCHESS And they will strew it
With a stark winding-sheet, and bitter herbs;
I think there are no roses in the grave,
Or if there are, they all are withered now
Since my lord went there.

GUIDO Ah! dear Beatrice
Your lips are roses that death cannot wither.

DUCHESS Nay, if we lie together, will not my lips
Fall into dust, and your enamoured eyes
Shrivel to sightless sockets, and the worms,
Which are our groomsmen, eat away your heart?

GUIDO I do not care: Death has no power on Love,
And so by Love's immortal sovereignty
I will die with you.

DUCHESS But the grave is black,
And the pit black, so I must go before
To light the candles for your coming hither.
No, no, I will not die, I will not die.
Love, you are strong, and young, and very brave,
Stand between me and the Angel of Death,
And wrestle with him for me.

(*thrusts* GUIDO *in front of her with his back to the audience*)

I will kiss you,
When you have o'erthrown him. Oh, have you no cordial,
To stay the workings of this poison in me?
Are there no rivers left in Italy
That you will not fetch me one cup of water
To quench this fire?

GUIDO O God!

DUCHESS You did not tell me
There was a drought in Italy, and no water,

Nothing but fire.

GUIDO O Love!

DUCHESS Send for a leech,
Not him who stanched my husband, but another;
We have no time: send for a leech, I say:
There is an antidote against each poison,
And he will sell it if we give him money.
Tell him that I will give him Padua,
For one short hour of life: I will not die.
Oh, I am sick to death: no, do not touch me,
This poison gnaws my heart: I did not know
It was such pain to die: I thought that life
Had taken all the agonies to itself;
It seems it is not so.

GUIDO O damnéd stars,
Quench your vile cresset-lights in tears, and bid
The moon, your mistress, shine no more tonight.

DUCHESS Guido, why are we here? I think this room
Is poorly furnished for a marriage chamber.
Let us get hence at once. Where are the horses?
We should be on our way to Venice now.
How cold the night is! We must ride faster.
That is our wedding-bell, is it not, Guido?
(MONKS *begin to chant outside*)
Music! It should be merrier; but grief
Is of the fashion now – I know not why.
You must not weep: do we not love each other? –
That is enough. Death, what do you here?
You were not bidden to this table, sir;
Away, we have no need of you: I tell you
It was in wine I pledged you, not in poison.
They lied who told you that I drank your poison.
It was spilt upon the ground, like my lord's blood;
You came too late.

GUIDO Sweet, there is nothing there:
These things are only unreal shadows.

DUCHESS Death,
Why do you tarry, get to the upper chamber;
The cold meats of my husband's funeral feast
Are set for you; this is a wedding feast.
You are out of place, sir: and, besides, 'tis summer.
We do not need these heavy fires now,

You scorch us. Guido, bid that gravedigger
Stop digging in the earth that empty grave.
I will not lie there. Oh, I am burned up,
Burned up and blasted by these fires within me.
Can you do nothing? Water, give me water,
Or else more poison. No: I feel no pain –
Is it not curious I should feel no pain? –
And Death has gone away, I am glad of that.
I thought he meant to part us. Tell me, Guido,
Are you not sorry that you ever saw me?

GUIDO I swear I would not have lived otherwise.
Why, in this dull and common world of ours,
Men have died looking for such moments as this
And have not found them.

DUCHESS Then you are not sorry?
How strange that seems.

GUIDO What, Beatrice, have I not
Stood face to face with beauty; that is enough
For one man's life. Why, love, I could be merry;
I have been often sadder at a feast,
But who were sad at such a feast as this,
When Love and Death are both our cupbearers;
We love and die together.

DUCHESS Oh, I have been
Guilty beyond all women, and indeed
Beyond all women punished. Do you think –
No, that could not be – Oh, do you think that love
Can wipe the bloody stain from off my hands,
Pour balm into my wounds, heal up my hurts,
And wash my scarlet sins as white as snow?
For I have sinned.

GUIDO They do not sin at all
Who sin for love.

DUCHESS No, I have sinned, and yet
Perchance my sin will be forgiven me.
I have loved much.

They kiss each other now for the first time in this Act, when suddenly the DUCHESS *leaps up in the dreadful spasm of death, tears in agony at her dress, and finally, with face twisted and distorted with pain, falls back dead in a chair.* GUIDO *seizing her dagger from her belt, kills himself; and, as he falls across her knees, clutches at the cloak which is on the back of the chair, and throws it entirely over her. There is a little pause. Then down the passage comes the tramp of* SOLDIERS; *the door is opened, and the* LORD JUSTICE, *the* HEADSMAN *and the* GUARD *enter and see this figure shrouded in black and* GUIDO *lying dead across her. The* LORD JUSTICE *rushes forward and drags the cloak off the* DUCHESS, *whose face is now the marble image of peace, the sign of God's forgiveness*

TABLEAU AND CURTAIN

SALOMÉ

THE PERSONS IN THE PLAY

HERODANTIPAS, *Tetrarch of Judaea*

JOKANAAN, *the Prophet*

THE YOUNG SYRIAN, *captain of the guard*

TIGELLINUS, *a young Roman*

A CAPPADOCIAN

A NUBIAN

FIRST SOLDIER

SECOND SOLDIER

THE PAGE OF HERODIAS

JEWS, NAZARENES, *etc.*

A SLAVE

NAAMAN, *the executioner*

HERODIAS, *wife of the Tetrarch*

SALOMÉ, *daughter of Herodias*

THE SLAVES OF SALOMÉ

SALOMÉ

A great terrace in the palace of Herod, set above the banqueting-hall. Some soldiers are leaning over the balcony. To the right there is a gigantic staircase, to the left, at the back, an old cistern surrounded by a wall of green bronze. Moonlight.

THE YOUNG SYRIAN: How beautiful is the Princess Salomé tonight!

THE PAGE OF HERODIAS: Look at the moon! How strange the moon seems! She is like a woman rising from a tomb. She is like a dead woman. You would fancy she was looking for dead things.

THE YOUNG SYRIAN: She has a strange look. She is like a little princess who wears a yellow veil and whose feet are of silver. She is like a princess who has little white doves for feet. You would fancy she was dancing.

THE PAGE OF HERODIAS: She is like a woman who is dead. She moves very slowly.

Noise in the banqueting-hall

FIRST SOLDIER: What an uproar! Who are those wild beasts howling!

SECOND SOLDIER: The Jews. They are always like that. They are disputing about their religion.

FIRST SOLDIER: Why do they dispute about their religion?

SECOND SOLDIER: I cannot tell. They are always doing it. The Pharisees, for instance, say that there are angels, and the Sadducees declare that angels do not exist.

FIRST SOLDIER: I think it is ridiculous to dispute about such things.

THE YOUNG SYRIAN: How beautiful is the Princess Salomé tonight!

THE PAGE OF HERODIAS: You are always looking at her. You look at her too much. It is dangerous to look at people in such fashion. Something terrible may happen.

THE YOUNG SYRIAN: SHE is very beautiful tonight.

FIRST SOLDIER: The Tetrarch has a sombre look.

SECOND SOLDIER: Yes, he has a sombre look.

FIRST SOLDIER: He is looking at something.

SECOND SOLDIER: He is looking at someone.

FIRST SOLDIER: At whom is he looking?

SECOND SOLDIER: I cannot tell.

THE YOUNG SYRIAN: How pale the princess is! Never have I seen her so pale. She is like the shadow of a white rose in a mirror of silver.

THE PAGE OF HERODIAS: You must not look at her. You look too much at her.

FIRST SOLDIER: Herodias has filled the cup of the Tetrarch.

THE CAPPADOCIAN: Is that the Queen Herodias, she who wears a black mitre sewn with pearls, and whose hair is powdered with blue dust?

FIRST SOLDIER: Yes, that is Herodias, the Tetrarch's wife.

SECOND SOLDIER: The Tetrarch is very fond of wine. He has wine of three sorts. One which is brought from the Island of Samothrace, and is purple like the cloak of Caesar.

THE CAPPADOCIAN: I have never seen Caesar.

SECOND SOLDIER: Another that comes from a town called Cyprus, and is yellow like gold.

THE CAPPADOCIAN: I love gold.

SECOND SOLDIER: And the third is a wine of Sicily. That wine is red like blood.

THE NUBIAN: The gods of my country are very fond of blood. Twice in the year we sacrifice to them young men and maidens; fifty young men and a hundred maidens. But it seems we never give them quite enough, for they are very harsh to us.

THE CAPPADOCIAN: In my country there are no gods left. The Romans have driven them out. There are some who say that they have hidden themselves in the mountains, but I do not believe it. Three nights I have been on the mountains seeking them everywhere. I did not find them. And at last I called them by their names, and they did not come. I think they are dead.

FIRST SOLDIER: The Jews worship a God that you cannot see.

THE CAPPADOCIAN: I cannot understand that.

FIRST SOLDIER: In fact, they only believe in things that you cannot see.

THE CAPPADOCIAN: That seems to me altogether ridiculous.

THE VOICE OF JOKANAAN: After me shall come another mightier than I. I am not worthy so much as to unloose the latchet of his shoes. When he cometh, the solitary places shall be glad. They shall blossom like the lily. The eyes of the blind shall see the day, and the ears of the deaf shall be opened. The newborn child shall put his hand upon the dragon's lair, he shall lead the lions by their manes.

SECOND SOLDIER: Make him be silent. He is always saying ridiculous things.

FIRST SOLDIER: No, no. He is a holy man. He is very gentle, too. Every day, when I give him to eat, he thanks me.

THE CAPPADOCIAN: Who is he?

FIRST SOLDIER: A prophet.

THE CAPPADOCIAN: What is his name?

FIRST SOLDIER: Jokanaan.

THE CAPPADOCIAN: Whence comes he?

FIRST SOLDIER: From the desert, where he fed on locusts and wild honey. He was clothed in camel's hair, and round his loins he had a leathern belt. He was very terrible to look upon. A great multitude used to follow him. He even had disciples.

THE CAPPADOCIAN: What is he talking of?

FIRST SOLDIER: We can never tell. Sometimes he says terrible things; but it is impossible to understand what he says.

THE CAPPADOCIAN: May one see him?

FIRST SOLDIER: No. The Tetrarch has forbidden it.

THE YOUNG SYRIAN: The princess has hidden her face behind her fan! Her little white hands are fluttering like doves that fly to their dovecots. They are like white butterflies. They are just like white butterflies.

THE PAGE OF HERODIAS: What is that to you! Why do you look at her? You must not look at her . . . Something terrible may happen.

THE CAPPADOCIAN (*pointing to the cistern*): What a strange prison!

SECOND SOLDIER: It is an old cistern.

THE CAPPADOCIAN: An old cistern! It must be very unhealthy.

SECOND SOLDIER: Oh, no! For instance, the Tetrarch's brother, his elder brother, the first husband of Herodias the Queen, was imprisoned there for twelve years. It did not kill him. At the end of the twelve years he had to be strangled.

THE CAPPADOCIAN: Strangled? Who dared to do that?

SECOND SOLDIER (*pointing to* THE EXECUTIONER, *a huge negro*): That man yonder, Naaman.

THE CAPPADOCIAN: He was not afraid?

SECOND SOLDIER: Oh, no! The Tetrarch sent him the ring.

THE CAPPADOCIAN: What ring?

SECOND SOLDIER: The death-ring. So he was not afraid.

THE CAPPADOCIAN: Yet it is a terrible thing to strangle a king.

FIRST SOLDIER: Why? Kings have but one neck, like other folk.

THE CAPPADOCIAN: I think it terrible.

THE YOUNG SYRIAN: The princess rises! She is leaving the table! She looks very troubled. Ah, she is coming this way. Yes, she is coming towards us. How pale she is! Never have I seen her so pale.

THE PAGE OF HERODIAS: Do not look at her. I pray you not to look at her.

THE YOUNG SYRIAN: She is like a dove that has strayed . . . She is like a narcissus trembling in the wind . . . She is like a silver flower.

Enter SALOMÉ

SALOMÉ: I will not stay. I cannot stay. Why does the Tetrarch look at me all the while with his mole's eyes under his shaking eyelids? It is strange that the husband of my mother looks at me like that. I know not what it means. In truth, yes, I know it.

THE YOUNG SYRIAN: You have just left the feast, princess?

SALOMÉ: How sweet the air is here! I can breathe here! Within there are Jews from Jerusalem who are tearing each other in pieces over their foolish ceremonies, and barbarians who drink and drink, and spill their wine on the pavement, and Greeks from Smyrna, with painted eyes and painted cheeks and frizzed hair curled in twisted coils, and silent, subtle Egyptians, with long nails of jade and russet cloaks, and Romans, brutal and coarse, with their uncouth jargon. Ah! how I loathe the Romans! They are rough and common, and they give themselves the airs of noble lords.

THE YOUNG SYRIAN: Will you be seated, princess?

THE PAGE OF HERODIAS: Why do you speak to her? Why do you look at her? Oh! something terrible will happen.

SALOMÉ: How good to see the moon. She is like a little piece of money, you would think she was a little silver flower. The moon is cold and chaste. I am sure she is a virgin, she has a virgin's beauty. Yes, she is a virgin. She has never defiled herself. She has never abandoned herself to men, like the other goddesses.

THE VOICE OF JOKANAAN: The Lord hath come. The Son of Man hath come. The centaurs have hidden themselves in the rivers, and the sirens have left the rivers and are lying beneath the leaves of the forest.

SALOMÉ: Who was that who cried out?

SECOND SOLDIER: The prophet, princess.

SALOMÉ: Ah, the prophet! He of whom the Tetrarch is afraid?

SECOND SOLDIER: We know nothing of that, princess. It was the prophet Jokanaan who cried out.

THE YOUNG SYRIAN: Is it your pleasure that I bid them bring your litter, princess? The night is fair in the garden.

SALOMÉ: He says terrible things about my mother, does he not!

SECOND SOLDIER: We never understand what he says, princess.

SALOMÉ: Yes; he says terrible things about her.

Enter A SLAVE

THE SLAVE: Princess, the Tetrarch prays you to return to the feast.

SALOMÉ: I will not go back.

THE YOUNG SYRIAN: Pardon me, princess, but if you do not return some misfortune may happen.

SALOMÉ: Is he an old man, this prophet?

THE YOUNG SYRIAN: Princess, it were better to return. Suffer me to lead you in.

SALOMÉ: This prophet . . . is he an old man?

FIRST SOLDIER: No, princess, he is quite a young man.

SECOND SOLDIER: You cannot be sure. There are those who say he is Elias.

SALOMÉ: Who is Elias?

SECOND SOLDIER: A very ancient prophet of this country, princess.

THE SLAVE: What answer may I give the Tetrarch from the princess?

THE VOICE OF JOKANAAN: Rejoice not thou, land of Palestine, because the rod of him who smote thee is broken. For from the seed of the serpent shall come forth a basilisk, and that which is born of it shall devour the birds.

SALOMÉ: What a strange voice! I would speak with him.

FIRST SOLDIER: I fear it is impossible, princess. The Tetrarch does not wish anyone to speak with him. He has even forbidden the high priest to speak with him.

SALOMÉ: I desire to speak with him.

FIRST SOLDIER: It is impossible, princess.

SALOMÉ: I will speak with him.

THE YOUNG SYRIAN: Would it not be better to return to the banquet?

SALOMÉ: Bring forth this prophet.

Exit THE SLAVE

FIRST SOLDIER: We dare not, princess.

SALOMÉ (*approaching the cistern and looking down into it*): How black it is, down there! It must be terrible to be in so black a pit! It is like a tomb . . . (*to* THE SOLDIERS): Did you not hear me? Bring out the prophet. I wish to see him.

SECOND SOLDIER: Princess, I beg you, do not require this of us.

SALOMÉ: You keep me waiting!

FIRST SOLDIER: Princess, our lives belong to you but we cannot do what you have asked of us. And, indeed, it is not of us that you should ask this thing.

SALOMÉ (*looking at* THE YOUNG SYRIAN): Ah!

THE PAGE OF HERODIAS: Oh! what is going to happen? I am sure that some misfortune will happen.

SALOMÉ (*going up to* THE YOUNG SYRIAN): You will do this thing for me, will you not, Narraboth? You will do this thing for me. I have always been kind to you. You will do it for me. I would but look at this strange prophet. Men have talked so much of him. Often have I heard the Tetrarch talk of him. I think the Tetrarch is afraid of him. Are you, even you, also afraid of him, Narraboth?

THE YOUNG SYRIAN: I fear him not, princess; there is no man I fear. But the Tetrarch has formally forbidden that any man should raise the cover of this well.

SALOMÉ: You will do this thing for me, Narraboth, and tomorrow when I pass in my litter beneath the gateway of the idol-sellers, I will let fall for you a little flower, a little green flower.

THE YOUNG SYRIAN: Princess, I cannot, I cannot.

SALOMÉ (*smiling*): You will do this thing for me, Narraboth. You know that you will do this thing for me. And tomorrow when I pass in my litter by the bridge of the idol-buyers, I will look at you through the muslin veils; I will look at you, Narraboth, it may be I will smile at you. Look at me, Narraboth, look at me. Ah! you know that you will do what I ask of you. You know it well . . . I know that you will do this thing.

THE YOUNG SYRIAN (*signing to* THE THIRD SOLDIER): Let the prophet come forth . . . The Princess Salomé desires to see him.

SALOMÉ: Ah!

THE PAGE OF HERODIAS: Oh! How strange the moon looks. You would think it was the hand of a dead woman who is seeking to cover herself with a shroud.

THE YOUNG SYRIAN: She has a strange look! She is like a little princess, whose eyes are eyes of amber. Through the clouds of muslin she is smiling like a little princess.

THE PROPHET *comes out of the cistern;* SALOMÉ *looks at him and steps slowly back*

JOKANAAN: Where is he whose cup of abominations is now full? Where is he who in a robe of silver shall one day die in the face of all the people? Bid him come forth, that he may hear the voice of him who has cried in the waste places and in the houses of kings.

SALOMÉ: Of whom is he speaking?

THE YOUNG SYRIAN: You can never tell, princess.

JOKANAAN: Where is she who, having seen the images of men painted on the walls, the images of the Chaldeans limned in colours, gave herself up unto the lust of her eyes, and sent ambassadors into Chaldea?

SALOMÉ: It is of my mother that he speaks.

THE YOUNG SYRIAN: Oh, no, princess.

SALOMÉ: Yes, it is of my mother that he speaks.

JOKANAAN: Where is she who gave herself unto the captains of Assyria, who have baldricks on their loins, and tiaras of divers colours on their heads? Where is she who hath given herself to the young men of Egypt, who are clothed in fine linen and purple, whose shields are of gold, whose helmets are of silver, whose bodies are mighty? Bid her rise up from the bed of her abominations, from the bed of her incestuousness, that she may hear the words of him who prepareth the way of the Lord, that she may repent her of her iniquities. Though she will never repent, but will stick fast in her abominations, bid her come, for the fan of the Lord is in His hand.

SALOMÉ: But he is terrible, he is terrible!

THE YOUNG SYRIAN: Do not stay here, princess, I beseech you.

SALOMÉ: It is his eyes above all that are terrible. They are like black holes burned by torches in a Tyrian tapestry. They are like black caverns where dragons dwell. They are like the black caverns of Egypt in which the dragons make their lairs. They are like black lakes troubled by fantastic moons . . . Do you think he will speak again?

THE YOUNG SYRIAN: Do not stay here, princess. I pray you do not stay here.

SALOMÉ: How wasted he is! He is like a thin ivory statue. He is like an image of silver. I am sure he is chaste as the moon is. He is like a moonbeam, like a shaft of silver. His flesh must be cool like ivory. I would look closer at him.

THE YOUNG SYRIAN: No, no, princess.

SALOMÉ: I must look at him closer.

THE YOUNG SYRIAN: Princess! Princess!

JOKANAAN: Who is this woman who is looking at me? I will not have her look at me. Wherefore doth she look at me with her golden eyes, under her gilded eyelids? I know not who she is. I do not wish to know who she is. Bid her begone. It is not to her that I would speak.

SALOMÉ: I am Salomé, daughter of Herodias, Princess of Judaea.

JOKANAAN: Back! Daughter of Babylon! Come not near the chosen of the Lord. Thy mother hath filled the earth with the wine of her iniquities, and the cry of her sins hath come up to the ears of God.

SALOMÉ: Speak again, Jokanaan. Thy voice is wine to me.

THE YOUNG SYRIAN: Princess! Princess! Princess!

SALOMÉ: Speak again! Speak again, Jokanaan, and tell me what I must do.

JOKANAAN: Daughter of Sodom, come not near me! But cover thy face with a veil, and scatter ashes upon thine head, and get thee to the desert and seek out the Son of Man.

SALOMÉ: Who is he, the Son of Man? Is he as beautiful as thou art, Jokanaan?

JOKANAAN: Get thee behind me! I hear in the palace the beating of the wings of the angel of death.

THE YOUNG SYRIAN: Princess, I beseech thee to go within.

JOKANAAN: Angel of the Lord God, what dost thou here with thy sword? Whom seekest thou in this foul palace? The day of him who shall die in a robe of silver has not yet come.

SALOMÉ: Jokanaan!

JOKANAAN: Who speaketh?

SALOMÉ: Jokanaan, I am amorous of thy body! Thy body is white like the lilies of a field that the mower hath never mowed. Thy body is white like the snows that lie on the mountains, like the snows that lie on the mountains of Judaea, and come down into the valleys. The roses in the garden of the Queen of Arabia are not so white as thy body. Neither the roses in the garden of the Queen of Arabia, nor the feet of the dawn when they light on the leaves, nor the breast of the moon when she lies on the breast of the sea . . . There is nothing in the world so white as thy body. Let me touch thy body.

JOKANAAN: Back! Daughter of Babylon! By woman came evil into the world. Speak not to me. I will not listen to thee. I listen but to the voice of the Lord God.

SALOMÉ: Thy body is hideous. It is like the body of a leper. It is like a plastered wall where vipers have crawled; like a plastered wall where the scorpions have made their nest. It is like a whitened sepulchre full of loathsome things. It is horrible, thy body is horrible. It is of thy hair that I am enamoured, Jokanaan. Thy hair is like clusters of grapes, like the clusters of black grapes that hang from the vine tree of Edom in the land of the Edomites. Thy hair is like the cedars of Lebanon, like the great cedars of Lebanon that give their shade to the lions and to the robbers who would hide themselves by day. The long black nights, when the moon hides her face, when the stars are afraid, are not so black. The silence that dwells in the forest is not so black. There is nothing in the world so black as thy hair . . . Let me touch thy hair.

JOKANAAN: Back, daughter of Sodom! Touch me not. Profane not the temple of the Lord God

SALOMÉ: Thy hair is horrible. It is covered with mire and dust. It is like a crown of thorns which they have placed on thy forehead. It is like a knot of black serpents writhing round thy neck. I love not thy hair . . . It is thy mouth that I desire, Jokanaan. Thy mouth is like a band of scarlet on a tower of ivory. It is like a pomegranate cut with a knife of ivory. The pomegranate flowers that blossom in the garden of Tyre, and are redder than roses, are not so red. The red blasts of trumpets that herald the approach of kings, and make afraid the enemy, are not so red. Thy mouth is redder than the feet of those who tread the wine in the winepress. Thy mouth is redder than the feet of the doves who haunt the temples and are fed by the priests. It is redder than the feet of him who cometh from a forest where he hath slain a lion, and seen gilded tigers. Thy mouth is like a branch of coral that fishers have found in the twilight of the sea, the coral that they keep for the kings . . . ! It is like the vermilion that the Moabites find in the mines of Moab, the vermilion that the kings take from them. It is like the bow of the King of the Persians, that is painted with vermilion, and is tipped with coral. There is nothing in the world so red as thy mouth . . . Let me kiss thy mouth.

JOKANAAN: Never, daughter of Babylon! Daughter of Sodom! Never.

SALOMÉ: I will kiss thy mouth, Jokanaan. I will kiss thy mouth.

THE YOUNG SYRIAN: Princess, princess, thou who art like a garden of myrrh, thou who art the dove of all doves, look not at this man, look not at him! Do not speak such words to him. I cannot suffer them . . . princess, princess, do not speak these things.

SALOMÉ: I will kiss thy mouth, Jokanaan.

THE YOUNG SYRIAN: Ah!

He kills himself and falls between SALOMÉ *and* JOKANAAN

THE PAGE OF HERODIAS: The young Syrian has slain himself! The young captain has slain himself! He has slain himself who was my friend! I gave him a little box of perfumes and earrings wrought in silver and now he has killed himself! Ah, did he not foretell that some misfortune would happen? I, too, foretold it, and it has happened. Well, I knew that the moon was seeking a dead thing, but I knew not that it was he whom she sought. Ah! why did I not hide him from the moon? If I had hidden him in a cavern she would not have seen him.

FIRST SOLDIER: Princess, the young captain has just killed himself.

SALOMÉ: Let me kiss thy mouth, Jokanaan.

JOKANAAN: Art thou not afraid, daughter of Herodias? Did I not tell thee that I had heard in the palace the beatings of the wings of the angel of death, and hath he not come, the angel of death?

SALOMÉ: Let me kiss thy mouth.

JOKANAAN: Daughter of adultery, there is but one who can save thee, it is He of whom I spake. Go seek Him. He is in a boat on the sea of Galilee and He talketh with His disciples. Kneel down on the shore of the sea, and call unto Him by His name. When he cometh to thee (and to all who call on Him He cometh) bow thyself at His feet and ask of Him the remission of thy sins.

SALOMÉ: Let me kiss thy mouth.

JOKANAAN: Cursed be thou! Daughter of an incestuous mother, be thou accursed!

SALOMÉ: I will kiss thy mouth, Jokanaan.

JOKANAAN: I do not wish to look at thee. I will not look at thee, thou art accursed, Salomé, thou art accursed.

He goes down into the cistern

SALOMÉ: I will kiss thy mouth, Jokanaan. I will kiss thy mouth.

FIRST SOLDIER: We must bear away the body to another place. The Tetrarch does not care to see dead bodies, save the bodies of those whom he himself has slain.

THE PAGE OF HERODIAS: He was my brother, and nearer to me than a brother. I gave him a little box full of perfumes, and a ring of agate that he wore always on his hand. In the evening we used to walk by the river, among the almond trees, and he would tell me of the things of his country. He spake ever very low. The sound of his voice was like the sound of the flute, of a flute player. Also he much loved to gaze at himself in the river. I used to reproach him for that.

SECOND SOLDIER: You are right; we must hide the body. The Tetrarch must not see it

FIRST SOLDIER: The Tetrarch will not come to this place. He never comes on the terrace. He is too much afraid of the prophet.

Enter HEROD, HERODIAS *and all the court*

HEROD: Where is Salomé? Where is the princess? Why did she not return to the banquet as I commanded her? Ah! There she is!

HERODIAS: You must not look at her! You are always looking at her!

HEROD: The moon has a strange look tonight. Has she not a strange look? She is like a mad woman, a mad woman who is seeking everywhere for lovers. She is naked, too. She is quite naked. The clouds are seeking to clothe her nakedness, but she will not let them. She shows herself naked in the sky. She reels through the clouds like a drunken woman . . . I am sure she is looking for lovers. Does she not reel like a drunken woman? She is like a mad woman, is she not?

HERODIAS: No; the moon is like the moon, that is all. Let us go within . . . You have nothing to do here.

HEROD: I will stay here! Manesseh, lay carpets there. Light torches, bring forth the ivory tables and the tables of jasper. The air here is delicious. I will drink more wine with my guests. We must show all honours to the ambassadors of Caesar.

HERODIAS: It is not because of them that you remain.

HEROD: Yes; the air is delicious. Come, Herodias, our guests await us. Ah! I have slipped! I have slipped in blood! It is an ill omen. It is a very evil omen. Wherefore is there blood here . . . ? And this body, what does this body here? Think you that I am like the King of Egypt, who gives no feast to his guests but that he shows them a corpse? Whose is it? I will not look on it.

FIRST SOLDIER: It is our captain, sire. He is the young Syrian whom you made captain only three days ago.

HEROD: I gave no order that he should be slain.

SECOND SOLDIER: He killed himself, sire.

HEROD: For what reason? I had made him captain.

SECOND SOLDIER: We do not know, sire. But he killed himself.

HEROD: That seems strange to me. I thought it was only the Roman philosophers who killed themselves. Is it not true, Tigellinus, that the philosophers at Rome kill themselves?

TIGELLINUS: There are some who kill themselves, sire. They are the Stoics. The Stoics are coarse people. They are ridiculous people. I myself regard them as being perfectly ridiculous.

HEROD: I also. It is ridiculous to kill oneself.

TIGELLINUS: Everybody at Rome laughs at them. The Emperor has written a satire against them. It is recited everywhere.

HEROD: Ah! he has written a satire against them? Caesar is wonderful. He can do everything . . . It is strange that the young Syrian has killed himself. I am sorry he has killed himself. I am very sorry, for he was fair to look upon. He was even very fair. He had very languorous eyes. I remember that I saw that he looked languorously at Salomé. Truly, I thought he looked too much at her.

HERODIAS: There are others who look at her too much.

HEROD: His father was a king. I drove him from his kingdom. And you made a slave of his mother, who was a queen, Herodias. So he was here as my guest, as it were, and for that reason I made him my captain. I am sorry he is dead. Ho! Why have you left the body here? I will not look at it – away with it. (*They take away the body*) It is cold here. There is a wind blowing. Is there not a wind blowing?

HERODIAS: No, there is no wind.

HEROD: I tell you there is a wind that blows . . . And I hear in the air something that is like the beating of wings, like the beating of vast wings. Do you not hear it?

HERODIAS: I hear nothing.

HEROD: I hear it no longer. But I heard it. It was the blowing of the wind, no doubt. It has passed away. But no, I hear it again. Do you not hear it? It is just like the beating of wings.

HERODIAS: I tell you there is nothing. You are ill. Let us go within.

HEROD: I am not ill. It is your daughter who is sick. She has the mien of a sick person. Never have I seen her so pale.

HERODIAS: I have told you not to look at her.

HEROD: Pour me forth wine. (*wine is brought*) Salomé, come drink a little wine with me. I have here a wine that is exquisite. Caesar himself sent it me. Dip into it thy little red lips, that I may drain the cup.

SALOMÉ: I am not thirsty, Tetrarch.

HEROD: You hear how she answers me, this daughter of yours?

HERODIAS: She does right. Why are you always gazing at her?

HEROD: Bring me ripe fruits. (*fruits are brought*) Salomé, come and eat fruit with me. I love to see in a fruit the mark of thy little teeth. Bite but a little of this fruit and then I will eat what is left.

SALOMÉ: I am not hungry, Tetrarch.

HEROD (*to* HERODIAS): You see how you have brought up this daughter of yours.

HERODIAS: My daughter and I come of a royal race. As for thee, thy father was a camel driver! He was also a robber!

HEROD: Thou liest!

HERODIAS: Thou knowest well that it is true.

HEROD: Salomé, come and sit next to me. I will give thee the throne of thy mother.

SALOMÉ: I am not tired, Tetrarch.

HERODIAS: You see what she thinks of you.

HEROD: Bring me – what is it that I desire? I forget. Ah! ah! I remember.

THE VOICE OF JOKANAAN: Lo! the time is come! That which I foretold has come to pass, saith the Lord God. Lo! the day of which I spoke.

HERODIAS: Bid him be silent. I will not listen to his voice. This man is forever vomiting insults against me.

HEROD: He has said nothing against you. Besides he is a very great prophet.

HERODIAS: I do not believe in prophets. Can a man tell what will come to pass? No man knows it. Moreover, he is forever insulting me. But I think you are afraid of him . . . I know well that you are afraid of him.

HEROD: I am not afraid of him. I am afraid of no man.

HERODIAS: I tell you, you are afraid of him. If you are not afraid of him why do you not deliver him to the Jews, who for these six months past have been clamouring for him?

A JEW: Truly, my lord, it were better to deliver him into our hands.

HEROD: Enough on this subject. I have already given you my answer. I will not deliver him into your hands. He is a holy man. He is a man who has seen God.

A JEW: That cannot be. There is no man who hath seen God since the prophet Elias. He is the last man who saw God. In these days God doth not show Himself. He hideth Himself. Therefore great evils have come upon the land.

ANOTHER JEW: Verily, no man knoweth if Elias the prophet did indeed see God. Peradventure it was but the shadow of God that he saw.

A THIRD JEW: God is at no time hidden. He showeth Himself at all times and in everything. God is in what is evil, even as He is in what is good.

A FOURTH JEW: That must not be said. It is a very dangerous doctrine. It is a doctrine that cometh from the schools at Alexandria, where men teach the philosophy of the Greeks. And the Greeks are Gentiles. They are not even circumcised.

A FIFTH JEW: No one can tell how God worketh. His ways are very mysterious. It may be that the things which we call evil are good, and that the things which we call good are evil. There is no knowledge of anything. We must needs submit to everything, for God is very strong. He breaketh in pieces the strong together with the weak, for He regardeth not any man

FIRST JEW: Thou speaketh truly. God is terrible. He breaketh the strong and the weak as a man brays corn in a mortar. But this man hath never seen God. No man hath seen God since the prophet Elias.

HERODIAS: Make them be silent. They weary me.

HEROD: But I have heard it said that Jokanaan himself is your prophet Elias.

THE JEW: That cannot be. It is more than three hundred years since the days of the prophet Elias.

HEROD: There be some who say that this man is the prophet Elias.

A NAZARENE: I am sure that he is the prophet Elias.

THE JEW: Nay, but he is not the prophet Elias.

THE VOICE OF JOKANAAN: So the day is come, the day of the Lord, and I hear upon the mountains the feet of Him who shall be the Saviour of the world.

HEROD: What does that mean? The Saviour of the world.

TIGELLINUS: It is a title that Caesar takes.

HEROD: But Caesar is not coming into Judaea. Only yesterday I received letters from Rome. They contained nothing concerning this matter. And you, Tigellinus, who were at Rome during the winter, you heard nothing concerning this matter, did you?

TIGELLINUS: Sire, I heard nothing concerning the matter. I was explaining the title. It is one of Caesar's titles.

HEROD: But Caesar cannot come. He is too gouty. They say that his feet are like the feet of an elephant. Also there are reasons of state. He who leaves Rome loses Rome. He will not come. Howbeit, Caesar is lord, he will come if he wishes. Nevertheless, I do not think he will come.

FIRST NAZARENE: It was not concerning Caesar that the prophet spake these words, sire.

HEROD: Not of Caesar?

FIRST NAZARENE: No, sire.

HEROD: Concerning whom, then, did he speak?

FIRST NAZARENE: Concerning Messias who has come.

A JEW: Messias hath not come.

FIRST NAZARENE: He hath come, and everywhere He worketh miracles.

HERODIAS: Ho! ho! miracles! I do not believe in miracles. I have seen too many. (*To* THE PAGE): My fan!

FIRST NAZARENE: This man worketh true miracles. Thus, at a marriage which took place in a little town of Galilee, a town of some importance, He changed water into wine. Certain persons who were present related it to me. Also He healed two lepers that were seated before the Gate of Capernaum simply by touching them.

SECOND NAZARENE: Nay, it was blind men that he healed at Capernaum.

FIRST NAZARENE: Nay, they were lepers. But He hath healed blind people also, and He was seen on a mountain talking with angels.

A SADDUCEE: Angels do not exist.

A PHARISEE: Angels exist, but I do not believe that this Man has talked with them.

FIRST NAZARENE: He was seen by a great multitude of people talking with angels.

A SADDUCEE: Not with angels.

HERODIAS: How these men weary me! They are ridiculous! (*To* THE PAGE): Well, my fan! (THE PAGE *gives her the fan*) You have a dreamer's look; you must not dream. It is only sick people who dream. (*she strikes* THE PAGE *with her fan*)

SECOND NAZARENE: There is also the miracle of the daughter of Jairus.

FIRST NAZARENE: Yes, that is sure. No man can gainsay it.

HERODIAS: These men are mad. They have looked too long on the moon. Command them to be silent.

HEROD: What is this miracle of the daughter of Jairus?

FIRST NAZARENE: The daughter of Jairus was dead. He raised her from the dead.

HEROD: He raises the dead?

FIRST NAZARENE: Yea, sire, He raiseth the dead.

HEROD: I do not wish Him to do that. I forbid Him to do that. I allow no man to raise the dead. This man must be found and told that I forbid Him to raise the dead. Where is this man at present?

SECOND NAZARENE: He is in every place, my lord, but it is hard to find Him.

FIRST NAZARENE: It is said that He is now in Samaria.

A JEW: It is easy to see that this is not Messias, if He is in Samaria. It is not to the Samaritans that Messias shall come. The Samaritans are accursed. They bring no offerings to the Temple.

SECOND NAZARENE: He left Samaria a few days since. I think that at the present moment He is in the neighbourhood of Jerusalem.

FIRST NAZARENE: No, He is not there. I have just come from Jerusalem. For two months they have had no tidings of Him.

HEROD: No matter! But let them find Him, and tell Him from me, I will not allow Him to raise the dead! To change water into wine, to heal the lepers and the blind . . . He may do these things if He will. I say nothing against these things. In truth I hold it a good deed to heal a leper. But I allow no man to raise the dead. It would be terrible if the dead came back.

THE VOICE OF JOKANAAN: Ah, the wanton! The harlot! Ah! the daughter of Babylon with her golden eyes and her gilded eyelids! Thus saith the Lord God, Let there come against her a multitude of men. Let the people take stones and stone her . . .

HERODIAS: Command him to be silent.

THE VOICE OF JOKANAAN: Let the war captains pierce her with their swords, let them crush her beneath their shields.

HERODIAS: Nay, but it is infamous.

THE VOICE OF JOKANAAN: It is thus that I will wipe out all wickedness from the earth, and that all women shall learn not to imitate her abominations.

HERODIAS: You hear what he says against me? You allow him to revile your wife?

HEROD: He did not speak your name.

HERODIAS: What does that matter? You know well that it is I whom he seeks to revile. And I am your wife, am I not?

HEROD: Of a truth, dear and noble Herodias, you are my wife, and before that you were the wife of my brother.

HERODIAS: It was you who tore me from his arms.

HEROD: Of a truth I was stronger . . . But let us not talk of that matter. I do not desire to talk of it. It is the cause of the terrible words that the prophet has spoken. Peradventure on account of it a misfortune will come. Let us not speak of this matter. Noble Herodias, we are not mindful of our guests. Fill thou my cup, my well-beloved. Fill with wine the great goblets of silver, and the great goblets of glass. I will drink to Caesar. There are Romans here; we must drink to Caesar.

ALL: Caesar! Caesar!

HEROD: Do you not see your daughter, how pale she is?

HERODIAS: What is it to you if she be pale or not?

HEROD: Never have I seen her so pale.

HERODIAS: You must not look at her.

THE VOICE OF JOKANAAN: In that day the sun shall become black like sackcloth of hair, and the moon shall become like blood, and the stars of the heavens shall fall upon the earth like ripe figs that fall from the fig tree, and the kings of the earth shall be afraid.

HERODIAS: Ah! Ah! I should like to see that day of which he speaks, when the moon shall become like blood, and when the stars shall fall upon the earth like ripe figs. This prophet talks like a drunken man . . . but I cannot suffer the sound of his voice. I hate his voice. Command him to be silent.

HEROD: I will not. I cannot understand what it is that he saith, but it may be an omen.

HERODIAS: I do not believe in omens. He speaks like a drunken man.

HEROD: It may be he is drunk with the wine of God.

HERODIAS: What wine is that, the wine of God? From what vineyards is it gathered? In what winepress may one find it?

HEROD (*from this point he looks all the while at* SALOMÉ): Tigellinus, when you were at Rome of late, did the Emperor speak with you on the subject of . . . ?

TIGELLINUS: On what subject, sire?

HEROD: On what subject? Ah! I asked you a question, did I not? I have forgotten what I would have asked you.

HERODIAS: You are looking again at my daughter. You must not look at her. I have already said so.

HEROD: You say nothing else.

HERODIAS: I say it again.

HEROD: And that restoration of the Temple about which they have talked so much, will anything be done? They say the veil of the Sanctuary has disappeared, do they not?

HERODIAS: It was thyself didst steal it. Thou speakest at random. I will not stay here. Let us go within.

HEROD: Dance for me, Salomé.

HERODIAS: I will not have her dance.

SALOMÉ: I have no desire to dance, Tetrarch.

HEROD: Salomé, daughter of Herodias, dance for me.

HERODIAS: Let her alone.

HEROD: I command thee to dance, Salomé.

SALOMÉ: I will not dance, Tetrarch.

HERODIAS (*laughing*): You see how she obeys you.

HEROD: What is it to me whether she dance or not? It is naught to me. Tonight I am happy, I am exceeding happy. Never have I been so happy.

FIRST SOLDIER: The Tetrarch has a sombre look. Has he not a sombre look?

SECOND SOLDIER: Yes, he has a sombre look

HEROD: Wherefore should I not be happy? Caesar who is lord of the world, who is lord of all things, loves me well. He has just sent me most precious gifts. Also he has promised me to summon to Rome the King of Cappadocia, who is my enemy. It may be that at Rome he will crucify him, for he is able to do all things that he wishes. Verily, Caesar is lord. Thus you see I have a right to be happy. Indeed, I am happy. I have never been so happy. There is nothing in the world that can mar my happiness

THE VOICE OF JOKANAAN: He shall be seated on this throne. He shall be clothed in scarlet and purple. In his hand he shall bear a golden cup full of his blasphemies. And the angel of the Lord shall smite him. He shall be eaten of worms.

HERODIAS: You hear what he says about you. He says that you will be eaten of worms.

HEROD: It is not of me that he speaks. He speaks never against me. It is of the King of Cappadocia that he speaks; the King of Cappadocia, who is mine enemy. It is he who shall be eaten of worms. It is not I. Never has he spoken a word against me, this prophet, save that I sinned in taking to wife the wife of my brother. It may be he is right. For, of a truth, you are sterile.

HERODIAS: I am sterile, I? You say that, you that are ever looking at my daughter, you that would have her dance for your pleasure? It is absurd to say that. I have borne a child. You have gotten no child, no, not even from one of your slaves. It is you who are sterile, not I.

HEROD: Peace, woman! I say that you are sterile. You have borne me no child, and the prophet says that our marriage is not a true marriage. He says that it is an incestuous marriage, a marriage that will bring evils . . . I fear he is right; I am sure that he is right. But it is not the moment to speak of such things. I would be happy at this moment. Of a truth, I am happy. There is nothing I lack.

HERODIAS: I am glad you are of so fair a humour tonight. It is not your custom. But it is late. Let us go within. Do not forget that we hunt at sunrise. All honours must be shown to Caesar's ambassadors, must they not?

SECOND SOLDIER: What a sombre look the Tetrarch wears.

FIRST SOLDIER: Yes, he wears a sombre look.

HEROD: Salomé, Salomé, dance for me. I pray thee dance for me. I am sad tonight. Yes, I am passing sad tonight. When I came hither I slipped in blood, which is an evil omen; and I heard, I am sure I heard in the air a beating of wings, a beating of giant wings. I cannot tell what they mean . . . I am sad tonight. Therefore dance for me. Dance for me, Salomé, I beseech you. If you dance for me you may ask of me what you will, and I will give it you, even unto the half of my kingdom.

SALOMÉ (*rising*): Will you indeed give me whatsoever I shall ask, Tetrarch?

HERODIAS: Do not dance, my daughter.

HEROD: Everything, even the half of my kingdom.

SALOMÉ: You swear it, Tetrarch?

HEROD: I swear it, Salomé.

HERODIAS: Do not dance, my daughter.

SALOMÉ: By what will you swear, Tetrarch?

HEROD: By my life, by my crown, by my gods. Whatsoever you desire I will give it you, even to the half of my kingdom, if you will but dance for me. O, Salomé, Salomé, dance for me!

SALOMÉ: You have sworn, Tetrarch.

HEROD: I have sworn, Salomé.

SALOMÉ: All that I ask, even the half of your kingdom?

HERODIAS: My daughter, do not dance.

HEROD: Even to the half of my kingdom. Thou wilt be passing fair as a queen, Salomé, if it please thee to ask for the half of my kingdom. Will she not be fair as a queen? Ah! it is cold here! There is an icy wind, and I hear . . . wherefore do I hear in the air this beating of wings? Ah! one might fancy a bird, a huge black bird that hovers over the terrace. Why can I not see it, this bird? The beat of its wings is terrible. The breath of the wind of its wings is terrible. It is a chill wind. Nay, but it is not cold it is hot. I am choking. Pour water on my hands. Give me snow to eat. Loosen my mantle. Quick, quick! Loosen my mantle. Nay, but leave it. It is my garland that hurts me, my garland of roses. The flowers are like fire. They have burned my forehead. (*he tears the wreath from his head and throws it on the table*) Ah! I can breathe now. How red those petals are! They are like stains of blood on the cloth. That does not matter. You must not find symbols in everything you see. It makes life impossible. It were better to say that stains of blood are as lovely as rose petals. It were better far to say that . . . But we will not speak of this. Now I am happy, I am passing happy. Have I not the right to be happy? Your daughter is going to dance for me. Will you not dance for me, Salomé? You have promised to dance for me.

HERODIAS: I will not have her dance.

SALOMÉ: I will dance for you, Tetrarch.

HEROD: You hear what your daughter says. She is going to dance for me. You do well to dance for me, Salomé. And when you have danced for me, forget not to ask of me whatsoever you wish. Whatsoever you wish I will give it you, even to the half of my kingdom. I have sworn it, have I not?

SALOMÉ: You have sworn it, Tetrarch.

HEROD: And I have never broken my word. I am not of those who break their oaths. I know not how to lie. I am the slave of my word, and my word is the word of a king. The King of Cappadocia always lies, but he is no true king. He is a coward. Also he owes me money that he will not repay. He has even insulted my ambassadors. He has spoken words that were wounding. But Caesar will crucify him when he comes to Rome. I am sure that Caesar will crucify him. And if not, yet will he die, being eaten of worms. The prophet has prophesied it. Well! wherefore dost thou tarry, Salomé?

SALOMÉ: I am awaiting until my slaves bring perfumes to me, and the seven veils, and take off my sandals. (SLAVES *bring perfumes, and the seven veils, and take off the sandals of Salomé*)

HEROD: Ah, you are going to dance with naked feet. 'Tis well! 'Tis well. Your little feet will be like white doves. They will be like little white flowers that dance upon the trees . . . No, no, she is going to dance on blood. There is blood spilt on the ground. She must not dance on blood. It were an evil omen.

HERODIAS: What is it to you if she dance on blood? Thou hast waded deep enough therein . . .

HEROD: What is it to me? Ah! Look at the moon! She has become red. She has become red as blood. Ah! the prophet prophesied truly. He prophesied that the moon would become red as blood. Did he not prophesy it? All of you heard him. And now the moon has become red as blood. Do ye not see it?

HERODIAS: Oh, yes, I see it well, and the stars are falling like ripe figs, are they not? And the sun is becoming black like sackcloth of hair, and the kings of the earth are afraid. That at least one can see. The prophet, for once in his life, was right; the kings of the earth are afraid . . . Let us go within. You are sick. They will say at Rome that you are mad. Let us go within, I tell you.

THE VOICE OF JOKANAAN: Who is this who cometh from Edom, who is this who cometh from Bozra, whose raiment is dyed with purple, who shineth in the beauty of his garments, who walketh mighty in his greatness? Wherefore is thy raiment stained with scarlet?

HERODIAS: Let us go within. The voice of that man maddens me. I will not have my daughter dance while he is continually crying out. I will not have her dance while you look at her in this fashion. In a word, I will not have her dance.

HEROD: Do not rise, my wife, my queen, it will avail thee nothing. I will not go within till she hath danced. Dance, Salomé, dance for me.

HERODIAS: Do not dance, my daughter.

SALOMÉ: I am ready, Tetrarch. (SALOMÉ *dances the dance of the seven veils*)

HEROD: Ah! Wonderful! Wonderful! You see that she has danced for me, your daughter. Come near, Salomé, come near, that I may give you your reward. Ah! I pay the dancers well. I will pay thee royally. I will give thee whatsoever thy soul desireth. What wouldst thou have? Speak.

SALOMÉ (*kneeling*): I would that they presently bring me in a silver charger . . .

HEROD (*laughing*): In a silver charger? Surely yes, in a silver charger. She is charming, is she not? What is it you would have in a silver charger, O sweet and fair Salomé, you who are fairer than all the daughters of Judaea? What would you have them bring thee in a silver charger? Tell me. Whatsoever it may be, they shall give it to you. My treasures belong to thee. What is it, Salomé?

SALOMÉ (*rising*): The head of Jokanaan.

HERODIAS: Ah! that is well said, my daughter.

HEROD: No, no!

HERODIAS: That is well said, my daughter.

HEROD: No, no, Salomé. You do not ask me that. Do not listen to your mother's voice. She is ever giving you evil counsel. Do not heed her.

SALOMÉ: I do not heed my mother. It is for mine own pleasure that I ask the head of Jokanaan in a silver charger. You have sworn, Herod. Forget not that you have sworn an oath.

HEROD: I know it. I have sworn by my gods. I know it well. But I pray you, Salomé, ask of me something else. Ask of me the half of my kingdom, and I will give it you. But ask not of me what you have asked.

SALOMÉ: I ask of you the head of Jokanaan.

HEROD: No, no, I do not wish it.

SALOMÉ: You have sworn, Herod.

HERODIAS: Yes, you have sworn. Everybody heard you. You swore it before everybody.

HEROD: Be silent! It is not to you I speak.

HERODIAS: My daughter has done well to ask the head of Jokanaan. He has covered me with insults. He has said monstrous things against me. One can see that she loves her mother well. Do not yield, my daughter. He has sworn, he has sworn.

HEROD: Be silent, speak not to me . . . ! Come, Salomé, be reasonable. I have never been hard to you. I have ever loved you . . . It may be that I have loved you too much. Therefore ask not this thing of me. This is a terrible thing, an awful thing to ask of me. Surely, I think you are jesting. The head of a man that is cut from his body is ill to look upon, is it not? It is not meet that the eyes of a virgin should look upon such a thing. What pleasure could you have in it? None. No, no, it is not what you desire. Hearken to me. I have an emerald, a great round emerald, which Caesar's minion sent me. If you look through this emerald you can see things which happen at a great distance. Caesar himself carries such an emerald when he goes to the circus. But my emerald is larger. I know well that it is larger. It is the largest emerald in the whole world. You would like that, would you not? Ask it of me and I will give it you.

SALOMÉ: I demand the head of Jokanaan.

HEROD: You are not listening. You are not listening. Suffer me to speak, Salomé.

SALOMÉ: The head of Jokanaan.

HEROD: No, no, you would not have that. You say that to trouble me, because I have looked at you all this evening. It is true, I have looked at you all evening. Your beauty troubled me. Your beauty has grievously troubled me, and I have looked at you too much. But I will look at you no more. Neither at things, nor at people should one look. Only in mirrors should one look, for mirrors do but show us masks. Oh! oh! bring wine! I thirst . . . Salomé, Salomé, let us be friends. Come now . . . ! Ah! what would I say? What was't? Ah! I remember . . . ! Salomé – nay, but come nearer to me; I fear you will not hear me – Salomé, you know my white peacocks, my beautiful white peacocks, that walk in the garden between the myrtles and the tall cypress trees. Their beaks are gilded with gold, and the grains that they eat are gilded with gold also, and their feet are stained with purple. When they cry out the rain comes, and the moon shows herself in the heavens when they spread their tails. Two by two they walk between the cypress trees and the black myrtles, and each has a slave to tend it. Sometimes they fly across the trees and anon they crouch in the grass, and round the lake. There are not in all the world birds so wonderful. There is no king in all the world who possesses such wonderful birds. I am sure that Caesar himself has no birds so fine as my birds. I will give you fifty of my peacocks. They will follow you whithersoever you go, and in the midst of them you will be like the moon in the midst of a great white cloud . . . I will give them all to you. I have but a hundred, and in the whole world there is no king who has peacocks like unto my peacocks. But I will give them all to you. Only you must loose me from my oath, and must not ask of me that which you have asked of me.

He empties the cup of wine

SALOMÉ: Give me the head of Jokanaan.

HERODIAS: Well said, my daughter! As for you, you are ridiculous with your peacocks.

HEROD: Be silent! You cry out always; you cry out like a beast of prey. You must not. Your voice wearies me. Be silent, I say . . . Salomé, think of what you are doing. This man comes perchance from God. He is a holy man. The finger of God has touched him. God has put into his mouth terrible words. In the palace as in the desert God is always with him . . . At least it is possible. One does not know. It is possible that God is for him and with him. Furthermore, if he died some misfortune might happen to me. In any case, he said that the day he dies a misfortune will happen to someone. That could only be to me. Remember, I slipped in blood when I entered. Also, I heard a beating of wings in the air, a beating of mighty wings. These are very evil omens, and there were others. I am sure there were others, though I did not see them. Well, Salomé, you do not wish a misfortune to happen to me? You do not wish that. Listen to me, then.

SALOMÉ: Give me the head of Jokanaan.

HEROD: Ah! you are not listening to me. Be calm. I – I am calm. I am quite calm. Listen. I have jewels hidden in this place – jewels that your mother even has never seen; jewels that are marvellous. I have a collar of pearls, set in four rows. They are like unto moons chained with rays of silver. They are like fifty moons caught in a golden net. On the ivory of her breast a queen has worn it. Thou shalt be as fair as a queen when thou wearest it. I have amethysts of two kinds, one that is black like wine and one that is red like wine which has been coloured with water. I have topazes, yellow as are the eyes of tigers, and topazes that are pink as the eyes of a woodpigeon, and green topazes that are as the eyes of cats. I have opals that burn always with an ice-like flame, opals that make sad men's minds, and are fearful of the shadows. I have onyxes like the eyeballs of a dead woman. I have moonstones that change when the moon changes, and are wan when they see the sun. I have sapphires big like eggs and as blue as blue flowers. The sea wanders within them and the moon comes never to trouble the blue of their waves. I have chrysolites and beryls and chrysoprases and rubies. I have sardonyx and hyacinth stones, and stones of chalcedony, and I will give them all to you, all, and other things will I add to them. The King of the Indies has but even now sent me four fans fashioned from the feathers of parrots, and the King of Numidia a garment of ostrich feathers. I have a crystal, into which it is not lawful for a woman to look, nor may young men behold it until they have been beaten with rods. In a coffer of nacre I have three wondrous turquoises. He who wears them on his forehead can imagine things which are not, and he who carries them in his hand can make women sterile. These are great treasures above all price. They are treasures without price. But this is not all. In an ebony coffer I have two cups of amber that are like apples of gold. If an enemy pour poison into these cups, they become like an apple of silver. In a coffer encrusted with amber I have sandals encrusted with glass. I have mantles that have been brought from the land of the Seres, and bracelets decked about with carbuncles and with jade that come from the city of Euphrates . . . What desirest thou more than this, Salomé? Tell me the thing that thou desirest, and I will give it thee. All that thou asketh I will give thee, save one thing. I will give thee all that is mine, save one life. I will give thee the mantle of the high priest. I will give thee the veil of the Sanctuary.

THE JEWS: Oh! Oh!

SALOMÉ: Give me the head of Jokanaan.

HEROD (*sinking back in his seat*): Let her be given what she asks! Of a truth she is her mother's child! (THE FIRST SOLDIER *approaches.* HERODIAS *draws from the hand of* THE TETRARCH *the ring of death and gives it to* THE SOLDIER, *who straightway bears it to*

THE EXECUTIONER. THE EXECUTIONER *looks scared)* Who has taken my ring? There was a ring on my right hand. Who has drunk my wine? There was wine in my cup. It was full of wine. Someone has drunk it! Oh! surely some evil will befall someone. (THE EXECUTIONER *goes down into the cistern*) Ah! Wherefore did I give my oath? Kings ought never to pledge their word. If they keep it not, it is terrible, and if they keep it, it is terrible also.

HERODIAS: My daughter has done well.

HEROD: I am sure that some misfortune will happen.

SALOMÉ (*leaning over the cistern and listening*): There is no sound. I hear nothing. Why does he not cry out, this man? Ah! if any man sought to kill me, I would cry out, I would struggle, I would not suffer. . . . Strike, strike, Naaman, strike, I tell you . . . No, I hear nothing. There is a silence, a terrible silence. Ah! something has fallen upon the ground. I heard something fall. It is the sword of the headsman. He is afraid, this slave. He has let his sword fall. He dare not kill him. He is a coward, this slave! Let soldiers be sent. (*She sees* THE PAGE *of Herodias and addresses him*) Come hither, thou wert the friend of him who is dead, is it not so? Well, I tell thee, there are not dead men enough. Go to the soldiers and bid them go down and bring me the thing I ask, the thing the Tetrarch has promised me, the thing that is mine. (THE PAGE *recoils. She turns to* THE SOLDIERS) Hither, ye soldiers. Get ye down into this cistern and bring me the head of this man. (THE SOLDIERS *recoil*) Tetrarch, Tetrarch, command your soldiers that they bring me the head of Jokanaan.

A huge black arm, the arm of THE EXECUTIONER, *comes forth from the cistern, bearing on a silver shield the head of* JOKANAAN. SALOMÉ *seizes it.* HEROD *hides his face with his cloak.* HERODIAS *smiles and fans herself.* THE NAZARENES *fall on their knees and begin to pray*

SALOMÉ: Ah! thou wouldst not suffer me to kiss thy mouth, Jokanaan. Well! I will kiss it now. I will bite it with my teeth as one bites a ripe fruit. Yes, I will kiss thy mouth, Jokanaan. I said it. Did I not say it? I said it. Ah! I will kiss it now . . . But wherefore dost thou not look at me, Jokanaan? Thine eyes that were so terrible, so full of rage and scorn, are shut now. Wherefore are they shut? Open thine eyes! Lift up thine eyelids, Jokanaan! Wherefore dost thou not look at me? Art thou afraid of me, Jokanaan, that thou wilt not look at me . . . ? And thy tongue, that was like a red snake darting poison, it moves no more, it says nothing now, Jokanaan, that scarlet viper that spat its venom upon me. It is strange, is it not? How is it that the red viper stirs no longer . . . ? Thou wouldst have none of me, Jokanaan. Thou didst reject me. Thou didst speak evil words against me. Thou didst treat me as a harlot, as a wanton, me, Salomé, daughter of Herodias, Princess of Judaea! Well, Jokanaan, I still live, but thou, thou art dead, and thy head belongs to me. I can do with it what I will. I can throw it to the dogs and to the birds of the air. That which the dogs leave, the birds of the air shall devour . . . Ah, Jokanaan, Jokanaan, thou wert the only man that I have loved. All other men are hateful to me. But thou, thou wert beautiful! Thy body was a column of ivory set on a silver socket. It was a garden full of doves and of silver lilies. It was a tower of silver decked with shields of ivory. There was nothing in the world so white as thy body. There was nothing in the world so black as thy hair. In the whole world there was nothing so red as thy mouth. Thy voice was a censer that scattered strange perfumes, and when I looked on thee I heard a strange music. Ah! wherefore didst thou not look at me, Jokanaan? Behind thine hands and thy curses thou didst hide thy face. Thou didst put upon thine eyes the covering of him who would see his God. Well, thou hast seen thy God, Jokanaan, but me, me, thou didst never see. If thou hadst seen me thou wouldst have loved me. I, I saw thee, Jokanaan, and I loved thee. Oh, how I loved thee! I love thee yet, Jokanaan, I love thee only . . . I am athirst for thy beauty; I am hungry for thy body; and neither wine nor fruits can appease my desire. What shall I do now, Jokanaan? Neither the floods nor the great waters can quench my passion. I was a princess, and thou didst scorn me. I was a virgin, and thou didst take my virginity from me. I was chaste, and thou didst fill my veins with fire . . . Ah! ah! wherefore didst thou not look at me, Jokanaan? If thou hadst looked at me thou hadst loved me. Well I know that thou wouldst have loved me, and the mystery of love is greater than the mystery of death. Love only should one consider.

HEROD: She is monstrous, thy daughter, she is altogether monstrous. In truth, what she has done is a great crime. I am sure that it was a crime against an unknown God.

HERODIAS: I approve of what my daughter has done. And I will stay here now.

HEROD (*rising*): Ah! There speaks the incestuous wife! Come! I will not stay here. Come, I tell thee. Surely some terrible thing will befall. Manasseh, Issachar, Ozias, put out the torches. I will not look at things, I will not suffer things to look at me. Put out the torches! Hide the moon! Hide the stars! Let us hide ourselves in our palace, Herodias. I begin to be afraid.

THE SLAVES *put out the torches. The stars disappear. A great black cloud crosses the moon and conceals it completely. The stage becomes very dark.* THE TETRARCH *begins to climb the staircase*

THE VOICE OF SALOMÉ: Ah! I have kissed thy mouth, Jokanaan. I have kissed thy mouth. There was a bitter taste on thy lips. Was it the taste of blood . . . ? But perchance it was the taste of love . . . They say that love hath a bitter taste . . . but what of that? What of that? I have kissed thy mouth, Jokanaan.

A moonbeam falls on SALOMÉ, *covering her with light*

HEROD (*turning round and seeing* SALOMÉ): Kill that woman!

THE SOLDIERS *rush forward and crush beneath their shields* SALOMÉ, *daughter of* HERODIAS, *Princess of Judaea*

CURTAIN

Aubrey Beardsley's tailpiece from the original published version of *Salomé*

LADY WINDERMERE'S FAN

To the dear memory of
ROBERT EARL OF LYTTON
in affection and admiration

PERSONS IN THE PLAY

LORD WINDERMERE
LORD DARLINGTON
LORD AUGUSTUS LORTON
MR DUMBY
MR CECIL GRAHAM
MR HOPPER
PARKER, *butler*
LADY WINDERMERE
THE DUCHESS OF BERWICK
LADY AGATHA CARLISLE
LADY PLYMDALE
LADY STUTFIELD
LADY JEDBURGH
MRS COWPER-COWPER
MRS ERLYNNE
ROSALIE, *maid*

THE SCENES OF THE PLAY

ACT ONE *Morning-room in Lord Windermere's house*
ACT TWO *Drawing-room in Lord Windermere's house*
ACT THREE *Lord Darlington's rooms*
ACT FOUR *Same as Act One*

TIME: *The Present*
PLACE: *London*

The action of the play takes place within twenty-four hours, beginning on a Tuesday afternoon at five o'clock, and ending the next day at 1.30 p.m.

FIRST PERFORMANCE

St James's Theatre, London, on 22 February 1892

LADY WINDERMERE'S FAN

ACT ONE

Morning-room of Lord Windermere's house in Carlton House Terrace. Doors C and R. Bureau with books and papers R. Sofa with small tea-table L. Window opening on to terrace L. Table R. Lady Windermere is at table R, arranging roses in a blue bowl.

Enter PARKER

PARKER: Is your ladyship at home this afternoon?

LADY WINDERMERE: Yes – who has called?

PARKER: Lord Darlington, my lady.

LADY WINDERMERE (*hesitates for a moment*): Show him up – and I'm at home to anyone who calls.

PARKER: Yes, my lady. (*exit*)

LADY WINDERMERE: It's best for me to see him before tonight. I'm glad he's come.

Enter PARKER

PARKER: Lord Darlington.

Enter LORD DARLINGTON

Exit PARKER

LORD DARLINGTON: How do you do, Lady Windermere?

LADY WINDERMERE: How do you do, Lord Darlington? No, I can't shake hands with you. My hands are all wet with these roses. Aren't they lovely? They came up from Selby this morning.

LORD DARLINGTON: They are quite perfect. (*Sees a fan lying on the table*) And what a wonderful fan! May I look at it?

LADY WINDERMERE: Do. Pretty, isn't it! It's got my name on it, and everything. I have only just seen it myself. It's my husband's birthday present to me. You know today is my birthday?

LORD DARLINGTON: No? Is it really?

LADY WINDERMERE: Yes, I'm of age today. Quite an important day in my life, isn't it? That is why I am giving this party tonight. Do sit down. (*still arranging flowers*)

LORD DARLINGTON (*sitting down*): I wish I had known it was your birthday, Lady Windermere. I would have covered the whole street in front of your house with flowers for you to walk on. They are made for you. (*a short pause*)

LADY WINDERMERE: Lord Darlington, you annoyed me last night at the Foreign Office. I am afraid you are going to annoy me again.

LORD DARLINGTON: I, Lady Windermere?

Enter PARKER *and footman, with tray and tea things*

LADY WINDERMERE: Put it there, Parker. That will do. (*Wipes her hands with her pocket-handkerchief, goes to tea-table and sits down*) Won't you come over, Lord Darlington?

Exit PARKER

LORD DARLINGTON (*takes chair and goes across*): I am quite miserable, Lady Windermere. You must tell me what I did. (*Sits down at table*)

LADY WINDERMERE: Well, you kept paying me elaborate compliments the whole evening.

LORD DARLINGTON (*smiling*): Ah, nowadays we are all of us so hard up, that the only pleasant things to pay are compliments. They're the only things we can pay.

Lady Windermere (*shaking her head*): No, I am talking very seriously. You mustn't laugh, I am quite serious. I don't like compliments, and I don't see why a man should think he is pleasing a woman enormously when he says to her a whole heap of things that he doesn't mean.

LORD DARLINGTON: Ah, but I did mean them. (*takes tea which she offers him*)

LADY WINDERMERE (*gravely*): I hope not. I should be sorry to have to quarrel with you, Lord Darlington. I like you very much, you know that. But I shouldn't like you at all if I thought you were what most other men are. Believe me, you are better than most other men, and I sometimes think you pretend to be worse.

LORD DARLINGTON: We all have our little vanities, Lady Windermere.

LADY WINDERMERE: Why do you make that your special one? (*still seated at table*)

LORD DARLINGTON (*still seated*): Oh, nowadays so many conceited people go about society pretending to be good that I think it shows rather a sweet and modest disposition to pretend to be bad. Besides, there is this to be said. If you pretend to be good, the world takes you very seriously. If you pretend to be bad, it doesn't. Such is the astounding stupidity of optimism.

LADY WINDERMERE: Don't you want the world to take you seriously then, Lord Darlington?

LORD DARLINGTON: No, not the world. Who are the people the world takes seriously? All the dull people one can think of, from the bishops down to the bores. I should like *you* to take me very seriously, Lady Windermere, *you* more than anyone else in life.

LADY WINDERMERE: Why – why me?

LORD DARLINGTON (*after a slight hesitation*): Because I think we might be great friends. Let us be great friends. You may want a friend someday.

LADY WINDERMERE: Why do you say that?

LORD DARLINGTON: Oh! – we all want friends at times.

LADY WINDERMERE: I think we're very good friends already, Lord Darlington. We can always remain so as long as you don't –

LORD DARLINGTON: Don't what?

LADY WINDERMERE: Don't spoil it by saying extravagant silly things to me. You think I am a puritan, I suppose? Well, I have something of the puritan in me. I was brought up like that. I am glad of it. My mother died when I was a mere child. I lived always with Lady Julia, my father's elder sister, you know. She was stern to me, but she taught me what the world is forgetting, the difference that there is between what is right and what is wrong. She allowed of no compromise. I allow of none.

LORD DARLINGTON: My dear Lady Windermere!

LADY WINDERMERE (*leaning back on the sofa*): You look on me as being behind the age – Well, I am! I should be sorry to be on the same level as an age like this.

LORD DARLINGTON: You think the age very bad?

LADY WINDERMERE: Yes. Nowadays people seem to look on life as a speculation. It is not a speculation. It is a sacrament. Its ideal is love. Its purification is sacrifice.

LORD DARLINGTON (*smiling*): Oh, anything is better than being sacrificed!

LADY WINDERMERE (*leaning forward*): Don't say that.

LORD DARLINGTON: I do say it. I feel it – I know it.

Enter PARKER

PARKER: The men want to know if they are to put the carpets on the terrace for tonight, my lady?

LADY WINDERMERE: You don't think it will rain, Lord Darlington, do you?

LORD DARLINGTON: I won't hear of its raining on your birthday.

LADY WINDERMERE: Tell them to do it at once, Parker.

Exit PARKER

LORD DARLINGTON (*still seated*): Do you think then – of course I am only putting an imaginary instance – do you think that in the case of a young married couple, say about two years married, if the husband suddenly becomes the intimate friend of a woman of – well, more than doubtful character – is always calling upon her, lunching with her, and probably paying her bills – do you think that the wife should not console herself?

LADY WINDERMERE (*frowning*): Console herself?

LORD DARLINGTON: Yes, I think she should – I think she has the right.

LADY WINDERMERE: Because the husband is vile – should the wife be vile also?

LORD DARLINGTON: Vileness is a terrible word, Lady Windermere.

LADY WINDERMERE: It is a terrible thing, Lord Darlington.

LORD DARLINGTON: Do you know I am afraid that good people do a great deal of harm in this world. Certainly the greatest harm they do is that they make badness of such extraordinary importance. It is absurd to divide people into good and bad. People are either charming or tedious. I take the side of the charming, and you, Lady Windermere, can't help belonging to them.

LADY WINDERMERE: Now, Lord Darlington. (*rising and crossing in front of him*) Don't stir, I am merely going to finish my flowers. (*goes to table*)

LORD DARLINGTON (*rising and moving chair*): And I must say I think you are very hard on modern life, Lady Windermere. Of course there is much against it, I admit. Most women, for instance, nowadays, are rather mercenary.

LADY WINDERMERE: Don't talk about such people.

LORD DARLINGTON: Well, then, setting mercenary people aside, who, of course, are dreadful, do you think seriously that women who have committed what the world calls a fault should never be forgiven?

LADY WINDERMERE (*standing at table*): I think they should never be forgiven.

LORD DARLINGTON: And men? Do you think that there should be the same laws for men as there are for women?

LADY WINDERMERE: Certainly!

LORD DARLINGTON: I think life too complex a thing to be settled by these hard and fast rules.

LADY WINDERMERE: If we had 'these hard and fast rules', we should find life much more simple.

LORD DARLINGTON: You allow of no exceptions?

LADY WINDERMERE: None!

LORD DARLINGTON: Ah, what a fascinating puritan you are, Lady Windermere!

LADY WINDERMERE: The adjective was unnecessary, Lord Darlington.

LORD DARLINGTON: I couldn't help it. I can resist everything except temptation.

LADY WINDERMERE: You have the modern affectation of weakness.

LORD DARLINGTON (*looking at her*): It's only an affectation, Lady Windermere.

Enter PARKER

PARKER: The Duchess of Berwick and Lady Agatha Carlisle.

Enter the DUCHESS OF BERWICK *and* LADY AGATHA CARLISLE

Exit PARKER

DUCHESS OF BERWICK: (*coming down centre stage and shaking hands*): Dear Margaret, I am so pleased to see you. You remember Agatha, don't you? How do you do, Lord Darlington? I won't let you know my daughter, you are far too wicked.

LORD DARLINGTON: Don't say that, duchess. As a wicked man I am a complete failure. Why, there are lots of people who say I have never really done anything wrong in the whole course of my life. Of course they only say it behind my back.

DUCHESS OF BERWICK: Isn't he dreadful? Agatha, this is Lord Darlington. Mind you don't believe a word he says. No, no tea, thank you, dear. (*crosses and sits on sofa*) We have just had tea at Lady Markby's. Such bad tea, too. It was quite undrinkable. I wasn't at all surprised. Her own son-in-law supplies it. Agatha is looking forward so much to your ball tonight, dear Margaret.

LADY WINDERMERE (*seated*): Oh, you mustn't think it is going to be a ball, duchess. It is only a dance in honour of my birthday. A small and early gathering.

LORD DARLINGTON (*standing*): Very small, very early, and very select, duchess.

DUCHESS OF BERWICK (*on sofa*): Of course it's going to be select. But we know *that*, dear Margaret, about *your* house. It is really one of the few houses in London where I can take Agatha, and where I feel perfectly secure about dear Berwick. I don't know what society is coming to. The most dreadful people seem to go everywhere. They certainly come to my parties – the men get quite furious if one doesn't ask them. Really, someone should make a stand against it.

LADY WINDERMERE: *I* will, duchess. I will have no one in my house about whom there is any scandal.

LORD DARLINGTON: Oh, don't say that, Lady Windermere. I should never be admitted! (*sitting*)

DUCHESS OF BERWICK: Oh, men don't matter. With women it is different. We're good. Some of us are, at least. But we are positively getting elbowed into the corner. Our husbands would really forget our existence if we didn't nag at them from time to time, just to remind them that we have a perfect legal right to do so.

LORD DARLINGTON: It's a curious thing, duchess, about the game of marriage – a game, by the way, that is going out of fashion – the wives hold all the honours, and invariably lose the odd trick.

DUCHESS OF BERWICK: The odd trick? Is that the husband, Lord Darlington?

LORD DARLINGTON: It would be rather a good name for the modern husband.

DUCHESS OF BERWICK: Dear Lord Darlington, how thoroughly depraved you are!

LADY WINDERMERE: Lord Darlington is trivial.

LORD DARLINGTON: Ah, don't say that, Lady Windermere.

LADY WINDERMERE: Why do you *talk* so trivially about life, then?

LORD DARLINGTON: Because I think that life is far too important a thing ever to talk seriously about it.

DUCHESS OF BERWICK: What does he mean? Do, as a concession to my poor wits, Lord Darlington, just explain to me what you really mean.

LORD DARLINGTON (*rising*): I think I had better not, duchess. Nowadays to be intelligible is to be found out. Goodbye! (*shakes hands with* DUCHESS) And now – (*goes up stage*) – Lady Windermere, goodbye. I may come tonight, mayn't I? Do let me come.

LADY WINDERMERE (*standing up stage with* LORD DARLINGTON): Yes, certainly. But you are not to say foolish, insincere things to people.

LORD DARLINGTON (*smiling*): Ah! you are beginning to reform me. It is a dangerous thing to reform anyone, Lady Windermere. (*bows and exits*)

DUCHESS OF BERWICK (*who has risen*): What a charming, wicked creature! I like him so much. I'm quite delighted he's gone!

How sweet you're looking! Where *do* you get your gowns? And now I must tell you how sorry I am for you, dear Margaret. (*crosses to sofa and sits with* LADY WINDERMERE) Agatha, darling!

LADY AGATHA: Yes, mamma. (*rises*)

DUCHESS OF BERWICK: Will you go and look over the photograph album that I see there?

LADY AGATHA: Yes, mamma. (*goes to table*)

DUCHESS OF BERWICK: Dear girl! She is so fond of photographs of Switzerland. Such a pure taste, I think. But I really am so sorry for you, Margaret.

LADY WINDERMERE (*smiling*): Why, duchess?

DUCHESS OF BERWICK: Oh, on account of that horrid woman. She dresses so well, too, which makes it much worse, sets such a dreadful example. Augustus – you know, my disreputable brother – such a trial to us all – well, Augustus is completely infatuated with her. It is quite scandalous, for she is absolutely inadmissible into society. Many a woman has a past, but I am told that she has at least a dozen, and that they all fit.

LADY WINDERMERE: Whom are you talking about, duchess?

DUCHESS OF BERWICK: About Mrs Erlynne.

LADY WINDERMERE: Mrs Erlynne? I never heard of her, duchess. And what *has* she to do with me?

DUCHESS OF BERWICK: My poor child! Agatha, darling!

LADY AGATHA: Yes, mamma.

DUCHESS OF BERWICK: Will you go out on the terrace and look at the sunset?

LADY AGATHA: Yes, mamma. (*exits through window*)

DUCHESS OF BERWICK: Sweet girl! So devoted to sunsets! Shows such refinement of feeling, does it not? After all, there is nothing like nature, is there?

LADY WINDERMERE: But what is it, duchess? Why do you talk to me about this person?

DUCHESS OF BERWICK: Don't you really know? I assure you we're all so distressed about it. Only last night at dear Lady Jansen's everyone was saying how extraordinary it was that, of all men in London, Windermere should behave in such a way.

LADY WINDERMERE: My husband – what has *he* got to do with any woman of that kind?

DUCHESS OF BERWICK: Ah, what indeed, dear? That is the point. He goes to see her continually, and stops for hours at a time, and while he is there she is not at home to anyone. Not that many ladies call on her, dear, but she has a great many disreputable men friends – my own brother particularly, as I told you – and that is what makes it so dreadful about Windermere. We looked upon *him* as being such a model husband, but I am afraid there is no doubt about it. My dear nieces – you know the Saville girls, don't you? – such nice domestic creatures – plain, dreadfully plain, but so good – well, they're always at the window doing fancy work, and making ugly things for the poor, which I think so useful of them in these dreadful socialistic days, and this terrible woman has taken a house in Curzon Street, right opposite them – such a respectable street, too! I don't know what we're coming to! And they tell me that Windermere goes there four and five times a week – they *see* him. They can't help it – and although they never talk scandal, they – well, of course – they remark on it to everyone. And the worst of it all is that I have been told that this woman has got a great deal of money out of somebody, for it seems that she came to London six months ago without anything at all to speak of, and now she has this charming house in Mayfair, drives her ponies in the park every afternoon, and all – well, all – since she has known poor dear Windermere.

LADY WINDERMERE: Oh, I can't believe it!

DUCHESS OF BERWICK: But it's quite true, my dear. The whole of London knows it. That is why I felt it was better to come and talk to you, and advise you to take Windermere away at once to Hamburg or to Aix, where he'll have something to amuse him, and where you can watch him all day long. I assure you, my dear, that on several occasions after I was first married, I had to pretend to be very ill, and was obliged to drink the most unpleasant mineral waters, merely to get Berwick out of town. He was so extremely susceptible. Though I am bound to say he never gave away any large sums of money to anybody. He is far too high-principled for that!

LADY WINDERMERE (*interrupting*): Duchess, duchess, it's impossible! (*rising and crossing stage*) We are only married two years. Our child is but six months old.

DUCHESS OF BERWICK: Ah, the dear pretty baby! How is the little darling? Is it a boy or a girl? I hope a girl – ah, no, I remember, it's a boy! I'm so sorry. Boys are so wicked. My boy is excessively immoral. You wouldn't believe at what hours he comes home. And he's only left Oxford a few months – I really don't know what they teach them there.

LADY WINDERMERE: Are *all* men bad?

DUCHESS OF BERWICK: Oh, all of them, my dear, all of them, without any exception, and they never grow any better. Men become old, but they never become good.

LADY WINDERMERE: Windermere and I married for love.

DUCHESS OF BERWICK: Yes, we begin like that. It was only Berwick's brutal and incessant threats of suicide that made me accept him at all, and before the year was out, he was running after all kinds of petticoats, every colour, every shape, every material. In fact, before the honeymoon was over, I caught him winking at my maid, a most pretty, respectable girl. I dismissed her at once without a character . . . No, I remember, I passed her on to my sister; poor dear Sir George is so short-sighted, I thought it wouldn't matter. But it did, though – it was most unfortunate. (*Rises.*) And now, my dear child, I must go, as we are dining out. And mind you don't take this little aberration of Windermere's too much to heart. Just take him abroad, and he'll come back to you all right.

LADY WINDERMERE: Come back to me?

DUCHESS OF BERWICK: Yes, dear, these wicked women get our husbands away from us, but they always come back, slightly damaged, of course. And don't make scenes, men hate them!

LADY WINDERMERE: It is very kind of you, duchess, to come and tell all this. But I can't believe that my husband is untrue to me.

DUCHESS OF BERWICK: Pretty child! I was like that once. Now I know that all men are monsters. (LADY WINDERMERE *rings bell*) The only thing to do is to feed the wretches well. A good cook does wonders, and that I know you have. My dear Margaret, you are not going to cry?

LADY WINDERMERE: You needn't be afraid, duchess, I never cry.

DUCHESS OF BERWICK: That's quite right, dear. Crying is the refuge of plain women but the ruin of pretty ones. Agatha, darling!

LADY AGATHA (*entering*): Yes, mamma.

DUCHESS OF BERWICK: Come and bid goodbye to Lady Windermere, and thank her for your charming visit. (*To* LADY WINDERMERE): And by the way, I must thank you for sending a card to Mr Hopper – he's that rich young Australian people are taking such notice of just at present. His father made a great fortune by selling some kind of food in circular tins – most palatable, I believe – I fancy it is the thing the servants always refuse to eat. But the son is quite interesting. I think he's attracted by dear Agatha's clever talk. Of course, we should be very sorry to lose her, but I think that a mother who doesn't part with a daughter every season has no real affection. We're coming tonight, dear. (PARKER *opens doors centre stage*) And remember my advice, take the poor fellow out of town at once, it is the only thing to do. Goodbye, once more; come, Agatha.

Exeunt DUCHESS *and* LADY AGATHA

LADY WINDERMERE: How horrible! I understand now what Lord Darlington meant by the imaginary instance of the couple not two years married. Oh! it can't be true – she spoke of enormous sums of money paid to this woman. I know where Arthur keeps his bank book – in one of the drawers of that desk. I might find out by that. I *will* find out. (*opens drawer*) No, it is some hideous mistake. Some silly scandal! He loves *me*! He loves *me*! But why should I not look? I am his wife, I have a right to look! (*returns to bureau, takes out book and examines it, page by page, smiles and gives a sigh of relief*) I knew it! there is not a word of truth in this stupid story. (*puts book back in drawer; as she does so, starts and takes out another book*) A second book – private – locked! (*tries to open it, but fails. Sees paper knife on bureau, and with it cuts cover from book. Begins to read at the first page*) 'Mrs Erlynne – £600 – Mrs Erlynne – £700 – Mrs Erlynne – £400.' Oh! it is true! It is true! How horrible! (*throws book on floor*)

Enter LORD WINDERMERE

LORD WINDERMERE: Well, dear, has the fan been sent home yet? (*sees book*) Margaret, you have cut open my bank book. You have no right to do such a thing!

LADY WINDERMERE: You think it wrong that you are found out, don't you?

LORD WINDERMERE: I think it wrong that a wife should spy on her husband.

LADY WINDERMERE: I did not spy on you. I never knew of this woman's existence till half an hour ago. Someone who pitied me was kind enough to tell me what everyone in London knows already – your daily visits to Curzon Street, your mad infatuation, the monstrous sums of money you squander on this infamous woman!

LORD WINDERMERE: Margaret! don't talk like that of Mrs Erlynne, you don't know how unjust it is!

LADY WINDERMERE (*turning to him*): You are very jealous of Mrs Erlynne's honour. I wish you had been as jealous of mine.

LORD WINDERMERE: Your honour is untouched, Margaret. You don't think for a moment that – (*puts book back into desk*)

LADY WINDERMERE: I think that you spend your money strangely.

That is all. Oh, don't imagine I mind about the money. As far as I am concerned you may squander everything we have. But what I *do* mind is that you who have loved me, you who have taught me to love you, should pass from the love that is given to the love that is bought. Oh, it's horrible! (*sits on sofa*) And it is I who feel degraded! *You* don't feel anything. I feel stained, utterly stained. You can't realise how hideous the last six months seems to me now – every kiss you have given me is tainted in my memory.

LORD WINDERMERE (*crossing to her*): Don't say that, Margaret. I never loved anyone in the whole world but you.

LADY WINDERMERE (*rises*): Who is this woman, then? Why do you take a house for her?

LORD WINDERMERE: I did not take a house for her.

LADY WINDERMERE: You gave her the money to do it, which is the same thing.

LORD WINDERMERE: Margaret, as far as I have known Mrs Erlynne –

LADY WINDERMERE: Is there a Mr Erlynne – or is he a myth?

LORD WINDERMERE: Her husband died many years ago. She is alone in the world.

LADY WINDERMERE: No relations? (*a pause*)

LORD WINDERMERE: None.

LADY WINDERMERE: Rather curious, isn't it?

LORD WINDERMERE: Margaret, I was saying to you – and I beg you to listen to me – that as far as I have known Mrs Erlynne, she has conducted herself well. If years ago –

LADY WINDERMERE: Oh! I don't want details about her life!

LORD WINDERMERE: I am not going to give you any details about her life. I tell you simply this – Mrs Erlynne was once honoured, loved, respected. She was well born, she had position – she lost everything – threw it away, if you like. That makes it all the more bitter. Misfortunes one can endure – they come from outside, they are accidents. But to suffer for one's own faults – ah! – there is the sting of life. It was twenty years ago, too. She was little more than a girl then. She had been a wife for even less time than you have.

LADY WINDERMERE: I am not interested in her – and – you should not mention this woman and me in the same breath. It is an error of taste. (*sitting at desk*)

LORD WINDERMERE: Margaret, you could save this woman. She wants to get back into society, and she wants you to help her. (*crossing to her*)

LADY WINDERMERE: Me!

LORD WINDERMERE: Yes, you.

LADY WINDERMERE: How impertinent of her! (*a pause*)

LORD WINDERMERE: Margaret, I came to ask you a great favour, and I still ask it of you, though you have discovered what I had intended you should never have known, that I have given Mrs Erlynne a large sum of money. I want you to send her an invitation for our party tonight.

LADY WINDERMERE: You are mad! (*rises*)

LORD WINDERMERE: I entreat you. People may chatter about her, do chatter about her, of course, but they don't know anything definite against her. She has been to several houses – not to houses where you would go, I admit, but still to houses where women who are in what is called society nowadays do go. That does not content her. She wants you to receive her once.

LADY WINDERMERE: As a triumph for her, I suppose?

LORD WINDERMERE: No; but because she knows that you are a good woman – and that if she comes here once she will have a chance of a happier, a surer life than she has had. She will make no further effort to know you. Won't you help a woman who is trying to get back?

LADY WINDERMERE: No! If a woman really repents, she never wishes to return to the society that has made or seen her ruin.

LORD WINDERMERE: I beg of you.

LADY WINDERMERE (*crossing to door*): I am going to dress for dinner, and don't mention the subject again this evening. Arthur – (*going to him*) – you fancy because I have no father or mother that I am alone in the world, and that you can treat me as you choose. You are wrong, I have friends, many friends.

LORD WINDERMERE: Margaret, you are talking foolishly, recklessly. I won't argue with you, but I insist upon your asking Mrs Erlynne tonight.

LADY WINDERMERE: I shall do nothing of the kind.

LORD WINDERMERE: You refuse?

LADY WINDERMERE: Absolutely!

LORD WINDERMERE: Ah, Margaret, do this for my sake; it is her last chance.

LADY WINDERMERE: What has that to do with me?

LORD WINDERMERE: How hard good women are!

LADY WINDERMERE: How weak bad men are!

LORD WINDERMERE: Margaret, none of us men may be good enough for the women we marry – that is quite true – but you don't imagine I would ever – oh, the suggestion is monstrous!

LADY WINDERMERE: Why should *you* be different from other men? I am told that there is hardly a husband in London who does not waste his life over *some* shameful passion.

LORD WINDERMERE: I am not one of them.

LADY WINDERMERE: I am not sure of that!

LORD WINDERMERE: You are sure in your heart. But don't make chasm after chasm between us. God knows the last few minutes have thrust us wide enough apart. Sit down and write the card.

LADY WINDERMERE: Nothing in the whole world would induce me.

LORD WINDERMERE (*crossing to bureau*): Then I will! (*rings electric bell, sits and writes card*)

LADY WINDERMERE: You are going to invite this woman? (*crossing to him*)

LORD WINDERMERE: Yes.

Pause; enter PARKER

Parker!

PARKER: Yes, my lord.

LORD WINDERMERE: Have this note sent to Mrs Erlynne at No. 84a Curzon Street. (*crossing and giving note to* PARKER) There is no answer!

Exit PARKER

LADY WINDERMERE: Arthur, if that woman comes here, I shall insult her.

LORD WINDERMERE: Margaret, don't say that.

LADY WINDERMERE: I mean it.

LORD WINDERMERE: Child, if you did such a thing, there's not a woman in London who wouldn't pity you.

LADY WINDERMERE: There is not a *good* woman in London who would not applaud me. We have been too lax. We must make an example. I propose to begin tonight. (*Picking up fan*) Yes, you gave me this fan today; it was your birthday present. If that woman crosses my threshold, I shall strike her across the face with it.

LORD WINDERMERE: Margaret, you couldn't do such a thing.

LADY WINDERMERE: You don't know me!

Enter PARKER

Parker!

PARKER: Yes, my lady.

LADY WINDERMERE: I shall dine in my own room. I don't want dinner, in fact. See that everything is ready by half-past ten.

And, Parker, be sure you pronounce the names of the guests very distinctly tonight. Sometimes you speak so fast that I miss them. I am particularly anxious to hear the names quite clearly so as to make no mistake. You understand, Parker?

PARKER: Yes, my lady.

LADY WINDERMERE: That will do!

Exit PARKER

(*Speaking to* LORD WINDERMERE): Arthur, if that woman comes here – I warn you –

LORD WINDERMERE: Margaret, you'll ruin us!

LADY WINDERMERE: Us! From this moment my life is separate from yours. But if you wish to avoid a public scandal, write at once to this woman, and tell her that I forbid her to come here!

LORD WINDERMERE: I will not – I cannot – she must come!

LADY WINDERMERE: Then I shall do exactly as I have said. You leave me no choice. (*exit*)

LORD WINDERMERE (*calling after her*): Margaret! Margaret! (*a pause*) My God! What shall I do? I dare not tell her who this woman really is. The shame would kill her. (*sinks down into a chair and buries his face in his hands*)

END OF ACT ONE

ACT TWO

Drawing-room in Lord Windermere's house. Door opening into ballroom, where band is playing. Door through which guests are entering. Door on to illuminated terrace. Palms, flowers and brilliant lights. Room crowded with guests. Lady Windermere is receiving them.

DUCHESS OF BERWICK: So strange Lord Windermere isn't here. Mr Hopper is very late, too. You have kept those five dances for him, Agatha?

LADY AGATHA: Yes, mamma.

DUCHESS OF BERWICK (*sitting on sofa*): Just let me see your card. I'm so glad Lady Windermere has revived cards – they're a mother's only safeguard. You dear simple little thing! (*scratches out two names.*) No nice girl should ever waltz with such particularly younger sons! It looks so fast! The last two dances you might pass on the terrace with Mr Hopper.

Enter MR DUMBY *and* LADY PLYMDALE *from the ballroom*

LADY AGATHA: Yes, mamma.

DUCHESS OF BERWICK (*fanning herself*): The air is so pleasant there.

PARKER: Mrs Cowper-Cowper. Lady Stutfield. Sir James Royston. Mr Guy Berkeley.

These people enter as announced

DUMBY: Good-evening, Lady Stutfield. I suppose this will be the last ball of the season?

LADY STUTFIELD: I suppose so, Mr Dumby. It's been a delightful season, hasn't it?

DUMBY: Quite delightful! Good-evening, duchess. I suppose this will be the last ball of the season?

DUCHESS OF BERWICK: I suppose so, Mr Dumby. It has been a very dull season, hasn't it?

DUMBY: Dreadfully dull! Dreadfully dull!

MRS COWPER-COWPER: Good-evening, Mr Dumby. I suppose this will be the last ball of the season?

DUMBY: Oh, I think not. There'll probably be two more. (*wanders back to* LADY PLYMDALE)

PARKER: Mr Rufford. Lady Jedburgh and Miss Graham. Mr Hopper.

These people enter as announced

HOPPER: How do you do, Lady Windermere? How do you do, duchess? (*bows to* LADY AGATHA)

DUCHESS OF BERWICK: Dear Mr Hopper, how nice of you to come so early. We all know how you are run after in London.

HOPPER: Capital place, London! They are not nearly so exclusive in London as they are in Sydney.

DUCHESS OF BERWICK: Ah! we know your value, Mr Hopper. We wish there were more like you. It would make life so much easier. Do you know, Mr Hopper, dear Agatha and I are so much interested in Australia. It must be so pretty with all the dear little kangaroos flying about. Agatha has found it on the map. What a curious shape it is! Just like a large packing case. However, it is a very young country, isn't it?

HOPPER: Wasn't it made at the same time as the others, duchess?

DUCHESS OF BERWICK: How clever you are, Mr Hopper. You have a cleverness quite of your own. Now I mustn't keep you.

HOPPER: But I should like to dance with Lady Agatha, duchess.

DUCHESS OF BERWICK: Well, I hope she has a dance left. Have you a dance left, Agatha?

LADY AGATHA: Yes, mamma.

DUCHESS OF BERWICK: The next one?

LADY AGATHA: Yes, mamma.

HOPPER: May I have the pleasure? (LADY AGATHA *bows*)

DUCHESS OF BERWICK: Mind you take great care of my little chatterbox, Mr Hopper.

LADY AGATHA *and* MR HOPPER *pass into ballroom*

Enter LORD WINDERMERE

LORD WINDERMERE: Margaret, I want to speak to you.

LADY WINDERMERE: In a moment. (*the music stops*)

PARKER: Lord Augustus Lorton.

Enter LORD AUGUSTUS

LORD AUGUSTUS: Good-evening, Lady Windermere.

DUCHESS OF BERWICK: Sir James, will you take me into the ballroom? Augustus has been dining with us tonight. I really have had quite enough of dear Augustus for the moment.

SIR JAMES ROYSTON *gives* DUCHESS *his arm and escorts her into the ballroom*

PARKER: Mr and Mrs Arthur Bowden. Lord and Lady Paisley. Lord Darlington.

These people enter as announced

LORD AUGUSTUS (*coming up to* LORD WINDERMERE): Want to speak to you particularly, dear boy. I'm worn to a shadow. Know I don't look it. None of us men do look what we really are. Demmed good thing, too. What I want to know is this. Who is she? Where does she come from? Why hasn't she got any demmed relations! Demmed nuisance, relations! But they make one so demmed respectable.

LORD WINDERMERE: You are talking of Mrs Erlynne, I suppose? I only met her six months ago. Till then, I never knew of her existence.

LORD AUGUSTUS: You have seen a good deal of her since then.

LORD WINDERMERE (*coldly*): Yes, I have seen a good deal of her since then. I have just seen her.

LORD AUGUSTUS: Egad! the women are very down on her. I have been dining with Arabella this evening! By Jove! you should have heard what she said about Mrs Erlynne. She didn't leave a rag on her . . . (*Aside*) Berwick and I told her that didn't matter much, as the lady in question must have an extremely fine figure. You should have seen Arabella's expression . . . But, look here, dear boy. I don't know what to do about Mrs Erlynne. Egad! I might be married to her; she treats me with such demmed indifference. She's deuced clever, too! She explains everything. Egad! she explains you. She has got any amount of explanations for you – and all of them different.

LORD WINDERMERE: No explanations are necessary about my friendship with Mrs Erlynne.

LORD AUGUSTUS: Hem! Well, look here, dear old fellow. Do you think she will ever get into this demmed thing called society? Would you introduce her to your wife? No use beating about the confounded bush. Would you do that?

LORD WINDERMERE: Mrs Erlynne is coming here tonight.

LORD AUGUSTUS: Your wife has sent her a card?

LORD WINDERMERE: Mrs Erlynne has received a card.

LORD AUGUSTUS: Then she's all right, dear boy. But why didn't you tell me that before? It would have saved me a heap of worry and demmed misunderstandings!

LADY AGATHA *and* MR HOPPER *cross and exit on to terrace*

PARKER: Mr Cecil Graham!

Enter MR CECIL GRAHAM

CECIL GRAHAM (*bows to* LADY WINDERMERE, *passes over and shakes hands with* LORD WINDERMERE): Good-evening, Arthur. Why don't you ask me how I am? I like people to ask me how I am. It shows a widespread interest in my health. Now, tonight I am not at all well. Been dining with my people. Wonder why it is one's people are always so tedious? My father would talk morality after dinner. I told him he was old enough to know better. But my experience is that as soon as people are old enough to know better, they don't know anything at all. Hullo, Tuppy! Hear you're going to be married again; thought you were tired of that game.

LORD AUGUSTUS: You're excessively trivial, my dear boy, excessively trivial!

CECIL GRAHAM: By the way, Tuppy, which is it? Have you been twice married and once divorced, or twice divorced and once married? I say you've been twice divorced and once married. It seems so much more probable.

LORD AUGUSTUS: I have a very bad memory. I really don't remember which. (*moves away*)

LADY PLYMDALE: Lord Windermere, I've something most particular to ask you.

LORD WINDERMERE: I am afraid – if you will excuse me – I must join my wife.

LADY PLYMDALE: Oh, you mustn't dream of such a thing. It's most dangerous nowadays for a husband to pay any attention to his wife in public. It always makes people think that he beats her when they're alone. The world has grown so suspicious of anything that looks like a happy married life. But I'll tell you what it is at supper. (*moves towards door of ballroom*)

LORD WINDERMERE: Margaret! I *must* speak to you.

LADY WINDERMERE: Will you hold my fan for me, Lord Darlington? Thanks. (*comes down to him*)

LORD WINDERMERE: (*crossing to her*): Margaret, what you said before dinner was, of course, impossible?

LADY WINDERMERE: That woman is not coming here tonight.

LORD WINDERMERE: Mrs Erlynne *is* coming here, and if you in any way annoy or wound her, you will bring shame and sorrow on us both. Remember that! Ah, Margaret, only trust me! A wife should trust her husband!

LADY WINDERMERE: London is full of women who trust their husbands. One can always recognise them. They look so thoroughly unhappy. I am not going to be one of them. (*moves up*) Lord Darlington, will you give me back my fan, please? Thanks . . . A useful thing a fan, isn't it ? . . . I want a friend tonight, Lord Darlington; I didn't know I would want one so soon.

LORD DARLINGTON: Lady Windermere! I knew the time would come someday; but why tonight?

LORD WINDERMERE: I will tell her. I must. It would be terrible if there were any scene. Margaret . . .

PARKER: Mrs Erlynne!

> LORD WINDERMERE *starts.* MRS ERLYNNE *enters, very beautifully dressed and very dignified.* LADY WINDERMERE *clutches at her fan, then lets it drop on the floor. She bows coldly to* MRS ERLYNNE, *who bows to her sweetly in turn, and sails into the room*

LORD DARLINGTON: You have dropped your fan, Lady Windermere. (*picks it up and hands it to her*)

MRS ERLYNNE: How do you do, again, Lord Windermere? How charming your sweet wife looks! Quite a picture!

LORD WINDERMERE (*in a low voice*): It was terribly rash of you to come!

MRS ERLYNNE (*smiling*): The wisest thing I ever did in my life. And, by the way, you must pay me a good deal of attention this evening. I am afraid of the women. You must introduce me to some of them. The men I can always manage. How do you do, Lord Augustus? You have quite neglected me lately. I have not seen you since yesterday. I am afraid you're faithless. Everyone told me so.

LORD AUGUSTUS: Now really, Mrs Erlynne, allow me to explain.

MRS ERLYNNE: No, dear Lord Augustus, you can't explain anything. It is your chief charm.

LORD AUGUSTUS: Ah! if you find charms in me, Mrs Erlynne –

> *They converse together.* LORD WINDERMERE *moves uneasily about the room watching* MRS ERLYNNE

LORD DARLINGTON (*to Lady Windermere*): How pale you are!

LADY WINDERMERE: Cowards are always pale!

LORD DARLINGTON: You look faint. Come out on the terrace.

LADY WINDERMERE: Yes. (*to* PARKER): Parker, send my cloak out.

MRS ERLYNNE (*crossing to her*): Lady Windermere, how beautifully your terrace is illuminated. Reminds me of Prince Doria's at Rome.

LADY WINDERMERE *bows coldly, and goes out with* LORD DARLINGTON

Oh, how do you do, Mr Graham? Isn't that your aunt, Lady Jedburgh? I should so much like to know her.

CECIL GRAHAM (*after a moment's hesitation and embarrassment*): Oh, certainly, if you wish it. Aunt Caroline, allow me to introduce Mrs Erlynne.

MRS ERLYNNE: So pleased to meet you, Lady Jedburgh. (*sits beside her on the sofa*) Your nephew and I are great friends. I am so much interested in his political career. I think he's sure to be a wonderful success. He thinks like a Tory, and talks like a Radical, and that's so important nowadays. He's such a brilliant talker, too. But we all know from whom he inherits that. Lord Allandale was saying to me only yesterday, in the park, that Mr Graham talks almost as well as his aunt.

LADY JEDBURGH: Most kind of you to say these charming things to me! (MRS ERLYNNE *smiles, and continues conversation*)

DUMBY (*to* CECIL GRAHAM): Did you introduce Mrs Erlynne to Lady Jedburgh?

CECIL GRAHAM: Had to, my dear fellow. Couldn't help it! That woman can make one do anything she wants. How, I don't know.

DUMBY: Hope to goodness she won't speak to me! (*saunters towards* LADY PLYMDALE)

MRS ERLYNNE (*to* LADY JEDBURGH): On Thursday? With great pleasure. (*Rises, and speaks to* LORD WINDERMERE, *laughing*) What a bore it is to have to be civil to these old dowagers! But they always insist on it!

LADY PLYMDALE (*to* MR DUMBY): Who is that well-dressed woman talking to Windermere?

DUMBY: Haven't got the slightest idea! Looks like an *édition de luxe* of a wicked French novel, meant specially for the English market.

MRS ERLYNNE: So that is poor Dumby with Lady Plymdale? I hear she is frightfully jealous of him. He doesn't seem anxious to speak to me tonight. I suppose he is afraid of her. Those straw-coloured women have dreadful tempers. Do you know, I think I'll dance with you first, Windermere. (LORD WINDERMERE *bites his lip and frowns*) It will make Lord Augustus so jealous! Lord Augustus! (LORD AUGUSTUS *comes down*) Lord Windermere insists on my dancing with him first, and, as it's his own house, I can't well refuse. You know I would much sooner dance with you.

LORD AUGUSTUS (*with a low bow*): I wish I could think so, Mrs Erlynne.

MRS ERLYNNE: You know it far too well. I can fancy a person dancing through life with you and finding it charming.

LORD AUGUSTUS (*placing his hand on his white waistcoat*): Oh, thank you, thank you. You are the most adorable of all ladies!

MRS ERLYNNE: What a nice speech! So simple and so sincere! Just the sort of speech I like. Well, you shall hold my bouquet. (*Goes towards ballroom on* LORD WINDERMERE'S *arm*) Ah, Mr Dumby, how are you? I am so sorry I have been out the last three times you have called. Come and lunch on Friday.

DUMBY (*with perfect nonchalance*): Delighted!

LADY PLYMDALE *glares with indignation at* MR DUMBY. LORD AUGUSTUS follows MRS ERLYNNE *and* LORD WINDERMERE *into the ballroom, holding bouquet*

LADY PLYMDALE (*to* MR DUMBY): What an absolute brute you are! I never can believe a word you say! Why did you tell me you didn't know her? What do you mean by calling on her three times running? You are not to go to lunch there; of course you understand that?

DUMBY: My dear Laura, I wouldn't dream of going!

LADY PLYMDALE: You haven't told me her name yet! Who is she?

DUMBY (*coughs slightly and smooths his hair*): She's a Mrs Erlynne.

LADY PLYMDALE: That woman!

DUMBY: Yes; that is what everyone calls her.

LADY PLYMDALE: How very interesting! How intensely interesting! I really must have a good stare at her. (*goes to door of ballroom and looks in*) I have heard the most shocking things about her. They say she is ruining poor Windermere. And Lady Windermere, who goes in for being so proper, invites her! How extremely amusing! It takes a thoroughly good woman to do a thoroughly stupid thing. You are to lunch there on Friday!

DUMBY: Why?

LADY PLYMDALE: Because I want you to take my husband with you. He has been so attentive lately that he has become a perfect nuisance. Now, this woman is just the thing for him. He'll dance attendance upon her as long as she lets him, and won't bother me. I assure you, women of that kind are most useful. They form the basis of other people's marriages.

DUMBY: What a mystery you are!

LADY PLYMDALE (*looking at him*): I wish *you* were!

DUMBY: I am – to myself. I am the only person in the world I should like to know thoroughly; but I don't see any chance of it just at present.

They pass into the ballroom, and LADY WINDERMERE *and* LORD DARLINGTON *enter from the terrace*

LADY WINDERMERE: Yes. Yes. Her coming here is monstrous, unbearable. I know now what you meant today at tea-time. Why didn't you tell me right out? You should have!

LORD DARLINGTON: I couldn't! A man can't tell these things about another man! But if I had known he was going to make you ask her here tonight, I think I would have told you. That insult, at any rate, you would have been spared.

LADY WINDERMERE: I did not ask her. He insisted on her coming – against my entreaties – against my commands. Oh! the house is tainted for me! I feel that every woman here sneers at me as she dances by with my husband. What have I done to deserve this? I gave him all my life. He took it – used it – spoiled it! I am degraded in my own eyes, and I lack courage – I am a coward! (*sits down on sofa*)

LORD DARLINGTON: If I know you at all, I know that you can't live with a man who treats you like this! What sort of life would you have with him? You would feel that he was lying to you every moment of the day. You would feel that the look in his eyes was false, his voice false, his touch false, his passion false. He would come to you when he was weary of others; you would have to comfort him. He would come to you when he was devoted to others; you would have to charm him. You would have to be to him the mask of his real life, the cloak to hide his secret.

LADY WINDERMERE: You are right – you are terribly right. But where am I to turn? You said you would be my friend, Lord Darlington – Tell me, what am I to do? Be my friend now.

LORD DARLINGTON: Between men and women there is no friendship possible. There is passion, enmity, worship, love, but no friendship. I love you –

LADY WINDERMERE: No, no! (*rises*)

LORD DARLINGTON: Yes, I love you! You are more to me than anything in the whole world. What does your husband give you? Nothing. Whatever is in him he gives to this wretched woman, whom he has thrust into your society, into your home, to shame you before everyone. I offer you my life –

LADY WINDERMERE: Lord Darlington!

LORD DARLINGTON: My life – my whole life. Take it, and do with it what you will . . . I love you – love you as I have never loved any living thing. From the moment I met you I loved you, loved you blindly, adoringly, madly! You did not know it then – you know it now! Leave this house tonight. I won't tell you that the world matters nothing, or the world's voice, or the voice of society. They matter a great deal. They matter far too much. But there are moments when one has to choose between living one's own life, fully, entirely, completely – or dragging out some false, shallow, degrading existence that the world in its hypocrisy demands. You have that moment now. Choose! Oh, my love, choose.

LADY WINDERMERE (*moving slowly away from him, and looking at him with startled eyes*): I have not the courage.

LORD DARLINGTON (*following her*): Yes; you have the courage. There may be six months of pain, of disgrace even, but when you no longer bear his name, when you bear mine, all will be well. Margaret, my love, my wife that shall be someday – yes, my wife! You know it! What are you now? This woman has the place that belongs by right to you. Oh! go – go out of this house, with head erect, with a smile upon your lips, with courage in your eyes. All London will know why you did it; and who will blame you? No one. If they do, what matter? Wrong? What is wrong? It's wrong for a man to abandon his wife for a shameless woman. It is wrong for a wife to remain with a man who so dishonours her. You said once you would make no compromise with things. Make none now. Be brave! Be yourself!

LADY WINDERMERE: I am afraid of being myself. Let me think. Let me wait! My husband may return to me. (*sits down on sofa*)

LORD DARLINGTON: And you would take him back! You are not what I thought you were. You are just the same as every other woman. You would stand anything rather than face the censure of a world, whose praise you would despise. In a week you will be driving with this woman in the park. She will be your constant guest – your dearest friend. You would endure anything rather than break with one blow this monstrous tie. You are right. You have no courage; none!

LADY WINDERMERE: Ah, give me time to think. I cannot answer you now. (*passes her hand nervously over her brow*)

LORD DARLINGTON: It must be now or not at all.

LADY WINDERMERE (*rising from the sofa*): Then, not at all! (*a pause*)

LORD DARLINGTON: You break my heart!

LADY WINDERMERE: Mine is already broken. (*a pause*)

LORD DARLINGTON: Tomorrow I leave England. This is the last time I shall ever look on you. You will never see me again. For one moment our lives met – our souls touched. They must never meet or touch again. Goodbye, Margaret. (*exit*)

LADY WINDERMERE: How alone I am in life. How terribly alone!

The music stops. Enter the DUCHESS OF BERWICK *and* LORD PAISLEY *laughing and talking. Other guests come in from ballroom*

DUCHESS OF BERWICK: Dear Margaret, I've just been having such a delightful chat with Mrs Erlynne. I am so sorry for what I said to you this afternoon about her. Of course, she must be all right if *you* invite her. A most attractive woman, and has such sensible views on life. Told me she entirely disapproved of people marrying more than once, so I feel quite safe about poor Augustus. Can't imagine why people speak against her. It's those horrid nieces of mine – the Saville girls – they're always talking scandal. Still, I should go to Homburg, dear, I really should. She is just a little too attractive. But where is Agatha? Oh there she is. (LADY AGATHA *and* MR HOPPER *enter from terrace*) Mr Hopper, I am very very angry with you. You have taken Agatha out on the terrace, and she is so delicate.

HOPPER: Awfully sorry, duchess. We went out for a moment and then got chatting together.

DUCHESS OF BERWICK: Ah, about dear Australia, I suppose?

HOPPER: Yes!

DUCHESS OF BERWICK: Agatha, darling! (*beckons her over*)

LADY AGATHA: Yes, mamma!

DUCHESS OF BERWICK (*aside*): Did Mr Hopper definitely –

LADY AGATHA: Yes, mamma.

DUCHESS OF BERWICK: And what answer did you give him, dear child?

LADY AGATHA: Yes, mamma.

DUCHESS OF BERWICK (*affectionately*): My dear one! You always say the right thing. Mr Hopper! James! Agatha has told me everything. How cleverly you have both kept your secret.

HOPPER: You don't mind my taking Agatha off to Australia, then, duchess?

DUCHESS OF BERWICK (*indignantly*): To Australia? Oh, don't mention that dreadful vulgar place.

HOPPER: But she said she'd like to come with me.

DUCHESS OF BERWICK (*severely*): Did you say that, Agatha?

LADY AGATHA: Yes, mamma.

DUCHESS OF BERWICK: Agatha, you say the most silly things possible. I think on the whole that Grosvenor Square would be a more healthy place to reside in. There are lots of vulgar people live in Grosvenor Square, but at any rate there are no horrid kangaroos crawling about. But we'll talk about that tomorrow. James, you can take Agatha down. You'll come to lunch, of course, James. At half-past one, instead of two. The duke will wish to say a few words to you, I am sure.

HOPPER: I should like to have a chat with the duke, duchess. He has not said a single word to me yet.

DUCHESS OF BERWICK: I think you'll find he will have a great deal to say to you tomorrow. (*Exit* LADY AGATHA *with* MR HOPPER) And now good-night, Margaret. I'm afraid it's the old, old story, dear. Love – well, not love at first sight, but love at the end of the season, which is so much more satisfactory.

LADY WINDERMERE: Good-night, duchess.

Exit DUCHESS OF BERWICK *on* LORD PAISLEY'S *arm*

LADY PLYMDALE: My dear Margaret, what a handsome woman your husband has been dancing with! I should be quite jealous if I were you! Is she a great friend of yours?

LADY WINDERMERE: No!

LADY PLYMDALE: Really? Good-night, dear. (*looks at* MR DUMBY *and exits*)

DUMBY: Awful manners young Hopper has!

CECIL GRAHAM: Ah! Hopper is one of nature's gentlemen, the worst type of gentleman I know.

DUMBY: Sensible woman, Lady Windermere. Lots of wives would have objected to Mrs Erlynne coming. But Lady Windermere has that uncommon thing called common sense.

CECIL GRAHAM: And Windermere knows that nothing looks so like innocence as an indiscretion.

DUMBY: Yes; dear Windermere is becoming almost modern. Never thought he would. (*bows to* LADY WINDERMERE *and exits*)

LADY JEDBURGH: Good-night, Lady Windermere. What a fascinating woman Mrs Erlynne is! She is coming to lunch on Thursday, won't you come too? I expect the bishop and dear Lady Merton.

LADY WINDERMERE: I am afraid I am engaged, Lady Jedburgh.

LADY JEDBURGH: So sorry. Come, dear.

Exeunt LADY JEDBURGH *and* MISS GRAHAM

Enter MRS ERLYNNE *and* LORD WINDERMERE

MRS ERLYNNE: Charming ball it has been! Quite reminds me of old days. (*sits on sofa*) And I see that there are just as many fools in society as there used to be. So pleased to find that nothing has altered! Except Margaret. She's grown quite pretty. The last time I saw her – twenty years ago – she was a fright in flannel. Positive fright, I assure you. The dear duchess! and that sweet Lady Agatha! Just the type of girl I like! Well, really, Windermere, if I am to be the Duchess's sister-in-law –

LORD WINDERMERE: But are you – ?

Exit MR CECIL GRAHAM *with rest of guests.* LADY WINDERMERE *watches, with a look of scorn and pain,* MRS ERLYNNE *and her husband. They are unconscious of her presence*

MRS ERLYNNE: Oh, yes! He's to call tomorrow at twelve o'clock! He wanted to propose tonight. In fact he did. He kept on proposing. Poor Augustus, you know how he repeats himself. Such a bad habit! But I told him I wouldn't give him an answer till tomorrow. Of course, I am going to take him. And I dare say I'll make him an admirable wife, as wives go. And there is a great deal of good in Lord Augustus. Fortunately it is all on the surface. Just where good qualities should be. Of course, you must help me in this matter.

LORD WINDERMERE: I am not called on to encourage Lord Augustus, I suppose?

MRS ERLYNNE: Oh, no! I do the encouraging. But you will make me a handsome settlement, Windermere, won't you?

LORD WINDERMERE (*frowning*): Is that what you want to talk to me about tonight?

MRS ERLYNNE: Yes.

LORD WINDERMERE (*with a gesture of impatience*): I will not talk of it here.

MRS ERLYNNE (*laughing*): Then we will talk of it on the terrace. Even business should have a picturesque background. Should it not, Windermere? With a proper background women can do anything.

LORD WINDERMERE: Won't tomorrow do as well?

MRS ERLYNNE: No; you see, tomorrow I am going to accept him. And I think it would be a good thing if I was able to tell him that I had – well, what shall I say? – two thousand pounds a year left to me by a third cousin – or a second husband – or some distant relative of that kind. It would be an additional attraction, wouldn't it? You have a delightful opportunity now of paying me a compliment, Windermere. But you are not very clever at paying compliments. I am afraid Margaret doesn't encourage you in that excellent habit. It's a great mistake on her part. When men give up saying what is charming, they give up thinking what is charming. But seriously, what do you say to two thousand pounds? Two thousand five hundred, I think. In modern life margin is everything. Windermere, don't you think the world an intensely amusing place? I do!

Exits on to terrace with LORD WINDERMERE. *Music strikes up in ballroom.*

LADY WINDERMERE: To stay in this house any longer is impossible. Tonight a man who loves me offered me his whole life. I refused it. It was foolish of me. I will offer him mine now. I will give him mine. I will go to him! (*Puts on cloak and goes to the door, then turns back. Sits down at table and writes a letter, puts it into an envelope, and leaves it on table*) Arthur has never understood me. When he reads this, he will. He may do as he chooses now with his life. I have done with mine as I think best, as I think right. It is he who has broken the bond of marriage – not I. I only break its bondage. (*exit*)

PARKER *enters and crosses towards the ballroom. Enter* MRS ERLYNNE

MRS ERLYNNE: Is Lady Windermere in the ballroom?

PARKER: Her ladyship has just gone out.

MRS ERLYNNE: Gone out? She's not on the terrace?

PARKER: No, madam. Her ladyship has just gone out of the house.

MRS ERLYNNE (*starts, and looks at the servant with a puzzled expression in her face*): Out of the house?

PARKER: Yes, madam – her ladyship told me she had left a letter for his lordship on the table.

MRS ERLYNNE: A letter for Lord Windermere?

PARKER: Yes, madam.

MRS ERLYNNE: Thank you.

Exit PARKER. *The music in the ballroom stops*

Gone out of her house! A letter addressed to her husband! (*goes over to bureau and looks at letter; takes it up and lays it down again with a shudder of fear*) No, no! It would be impossible! Life doesn't repeat its tragedies like that! Oh, why does this horrible fancy come across me? Why do I remember now the one moment of my life I most wish to forget? Does life repeat its tragedies? (*tears letter open and reads it, then sinks down into a chair with a gesture of anguish*) Oh, how terrible! The same words that twenty years ago I wrote to her father! and how bitterly I have been punished for it! No, my punishment, my real punishment is tonight, is now!

Enter LORD WINDERMERE

LORD WINDERMERE: Have you said good-night to my wife?

MRS ERLYNNE (*crushing letter in her hand*): Yes.

LORD WINDERMERE: Where is she?

MRS ERLYNNE: She is very tired. She has gone to bed. She said she had a headache.

LORD WINDERMERE: I must go to her. You'll excuse me?

MRS ERLYNNE (*rising hurriedly*): Oh, no! It's nothing serious. She's only very tired, that is all. Besides, there are people still in the supper-room. She wants you to make her apologies to them. She said she didn't wish to be disturbed. (*drops letter*) She asked me to tell you!

LORD WINDERMERE (*picks up letter*): You have dropped something.

MRS ERLYNNE: Oh yes, thank you, that is mine. (*puts out her hand to take it*)

LORD WINDERMERE (*still looking at letter*): But it's my wife's handwriting, isn't it?

MRS ERLYNNE (*takes the letter quickly*): Yes, it's – an address. Will you ask them to call my carriage, please?

LORD WINDERMERE: Certainly. (*exit*)

MRS ERLYNNE: Thanks! What can I do? What can I do? I feel a passion awakening within me that I never felt before. What can it mean? The daughter must not be like the mother – that would be terrible. How can I save her? How can I save my child? A moment may ruin a life. Who knows that better than I? Windermere must be got out of the house; that is absolutely necessary. But how shall I do it? It must be done somehow. Ah!

Enter LORD AUGUSTUS *carrying bouquet*

LORD AUGUSTUS: Dear lady, I am in such suspense! May I not have an answer to my request?

MRS ERLYNNE: Lord Augustus, listen to me. You are to take Lord Windermere down to your club at once, and keep him there as long as possible. You understand?

LORD AUGUSTUS: But you said you wished me to keep early hours!

MRS ERLYNNE (*nervously*): Do what I tell you. Do what I tell you.

LORD AUGUSTUS: And my reward?

MRS ERLYNNE: Your reward? Your reward? Oh! ask me that tomorrow. But don't let Windermere out of your sight tonight. If you do I will never forgive you. I will never speak to you again. I'll have nothing to do with you. Remember you are to keep Windermere at your club, and don't let him come back tonight. (*exit*)

LORD AUGUSTUS: Well, really, I might be her husband already, positively I might. (*follows her in a bewildered manner*)

END OF ACT TWO

ACT THREE

LORD DARLINGTON's rooms. A large sofa is in front of fireplace R. At the back of the stage a curtain is drawn across the window. Doors L and R. Table R with writing materials. Table C with syphons, glasses and tantalus frame. Table L with cigar and cigarette box. Lamps lit.

LADY WINDERMERE (*standing by the fireplace*): Why doesn't he come? This waiting is horrible. He should be here. Why is he not here, to wake by passionate words some fire within me? I am cold – cold as a loveless thing. Arthur must have read my letter by this time. If he cared for me, he would have come after me, would have taken me back by force. But he doesn't care. He's entrammelled by this woman – fascinated by her – dominated by her. If a woman wants to hold a man, she has merely to appeal to what is worst in him. We make gods of men and they leave us. Others make brutes of them and they fawn and are faithful. How hideous life is! . . . Oh! it was mad of me to come here, horribly mad. And yet, which is the worst, I wonder, to be at the mercy of a man who loves one, or the wife of a man who in one's own house dishonours one? What woman knows? What woman in the whole world? But will he love me always, this man to whom I am giving my life? What do I bring him? Lips that have lost the note of joy, eyes that are blinded by tears, chill hands and icy heart. I bring him nothing. I must go back – no; I can't go back, my letter has put me in their power – Arthur would not take me back! That fatal letter! No! Lord Darlington leaves England tomorrow. I will go with him – I have no choice. (*sits down for a few moments, then starts up and puts on her cloak*) No, no! I will go back, let Arthur do with me what he pleases. I can't wait here. It has been madness my coming. I must go at once. As for Lord Darlington – Oh! here he is! What shall I do? What can I say to him? Will he let me go away at all? I have heard that men are brutal, horrible . . . Oh! (*hides her face in her hands*)

Enter MRS ERLYNNE

MRS ERLYNNE: Lady Windermere! (LADY WINDERMERE *starts and looks up; then recoils in contempt*) Thank heaven I am in time. You must go back to your husband's house immediately.

LADY WINDERMERE: Must?

MRS ERLYNNE (*authoritatively*): Yes, you must! There is not a second to be lost. Lord Darlington may return at any moment.

LADY WINDERMERE: Don't come near me!

MRS ERLYNNE: Oh! You are on the brink of ruin, you are on the brink of a hideous precipice. You must leave this place at once, my carriage is waiting at the corner of the street. You must come with me and drive straight home.

LADY WINDERMERE *throws off her cloak and flings it on the sofa*

What are you doing?

LADY WINDERMERE: Mrs Erlynne – if you had not come here, I would have gone back. But now that I see you, I feel that nothing in the whole world would induce me to live under the same roof as Lord Windermere. You fill me with horror. There is something about you that stirs the wildest rage within me. And I know why you are here. My husband sent you to lure me back that I might serve as a blind to whatever relations exist between you and him.

MRS ERLYNNE: Oh! You don't think that – you can't.

LADY WINDERMERE: Go back to my husband, Mrs Erlynne. He belongs to you and not to me. I suppose he is afraid of a scandal. Men are such cowards. They outrage every law of the world, and are afraid of the world's tongue. But he had better prepare himself. He shall have a scandal. He shall have the worst scandal there has been in London for years. He shall see his name in every vile paper, mine on every hideous placard.

MRS ERLYNNE: No – no –

LADY WINDERMERE: Yes! he shall. Had he come himself, I admit I would have gone back to the life of degradation you and he had prepared for me – I was going back – but to stay himself at home, and to send you as his messenger – oh! it was infamous – infamous.

MRS ERLYNNE: Lady Windermere, you wrong me horribly – you wrong your husband horribly. He doesn't know you are here – he thinks you are safe in your own house. He thinks you are asleep in your own room. He never read the mad letter you wrote to him!

LADY WINDERMERE: Never read it!

MRS ERLYNNE: No – he knows nothing about it.

LADY WINDERMERE: How simple you think me! (*going to her*) You are lying to me!

MRS ERLYNNE (*restraining herself*): I am not. I am telling you the truth.

LADY WINDERMERE: If my husband didn't read my letter, how is it that you are here? Who told you I had left the house you were shameless enough to enter? Who told you where I had gone to? My husband told you, and sent you to decoy me back.

MRS ERLYNNE: You husband has never seen the letter. I – saw it, I opened it. I – read it.

LADY WINDERMERE (*turning to her*): You opened a letter of mine to my husband? You wouldn't dare!

MRS ERLYNNE: Dare! Oh! to save you from the abyss into which you are falling, there is nothing in the world I would not dare, nothing in the whole world. Here is the letter. Your husband has never read it. He never shall read it. (*going to fireplace*) It should never have been written. (*tears it up and throws it into the fire*)

LADY WINDERMERE (*with infinite contempt in her voice and look*): How do I know that that was my letter after all? You seem to think the commonest device can take me in!

MRS ERLYNNE: Oh! why do you disbelieve everything I tell you? What object do you think I have in coming here, except to save you from utter ruin, to save you from the consequence of a hideous mistake? That letter that is burnt now was your letter. I swear it to you!

LADY WINDERMERE (*slowly*): You took good care to burn it before I had examined it. I cannot trust you. You, whose whole life is a lie, how could you speak the truth about anything? (*sits down*)

MRS ERLYNNE (*hurriedly*): Think as you like about me – say what you choose against me, but go back, go back to the husband you love.

LADY WINDERMERE (*sullenly*): I do *not* love him!

MRS ERLYNNE: You do, and you know that he loves you.

LADY WINDERMERE: He does not understand what love is. He understands it as little as you do – but I see what you want. It would be a great advantage for you to get me back. Dear heaven! what a life I would have then! Living at the mercy of a woman who has neither mercy nor pity in her, a woman whom it is an infamy to meet, a degradation to know, a vile woman, a woman who comes between husband and wife!

MRS ERLYNNE (*with a gesture of despair*): Lady Windermere, Lady

Windermere, don't say such terrible things. You don't know how terrible they are, how terrible and how unjust. Listen, you must listen! Only go back to your husband, and I promise you never to communicate with him again on any pretext – never to see him – never to have anything to do with his life or yours. The money that he gave me, he gave me not through love, but through hatred, not in worship, but in contempt. The hold I have over him –

LADY WINDERMERE (*rising*): Ah! you admit you have a hold!

MRS ERLYNNE: Yes, and I will tell you what it is. It is his love for you, Lady Windermere.

LADY WINDERMERE: You expect me to believe that?

MRS ERLYNNE: You must believe it! it is true. It is his love for you that has made him submit to – oh! call it what you like, tyranny, threats, anything you choose. But it is his love for you. His desire to spare you – shame, yes, shame and disgrace.

LADY WINDERMERE: What do you mean? You are insolent! What have I to do with you?

MRS ERLYNNE (*humbly*): Nothing. I know it – but I tell you that your husband loves you – that you may never meet with such love again in your whole life – that such love you will never meet – and that if you throw it away, the day may come when you will starve for love and it will not be given to you, beg for love and it will be denied you – Oh! Arthur loves you!

LADY WINDERMERE: Arthur? And you tell me there is nothing between you?

MRS ERLYNNE: Lady Windermere, before heaven your husband is guiltless of all offence towards you! And I – I tell you that had it ever occurred to me that such a monstrous suspicion would have entered your mind, I would have died rather than have crossed your life or his – oh! died, gladly died! (*moves away to sofa*)

LADY WINDERMERE: You talk as if you had a heart. Women like you have no hearts. Heart is not in you. You are bought and sold. (*sits*)

MRS ERLYNNE (*starts, with a gesture of pain. Then restrains herself, and comes over to where* LADY WINDERMERE *is sitting. As she speaks, she stretches out her hands towards her, but does not dare to touch her*): Believe what you choose about me. I am not worth a moment's sorrow. But don't spoil your beautiful young life on my account! You don't know what may be in store for you, unless you leave this house at once. You don't know what it is to fall into the pit, to be despised, mocked, abandoned, sneered at – to be an outcast! to find the door shut against one, to have to creep in by hideous byways, afraid every moment lest the mask should be stripped from one's face, and all the while to hear the laughter, the horrible laughter of the world, a thing more tragic than all the tears the world has ever shed. You don't know what it is. One pays for one's sin, and then one pays again, and all one's life one pays. You must never know that. As for me, if suffering be an expiation, then at this moment I have expiated all my faults, whatever they have been; for tonight you have made a heart in one who had it not, made it and broken it. But let that pass. I may have wrecked my own life, but I will not let you wreck yours. You – why, you are a mere girl, you would be lost. You haven't got the kind of brains that enables a woman to get back. You have neither the wit nor the courage. You couldn't stand dishonour! No! Go back, Lady Windermere, to the husband who loves you, whom you love. You have a child, Lady Windermere. Go back to that child who even now, in pain or in joy, may be calling to you. (LADY WINDERMERE *rises*) God gave you that child. He will require from you that you make his life fine, that you watch over him. What answer will you make to God if his life is ruined through you? Back to your house, Lady Windermere – your husband loves you! He has never swerved for a moment from the love he bears you. But even if he had a thousand loves, you must stay with your child. If he was harsh to you, you must stay with your child. If he ill-treated you, you must stay with your child. If he abandoned you, your place is with your child.

LADY WINDERMERE *bursts into tears and buries her face in her hands*

(*rushing to her*): Lady Windermere!

LADY WINDERMERE (*holding out her hands to her helplessly, as a child might do*): Take me home. Take me home.

MRS ERLYNNE (*is about to embrace her. Then restrains herself. There is a look of wonderful joy in her face*): Come! Where is your cloak? (*getting it from sofa*) Here. Put it on. Come at once!

They go to the door

LADY WINDERMERE: Stop! Don't you hear voices?

MRS ERLYNNE: No, no! There is no one!

LADY WINDERMERE: Yes, there is! Listen! Oh! that is my husband's voice! He is coming in! Save me! Oh, it's some plot! You have sent for him.

Voices outside

MRS ERLYNNE: Silence! I'm here to save you, if I can. But I fear it is too late! There! (*points to the curtain across the window*) The first chance you have slip out, if you ever get a chance!

LADY WINDERMERE: But you?

MRS ERLYNNE: Oh! never mind me. I'll face them.

LADY WINDERMERE *hides herself behind the curtain*

LORD AUGUSTUS (*outside*): Nonsense, dear Windermere, you must not leave me!

MRS ERLYNNE: Lord Augustus! Then it is I who am lost! (*hesitates for a moment, then looks round and sees door, and exits through it*)

Enter LORD DARLINGTON, MR DUMBY, LORD WINDERMERE, LORD AUGUSTUS LORTON *and* MR CECIL GRAHAM

DUMBY: What a nuisance their turning us out of the club at this hour! It's only two o'clock. (*sinks into a chair*) The lively part of the evening is only just beginning. (*yawns and closes his eyes*)

LORD WINDERMERE: It is very good of you, Lord Darlington, allowing Augustus to force our company on you, but I'm afraid I can't stay long.

LORD DARLINGTON: Really! I am so sorry! You'll take a cigar, won't you?

LORD WINDERMERE: Thanks! (*sits down*)

LORD AUGUSTUS (*to* LORD WINDERMERE): My dear boy, you must not dream of going. I have a great deal to talk to you about, of demmed importance, too. (*sits down with him at table*)

CECIL GRAHAM: Oh! We all know what that is! Tuppy can't talk about anything but Mrs Erlynne.

LORD WINDERMERE: Well, that is no business of yours, is it, Cecil?

CECIL GRAHAM: None! That is why it interests me. My own business always bores me to death. I prefer other people's.

LORD DARLINGTON: Have something to drink, you fellows. Cecil, you'll have a whisky and soda?

CECIL GRAHAM: Thanks. (*goes to table with* LORD DARLINGTON) Mrs Erlynne looked very handsome tonight, didn't she?

LORD DARLINGTON: I am not one of her admirers.

CECIL GRAHAM: I usen't to be, but I am now. Why! she actually made me introduce her to poor dear Aunt Caroline. I believe she is going to lunch there.

LORD DARLINGTON (*in surprise*): No?

CECIL GRAHAM: She is, really.

LORD DARLINGTON: Excuse me, you fellows. I'm going away to-morrow and I have to write a few letters. (*goes to writing-table and sits down*)

DUMBY: Clever woman, Mrs Erlynne.

CECIL GRAHAM: Hallo, Dumby! I thought you were asleep.

DUMBY: I am, I usually am!

LORD AUGUSTUS: A very clever woman. Knows perfectly well what a demmed fool I am – knows it as well as I do myself.

CECIL GRAHAM *comes towards him laughing*

Ah, you may laugh, my boy, but it is a great thing to come across a woman who thoroughly understands one.

DUMBY: It is an awfully dangerous thing. They always end by marrying one.

CECIL GRAHAM: But I thought, Tuppy, you were never going to see her again! Yes! you told me so yesterday evening at the club. You said you'd heard –

whispering to him

LORD AUGUSTUS: Oh, she's explained that.

CECIL GRAHAM: And the Wiesbaden affair?

LORD AUGUSTUS: She's explained that too.

DUMBY: And her income, Tuppy? Has she explained that?

LORD AUGUSTUS (*in a very serious voice*): She's going to explain that tomorrow.

CECIL GRAHAM *goes back to table*

DUMBY: Awfully commercial, women nowadays. Our grandmothers threw their caps over the mills, of course, but, by Jove, their granddaughters only throw their caps over mills that can raise the wind for them.

LORD AUGUSTUS: You want to make her out a wicked woman. She is not!

CECIL GRAHAM: Oh! Wicked women bother one. Good women bore one. That is the only difference between them.

LORD AUGUSTUS (*puffing a cigar*): Mrs Erlynne has a future before her.

DUMBY: Mrs Erlynne has a past before her.

LORD AUGUSTUS: I prefer women with a past. They're always so demmed amusing to talk to.

CECIL GRAHAM: Well, you'll have lots of topics of conversation with her, Tuppy. (*rising and going to him*)

LORD AUGUSTUS: You're getting annoying, dear boy; you're getting demmed annoying.

CECIL GRAHAM (*puts his hands on his shoulders*): Now, Tuppy, you've lost your figure and you've lost your character. Don't lose your temper; you have only got one.

LORD AUGUSTUS: My dear boy, if I wasn't the most good-natured man in London –

CECIL GRAHAM: We'd treat you with more respect, wouldn't we, Tuppy? (*strolls away*)

DUMBY: The youth of the present day are quite monstrous. They have absolutely no respect for dyed hair.

LORD AUGUSTUS *looks round angrily*

CECIL GRAHAM: Mrs Erlynne has a very great respect for dear Tuppy.

DUMBY: Then Mrs Erlynne sets an admirable example to the rest of her sex. It is perfectly brutal the way most women nowadays behave to men who are not their husbands.

LORD WINDERMERE: Dumby, you are ridiculous, and Cecil, you let your tongue run away with you. You must leave Mrs Erlynne alone. You don't really know anything about her, and you're always talking scandal against her.

CECIL GRAHAM (*coming towards him*): My dear Arthur, I never talk scandal. I only talk gossip.

LORD WINDERMERE: What is the difference between scandal and gossip?

CECIL GRAHAM: Oh! gossip is charming! History is merely gossip. But scandal is gossip made tedious by morality. Now, I never moralise. A man who moralises is usually a hypocrite, and a woman who moralises is invariably plain. There is nothing in the whole world so unbecoming to a woman as a Nonconformist conscience. And most women know it, I'm glad to say.

LORD AUGUSTUS: Just my sentiments, dear boy, just my sentiments.

CECIL GRAHAM: Sorry to hear it, Tuppy; whenever people agree with me, I always feel I must be wrong.

LORD AUGUSTUS: My dear boy, when I was your age –

CECIL GRAHAM: But you never were, Tuppy, and you never will be. I say, Darlington, let us have some cards. You'll play, Arthur, won't you?

LORD WINDERMERE: No, thanks, Cecil.

DUMBY (*with a sigh*): Good heavens! how marriage ruins a man! It's as demoralising as cigarettes, and far more expensive.

CECIL GRAHAM: You'll play, of course, Tuppy?

LORD AUGUSTUS (*pouring himself out a brandy and soda at the table*): Can't, dear boy. Promised Mrs Erlynne never to play or drink again.

CECIL GRAHAM: Now, my dear Tuppy, don't be led astray into the paths of virtue. Reformed, you would be perfectly tedious. That is the worst of women. They always want one to be good. And if we are good, when they meet us, they don't love us at all. They like to find us quite irretrievably bad, and to leave us quite unattractively good.

LORD DARLINGTON (*rising from table, where he has been writing letters*): They always do find us bad!

DUMBY: I don't think we are bad. I think we are all good, except Tuppy.

LORD DARLINGTON: No, we are all in the gutter, but some of us are looking at the stars. (*sits down at table*)

DUMBY: We are all in the gutter, but some of us are looking at the stars? Upon my word, you are very romantic tonight, Darlington.

CECIL GRAHAM: Too romantic! You must be in love. Who is the girl?

LORD DARLINGTON: The woman I love is not free, or thinks she isn't. (*glances instinctively at* LORD WINDERMERE *while he speaks*)

CECIL GRAHAM: A married woman, then! Well, there's nothing in the world like the devotion of a married woman. It's a thing no married man knows anything about.

LORD DARLINGTON: Oh! she doesn't love me. She is a good woman. She is the only good woman I have ever met in my life.

CECIL GRAHAM: The only good woman you have ever met in your life?

LORD DARLINGTON: Yes!

CECIL GRAHAM (*lighting a cigarette*): Well, you are a lucky fellow! Why, I have met hundreds of good women. I never seem to meet any but good women. The world is perfectly packed with good women. To know them is a middle-class education.

LORD DARLINGTON: This woman has purity and innocence. She has everything we men have lost.

CECIL GRAHAM: My dear fellow, what on earth should we men do, going about with purity and innocence? A carefully thought-out buttonhole is much more effective.

DUMBY: She doesn't really love you then?

LORD DARLINGTON: No, she does not!

DUMBY: I congratulate you, my dear fellow. In this world there are only two tragedies. One is not getting what one wants, and the other is getting it. The last is much the worst; the last is a real tragedy! But I am interested to hear she does not love you. How long could you love a woman who didn't love you, Cecil?

CECIL GRAHAM: A woman who didn't love me? Oh, all my life!

DUMBY: So could I. But it's so difficult to meet one.

LORD DARLINGTON: How can you be so conceited, Dumby?

DUMBY: I didn't say it as a matter of conceit. I said it as a matter of regret. I have been wildly, madly adored. I am sorry I have. It has been an immense nuisance. I should like to be allowed a little time to myself now and then.

LORD AUGUSTUS (*looking round*): Time to educate yourself, I suppose.

DUMBY: No, time to forget all I have learned. That is much more important, dear Tuppy.

LORD AUGUSTUS *moves uneasily in his chair*

LORD DARLINGTON: What cynics you fellows are!

CECIL GRAHAM: What is a cynic? (*Sitting on the back of the sofa*)

LORD DARLINGTON: A man who knows the price of everything and the value of nothing.

CECIL GRAHAM: And a sentimentalist, my dear Darlington, is a man who sees an absurd value in everything, and doesn't know the market price of any single thing.

LORD DARLINGTON: You always amuse me, Cecil. You talk as if you were a man of experience.

CECIL GRAHAM: I am. (*moves to front of fireplace*)

LORD DARLINGTON: You are far too young!

CECIL GRAHAM: That is a great error. Experience is a question of instinct about life. I have got it. Tuppy hasn't. Experience is the name Tuppy gives to his mistakes. That is all.

LORD AUGUSTUS *looks round indignantly*

DUMBY: Experience is the name everyone gives to their mistakes.

CECIL GRAHAM (*standing with his back to the fireplace*): One shouldn't commit any. (*sees* LADY WINDERMERE'*s fan on sofa*)

DUMBY: Life would be very dull without them.

CECIL GRAHAM: Of course you are quite faithful to this woman you are in love with, Darlington, to this good woman?

LORD DARLINGTON: Cecil, if one really loves a woman, all other women in the world become absolutely meaningless to one. Love changes one – I am changed.

CECIL GRAHAM: Dear me! How very interesting! Tuppy, I want to talk to you.

LORD AUGUSTUS *takes no notice*

DUMBY: It's no use talking to Tuppy. You might just as well talk to a brick wall.

CECIL GRAHAM: But I like talking to a brick wall – it's the only thing in the world that never contradicts me! Tuppy!

LORD AUGUSTUS: Well, what is it? What is it? (*rising and going over to* CECIL GRAHAM)

CECIL GRAHAM: Come over here. I want you particularly. (*Aside*) Darlington has been moralising and talking about the purity of love, and that sort of thing, and he has got some woman in his rooms all the time.

LORD AUGUSTUS: No, really! really!

CECIL GRAHAM (*in a low voice*): Yes, here is her fan. (*points to the fan*)

LORD AUGUSTUS (*chuckling*): By Jove! By Jove!

LORD WINDERMERE (*up by door*): I am really off now, Lord Darlington. I am sorry you are leaving England so soon. Pray call on us when you come back! My wife and I will be charmed to see you!

LORD DARLINGTON (*up stage with* LORD WINDERMERE): I am afraid I shall be away for many years. Good-night!

CECIL GRAHAM: Arthur!

LORD WINDERMERE: What?

CECIL GRAHAM: I want to speak to you for a moment. No, do come!

LORD WINDERMERE (*putting on his coat*): I can't – I'm off.

CECIL GRAHAM: It is something very particular. It will interest you enormously.

LORD WINDERMERE (*smiling*): It is some of your nonsense, Cecil.

CECIL GRAHAM: It isn't! It isn't really.

LORD AUGUSTUS(*going to him*): My dear fellow, you mustn't go yet. I have a lot to talk to you about. And Cecil has something to show you.

LORD WINDERMERE (*walking over*): Well, what is it?

CECIL GRAHAM: Darlington has got a woman here in his rooms. Here is her fan. Amusing, isn't it? (*a pause*)

LORD WINDERMERE: Good God! (*seizes the fan* – DUMBY *rises*)

CECIL GRAHAM: What is the matter?

LORD WINDERMERE: Lord Darlington!

LORD DARLINGTON (*turning round*): Yes!

LORD WINDERMERE: What is my wife's fan doing here in your rooms? Hands off, Cecil. Don't touch me.

LORD DARLINGTON: Your wife's fan?

LORD WINDERMERE: Yes, here it is.

LORD DARLINGTON (*walking towards him*): I don't know!

LORD WINDERMERE: You must know. I demand an explanation. Don't hold me, you fool (*to* CECIL GRAHAM).

LORD DARLINGTON (*aside*): She is here after all!

LORD WINDERMERE: Speak, sir! Why is my wife's fan here? Answer me! By God! I'll search your rooms, and if my wife's here, I'll –

LORD DARLINGTON: You shall not search my rooms. You have no right to do so. I forbid you!

LORD WINDERMERE: You scoundrel! I'll not leave your room till I have searched every corner of it! What moves behind that curtain? (*rushes towards the curtain*)

MRS ERLYNNE (*entering*): Lord Windermere!

LORD WINDERMERE: Mrs Erlynne!

Everyone starts and turns round. LADY WINDERMERE *slides out from behind the curtain and glides from the room*

MRS ERLYNNE: I am afraid I took your wife's fan in mistake for my own, when I was leaving your house tonight. I am so sorry. (*takes fan from him.* LORD WINDERMERE *looks at her in contempt.* LORD DARLINGTON *in mingled astonishment and anger.* LORD AUGUSTUS *turns away. The other men smile at each other*)

END OF ACT THREE

ACT FOUR

Scene as in Act One

LADY WINDERMERE (*lying on sofa*): How can I tell him? I can't tell him. It would kill me. I wonder what happened after I escaped from that horrible room. Perhaps she told them the true reason of her being there, and the real meaning of that – fatal fan of mine. Oh, if he knows – how can I look him in the face again? He would never forgive me. (*touches bell*) How securely one thinks one lives out of reach of temptation, sin, folly. And then suddenly – Oh! Life is terrible. It rules us, we do not rule it.

Enter ROSALIE

ROSALIE: Did your ladyship ring for me?

LADY WINDERMERE: Yes. Have you found out at what time Lord Windermere came in last night?

ROSALIE: His lordship did not come in till five o'clock.

LADY WINDERMERE: Five o'clock? He knocked at my door this morning, didn't he?

ROSALIE: Yes, my lady – at half-past nine. I told him your ladyship was not awake yet.

LADY WINDERMERE: Did he say anything?

ROSALIE: Something about your ladyship's fan. I didn't quite catch what his lordship said. Has the fan been lost, my lady? I can't find it, and Parker says it was not left in any of the rooms. He has looked in all of them and on the terrace as well.

LADY WINDERMERE: It doesn't matter. Tell Parker not to trouble. That will do.

Exit ROSALIE

LADY WINDERMERE (*rising*): She is sure to tell him. I can fancy a person doing a wonderful act of self-sacrifice, doing it spontaneously, recklessly, nobly – and afterwards finding out that it costs too much. Why should she hesitate between her ruin and mine? . . . How strange! I would have publicly disgraced her in my own house. She accepts public disgrace in the house of another to save me . . . There is a bitter irony in things, a bitter irony in the way we talk of good and bad women . . . Oh, what a lesson! and what a pity that in life we only get our lessons when they are of no use to us! For even if she doesn't tell, I must. Oh! the shame of it, the shame of it. To tell it is to live through it all again. Actions are the first tragedy in life, words are the second. Words are perhaps the worst. Words are merciless . . . Oh! (*starts as* LORD WINDERMERE *enters*)

LORD WINDERMERE (*kisses her*): Margaret – how pale you look!

LADY WINDERMERE: I slept very badly.

LORD WINDERMERE (*sitting on sofa with her*): I am so sorry. I came in dreadfully late, and didn't like to wake you. You are crying, dear.

LADY WINDERMERE: Yes, I am crying, for I have something to tell you, Arthur.

LORD WINDERMERE: My dear child, you are not well. You've been doing too much. Let us go away to the country. You'll be all right at Selby. The season is almost over. There is no use staying on. Poor darling! We'll go away today, if you like. (*rises*) We can easily catch the 3.40. I'll send a wire to Fannen. (*crosses and sits down at table to write a telegram*)

LADY WINDERMERE: Yes; let us go away today. No; I can't go today, Arthur. There is someone I must see before I leave town – someone who has been kind to me.

LORD WINDERMERE (*rising and leaning over sofa*): Kind to you?

LADY WINDERMERE: Far more than that. (*rises and goes to him.*) I will tell you, Arthur, but only love me, love me as you used to love me.

LORD WINDERMERE: Used to? You are not thinking of that wretched woman who came here last night? (*coming round and sitting beside her*) You don't still imagine – no, you couldn't.

LADY WINDERMERE: I don't. I know now I was wrong and foolish.

LORD WINDERMERE: It was very good of you to receive her last night – but you are never to see her again.

LADY WINDERMERE: Why do you say that? (*a pause*)

LORD WINDERMERE (*holding her hand*): Margaret, I thought Mrs Erlynne was a woman more sinned against than sinning, as the phrase goes. I thought she wanted to be good, to get back into a place that she had lost by a moment's folly, to lead again a decent life. I believed what she told me – I was mistaken in her. She is bad – as bad as a woman can be.

LADY WINDERMERE: Arthur, Arthur, don't talk so bitterly about any woman. I don't think now that people can be divided into the good and the bad as though they were two separate races or creations. What are called good women may have terrible things in them, mad moods of recklessness, assertion, jealousy, sin. Bad women, as they are termed, may have in them sorrow, repentance, pity, sacrifice. And I don't think Mrs Erlynne a bad woman – I know she's not.

LORD WINDERMERE: My dear child, the woman's impossible. No matter what harm she tries to do us, you must never see her again. She is inadmissible anywhere.

LADY WINDERMERE: But I want to see her. I want her to come here.

LORD WINDERMERE: Never!

LADY WINDERMERE: She came here once as *your* guest. She must come now as *mine*. That is but fair.

LORD WINDERMERE: She should never have come here.

LADY WINDERMERE (*rising*): It is too late, Arthur, to say that now. (*moves away*)

LORD WINDERMERE (*rising*): Margaret, if you knew where Mrs Erlynne went last night, after she left this house, you would not sit in the same room with her. It was absolutely shameless, the whole thing.

LADY WINDERMERE: Arthur, I can't bear it any longer. I must tell you. Last night –

Enter PARKER *with a tray on which lie* LADY WINDERMERE'S *fan and a card*

PARKER: Mrs Erlynne has called to return your ladyship's fan which she took away by mistake last night. Mrs Erlynne has written a message on the card.

LADY WINDERMERE: Oh, ask Mrs Erlynne to be kind enough to come up. (*reads card*) Say I shall be very glad to see her.

Exit PARKER

She wants to see me, Arthur.

LORD WINDERMERE (*takes card and looks at it*): Margaret, I beg you not to. Let me see her first, at any rate. She's a dangerous woman. She is the most dangerous woman I know. You don't realise what you're doing.

LADY WINDERMERE: It is right that I should see her.

LORD WINDERMERE: My child, you may be on the brink of a great sorrow. Don't go to meet it. It is absolutely necessary that I should see her before you do.

LADY WINDERMERE: Why should it be necessary?

Enter PARKER

PARKER: Mrs Erlynne.

Enter MRS ERLYNNE; *exit* PARKER

MRS ERLYNNE: How do you do, Lady Windermere? (*to* LORD WINDERMERE): How do you do? Do you know, Lady Windermere, I am so sorry about your fan. I can't imagine how I made such a silly mistake. Most stupid of me. And as I was driving in your direction, I thought I would take the opportunity of returning your property in person with many apologies for my carelessness, and of bidding you goodbye.

LADY WINDERMERE: Goodbye? (*moves towards sofa with* MRS ERLYNNE *and sits down beside her*) Are you going away, then, Mrs Erlynne?

MRS ERLYNNE: Yes; I am going to live abroad again. The English climate doesn't suit me. My – heart is affected here, and that I don't like. I prefer living in the south. London is too full of fogs and – and serious people, Lord Windermere. Whether the fogs produce the serious people or whether the serious people produce the fogs, I don't know, but the whole thing rather gets on my nerves, and so I'm leaving this afternoon by the Club Train.

LADY WINDERMERE: This afternoon? But I wanted so much to come and see you.

MRS ERLYNNE: How kind of you! But I am afraid I have to go.

LADY WINDERMERE: Shall I never see you again, Mrs Erlynne?

MRS ERLYNNE: I am afraid not. Our lives lie too far apart. But there is a little thing I would like you to do for me. I want a photograph of you, Lady Windermere – would you give me one? You don't know how gratified I should be.

LADY WINDERMERE: Oh, with pleasure. There is one on that table. I'll show it to you. (*goes across to the table*)

LORD WINDERMERE (*coming up to* MRS ERLYNNE *and speaking in a low voice*): It is monstrous your intruding yourself here after your conduct last night.

MRS ERLYNNE (*with an amused smile*): My dear Windermere, manners before morals!

LADY WINDERMERE (*returning*): I'm afraid it is very flattering – I am not so pretty as that. (*showing photograph*)

MRS ERLYNNE: You are much prettier. But haven't you got one of yourself with your little boy?

LADY WINDERMERE: I have. Would you prefer one of those?

MRS ERLYNNE: Yes.

LADY WINDERMERE: I'll go and get it for you, if you'll excuse me for a moment. I have one upstairs.

MRS ERLYNNE: So sorry, Lady Windermere, to give you so much trouble.

LADY WINDERMERE (*moves to door*): No trouble at all, Mrs Erlynne.

MRS ERLYNNE: Thanks so much.

Exit LADY WINDERMERE

You seem rather out of temper this morning, Windermere. Why should you be? Margaret and I get on charmingly together.

LORD WINDERMERE: I can't bear to see you with her. Besides, you have not told me the truth, Mrs Erlynne.

MRS ERLYNNE: I have not told *her* the truth, you mean.

LORD WINDERMERE (*standing*): I sometimes wish you had. I should have been spared then the misery, the anxiety, the annoyance of the last six months. But rather than my wife should know that the mother whom she was taught to consider as dead, the mother whom she has mourned as dead, is living – a divorced woman, going about under an assumed name, a bad woman preying upon life, as I know you now to be – rather than that, I was ready to supply you with money to pay bill after bill, extravagance after extravagance, to risk what occurred yesterday, the first quarrel I have ever had with my wife. You don't understand what that means to me. How could you? But I tell you that the only bitter words that ever came from those sweet lips of hers were on your account, and I hate to see you next her. You sully the innocence that is in her. – And I used to think that with all your faults you were frank and honest. You are not.

MRS ERLYNNE: Why do you say that?

LORD WINDERMERE: You made me get you an invitation to my wife's ball.

MRS ERLYNNE: For my daughter's ball – yes.

LORD WINDERMERE: You came, and within an hour of your leaving the house you are found in a man's rooms – you are disgraced before everyone. (*goes up stage*)

MRS ERLYNNE: Yes.

LORD WINDERMERE (*turning round on her*): Therefore I have a right to look upon you as what you are – a worthless, vicious woman. I have the right to tell you never to enter this house, never to attempt to come near my wife –

MRS ERLYNNE (*coldly*): My daughter, you mean.

LORD WINDERMERE: You have no right to claim her as your daughter. You left her, abandoned her when she was but a child in the cradle, abandoned her for your lover, who abandoned you in turn.

MRS ERLYNNE (*rising*): Do you count that to his credit, Lord Windermere – or to mine?

LORD WINDERMERE: To his, now that I know you.

MRS ERLYNNE: Take care – you had better be careful.

LORD WINDERMERE: Oh, I am not going to mince words for you. I know you thoroughly.

MRS ERLYNNE (*looking steadily at him*): I question that.

LORD WINDERMERE: I *do* know you. For twenty years of your life you lived without your child, without a thought of your child. One day you read in the papers that she had married a rich man. You saw your hideous chance. You knew that to spare her the ignominy of learning that a woman like you was her mother, I would endure anything. You began your blackmailing.

MRS ERLYNNE (*shrugging her shoulders*): Don't use ugly words, Windermere. They are vulgar. I saw my chance, it is true, and took it.

LORD WINDERMERE: Yes, you took it – and spoiled it all last night by being found out.

MRS ERLYNNE (*with a strange smile*): You are quite right, I spoiled it all last night.

LORD WINDERMERE: And as for your blunder in taking my wife's fan from here and then leaving it about in Darlington's rooms, it is unpardonable. I can't bear the sight of it now. I shall never let my wife use it again. The thing is soiled for me. You should have kept it and not brought it back.

MRS ERLYNNE: I think I *shall* keep it. (*goes up*) It's extremely pretty. (*takes up fan*) I shall ask Margaret to give it to me.

LORD WINDERMERE: I hope my wife will give it you.

MRS ERLYNNE: Oh, I'm sure she will have no objection.

LORD WINDERMERE: I wish that at the same time she would give you a miniature she kisses every night before she prays. It's the miniature of a young innocent-looking girl with beautiful dark hair.

MRS ERLYNNE: Ah, yes, I remember. How long ago that seems! (*goes to sofa and sits down*) It was done before I was married. Dark hair and an innocent expression were the fashion then, Windermere! (*a pause*)

LORD WINDERMERE: What do you mean by coming here this morning? What is your object?

MRS ERLYNNE (*with a note of irony in her voice*): To bid goodbye to my dear daughter, of course.

LADY WINDERMERE *bites his underlip in anger.* MRS ERLYNNE *looks at him, and her voice and manner become serious. In her accents as she talks there is a note of deep tragedy. For a moment she reveals herself*

Oh, don't imagine I am going to have a pathetic scene with her, weep on her neck and tell her who I am, and all that kind of thing. I have no ambition to play the part of a mother. Only once in my life have I known a mother's feelings. That was last night. They were terrible – they made me suffer – they made me suffer too much. For twenty years, as you say, I have lived childless – I want to live childless still. (*hiding her feelings with a trivial laugh*) Besides, my dear Windermere, how on earth could I pose as a mother with a grown-up daughter? Margaret is twenty-one, and I have never admitted that I am more than twenty-nine, or thirty at the most. Twenty-nine when there are pink shades, thirty when there are not. So you see what difficulties it would involve. No, as far as I am concerned, let your wife cherish the memory of this dead, stainless mother. Why should I interfere with her illusions? I find it hard enough to keep my own. I lost one illusion last night. I thought I had no heart. I find I have, and a heart doesn't suit me, Windermere. Somehow it doesn't go with modern dress. It makes one look old. (*takes up hand-mirror from table and looks into it*) And it spoils one's career at critical moments.

LORD WINDERMERE: You fill me with horror – with absolute horror.

MRS ERLYNNE (*rising*): I suppose, Windermere, you would like me to retire into a convent, or become a hospital nurse, or something of that kind, as people do in silly modern novels. That is stupid of you, Arthur; in real life we don't do such things – not as long as we have any good looks left, at any rate. No – what consoles one nowadays is not repentance, but pleasure. Repentance is quite out of date. And besides, if a woman really repents, she has to go to a bad dressmaker, otherwise no one believes in her. And nothing in the world would induce me to do that. No; I am going to pass entirely out of your two lives. My coming into them has been a mistake – I discovered that last night.

LORD WINDERMERE: A fatal mistake.

MRS ERLYNNE (*smiling*): Almost fatal.

LORD WINDERMERE: I am sorry now I did not tell my wife the whole thing at once.

MRS ERLYNNE: I regret my bad actions. You regret your good ones – that is the difference between us.

LORD WINDERMERE: I don't trust you. I *will* tell my wife. It's better for her to know, and from me. It will cause her infinite pain – it will humiliate her terribly, but it's right that she should know.

MRS ERLYNNE: You propose to tell her?

LORD WINDERMERE: I am going to tell her.

MRS ERLYNNE (*going up to him*): If you do, I will make my name so infamous that it will mar every moment of her life. It will ruin her, and make her wretched. If you dare to tell her, there is no depth of degradation I will not sink to, no pit of shame I will not enter. You shall not tell her – I forbid you.

LORD WINDERMERE: Why?

MRS ERLYNNE (*after a pause*): If I said to you that I cared for her, perhaps loved her even – you would sneer at me, wouldn't you?

LORD WINDERMERE: I should feel it was not true. A mother's love means devotion, unselfishness, sacrifice. What could you know of such things?

MRS ERLYNNE: You are right. What could I know of such things? Don't let us talk any more about it – as for telling my daughter who I am, that I do not allow. It is my secret it is not yours. If I make up my mind to tell her, and I think I will, I shall tell her before I leave the house – if not, I shall never tell her.

LORD WINDERMERE (*angrily*): Then let me beg of you to leave our house at once. I will make your excuses to Margaret.

Enter LADY WINDERMERE. *She goes over to* MRS ERLYNNE *with the photograph in her hand.* LORD WINDERMERE *moves to back of sofa, and anxiously watches* MRS ERLYNNE *as the scene progresses*

LADY WINDERMERE: I am so sorry, Mrs Erlynne, to have kept you waiting. I couldn't find the photograph anywhere. At last I discovered it in my husband's dressing-room – he had stolen it.

MRS ERLYNNE (*takes the photograph from her and looks at it*): I am not surprised – it is charming. (*Goes over to sofa with* LADY WINDERMERE, *and sits down beside her. Looks again at the photograph*) And so that is your little boy! What is he called?

LADY WINDERMERE: Gerard, after my dear father.

MRS ERLYNNE (*laying the photograph down*): Really?

LADY WINDERMERE: Yes. If it had been a girl, I would have called her after my mother. My mother had the same name as myself – Margaret.

MRS ERLYNNE: My name is Margaret too.

LADY WINDERMERE: Indeed!

MRS ERLYNNE: Yes. (*pause*) You are devoted to your mother's memory, Lady Windermere, your husband tells me.

LADY WINDERMERE: We all have ideals in life. At least we all should have. Mine is my mother.

MRS ERLYNNE: Ideals are dangerous things. Realities are better. They wound, but they're better.

LADY WINDERMERE (*shaking her head*): If I lost my ideals, I should lose everything.

MRS ERLYNNE: Everything?

LADY WINDERMERE: Yes. (*pause*)

MRS ERLYNNE: Did your father often speak to you of your mother?

LADY WINDERMERE: No, it gave him too much pain. He told me how my mother had died a few months after I was born. His eyes filled with tears as he spoke. Then he begged me never to mention her name to him again. It made him suffer even to hear it. My father – my father really died of a broken heart. His was the most ruined life I know.

MRS ERLYNNE (*rising*): I am afraid I must go now, Lady Windermere.

LADY WINDERMERE (*rising*): Oh no, don't.

MRS ERLYNNE: I think I had better. My carriage must have come back by this time. I sent it to Lady Jedburgh's with a note.

LADY WINDERMERE: Arthur, would you mind seeing if Mrs Erlynne's carriage has come back?

MRS ERLYNNE: Pray don't trouble, Lord Windermere.

LADY WINDERMERE: Yes, Arthur, do go, please.

> LORD WINDERMERE *hesitates for a moment and looks at* MRS ERLYNNE. *She remains quite impassive. He leaves the room*

(*to* MRS ERLYNNE): Oh! What am I to say to you? You saved me last night! (*goes towards her*)

MRS ERLYNNE: Hush – don't speak of it.

LADY WINDERMERE: I must speak of it. I can't let you think that I am going to accept this sacrifice. I am not. It is too great. I am going to tell my husband everything. It is my duty.

MRS ERLYNNE: It is not your duty – at least you have duties to others besides him. You say you owe me something?

LADY WINDERMERE: I owe you everything.

MRS ERLYNNE: Then pay your debt by silence. That is the only way in which it can be paid. Don't spoil the one good thing I have done in my life by telling it to anyone. Promise me that what passed last night will remain a secret between us. You must not bring misery into your husband's life. Why spoil his love? You must not spoil it. Love is easily killed. Oh! how easily love is killed. Pledge me your word, Lady Windermere, that you will never tell him. I insist upon it.

LADY WINDERMERE (*with bowed head*): It is your will, not mine.

MRS ERLYNNE: Yes, it is my will. And never forget your child – I like to think of you as a mother. I like you to think of yourself as one.

LADY WINDERMERE (*looking up*): I always will now. Only once in my life have I forgotten my own mother – that was last night. Oh, if I had remembered her I should not have been so foolish, so wicked.

MRS ERLYNNE (*with a slight shudder*): Hush, last night is quite over.

Enter LORD WINDERMERE

LORD WINDERMERE: Your carriage has not come back yet, Mrs Erlynne.

MRS ERLYNNE: It makes no matter. I'll take a hansom. There is nothing in the world so respectable as a good Shrewsbury and Talbot. And now, dear Lady Windermere, I am afraid it is really goodbye. (*moves up centre stage*) Oh, I remember. You'll think me absurd, but do you know I've taken a great fancy to this fan that I was silly enough to run away with last night from your ball. Now, I wonder would you give it to me? Lord Windermere says you may. I know it is his present.

LADY WINDERMERE: Oh, certainly, if it will give you any pleasure. But it has my name on it. It has 'Margaret' on it.

MRS ERLYNNE: But we have the same Christian name.

LADY WINDERMERE: Oh, I forgot. Of course, do have it. What a wonderful chance our names being the same!

MRS ERLYNNE: Quite wonderful. Thanks – it will always remind me of you. (*shakes hands with her*)

Enter PARKER

PARKER: Lord Augustus Lorton. Mrs Erlynne's carriage has come.

Enter LORD AUGUSTUS

LORD AUGUSTUS: Good-morning, dear boy. Good-morning, Lady Windermere. (*sees* MRS ERLYNNE) Mrs Erlynne!

MRS ERLYNNE: How do you do, Lord Augustus? Are you quite well this morning?

LORD AUGUSTUS (*coldly*): Quite well, thank you, Mrs Erlynne.

MRS ERLYNNE: You don't look at all well, Lord Augustus. You stop up too late – it is so bad for you. You really should take more care of yourself. Goodbye, Lord Windermere. (*Goes towards door with a bow to* LORD AUGUSTUS. *Suddenly smiles and looks back at him*) Lord Augustus! Won't you see me to my carriage? You might carry the fan.

LORD WINDERMERE: Allow me!

MRS ERLYNNE: No; I want Lord Augustus. I have a special message for the dear duchess. Won't you carry the fan, Lord Augustus?

LORD AUGUSTUS: If you really desire it, Mrs Erlynne.

MRS ERLYNNE (*laughing*): Of course I do. You'll carry it so gracefully. You would carry off anything gracefully, dear Lord Augustus. (*When she reaches the door she looks back for a moment at* LADY WINDERMERE. *Their eyes meet. Then she turns and exits, followed by* LORD AUGUSTUS)

LADY WINDERMERE: You will never speak against Mrs Erlynne again, Arthur, will you?

LORD WINDERMERE (*gravely*): She is better than one thought her.

LADY WINDERMERE: She is better than I am.

LORD WINDERMERE (*smiling as he strokes her hair*): Child, you and she belong to different worlds. Into your world evil has never entered.

LADY WINDERMERE: Don't say that, Arthur. There is the same world for all of us, and good and evil, sin and innocence, go through it hand in hand. To shut one's eyes to half of life that one may live securely is as though one blinded oneself that one might walk with more safety in a land of pit and precipice.

LORD WINDERMERE (*moves down stage with her*): Darling, why do you say that?

LADY WINDERMERE (*sits on sofa*): Because I, who had shut my eyes to life, came to the brink. And one who had separated us –

LORD WINDERMERE: We were never separated.

LADY WINDERMERE: We never must be again. Oh, Arthur, don't love me less, and I will trust you more. I will trust you absolutely. Let us go to Selby. In the rose garden at Selby the roses are white and red.

Enter LORD AUGUSTUS

LORD AUGUSTUS: Arthur, she has explained everything!

LADY WINDERMERE *looks horribly frightened at this.* LORD WINDERMERE *starts.* LORD AUGUSTUS *takes* LORD WINDERMERE *by the arm and brings him to front of stage. He talks rapidly and in a low voice.* LADY WINDERMERE *stands watching them in terror*

My dear fellow, she has explained every demmed thing. We all wronged her immensely. It was entirely for my sake she went to Darlington's rooms. Called first at the club – fact is, wanted to put me out of suspense – and being told I had gone on – followed – naturally frightened when she heard a lot of us coming in – retired to another room – I assure you, most gratifying to me, the whole thing. We all behaved brutally to her. She is just the woman for me. Suits me down to the ground. All the conditions she makes are that we live entirely out of England. A very good thing too. Demmed clubs, demmed climate, demmed cooks, demmed everything. Sick of it all!

LADY WINDERMERE (*frightened*): Has Mrs Erlynne – ?

LORD AUGUSTUS (*advancing towards her with a low bow*): Yes, Lady Windermere – Mrs Erlynne has done me the honour of accepting my hand.

LORD WINDERMERE: Well, you are certainly marrying a very clever woman!

LADY WINDERMERE (*taking her husband's hand*): Ah, you're marrying a very good woman!

CURTAIN

A WOMAN OF NO IMPORTANCE

To
GLADYS COUNTESS DE GREY

PERSONS IN THE PLAY

LORD ILLINGWORTH
SIR JOHN PONTEFRACT
LORD ALFRED RUFFORD
MR KEVIL MP
THE VENERABLE ARCHDEACON DAUBENY DD
GERALD ARBUTHNOT
FARQUHAR, *butler*
FRANCIS, *footman*
LADY HUNSTANTON
LADY CAROLINE PONTEFRACT
LADY STUTFIELD
MRS ALLONBY
MISS HESTER WORSLEY
ALICE, *maid*
MRS ARBUTHNOT

THE SCENES OF THE PLAY

ACT ONE *The terrace at Hunstanton Chase*
ACT TWO *The drawing-room at Hunstanton Chase*
ACT THREE *The picture gallery at Hunstanton Chase*
ACT FOUR *Sitting-room in Mrs Arbuthnot's house at Wrockley*

TIME: *The Present*
PLACE: *The Shires*

The action of the play takes place within twenty-four hours

FIRST PERFORMANCE

Haymarket Theatre, London, on 19 April 1893

A WOMAN OF NO IMPORTANCE

ACT ONE

Lawn in front of the terrace at Hunstanton. SIR JOHN *and* LADY CAROLINE PONTEFRACT, MISS WORSLEY, *on chairs under large yew tree.*

LADY CAROLINE: I believe this is the first English country house you have stayed at, Miss Worsley?

HESTER: Yes, Lady Caroline.

LADY CAROLINE: You have no country houses, I am told, in America?

HESTER: We have not many.

LADY CAROLINE: Have you any country? What we should call country?

HESTER (*smiling*): We have the largest country in the world, Lady Caroline. They used to tell us at school that some of our states are as big as France and England put together.

LADY CAROLINE: Ah! you must find it very draughty, I should fancy. (*To* SIR JOHN): John, you should have your muffler. What is the use of my always knitting mufflers for you if you won't wear them?

SIR JOHN: I am quite warm, Caroline, I assure you.

LADY CAROLINE: I think not, John. Well, you couldn't come to a more charming place than this, Miss Worsley, though the house is excessively damp, quite unpardonably damp, and dear Lady Hunstanton is sometimes a little lax about the people she asks down here. (*To* SIR JOHN): Jane mixes too much. Lord Illingworth, of course, is a man of high distinction. It is a privilege to meet him. And that Member of Parliament, Mr Kettle –

SIR JOHN: Kelvil, my love, Kelvil.

LADY CAROLINE: He must be quite respectable. One has never heard his name before in the whole course of one's life, which speaks volumes for a man, nowadays. But Mrs Allonby is hardly a very suitable person.

HESTER: I dislike Mrs Allonby. I dislike her more than I can say.

LADY CAROLINE: I am not sure, Miss Worsley, that foreigners like yourself should cultivate likes or dislikes about the people they are invited to meet. Mrs Allonby is very well born. She is a niece of Lord Brancaster's. It is said, of course, that she ran away twice before she was married. But you know how unfair people often are. I myself don't believe she ran away more than once.

HESTER: Mr Arbuthnot is very charming.

LADY CAROLINE: Ah, yes! the young man who has a post in a bank. Lady Hunstanton is most kind in asking him here, and Lord Illingworth seems to have taken quite a fancy to him. I am not sure, however, that Jane is right in taking him out of his position. In my young days, Miss Worsley, one never met anyone in society who worked for their living. It was not considered the thing.

HESTER: In America those are the people we respect most.

LADY CAROLINE: I have no doubt of it.

HESTER: Mr Arbuthnot has a beautiful nature! He is so simple, so sincere. He has one of the most beautiful natures I have ever come across. It is a privilege to meet *him*.

LADY CAROLINE: It is not customary in England, Miss Worsley, for a young lady to speak with such enthusiasm of any person of the opposite sex. English women conceal their feelings till after they are married. They show them then.

HESTER: Do you, in England, allow no friendship to exist between a young man and a young girl?

Enter LADY HUNSTANTON, *followed by* FOOTMAN *with shawls and a cushion*

LADY CAROLINE: We think it very inadvisable. Jane, I was just saying what a pleasant party you have asked us to meet. You have a wonderful power of selection. It is quite a gift.

LADY HUNSTANTON: Dear Caroline, how kind of you! I think we all do fit in very nicely together. And I hope our charming American visitor will carry back pleasant recollections of our English country life. (*To* FOOTMAN): The cushion, there, Francis. And my shawl. The Shetland. Get the Shetland.

Exit FOOTMAN *for shawl*

Enter GERALD ARBUTHNOT

GERALD: Lady Hunstanton, I have such good news to tell you. Lord Illingworth has just offered to make me his secretary.

LADY HUNSTANTON: His secretary? That is good news indeed, Gerald. It means a very brilliant future in store for you. Your dear mother will be delighted. I really must try and induce her to come up here tonight. Do you think she would, Gerald? I know how difficult it is to get her to go anywhere.

GERALD: Oh! I am sure she would, Lady Hunstanton, if she knew Lord Illingworth had made me such an offer.

Enter FOOTMAN *with shawl*

LADY HUNSTANTON: I will write and tell her about it and ask her to come up and meet him. (*To* FOOTMAN): Just wait, Francis. (*writes letter*)

LADY CAROLINE: That is a very wonderful opening for so young a man as you are, Mr Arbuthnot.

GERALD: It is indeed, Lady Caroline. I trust I shall be able to show myself worthy of it.

LADY CAROLINE: I trust so.

GERALD (*to* HESTER): *You* have not congratulated me yet, Miss Worsley.

HESTER: Are you very pleased about it?

GERALD: Of course I am. It means everything to me – things that were out of the reach of hope before may be within hope's reach now.

HESTER: Nothing should be out of the reach of hope. Life is a hope.

LADY HUNSTANTON: I fancy, Caroline, that diplomacy is what Lord Illingworth is aiming at. I heard that he was offered Vienna. But that may not be true.

LADY CAROLINE: I don't think that England should be represented abroad by an unmarried man, Jane. It might lead to complications.

LADY HUNSTANTON: You are too nervous, Caroline. Believe me, you are too nervous. Besides, Lord Illingworth may marry any day. I was in hopes he would have married Lady Kelso. But I believe he said her family was too large. Or was it her feet? I forget which. I regret it very much. She was made to be an ambassador's wife.

LADY CAROLINE: She certainly has a wonderful faculty for remembering people's names, and forgetting their faces.

LADY HUNSTANTON: Well, that is very natural, Caroline, is it not? (*To* FOOTMAN): Tell Henry to wait for an answer. I have written a line to your dear mother, Gerald, to tell her your good news, and to say she really must come to dinner.

Exit FOOTMAN

GERALD: That is awfully kind of you, Lady Hunstanton. (*To* HESTER): Will you come for a stroll, Miss Worsley?

HESTER: With pleasure. (*exit with* GERALD)

LADY HUNSTANTON: I am very much gratified at Gerald Arbuthnot's good fortune. He is quite a *protégé* of mine. And I am particularly pleased that Lord Illingworth should have made the offer of his own accord without my suggesting anything. Nobody likes to be asked favours. I remember poor Charlotte Pagden making herself quite unpopular one season because she had a French governess she wanted to recommend to everyone.

LADY CAROLINE: I saw the governess, Jane. Lady Pagden sent her to me. It was before Eleanor came out. She was far too good-looking to be in any respectable household. I don't wonder Lady Pagden was so anxious to get rid of her.

LADY HUNSTANTON: Ah, that explains it.

LADY CAROLINE: John, the grass is too damp for you. You had better go and put on your overshoes at once.

SIR JOHN: I am quite comfortable, Caroline, I assure you.

LADY CAROLINE: You must allow me to be the best judge of that, John. Pray do as I tell you.

SIR JOHN *gets up and goes off*

LADY HUNSTANTON: You spoil him, Caroline, you do indeed!

Enter MRS ALLONBY *and* LADY STUTFIELD

(*To* MRS ALLONBY): Well, dear, I hope you like the park. It is said to be well timbered.

MRS ALLONBY: The trees are wonderful, Lady Hunstanton.

LADY STUTFIELD: Quite, quite wonderful.

MRS ALLONBY: But, somehow, I feel sure that if I lived in the country for six months, I should become so unsophisticated that no one would take the slightest notice of me.

LADY HUNSTANTON: I assure you, dear, that the country has not that effect at all. Why, it was from Melthorpe, which is only two miles from here, that Lady Belton eloped with Lord Fethersdale. I remember the occurrence perfectly. Poor Lord Belton died three days afterwards of joy, or gout. I forget which. We had a large party staying here at the time so we were all very much interested in the whole affair.

MRS ALLONBY: I think to elope is cowardly. It's running away from danger. And danger has become so rare in modern life.

LADY CAROLINE: As far as I can make out, the young women of the present day seem to make it the sole object of their lives to be always playing with fire.

MRS ALLONBY: The one advantage of playing with fire, Lady Caroline, is that one never gets even singed. It is the people who don't know how to play with it who get burned up.

LADY STUTFIELD: Yes; I see that. It is very, very helpful.

LADY HUNSTANTON: I don't know how the world would get on with such a theory as that, dear Mrs Allonby.

LADY STUTFIELD: Ah! The world was made for men and not for women.

MRS ALLONBY: Oh, don't say that, Lady Stutfield. We have a much better time than they have. There are far more things forbidden to us than are forbidden to them.

LADY STUTFIELD: Yes; that is quite, quite true. I had not thought of that.

Enter SIR JOHN *and* MR KELVIL

LADY HUNSTANTON: Well, Mr Kelvil, have you got through your work?

KELVIL: I have finished my writing for the day, Lady Hunstanton. It has been an arduous task. The demands on the time of a public man are very heavy nowadays, very heavy indeed. And I don't think they meet with adequate recognition.

LADY CAROLINE: John, have you got your overshoes on?

SIR JOHN: Yes, my love.

LADY CAROLINE: I think you had better come over here, John. It is more sheltered.

SIR JOHN: I am quite comfortable, Caroline.

LADY CAROLINE: I think not, John. You had better sit beside me.

SIR JOHN *rises and goes across*

LADY STUTFIELD: And what have you been writing about this morning, Mr Kelvil?

KELVIL: On the usual subject, Lady Stutfield. On purity.

LADY STUTFIELD: That must be such a very, very interesting thing to write about.

KELVIL: It is the one subject of really national importance, nowadays, Lady Stutfield. I purpose addressing my constituents on the question before Parliament meets. I find that the poorer classes of this country display a marked desire for a higher ethical standard.

LADY STUTFIELD: How quite, quite nice of them.

LADY CAROLINE: Are you in favour of women taking part in politics, Mr Kettle?

SIR JOHN: Kelvil, my love, Kelvil.

KELVIL: The growing influence of women is the one reassuring thing in our political life, Lady Caroline. Women are always on the side of morality, public and private.

LADY STUTFIELD: It is so very, very gratifying to hear you say that.

LADY HUNSTANTON: Ah, yes! – the moral qualities in women – that is the important thing. I am afraid, Caroline, that dear Lord Illingworth doesn't value the moral qualities in women as much as he should.

Enter LORD ILLINGWORTH

LADY STUTFIELD: The world says that Lord Illingworth is very, very wicked.

LORD ILLINGWORTH: But what world says that, Lady Stutfield? It must be the next world. This world and I are on excellent terms. (*sits down beside* MRS ALLONBY)

LADY STUTFIELD: Everyone I know says you are very, very wicked.

LORD ILLINGWORTH: It is perfectly monstrous the way people go about, nowadays, saying things against one behind one's back that are absolutely and entirely true.

LADY HUNSTANTON: Dear Lord Illingworth is quite hopeless, Lady Stutfield. I have given up trying to reform him. It would take a public company with a board of directors and a paid secretary to do that. But you have the secretary already, Lord Illingworth, haven't you? Gerald Arbuthnot has told us of his good fortune; it is really most kind of you.

LORD ILLINGWORTH: Oh, don't say that, Lady Hunstanton. Kind is a dreadful word. I took a great fancy to young Arbuthnot the moment I met him, and he'll be of considerable use to me in something I am foolish enough to think of doing.

LADY HUNSTANTON: He is an admirable young man. And his mother is one of my dearest friends. He has just gone for a walk with our pretty American. She is very pretty, is she not?

LADY CAROLINE: Far too pretty. These American girls[1] carry off all the good matches. Why can't they stay in their own country? They are always telling us it is the paradise of women.

LORD ILLINGWORTH: It is, Lady Caroline. That is why, like Eve, they are so extremely anxious to get out of it.

LADY CAROLINE: Who are Miss Worsley's parents?

LORD ILLINGWORTH: American women are wonderfully clever in concealing their parents.

LADY HUNSTANTON: My dear Lord Illingworth, what do you mean? Miss Worsley, Caroline, is an orphan. Her father was a very wealthy millionaire or philanthropist, or both, I believe, who entertained my son quite hospitably, when he visited Boston. I don't know how he made his money, originally.

KELVIL: I fancy in American dry goods.

LADY HUNSTANTON: What are American dry goods?

LORD ILLINGWORTH: American novels.

LADY HUNSTANTON: How very singular! . . . Well, from whatever source her large fortune came, I have a great esteem for Miss Worsley. She dresses exceedingly well. All Americans do dress well. They get their clothes in Paris.

MRS ALLONBY: They say, Lady Hunstanton, that when good Americans die they go to Paris.

LADY HUNSTANTON: Indeed? And when bad Americans die, where do they go to?

LORD ILLINGWORTH: Oh, they go to America.

KELVIL: I am afraid you don't appreciate America, Lord Illingworth. It is a very remarkable country, especially considering its youth.

LORD ILLINGWORTH: The youth of America is their oldest tradition. It has been going on now for three hundred years. To hear them talk one would imagine they were in their first childhood. As far as civilisation goes they are in their second.

KELVIL: There is undoubtedly a great deal of corruption in American politics. I suppose you allude to that?

LORD ILLINGWORTH: I wonder.

LADY HUNSTANTON: Politics are in a sad way everywhere, I am told. They certainly are in England. Dear Mr Cardew is ruining the country. I wonder Mrs Cardew allows him. I am sure, Lord Illingworth, you don't think that uneducated people should be allowed to have votes?

LORD ILLINGWORTH: I think they are the only people who should.

KELVIL: Do you take no side then in modern politics, Lord Illingworth?

LORD ILLINGWORTH: One should never take sides in anything, Mr Kelvil. Taking sides is the beginning of sincerity, and earnestness follows shortly afterwards and the human being becomes a bore. However, the House of Commons really does very little harm. You can't make people good by Act of Parliament – that is something.

KELVIL: You cannot deny that the House of Commons has always shown great sympathy with the sufferings of the poor.

LORD ILLINGWORTH: That is its special vice. That is the special vice of the age. One should sympathise with the joy, the beauty, the colour of life. The less said about life's sores the better, Mr Kelvil.

KELVIL: Still our East End is a very important problem.

LORD ILLINGWORTH: Quite so. It is the problem of slavery. And we are trying to solve it by amusing the slaves.

LADY HUNSTANTON: Certainly, a great deal may be done by means of cheap entertainments, as you say, Lord Illingworth. Dear Dr Daubeny, our rector here, provides, with the assistance of his curates, really admirable recreations for the poor during the winter. And much good may be done by means of a magic lantern, or a missionary, or some popular amusement of that kind.

LADY CAROLINE: I am not at all in favour of amusements for the poor, Jane. Blankets and coals are sufficient. There is too much love of pleasure amongst the upper classes as it is. Health is what we want in modern life. The tone is not healthy, not healthy at all.

KELVIL: You are quite right, Lady Caroline.

LADY CAROLINE: I believe I am usually right.

MRS ALLONBY: Horrid word 'health'.

LORD ILLINGWORTH: Silliest word in our language, and one knows so well the popular idea of health. The English country gentleman galloping after a fox – the unspeakable in full pursuit of the uneatable.

KELVIL: May I ask, Lord Illingworth, if you regard the House of Lords as a better institution than the House of Commons?

LORD ILLINGWORTH: A much better institution, of course. We in the House of Lords are never in touch with public opinion. That makes us a civilised body.

KELVIL: Are you serious in putting forward such a view?

LORD ILLINGWORTH: Quite serious, Mr Kelvil. (*To* MRS ALLONBY): Vulgar habit that is people have nowadays of asking one, after one has given them an idea, whether one is serious or not. Nothing is serious except passion. The intellect is not a serious thing, and never has been. It is an instrument on which one plays, that is all. The only serious form of intellect I know is the British intellect. And on the British intellect the illiterates play the drum.

LADY HUNSTANTON: What are you saying, Lord Illingworth, about the drum?

LORD ILLINGWORTH: I was merely talking to Mrs Allonby about the leading articles in the London newspapers.

LADY HUNSTANTON: But do you believe all that is written in the newspapers?

LORD ILLINGWORTH: I do. Nowadays it is only the unreadable that occurs. (*rises with* MRS ALLONBY)

LADY HUNSTANTON: Are you going, Mrs Allonby?

MRS ALLONBY: Just as far as the conservatory. Lord Illingworth told me this morning that there was an orchid there as beautiful as the seven deadly sins.

LADY HUNSTANTON: My dear, I hope there is nothing of the kind. I will certainly speak to the gardener.

Exit MRS ALLONBY *with* LORD ILLINGWORTH

LADY CAROLINE: Remarkable type, Mrs Allonby.

LADY HUNSTANTON: She lets her clever tongue run away with her sometimes.

LADY CAROLINE: Is that the only thing, Jane, Mrs Allonby allows to run away with her?

LADY HUNSTANTON: I hope so, Caroline, I am sure.

Enter LORD ALFRED

Dear Lord Alfred, do join us.

LORD ALFRED *sits down beside* LADY STUTFIELD

LADY CAROLINE: You believe good of everyone, Jane. It is a great fault.

LADY STUTFIELD: Do you really, really think, Lady Caroline, that one should believe evil of everyone?

LADY CAROLINE: I think it is much safer to do so, Lady Stutfield. Until, of course, people are found out to be good. But that requires a great deal of investigation nowadays.

LADY STUTFIELD: But there is so much unkind scandal in modern life.

LADY CAROLINE: Lord Illingworth remarked to me last night at dinner that the basis of every scandal is an absolutely immoral certainty.

KELVIL: Lord Illingworth is, of course, a very brilliant man, but he seems to me to be lacking in that fine faith in the nobility and purity of life which is so important in this century.

LADY STUTFIELD: Yes, quite, quite important, is it not?

KELVIL: He gives me the impression of a man who does not appreciate the beauty of our English home-life. I would say that he was tainted with foreign ideas on the subject.

LADY STUTFIELD: There is nothing, nothing like the beauty of home-life, is there?

KELVIL: It is the mainstay of our moral system in England, Lady Stutfield. Without it we would become like our neighbours.

LADY STUTFIELD: That would be so, so sad, would it not?

KELVIL: I am afraid, too, that Lord Illingworth regards woman simply as a toy. Now, I have never regarded woman as a toy. Woman is the intellectual helpmeet of man in public as in private life. Without her we should forget the true ideals. (*sits down beside* LADY STUTFIELD)

LADY STUTFIELD: I am so very, very glad to hear you say that.

LADY CAROLINE: You a married man, Mr Kettle?

SIR JOHN: Kelvil, dear, Kelvil.

KELVIL: I am married, Lady Caroline.

LADY CAROLINE: Family?

KELVIL: Yes.

LADY CAROLINE: How many?

KELVIL: Eight.

LADY STUTFIELD *turns her attention to* LORD ALFRED

LADY CAROLINE: Mrs Kettle and the children are, I suppose, at the seaside?

SIR JOHN *shrugs his shoulders*

KELVIL: My wife is at the seaside with the children, Lady Caroline.

LADY CAROLINE: You will join them later on, no doubt?

KELVIL: If my public engagements permit me.

LADY CAROLINE: Your public life must be a great source of gratification to Mrs Kettle.

SIR JOHN: Kelvil, my love, Kelvil.

LADY STUTFIELD (*to* LORD ALFRED): How very, very charming those gold-tipped cigarettes of yours are, Lord Alfred.

LORD ALFRED: They are awfully expensive. I can only afford them when I'm in debt.

LADY STUTFIELD: It must be terribly, terribly distressing to be in debt.

LORD ALFRED: One must have some occupation nowadays. If I hadn't my debts I shouldn't have anything to think about. All the chaps I know are in debt.

LADY STUTFIELD: But don't the people to whom you owe the money give you a great, great deal of annoyance?

Enter FOOTMAN

LORD ALFRED: Oh, no, they write; I don't.

LADY STUTFIELD: How very, very strange.

LADY HUNSTANTON: Ah, here is a letter, Caroline, from dear Mrs Arbuthnot. She won't dine. I am so sorry. But she will come in the evening. I am very pleased, indeed. She is one of the sweetest of women. Writes a beautiful hand, too, so large, so firm. (*hands letter to* LADY CAROLINE)

LADY CAROLINE (*looking at it*): A little lacking in femininity, Jane. Femininity is the quality I admire most in women.

LADY HUNSTANTON (*taking back letter and leaving it on table*): Oh ! she is very feminine, Caroline, and so good, too. You should hear what the Archdeacon says of her. He regards her as his right hand in the parish. (FOOTMAN *speaks to her*) In the yellow drawing-room. Shall we all go in? Lady Stutfield, shall we go in to tea?

LADY STUTFIELD: With pleasure, Lady Hunstanton.

They rise and proceed to go off. SIR JOHN *offers to carry* LADY STUTFIELD'S *cloak*

LADY CAROLINE: John! If you would allow your nephew to look after Lady Stutfield's cloak, you might help me with my workbasket.

Enter LORD ILLINGWORTH *and* MRS ALLONBY

SIR JOHN: Certainly, my love.

Exeunt

MRS ALLONBY: Curious thing, plain women are always jealous of their husbands, beautiful women never are!

LORD ILLINGWORTH: Beautiful women never have time. They are always so occupied in being jealous of other people's husbands.

MRS ALLONBY: I should have thought Lady Caroline would have grown tired of conjugal anxiety by this time! Sir John is her fourth!

LORD ILLINGWORTH: So much marriage is certainly not becoming. Twenty years of romance make a woman look like a ruin; but twenty years of marriage make her something like a public building.

MRS ALLONBY: Twenty years of romance! Is there such a thing?

LORD ILLINGWORTH: Not in our day. Women have become too brilliant. Nothing spoils a romance so much as a sense of humour in the woman.

MRS ALLONBY: Or the want of it in the man.

LORD ILLINGWORTH: You are quite right. In a temple everyone should be serious, except the thing that is worshipped.

MRS ALLONBY: And that should be man?

LORD ILLINGWORTH: Women kneel so gracefully; men don't.

MRS ALLONBY: You are thinking of Lady Stutfield!

LORD ILLINGWORTH: I assure you I have not thought of Lady Stutfield for the last quarter of an hour.

MRS ALLONBY: Is she such a mystery?

LORD ILLINGWORTH: She is more than a mystery – she is a mood.

MRS ALLONBY: Moods don't last.

LORD ILLINGWORTH: It is their chief charm.

Enter HESTER *and* GERALD

GERALD: Lord Illingworth, everyone has been congratulating me – Lady Hunstanton and Lady Caroline, and . . . everyone. I hope I shall make a good secretary.

LORD ILLINGWORTH: You will be the pattern secretary, Gerald. (*talks to him*)

MRS ALLONBY: You enjoy country life, Miss Worsley?

HESTER: Very much indeed.

MRS ALLONBY: Don't you find yourself longing for a London dinner-party?

HESTER: I dislike London dinner-parties.

MRS ALLONBY: I adore them. The clever people never listen, and the stupid people never talk.

HESTER: I think the stupid people talk a great deal.

MRS ALLONBY: Ah, I never listen!

LORD ILLINGWORTH: My dear boy, if I didn't like you I wouldn't have made you the offer. It is because I like you so much that I want to have you with me.

Exit HESTER *with* GERALD

Charming fellow, Gerald Arbuthnot!

MRS ALLONBY: He is very nice; very nice indeed. But I can't stand the American young lady.

LORD ILLINGWORTH: Why?

MRS ALLONBY: She told me yesterday, and in quite a loud voice too, that she was only eighteen. It was most annoying.

LORD ILLINGWORTH: One should never trust a woman who tells one her real age. A woman who would tell one that, would tell one anything.

MRS ALLONBY: She is a puritan besides –

LORD ILLINGWORTH: Ah, that is inexcusable. I don't mind plain women being puritans. It is the only excuse they have for being plain. But she is decidedly pretty. I admire her immensely. (*looks steadfastly at* MRS ALLONBY)

MRS ALLONBY: What a thoroughly bad man you must be!

LORD ILLINGWORTH: What do you call a bad man?

MRS ALLONBY: The sort of man who admires innocence.

LORD ILLINGWORTH: And a bad woman?

MRS ALLONBY: Oh ! the sort of woman a man never gets tired of.

LORD ILLINGWORTH: You are severe – on yourself.

MRS ALLONBY: Define us as a sex.

LORD ILLINGWORTH: Sphinxes without secrets.

MRS ALLONBY: Does that include the puritan women?

LORD ILLINGWORTH: Do you know, I don't believe in the existence of puritan women! I don't think there is a woman in the world who would not be a little flattered if one made love to her. It is that which makes women so irresistibly adorable.

MRS ALLONBY: You think there is no woman in the world who would object to being kissed?

LORD ILLINGWORTH: Very few.

MRS ALLONBY: Miss Worsley would not let you kiss her.

LORD ILLINGWORTH: Are you sure?

MRS ALLONBY: Quite.

LORD ILLINGWORTH: What do you think she'd do if I kissed her?

MRS ALLONBY: Either marry you, or strike you across the face with her glove. What would you do if she struck you across the face with her glove?

LORD ILLINGWORTH: Fall in love with her, probably.

MRS ALLONBY: Then it is lucky you are not going to kiss her!

LORD ILLINGWORTH: Is that a challenge?

MRS ALLONBY: It is an arrow shot into the air.

LORD ILLINGWORTH: Don't you know that I always succeed in whatever I try?

MRS ALLONBY: I am sorry to hear it. We women adore failures. They lean on us.

LORD ILLINGWORTH: You worship successes. You cling to them.

MRS ALLONBY: We are the laurels to hide their baldness.

LORD ILLINGWORTH: And they need you always, except at the moment of triumph.

MRS ALLONBY: They are uninteresting then.

LORD ILLINGWORTH: How tantalising you are! (*a pause*)

MRS ALLONBY: Lord Illingworth, there is one thing I shall always like you for.

LORD ILLINGWORTH: Only one thing? And I have so many bad qualities.

MRS ALLONBY: Ah, don't be too conceited about them. You may lose them as you grow old.

LORD ILLINGWORTH: I never intend to grow old. The soul is born old but grows young. That is the comedy of life.

MRS ALLONBY: And the body is born young and grows old. That is life's tragedy.

LORD ILLINGWORTH: Its comedy also, sometimes. But what is the mysterious reason why you will always like me?

MRS ALLONBY: It is that you have never made love to me.

LORD ILLINGWORTH: I have never done anything else.

MRS ALLONBY: Really? I have not noticed it.

LORD ILLINGWORTH: How unfortunate! It might have been a tragedy for both of us.

MRS ALLONBY: We should each have survived.

LORD ILLINGWORTH: One can survive everything nowadays, except death, and live down anything except a good reputation.

MRS ALLONBY: Have you tried a good reputation?

LORD ILLINGWORTH: It is one of the many annoyances to which I have never been subjected.

MRS ALLONBY: It may come.

LORD ILLINGWORTH: Why do you threaten me?

MRS ALLONBY: I will tell you when you have kissed the puritan.

Enter FOOTMAN

FRANCIS: Tea is served in the yellow drawing-room, my lord.

LORD ILLINGWORTH: Tell her ladyship we are coming in.

FRANCIS: Yes, my lord. (*exit*)

LORD ILLINGWORTH: Shall we go in to tea?

MRS ALLONBY: Do you like such simple pleasures?

LORD ILLINGWORTH: I adore simple pleasures. They are the last refuge of the complex. But, if you wish, let us stay here. Yes, let us stay here. The *Book of Life* begins with a man and a woman in a garden.

MRS ALLONBY: It ends with Revelations.

LORD ILLINGWORTH: You fence divinely. But the button has come off your foil.

MRS ALLONBY: I have still the mask.

LORD ILLINGWORTH: It makes your eyes lovelier.

MRS ALLONBY: Thank you. Come.

LORD ILLINGWORTH (*sees* MRS ARBUTHNOT'S *letter on table, and takes it up and looks at envelope*): What a curious handwriting! It reminds me of the handwriting of a woman I used to know years ago.

MRS ALLONBY: Who?

LORD ILLINGWORTH: Oh! no one. No one in particular. A woman of no importance. (*Throws letter down, and passes up the steps of the terrace with* MRS ALLONBY. *They smile at each other*)

END OF ACT ONE

ACT TWO

Drawing-room at Hunstanton, after dinner, lamps lit. Ladies seated on sofa.

MRS ALLONBY: What a comfort it is to have got rid of the men for a little!

LADY STUTFIELD: Yes; men persecute us dreadfully, don't they?

MRS ALLONBY: Persecute us? I wish they did.

LADY HUNSTANTON: My dear!

MRS ALLONBY: The annoying thing is that the wretches can be perfectly happy without us. That is why I think it is every woman's duty never to leave them alone for a single moment, except during this short breathing space after dinner; without which, I believe, we poor women would be absolutely worn to shadows.

Enter servants with coffee

LADY HUNSTANTON: Worn to shadows, dear?

MRS ALLONBY: Yes, Lady Hunstanton. It is such a strain keeping men up to the mark. They are always trying to escape from us.

LADY STUTFIELD: It seems to me that it is we who are always trying to escape from them. Men are so very, very heartless. They know their power and use it.

LADY CAROLINE (*takes coffee from servant*): What stuff and nonsense all this about men is! The thing to do is to keep men in their proper place.

MRS ALLONBY: But what is their proper place, Lady Caroline?

LADY CAROLINE: Looking after their wives, Mrs Allonby.

MRS ALLONBY (*takes coffee from servant*): Really. And if they're not married?

LADY CAROLINE: If they are not married, they should be looking after a wife. It's perfectly scandalous, the amount of bachelors who are going about society. There should be a law passed to compel them all to marry within twelve months.

LADY STUTFIELD (*refuses coffee*): But if they're in love with someone who, perhaps, is tied to another?

LADY CAROLINE: In that case, Lady Stutfield, they should be married off in a week to some plain respectable girl, in order to teach them not to meddle with other people's property.

MRS ALLONBY: I don't think that we should ever be spoken of as other people's property. All men are married women's property.[2] That is the only true definition of what married women's property really is. But we don't belong to anyone.

LADY STUTFIELD: Oh, I am so very, very glad to hear you say so.

LADY HUNSTANTON: But do you really think, dear Caroline, that legislation would improve matters in any way? I am told that, nowadays, all the married men live like bachelors, and all the bachelors like married men.

MRS ALLONBY: I certainly never know one from the other.

LADY STUTFIELD: Oh, I think one can always know at once whether a man has home claims upon his life or not. I have noticed a very, very sad expression in the eyes of so many married men.

MRS ALLONBY: Ah, all that I have noticed is that they are horribly tedious when they are good husbands, and abominably conceited when they are not.

LADY HUNSTANTON: Well, I suppose the type of husband has completely changed since my young days, but I am bound to state that poor dear Hunstanton was the most delightful of creatures, and as good as gold.

MRS ALLONBY: Ah, my husband is a sort of promise note; I'm tired of meeting him.

LADY CAROLINE: But you renew him from time to time, don't you?

MRS ALLONBY: Oh no, Lady Caroline. I have only had one husband as yet. I suppose you look upon me as quite an amateur.

LADY CAROLINE: With your views on life I wonder you married at all.

MRS ALLONBY: So do I.

LADY HUNSTANTON: My dear child, I believe you are really very happy in your married life, but that you like to hide your happiness from others.

MRS ALLONBY: I assure you I was horribly deceived in Ernest.

LADY HUNSTANTON: Oh, I hope not, dear. I knew his mother quite well. She was a Stratton, Caroline, one of Lord Crowland's daughters.

LADY CAROLINE: Victoria Stratton? I remember her perfectly. A silly, fair-haired woman with no chin.

MRS ALLONBY: Ah, Ernest has a chin. He has a very strong chin, a square chin. Ernest's chin is far too square.

LADY STUTFIELD: But do you really think a man's chin can be too square? I think a man should look very, very strong, and that his chin should be quite, quite square.

MRS ALLONBY: Then you should certainly know Ernest, Lady Stutfield. It is only fair to tell you beforehand he has got no conversation at all.

LADY STUTFIELD: I adore silent men.

MRS ALLONBY: Oh, Ernest isn't silent. He talks the whole time. But he has got no conversation. What he talks about I don't know. I haven't listened to him for years.

LADY STUTFIELD: Have you never forgiven him then? How sad that seems! But all life is very, very sad, is it not?

MRS ALLONBY: Life, Lady Stutfield, is simply a *mauvais quart d'heure* made up of exquisite moments.

LADY STUTFIELD: Yes, there are moments, certainly. But was it something very, very wrong that Mr Allonby did? Did he become angry with you, and say anything that was unkind or true?

MRS ALLONBY: Oh, dear, no. Ernest is invariably calm. That is one of the reasons he always gets on my nerves. Nothing is so aggravating as calmness. There is something positively brutal about the good temper of most modern men. I wonder we women stand it as well as we do.

LADY STUTFIELD: Yes; men's good temper shows they are not so sensitive as we are, not so finely strung. It makes a great barrier often between husband and wife, does it not? But I would so much like to know what was the wrong thing Mr Allonby did.

MRS ALLONBY: Well, I will tell you, if you solemnly promise to tell everybody else.

LADY STUTFIELD: Thank you, thank you. I will make a point of repeating it.

MRS ALLONBY: When Ernest and I were engaged, he swore to me positively on his knees that he had never loved anyone before in the whole course of his life. I was very young at the time, so I didn't believe him, I needn't tell you. Unfortunately, however, I made no enquiries of any kind till after I had been actually married four or five months. I found out then that what he had told me was perfectly true. And that sort of thing makes a man so absolutely uninteresting.

LADY HUNSTANTON: My dear!

MRS ALLONBY: Men always want to be a woman's first love. That is their clumsy vanity. We women have a more subtle instinct about things. What we like is to be a man's last romance.

LADY STUTFIELD: I see what you mean. It's very, very beautiful.

LADY HUNSTANTON: My dear child, you don't mean to tell me that you won't forgive your husband because he never loved anyone else? Did you ever hear such a thing, Caroline? I am quite surprised.

LADY CAROLINE: Oh, women have become so highly educated, Jane, that nothing should surprise us nowadays, except happy marriages. They apparently are getting remarkably rare.

MRS ALLONBY: Oh, they're quite out of date.

LADY STUTFIELD: Except amongst the middle classes, I have been told.

MRS ALLONBY: How like the middle classes!

LADY STUTFIELD: Yes – is it not? – very, very like them.

LADY CAROLINE: If what you tell us about the middle classes is true, Lady Stutfield, it redounds greatly to their credit. It is much to be regretted that in our rank of life the wife should be so persistently frivolous, under the impression apparently that it is the proper thing to be. It is to that I attribute the unhappiness of so many marriages we all know of in society.

MRS ALLONBY: Do you know, Lady Caroline, I don't think the frivolity of the wife has ever anything to do with it. More marriages are ruined nowadays by the common sense of the husband than by anything else. How can a woman be expected to be happy with a man who insists on treating her as if she was a perfectly rational being?

LADY HUNSTANTON: My dear!

MRS ALLONBY: Man, poor, awkward, reliable, necessary man belongs to a sex that has been rational for millions and millions of years. He can't help himself. It is in his race. The history of woman is very different. We have always been picturesque protests against the mere existence of common sense. We saw its dangers from the first.

LADY STUTFIELD: Yes, the common sense of husbands is certainly most, most trying. Do tell me your conception of the Ideal Husband. I think it would be so very, very helpful.

MRS ALLONBY: The Ideal Husband? There couldn't be such a thing. The institution is wrong.

LADY STUTFIELD: The Ideal Man, then, in his relations to *us*.

LADY CAROLINE: He would probably be extremely realistic.

MRS ALLONBY: The Ideal Man! Oh, the Ideal Man should talk to us as if we were goddesses, and treat us as if we were children. He should refuse all our serious requests, and gratify every one of our whims. He should encourage us to have caprices, and forbid us to have missions. He should always say much more than he means, and always mean much more than he says.

LADY HUNSTANTON: But how could he do both, dear?

MRS ALLONBY: He should never run down other pretty women. That would show he had no taste, or make one suspect that he had too much. No, he should be nice about them all, but say that somehow they don't attract him.

LADY STUTFIELD: Yes, that is always very, very pleasant to hear about other women.

MRS ALLONBY: If we ask him a question about anything, he should give us an answer all about ourselves. He should invariably praise us for whatever qualities he knows we haven't got. But he should be pitiless, quite pitiless, in reproaching us for the virtues that we have never dreamed of possessing. He should never believe that we know the use of useful things. That would be unforgivable. But he should shower on us everything we don't want.

LADY CAROLINE: As far as I can see, he is to do nothing but pay bills and compliments.

MRS ALLONBY: He should persistently compromise us in public, and treat us with absolute respect when we are alone. And yet he should be always ready to have a perfectly terrible scene, whenever we want one, and to become miserable, absolutely miserable, at a moment's notice, and to overwhelm us with just reproaches in less than twenty minutes, and to be positively violent at the end of half an hour, and to leave us for ever at a quarter to eight, when we have to go and dress for dinner. And when, after that, one has seen him for really the last time, and he has refused to take back the little things he has given one, and promised never to communicate with one again, or to write one any foolish letters, he should be perfectly broken-hearted, and telegraph to one all day long, and send one little notes every half-hour by a private hansom, and dine quite alone at the club, so that everyone should know how unhappy he was. And after a whole dreadful week, during which one has gone about everywhere with one's husband, just to show how absolutely lonely one was, he may be given a third last parting, in the evening, and then, if his conduct has been quite irreproachable, and one has behaved really badly to him, he should be allowed to admit that he has been entirely in the wrong, and when he has admitted that, it becomes a woman's duty to forgive, and one can do it all over again from the beginning, with variations.

LADY HUNSTANTON: How clever you are, my dear! You never mean a single word you say.

LADY STUTFIELD: Thank you, thank you. It has been quite, quite entrancing. I must try and remember it all. There are such a number of details that are so very, very important.

LADY CAROLINE: But you have not told us yet what the reward of the Ideal Man is to be.

MRS ALLONBY: His reward? Oh, infinite expectation. That is quite enough for him.

LADY STUTFIELD: But men are so terribly, terribly exacting, are they not?

MRS ALLONBY: That makes no matter. One should never surrender.

LADY STUTFIELD: Not even to the Ideal Man?

MRS ALLONBY: Certainly not to him. Unless, of course, one wants to grow tired of him.

LADY STUTFIELD: Oh! . . . Yes. I see that. It is very, very helpful. Do you think, Mrs Allonby, I shall ever meet the Ideal Man? Or are there more than one?

MRS ALLONBY: There are just four in London, Lady Stutfield.

LADY HUNSTANTON: Oh, my dear!

MRS ALLONBY (*going over to her*): What has happened? Do tell me.

LADY HUNSTANTON (*in a low voice*): I had completely forgotten that the American young lady has been in the room all the time. I am afraid some of this clever talk may have shocked her a little.

MRS ALLONBY: Ah, that will do her so much good!

LADY HUNSTANTON: Let us hope she didn't understand much. I think I had better go over and talk to her. (*rises and goes across to* HESTER WORSLEY) Well, dear Miss Worsley. (*sitting down beside her*) How quiet you have been in your nice little corner all this time! I suppose you have been reading a book? There are so many books here in the library.

HESTER: No, I have been listening to the conversation.

LADY HUNSTANTON: You mustn't believe everything that was said, you know, dear.

HESTER: I didn't believe any of it.

LADY HUNSTANTON: That is quite right, dear.

HESTER (*continuing*): I couldn't believe that any women could really hold such views of life as I have heard tonight from some of your guests. (*an awkward pause*)

LADY HUNSTANTON: I hear you have such pleasant society in America. Quite like our own in places, my son wrote to me.

HESTER: There are cliques in America as elsewhere, Lady Hunstanton. But true American society consists simply of all the good women and good men we have in our country.

LADY HUNSTANTON: What a sensible system, and I dare say quite pleasant, too. I am afraid in England we have too many artificial social barriers. We don't see as much as we should of the middle and lower classes.

HESTER: In America we have no lower classes.

LADY HUNSTANTON: Really? What a very strange arrangement!

MRS ALLONBY: What is that dreadful girl talking about?

LADY STUTFIELD: She is painfully natural, is she not?

LADY CAROLINE: There are a great many things you haven't got in America, I am told, Miss Worsley. They say you have no ruins, and no curiosities.

MRS ALLONBY (*to* LADY STUTFIELD): What nonsense! They have their mothers and their manners.

HESTER: The English aristocracy supply us with our curiosities, Lady Caroline. They are sent over to us every summer, regularly, in the steamers, and propose to us the day after they land. As for ruins, we are trying to build up something that will last longer than brick or stone. (*Gets up to take her fan from table*)

LADY HUNSTANTON: What is that, dear? Ah, yes, an iron exhibition, is it not, at that place that has the curious name?

HESTER (*standing by table*): We are trying to build up life, Lady Hunstanton, on a better, truer, purer basis than life rests on here. This sounds strange to you all, no doubt. How could it sound other than strange? You rich people in England, you don't know how you are living. How could you know? You shut out from your society the gentle and the good. You laugh at the simple and the pure. Living, as you all do, on others and by them, you sneer at self-sacrifice, and if you throw bread to the poor, it is merely to keep them quiet for a season. With all your pomp and wealth and art you don't know how to live – you don't even know that. You love the beauty that you can see and touch and handle, the beauty that you can destroy, and do destroy, but of the unseen beauty of life, of the unseen beauty of a higher life, you know nothing. You have lost life's secret. Oh, your English society seems to me shallow, selfish, foolish. It has blinded its eyes, and stopped its ears. It lies, like a leper in purple. It sits like a dead thing smeared with gold. It is all wrong, all wrong.

LADY STUTFIELD: I don't think one should know of these things. It is not very, very nice, is it?

LADY HUNSTANTON: My dear Miss Worsley, I thought you liked English society so much. You were such a success in it. And you were so much admired by the best people. I quite forget what Lord Henry Weston said of you – but it was most complimentary, and you know what an authority he is on beauty.

HESTER: Lord Henry Weston! I remember him, Lady Hunstanton. A man with a hideous smile and a hideous past. He is asked everywhere. No dinner party is complete without him. What of those whose ruin is due to him? They are outcasts. They are nameless. If you met them in the street you would turn your head away. I don't complain of their punishment. Let all women who have sinned be punished.

MRS ARBUTHNOT *enters from terrace behind in a cloak with a lace veil over her head. She hears the last words and starts*

LADY HUNSTANTON: My dear young lady!

HESTER: It is right that they should be punished, but don't let them be the only ones to suffer. If a man and woman have sinned, let them both go forth into the desert to love or loathe each other there. Let them both be branded. Set a mark, if you wish, on each, but don't punish the one and let the other go free. Don't have one law for men and another for women. You are unjust to women in England. And till you count what is a shame in a woman to be infamy in a man, you will always be unjust, and Right, that pillar of fire, and Wrong, that pillar of cloud, will be made dim to your eyes, or be not seen at all, or if seen, not regarded.

LADY CAROLINE: Might I, dear Miss Worsley, as you are standing up, ask you for my cotton that is just behind you? Thank you.

LADY HUNSTANTON: My dear Mrs Arbuthnot! I am so pleased you have come up. But I didn't hear you announced.

MRS ARBUTHNOT: Oh, I came straight in from the terrace, Lady Hunstanton, just as I was. You didn't tell me you had a party.

LADY HUNSTANTON: Not a party. Only a few guests who are staying in the house, and whom you must know. Allow me. (*Tries to help her. Rings bell*) Caroline, this is Mrs Arbuthnot, one of my sweetest friends. Lady Caroline Pontefract, Lady Stutfield, Mrs Allonby, amd my young American friend, Miss Worsley, who has just been telling us all how wicked we are.

HESTER: I am afraid you think I spoke too strongly, Lady Hunstanton. But there are some things in England –

LADY HUNSTANTON: My dear young lady, there was a great deal of truth, I dare say, in what you said, and you looked very pretty while you said it, which is much more important, Lord Illingworth would tell us. The only point where I thought you were a little hard was about Lady Caroline's brother, about poor Lord Henry. He is really such good company.

Enter FOOTMAN

Take Mrs Arbuthnot's things.

Exit FOOTMAN *with wraps*

HESTER: Lady Caroline, I had no idea it was your brother. I am sorry for the pain I must have caused you – I –

LADY CAROLINE: My dear Miss Worsley, the only part of your little speech, if I may so term it, with which I thoroughly agreed, was the part about my brother. Nothing that you could possibly say could be too bad for him. I regard Henry as infamous, absolutely infamous. But I am bound to state, as you were remarking, Jane, that he is excellent company, and he has one of the best cooks in London, and after a good dinner one can forgive anybody, even one's own relations.

LADY HUNSTANTON (*to* MISS WORSLEY): Now, do come, dear, and make friends with Mrs Arbuthnot. She is one of the good, sweet, simple people you told us we never admitted into society. I am sorry to say Mrs Arbuthnot comes very rarely to me. But that is not my fault.

MRS ALLONBY: What a bore it is the men staying so long after dinner! I expect they are saying the most dreadful things about us.

LADY STUTFIELD: Do you really think so?

MRS ALLONBY: I am sure of it.

LADY STUTFIELD: How very, very horrid of them! Shall we go on to the terrace?

MRS ALLONBY: Oh, anything to get away from the dowagers and the dowdies. (*rises and goes with* LADY STUTFIELD *to door*) We are only going to look at the stars, Lady Hunstanton.

LADY HUNSTANTON: You will find a great many, dear, a great many. But don't catch cold. (*To* MRS ARBUTHNOT): We shall all miss Gerald so much, dear Mrs Arbuthnot.

MRS ARBUTHNOT: But has Lord Illingworth really offered to make Gerald his secretary?

LADY HUNSTANTON: Oh, yes! He has been most charming about it. He has the highest possible opinion of your boy. You don't know Lord Illingworth, I believe, dear.

MRS ARBUTHNOT: I have never met him.

LADY HUNSTANTON: You know him by name, no doubt?

MRS ARBUTHNOT: I am afraid I don't. I live so much out of the world, and see so few people. I remember hearing years ago of an old Lord Illingworth who lived in Yorkshire, I think.

LADY HUNSTANTON: Ah, yes. That would be the last earl but one. He was a very curious man. He wanted to marry beneath him. Or wouldn't, I believe. There was some scandal about it. The present Lord Illingworth is quite different. He is very distinguished. He does – well, he does nothing, which I am afraid our pretty American visitor here thinks very wrong of anybody, and I don't know that he cares much for the subjects in which you are so interested, dear Mrs Arbuthnot. Do you think, Caroline, that Lord Illingworth is interested in the housing of the poor?

LADY CAROLINE: I should fancy not at all, Jane.

LADY HUNSTANTON: We all have our different tastes, have we not? But Lord Illingworth has a very high position, and there is nothing he couldn't get if he chose to ask for it. Of course, he is comparatively a young man still, and he has only come to his title within – how long exactly is it, Caroline, since Lord Illingworth succeeded?

LADY CAROLINE: About four years, I think, Jane. I know it was the same year in which my brother had his last exposure in the evening newspapers.

LADY HUNSTANTON: Ah, I remember. That would be about four years ago. Of course, there were a great many people between the present Lord Illingworth and the title, Mrs Arbuthnot. There was – who was there, Caroline?

LADY CAROLINE: There was poor Margaret's baby. You remember how anxious she was to have a boy, and it was a boy, but it died, and her husband died shortly afterwards, and she married almost immediately one of Lord Ascot's sons, who, I am told, beats her.

LADY HUNSTANTON: Ah, that is in the family, dear, that is in the family. And there was also, I remember, a clergyman who wanted to be a lunatic, or a lunatic who wanted to be a clergyman, I forget which, but I know the Court of Chancery investigated the matter, and decided that he was quite insane. And I saw him afterwards at poor Lord Plumstead's with straws in his hair, or something very odd about him. I can't recall what. I often regret, Caroline, that dear Lady Cecilia never lived to see her son get the title.

MRS ARBUTHNOT: Lady Cecilia?

LADY HUNSTANTON: Lord Illingworth's mother, dear Mrs Arbuthnot, was one of the Duchess of Jerningham's pretty daughters, and she married Sir Thomas Harford, who wasn't considered a very good match for her at the time, though he was said to be the handsomest man in London. I knew them all quite intimately, and both the sons, Arthur and George.

MRS ARBUTHNOT: It was the elder son who succeeded, of course, Lady Hunstanton?

LADY HUNSTANTON: No, dear, he was killed in the hunting field. Or was it fishing, Caroline? I forget. But George came in for everything. I always tell him that no younger son has ever had such good luck as he has had.

MRS ARBUTHNOT: Lady Hunstanton, I want to speak to Gerald at once. Might I see him? Can he be sent for?

LADY HUNSTANTON: Certainly, dear. I will send one of the servants into the dining-room to fetch him. I don't know what keeps the gentlemen so long. (*rings bell*) When I knew Lord Illingworth first as plain George Harford, he was simply a very brilliant young man about town, with not a penny of money except what poor dear Lady Cecilia gave him. She was quite devoted to him. Chiefly, I fancy, because he was on bad terms with his father. Oh, here is the dear Archdeacon. (*To servant*) It doesn't matter.

Enter SIR JOHN *and* DR DAUBENY. SIR JOHN *goes over to* LADY STUTFIELD, DR DAUBENY *to* LADY HUNSTANTON

DR DAUBENY: Lord Illingworth has been most entertaining. I have never enjoyed myself more. (*Sees* MRS ARBUTHNOT) Ah, Mrs Arbuthnot.

LADY HUNSTANTON (*to* DR DAUBENY): You see I have got Mrs Arbuthnot to come to me at last.

DR DAUBENY: That is a great honour, Lady Hunstanton. Mrs Daubeny will be quite jealous of you.

LADY HUNSTANTON: Ah, I am so sorry Mrs Daubeny could not come with you tonight. Headache as usual, I suppose.

DR DAUBENY: Yes, Lady Hunstanton; a perfect martyr. But she is happiest alone. She is happiest alone.

LADY CAROLINE (*to her husband*): John!

SIR JOHN *goes over to his wife.* DR DAUBENY *talks to* LADY HUNSTANTON *and* MRS ARBUTHNOT. MRS ARBUTHNOT *watches* LORD ILLINGWORTH *the whole time. He has passed across the room without noticing her, and approaches* MRS ALLONBY, *who with* LADY STUTFIELD *is standing by the door looking on to the terrace*

LORD ILLINGWORTH: How is the most charming woman in the world?

MRS ALLONBY (*taking* LADY STUTFIELD by the hand): We are both quite well, thank you, Lord Illingworth. But what a short time you have been in the dining-room! It seems as if we had only just left.

LORD ILLINGWORTH: I was bored to death. Never opened my lips the whole time. Absolutely longing to come in to you.

MRS ALLONBY: You should have. The American girl has been giving us a lecture.

LORD ILLINGWORTH: Really? All Americans lecture, I believe. I suppose it is something in their climate. What did she lecture about?

MRS ALLONBY: Oh, puritanism, of course.

LORD ILLINGWORTH: I am going to convert her, am I not? How long do you give me?

MRS ALLONBY: A week.

LORD ILLINGWORTH: A week is more than enough.

Enter GERALD *and* LORD ALFRED

GERALD (*going to* MRS ARBUTHNOT): Dear mother!

MRS ARBUTHNOT: Gerald, I don't feel at all well. See me home, Gerald. I shouldn't have come.

GERALD: I am so sorry, mother. Certainly. But you must know Lord Illingworth first. (*Goes across room*)

MRS ARBUTHNOT: Not tonight, Gerald.

GERALD: Lord Illingworth, I want you so much to know my mother.

LORD ILLINGWORTH: With the greatest pleasure. (*To* MRS ALLONBY): I'll be back in a moment. People's mothers always bore me to death. All women become like their mothers. That is their tragedy.

MRS ALLONBY: No man does. That is his.

LORD ILLINGWORTH: What a delightful mood you are in tonight! (*Turns round and goes across with* GERALD *to* MRS ARBUTHNOT. *When he sees her, he starts back in wonder. Then slowly his eyes turn towards* GERALD)

GERALD: Mother, this is Lord Illingworth, who has offered to take me as his private secretary.

MRS ARBUTHNOT *bows coldly*

It is a wonderful opening for me, isn't it? I hope he won't be disappointed in me, that is all. You'll thank Lord Illingworth, mother, won't you?

MRS ARBUTHNOT: Lord Illingworth is very good, I am sure, to interest himself in you for the moment.

LORD ILLINGWORTH (*putting his hand on* GERALD'S *shoulder*): Oh, Gerald and I are great friends already, Mrs . . . Arbuthnot.

MRS ARBUTHNOT: There can be nothing in common between you and my son, Lord Illingworth.

GERALD: Dear mother, how can you say so? Of course, Lord Illingworth is awfully clever and that sort of thing. There is nothing Lord Illingworth doesn't know.

LORD ILLINGWORTH: My dear boy!

GERALD: He knows more about life than anyone I have ever met. I feel an awful duffer when I am with you, Lord Illingworth. Of course, I have had so few advantages. I have not been to Eton or Oxford like other chaps. But Lord Illingworth doesn't seem to mind that. He has been awfully good to me, mother.

MRS ARBUTHNOT: Lord Illingworth may change his mind. He may not really want you as his secretary.

GERALD: Mother!

MRS ARBUTHNOT: You must remember, as you said yourself, you have had so few advantages.

MRS ALLONBY: Lord Illingworth, I want to speak to you for a moment. Do come over.

LORD ILLINGWORTH: Will you excuse me, Mrs Arbuthnot? Now, don't let your charming mother make any more difficulties, Gerald. The thing is quite settled, isn't it?

GERALD: I hope so.

LORD ILLINGWORTH *goes across to* MRS ALLONBY

MRS ALLONBY: I thought you were never going to leave the lady in black velvet.

LORD ILLINGWORTH: She is excessively handsome. (*Looks at* MRS ARBUTHNOT)

LADY HUNSTANTON: Caroline, shall we all make a move to the music-room? Miss Worsley is going to play. You'll come too, dear Mrs Arbuthnot, won't you? You don't know what a treat is in store for you. (*To* DR DAUBENY): I must really take Miss Worsley down some afternoon to the rectory. I should so much like dear Mrs Daubeny to hear her on the violin. Ah, I forgot. Dear Mrs Daubeny's hearing is a little defective, is it not?

DR DAUBENY: Her deafness is a great privation to her. She can't even hear my sermons now. She reads them at home. But she has many resources in herself, many resources.

LADY HUNSTANTON: She reads a good deal, I suppose?

DR DAUBENY: Just the very largest print. The eyesight is rapidly going. But she's never morbid, never morbid.

GERALD (*to Lord Illingworth*): Do speak to my mother, Lord Illingworth, before you go into the music-room. She seems to think, somehow, you don't mean what you said to me.

MRS ALLONBY: Aren't you coming?

LORD ILLINGWORTH: In a few moments. Lady Hunstanton, if Mrs Arbuthnot would allow me, I would like to say a few words to her, and we will join you later on.

LADY HUNSTANTON: Ah, of course. You will have a great deal to say to her, and she will have a great deal to thank you for. It is not every son who gets such an offer, Mrs Arbuthnot. But I know you appreciate that, dear.

LADY CAROLINE: John!

LADY HUNSTANTON: Now, don't keep Mrs Arbuthnot too long, Lord Illingworth. We can't spare her. (*Exit following the other guests. Sound of violin heard from music-room*)

LORD ILLINGWORTH: So that is our son, Rachel! Well, I am very proud of him. He is a Harford, every inch of him. By the way, why Arbuthnot, Rachel?

MRS ARBUTHNOT: One name is as good as another, when one has no right to any name.

LORD ILLINGWORTH: I suppose so – but why Gerald?

MRS ARBUTHNOT: After a man whose heart I broke – after my father.

LORD ILLINGWORTH: Well, Rachel, what is over is over. All I have got to say now is that I am very, very much pleased with our boy. The world will know him merely as my private secretary, but to me he will be something very near, and very dear. It is a curious thing, Rachel; my life seemed to be quite complete. It was not so. It lacked something, it lacked a son. I have found my son now. I am glad I have found him.

MRS ARBUTHNOT: You have no right to claim him, or the smallest part of him. The boy is entirely mine, and shall remain mine.

LORD ILLINGWORTH: My dear Rachel, you have had him to yourself for over twenty years. Why not let me have him for a little now? He is quite as much mine as yours.

MRS ARBUTHNOT: Are you talking of the child you abandoned? Of the child who, as far as you are concerned, might have died of hunger and of want?

LORD ILLINGWORTH: You forget, Rachel, it was you who left me. It was not I who left you.

MRS ARBUTHNOT: I left you because you refused to give the child a name. Before my son was born, I implored you to marry me.

LORD ILLINGWORTH: I had no expectations then. And, besides,

Rachel, I wasn't much older than you were. I was only twenty-two. I was twenty-one, I believe, when the whole thing began in your father's garden.

MRS ARBUTHNOT: When a man is old enough to do wrong he should be old enough to do right also.

LORD ILLINGWORTH: My dear Rachel, intellectual generalities are always interesting, but generalities in morals mean absolutely nothing. As for saying I left our child to starve, that, of course, is untrue and silly. My mother offered you six hundred a year. But you wouldn't take anything. You simply disappeared, and carried the child away with you.

MRS ARBUTHNOT: I wouldn't have accepted a penny from her. Your father was different. He told you, in my presence, when we were in Paris, that it was your duty to marry me.

LORD ILLINGWORTH: Oh, duty is what one expects from others, it is not what one does oneself. Of course, I was influenced by my mother. Every man is when he is young.

MRS ARBUTHNOT: I am glad to hear you say so. Gerald shall certainly not go away with you.

LORD ILLINGWORTH: What nonsense, Rachel!

MRS ARBUTHNOT: Do you think I would allow my son –

LORD ILLINGWORTH: *Our* son.

MRS ARBUTHNOT: My son – (LORD ILLINGWORTH *shrugs his shoulders*) – to go away with the man who spoiled my youth, who ruined my life, who has tainted every moment of my days? You don't realise what my past has been in suffering and in shame.

LORD ILLINGWORTH: My dear Rachel, I must candidly say that I think Gerald's future considerably more important than your past.

MRS ARBUTHNOT: Gerald cannot separate his future from my past.

LORD ILLINGWORTH: That is exactly what he should do. That is exactly what you should help him to do. What a typical woman you are! You talk sentimentally, and you are thoroughly selfish the whole time. But don't let us have a scene. Rachel, I want you to look at this matter from the common-sense point of view, from the point of view of what is best for our son, leaving you and me out of the question. What is our son at present? An underpaid clerk in a small provincial bank in a third-rate English town. If you imagine he is quite happy in such a position, you are mistaken. He is thoroughly discontented.

MRS ARBUTHNOT: He was not discontented till he met you. You have made him so.

LORD ILLINGWORTH: Of course, I made him so. Discontent is the first step in the progress of a man or a nation. But I did not leave him with a mere longing for things he could not get. No, I made him a charming offer. He jumped at it, I need hardly say. Any young man would. And now, simply because it turns out that I am the boy's own father and he my own son, you propose practically to ruin his career. That is to say, if I were a perfect stranger, you would allow Gerald to go away with me, but as he is my own flesh and blood you won't. How utterly illogical you are!

MRS ARBUTHNOT: I will not allow him to go.

LORD ILLINGWORTH: How can you prevent it? What excuse can you give to him for making him decline such an offer as mine? I won't tell him in what relation I stand to him, I need hardly say. But you daren't tell him. You know that. Look how you have brought him up.

MRS ARBUTHNOT: I have brought him up to be a good man.

LORD ILLINGWORTH: Quite so. And what is the result? You have educated him to be your judge if he ever finds you out. And a bitter, an unjust judge he will be to you. Don't be deceived, Rachel. Children begin by loving their parents. After a time they judge them. Rarely, if ever, do they forgive them.

MRS ARBUTHNOT: George, don't take my son away from me. I have had twenty years of sorrow, and I have only had one thing to love me, only one thing to love. You have had a life of joy, and pleasure, and success. You have been quite happy, you have never thought of us. There was no reason, according to your views of life, why you should have remembered us at all. Your meeting us was a mere accident, a horrible accident. Forget it. Don't come now, and rob me of – of all I have in the whole world. You are so rich in other things. Leave me the little vineyard of my life; leave me the walled-in garden and the well of water; the ewe-lamb God sent me, in pity or in wrath, oh! leave me that. George, don't take Gerald from me.

LORD ILLINGWORTH: Rachel, at the present moment you are not necessary to Gerald's career; I am. There is nothing more to be said on the subject.

MRS ARBUTHNOT: I will not let him go.

LORD ILLINGWORTH: Here is Gerald. He has a right to decide for himself.

Enter GERALD

GERALD: Well, dear mother, I hope you have settled it all with Lord Illingworth?

MRS ARBUTHNOT: I have not, Gerald.

LORD ILLINGWORTH: Your mother seems not to like your coming with me, for some reason.

GERALD: Why, mother?

MRS ARBUTHNOT: I thought you were quite happy here with me, Gerald. I didn't know you were so anxious to leave me.

GERALD: Mother, how can you talk like that? Of course I have been quite happy with you. But a man can't stay always with his mother. No chap does. I want to make myself a position, to do something. I thought you would have been proud to see me Lord Illingworth's secretary.

MRS ARBUTHNOT: I do not think you would be suitable as a private secretary to Lord Illingworth. You have no qualifications.

LORD ILLINGWORTH: I don't wish to seem to interfere for a moment, Mrs Arbuthnot, but as far as your last objection is concerned, I surely am the best judge. And I can only tell you that your son has all the qualifications I had hoped for. He has more, in fact, than I had even thought of. Far more. (MRS ARBUTHNOT *remains silent*) Have you any other reason, Mrs Arbuthnot, why you don't wish your son to accept this post?

GERALD: Have you, mother? Do answer.

LORD ILLINGWORTH: If you have, Mrs Arbuthnot, pray, pray say it. We are quite by ourselves here. Whatever it is, I need not say I will not repeat it.

GERALD: Mother?

LORD ILLINGWORTH: If you would like to be alone with your son, I will leave you. You may have some other reason you don't wish me to hear.

MRS ARBUTHNOT: I have no other reason.

LORD ILLINGWORTH: Then, my dear boy, we may look on the thing as settled. Come, you and I will smoke a cigarette on the terrace together. And, Mrs Arbuthnot, pray let me tell you that I think you have acted very, very wisely.

Exit with GERALD. MRS ARBUTHNOT *is left alone. She stands immobile with a look of unutterable sorrow on her face.*

END OF ACT TWO

ACT THREE

The picture gallery at Hunstanton Chase. Door at back leading on to terrace. LORD ILLINGWORTH *and* GERALD. LORD ILLINGWORTH *lolling on a sofa.* GERALD *in a chair.*

LORD ILLINGWORTH: Thoroughly sensible woman, your mother, Gerald. I knew she would come round in the end.

GERALD: My mother is awfully conscientious, Lord Illingworth, and I know she doesn't think I am educated enough to be your secretary. She is perfectly right, too. I was fearfully idle when I was at school, and I couldn't pass an examination now to save my life.

LORD ILLINGWORTH: My dear Gerald, examinations are of no value whatsoever. If a man is a gentleman, he knows quite enough, and if he is not a gentleman, whatever he knows is bad for him.

GERALD: But I am so ignorant of the world, Lord Illingworth.

LORD ILLINGWORTH: Don't be afraid, Gerald. Remember that you've got on your side the most wonderful thing in the world – youth! There is nothing like youth. The middle-aged are mortgaged to life. The old are in life's lumber-room. But youth is the lord of life. Youth has a kingdom waiting for it. Everyone is born a king, and most people die in exile like most kings. To win back my youth, Gerald, there is nothing I wouldn't do – except take exercise, get up early or be a useful member of the community.

GERALD: But you don't call yourself old, Lord Illingworth?

LORD ILLINGWORTH: I am old enough to be your father, Gerald.

GERALD: I don't remember my father; he died years ago.

LORD ILLINGWORTH: So Lady Hunstanton told me.

GERALD: It is very curious, my mother never talks to me about my father. I sometimes think she must have married beneath her.

LORD ILLINGWORTH (*winces slightly*): Really? (*goes over and puts his hand on* GERALD'*s shoulder*) You have missed not having a father, I suppose, Gerald?

GERALD: Oh, no; my mother has been so good to me. No one ever had such a mother as I have had.

LORD ILLINGWORTH: I am quite sure of that. Still I should imagine that most mothers don't quite understand their sons. Don't realise, I mean, that a son has ambitions, a desire to see life, to make himself a name. After all, Gerald, you couldn't be expected to pass all your life in such a hole as Wrockley, could you?

GERALD: Oh, no! It would be dreadful!

LORD ILLINGWORTH: A mother's love is very touching, of course, but it is often curiously selfish. I mean there is a good deal of selfishness in it.

GERALD (*slowly*): I suppose there is.

LORD ILLINGWORTH: Your mother is a thoroughly good woman. But good women have such limited views of life, their horizon is so small, their interests are so petty, aren't they?

GERALD: They are awfully interested, certainly, in things we don't care much about.

LORD ILLINGWORTH: I suppose your mother is very religious, and that sort of thing.

GERALD: Oh, yes, she's always going to church.

LORD ILLINGWORTH: Ah! she is not modern, and to be modern is the only thing worth being nowadays. You want to be modern, don't you, Gerald? You want to know life as it really is. Not to be put off with any old-fashioned theories about life. Well, what you have to do at present is simply to fit yourself for the best society. A man who can dominate a London dinner-table can dominate the world. The future belongs to the dandy. It is the exquisites who are going to rule.

GERALD: I should like to wear nice things awfully, but I have always been told that a man should not think so much about his clothes.

LORD ILLINGWORTH: People nowadays are so absolutely superficial that they don't understand the philosophy of the superficial. By the way, Gerald, you should learn how to tie your tie better. Sentiment is all very well for the buttonhole. But the essential thing for a necktie is style. A well-tied tie is the first serious step in life.

GERALD (*laughing*): I might be able to learn how to tie a tie, Lord Illingworth, but I should never be able to talk as you do. I don't know how to talk.

LORD ILLINGWORTH: Oh! talk to every woman as if you loved her, and to every man as if he bored you, and at the end of your first season you will have the reputation of possessing the most perfect social tact.

GERALD: But it is very difficult to get into society, isn't it?

LORD ILLINGWORTH: To get into the best society, nowadays, one has either to feed people, amuse people, or shock people – that is all!

GERALD: I suppose society is wonderfully delightful!

LORD ILLINGWORTH: To be in it is merely a bore. But to be out of it simply a tragedy. Society is a necessary thing. No man has any real success in this world unless he has got women to back him, and women rule society. If you have not got women on your side you are quite over. You might just as well be a barrister or a stockbroker or a journalist at once.

GERALD: It is very difficult to understand women, is it not?

LORD ILLINGWORTH: You should never try to understand them. Women are pictures. Men are problems. If you want to know what a woman really means – which, by the way, is always a dangerous thing to do – look at her, don't listen to her.

GERALD: But women are awfully clever, aren't they?

LORD ILLINGWORTH: One should always tell them so. But to the philosopher, my dear Gerald, women represent the triumph of matter over mind – just as men represent the triumph of mind over morals.

GERALD: How then can women have so much power as you say they have?

LORD ILLINGWORTH: The history of women is the history of the worst form of tyranny the world has ever known. The tyranny of the weak over the strong. It is the only tyranny that lasts.

GERALD: But haven't women got a refining influence?

LORD ILLINGWORTH: Nothing refines but the intellect.

GERALD: Still, there are many different kinds of women, aren't there?

LORD ILLINGWORTH: Only two kinds in society: the plain and the coloured.

GERALD: But there are good women in society, aren't there?

LORD ILLINGWORTH: Far too many.

GERALD: But do you think women shouldn't be good?

LORD ILLINGWORTH: One should never tell them so, they'd all become good at once. Women are a fascinatingly wilful sex. Every woman is a rebel, and usually in wild revolt against herself.

GERALD: You have never been married, Lord Illingworth, have you?

LORD ILLINGWORTH: Men marry because they are tired; women because they are curious. Both are disappointed.

GERALD: But don't you think one can be happy when one is married?

LORD ILLINGWORTH: Perfectly happy. But the happiness of a married man, my dear Gerald, depends on the people he has not married.

GERALD: But if one is in love?

LORD ILLINGWORTH: One should always be in love. That is the reason one should never marry.

GERALD: Love is a very wonderful thing, isn't it?

LORD ILLINGWORTH: When one is in love one begins by deceiving oneself. And one ends by deceiving others. That is what the world calls a romance. But a really *grande passion* is comparatively rare nowadays. It is the privilege of people who have nothing to do. That is the one use of the idle classes in a country, and the only possible explanation of us Harfords.

GERALD: Harfords, Lord Illingworth?

LORD ILLINGWORTH: That is my family name. You should study the *Peerage*, Gerald. It is the one book a young man about town should know thoroughly, and it is the best thing in fiction the English have ever done. And now, Gerald, you are going into a perfectly new life with me, and I want you to know how to live.

MRS ARBUTHNOT *appears on terrace behind*

For the world has been made by fools that wise men should live in it!

Enter LADY HUNSTANTON *and* DR DAUBENY

LADY HUNSTANTON: Ah! here you are, dear Lord Illingworth. Well, I suppose you have been telling our young friend, Gerald, what his new duties are to be, and giving him a great deal of good advice over a pleasant cigarette.

LORD ILLINGWORTH: I have been giving him the best of advice, Lady Hunstanton, and the best of cigarettes.

LADY HUNSTANTON: I am so sorry I was not here to listen to you, but I suppose I am too old now to learn. Except from you, dear Archdeacon, when you are in your nice pulpit. But then I always know what you are going to say, so I don't feel alarmed. (*Sees* MRS ARBUTHNOT) Ah! dear Mrs Arbuthnot, do come and join us. Come, dear.

Enter MRS ARBUTHNOT

Gerald has been having such a long talk with Lord Illingworth; I am sure you must feel very much flattered at the pleasant way in which everything has turned out for him. Let us sit down. (*they sit down*) And how is your beautiful embroidery going on?

MRS ARBUTHNOT: I am always at work, Lady Hunstanton.

LADY HUNSTANTON: Mrs Daubeny embroiders a little, too, doesn't she?

DR DAUBENY: She was very deft with her needle once, quite a Dorcas. But the gout has crippled her fingers a good deal. She has not touched the tambour frame for nine or ten years. But she has many other amusements. She is very much interested in her own health.

LADY HUNSTANTON: Ah! that is always a nice distraction, is it not? Now, what are you talking about, Lord Illingworth? Do tell us.

LORD ILLINGWORTH: I was on the point of explaining to Gerald that the world has always laughed at its own tragedies, that being the only way in which it has been able to bear them. And that, consequently, whatever the world has treated seriously belongs to the comedy side of things.

LADY HUNSTANTON: Now I am quite out of my depth. I usually am when Lord Illingworth says anything. And the Humane Society is most careless. They never rescue me. I am left to sink. I have a dim idea, dear Lord Illingworth, that you are always on the side of the sinners, and I know I always try to be on the side of the saints, but that is as far as I get. And, after all, it may be merely the fancy of a drowning person.

LORD ILLINGWORTH: The only difference between the saint and the sinner is that every saint has a past, and every sinner has a future.

LADY HUNSTANTON: Ah! that quite does for me. I haven't a word to say. You and I, dear Mrs Arbuthnot, are behind the age. We can't follow Lord Illingworth. Too much care was taken with our education, I am afraid. To have been well brought up is a great drawback nowadays. It shuts one out from so much.

MRS ARBUTHNOT: I should be sorry to follow Lord Illingworth in any of his opinions.

LADY HUNSTANTON: You are quite right, dear.

GERALD *shrugs his shoulders and looks irritably over at his mother. Enter* LADY CAROLINE

LADY CAROLINE: Jane, have you seen John anywhere?

LADY HUNSTANTON: You needn't be anxious about him, dear. He is with Lady Stutfield; I saw them some time ago, in the yellow drawing-room. They seem quite happy together. You are not going, Caroline? Pray sit down.

LADY CAROLINE: I think I had better look after John.

Exit LADY CAROLINE

LADY HUNSTANTON: It doesn't do to pay men so much attention. And Caroline has really nothing to be anxious about. Lady

Stutfield is very sympathetic. She is just as sympathetic about one thing as she is about another. A beautiful nature.

Enter SIR JOHN *and* MRS ALLONBY

Ah! here is Sir John! And with Mrs Allonby too! I suppose it was Mrs Allonby I saw him with. Sir John, Caroline has been looking everywhere for you.

MRS ALLONBY: We have been waiting for her in the music-room, dear Lady Hunstanton.

LADY HUNSTANTON: Ah! the music-room, of course. I thought it was the yellow drawing-room, my memory is getting so defective. (*To the* ARCHDEACON) Mrs Daubeny has a wonderful memory, hasn't she?

DR DAUBENY: She used to be quite remarkable for her memory, but since her last attack she recalls chiefly the events of her early childhood. But she finds great pleasure in such retrospections, great pleasure.

Enter LADY STUTFIELD *and* MR KELVIL

LADY HUNSTANTON: Ah! dear Lady Stutfield! and what has Mr Kelvil been talking to you about?

LADY STUTFIELD: About bimetallism, as well as I remember.

LADY HUNSTANTON: Bimetallism! Is that quite a nice subject? However, I know people discuss everything very freely nowadays. What did Sir John talk to you about, dear Mrs Allonby?

MRS ALLONBY: About Patagonia.

LADY HUNSTANTON: Really? What a remote topic! But very improving, I have no doubt.

MRS ALLONBY: He has been most interesting on the subject of Patagonia. Savages seem to have quite the same views as cultured people on almost all subjects. They are excessively advanced.

LADY HUNSTANTON: What do they do?

MRS ALLONBY: Apparently everything.

LADY HUNSTANTON: Well, it is very gratifying, dear Archdeacon, is it not, to find that human nature is permanently one. On the whole, the world is the same world, is it not?

LORD ILLINGWORTH: The world is simply divided into two classes – those who believe the incredible, like the public – and those who do the improbable –

MRS ALLONBY: Like yourself?

LORD ILLINGWORTH: Yes; I am always astonishing myself. It is the only thing that makes life worth living.

LADY STUTFIELD: And what have you been doing lately that astonishes you?

LORD ILLINGWORTH: I have been discovering all kinds of beautiful qualities in my own nature.

MRS ALLONBY: Ah! don't become quite perfect all at once. Do it gradually!

LORD ILLINGWORTH: I don't intend to grow perfect at all. At least, I hope I shan't. It would be most inconvenient. Women love us for our defects. If we have enough of them, they will forgive us everything, even our gigantic intellects.

MRS ALLONBY: It is premature to ask us to forgive analysis. We forgive adoration; that is quite as much as should be expected from us.

Enter LORD ALFRED. *He joins* LADY STUTFIELD

LADY HUNSTANTON: Ah! we women should forgive everything, shouldn't we, dear Mrs Arbuthnot? I am sure you agree with me in that.

MRS ARBUTHNOT: I do not, Lady Hunstanton. I think there are many things women should never forgive.

LADY HUNSTANTON: What sort of things?

MRS ARBUTHNOT: The ruin of another woman's life. (*moves slowly away to back of stage*)

LADY HUNSTANTON: Ah! those things are very sad, no doubt, but I believe there are admirable homes where people of that kind are looked after and reformed, and I think on the whole that the secret of life is to take things very, very easily.

MRS ALLONBY: The secret of life is never to have an emotion that is unbecoming.

LADY STUTFIELD: The secret of life is to appreciate the pleasure of being terribly, terribly deceived.

KELVIL: The secret of life is to resist temptation, Lady Stutfield.

LORD ILLINGWORTH: There is no secret of life. Life's aim, if it has one, is simply to be always looking for temptations. There are not nearly enough. I sometimes pass a whole day without coming across a single one. It is quite dreadful. It makes one so nervous about the future.

LADY HUNSTANTON (*shakes her fan at him*): I don't know how it is, dear Lord Illingworth, but everything you have said today seems to me excessively immoral. It has been most interesting, listening to you.

LORD ILLINGWORTH: All thought is immoral. Its very essence is destruction. If you think of anything, you kill it. Nothing survives being thought of.

LADY HUNSTANTON: I don't understand a word, Lord Illingworth. But I have no doubt it is all quite true. Personally, I have very little to reproach myself with, on the score of thinking. I don't believe in women thinking too much. Women should think in moderation, as they should do all things in moderation.

LORD ILLINGWORTH: Moderation is a fatal thing, Lady Hunstanton. Nothing succeeds like excess.

LADY HUNSTANTON: I hope I shall remember that. It sounds an admirable maxim. But I'm beginning to forget everything. It's a great misfortune.

LORD ILLINGWORTH: It is one of your most fascinating qualities, Lady Hunstanton. No woman should have a memory. Memory in a woman is the beginning of dowdiness. One can always tell from a woman's bonnet whether she has got a memory or not.

LADY HUNSTANTON: How charming you are, dear Lord Illingworth. You always find out that one's most glaring fault is one's most important virtue. You have the most comforting view of life.

Enter FARQUHAR

FARQUHAR: Dr Daubeny's carriage!

LADY HUNSTANTON: My dear Archdeacon! It is only half-past ten.

DR DAUBENY (*rising*): I am afraid I must go, Lady Hunstanton. Tuesday is always one of Mrs Daubeny's bad nights.

LADY HUNSTANTON (*rising*): Well, I won't keep you from her. (*goes with him towards door*) I have told Farquhar to put a brace of partridge into the carriage. Mrs Daubeny may fancy them.

DR DAUBENY: It is very kind of you, but Mrs Daubeny never touches solids now. Lives entirely on jellies. But she is wonderfully cheerful, wonderfully cheerful. She has nothing to complain of.

Exit with LADY HUNSTANTON

MRS ALLONBY (*goes over to* LORD ILLINGWORTH): There is a beautiful moon tonight.

LORD ILLINGWORTH: Let us go and look at it. To look at anything that is inconstant is charming nowadays.

MRS ALLONBY: You have your looking-glass.

LORD ILLINGWORTH: It is unkind. It merely shows me my wrinkles.

MRS ALLONBY: Mine is better behaved. It never tells me the truth.

LORD ILLINGWORTH: Then it is in love with you.

SIR JOHN, LADY STUTFIELD, MR KELVIL *and* LORD ALFRED *exeunt*

GERALD (*to Lord Illingworth*): May I come too?

LORD ILLINGWORTH: Do, my dear boy. (*moves towards door with* MRS ALLONBY *and* GERALD)

LADY CAROLINE *enters, looks rapidly round and goes out in opposite direction to that taken by* SIR JOHN *and* LADY STUTFIELD

MRS ARBUTHNOT: Gerald!

GERALD: What, mother!

Exit LORD ILLINGWORTH *with* MRS ALLONBY

MRS ARBUTHNOT: It is getting late. Let us go home.

GERALD: My dear mother. Do let us wait a little longer. Lord Illingworth is so delightful, and, by the way, mother, I have a great surprise for you. We are starting for India at the end of this month.

MRS ARBUTHNOT: Let us go home.

GERALD: If you really want to, of course, mother, but I must bid goodbye to Lord Illingworth first. I'll be back in five minutes. (*exit*)

MRS ARBUTHNOT: Let him leave me if he chooses, but not with him – not with him! I couldn't bear it. (*walks up and down*)

Enter HESTER

HESTER: What a lovely night it is, Mrs Arbuthnot.

MRS ARBUTHNOT: Is it?

HESTER: Mrs Arbuthnot, I wish you would let us be friends. You are so different from the other women here. When you came into the drawing-room this evening, somehow you brought with you a sense of what is good and pure in life. I had been foolish. There are things that are right to say but that may be said at the wrong time and to the wrong people.

MRS ARBUTHNOT: I heard what you said. I agree with it, Miss Worsley.

HESTER: I didn't know you had heard it. But I knew you would agree with me. A woman who has sinned should be punished, shouldn't she?

MRS ARBUTHNOT: Yes.

HESTER: She shouldn't be allowed to come into the society of good men and women?

MRS ARBUTHNOT: She should not.

HESTER: And the man should be punished in the same way?

MRS ARBUTHNOT: In the same way. And the children, if there are children, in the same way also?

HESTER: Yes, it is right that the sins of the parents should be visited on the children. It is a just law. It is God's law.

MRS ARBUTHNOT: It is one of God's terrible laws. (*moves away to fireplace*)

HESTER: You are distressed about your son leaving you, Mrs Arbuthnot?

MRS ARBUTHNOT: Yes.

HESTER: Do you like him going away with Lord Illingworth? Of course there is position, no doubt, and money, but position and money are not everything, are they?

MRS ARBUTHNOT: They are nothing; they bring misery.

HESTER: Then why do you let your son go with him?

MRS ARBUTHNOT: He wishes it himself.

HESTER: But if you asked him he would stay, would he not?

MRS ARBUTHNOT: He has set his heart on going.

HESTER: He couldn't refuse you anything. He loves you too much. Ask him to stay. Let me send him to you. He is on the terrace at this moment with Lord Illingworth. I heard them laughing together as I passed through the music-room.

MRS ARBUTHNOT: Don't trouble, Miss Worsley, I can wait. It is of no consequence.

HESTER: No, I'll tell him you want him. Do – do ask him to stay.

Exit HESTER

MRS ARBUTHNOT: He won't come – I know he won't come.

Enter LADY CAROLINE. *She looks round anxiously. Enter* GERALD

LADY CAROLINE: Mr Arbuthnot, may I ask you is Sir John anywhere on the terrace?

GERALD: No, Lady Caroline, he is not on the terrace.

LADY CAROLINE: It is very curious. It is time for him to retire.

Exit LADY CAROLINE

GERALD: Dear mother, I am afraid I kept you waiting. I forgot all about it. I am so happy tonight, mother; I have never been so happy.

MRS ARBUTHNOT: At the prospect of going away?

GERALD: Don't put it like that, mother. Of course I am sorry to leave you. Why, you are the best mother in the whole world. But after all, as Lord Illingworth says, it is impossible to live in such a place as Wrockley. You don't mind it. But I'm ambitious; I want something more than that. I want to have a career. I want to do something that will make you proud of me, and Lord Illingworth is going to help me. He is going to do everything for me.

MRS ARBUTHNOT: Gerald, don't go away with Lord Illingworth. I implore you not to. Gerald, I beg you!

GERALD: Mother, how changeable you are! You don't seem to know your own mind for a single moment. An hour and a half ago in the drawing-room you agreed to the whole thing; now you turn round and make objections, and try to force me to give up my one chance in life. Yes, my one chance. You don't suppose that men like Lord Illingworth are to be found every day, do you, mother? It is very strange that when I have had such a wonderful piece of good luck, the one person to put difficulties in my way should be my own mother. Besides, you know, mother, I love Hester Worsley. Who could help loving her? I love her more than I have ever told you, far more. And if I had a position, if I had prospects, I could – I could ask her to . . . Don't you understand now, mother, what it means to me to be Lord Illingworth's secretary? To start like that is to find a career ready for one – before one – waiting for one. If I were Lord Illingworth's secretary I could ask Hester to be my wife. As a wretched bank clerk with a hundred a year it would be an impertinence.

MRS ARBUTHNOT: I fear you need have no hopes of Miss Worsley. I know her views on life. She has just told them to me. (*a pause*)

GERALD: Then I have my ambition left, at any rate. That is something – I am glad I have that! You have always tried to crush my ambition, mother – haven't you? You have told me that the world is a wicked place, that success is not worth having, that society is shallow, and all that sort of thing – well, I don't believe it, mother. I think the world must be delightful. I think society must be exquisite. I think success is a thing worth having. You have been wrong in all that you have taught me, mother, quite wrong. Lord Illingworth is a successful man. He is a fashionable man. He is a man who lives in the world and for it. Well, I would give anything to be just like Lord Illingworth.

MRS ARBUTHNOT: I would sooner see you dead.

GERALD: Mother, what is your objection to Lord Illingworth? Tell me – tell me right out. What is it?

MRS ARBUTHNOT: He is a bad man.

GERALD: In what way bad? I don't understand what you mean.

MRS ARBUTHNOT: I will tell you.

GERALD: I suppose you think him bad, because he doesn't believe the same things as you do. Well, men are different from women, mother. It is natural that they should have different views.

MRS ARBUTHNOT: It is not what Lord Illingworth believes, or what he does not believe, that makes him bad. It is what he is.

GERALD: Mother, is it something you know of him? Something you actually know?

MRS ARBUTHNOT: It is something I know.

GERALD: Something you are quite sure of?

MRS ARBUTHNOT: Quite sure of.

GERALD: How long have you known it?

MRS ARBUTHNOT: For twenty years.

GERALD: Is it fair to go back twenty years in any man's career? And what have you or I to do with Lord Illingworth's early life? What business is it of ours?

MRS ARBUTHNOT: What this man has been, he is now, and will be always.

GERALD: Mother, tell me what Lord Illingworth did? If he did anything shameful, I will not go away with him. Surely you know me well enough for that?

MRS ARBUTHNOT: Gerald, come near to me. Quite close to me, as you used to do when you were a little boy, when you were mother's own boy.

GERALD *sits down beside his mother. She runs her fingers through his hair, and strokes his hands*

Gerald, there was a girl once, she was very young, she was little over eighteen at the time. George Harford – that was Lord Illingworth's name then – George Harford met her. She knew nothing about life. He – knew everything. He made this girl love him. He made her love him so much that she left her father's house with him one morning. She loved him so much, and he had promised to marry her! He had solemnly promised to marry her, and she had believed him. She was very young, and – and ignorant of what life really is. But he put the marriage off from week to week, and month to month. She trusted in him all the while. She loved him. Before her child was born – for she had a child – she implored him for the child's sake to marry her, that the child might have a name, that her sin might not be visited on the child, who was innocent. He refused. After the child was born she left him, taking the child away, and her life was ruined, and her soul ruined, and all that was sweet, and good, and pure in her ruined also. She suffered terribly – she suffers now. She will always suffer. For her there is no joy, no peace, no atonement. She is a woman who drags a chain like a guilty thing. She is a woman who wears a mask, like a thing that is a leper. The fire cannot purify her. The waters cannot quench her anguish. Nothing can heal her! no anodyne can give her sleep! no poppies forgetfulness! She is lost! She is a lost soul! – That is why I call Lord Illingworth a bad man. That is why I don't want my boy to be with him.

GERALD: My dear mother, it all sounds very tragic, of course. But I dare say the girl was just as much to blame as Lord Illingworth was. After all, would a really nice girl, a girl with any nice feelings at all, go away from her home with a man to whom she was not married, and live with him as his wife? No nice girl would.

MRS ARBUTHNOT (*after a pause*): Gerald, I withdraw all my objections. You are at liberty to go away with Lord Illingworth, when and where you choose.

GERALD: Dear mother, I knew you wouldn't stand in my way. You are the best woman God ever made. And, as for Lord Illingworth, I don't believe he is capable of anything infamous or base. I can't believe it of him – I can't.

HESTER (*outside*): Let me go! Let me go!

Enter HESTER *in terror, and rushes over to* GERALD *and flings herself in his arms*

HESTER: Oh! save me – save me from him!

GERALD: From whom?

HESTER: He has insulted me! Horribly insulted me! Save me!

GERALD: Who? Who has dared?

LORD ILLINGWORTH *enters at back of stage.* HESTER *breaks from* GERALD's *arms and points to him.*

GERALD (*he is quite beside himself with rage and indignation*): Lord Illingworth, you have insulted the purest thing on God's earth, a thing as pure as my own mother. You have insulted the woman I love most in the world, with my own mother. As there is a God in heaven, I will kill you!

MRS ARBUTHNOT (*rushing across and catching hold of him*): No! no!

GERALD (*thrusting her back*): Don't hold me, mother. Don't hold me – I'll kill him!

MRS ARBUTHNOT: Gerald!

GERALD: Let me go, I say!

MRS ARBUTHNOT: Stop, Gerald, stop! He is your own father!

> GERALD *clutches his mother's hands and looks into her face. She sinks slowly on the ground in shame.* HESTER *steals towards the door.* LORD ILLINGWORTH *frowns and bites his lip. After a time,* GERALD *raises his mother up, puts his arm round her, and leads her from the room*

END OF ACT THREE

ACT FOUR

Sitting-room at Mrs Arbuthnot's. Large open French window at back, looking on to garden. Doors right and left. GERALD ARBUTHNOT *writing at table. Enter* ALICE *followed by* LADY HUNSTANTON *and* MRS ALLONBY.

ALICE: Lady Hunstanton and Mrs Allonby. (*exit*)

LADY HUNSTANTON: Good-morning, Gerald.

GERALD (*rising*): Good-morning, Lady Hunstanton. Good-morning, Mrs Allonby.

LADY HUNSTANTON (*sitting down*): We came to enquire for your dear mother, Gerald. I hope she is better?

GERALD: My mother has not come down yet, Lady Hunstanton.

LADY HUNSTANTON: Ah, I am afraid the heat was too much for her last night. I think there must have been thunder in the air. Or perhaps it was the music. Music makes one feel so romantic – at least it always gets on one's nerves.

MRS ALLONBY: It's the same thing, nowadays.

LADY HUNSTANTON: I am so glad I don't know what you mean, dear. I am afraid you mean something wrong. Ah, I see you're examining Mrs Arbuthnot's pretty room. Isn't it nice and old-fashioned?

MRS ALLONBY (*surveying the room through her lorgnette*): It looks quite the happy English home.

LADY HUNSTANTON: That's just the word, dear; that just describes it. One feels your mother's good influence in everything she has about her, Gerald.

MRS ALLONBY: Lord Illingworth says that all influence is bad, but that a good influence is the worst in the world.

LADY HUNSTANTON: When Lord Illingworth knows Mrs Arbuthnot better he will change his mind. I must certainly bring him here.

MRS ALLONBY: I should like to see Lord Illingworth in a happy English home.

LADY HUNSTANTON: It would do him a great deal of good, dear. Most women in London, nowadays, seem to furnish their rooms with nothing but orchids, foreigners and French novels. But here we have the room of a sweet saint. Fresh natural flowers, books that don't shock one, pictures that one can look at without blushing.

MRS ALLONBY: But I like blushing.

LADY HUNSTANTON: Well, there is a good deal to be said for blushing, if one can do it at the proper moment. Poor dear Hunstanton used to tell me I didn't blush nearly often enough. But then he was so very particular. He wouldn't let me know any of his men friends, except those who were over seventy, like poor Lord Ashton; who afterwards, by the way, was brought into the divorce court. A most unfortunate case.

MRS ALLONBY: I delight in men over seventy. They always offer one the devotion of a lifetime. I think seventy an ideal age for a man.

LADY HUNSTANTON: She is quite incorrigible, Gerald, isn't she? By the by, Gerald, I hope your dear mother will come and see me more often now. You and Lord Illingworth start almost immediately, don't you?

GERALD: I have given up my intention of being Lord Illingworth's secretary.

LADY HUNSTANTON: Surely not, Gerald! It would be most unwise of you. What reason can you have?

GERALD: I don't think I should be suitable for the post.

MRS ALLONBY: I wish Lord Illingworth would ask me to be his secretary. But he says I am not serious enough.

LADY HUNSTANTON: My dear, you really mustn't talk like that in this house. Mrs Arbuthnot doesn't know anything about the wicked society in which we all live. She won't go into it. She is far too good. I consider it was a great honour her coming to me last night. It gave quite an atmosphere of respectability to the party.

MRS ALLONBY: Ah, that must have been what you thought was thunder in the air.

LADY HUNSTANTON: My dear, how can you say that? There is no resemblance between the two things at all. But really, Gerald, what do you mean by not being suitable?

GERALD: Lord Illingworth's views of life and mine are too different.

LADY HUNSTANTON: But, my dear Gerald, at your age you shouldn't have any views of life. They are quite out of place. You must be guided by others in this matter. Lord Illingworth has made you the most flattering offer, and travelling with him you would see the world – as much of it, at least, as one should look at – under the best auspices possible, and stay with all the right people, which is so important at this solemn moment in your career.

GERALD: I don't want to see the world, I've seen enough of it.

MRS ALLONBY: I hope you don't think you have exhausted life, Mr Arbuthnot. When a man says that, one knows that life has exhausted him.

GERALD: I don't wish to leave my mother.

LADY HUNSTANTON: Now, Gerald, that is pure laziness on your part. Not leave your mother! If I were your mother I would insist on your going.

Enter ALICE

ALICE: Mrs Arbuthnot's compliments, my lady, but she has a bad headache, and cannot see anyone this morning. (*exit*)

LADY HUNSTANTON (*rising*): A bad headache! I am so sorry! Perhaps you'll bring her up to Hunstanton this afternoon, if she is better, Gerald.

GERALD: I am afraid not this afternoon, Lady Hunstanton.

LADY HUNSTANTON: Well, tomorrow, then. Ah, if you had a father, Gerald, he wouldn't let you waste your life here. He would send you off with Lord Illingworth at once. But mothers are so weak. They give up to their sons in everything. We are all heart, all heart. Come, dear, I must call at the rectory and enquire for Mrs Daubeny, who, I am afraid, is far from well. It is wonderful how the Archdeacon bears up, quite wonderful. He is the most sympathetic of husbands. Quite a model. Goodbye, Gerald, give my fondest love to your mother.

MRS ALLONBY: Goodbye, Mr Arbuthnot.

GERALD: Goodbye.

Exeunt LADY HUNSTANTON *and* MRS ALLONBY. GERALD *sits down and reads over his letter*

GERALD: What name can I sign? I, who have no right to any name. (*Signs name, puts letter into envelope, addresses it, and is about to seal it, when door opens and* MRS ARBUTHNOT *enters.* GERALD *lays down sealing-wax. Mother and son look at each other*)

LADY HUNSTANTON (*through French window at the back*): Goodbye again, Gerald. We are taking the short cut across your pretty garden. Now, remember my advice to you – start at once with Lord Illingworth.

MRS ALLONBY: *Au revoir*, Mr Arbuthnot. Mind you bring me back something nice from your travels – not an Indian shawl – on no account an Indian shawl. (*exeunt*)

GERALD: Mother, I have just written to him.

MRS ARBUTHNOT: To whom?

GERALD: To my father. I have written to tell him to come here at four o'clock this afternoon.

MRS ARBUTHNOT: He shall not come here. He shall not cross the threshold of my house.

GERALD: He must come.

MRS ARBUTHNOT: Gerald, if you are going away with Lord Illingworth, go at once. Go before it kills me; but don't ask me to meet him.

GERALD: Mother, you don't understand. Nothing in the world would induce me to go away with Lord Illingworth, or to leave you. Surely you know me well enough for that. No, I have written to him to say –

MRS ARBUTHNOT: What can you have to say to him?

GERALD: Can't you guess, mother, what I have written in this letter?

MRS ARBUTHNOT: No.

GERALD: Mother, surely you can. Think, think what must be done, now, at once, within the next few days.

MRS ARBUTHNOT: There is nothing to be done.

GERALD: I have written to Lord Illingworth to tell him that he must marry you.

MRS ARBUTHNOT: Marry me?

GERALD: Mother, I will force him to do it. The wrong that has been done you must be repaired. Atonement must be made. Justice may be slow, mother, but it comes in the end. In a few days you shall be Lord Illingworth's lawful wife.

MRS ARBUTHNOT: But, Gerald –

GERALD: I will insist upon his doing it. I will make him do it, he will not dare to refuse.

MRS ARBUTHNOT: But, Gerald, it is I who refuse. I will not marry Lord Illingworth.

GERALD: Not marry him? Mother!

MRS ARBUTHNOT: I will not marry him.

GERALD: But you don't understand: it is for your sake I am talking, not for mine. This marriage, this necessary marriage, this marriage which for obvious reasons must inevitably take place, will not help me, will not give me a name that will be really, rightly mine to bear. But surely it will be something for you, that you, my mother, should, however late, become the wife of the man who is my father. Will not that be something?

MRS ARBUTHNOT: I will not marry him.

GERALD: Mother, you must.

MRS ARBUTHNOT: I will not. You talk of atonement for a wrong done. What atonement can be made to me? There is no atonement possible. I am disgraced; he is not. That is all. It is the usual history of a man and a woman as it usually happens, as it always happens. And the ending is the ordinary ending. The woman suffers. The man goes free.

GERALD: I don't know if that is the ordinary ending, mother; I hope it is not. But your life, at any rate, shall not end like that. The man shall make whatever reparation is possible. It is not enough. It does not wipe out the past, I know that. But at least it makes the future better, better for you, mother.

MRS ARBUTHNOT: I refuse to marry Lord Illingworth.

GERALD: If he came to you himself and asked you to be his wife you would give him a different answer. Remember, he is my father.

MRS ARBUTHNOT: If he came himself, which he will not do, my answer would be the same. Remember I am your mother.

GERALD: Mother, you make it terribly difficult for me by talking like that; and I can't understand why you won't look at this matter from the right, from the only proper standpoint. It is to take away the bitterness out of your life, to take away the shadow that lies on your name, that this marriage must take place. There is no alternative; and after the marriage you and I can go away together. But the marriage must take place first. It is a duty that you owe, not merely to yourself, but to all other women – yes; to all the other women in the world, lest he betray more.

MRS ARBUTHNOT: I owe nothing to other women. There is not one of them to help me. There is not one woman in the world to whom I could go for pity, if I would take it, or for sympathy, if I could win it. Women are hard on each other. That girl, last night, good though she is, fled from the room as though I were a tainted thing. She was right. I am a tainted thing. But my wrongs are my own, and I will bear them alone. I must bear them alone. What have women who have not sinned to do with me, or I with them? We do not understand each other.

Enter HESTER *behind*

GERALD: I implore you to do what I ask you.

MRS ARBUTHNOT: What son has ever asked of his mother to make so hideous a sacrifice? None.

GERALD: What mother has ever refused to marry the father of her own child? None.

MRS ARBUTHNOT: Let me be the first, then. I will not do it.

GERALD: Mother, you believe in religion, and you brought me up to believe in it also. Well, surely your religion, the religion that you taught me when I was a boy, mother, must tell you that I am right. You know it, you feel it.

MRS ARBUTHNOT: I do not know it. I do not feel it, nor will I ever stand before God's altar and ask God's blessing on so hideous a mockery as a marriage between me and George Harford. I will not say the words the church bids us to say. I will not say them. I dare not. How could I swear to love the man I loathe, to honour him who wrought you dishonour, to obey him who, in his mastery, made me to sin? No; marriage is a sacrament for those who love each other. It is not for such as him, or such as me. Gerald, to save you from the world's sneers and taunts I have lied to the world. For twenty years I have lied to the world. I could not tell the world the truth. Who can, ever? But not for my own sake will I lie to God, and in God's presence. No, Gerald, no ceremony, church-hallowed or state-made, shall ever bind me to George Harford. It may be that I am too bound to him already, who, robbing me, yet left me richer, so that in the mire of my life I found the pearl of price, or what I thought would be so.

GERALD: I don't understand you now.

MRS ARBUTHNOT: Men don't understand what mothers are. I am no different from other women except in the wrong done me and the wrong I did, and my very heavy punishments and great disgrace. And yet, to bear you I had to look on death. To nurture you I had to wrestle with it. Death fought with me for you. All women have to fight with death to keep their children. Death, being childless, wants our children from us. Gerald, when you were naked I clothed you, when you were hungry I gave you food. Night and day all that long winter I tended you. No office is too mean, no care too lowly for the thing we women love – and oh! how I loved you. Not Hannah, Samuel more. And you needed love, for you were weakly, and only love could have kept you alive. Only love can keep anyone alive. And boys are careless often, and without thinking give pain, and we always fancy that when they come to man's estate and know us better they will repay us. But it is not so. The world draws them from our side, and they make friends with whom they are happier than they are with us, and have amusements from which we are barred, and interests that are not ours; and they are unjust to us often, for when they find life bitter they blame us for it, and when they find it sweet we do not taste its sweetness with them . . . You made many friends and went into their houses and were glad with them, and I, knowing my secret, did not dare to follow but stayed at home and closed the door, shut out the sun and sat in darkness. What should I have done in honest households? My past was ever with me . . . And you thought I didn't care for the pleasant things of life. I tell you I longed for them, but did not dare to touch them, feeling I had no right. You thought I was happier working amongst the poor. That was my mission, you imagined. It was not, but where else was I to go? The sick do not ask if the hand that smooths their pillow is pure, nor the dying care if the lips that touch their brow have known the kiss of sin. It was you I thought of all the time; I gave to them the love you did not need; lavished on them a love that was not theirs . . . And you thought I spent too much of my time in going to church, and in church duties. But where else could I turn? God's house is the only house where sinners are made welcome, and you were always in my heart, Gerald, too much in my heart. For, though day after day, at morn or evensong, I have knelt in God's house, I have never repented of my sin. How could I repent of my sin when you, my love, were its fruit. Even now that you are bitter to me I cannot repent. I do not. You are more to me than innocence. I would rather be your mother – oh! much rather! – than have been always pure . . . Oh, don't you see? don't you understand? It is my dishonour that has made you so dear to me. It is my disgrace that has bound you so closely to me. It is the price I paid for you – the price of soul and body – that makes me love you as I do. Oh, don't ask me to do this horrible thing. Child of my shame, be still the child of my shame!

GERALD: Mother, I didn't know you loved me so much as that. And I will be a better son to you than I have been. And you and I must never leave each other . . . but, mother . . . I can't help it . . . you must become my father's wife. You must marry him. It is your duty.

HESTER (*running forward and embracing* MRS ARBUTHNOT): No, no; you shall not. That would be real dishonour: the first you have ever known. That would be real disgrace: the first to touch you. Leave him and come with me. There are other countries than England . . . Oh! other countries over sea, better, wiser and less unjust lands. The world is very wide and very big.

MRS ARBUTHNOT: No, not for me. For me the world is shrivelled to a palm's breadth, and where I walk there are thorns.

HESTER: It shall not be so. We shall somewhere find green valleys and fresh waters, and if we weep well, we shall weep together. Have we not both loved him?

GERALD: Hester!

HESTER (*waving him back*): Don't, don't! You cannot love me at all unless you love her also. You cannot honour me, unless she's holier to you. In her all womanhood is martyred. Not she alone, but all of us are stricken in her house.

GERALD: Hester, Hester, what shall I do?

HESTER: Do you respect the man who is your father?

GERALD: Respect him? I despise him! He is infamous.

HESTER: I thank you for saving me from him last night.

GERALD: Ah, that is nothing. I would die to save you. But you don't tell me what to do now!

HESTER: Have I not thanked you for saving me?

GERALD: But what should I do?

HESTER: Ask your own heart, not mine. I never had a mother to save, or shame.

MRS ARBUTHNOT: He is hard – he is hard. Let me go away.

GERALD (*rushes over and kneels down beside his mother*): Mother, forgive me; I have been to blame.

MRS ARBUTHNOT: Don't kiss my hands; they are cold. My heart is cold; something has broken it.

HESTER: Ah, don't say that. Hearts live by being wounded. Pleasure may turn a heart to stone, riches may make it callous, but sorrow – oh, sorrow cannot break it. Besides, what sorrows have you now? Why, at this moment you are more dear to him than ever, dear though you have been, and oh! how dear you *have* been always. Ah! be kind to him.

GERALD: You are my mother and my father all in one. I need no second parent. It was for you I spoke, for you alone. Oh, say something, mother. Have I but found one love to lose another? Don't tell me that. Oh mother, you are cruel. (*gets up and flings himself sobbing on a sofa*)

MRS ARBUTHNOT (*to* HESTER): But has he found indeed another love?

HESTER: You know I have loved him always.

MRS ARBUTHNOT: But we are very poor.

HESTER: Who, being loved, is poor? Oh, no one. I hate my riches. They are a burden. Let him share them with me.

MRS ARBUTHNOT: But we are disgraced. We rank among the outcasts. Gerald is nameless. The sins of the parents should be visited on the children. It is God's law.

HESTER: I was wrong. God's law is only love.

MRS ARBUTHNOT (*rises, and taking* HESTER *by the hand goes slowly over to where* GERALD *is lying on the sofa with his head buried in his hands. She touches him and he looks up*): Gerald, I cannot give you a father, but I have brought you a wife.

GERALD: Mother, I am not worthy either of her or you.

MRS ARBUTHNOT: So she comes first, you are worthy. And when you are away, Gerald . . . with . . . her – oh, think of me sometimes.

Don't forget me. And when you pray, pray for me. We should pray when we are happiest, and you will be happy, Gerald.

HESTER: Oh, you don't think of leaving us?

GERALD: Mother, you won't leave us?

MRS ARBUTHNOT: I might bring shame upon you!

GERALD: Mother!

MRS ARBUTHNOT: For a little then; and if you let me, near you always.

HESTER (*to* MRS ARBUTHNOT): Come out with us to the garden.

MRS ARBUTHNOT: Later on, later on.

Exeunt HESTER *and* GERALD. MRS ARBUTHNOT *goes towards door. Stops at looking-glass over mantelpiece and looks into it. Enter* ALICE

ALICE: A gentleman to see you, ma'am.

MRS ARBUTHNOT: Say I am not at home. Show me the card. (*takes card from salver and looks at it*) Say I will not see him.

LORD ILLINGWORTH *enters.* MRS ARBUTHNOT *sees him in the glass and starts, but does not turn round. Exit* ALICE

What can you have to say to me today, George Harford? You can have nothing to say to me. You must leave this house.

LORD ILLINGWORTH: Rachel, Gerald knows everything about you and me now, so some arrangement must be come to that will suit us all three. I assure you, he will find in me the most charming and generous of fathers.

MRS ARBUTHNOT: My son may come in at any moment. I saved you last night. I may not be able to save you again. My son feels my dishonour strongly, terribly strongly. I beg you to go.

LORD ILLINGWORTH (*sitting down*): Last night was excessively unfortunate. That silly puritan girl making a scene merely because I wanted to kiss her. What harm is there in a kiss?

MRS ARBUTHNOT (*turning round*): A kiss may ruin a human life, George Harford. I know that. I know that too well.

LORD ILLINGWORTH: We won't discuss that at present. What is of importance today, as yesterday, is still our son. I am extremely fond of him, as you know, and odd though it may seem to you, I admired his conduct last night immensely. He took up the cudgels for that pretty prude with wonderful promptitude. He is just what I should have liked a son of mine to be. Except that no son of mine should ever take the side of the puritans; that is always an error. Now, what I propose is this.

MRS ARBUTHNOT: Lord Illingworth, no proposition of yours interests me.

LORD ILLINGWORTH: According to our ridiculous English laws, I can't legitimise Gerald. But I can leave him my property. Illingworth is entailed, of course, but it is a tedious barrack of a place. He can have Ashby, which is much prettier, Harborough, which has the best shooting in the north of England, and the house in St James's Square. What more can a gentleman desire in this world?

MRS ARBUTHNOT: Nothing more, I am quite sure.

LORD ILLINGWORTH: As for a title, a title is really rather a nuisance in these democratic days. As George Harford I had everything I wanted. Now I have merely everything that other people want, which isn't nearly so pleasant. Well, my proposal is this.

MRS ARBUTHNOT: I told you I was not interested, and I beg you to go.

LORD ILLINGWORTH: The boy is to be with you for six months in the year, and with me for the other six. That is perfectly fair, is it not? You can have whatever allowance you like, and live where you choose. As for your past, no one knows anything about it except myself and Gerald. There is the puritan, of course, the puritan in white muslin, but she doesn't count. She couldn't tell the story without explaining that she objected to being kissed, could she? And all the women would think her a fool and the men think her a bore. And you need not be afraid that Gerald won't be my heir. I needn't tell you I have not the slightest intention of marrying.

MRS ARBUTHNOT: You come too late. My son has no need of you. You are not necessary.

LORD ILLINGWORTH: What do you mean, Rachel?

MRS ARBUTHNOT: That you are not necessary to Gerald's career. He does not require you.

LORD ILLINGWORTH: I do not understand you.

MRS ARBUTHNOT: Look into the garden. (LORD ILLINGWORTH *rises and goes towards window*) You had better not let them see you; you bring unpleasant memories. (LORD ILLINGWORTH *looks out and starts*) She loves him. They love each other. We are safe from you, and we are going away.

LORD ILLINGWORTH: Where?

MRS ARBUTHNOT: We will not tell you, and if you find us we will not know you. You seem surprised. What welcome would you get from the girl whose lips you tried to soil, from the boy whose life you have shamed, from the mother whose dishonour comes from you?

LORD ILLINGWORTH: You have grown hard, Rachel.

MRS ARBUTHNOT: I was too weak once. It is well for me that I have changed.

LORD ILLINGWORTH: I was very young at the time. We men know life too early.

MRS ARBUTHNOT: And we women know life too late. That is the difference between men and women. (*a pause*)

LORD ILLINGWORTH: Rachel, I want my son. My money may be of no use to him now. I may be of no use to him, but I want my son. Bring us together, Rachel. You can do it if you choose. (*sees letter on table*)

MRS ARBUTHNOT: There is no room in my boy's life for you. He is not interested in you.

LORD ILLINGWORTH: Then why does he write to me?

MRS ARBUTHNOT: What do you mean?

LORD ILLINGWORTH: What letter is this? (*takes up letter*)

MRS ARBUTHNOT: That – is nothing. Give it to me.

LORD ILLINGWORTH: It is addressed to me.

MRS ARBUTHNOT: You are not to open it. I forbid you to open it.

LORD ILLINGWORTH: And in Gerald's handwriting.

MRS ARBUTHNOT: It was not to have been sent. It is a letter he wrote to you this morning, before he saw me. But he is sorry now he wrote it, very sorry. You are not to open it. Give it to me.

LORD ILLINGWORTH: It belongs to me. (*opens it, sits down and reads it slowly.* MRS ARBUTHNOT *watches him all the time*) You have read this letter, I suppose, Rachel?

MRS ARBUTHNOT: No.

LORD ILLINGWORTH: You know what is in it?

MRS ARBUTHNOT: Yes!

LORD ILLINGWORTH: I don't admit for a moment that the boy is right in what he says. I don't admit that it is any duty of mine to marry you. I deny it entirely. But to get my son back I am ready – yes, I am ready to marry you, Rachel – and to treat you always with the deference and respect due to my wife. I will marry you as soon as you choose. I give you my word of honour.

MRS ARBUTHNOT: You made that promise to me once before and broke it.

LORD ILLINGWORTH: I will keep it now. And that will show you that I love my son, at least as much as you love him. For when I marry you, Rachel, there are some ambitions I shall have to surrender. High ambitions, too, if any ambition is high.

MRS ARBUTHNOT: I decline to marry you, Lord Illingworth.

LORD ILLINGWORTH: Are you serious?

MRS ARBUTHNOT: Yes.

LORD ILLINGWORTH: Do tell me your reasons. They would interest me enormously.

MRS ARBUTHNOT: I have already explained them to my son.

LORD ILLINGWORTH: I suppose they were intensely sentimental, weren't they? You women live by your emotions and for them. You have no philosophy of life.

MRS ARBUTHNOT: You are right. We women live by our emotions and for them. By our passions, and for them, if you will. I have two passions, Lord Illingworth: my love of him, my hate of you. You cannot kill those. They feed each other.

LORD ILLINGWORTH: What sort of love is that which needs to have hate as its brother?

MRS ARBUTHNOT: It is the sort of love I have for Gerald. Do you think that terrible? Well, it is terrible. All love is terrible. All love is a tragedy. I loved you once, Lord Illingworth. Oh, what a tragedy for a woman to have loved you!

LORD ILLINGWORTH: So you really refuse to marry me?

MRS ARBUTHNOT: Yes.

LORD ILLINGWORTH: Because you hate me?

MRS ARBUTHNOT: Yes.

LORD ILLINGWORTH: And does my son hate me as you do?

MRS ARBUTHNOT: No.

LORD ILLINGWORTH: I am glad of that, Rachel.

MRS ARBUTHNOT: He merely despises you.

LORD ILLINGWORTH: What a pity! What a pity for him, I mean.

MRS ARBUTHNOT: Don't be deceived, George. Children begin by loving their parents. After a time they judge them. Rarely if ever do they forgive them.

LORD ILLINGWORTH (*reads letter over again, very slowly*): May I ask by what arguments you made the boy who wrote this letter, this beautiful, passionate letter, believe that you should not marry his father, the father of your own child?

MRS ARBUTHNOT: It was not I who made him see it. It was another.

LORD ILLINGWORTH: What *fin-de-siècle* person?

MRS ARBUTHNOT: The puritan, Lord Illingworth. (*a pause*)

LORD ILLINGWORTH (*winces, then rises slowly and goes over to table where his hat and gloves are.* MRS ARBUTHNOT *is standing close to the table. He picks up one of the gloves, and begins putting it on*): There is not much then for me to do here, Rachel?

MRS ARBUTHNOT: Nothing.

LORD ILLINGWORTH: It is goodbye, is it?

MRS ARBUTHNOT: For ever, I hope, this time, Lord Illingworth.

LORD ILLINGWORTH: How curious! At this moment you look exactly as you looked the night you left me twenty years ago. You have just the same expression in your mouth. Upon my word, Rachel, no woman ever loved me as you did. Why, you gave yourself to me like a flower, to do anything I liked with. You were the prettiest of playthings, the most fascinating of small romances . . . (*Pulls out watch*) Quarter to two! Must be strolling back to Hunstanton. Don't suppose I shall see you there again. I'm sorry, I am, really. It's been an amusing experience to have met amongst people of one's own rank, and treated quite seriously too, one's mistress and one's –

MRS ARBUTHNOT *snatches up glove and strikes* LORD ILLINGWORTH *across the face with it.* LORD ILLINGWORTH *starts. He is dazed by the insult of his punishment. Then he controls himself and goes to window and looks out at his son. Sighs and leaves the room*

MRS ARBUTHNOT (*falls sobbing on the sofa*): He would have said it. He would have said it.

Enter GERALD *and* HESTER *from the garden*

GERALD: Well, dear mother. You never came out after all. So we have come in to fetch you. Mother, you have not been crying? (*kneels down beside her*)

MRS ARBUTHNOT: My boy! My boy! My boy! (*running her fingers through his hair*)

HESTER (*coming over*): But you have two children now. You'll let me be your daughter?

MRS ARBUTHNOT (*looking up*): Would you choose me for a mother?

HESTER: You of all women I have ever known.

They move towards the door leading into garden with their arms round each other's waists. GERALD *goes to the table for his hat. On turning round he sees* LORD ILLINGWORTH'S *glove lying on the floor, and picks it up.*

GERALD: Hallo, mother, whose glove is this? You have had a visitor. Who was it?

MRS ARBUTHNOT (*turning round*): Oh! no one. No one in particular. A man of no importance.

CURTAIN

AN IDEAL HUSBAND

To
FRANK HARRIS
a slight tribute to his power and
distinction as an artist, his chivalry
and his nobility as a friend

PERSONS IN THE PLAY

THE EARL OF CAVERSHAM KG
VISCOUNT GORING, *his son*
SIR ROBERT CHILTERN BART, *Under-Secretary for Foreign Affairs*
VICOMTE DE NANJAC, *attaché at the French Embassy in London*
MR MONTFORD
MASON, *butler to Sir Robert Chiltern*
PHIPPS, *Lord Goring's servant*
JAMES, *footman*
HAROLD, *footman*
LADY CHILTERN
LADY MARKBY
THE COUNTESS OF BASILDON
MRS MARCHMONT
MISS MABEL CHILTERN, *Sir Robert Chiltern's sister*
MRS CHEVELEY

THE SCENES OF THE PLAY

ACT ONE *The octagon room in Sir Robert Chiltern's house in Grosvenor Square*
ACT TWO *The morning-room in Sir Robert Chiltern's house*
ACT THREE *The library of Lord Goring's house in Curzon Street*
ACT FOUR *Same as Act Two*

TIME: *The Present*
PLACE: *London*

The action of the play is completed within twenty-four hours

FIRST PERFORMANCE

Theatre Royal, Haymarket, London, on 3 January 1895

AN IDEAL HUSBAND

ACT ONE

The octagon room at Sir Robert Chiltern's house in Grosvenor Square. The room is brilliantly lighted and full of guests. At the top of the staircase stands LADY CHILTERN, *a woman of grave Greek beauty, about twenty-seven years of age. She receives the guests as they come up. Over the well of the staircase hangs a great chandelier with wax lights which illumine a large eighteenth-century French tapestry – representing the* Triumph of Love, *from a design by Boucher – that is stretched on the staircase wall. On the right is the entrance to the music-room. The sound of a string quartet is faintly heard. The entrance on the left leads to other reception rooms.* MRS MARCHMONT *and* LADY BASILDON, *two very pretty women, are seated together on a Louis-Seize sofa. They are types of exquisite fragility. Their affectation of manner has a delicate charm. Watteau would have loved to paint them.*

MRS MARCHMONT: Going on to the Hartlocks, tonight, Margaret?

LADY BASILDON: I suppose so. Are you?

MRS MARCHMONT: Yes. Horribly tedious parties they give, don't they?

LADY BASILDON: Horribly tedious! Never know why I go. Never know why I go anywhere.

MRS MARCHMONT: I come here to be educated.

LADY BASILDON: Ah! I hate being educated!

MRS MARCHMONT: So do I. It puts one almost on a level with the commercial classes, doesn't it? But dear Gertrude Chiltern is always telling me that I should have some serious purpose in life. So I come here to try to find one.

LADY BASILDON (*looking round through her lorgnette*): I don't see anybody here tonight whom one could possibly call a serious purpose. The man who took me in to dinner talked to me about his wife the whole time.

MRS MARCHMONT: How very trivial of him!

LADY BASILDON: Terribly trivial! What did your man talk about?

MRS MARCHMONT: About myself.
LADY BASILDON (*languidly*): And were you interested?
MRS MARCHMONT (*shaking her head*): Not in the smallest degree.
LADY BASILDON: What martyrs we are, dear Margaret!
MRS MARCHMONT (*rising*): And how well it becomes us, Olivia!

They rise and go towards the music-room. The VICOMTE DE NANJAC, *a young attaché known for his neckties and his Anglomania, approaches with a low bow and enters into conversation*

MASON (*announcing guests from the top of the staircase*): Mr and Lady Jane Barford. Lord Caversham.

Enter LORD CAVERSHAM, *an old gentleman of seventy, wearing the riband and star of the Garter. A fine Whig type. Rather like a portrait by Lawrence.*

LORD CAVERSHAM: Good-evening, Lady Chiltern! Has my good-for-nothing young son been here?
LADY CHILTERN (*smiling*): I don't think Lord Goring has arrived yet.
MABEL CHILTERN (*coming up to* LORD CAVERSHAM): Why do you call Lord Goring good-for-nothing?

MABEL CHILTERN *is a perfect example of the English type of prettiness, the apple-blossom type. She has all the fragrance and freedom of a flower. There is ripple after ripple of sunlight in her hair, and the little mouth, with its parted lips, is expectant, like the mouth of a child. She has the fascinating tyranny of youth, and the astonishing courage of innocence. To sane people she is not reminiscent of any work of art. But she is really like a Tanagra statuette, and would be rather annoyed if she were told so.*

LORD CAVERSHAM: Because he leads such an idle life.
MABEL CHILTERN: How can you say such a thing? Why, he rides in the Row at ten o'clock in the morning, goes to the opera three times a week, changes his clothes at least five times a day, and dines out every night of the season. You don't call that leading an idle life, do you?
LORD CAVERSHAM (*looking at her with a kindly twinkle in his eyes*): You are a very charming young lady!
MABEL CHILTERN: How sweet of you to say that, Lord Caversham! Do come to us more often. You know we are always at home on Wednesdays, and you look so well with your star!
LORD CAVERSHAM: Never go anywhere now. Sick of London society.

Shouldn't mind being introduced to my own tailor; he always votes on the right side. But object strongly to being sent down to dinner with my wife's milliner. Never could stand Lady Caversham's bonnets.

MABEL CHILTERN: Oh, I love London society! I think it has immensely improved. It is entirely composed now of beautiful idiots and brilliant lunatics. Just what society should be.

LORD CAVERSHAM: Hum! Which is Goring? Beautiful idiot or the other thing?

MABEL CHILTERN (*gravely*): I have been obliged for the present to put Lord Goring into a class quite by himself. But he is developing charmingly!

LORD CAVERSHAM: Into what?

MABEL CHILTERN (*with a little curtsey*): I hope to let you know very soon, Lord Caversham!

MASON (*announcing guests*): Lady Markby. Mrs Cheveley.

Enter LADY MARKBY *and* MRS CHEVELEY. LADY MARKBY *is a pleasant, kindly, popular woman, with grey hair* à la marquise *and good lace.* MRS CHEVELEY, *who accompanies her, is tall and rather slight. Lips very thin and highly-coloured, a line of scarlet on a pallid face. Venetian red hair, aquiline nose and long throat. Rouge accentuates the natural paleness of her complexion. Grey-green eyes that move restlessly. She is in heliotrope, with diamonds. She looks rather like an orchid, and makes great demands on one's curiosity. In all her movements she is extremely graceful. A work of art, on the whole, but showing the influence of too many schools.*

LADY MARKBY: Good-evening, dear Gertrude! So kind of you to let me bring my friend Mrs Cheveley. Two such charming women should know each other!

LADY CHILTERN (*advances towards* MRS CHEVELEY *with a sweet smile. Then suddenly stops, and bows rather distantly*): I think Mrs Cheveley and I have met before. I did not know she had married a second time.

LADY MARKBY (*genially*): Ah, nowadays people marry as often as they can, don't they? It is most fashionable. (*To* DUCHESS OF MARYBOROUGH): Dear duchess, and how is the duke? Brain still weak, I suppose? Well, that is only to be expected, is it not? His good father was just the same. There is nothing like race, is there.

MRS CHEVELEY (*playing with her fan*): But have we really met before,

Lady Chiltern? I can't remember where. I have been out of England for so long.

LADY CHILTERN: We were at school together, Mrs Cheveley.

MRS CHEVELEY (*superciliously*): Indeed? I have forgotten all about my schooldays. I have a vague impression that they were detestable.

LADY CHILTERN (*coldly*): I am not surprised!

MRS CHEVELEY (*in her sweetest manner*): Do you know, I am quite looking forward to meeting your clever husband, Lady Chiltern. Since he has been at the Foreign Office, he has been so much talked of in Vienna. They actually succeed in spelling his name right in the newspapers. That in itself is fame, on the continent.

LADY CHILTERN: I hardly think there will be much in common between you and my husband, Mrs Cheveley! (*moves away.*)

VICOMTE DE NANJAC: Ah, chère madame, quelle surprise! I have not seen you since Berlin!

MRS CHEVELEY: Not since Berlin, vicomte. Five years ago!

VICOMTE DE NANJAC: And you are younger and more beautiful than ever. How do you manage it?

MRS CHEVELEY: By making it a rule only to talk to perfectly charming people like yourself.

VICOMTE DE NANJAC: Ah! you flatter me. You butter me, as they say here.

MRS CHEVELEY: Do they say that here? How dreadful of them!

VICOMTE DE NANJAC: Yes, they have a wonderful language. It should be more widely known.

SIR ROBERT CHILTERN *enters. A man of forty but looking somewhat younger. Clean-shaven, with finely cut features, dark-haired and dark-eyed. A personality of mark. Not popular – few personalities are. But intensely admired by the few, and deeply respected by the many. The note of his manner is that of perfect distinction, with a slight touch of pride. One feels that he is conscious of the success he has made in life. A nervous temperament, with a tired look. The firmly chiselled mouth and chin contrast strikingly with the romantic expression in the deep-set eyes. The variance is suggestive of an almost complete separation of passion and intellect, as though thought and emotion were each isolated in its own sphere through some violence of willpower. There is nervousness in the nostrils, and in the pale, thin, pointed hands. It would be inaccurate to call him picturesque. Picturesqueness cannot survive the House of Commons. But Van Dyck would have liked to have painted his head.*

SIR ROBERT CHILTERN: Good-evening, Lady Markby. I hope you have brought Sir John with you?

LADY MARKBY: Oh! I have brought a much more charming person than Sir John. Sir John's temper since he has taken seriously to politics has become quite unbearable. Really, now that the House of Commons is trying to become useful, it does a great deal of harm.

SIR ROBERT CHILTERN: I hope not, Lady Markby. At any rate we do our best to waste the public time, don't we? But who is this charming person you have been kind enough to bring to us?

LADY MARKBY: Her name is Mrs Cheveley! One of the Dorsetshire Cheveleys, I suppose. But I really don't know. Families are so mixed nowadays. Indeed, as a rule, everybody turns out to be somebody else.

SIR ROBERT CHILTERN: Mrs Cheveley? I seem to know the name.

LADY MARKBY: She has just arrived from Vienna.

SIR ROBERT CHILTERN: Ah! yes. I think I know whom you mean.

LADY MARKBY: Oh! she goes everywhere there, and has such pleasant scandals about all her friends. I really must go to Vienna next winter. I hope there is a good chef at the embassy.

SIR ROBERT CHILTERN: If there is not, the ambassador will certainly have to be recalled. Pray point out Mrs Cheveley to me. I should like to see her.

LADY MARKBY: Let me introduce you. (*To* MRS CHEVELEY.) My dear, Sir Robert Chiltern is dying to know you!

SIR ROBERT CHILTERN (*bowing*): Everyone is dying to know the brilliant Mrs Cheveley. Our attachés at Vienna write to us about nothing else.

MRS CHEVELEY: Thank you, Sir Robert. An acquaintance that begins with a compliment is sure to develop into a real friendship. It starts in the right manner. And I find that I know Lady Chiltern already.

SIR ROBERT CHILTERN: Really?

MRS CHEVELEY: Yes. She has just reminded me that we were at school together. I remember it perfectly now. She always got the good conduct prize. I have a distinct recollection of Lady Chiltern always getting the good conduct prize!

SIR ROBERT CHILTERN (*smiling*): And what prizes did you get, Mrs Cheveley?

MRS CHEVELEY: My prizes came a little later on in life. I don't think any of them were for good conduct. I forget!

SIR ROBERT CHILTERN: I am sure they were for something charming!

MRS CHEVELEY: I don't know that women are always rewarded for being charming. I think they are usually punished for it! Certainly, more women grow old nowadays through the faithfulness of their admirers than through anything else! At least that is the only way I can account for the terribly haggard look of most of your pretty women in London!

SIR ROBERT CHILTERN: What an appalling philosophy that sounds! To attempt to classify you, Mrs Cheveley, would be an impertinence. But may I ask, at heart, are you an optimist or a pessimist? Those seem to be the only two fashionable religions left to us nowadays.

MRS CHEVELEY: Oh, I'm neither. Optimism begins in a broad grin, and Pessimism ends with blue spectacles. Besides, they are both of them merely poses.

SIR ROBERT CHILTERN: You prefer to be natural?

MRS CHEVELEY: Sometimes. But it is such a very difficult pose to keep up.

SIR ROBERT CHILTERN: What would those modern psychological novelists, of whom we hear so much, say to such a theory as that?

MRS CHEVELEY: Ah! the strength of women comes from the fact that psychology cannot explain us. Men can be analysed, women . . . merely adored.

SIR ROBERT CHILTERN: You think science cannot grapple with the problem of women?

MRS CHEVELEY: Science can never grapple with the irrational. That is why it has no future before it, in this world.

SIR ROBERT CHILTERN: And women represent the irrational.

MRS CHEVELEY: Well-dressed women do.

SIR ROBERT CHILTERN (*with a polite bow*): I fear I could hardly agree with you there. But do sit down. And now tell me, what makes you leave your brilliant Vienna for our gloomy London – or perhaps the question is indiscreet?

MRS CHEVELEY: Questions are never indiscreet. Answers sometimes are.

SIR ROBERT CHILTERN: Well, at any rate, may I know if it is politics or pleasure?

MRS CHEVELEY: Politics are my only pleasure. You see nowadays it is not fashionable to flirt till one is forty, or to be romantic till one is forty-five, so we poor women who are under thirty, or say we are, have nothing open to us but politics or philanthropy. And philanthropy seems to me to have become simply the refuge of people who wish to annoy their fellow creatures. I prefer politics. I think they are more . . . becoming!

SIR ROBERT CHILTERN: A political life is a noble career!

MRS CHEVELEY: Sometimes. And sometimes it is a clever game, Sir Robert. And sometimes it is a great nuisance.

SIR ROBERT CHILTERN: Which do you find it?

MRS CHEVELEY: A combination of all three. (*drops her fan*)

SIR ROBERT CHILTERN (*picks up fan*): Allow me!

MRS CHEVELEY: Thanks.

SIR ROBERT CHILTERN: But you have not told me yet what makes you honour London so suddenly. Our season is almost over.

MRS CHEVELEY: Oh! I don't care about the London season! It is too matrimonial. People are either hunting for husbands, or hiding from them. I wanted to meet you. It is quite true. You know what a woman's curiosity is. Almost as great as a man's! I wanted immensely to meet you, and . . . to ask you to do something for me.

SIR ROBERT CHILTERN: I hope it is not a little thing, Mrs Cheveley. I find that little things are so very difficult to do.

MRS CHEVELEY (*after a moment's reflection*): No, I don't think it is quite a little thing.

SIR ROBERT CHILTERN: I am so glad. Do tell me what it is.

MRS CHEVELEY: Later on. (*rises.*) And now may I walk through your beautiful house? I hear your pictures are charming. Poor Baron Arnheim – you remember the baron? – used to tell me you had some wonderful Corots.

SIR ROBERT CHILTERN (*with an almost imperceptible start*): Did you know Baron Arnheim well?

MRS CHEVELEY (*smiling*): Intimately. Did you?

SIR ROBERT CHILTERN: At one time.

MRS CHEVELEY: Wonderful man, wasn't he?

SIR ROBERT CHILTERN (*after a pause*): He was very remarkable, in many ways.

MRS CHEVELEY: I often think it such a pity he never wrote his memoirs. They would have been most interesting.

SIR ROBERT CHILTERN: Yes: he knew men and cities well, like the old Greek.

MRS CHEVELEY: Without the dreadful disadvantage of having a Penelope waiting at home for him.

MASON: Lord Goring.

Enter LORD GORING. *Thirty-four, but always says he is younger. A well-bred, expressionless face. He is clever, but would not like to be thought so. A flawless dandy, he would be annoyed if he were considered romantic. He plays with life, and is on perfectly good terms with the world. He is fond of being misunderstood. It gives him a post of vantage.*

SIR ROBERT CHILTERN: Good-evening, my dear Arthur! Mrs Cheveley, allow me to introduce to you Lord Goring, the idlest man in London.

MRS CHEVELEY: I have met Lord Goring before.

LORD GORING (*bowing*): I did not think you would remember me, Mrs Cheveley.

MRS CHEVELEY: My memory is under admirable control. And are you still a bachelor?

LORD GORING: I . . . believe so.

MRS CHEVELEY: How very romantic!

LORD GORING: Oh! I am not at all romantic. I am not old enough. I leave romance to my seniors.

SIR ROBERT CHILTERN: Lord Goring is the result of Boodle's Club, Mrs Cheveley.

MRS CHEVELEY: He reflects every credit on the institution.

LORD GORING: May I ask are you staying in London long?

MRS CHEVELEY: That depends partly on the weather, partly on the cooking, and partly on Sir Robert.

SIR ROBERT CHILTERN: You are not going to plunge us into a European war, I hope?

MRS CHEVELEY: There is no danger, at present!

She nods to LORD GORING, *with a look of amusement in her eyes, and goes out with* SIR ROBERT CHILTERN. LORD GORING *saunters over to* MABEL CHILTERN.

MABEL CHILTERN: You are very late!

LORD GORING: Have you missed me?

MABEL CHILTERN: Awfully!

LORD GORING: Then I am sorry I did not stay away longer. I like being missed.

MABEL CHILTERN: How very selfish of you!

LORD GORING: I am very selfish.

MABEL CHILTERN: You are always telling me of your bad qualities, Lord Goring.

LORD GORING: I have only told you half of them as yet, Miss Mabel!

MABEL CHILTERN: Are the others very bad?

LORD GORING: Quite dreadful! When I think of them at night I go to sleep at once.

MABEL CHILTERN: Well, I delight in your bad qualities. I wouldn't have you part with one of them.

LORD GORING: How very nice of you! But then you are always nice. By the way, I want to ask you a question, Miss Mabel. Who brought Mrs Cheveley here? That woman in heliotrope, who has just gone out of the room with your brother?

MABEL CHILTERN: Oh, I think Lady Markby brought her. Why do you ask?

LORD GORING: I haven't seen her for years, that is all.

MABEL CHILTERN: What an absurd reason!

LORD GORING: All reasons are absurd.

MABEL CHILTERN: What sort of a woman is she?

LORD GORING: Oh! a genius in the daytime and a beauty at night!

MABEL CHILTERN: I dislike her already.

LORD GORING: That shows your admirable good taste.

VICOMTE DE NANJAC (*approaching*): Ah, the English young lady is the dragon of good taste, is she not? Quite the dragon of good taste.

LORD GORING: So the newspapers are always telling us.

VICOMTE DE NANJAC: I read all your English newspapers. I find them so amusing.

LORD GORING: Then, my dear Nanjac, you must certainly read between the lines.

VICOMTE DE NANJAC: I should like to, but my professor objects. (*To* MABEL CHILTERN): May I have the pleasure of escorting you to the music-room, mademoiselle?

MABEL CHILTERN (*looking very disappointed*): Delighted, vicomte, quite delighted! (*Turning to* LORD GORING): Aren't you coming to the music-room?

LORD GORING: Not if there is any music going on, Miss Mabel.

MABEL CHILTERN (*severely*): The music is in German. You would not understand it.

Goes out with the VICOMTE DE NANJAC. LORD CAVERSHAM *comes up to his son*

LORD CAVERSHAM: Well, sir! what are you doing here? Wasting your life as usual! You should be in bed, sir. You keep too late hours! I heard of you the other night at Lady Rufford's dancing till four o'clock in the morning!

LORD GORING: Only a quarter to four, father.

LORD CAVERSHAM: Can't make out how you stand London society.

The thing has gone to the dogs, a lot of damned nobodies talking about nothing.

LORD GORING: I love talking about nothing, father. It is the only thing I know anything about.

LORD CAVERSHAM: You seem to me to be living entirely for pleasure.

LORD GORING: What else is there to live for, father? Nothing ages like happiness.

LORD CAVERSHAM: You are heartless, sir, very heartless.

LORD GORING: I hope not, father. Good-evening, Lady Basildon!

LADY BASILDON (*arching two pretty eyebrows*): Are you here? I had no idea you ever came to political parties.

LORD GORING: I adore political parties. They are the only place left to us where people don't talk politics.

LADY BASILDON: I delight in talking politics. I talk them all day long. But I can't bear listening to them. I don't know how the unfortunate men in the House stand these long debates.

LORD GORING: By never listening.

LADY BASILDON: Really?

LORD GORING (*in his most serious manner*): Of course. You see, it is a very dangerous thing to listen. If one listens one may be convinced; and a man who allows himself to be convinced by an argument is a thoroughy unreasonable person.

LADY BASILDON: Ah! that accounts for so much in men that I have never understood, and so much in women that their husbands never appreciate in them!

MRS MARCHMONT (*with a sigh*): Our husbands never appreciate anything in us. We have to go to others for that!

LADY BASILDON (*emphatically)*: Yes, always to others, have we not?

LORD GORING (*smiling*): And those are the views of the two ladies who are known to have the most admirable husbands in London.

MRS MARCHMONT: That is exactly what we can't stand. My Reginald is quite hopelessly faultless. He is really unendurably so, at times! There is not the smallest element of excitement in knowing him.

LORD GORING: How terrible! Really, the thing should be more widely known!

LADY BASILDON: Basildon is quite as bad; he is as domestic as if he was a bachelor.

MRS MARCHMONT (*pressing* LADY BASILDON'S *hand*): My poor Olivia! We have married perfect husbands, and we are well punished for it.

LORD GORING: I should have thought it was the husbands who were punished.

MRS MARCHMONT (*drawing herself up*): Oh, dear no! They are as happy as possible! And as for trusting us, it is tragic how much they trust us.

LADY BASILDON: Perfectly tragic!

LORD GORING: Or comic, Lady Basildon?

LADY BASILDON: Certainly not comic, Lord Goring. How unkind of you to suggest such a thing!

MRS MARCHMONT: I am afraid Lord Goring is in the camp of the enemy, as usual. I saw him talking to that Mrs Cheveley when he came in.

LORD GORING: Handsome woman, Mrs Cheveley!

LADY BASILDON (*stiffly*): Please don't praise other women in our presence. You might wait for us to do that!

LORD GORING: I did wait.

MRS MARCHMONT: Well, we are not going to praise her. I hear she went to the opera on Monday night, and told Tommy Rufford at supper that, as far as she could see, London society was entirely made up of dowdies and dandies.

LORD GORING: She is quite right, too. The men are all dowdies and the women are all dandies, aren't they?

MRS MARCHMONT (*after a pause*): Oh! do you really think that is what Mrs Cheveley meant?

LORD GORING: Of course. And a very sensible remark for Mrs Cheveley to make, too.

Enter MABEL CHILTERN. *She joins the group*

MABEL CHILTERN: Why are you talking about Mrs Cheveley? Everybody is talking about Mrs Cheveley! Lord Goring, says – what did you say, Lord Goring about Mrs Cheveley? Oh! I remember, that she was a genius in the daytime and a beauty at night.

LADY BASILDON: What a horrid combination! So very unnatural!

MRS MARCHMONT (*in her most dreamy manner*): I like looking at geniuses, and listening to beautiful people!

LORD GORING: Ah! that is morbid of you, Mrs Marchmont!

MRS MARCHMONT (*brightening to a look of real pleasure*): I am so glad to hear you say that. Marchmont and I have been married for seven years, and he has never once told me that I was morbid. Men are so painfully unobservant.

LADY BASILDON (*turning to her*): I have always said, dear Margaret, that you were the most morbid person in London.

MRS MARCHMONT: Ah! but you are always sympathetic, Olivia!

MABEL CHILTERN: Is it morbid to have a desire for food? I have a great desire for food. Lord Goring, will you give me some supper?

LORD GORING: With pleasure, Miss Mabel. (*moves away with her*)

MABEL CHILTERN: How horrid you have been! You have never talked to me the whole evening!

LORD GORING: How could I? You went away with the child-diplomatist.

MABEL CHILTERN: You might have followed us. Pursuit would have been only polite. I don't think I like you at all this evening!

LORD GORING: I like you immensely.

MABEL CHILTERN: Well, I wish you'd show it in a more marked way!

They go downstairs

MRS MARCHMONT: Olivia, I have a curious feeling of absolute faintness. I think I should like some supper very much. I know I should like some supper.

LADY BASILDON: I am positively dying for supper, Margaret!

MRS MARCHMONT: Men are so horribly selfish, they never think of these things.

LADY BASILDON: Men are grossly material, grossly material!

The VICOMTE DE NANJAC *enters from the music-room with some other guests. After having carefully examined all the people present, he approaches* LADY BASILDON

VICOMTE DE NANJAC: May I have the honour of taking you down to supper, Comtesse?

LADY BASILDON (*coldly*): I never take supper, thank you, vicomte. (*The* VICOMTE DE NANJAC *is about to retire.* LADY BASILDON, *seeing this, rises at once and takes his arm*) But I will come down with you with pleasure.

VICOMTE DE NANJAC: I am so fond of eating! I am very English in all my tastes.

LADY BASILDON: You look quite English, vicomte, quite English.

They pass out. MR MONTFORD, *a perfectly groomed young dandy, approaches* MRS MARCHMONT

MR MONTFORD: Like some supper, Mrs Marchmont?

MRS MARCHMONT (*languidly*): Thank you, Mr Montford, I never touch supper. (*rises hastily and takes his arm*) But I will sit beside you, and watch you.

MR MONTFORD: I don't know that I like being watched when I am eating!

MRS MARCHMONT: Then I will watch someone else.

MR MONTFORD: I don't know that I should like that either.

MRS MARCHMONT (*severely*): Pray, Mr Montford, do not make these painful scenes of jealousy in public!

They go downstairs with the other guests, passing SIR ROBERT CHILTERN *and* MRS CHEVELEY, *who now enter*

SIR ROBERT CHILTERN: And are you going to any of our country houses before you leave England, Mrs Cheveley?

MRS CHEVELEY: Oh, no! I can't stand your English house-parties. In England people actually try to be brilliant at breakfast. That is so dreadful of them! Only dull people are brilliant at breakfast. And then the family skeleton is always reading family prayers. My stay in England really depends on you, Sir Robert. (*sits down on the sofa*)

SIR ROBERT CHILTERN (*taking a seat beside her*): Seriously?

MRS CHEVELEY: Quite seriously. I want to talk to you about a great political and financial scheme, about this Argentine Canal Company, in fact.

SIR ROBERT CHILTERN: What a tedious, practical subject for you to talk about, Mrs Cheveley!

MRS CHEVELEY: Oh, I like tedious, practical subjects. What I don't like are tedious, practical people. There is a wide difference. Besides, you are interested, I know, in international canal schemes. You were Lord Radley's secretary, weren't you, when the government bought the Suez Canal shares?

SIR ROBERT CHILTERN: Yes. But the Suez Canal was a very great and splendid undertaking. It gave us our direct route to India. It had imperial value. It was necessary that we should have control. This Argentine scheme is a commonplace Stock Exchange swindle.

MRS CHEVELEY: A speculation, Sir Robert! A brilliant, daring speculation.

SIR ROBERT CHILTERN: Believe me, Mrs Cheveley, it is a swindle. Let us call things by their proper names. It makes matters simpler. We have all the information about it at the Foreign Office. In fact, I sent out a special commission to enquire into the matter privately, and they report that the works are hardly begun, and as for the money already subscribed, no one seems to know what has become of it. The whole thing is a second Panama, and with not a quarter of the chance of success that miserable affair ever had. I hope you have not invested in it. I am sure you are far too clever to have done that.

MRS CHEVELEY: I have invested very largely in it.

SIR ROBERT CHILTERN: Who could have advised you to do such a foolish thing?

MRS CHEVELEY: Your old friend – and mine.

SIR ROBERT CHILTERN: Who?

MRS CHEVELEY: Baron Arnheim.

SIR ROBERT CHILTERN (*frowning*): Ah! yes. I remember hearing, at the time of his death, that he had been mixed up in the whole affair.

MRS CHEVELEY: It was his last romance. His last but one, to do him justice.

SIR ROBERT CHILTERN (*rising*): But you have not seen my Corots yet. They are in the music-room. Corots seem to go with music, don't they? May I show them to you?

MRS CHEVELEY (*shaking her head*): I am not in a mood tonight for silver twilights, or rose-pink dawns. I want to talk business. (*motions to him with her fan to sit down again beside her*)

SIR ROBERT CHILTERN: I fear I have no advice to give you, Mrs Cheveley, except to interest yourself in something less dangerous. The success of the canal depends, of course, on the attitude of England, and I am going to lay the report of the commissioners before the House tomorrow night.

MRS CHEVELEY: That you must not do. In your own interests, Sir Robert, to say nothing of mine, you must not do that.

SIR ROBERT CHILTERN (*looking at her in wonder*): In my own interests? My dear Mrs Cheveley, what do you mean? (*sits down beside her*)

MRS CHEVELEY: Sir Robert, I will be quite frank with you. I want you to withdraw the report that you had intended to lay before the House, on the ground that you have reasons to believe that the commissioners have been prejudiced, or misinformed, or something. Then I want you to say a few words to the effect that the government is going to reconsider the question, and that you have reason to believe that the canal, if completed, will be of great international value. You know the sort of things ministers say in cases of this kind. A few ordinary platitudes will do. In modern life nothing produces such an effect as a good platitude. It makes the whole world kin. Will you do that for me?

SIR ROBERT CHILTERN: Mrs Cheveley, you cannot be serious in making me such a proposition!

MRS CHEVELEY: I am quite serious.

SIR ROBERT CHILTERN (*coldly*): Pray allow me to believe that you are not.

MRS CHEVELEY (*speaking with great deliberation and emphasis*): Ah! but I am. And if you do what I ask you, I . . . will pay you very handsomely!

SIR ROBERT CHILTERN: Pay me!

MRS CHEVELEY: Yes.

SIR ROBERT CHILTERN: I am afraid I don't quite understand what you mean.

MRS CHEVELEY (*leaning back on the sofa and looking at him*): How very disappointing! And I have come all the way from Vienna in order that you should thoroughly understand me.

SIR ROBERT CHILTERN: I fear I don't.

MRS CHEVELEY (*in her most nonchalant manner*): My dear Sir Robert, you are a man of the world, and you have your price, I suppose. Everybody has nowadays. The drawback is that most people are so dreadfully expensive. I know I am. I hope you will be more reasonable in your terms.

SIR ROBERT CHILTERN (*rises indignantly*): If you will allow me, I will call your carriage for you. You have lived so long abroad, Mrs Cheveley, that you seem to be unable to realise that you are talking to an English gentleman.

MRS CHEVELEY (*detains him by touching his arm with her fan, and keeping it there while she is talking*): I realise that I am talking to a man who laid the foundation of his fortune by selling to a Stock Exchange speculator a cabinet secret.

SIR ROBERT CHILTERN (*biting his lip*): What do you mean?

MRS CHEVELEY (*rising and facing him*): I mean that I know the real origin of your wealth and your career, and I have got your letter, too.

SIR ROBERT CHILTERN: What letter?

MRS CHEVELEY (*contemptuously*): The letter you wrote to Baron Arnheim, when you were Lord Radley's secretary, telling the baron to buy Suez Canal shares – a letter written three days before the government announced its own purchase.

SIR ROBERT CHILTERN (*hoarsely*): It is not true.

MRS CHEVELEY: You thought that letter had been destroyed. How foolish of you! It is in my possession.

SIR ROBERT CHILTERN: The affair to which you allude was no more than a speculation. The House of Commons had not yet passed the bill; it might have been rejected.

MRS CHEVELEY: It was a swindle, Sir Robert. Let us call things by their proper names. It makes everything simpler. And now I am going to sell you that letter, and the price I ask for it is your public support of the Argentine scheme. You made your own fortune out of one canal. You must help me and my friends to make our fortunes out of another!

SIR ROBERT CHILTERN: It is infamous, what you propose – infamous!

MRS CHEVELEY: Oh, no! This is the game of life as we all have to play it, Sir Robert, sooner or later!

SIR ROBERT CHILTERN: I cannot do what you ask me.

MRS CHEVELEY: You mean you cannot help doing it. You know you are standing on the edge of a precipice. And it is not for you to make terms. It is for you to accept them. Supposing you refuse –

SIR ROBERT CHILTERN: What then?

MRS CHEVELEY: My dear Sir Robert, what then? You are ruined, that is all! Remember to what a point your puritanism in England has brought you. In the old days nobody pretended to be a bit better than his neighbours. In fact, to be a bit better than one's neighbours was considered excessively vulgar and middle-class. Nowadays, with our modern mania for morality, everyone has to pose as a paragon of purity, incorruptibility and all the other seven deadly virtues – and what is the result? You all go over like ninepins – one after the other. Not a year passes in England without somebody disappearing. Scandals used to lend charm, or at least interest, to a man – now they crush him. And yours is a very nasty scandal. You couldn't survive it. If it were known that as a young man, secretary to a great and important minister, you sold a cabinet secret for a large sum of money, and that was the origin of your wealth and career, you would be hounded out of public life, you would disappear completely. And after all, Sir Robert, why should you sacrifice your entire future rather than deal diplomatically with your enemy? For the moment I am your enemy. I admit it! And I am much stronger than you are. The big battalions are on my side. You have a splendid position, but it is your splendid position that makes you so vulnerable. You can't defend it! And I am in attack. Of course I have not talked morality to you. You must admit in fairness that I have spared you that. Years ago you did a clever, unscrupulous thing; it turned out a great success. You owe to it your fortune and position. And now you have got to pay for it. Sooner or later we have all to pay for what we do. You have to pay now. Before I leave you tonight, you have got to promise me to suppress your report, and to speak in the House in favour of this scheme.

SIR ROBERT CHILTERN: What you ask is impossible.

MRS CHEVELEY: You must make it possible. You are going to make it possible. Sir Robert, you know what your English newspapers are like. Suppose that when I leave this house I drive down to some newspaper office, and give them this scandal and the proofs of it! Think of their loathsome joy, of the delight they would have in dragging you down, of the mud and mire they would plunge you in. Think of the hypocrite with his greasy smile penning his leading article, and arranging the foulness of the public placard.

SIR ROBERT CHILTERN: Stop! You want me to withdraw the report and to make a short speech stating that I believe there are possibilities in the scheme?

MRS CHEVELEY (*sitting down on the sofa*): Those are my terms.

SIR ROBERT CHILTERN (*in a low voice*): I will give you any sum of money you want.

MRS CHEVELEY: Even you are not rich enough, Sir Robert, to buy back your past. No man is.

SIR ROBERT CHILTERN: I will not do what you ask me. I will not.

MRS CHEVELEY: You have to. If you don't . . . (*rises from the sofa*)

SIR ROBERT CHILTERN (*bewildered and unnerved*): Wait a moment! What did you propose? You said that you would give me back my letter, didn't you?

MRS CHEVELEY: Yes. That is agreed. I will be in the Ladies' Gallery tomorrow night at half-past eleven. If by that time – and you will have had heaps of opportunity – you have made an announcement to the House in the terms I wish, I shall hand you back your letter with the prettiest thanks, and the best, or at any rate the most suitable, compliment I can think of. I intend to play quite fairly with you. One should always play fairly . . . when one has the winning cards. The baron taught me that . . . amongst other things.

SIR ROBERT CHILTERN: You must let me have time to consider your proposal.

MRS CHEVELEY: No; you must settle now!

SIR ROBERT CHILTERN: Give me a week – three days!

MRS CHEVELEY: Impossible! I have got to telegraph to Vienna tonight.

SIR ROBERT CHILTERN: My God! what brought you into my life?

MRS CHEVELEY: Circumstances. (*moves towards the door*)

SIR ROBERT CHILTERN: Don't go. I consent. The report shall be withdrawn. I will arrange for a question to be put to me on the subject.

MRS CHEVELEY: Thank you. I knew we should come to an amicable agreement. I understood your nature from the first. I analysed you, though you did not adore me. And now you can get my carriage for me, Sir Robert. I see the people coming up from supper, and Englishmen always get romantic after a meal, and that bores me dreadfully. (*Exit* SIR ROBERT CHILTERN.)

Enter LADY CHILTERN, LADY MARKBY, LORD CAVERSHAM, LADY BASILDON, MRS MARCHMONT, VICOMTE DE NANJAC, MR MONTFORD

LADY MARKBY: Well, dear Mrs Cheveley, I hope you have enjoyed yourself. Sir Robert is very entertaining, is he not?

MRS CHEVELEY: Most entertaining! I have enjoyed my talk with him immensely.

LADY MARKBY: He has had a very interesting and brilliant career. And he has married a most admirable wife. Lady Chiltern is a woman of the very highest principles, I am glad to say. I am a little too old now myself, to trouble about setting a good example, but I always admire people who do. And Lady Chiltern has a very ennobling effect on life, though her dinner-parties are rather dull sometimes. But one can't have everything, can one? And now I must go, dear. Shall I call for you tomorrow?

MRS CHEVELEY: Thanks.

LADY MARKBY: We might drive in the park at five. Everything looks so fresh in the park now!

MRS CHEVELEY: Except the people!

LADY MARKBY: Perhaps the people are a little jaded. I have often observed that the season as it goes on produces a kind of softening of the brain. However, I think anything is better than high intellectual pressure. That is the most unbecoming thing there is. It makes the noses of the young girls so particularly large. And there is nothing so difficult to marry as a large nose; men don't like them. Good-night, dear! (*To* LADY CHILTERN): Good-night, Gertrude! (*goes out on* LORD CAVERSHAM'S *arm*)

MRS CHEVELEY: What a charming house you have, Lady Chiltern! I have spent a delightful evening. It has been so interesting getting to know your husband.

LADY CHILTERN: Why did you wish to meet my husband, Mrs Cheveley?

MRS CHEVELEY: Oh, I will tell you. I wanted to interest him in this Argentine Canal Scheme, of which I dare say you have heard. And I found him most susceptible – susceptible to reason, I mean. A rare thing in a man. I converted him in ten minutes. He is going to make a speech in the House tomorrow night in favour of the idea. We must go to the Ladies' Gallery and hear him! It will be a great occasion!

LADY CHILTERN: There must be some mistake. That scheme could never have my husband's support.

MRS CHEVELEY: Oh, I assure you it's all settled. I don't regret my tedious journey from Vienna now. It has been a great success. But, of course, for the next twenty-four hours the whole thing is a dead secret.

LADY CHILTERN (*gently*): A secret? Between whom?

MRS CHEVELEY (*with a flash of amusement in her eyes*): Between your husband and myself.

SIR ROBERT CHILTERN (*entering*): Your carriage is here, Mrs Cheveley!

MRS CHEVELEY: Thanks! Good-evening, Lady Chiltern! Good-night, Lord Goring! I am at Claridge's. Don't you think you might leave a card?

LORD GORING: If you wish it, Mrs Cheveley!

MRS CHEVELEY: Oh, don't be so solemn about it, or I shall be obliged to leave a card on you. In England I suppose that would hardly be considered *en règle*. Abroad, we are more civilised. Will you see me down, Sir Robert? Now that we have both the same interests at heart we shall be great friends, I hope!

Sails out on SIR ROBERT CHILTERN*'s arm.* LADY CHILTERN *goes to the top of the staircase and looks down at them as they descend. Her expression is troubled. After a little time she is joined by some of the guests, and passes with them into another reception room.*

MABEL CHILTERN: What a horrid woman!

LORD GORING: You should go to bed, Miss Mabel.

MABEL CHILTERN: Lord Goring!

LORD GORING: My father told me to go to bed an hour ago. I don't see why I shouldn't give you the same advice. I always pass on good advice. It is the only thing to do with it. It is never of any use to oneself.

MABEL CHILTERN: Lord Goring, you are always ordering me out of the room. I think it most courageous of you. Especially as I am not going to bed for hours. (*goes over to the sofa*) You can come and sit down if you like, and talk about anything in the world, except the Royal Academy, Mrs Cheveley or novels in Scotch dialect. They are not improving subjects. (*catches sight of something that is lying on the sofa half-hidden by the cushion*) What is this? Someone has dropped a diamond brooch! Quite beautiful, isn't it? (*shows it to him*) I wish it was mine, but Gertrude won't let me wear anything but pearls, and I am thoroughly sick of pearls. They make one look so plain, so good and so intellectual. I wonder whom the brooch belongs to.

LORD GORING: I wonder who dropped it.

MABEL CHILTERN: It is a beautiful brooch.

LORD GORING: It is a handsome bracelet.

MABEL CHILTERN: It isn't a bracelet. It's a brooch.

LORD GORING: It can be used as a bracelet. (*takes it from her, and, pulling out a green letter-case, puts the ornament carefully in it, and replaces the whole thing in his breast-pocket with the most perfect* sang froid)

MABEL CHILTERN: What are you doing?

LORD GORING: Miss Mabel, I am going to make a rather strange request to you.

MABEL CHILTERN (*eagerly*): Oh, pray do! I have been waiting for it all the evening.

LORD GORING (*is a little taken aback, but recovers himself*): Don't mention to anybody that I have taken charge of this brooch. Should anyone write and claim it, let me know at once.

MABEL CHILTERN: That is a strange request.

LORD GORING: Well, you see I gave this brooch to somebody once, years ago.

MABEL CHILTERN: You did?

LORD GORING: Yes.

LADY CHILTERN *enters alone. The other guests have gone*

MABEL CHILTERN: Then I shall certainly bid you good-night. Good-night, Gertrude! (*exit*)

LADY CHILTERN: Good-night, dear! (*To* LORD GORING): You saw whom Lady Markby brought here tonight?

LORD GORING: Yes. It was an unpleasant surprise. What did she come here for?

LADY CHILTERN: Apparently to try and lure Robert to uphold some fraudulent scheme in which she is interested. The Argentine canal, in fact.

LORD GORING: She has mistaken her man, hasn't she?

LADY CHILTERN: She is incapable of understanding an upright nature like my husband's!

LORD GORING: Yes. I should fancy she came to grief if she tried to get Robert into her toils. It is extraordinary what astounding mistakes clever women make.

LADY CHILTERN: I don't call women of that kind clever. I call them stupid!

LORD GORING: Same thing often. Good-night, Lady Chiltern!

LADY CHILTERN: Good-night!

Enter SIR ROBERT CHILTERN

SIR ROBERT CHILTERN: My dear Arthur, you are not going? Do stop a little!

LORD GORING: Afraid I can't, thanks. I have promised to look in at the Hartlocks. I believe they have got a mauve Hungarian band that plays mauve Hungarian music. See you soon. Goodbye! (*exit*)

SIR ROBERT CHILTERN: How beautiful you look tonight, Gertrude!

LADY CHILTERN: Robert, it is not true, is it? You are not going to lend your support to this Argentine speculation? You couldn't!

SIR ROBERT CHILTERN (*starting*): Who told you I intended to do so?

LADY CHILTERN: That woman who has just gone out, Mrs Cheveley, as she calls herself now. She seemed to taunt me with it. Robert, I know this woman. You don't. We were at school together. She was untruthful, dishonest, an evil influence on everyone whose trust or friendship she could win. I hated, I despised her. She stole things, she was a thief. She was sent away for being a thief. Why do you let her influence you?

SIR ROBERT CHILTERN: Gertrude, what you tell me may be true, but it happened many years ago. It is best forgotten! Mrs Cheveley may have changed since then. No one should be entirely judged by their past.

LADY CHILTERN (*sadly*): One's past is what one is. It is the only way by which people should be judged.

SIR ROBERT CHILTERN: That is a hard saying, Gertrude!

LADY CHILTERN: It is a true saying, Robert. And what did she mean by boasting that she had got you to lend your support, your name, to a thing I have heard you describe as the most dishonest and fraudulent scheme there has ever been in political life?

SIR ROBERT CHILTERN (*biting his lip*): I was mistaken in the view I took. We all may make mistakes.

LADY CHILTERN: But you told me yesterday that you had received the report from the commission, and that it entirely condemned the whole thing.

SIR ROBERT CHILTERN (*walking up and down*): I have reasons now to believe that the commission was prejudiced, or, at any rate, misinformed. Besides, Gertrude, public and private life are different things. They have different laws, and move on different lines.

LADY CHILTERN: They should both represent man at his highest. I see no difference between them.

SIR ROBERT CHILTERN (*stopping*): In the present case, on a matter of practical politics, I have changed my mind. That is all.

LADY CHILTERN: All!

SIR ROBERT CHILTERN (*sternly*): Yes!

LADY CHILTERN: Robert! Oh! it is horrible that I should have to ask you such a question – Robert, are you telling me the whole truth?

SIR ROBERT CHILTERN: Why do you ask me such a question?

LADY CHILTERN (*after a pause*): Why do you not answer it?

SIR ROBERT CHILTERN (*sitting down*): Gertrude, truth is a very complex thing, and politics is a very complex business. There are wheels within wheels. One may be under certain obligations to people that one must pay. Sooner or later in political life one has to compromise. Everyone does.

LADY CHILTERN: Compromise? Robert, why do you talk so differently tonight from the way I have always heard you talk? Why are you changed?

SIR ROBERT CHILTERN: I am not changed. But circumstances alter things.

LADY CHILTERN: Circumstances should never alter principles.

SIR ROBERT CHILTERN: But if I told you –

LADY CHILTERN: What?

SIR ROBERT CHILTERN: That it was necessary, vitally necessary?

LADY CHILTERN: It can never be necessary to do what is not honourable. Or if it be necessary, then what is it that I have loved! But it is not, Robert; tell me it is not. Why should it be? What gain would you get? Money? We have no need of that! And money that comes from a tainted source is a degradation. Power? But Power is nothing in itself. It is power to do good that is fine – that, and that only. What is it, then? Robert, tell me why you are going to do this dishonourable thing!

SIR ROBERT CHILTERN: Gertrude, you have no right to use that word. I told you it was a question of rational compromise. It is no more than that.

LADY CHILTERN: Robert, that is all very well for other men, for men who treat life simply as a sordid speculation; but not for you, Robert, not for you. You are different. All your life you have stood apart from others. You have never let the world soil you. To the world, as to myself, you have been an ideal always. Oh! be that ideal still. That great inheritance throw not away – that tower of ivory do not destroy. Robert, men can love what is beneath them – things unworthy, stained, dishonoured. We women worship when we love; and when we lose our worship, we lose everything. Oh! don't kill my love for you, don't kill that!

SIR ROBERT CHILTERN: Gertrude!

LADY CHILTERN: I know that there are men with horrible secrets in their lives – men who have done some shameful thing, and who in some critical moment have to pay for it, by doing some other act of shame – oh! don't tell me you are such as they are! Robert, is there in your life any secret dishonour or disgrace? Tell me, tell me at once, that –

SIR ROBERT CHILTERN: That what?

LADY CHILTERN (*speaking very slowly*): That our lives may drift apart.

SIR ROBERT CHILTERN: Drift apart?

LADY CHILTERN: That they may entirely separate. It would be better for us both.

SIR ROBERT CHILTERN: Gertrude, there is nothing in my past life that you might not know.

LADY CHILTERN: I was sure of it, Robert, I was sure of it. But why did you say those dreadful things, things so unlike your real self? Don't let us ever talk about the subject again. You will write, won't you, to Mrs Cheveley, and tell her that you cannot support this scandalous scheme of hers? If you have given her any promise you must take it back, that is all!

SIR ROBERT CHILTERN: Must I write and tell her that?

LADY CHILTERN: Surely, Robert! What else is there to do?

SIR ROBERT CHILTERN: I might see her personally. It would be better.

LADY CHILTERN: You must never see her again, Robert. She is not a woman you should ever speak to. She is not worthy to talk to a man like you. No; you must write to her at once, now, this moment, and let your letter show her that your decision is quite irrevocable!

SIR ROBERT CHILTERN: Write this moment!

LADY CHILTERN: Yes.

SIR ROBERT CHILTERN: But it is so late. It is close on twelve.

LADY CHILTERN: That makes no matter. She must know at once that she has been mistaken in you – and that you are not a man to do anything base or underhand or dishonourable. Write here, Robert. Write that you decline to support this scheme of hers, as you hold it to be a dishonest scheme. Yes – write the word dishonest. She knows what that word means. (SIR ROBERT CHILTERN *sits down and writes a letter. His wife takes it up and reads it.*) Yes; that will do. (*rings bell*) And now the envelope. (*he writes the envelope slowly. Enter* MASON) Have this letter sent at once to Claridge's Hotel. There is no answer. (*exit* MASON. LADY CHILTERN *kneels down beside her husband and puts her arms around him*) Robert, love gives one an instinct to things. I feel tonight that I have saved you from something that might have been a danger to you, from something that might have made men honour you less than they do. I don't think you realise sufficiently, Robert, that you have brought into the political life of our time a nobler atmosphere, a finer attitude towards life, a freer air of purer aims and higher ideals – I know it, and for that I love you, Robert.

SIR ROBERT CHILTERN: Oh, love me always, Gertrude, love me always!

LADY CHILTERN: I will love you always, because you will always be worthy of love. We needs must love the highest when we see it! (*kisses him and rises and goes out*)

SIR ROBERT CHILTERN *walks up and down for a moment; then sits down and buries his face in his hands. The servant enters and begins putting out the lights.* SIR ROBERT CHILTERN *looks up*

SIR ROBERT CHILTERN: Put out the lights, Mason, put out the lights!

The servant puts out the lights. The room becomes almost dark. The only light there is comes from the great chandelier that hangs over the staircase and illumines the tapestry of the Triumph of Love

END OF ACT ONE

ACT TWO

The morning-room at Sir Robert Chiltern's house. LORD GORING, *dressed in the height of fashion, is lounging in an armchair.* SIR ROBERT CHILTERN *is standing in front of the fireplace. He is evidently in a state of great mental excitement and distress. As the scene progresses he paces nervously up and down the room.*

LORD GORING: My dear Robert, it's a very awkward business, very awkward indeed. You should have told your wife the whole thing. Secrets from other people's wives are a necessary luxury in modern life. So, at least, I am always told at the club by people who are bald enough to know better. But no man should have a secret from his own wife. She invariably finds it out. Women have a wonderful instinct about things. They can discover everything except the obvious.

SIR ROBERT CHILTERN: Arthur, I couldn't tell my wife. When could I have told her? Not last night. I would have made a life-long separation between us, and I would have lost the love of the one woman in the world I worship, of the only woman who has ever stirred love within me. Last night it would have been quite impossible. She would have turned from me in horror . . . in horror and in contempt.

LORD GORING: Is Lady Chiltern as perfect as all that?

SIR ROBERT CHILTERN: Yes; my wife is as perfect as all that.

LORD GORING (*taking off his left-hand glove*): What a pity! I beg your pardon, my dear fellow, I didn't quite mean that. But if what you tell me is true, I should like to have a serious talk about life with Lady Chiltern.

SIR ROBERT CHILTERN: It would be quite useless.

LORD GORING: May I try?

SIR ROBERT CHILTERN: Yes, but nothing could make her alter her views.

LORD GORING: Well, at the worst it would simply be a psychological experiment.

SIR ROBERT CHILTERN: All such experiments are terribly dangerous.

LORD GORING: Everything is dangerous, my dear fellow. If it wasn't so, life wouldn't be worth living . . . Well, I am bound to say that I think you should have told her years ago.

SIR ROBERT CHILTERN: When? When we were engaged? Do you think she would have married me if she had known that the origin of my fortune is such as it is, the basis of my career such as it is, and that I had done a thing that I suppose most men would call shameful and dishonourable?

LORD GORING (*slowly*): Yes; most men would call it ugly names. There is no doubt of that.

SIR ROBERT CHILTERN (*bitterly*): Men who every day do something of the same kind themselves. Men who, each one of them, have worse secrets in their own lives.

LORD GORING: That is the reason they are so pleased to find out other people's secrets. It distracts public attention from their own.

SIR ROBERT CHILTERN: And, after all, whom did I wrong by what I did? No one.

LORD GORING (*looking at him steadily*): Except yourself, Robert.

SIR ROBERT CHILTERN (*after a pause*): Of course I had private information about a certain transaction contemplated by the government of the day, and I acted on it. Private information is practically the source of every large modern fortune.

LORD GORING (*tapping his boot with his cane*): And public scandal invariably the result.

SIR ROBERT CHILTERN (*pacing up and down the room*): Arthur, do you think that what I did nearly eighteen years ago should be brought up against me now? Do you think it fair that a man's whole career should be ruined for a fault done in his boyhood almost? I was twenty-two at the time, and I had the double misfortune of being well born and poor, two unforgivable things nowadays. Is it fair that the folly, the sin of one's youth, if men choose to call it a sin, should wreck a life like mine, should place me in the pillory, should shatter all that I have worked for, all that I have built up? Is it fair, Arthur?

LORD GORING: Life is never fair, Robert. And perhaps it is a good thing for most of us that it is not.

SIR ROBERT CHILTERN: Every man of ambition has to fight his century with its own weapons. What this century worships is wealth. The god of this century is wealth. To succeed one must have wealth. At all costs one must have wealth.

LORD GORING: You underrate yourself, Robert. Believe me, without wealth you could have succeeded just as well.

SIR ROBERT CHILTERN: When I was old, perhaps. When I had lost my passion for power, or could not use it. When I was tired, worn out, disappointed. I wanted my success when I was young. Youth is the time for success. I couldn't wait.

LORD GORING: Well, you certainly have had your success while you are still young. No one in our day has had such a brilliant success. Under-Secretary for Foreign Affairs at the age of forty – that's good enough for anyone, I should think.

SIR ROBERT CHILTERN: And if it is all taken away from me now? If I lose everything over a horrible scandal? If I am hounded from public life?

LORD GORING: Robert, how could you have sold yourself for money?

SIR ROBERT CHILTERN (*excitedly*): I did not sell myself for money. I bought success at a great price. That is all.

LORD GORING (*gravely*): Yes; you certainly paid a great price for it. But what first made you think of doing such a thing?

SIR ROBERT CHILTERN: Baron Arnheim.

LORD GORING: Damned scoundrel!

SIR ROBERT CHILTERN: No; he was a man of a most subtle and refined intellect. A man of culture, charm, and distinction. One of the most intellectual men I ever met.

LORD GORING: Ah! I prefer a gentlemanly fool any day. There is more to be said for stupidity than people imagine. Personally I have a great admiration for stupidity. It is a sort of fellow-feeling, I suppose. But how did he do it? Tell me the whole thing.

SIR ROBERT CHILTERN (*throws himself into an armchair by the writing-table*): One night after dinner at Lord Radley's the baron began talking about success in modern life as something that one could reduce to an absolutely definite science. With that wonderfully fascinating quiet voice of his he expounded to us the most terrible of all philosophies, the philosophy of power, preached to us the most marvellous of all gospels, the gospel of gold. I think he saw the effect he had produced on me, for some days afterwards he wrote and asked me to come and see him. He was living then in Park Lane, in the house Lord Woolcomb has now. I remember so well how, with a strange smile on his pale, curved lips, he led me through his wonderful picture gallery, showed me his tapestries, his enamels, his jewels, his carved ivories, made me wonder at the strange loveliness of the luxury in which he lived; and then told me that luxury was nothing but a background, a painted scene in a play, and that power, power over other men, power over the world, was the one thing worth having, the one supreme pleasure worth knowing, the one joy one never tired of, and that in our century only the rich possessed it.

LORD GORING (*with great deliberation*): A thoroughly shallow creed.

SIR ROBERT CHILTERN (*rising*): I didn't think so then. I don't think so now. Wealth has given me enormous power. It gave me at the very outset of my life freedom, and freedom is everything. You have never been poor, and never known what ambition is. You cannot understand what a wonderful chance the baron gave me. Such a chance as few men get.

LORD GORING: Fortunately for them, if one is to judge by results. But tell me definitely, how did the baron finally persuade you to – well, to do what you did?

SIR ROBERT CHILTERN: When I was going away he said to me that if I ever could give him any private information of real value he would make me a very rich man. I was dazed at the prospect he held out to me, and my ambition and my desire for power were at that time boundless. Six weeks later certain private documents passed through my hands.

LORD GORING (*keeping his eyes steadily fixed on the carpet*): State documents?

SIR ROBERT CHILTERN: Yes.

LORD GORING *sighs, then passes his hand across his forehead and looks up*

LORD GORING: I had no idea that you, of all men in the world, could have been so weak, Robert, as to yield to such a temptation as Baron Arnheim held out to you.

SIR ROBERT CHILTERN: Weak? Oh, I am sick of hearing that phrase. Sick of using it about others. Weak! Do you really think, Arthur, that it is weakness that yields to temptation? I tell you that there are terrible temptations that it requires strength, strength and courage, to yield to. To stake all one's life on a single moment, to risk everything on one throw, whether the stake be power or pleasure, I care not – there is no weakness in that. There is a horrible, a terrible courage. I had that courage. I sat down the same afternoon and wrote Baron Arnheim the letter this woman now holds. He made three-quarters of a million over the transaction.

LORD GORING: And you?

SIR ROBERT CHILTERN: I received from the baron a hundred and ten thousand pounds.

LORD GORING: You were worth more, Robert.

SIR ROBERT CHILTERN: No; that money gave me exactly what I wanted, power over others. I went into the House immediately.

The baron advised me in finance from time to time. Before five years I had almost trebled my fortune. Since then everything that I have touched has turned out a success. In all things connected with money I have had a luck so extraordinary that sometimes it has made me almost afraid. I remember having read somewhere, in some strange book, that when the gods wish to punish us they answer our prayers.

LORD GORING: But tell me, Robert, did you never suffer any regret for what you had done?

SIR ROBERT CHILTERN: No. I felt that I had fought the century with its own weapons, and won.

LORD GORING (*sadly*): You thought you had won.

SIR ROBERT CHILTERN: I thought so. (*after a long pause*) Arthur, do you despise me for what I have told you?

LORD GORING (*with deep feeling in his voice*): I am very sorry for you, Robert, very sorry indeed.

SIR ROBERT CHILTERN: I don't say that I suffered any remorse. I didn't. Not remorse in the ordinary, rather silly sense of the word. But I have paid conscience money many times. I had a wild hope that I might disarm destiny. The sum Baron Arnheim gave me I have distributed twice over in public charities since then.

LORD GORING (*looking up*): In public charities? Dear me! what a lot of harm you must have done, Robert!

SIR ROBERT CHILTERN: Oh, don't say that, Arthur; don't talk like that!

LORD GORING: Never mind what I say, Robert! I am always saying what I shouldn't say. In fact, I usually say what I really think. A great mistake nowadays. It makes one so liable to be understood. As regards this dreadful business, I will help you in whatever way I can. Of course you know that.

SIR ROBERT CHILTERN: Thank you, Arthur, thank you. But what is to be done? What can be done?

LORD GORING (*leaning back with his hands in his pockets*): Well, the English can't stand a man who is always saying he is in the right, but they are very fond of a man who admits that he has been in the wrong. It is one of the best things in them. However, in your case, Robert, a confession would not do. The money, if you will allow me to say so, is . . . awkward. Besides, if you did make a clean breast of the whole affair, you would never be able to talk morality again. And in England a man who can't talk morality twice a week to a large, popular, immoral audience is quite over as a serious politician. There would be nothing left for him as a profession except botany or the church. A confession would be of no use. It would ruin you.

SIR ROBERT CHILTERN: It would ruin me. Arthur, the only thing for me to do now is to fight the thing out.

LORD GORING (*rising from his chair*): I was waiting for you to say that, Robert. It is the only thing to do now. And you must begin by telling your wife the whole story.

SIR ROBERT CHILTERN: That I will not do.

LORD GORING: Robert, believe me, you are wrong.

SIR ROBERT CHILTERN: I couldn't do it. It would kill her love for me. And now about this woman, this Mrs Cheveley. How can I defend myself against her? You knew her before, Arthur, apparently.

LORD GORING: Yes.

SIR ROBERT CHILTERN: Did you know her well?

LORD GORING (*arranging his necktie*): So little that I got engaged to be married to her once, when I was staying at the Tenbys. The affair lasted for three days . . . nearly.

SIR ROBERT CHILTERN: Why was it broken off?

LORD GORING (*airily*): Oh, I forget. At least, it makes no matter. By the way, have you tried her with money? She used to be confoundedly fond of money.

SIR ROBERT CHILTERN: I offered her any sum she wanted. She refused.

LORD GORING: Then the marvellous gospel of gold breaks down sometimes. The rich can't do everything, after all.

SIR ROBERT CHILTERN: Not everything. I suppose you are right. Arthur, I feel that public disgrace is in store for me. I feel certain of it. I never knew what terror was before. I know it now. It is as if a hand of ice were laid upon one's heart. It is as if one's heart were beating itself to death in some empty hollow.

LORD GORING (*striking the table*): Robert, you must fight her. You must fight her.

SIR ROBERT CHILTERN: But how?

LORD GORING: I can't tell you how at present. I have not the smallest idea. But everyone has some weak point. There is some flaw in each one of us. (*strolls over to the fireplace and looks at himself in the glass*) My father tells me that even I have faults. Perhaps I have. I don't know.

SIR ROBERT CHILTERN: In defending myself against Mrs Cheveley, I have a right to use any weapon I can find, have I not?

LORD GORING (*still looking in the glass*): In your place I don't think I should have the smallest scruple in doing so. She is thoroughly well able to take care of herself.

SIR ROBERT CHILTERN (*sits down at the table and takes a pen in his hand*): Well, I shall send a cipher telegram to the embassy at Vienna, to enquire if there is anything known against her. There may be some secret scandal she might be afraid of.

LORD GORING (*settling his buttonhole*): Oh, I should fancy Mrs Cheveley is one of those very modern women of our time who find a new scandal as becoming as a new bonnet, and air them both in the park every afternoon at five-thirty. I am sure she adores scandals, and that the sorrow of her life at present is that she can't manage to have enough of them.

SIR ROBERT CHILTERN (*writing*): Why do you say that?

LORD GORING (*turning round*): Well, she wore far too much rouge last night, and not quite enough clothes. That is always a sign of despair in a woman.

SIR ROBERT CHILTERN (*striking a bell*): But it is worthwhile my wiring to Vienna, is it not?

LORD GORING: It is always worthwhile asking a question, though it is not always worthwhile answering one.

Enter MASON

SIR ROBERT CHILTERN: Is Mr Trafford in his room?

MASON: Yes, Sir Robert.

SIR ROBERT CHILTERN (*puts what he has written into an envelope, which he then carefully closes*): Tell him to have this sent off in cipher at once. There must not be a moment's delay.

MASON: Yes, Sir Robert.

SIR ROBERT CHILTERN: Oh! just give that back to me again.

Writes something on the envelope. MASON *then goes out with the letter*

SIR ROBERT CHILTERN: She must have had some curious hold over Baron Arnheim. I wonder what it was.

LORD GORING (*smiling*): I wonder.

SIR ROBERT CHILTERN: I will fight her to the death, as long as my wife knows nothing.

LORD GORING (*strongly*): Oh, fight in any case – in any case.

SIR ROBERT CHILTERN (*with a gesture of despair*): If my wife found out, there would be little left to fight for. Well, as soon as I hear from Vienna, I shall let you know the result. It is a chance, just a chance, but I believe in it. And as I fought the age with its own weapons, I will fight her with her weapons. It is only fair, and she looks like a woman with a past, doesn't she?

LORD GORING: Most pretty women do. But there is a fashion in pasts just as there is a fashion in frocks. Perhaps Mrs Cheveley's past is merely a slightly *décolleté* one, and they are excessively popular nowadays. Besides, my dear Robert, I should not build too high hopes on frightening Mrs Cheveley. I should not fancy Mrs Cheveley is a woman who would be easily frightened. She has survived all her creditors, and she shows wonderful presence of mind.

SIR ROBERT CHILTERN: Oh! I live on hopes now. I clutch at every chance. I feel like a man on a ship that is sinking. The water is round my feet, and the very air is bitter with storm. Hush! I hear my wife's voice.

Enter LADY CHILTERN *in walking dress*

LADY CHILTERN: Good-afternoon, Lord Goring.

LORD GORING: Good-afternoon, Lady Chiltern! Have you been in the park?

LADY CHILTERN: No; I have just come from the Woman's Liberal Association, where, by the way, Robert, your name was received with loud applause, and now I have come in to have my tea. (*To* LORD GORING): You will wait and have some tea, won't you?

LORD GORING: I'll wait for a short time, thanks.

LADY CHILTERN: I will be back in a moment. I am only going to take my hat off.

LORD GORING (*in his most earnest manner*): Oh! please don't. It is so pretty. One of the prettiest hats I ever saw. I hope the Woman's Liberal Association received it with loud applause.

LADY CHILTERN (*with a smile*): We have much more important work to do than look at each other's bonnets, Lord Goring.

LORD GORING: Really? What sort of work?

LADY CHILTERN: Oh! dull, useful, delightful things, Factory Acts, Female Inspectors, the Eight Hours Bill, the Parliamentary Franchise . . . Everything in fact, that you would find thoroughly uninteresting.

LORD GORING: And never bonnets?

LADY CHILTERN (*with mock indignation*): Never bonnets, never!

LADY CHILTERN *goes out through the door leading to her boudoir*

SIR ROBERT CHILTERN (*takes* LORD GORING'S *hand*): You have been a good friend to me, Arthur, a thoroughly good friend.

LORD GORING: I don't know that I have been able to do much for you, Robert, as yet. In fact, I have not been able to do anything for you, as far as I can see. I am thoroughly disappointed with myself.

SIR ROBERT CHILTERN: You have enabled me to tell you the truth. That is something. The truth has always stifled me.

LORD GORING: Ah! the truth is a thing I get rid of as soon as possible! Bad habit, by the way. Makes one very unpopular at the club . . . with the older members. They call it being conceited. Perhaps it is.

SIR ROBERT CHILTERN: I would to God that I had been able to tell the truth . . . to live the truth. Ah! that is the great thing in life, to live the truth. (*sighs, and goes towards the door*) I'll see you soon again, Arthur, shan't I?

LORD GORING: Certainly. Whenever you like. I'm going to look in at the Bachelors' Ball tonight, unless I find something better to do. But I'll come round tomorrow morning. If you should want me tonight by any chance, send round a note to Curzon Street.

SIR ROBERT CHILTERN: Thank you.

As he reaches the door, LADY CHILTERN *enters from her boudoir*

LADY CHILTERN: You are not going, Robert?

SIR ROBERT CHILTERN: I have some letters to write, dear.

LADY CHILTERN (*going to him*): You work too hard, Robert. You seem never to think of yourself, and you are looking so tired.

SIR ROBERT CHILTERN: It is nothing, dear, nothing. (*he kisses her and goes out*)

LADY CHILTERN (*to* LORD GORING): Do sit down. I am so glad you have called. I want to talk to you about . . . well, not about bonnets, or the Woman's Liberal Association. You take far too much interest in the first subject; and not nearly enough in the second.

LORD GORING: You want to talk to me about Mrs Cheveley?

LADY CHILTERN: Yes. You have guessed it. After you left last night I found out that what she had said was really true. Of course I made Robert write her a letter at once, withdrawing his promise.

LORD GORING: So he gave me to understand.

LADY CHILTERN: To have kept it would have been the first stain on a career that has been stainless always. Robert must be above reproach. He is not like other men. He cannot afford to do what other men do. (*she looks at* LORD GORING, *who remains silent*) Don't you agree with me? You are Robert's greatest friend. You are our greatest friend, Lord Goring. No one, except myself, knows Robert better than you do. He has no secrets from me, and I don't think he has any from you.

LORD GORING: He certainly has no secrets from me. At least I don't think so.

LADY CHILTERN: Then am I not right in my estimate of him? I know I am right. But speak to me frankly.

LORD GORING (*looking straight at her*): Quite frankly?

LADY CHILTERN: Surely. You have nothing to conceal, have you?

LORD GORING: Nothing. But, my dear Lady Chiltern, I think, if you will allow me to say so, that in practical life –

LADY CHILTERN (*smiling*): Of which you know so little, Lord Goring –

LORD GORING: Of which I know nothing by experience, though I know something by observation. I think that in practical life there is something about success, actual success, that is a little unscrupulous, something about ambition that is unscrupulous always. Once a man has set his heart and soul on getting to a certain point, if he has to climb the crag, he climbs the crag; if he has to walk in the mire –

LADY CHILTERN: Well?

LORD GORING: He walks in the mire. Of course I am only talking generally about life.

LADY CHILTERN (*gravely*): I hope so. Why do you look at me so strangely, Lord Goring?

LORD GORING: Lady Chiltern, I have sometimes thought that . . . perhaps you are a little hard in some of your views on life. I think that . . . often you don't make sufficient allowances. In every nature there are elements of weakness, or worse than weakness. Supposing, for instance, that – that any public man, my father, or Lord Merton, or Robert, say, had, years ago, written some foolish letter to someone . . .

LADY CHILTERN: What do you mean by a foolish letter?

LORD GORING: A letter gravely compromising one's position. I am only putting an imaginary case.

LADY CHILTERN: Robert is as incapable of doing a foolish thing as he is of doing a wrong thing.

LORD GORING (*after a long pause*): Nobody is incapable of doing a foolish thing. Nobody is incapable of doing a wrong thing.

LADY CHILTERN: Are you a Pessimist? What will the other dandies say? They will all have to go into mourning.

LORD GORING (*rising*): No, Lady Chiltern, I am not a Pessimist. Indeed I am not sure that I quite know what pessimism really means. All I do know is that life cannot be understood without much charity, cannot be lived without much charity. It is love, and not German philosophy, that is the true explanation of this world, whatever may be the explanation of the next. And if you are ever in trouble, Lady Chiltern, trust me absolutely, and I will help you in every way I can. If you ever want me, come to me for my assistance, and you shall have it. Come at once to me.

LADY CHILTERN (*looking at him in surprise*): Lord Goring, you are talking quite seriously. I don't think I ever heard you talk seriously before.

LORD GORING (*laughing*): You must excuse me, Lady Chiltern. It won't occur again, if I can help it.

LADY CHILTERN: But I like you to be serious.

Enter MABEL CHILTERN, *in the most ravishing frock*

MABEL CHILTERN: Dear Gertrude, don't say such a dreadful thing to Lord Goring. Seriousness would be very unbecoming to him. Good-afternoon, Lord Goring! Pray be as trivial as you can.

LORD GORING: I should like to, Miss Mabel, but I am afraid I am . . . a little out of practice this morning; and, besides, I have to be going now.

MABEL CHILTERN: Just when I have come in! What dreadful manners you have! I am sure you were very badly brought up.

LORD GORING: I was.

MABEL CHILTERN: I wish I had brought you up!

LORD GORING: I am so sorry you didn't.

MABEL CHILTERN: It is too late now, I suppose?

LORD GORING (*smiling*): I am not so sure.

MABEL CHILTERN: Will you ride tomorrow morning?

LORD GORING: Yes, at ten.

MABEL CHILTERN: Don't forget.

LORD GORING: Of course I shan't. By the way, Lady Chiltern, there is no list of your guests in the *Morning Post* of today. It has apparently been crowded out by the County Council, or the Lambeth Conference, or something equally boring. Could you let me have a list? I have a particular reason for asking you.

LADY CHILTERN: I am sure Mr Trafford will be able to give you one.

LORD GORING: Thanks, so much.

MABEL CHILTERN: Tommy is the most useful person in London.

LORD GORING (*turning to her*): And who is the most ornamental?

MABEL CHILTERN (*triumphantly*): I am.

LORD GORING: How clever of you to guess it! (*takes up his hat and cane*) Goodbye, Lady Chiltern! You will remember what I said to you, won't you?

LADY CHILTERN: Yes; but I don't know why you said it to me.

LORD GORING: I hardly know myself. Goodbye, Miss Mabel!

MABEL CHILTERN (*with a little moue of disappointment*): I wish you were not going. I have had four wonderful adventures this morning, four and a half, in fact. You might stop and listen to some of them.

LORD GORING: How very selfish of you to have four and a half! There won't be any left for me.

MABEL CHILTERN: I don't want you to have any. They would not be good for you.

LORD GORING: That is the first unkind thing you have ever said to me. How charmingly you said it! Ten tomorrow.

MABEL CHILTERN: Sharp.

LORD GORING: Quite sharp. But don't bring Mr Trafford.

MABEL CHILTERN (*with a little toss of the head*): Of course I shan't bring Tommy Trafford. Tommy Trafford is in great disgrace.

LORD GORING: I am delighted to hear it. (*bows and goes out*)

MABEL CHILTERN: Gertrude, I wish you would speak to Tommy Trafford.

LADY CHILTERN: What has poor Mr Trafford done this time? Robert says he is the best secretary he has ever had.

MABEL CHILTERN: Well, Tommy has proposed to me again. Tommy really does nothing but propose to me. He proposed to me last night in the music-room, when I was quite unprotected as there was an elaborate trio going on. I didn't dare to make the smallest repartee, I need hardly tell you. If I had, it would have stopped the music at once. Musical people are so absurdly unreasonable. They always want one to be perfectly dumb at the very moment when one is longing to be absolutely deaf. Then he proposed to me in broad daylight this morning, in front of that dreadful statue of Achilles. Really, the things that go on in front of that work of art are quite appalling. The police should interfere. At luncheon I saw by the glare in his eye that he was going to propose again, and I just managed to check him in time by assuring him that I was a bimetallist. Fortunately I don't know what bimetallism means. And I don't believe anybody else does either. But the observation crushed Tommy for ten minutes. He looked quite shocked. And then Tommy is so annoying in the way he proposes. If he proposed at the top of his voice, I should not mind so much. That might produce some effect on the public. But he does it in a horrid confidential way. When Tommy wants to be romantic he talks to one just like a doctor. I am very fond of Tommy, but his methods of proposing are quite out of date. I wish, Gertrude, you would speak to him, and tell him that once a week is quite often enough to propose to anyone, and that it should always be done in a manner that attracts some attention.

LADY CHILTERN: Dear Mabel, don't talk like that. Besides, Robert thinks very highly of Mr Trafford. He believes he has a brilliant future before him.

MABEL CHILTERN: Oh! I wouldn't marry a man with a future before him for anything under the sun.

LADY CHILTERN: Mabel!

MABEL CHILTERN: I know, dear. You married a man with a future, didn't you? But then Robert was a genius, and you have a noble, self-sacrificing character. You can stand geniuses. I have no character at all, and Robert is the only genius I could ever bear. As a rule, I think they are quite impossible. Geniuses talk so much, don't they? Such a bad habit! And they are always thinking about themselves, when I want them to be thinking about me. I must go round now and rehearse at Lady Basildon's. You remember, we are having tableaux, don't you? The Triumph of something, I don't know what! I hope it will be triumph of me. Only triumph I am really interested in at present. (*kisses* LADY CHILTERN *and goes out; then comes running back*) Oh, Gertrude, do you know who is coming to see you? That dreadful Mrs Cheveley, in a most lovely gown. Did you ask her?

LADY CHILTERN (*rising*): Mrs Cheveley! Coming to see me? Impossible!

MABEL CHILTERN: I assure you she is coming upstairs as large as life and not nearly so natural.

LADY CHILTERN: You need not wait, Mabel. Remember, Lady Basildon is expecting you.

MABEL CHILTERN: Oh! I must shake hands with Lady Markby. She is delightful. I love being scolded by her.

Enter MASON

MASON: Lady Markby. Mrs Cheveley.

Enter LADY MARKBY *and* MRS CHEVELEY

LADY CHILTERN (*advancing to meet them*): Dear Lady Markby, how nice of you to come and see me! (*shakes hands with her, and bows somewhat distantly to* MRS CHEVELEY) Won't you sit down, Mrs Cheveley?

MRS CHEVELEY: Thanks. Isn't that Miss Chiltern? I should like so much to know her.

LADY CHILTERN: Mabel, Mrs Cheveley wishes to know you. (MABEL CHILTERN *gives a little nod*)

MRS CHEVELEY (*sitting down*): I thought your frock so charming last night, Miss Chiltern. So simple and . . . suitable.

MABEL CHILTERN: Really? I must tell my dressmaker. It will be such a surprise to her. Goodbye, Lady Markby!

LADY MARKBY: Going already?

MABEL CHILTERN: I am so sorry but I am obliged to. I am just off to rehearsal. I have got to stand on my head in some tableaux.

LADY MARKBY: On your head, child? Oh! I hope not. I believe it is most unhealthy. (*takes a seat on the sofa next to* LADY CHILTERN)

MABEL CHILTERN: But it is for an excellent charity in aid of the Undeserving, the only people I am really interested in. I am the secretary, and Tommy Trafford is treasurer.

MRS CHEVELEY: And what is Lord Goring?

MABEL CHILTERN: Oh! Lord Goring is president.

MRS CHEVELEY: The post should suit him admirably, unless he has deteriorated since I knew him first.

LADY MARKBY (*reflecting*): You are remarkably modern, Mabel. A little too modern, perhaps. Nothing is so dangerous as being too modern. One is apt to grow old-fashioned quite suddenly. I have known many instances of it.

MABEL CHILTERN: What a dreadful prospect!

LADY MARKBY: Ah! my dear, you need not be nervous. You will always be as pretty as possible. That is the best fashion there is, and the only fashion that England succeeds in setting.

MABEL CHILTERN (*with a curtsey*): Thank you so much, Lady Markby, for England . . . and myself. (*goes out*)

LADY MARKBY (*turning to* LADY CHILTERN): Dear Gertrude, we just called to know if Mrs Cheveley's diamond brooch has been found.

LADY CHILTERN: Here?

MRS CHEVELEY: Yes. I missed it when I got back to Claridge's, and I thought I might possibly have dropped it here.

LADY CHILTERN: I have heard nothing about it. But I will send for the butler and ask. (*touches the bell*)

MRS CHEVELEY: Oh, pray don't trouble, Lady Chiltern. I dare say I lost it at the opera, before we came on here.

LADY MARKBY: Ah yes, I suppose it must have been at the opera. The fact is, we all scramble and jostle so much nowadays that I wonder we have anything at all left on us at the end of an evening. I know myself that, when I am coming back from the drawing room, I always feel as if I hadn't a shred on me, except a small shred of decent reputation, just enough to prevent the lower classes making painful observations through the windows of the carriage. The fact is that our society is terribly over-populated. Really, someone should arrange a proper scheme of assisted emigration. It would do a great deal of good.

MRS CHEVELEY: I quite agree with you, Lady Markby. It is nearly six years since I have been in London for the season, and I must say society has become dreadfully mixed. One sees the oddest people everywhere.

LADY MARKBY: That is quite true, dear. But one needn't know them. I'm sure I don't know half the people who come to my house. Indeed, from all I hear, I shouldn't like to.

Enter MASON

LADY CHILTERN: What sort of a brooch was it that you lost, Mrs Cheveley?

MRS CHEVELEY: A diamond snake-brooch with a ruby, a rather large ruby.

LADY MARKBY: I thought you said there was a sapphire on the head, dear?

MRS CHEVELEY (*smiling*): No, Lady Markby – a ruby.

LADY MARKBY (*nodding her head*): And very becoming, I am quite sure.

LADY CHILTERN: Has a ruby and diamond brooch been found in any of the rooms this morning, Mason?

MASON: No, my lady.

MRS CHEVELEY: It really is of no consequence, Lady Chiltern. I am so sorry to have put you to any inconvenience.

LADY CHILTERN (*coldly*): Oh, it has been no inconvenience. That will do, Mason. You can bring tea. (*Exit* MASON.)

LADY MARKBY: Well, I must say it is most annoying to lose anything. I remember once at Bath, years ago, losing in the Pump Room an exceedingly handsome cameo bracelet that Sir John had given me. I don't think he has ever given me anything since, I am sorry to say. He has sadly degenerated. Really, this horrid House of Commons quite ruins our husbands for us. I think the Lower House by far the greatest blow to a happy married life that there has been since that terrible thing called the Higher Education of Women was invented.

LADY CHILTERN: Ah! it is heresy to say that in this house, Lady Markby. Robert is a great champion of the Higher Education of Woman, and so, I am afraid, am I.

MRS CHEVELEY: The higher education of men is what I should like to see. Men need it so sadly.

LADY MARKBY: They do, dear. But I am afraid such a scheme would be quite unpractical. I don't think man has much capacity for development. He has got as far as he can, and that is not far, is it? With regard to women, well, dear Gertrude, you belong to the younger generation, and I am sure it is all right if you approve of it. In my time, of course, we were taught not to understand anything. That was the old system, and wonderfully interesting it was. I assure you that the amount of things I and my poor dear sister were taught not to understand was quite extraordinary. But modern women understand everything, I am told.

MRS CHEVELEY: Except their husbands. That is the one thing the modern woman never understands.

LADY MARKBY: And a very good thing too, dear, I dare say. It might break up many a happy home if they did. Not yours, I need hardly say, Gertrude. You have married a pattern husband. I wish I could say as much for myself. But since Sir John has taken to attending the debates regularly, which he never used to do in the good old days, his language has become quite impossible. He always seems to think that he is addressing the House, and consequently whenever he discusses the state of the agricultural labourer, or the Welsh church, or something quite improper of that kind, I am obliged to send all the servants out of the room. It is not pleasant to see one's own butler, who has been with one for twenty-three years, actually blushing at the sideboard, and the footmen making contortions in corners like persons in circuses. I assure you my life will be quite ruined unless they send John at once to the Upper House. He won't take any interest in politics then, will he? The House of Lords is so sensible. An assembly of gentlemen. But in his present state, Sir John is really a great trial. Why, this morning before breakfast was half over, he stood up on the hearth-rug, put his hands in his pockets, and appealed to the country at the top of his voice. I left the table as soon as I had had my second cup of tea, I need hardly say. But his violent language could be heard all over the house! I trust, Gertrude, that Sir Robert is not like that?

LADY CHILTERN: But I am very much interested in politics, Lady Markby. I love to hear Robert talk about them.

LADY MARKBY: Well, I hope he is not as devoted to Blue Books as Sir John is. I don't think they can be quite improving reading for anyone.

MRS CHEVELEY (*languidly*): I have never read a Blue Book. I prefer books . . . in yellow covers.

LADY MARKBY (*genially unconscious*): Yellow is a gayer colour, is it not? I used to wear yellow a good deal in my early days, and would do so now if Sir John was not so painfully personal in his observations, and a man on the question of dress is always ridiculous, is he not?

MRS CHEVELEY: Oh, no! I think men are the only authorities on dress.

LADY MARKBY: Really? One wouldn't say so from the sort of hats they wear, would one?

THE BUTLER *enters, followed by* THE FOOTMAN. *Tea is set on a small table close to* LADY CHILTERN

LADY CHILTERN: May I give you some tea, Mrs Cheveley.

MRS CHEVELEY: Thanks. (THE BUTLER *hands* MRS CHEVELEY *a cup of tea on a salver*)

LADY CHILTERN: Some tea, Lady Markby?

LADY MARKBY: No thanks, dear. (THE SERVANTS *go out*) The fact is, I have promised to go round for ten minutes to see poor Lady Brancaster, who is in very great trouble. Her daughter, quite a well-brought-up girl, too, has actually become engaged to be married to a curate in Shropshire. It is very sad, very sad indeed. I can't understand this modern mania for curates. In my time we girls saw them, of course, running about the place like rabbits. But we never took any notice of them, I need hardly say. But I am told that nowadays country society is quite honeycombed with them. I think it most irreligious. And then the eldest son has quarrelled with his father, and it is said that when they meet at the club Lord Brancaster always hides himself behind the money article in *The Times.* However, I believe that is quite a common occurrence nowadays and that they have to take in extra copies of *The Times* at all the clubs in St James's Street, there are so many sons who won't have anything to do with their fathers, and so many fathers who won't speak to their sons. I think, myself, it is very much to be regretted.

MRS CHEVELEY: So do I. Fathers have so much to learn from their sons nowadays.

LADY MARKBY: Really, dear? What?

MRS CHEVELEY: The art of living. The only really fine art we have produced in modern times.

LADY MARKBY (*shaking her head*): Ah! I am afraid Lord Brancaster knew a good deal about that. More than his poor wife ever did. (*Turning to* LADY CHILTERN) You know Lady Brancaster, don't you, dear?

LADY CHILTERN: Just slightly. She was staying at Langton last autumn, when we were there.

LADY MARKBY: Well, like all stout women, she looks the very picture of happiness, as no doubt you noticed. But there are many tragedies in her family, besides this affair of the curate. Her own sister, Mrs Jekyll, had a most unhappy life; through no fault of her own, I am sorry to say. She ultimately was so broken-hearted that she went into a convent, or on to the operatic stage, I forget which. No; I think it was decorative art-needlework she took up. I know she had lost all sense of pleasure in life. (*Rising*) And now, Gertrude, if you will allow me, I shall leave Mrs Cheveley in your charge and call back for her in a quarter of an hour. Or perhaps, dear Mrs Cheveley, you wouldn't mind waiting in the carriage while I am with Lady Brancaster. As I intend it to be a visit of condolence, I shan't stay long.

MRS CHEVELEY (*rising*): I don't mind waiting in the carriage at all, provided there is somebody to look at one.

LADY MARKBY: Well, I hear the curate is always prowling about the house.

MRS CHEVELEY: I am afraid I am not fond of girl friends.

LADY CHILTERN (*rising*): Oh, I hope Mrs Cheveley will stay here a little. I should like to have a few minutes' conversation with her.

MRS CHEVELEY: How very kind of you, Lady Chiltern! Believe me, nothing would give me greater pleasure.

LADY MARKBY: Ah! no doubt you both have many pleasant reminiscences of your schooldays to talk over together. Goodbye, dear Gertrude! Shall I see you at Lady Bonar's tonight? She has discovered a wonderful new genius. He does . . . nothing at all, I believe. That is a great comfort, is it not?

LADY CHILTERN: Robert and I are dining at home by ourselves tonight, and I don't think I shall go anywhere afterwards. Robert, of course, will have to be in the House. But there is nothing interesting on.

LADY MARKBY: Dining at home by yourselves? Is that quite prudent? Ah, I forgot, your husband is an exception. Mine is the general rule, and nothing ages a woman so rapidly as having married the general rule.

Exit LADY MARKBY

MRS CHEVELEY: Wonderful woman, Lady Markby, isn't she? Talks more and says less than anybody I ever met. She is made to be a public speaker. Much more so than her husband, though he is a typical Englishman, always dull and usually violent.

LADY CHILTERN (*makes no answer, but remains standing. There is a pause. Then the eyes of the two women meet.* LADY CHILTERN *looks stern and pale.* MRS CHEVELEY *seems rather amused*): Mrs Cheveley, I think it is right to tell you quite frankly that, had I known who you really were, I should not have invited you to my house last night.

MRS CHEVELEY (*with an impertinent smile*): Really?

LADY CHILTERN: I could not have done so.

MRS CHEVELEY: I see that after all these years you have not changed a bit, Gertrude.

LADY CHILTERN: I never change.

MRS CHEVELEY (*elevating her eyebrows*): Then life has taught you nothing?

LADY CHILTERN: It has taught me that a person who has once been guilty of a dishonest and dishonourable action may be guilty of it a second time, and should be shunned.

MRS CHEVELEY: Would you apply that rule to everyone?

LADY CHILTERN: Yes, to everyone, without exception.

MRS CHEVELEY: Then I am sorry for you, Gertrude, very sorry for you.

LADY CHILTERN: You see now, I am sure, that for many reasons any further acquaintance between us during your stay in London is quite impossible?

MRS CHEVELEY (*leaning back in her chair*): Do you know, Gertrude, I don't mind your talking morality a bit. Morality is simply the attitude we adopt towards people whom we personally dislike. You dislike me. I am quite aware of that. And I have always detested you. And yet I have come here to do you a service.

LADY CHILTERN (*contemptuously*): Like the service you wished to render my husband last night, I suppose. Thank heaven, I saved him from that.

MRS CHEVELEY (*starting to her feet*): It was you who made him write that insolent letter to me? It was you who made him break his promise?

LADY CHILTERN: Yes.

MRS CHEVELEY: Then you must make him keep it. I give you till tomorrow morning – no more. If by that time your husband does not solemnly bind himself to help me in this great scheme in which I am interested –

LADY CHILTERN: This fraudulent speculation –

MRS CHEVELEY: Call it what you choose. I hold your husband in the hollow of my hand, and if you are wise you will make him do what I tell him.

LADY CHILTERN (*rising and going towards her*): You are impertinent. What has my husband to do with you? With a woman like you?

MRS CHEVELEY (*with a bitter laugh*): In this world like meets with like. It is because your husband is himself fraudulent and dishonest that we pair so well together. Between you and him there are chasms. He and I are closer than friends. We are enemies linked together. The same sin binds us.

LADY CHILTERN: How dare you class my husband with yourself? How dare you threaten him or me? Leave my house. You are unfit to enter it.

SIR ROBERT CHILTERN *enters from behind. He hears his wife's last words, and sees to whom they are addressed. He grows deadly pale.*

MRS CHEVELEY: Your house! A house bought with the price of dishonour. A house, everything in which has been paid for by fraud. (*turns round and sees* SIR ROBERT CHILTERN) Ask him what the origin of his fortune is! Get him to tell you how he sold to a stockbroker a cabinet secret. Learn from him to what you owe your position.

LADY CHILTERN: It is not true! Robert! It is not true!

MRS CHEVELEY (*pointing at him with outstretched finger*): Look at him! Can he deny it? Does he dare to?

SIR ROBERT CHILTERN: Go! Go at once. You have done your worst now.

MRS CHEVELEY: My worst? I have not yet finished with you, with either of you. I give you both till tomorrow at noon. If by then you don't do what I bid you to do, the whole world shall know the origin of Robert Chiltern.

SIR ROBERT CHILTERN *strikes the bell. Enter* MASON

SIR ROBERT CHILTERN: Show Mrs Cleveley out.

MRS CHEVELEY *starts; then bows with somewhat exaggerated politeness to* LADY CHILTERN, *who makes no sign of response. As she passes by* SIR ROBERT CHILTERN, *who is standing close to the door, she pauses for a moment and looks him straight in the face. She then goes out, followed by the servant, who closes the door after him. The husband*

and wife are left alone. LADY CHILTERN *stands like someone in a dreadful dream. Then she turns round and looks at her husband. She looks at him with strange eyes, as though she was seeing him for the first time.*

LADY CHILTERN: You sold a cabinet secret for money! You began your life with fraud! You built up your career on dishonour! Oh, tell me it is not true! Lie to me! Lie to me! Tell me it is not true.

SIR ROBERT CHILTERN: What this woman said is quite true. But, Gertrude, listen to me. You don't realise how I was tempted. Let me tell you the whole thing. (*goes towards her*)

LADY CHILTERN: Don't come near me. Don't touch me. I feel as if you had soiled me for ever. Oh! what a mask you have been wearing all these years! A horrible painted mask! You sold yourself for money. Oh! a common thief were better. You put yourself up for sale to the highest bidder! You were bought in the market. You lied to the whole world. And yet you will not lie to me.

SIR ROBERT CHILTERN (*rushing towards her*): Gertrude! Gertrude!

LADY CHILTERN (*thrusting him back with outstretched hands*): No, don't speak! Say nothing! Your voice wakes terrible memories – memories of things that made me love you – memories of words that made me love you – memories that now are horrible to me. And how I worshipped you! You were to me something apart from common life, a thing pure, noble, honest, without stain. The world seemed to me finer because you were in it, and goodness more real because you lived. And now – oh, when I think that I made of a man like you my ideal! the ideal of my life!

SIR ROBERT CHILTERN: There was your mistake. There was your error. The error all women commit. Why can't you women love us, faults and all? Why do you place us on monstrous pedestals? We have all feet of clay, women as well as men; but when we men love women, we love them knowing their weaknesses, their follies, their imperfections, love them all the more, it may be, for that reason. It is not the perfect, but the imperfect, who have need of love. It is when we are wounded by our own hands, or by the hands of others, that love should come to cure us – else what use is love at all? All sins, except a sin against itself, love should forgive. All lives, save loveless lives, true love should pardon. A man's love is like that. It is wider, larger, more human than a woman's. Women think that they are making ideals of men. What they are making of us are false idols merely. You made your false idol of me, and I had not the courage to come down, show you my wounds, tell you my weaknesses. I was afraid that I might lose your love, as I have lost it now. And so, last night you ruined my life for me – yes, ruined it! What this woman asked of me was nothing compared to what she offered to me. She offered security, peace, stability. The sin of my youth, that I had thought was buried, rose up in front of me, hideous, horrible, with its hands at my throat. I could have killed it for ever, sent it back into its tomb, destroyed its record, burned the one witness against me. You prevented me. No one but you, you know it. And now what is there before me but public disgrace, ruin, terrible shame, the mockery of the world, a lonely dishonoured life – a lonely dishonoured death, it may be, someday? Let women make no more ideals of men! let them not put them on altars and bow before them, or they may ruin other lives as completely as you – you whom I have so wildly loved – have ruined mine!

He passes from the room. LADY CHILTERN *rushes towards him, but the door is closed when she reaches it. Pale with anguish, bewildered, helpless, she sways like a plant in the water. Her hands, outstretched, seem to tremble in the air like blossoms in the wind. Then she flings herself down beside a sofa and buries her face. Her sobs are like the sobs of a child.*

END OF ACT TWO

ACT THREE

The library in Lord Goring's house. An Adam room. On the right is the door leading into the hall. On the left, the door of the smoking-room. A pair of folding doors at the back open into the drawing-room. The fire is lit. PHIPPS, *the butler, is arranging some newspapers on the writing-table. The distinction of Phipps is his impassivity. He has been termed by enthusiasts the Ideal Butler. The Sphinx is not so incommunicable. He is a mask with a manner. Of his intellectual or emotional life, history knows nothing. He represents the dominance of form.*

Enter LORD GORING *in evening dress with a buttonhole. He is wearing a silk hat and Inverness cape. White-gloved, he carries a Louis-Seize cane. His are all the delicate fopperies of fashion. One sees that he stands in immediate relation to modern life, makes it indeed, and so masters it. He is the first well-dressed philosopher in the history of thought.*

LORD GORING: Got my second buttonhole for me, Phipps?

PHIPPS: Yes, my lord. (*takes his hat, cane and cape, and presents new buttonhole on salver*)

LORD GORING: Rather distinguished thing, Phipps. I am the only person of the smallest importance in London at present who wears a buttonhole.

PHIPPS: Yes, my lord. I have observed that.

LORD GORING (*taking out old buttonhole*): You see, Phipps, fashion is what one wears oneself. What is unfashionable is what other people wear.

PHIPPS: Yes, my lord.

LORD GORING: Just as vulgarity is simply the conduct of other people.

PHIPPS: Yes, my lord.

LORD GORING (*putting in new buttonhole*): And falsehoods the truths of other people.

PHIPPS: Yes, my lord.

LORD GORING: Other people are quite dreadful. The only possible society is oneself.

PHIPPS: Yes, my lord.

LORD GORING: To love oneself is the beginning of a lifelong romance, Phipps.

PHIPPS: Yes, my lord.

LORD GORING (*looking at himself in the glass*): Don't think I quite like this buttonhole, Phipps. Makes me look a little too old. Makes me almost in the prime of life, eh, Phipps?

PHIPPS: I don't observe any alteration in your lordship's appearance.

LORD GORING: You don't, Phipps?

PHIPPS: No, my lord.

LORD GORING: I am not quite sure. For the future a more trivial buttonhole, Phipps, on Thursday evenings.

PHIPPS: I will speak to the florist, my lord. She has had a loss in her family lately, which perhaps accounts for the lack of trivality your lordship complains of in the buttonhole.

LORD GORING: Extraordinary thing about the lower classes in England – they are always losing their relations.

PHIPPS: Yes, my lord! They are extremely fortunate in that respect.

LORD GORING (*turns round and looks at him.* PHIPPS *remains impassive*): Hum! Any letters, Phipps?

PHIPPS: Three, my lord. (*hands letters on a salver*)

LORD GORING (*takes letters*): Want my cab round in twenty minutes.

PHIPPS: Yes, my lord. (*goes towards door*)

LORD GORING (*holds up letter in pink envelope*): Ahem, Phipps, when did this letter arrive?

PHIPPS: It was brought by hand just after your lordship went to the club.

LORD GORING: That will do. (*Exit* PHIPPS) Lady Chiltern's handwriting on Lady Chiltern's pink notepaper. That is rather curious. I thought Robert was to write. Wonder what Lady Chiltern has got to say to me? (*sits at bureau, opens letter and reads it*) 'I want you. I trust you. I am coming to you. Gertrude.' (*puts down the letter with a puzzled look; then takes it up, and reads it again slowly*) 'I want you. I trust you. I am coming to you.' So she has found out everything! Poor woman! Poor woman! (*pulls out watch and looks at it*) But what an hour to call! Ten o'clock! I shall have to give up going to the Berkshires. However, it is always nice to be expected, and not to arrive. I am not expected at the Bachelors', so I shall certainly go there. Well, I will make her stand by her husband. That is the only thing for any woman to do. It is the growth of the moral sense in women that makes marriage such a hopeless, one-sided institution. Ten o'clock.

She should be here soon. I must tell Phipps I am not in to anyone else. (*goes towards bell*)

Enter PHIPPS

PHIPPS: Lord Caversham.

LORD GORING: Oh, why will parents always appear at the wrong time? Some extraordinary mistake in nature, I suppose. (*enter* LORD CAVERSHAM) Delighted to see you, my dear father. (*goes to meet him*)

LORD CAVERSHAM: Take my cloak off.

LORD GORING: Is it worthwhile, father?

LORD CAVERSHAM: Of course it is worthwhile, sir. Which is the most comfortable chair?

LORD GORING: This one, father. It is the chair I use myself, when I have visitors.

LORD CAVERSHAM: Thank ye. No draught, I hope, in this room?

LORD GORING: No, father.

LORD CAVERSHAM (*sitting down*): Glad to hear it. Can't stand draughts. No draughts at home.

LORD GORING: Good many breezes, father.

LORD CAVERSHAM: Eh? Eh? Don't understand what you mean. Want to have a serious conversation with you, sir.

LORD GORING: My dear father! At this hour?

LORD CAVERSHAM: Well, sir, it is only ten o'clock. What is your objection to the hour? I think the hour is an admirable hour!

LORD GORING: Well, the fact is, father, this is not my day for talking seriously. I am very sorry, but it is not my day.

LORD CAVERSHAM: What do you mean, sir?

LORD GORING: During the season, father, I only talk seriously on the first Tuesday in every month, from four to seven.

LORD CAVERSHAM: Well, make it Tuesday, sir, make it Tuesday.

LORD GORING: But it is after seven, father, and my doctor says I must not have any serious conversation after seven. It makes me talk in my sleep.

LORD CAVERSHAM: Talk in your sleep, sir? What does that matter? You are not married.

LORD GORING: No, father, I am not married.

LORD CAVERSHAM: Hum! That is what I have come to talk to you about, sir. You have got to get married, and at once. Why, when I was your age, sir, I had been an inconsolable widower for three months and was already paying my addresses to your admirable mother. Damme, sir, it is your duty to get married. You can't be always living for pleasure. Every man of position is married nowadays. Bachelors are not fashionable any more. They are a damaged lot. Too much is known about them. You must get a wife, sir. Look where your friend Robert Chiltern has got to by probity, hard work and a sensible marriage with a good woman. Why don't you imitate him, sir? Why don't you take him for your model?

LORD GORING: I think I shall, father.

LORD CAVERSHAM: I wish you would, sir. Then I should be happy. At present I make your mother's life miserable on your account. You are heartless, sir, quite heartless.

LORD GORING: I hope not, father.

LORD CAVERSHAM: And it is high time for you to get married. You are thirty-four years of age, sir.

LORD GORING: Yes, father, but I only admit to thirty-two – thirty-one and a half when I have a really good buttonhole. This buttonhole is not . . . trivial enough.

LORD CAVERSHAM: I tell you you are thirty-four, sir. And there is a draught in your room, besides, which makes your conduct worse. Why did you tell me there was no draught, sir? I feel a draught, sir, I feel it distinctly.

LORD GORING: So do I, father. It is a dreadful draught. I will come and see you tomorrow, father. We can talk over anything you like. Let me help you on with your cloak, father.

LORD CAVERSHAM: No, sir; I have called this evening for a definite purpose, and I am going to see it through at all costs to my health or yours. Put down my cloak, sir.

LORD GORING: Certainly, father. But let us go into another room. (*rings bell*) There is a dreadful draught here. (*Enter* PHIPPS) Phipps, is there a good fire in the smoking-room?

PHIPPS: Yes, my lord.

LORD GORING: Come in there, father. Your sneezes are quite heartrending.

LORD CAVERSHAM: Well, sir, I suppose I have a right to sneeze when I choose?

LORD GORING (*apologetically*): Quite so, father. I was merely expressing sympathy.

LORD CAVERSHAM: Oh, damn sympathy. There is a great deal too much of that sort of thing going on nowadays.

LORD GORING: I quite agree with you, father. If there was less sympathy in the world there would be less trouble in the world.

LORD CAVERSHAM (*going towards the smoking-room*): That is a paradox, sir. I hate paradoxes.

LORD GORING: So do I, father. Everybody one meets is a paradox nowadays. It is a great bore. It makes society so obvious.

LORD CAVERSHAM (*turning round, and looking at his son beneath his bushy eyebrows*): Do you always really understand what you say, sir?

LORD GORING (*after some hesitation*): Yes, father, if I listen attentively.

LORD CAVERSHAM (*indignantly*): If you listen attentively! . . . Conceited young puppy!

Goes out grumbling into the smoking-room. PHIPPS *enters*

LORD GORING: Phipps, there is a lady coming to see me this evening on particular business. Show her into the drawing-room when she arrives. You understand?

PHIPPS: Yes, my lord.

LORD GORING: It is a matter of the gravest importance, Phipps.

PHIPPS: I understand, my lord.

LORD GORING: No one else is to be admitted, under any circumstances.

PHIPPS: I understand, my lord. (*Bell rings*)

LORD GORING: Ah! that is probably the lady. I shall see her myself.

Just as he is going towards the door LORD CAVERSHAM *enters from the smoking-room*

LORD CAVERSHAM: Well, sir? am I to wait attendance on you?

LORD GORING (*considerably perplexed*): In a moment, father. Do excuse me. (LORD CAVERSHAM *goes back*) Well, remember my instructions, Phipps – into that room.

PHIPPS: Yes, my lord.

LORD GORING *goes into the smoking-room*

HAROLD, *the footman, shows* MRS CHEVELEY *in. Lamia-like, she is in green and silver. She has a cloak of black satin, lined with dead rose-leaf silk.*

HAROLD: What name, madam?

MRS CHEVELEY (*to* PHIPPS, *who advances towards her*): Is Lord Goring not here? I was told he was at home?

PHIPPS: His lordship is engaged at present with Lord Caversham, madam. (*turns a cold, glassy eye on* HAROLD, *who at once retires*)

MRS CHEVELEY (*to herself*): How very filial!

PHIPPS: His lordship told me to ask you, madam, to be kind enough to wait in the drawing-room for him. His lordship will come to you there.

MRS CHEVELEY (*with a look of surprise*): Lord Goring expects me?

PHIPPS: Yes, madam.

MRS CHEVELEY: Are you quite sure?

PHIPPS: His lordship told me that if a lady called I was to ask her to wait in the drawing-room. (*goes to the door of the drawing-room and opens it*) His lordship's directions on the subject were very precise.

MRS CHEVELEY (*to herself*): How thoughtful of him! To expect the unexpected shows a thoroughly modern intellect. (*goes towards the drawing-room and looks in*) Ugh! How dreary a bachelor's drawing-room always looks. I shall have to alter all this. (PHIPPS *brings the lamp from the writing-table.*) No, I don't care for that lamp. It is far too glaring. Light some candles.

PHIPPS (*replaces lamp*): Certainly, madam.

MRS CHEVELEY: I hope the candles have very becoming shades.

PHIPPS: We have had no complaints about them, madam, as yet.

Passes into the drawing-room and begins to light the candles

MRS CHEVELEY (*to herself*): I wonder what woman he is waiting for tonight. It will be delightful to catch him. Men always look so silly when they are caught. And they are always being caught. (*Looks about room and approaches the writing-table*) What a very interesting room! What a very interesting picture! Wonder what his correspondence is like. (*takes up letters*) Oh, what a very uninteresting correspondence! Bills and cards, debts and dowagers! Who on earth writes to him on pink paper? How silly to write on pink paper! It looks like the beginning of a middle-class romance. Romance should never begin with sentiment. It should begin with science and end with a settlement. (*puts letter down, then takes it up again*) I know that handwriting. That is Gertrude Chiltern's. I remember it perfectly. The ten commandments in every stroke of the pen, and the moral law all over the page. Wonder what Gertrude is writing to him about? Something horrid about me, I suppose. How I detest that woman! (*reads it*) 'I trust you. I want you. I am coming to you. Gertrude.' 'I trust you. I want you. I am coming to you.'

A look of triumph comes over her face. She is just about to steal the letter, when PHIPPS *comes in*

PHIPPS: The candles in the drawing-room are lit, madam, as you directed.

MRS CHEVELEY: Thank you. (*rises hastily and slips the letter under a large silver-cased blotting-book that is lying on the table*)

PHIPPS: I trust the shades will be to your liking, madam. They are the most becoming we have. They are the same as his lordship uses himself when he is dressing for dinner.

MRS CHEVELEY (*with a smile*): Then I am sure they will be perfectly right.

PHIPPS (*gravely*): Thank you, madam.

MRS CHEVELEY *goes into the drawing-room.* PHIPPS *closes the door and retires. The door is then slowly opened, and* MRS CHEVELEY *comes out and creeps stealthily towards the writing-table. Suddenly voices are heard from the smoking-room.* MRS CHEVELEY *grows pale, and stops. The voices grow louder, and she goes back into the drawing-room, biting her lip.*

Enter LORD GORING *and* LORD CAVERSHAM

LORD GORING (*expostulating*): My dear father, if I am to get married, surely you will allow me to choose the time, place and person? Particularly the person.

LORD CAVERSHAM (*testily*): That is a matter for me, sir. You would probably make a very poor choice. It is I who should be consulted, not you. There is property at stake. It is not a matter for affection. Affection comes later on in married life.

LORD GORING: Yes. In married life affection comes when people thoroughly dislike each other, father, doesn't it? (*puts on* LORD CAVERSHAM's *cloak for him*)

LORD CAVERSHAM: Certainly, sir. I mean certainly not, sir. You are talking very foolishly tonight. What I say is that marriage is a matter for common sense.

LORD GORING: But women who have common sense are so curiously plain, father, aren't they? Of course I only speak from hearsay.

LORD CAVERSHAM: No woman, plain or pretty, has any common sense at all, sir. Common sense is the privilege of our sex.

LORD GORING: Quite so. And we men are so self-sacrificing that we never use it, do we, father?

LORD CAVERSHAM: I use it, sir. I use nothing else.

LORD GORING: So my mother tells me.

LORD CAVERSHAM: It is the secret of your mother's happiness. You are very heartless, sir, very heartless.

LORD GORING: I hope not, father.

Goes out for a moment. Then returns, looking rather put out, with SIR ROBERT CHILTERN

SIR ROBERT CHILTERN: My dear Arthur, what a piece of good luck meeting you on the doorstep! Your servant had just told me you were not at home. How extraordinary!

LORD GORING: The fact is, I am horribly busy tonight, Robert, and I gave orders I was not at home to anyone. Even my father had a comparatively cold reception. He complained of a draught the whole time.

SIR ROBERT CHILTERN: Ah! you must be at home to me, Arthur. You are my best friend. Perhaps by tomorrow you will be my only friend. My wife has discovered everything.

LORD GORING: Ah! I guessed as much!

SIR ROBERT CHILTERN (*looking at him*): Really! How!

LORD GORING (*after some hesitation*): Oh, merely by something in the expression of your face as you came in. Who told her?

SIR ROBERT CHILTERN: Mrs Cheveley herself. And the woman I love knows that I began my career with an act of low dishonesty, that I built up my life upon sands of shame – that I sold, like a common huckster, the secret that had been entrusted to me as a man of honour. I thank heaven poor Lord Radley died without knowing that I betrayed him. I would to God I had died before I had been so horribly tempted, or had fallen so low. (*burying his face in his hands*)

LORD GORING (*after a pause*): You have heard nothing from Vienna yet, in answer to your wire?

SIR ROBERT CHILTERN (*looking up*): Yes; I got a telegram from the first secretary at eight o'clock tonight.

LORD GORING: Well?

SIR ROBERT CHILTERN: Nothing is absolutely known against her. On the contrary, she occupies a rather high position in society. It is a sort of open secret that Baron Arnheim left her the greater portion of his immense fortune. Beyond that I can learn nothing.

LORD GORING: She doesn't turn out to be a spy, then?

SIR ROBERT CHILTERN: Oh! spies are of no use nowadays. Their profession is over. The newspapers do their work instead.

LORD GORING: And thunderingly well they do it.

SIR ROBERT CHILTERN: Arthur, I am parched with thirst. May I ring for something? Some hock and seltzer?

LORD GORING: Certainly. Let me. (*rings the bell*)

SIR ROBERT CHILTERN: Thanks! I don't know what to do, Arthur, I don't know what to do, and you are my only friend. But what a friend you are – the one friend I can trust. I can trust you absolutely, can't I?

Enter PHIPPS

LORD GORING: My dear Robert, of course. (*To* PHIPPS): Bring some hock and seltzer.

PHIPPS: Yes, my lord.

LORD GORING: And Phipps!

PHIPPS: Yes, my lord.

LORD GORING: Will you excuse me for a moment, Robert? I want to give some directions to my servant

SIR ROBERT CHILTERN: Certainly.

LORD GORING: When that lady calls, tell her that I am not expected home this evening. Tell her that I have been suddenly called out of town. You understand?

PHIPPS: The lady is in that room, my lord. You told me to show her into that room, my lord.

LORD GORING: You did perfectly right. (*exit* PHIPPS) What a mess I am in. No; I think I shall get through it. I'll give her a lecture through the door. Awkward thing to manage, though.

SIR ROBERT CHILTERN: Arthur, tell me what I should do. My life seems to have crumbled about me. I am a ship without a rudder in a night without a star.

LORD GORING: Robert, you love your wife, don't you?

SIR ROBERT CHILTERN: I love her more than anything in the world. I used to think ambition the great thing. It is not. Love is the great thing in the world. There is nothing but love, and I love her. But I am defamed in her eyes. I am ignoble in her eyes. There is a wide gulf between us now. She has found me out, Arthur, she has found me out.

LORD GORING: Has she never in her life done some folly – some indiscretion – that she should not forgive your sin?

SIR ROBERT CHILTERN: My wife! Never! She does not know what weakness or temptation is. I am of clay like other men. She stands apart as good women do – pitiless in her perfection – cold and stern and without mercy. But I love her, Arthur. We are childless, and I have no one else to love, no one else to love me. Perhaps if God had sent us children she might have been kinder to me. But God has given us a lonely house. And she has cut my heart in two. Don't let us talk of it. I was brutal to her this evening. But I suppose when sinners talk to saints they are brutal always. I said to her things that were hideously true, on my side, from my standpoint, from the standpoint of men. But don't let us talk of that.

LORD GORING: Your wife will forgive you. Perhaps at this moment she is forgiving you. She loves you, Robert. Why should she not forgive?

SIR ROBERT CHILTERN: God grant it! God grant it! (*buries his face in his hands*) But there is something more I have to tell you, Arthur.

Enter PHIPPS *with drinks*

PHIPPS (*hands hock and seltzer to* SIR ROBERT CHILTERN): Hock and seltzer, sir.

SIR ROBERT CHILTERN: Thank you.

LORD GORING: Is your carriage here, Robert?

SIR ROBERT CHILTERN: No, I walked from the club.

LORD GORING: Sir Robert will take my cab, Phipps.

PHIPPS: Yes, my lord. (*exit*)

LORD GORING: Robert, you don't mind my sending you away?

SIR ROBERT CHILTERN: Arthur, you must let me stay for five minutes. I have made up my mind what I am going to do tonight in the House. The debate on the Argentine canal is to begin at eleven. (*A chair falls in the drawing-room*) What is that?

LORD GORING: Nothing.

SIR ROBERT CHILTERN: I heard a chair fall in the next room. Someone has been listening.

LORD GORING: No, no; there is no one there.

SIR ROBERT CHILTERN: There is someone. There are lights in the room, and the door is ajar. Someone has been listening to every secret of my life. Arthur, what does this mean?

LORD GORING: Robert, you are excited, unnerved. I tell you there is no one in that room. Sit down, Robert.

SIR ROBERT CHILTERN: Do you give me your word that there is no one there?

LORD GORING: Yes.

SIR ROBERT CHILTERN: Your word of honour? (*sits down*)

LORD GORING: Yes.

SIR ROBERT CHILTERN (*rises*): Arthur, let me see for myself.

LORD GORING: No, no.

SIR ROBERT CHILTERN: If there is no one there why should I not look in that room? Arthur, you must let me go into that room and satisfy myself. Let me know that no eavesdropper has heard my life's secret. Arthur, you don't realise what I am going through.

LORD GORING: Robert, this must stop. I have told you that there is no one in that room – that is enough.

SIR ROBERT CHILTERN (*rushes to the door of the room*): It is not enough. I insist on going into this room. You have told me there is no one there, so what reason can you have for refusing me?

LORD GORING: For God's sake, don't! There is someone there. Someone whom you must not see.

SIR ROBERT CHILTERN: Ah, I thought so!

LORD GORING: I forbid you to enter that room.

SIR ROBERT CHILTERN: Stand back. My life is at stake. And I don't care who is there. I will know who it is to whom I have told my secret and my shame. (*enters room*)

LORD GORING: Great heavens! his own wife!

SIR ROBERT CHILTERN *comes back, with a look of scorn and anger on his face*

SIR ROBERT CHILTERN: What explanation have you to give for the presence of that woman here?

LORD GORING: Robert, I swear to you on my honour that that lady is stainless and guiltless of all offence towards you.

SIR ROBERT CHILTERN: She is a vile, an infamous thing!

LORD GORING: Don't say that, Robert! It was for your sake she came here. It was to try and save you she came here. She loves you and no one else.

SIR ROBERT CHILTERN: You are mad. What have I to do with her intrigues with you? Let her remain your mistress! You are well suited to each other. She, corrupt and shameful – you, false as a friend, treacherous as an enemy even –

LORD GORING: It is not true, Robert. Before heaven, it is not true. In her presence and in yours I will explain all.

SIR ROBERT CHILTERN: Let me pass, sir. You have lied enough upon your word of honour.

SIR ROBERT CHILTERN *goes out.* LORD GORING *rushes to the door of the drawing-room, when* MRS CHEVELEY *comes out, looking radiant and much amused*

MRS CHEVELEY (*with a mock curtsey*): Good-evening, Lord Goring!

LORD GORING: Mrs Cheveley! Great heavens! . . . May I ask what you were doing in my drawing-room?

MRS CHEVELEY: Merely listening. I have a perfect passion for listening through keyholes. One always hears such wonderful things through them.

LORD GORING: Doesn't that sound rather like tempting Providence?

MRS CHEVELEY: Oh! surely Providence can resist temptation by this time. (*makes a sign to him to take her cloak off, which he does*)

LORD GORING: I am glad you have called. I am going to give you some good advice.

MRS CHEVELEY: Oh! pray don't. One should never give a woman anything that she can't wear in the evening.

LORD GORING: I see you are quite as wilful as you used to be.

MRS CHEVELEY: Far more! I have greatly improved. I have had more experience.

LORD GORING: Too much experience is a dangerous thing. Pray have a cigarette. Half the pretty women in London smoke cigarettes. Personally I prefer the other half.

MRS CHEVELEY: Thanks. I never smoke. My dressmaker wouldn't like it, and a woman's first duty in life is to her dressmaker, isn't it? What the second duty is, no one has as yet discovered.

LORD GORING: You have come here to sell me Robert Chiltern's letter, haven't you?

MRS CHEVELEY: To offer it to you on conditions! How did you guess that?

LORD GORING: Because you haven't mentioned the subject. Have you got it with you?

MRS CHEVELEY (*sitting down*): Oh, no! A well-made dress has no pockets.

LORD GORING: What is your price for it?

MRS CHEVELEY: How absurdly English you are! The English think that a cheque-book can solve every problem in life. Why, my dear Arthur, I have very much more money than you have, and quite as much as Robert Chiltern has got hold of. Money is not what I want.

LORD GORING: What do you want then, Mrs Cheveley?

MRS CHEVELEY: Why don't you call me Laura?

LORD GORING: I don't like the name.

MRS CHEVELEY: You used to adore it.

LORD GORING: Yes; that's why. (MRS CHEVELEY *motions to him to sit down beside her. He smiles, and does so*)

MRS CHEVELEY: Arthur, you loved me once.

LORD GORING: Yes.

MRS CHEVELEY: And you asked me to be your wife.

LORD GORING: That was the natural result of my loving you.

MRS CHEVELEY: And you threw me over because you saw, or said you saw, poor old Lord Mortlake trying to have a violent flirtation with me in the conservatory at Tenby.

LORD GORING: I am under the impression that my lawyer settled that matter with you on certain terms . . . dictated by yourself.

MRS CHEVELEY: At that time I was poor; you were rich.

LORD GORING: Quite so. That is why you pretended to love me.

MRS CHEVELEY (*shrugging her shoulders*): Poor old Lord Mortlake, who had only two topics of conversation, his gout and his wife! I never could quite make out which of the two he was talking about. He used the most horrible language about them both. Well, you were silly, Arthur. Why, Lord Mortlake was never anything more to me than an amusement. One of those utterly tedious amusements one only finds at an English country house on an English country Sunday. I don't think anyone at all morally responsible for what he or she does at an English country house.

LORD GORING: Yes. I know lots of people think that.

MRS CHEVELEY: I loved you, Arthur.

LORD GORING: My dear Mrs Cheveley, you have always been far too clever to know anything about love.

MRS CHEVELEY: I did love you. And you loved me. You know you loved me; and love is a very wonderful thing. I suppose that when a man has once loved a woman, he will do anything for her, except continue to love her? (*puts her hand on his*)

LORD GORING (*taking his hand away quietly*): Yes; except that.

MRS CHEVELEY (*after a pause*): I am tired of living abroad. I want to come back to London. I want to have a charming house here. I want to have a salon. If one could only teach the English how to talk, and the Irish how to listen, society here would be quite civilised. Besides, I have arrived at the romantic stage. When I saw you last night at the Chilterns, I knew you were the only person I had ever cared for, if I ever have cared for anybody, Arthur. And so, on the morning of the day you marry me, I will give you Robert Chiltern's letter. That is my offer. I will give it to you now, if you promise to marry me.

LORD GORING: Now?

MRS CHEVELEY (*smiling*): Tomorrow.

LORD GORING: Are you really serious?

MRS CHEVELEY: Yes, quite serious.

LORD GORING: I should make you a very bad husband.

MRS CHEVELEY: I don't mind bad husbands. I have had two. They amused me immensely.

LORD GORING: You mean that you amused yourself immensely, don't you?

MRS CHEVELEY: What do you know about my married life?

LORD GORING: Nothing; but I can read it like a book.

MRS CHEVELEY: What book?

LORD GORING (*rising*): The Book of Numbers.

MRS CHEVELEY: Do you think it is quite charming of you to be so rude to a woman in your own house?

LORD GORING: In the case of very fascinating women, sex is a challenge, not a defence.

MRS CHEVELEY: I suppose that is meant for a compliment. My dear Arthur, women are never disarmed by compliments. Men always are. That is the difference between the two sexes.

LORD GORING: Women are never disarmed by anything, as far as I know them.

MRS CHEVELEY (*after a pause*): Then you are going to allow your greatest friend, Robert Chiltern, to be ruined, rather than marry someone who really has considerable attractions left. I thought you would have risen to some great height of self-sacrifice, Arthur. I think you should. And the rest of your life you could spend in contemplating your own perfections.

LORD GORING: Oh! I do that as it is. And self-sacrifice is a thing that should be put down by law. It is so demoralising to the people for whom one sacrifices oneself. They always go to the bad.

MRS CHEVELEY: As if anything could demoralise Robert Chiltern! You seem to forget that I know his real character.

LORD GORING: What you know about him is not his real character. It was an act of folly done in his youth, dishonourable, I admit, shameful, I admit, unworthy of him, I admit, and therefore . . . not his true character.

MRS CHEVELEY: How you men stand up for each other!

LORD GORING: How you women war against each other!

MRS CHEVELEY (*bitterly*): I only war against one woman, against Gertrude Chiltern. I hate her. I hate her now more than ever.

LORD GORING: Because you have brought a real tragedy into her life, I suppose.

MRS CHEVELEY (*with a sneer*): Oh, there is only one real tragedy in a woman's life. The fact that her past is always her lover, and her future invariably her husband.

LORD GORING: Lady Chiltern knows nothing of the kind of life to which you are alluding.

MRS CHEVELEY: A woman whose size in gloves is seven and three-quarters never knows much about anything. You know Gertrude has always worn seven and three-quarters? That is one of the reasons why there was never any moral sympathy between us . . . Well, Arthur, I suppose this romantic interview may be regarded as at an end. You admit it was romantic, don't you? For the privilege of being your wife I was ready to surrender a great prize, the climax of my diplomatic career. You decline. Very well. If Sir Robert doesn't uphold my Argentine scheme, I expose him. *Voilà tout.*

LORD GORING: You mustn't do that. It would be vile, horrible, infamous.

MRS CHEVELEY (*shrugging her shoulders*): Oh! don't use big words. They mean so little. It is a commercial transaction. That is all. There is no good mixing up sentimentality in it. I offered to sell Robert Chiltern a certain thing. If he won't pay me my price, he will have to pay the world a greater price. There is no more to be said. I must go. Goodbye. Won't you shake hands?

LORD GORING: With you? No. Your transaction with Robert Chiltern may pass as a loathsome commercial transaction of a loathsome commercial age; but you seem to have forgotten that you came here tonight to talk of love; you whose lips desecrate the word love, you to whom the thing is a book closely sealed, went this afternoon to the house of one of the most noble and gentle women in the world to degrade her husband in her eyes, to try and kill her love for him, to put poison in her heart, and bitterness in her life, to break her idol, and, it may be, spoil her soul. That I cannot forgive you. That was horrible. For that there can be no forgiveness.

MRS CHEVELEY: Arthur, you are unjust to me. Believe me, you are quite unjust to me. I didn't go to taunt Gertrude at all. I had no idea of doing anything of the kind when I entered. I called with Lady Markby simply to ask whether an ornament, a jewel, that I lost somewhere last night, had been found at the Chilterns'. If you don't believe me, you can ask Lady Markby. She will tell you it is true. The scene that occurred happened after Lady Markby had left, and was really forced on me by Gertrude's rudeness and sneers. I called, oh! – a little out of malice if you like – but really to ask if a diamond brooch of mine had been found. That was the origin of the whole thing.

LORD GORING: A diamond snake-brooch with a ruby?

MRS CHEVELEY: Yes. How do you know?

LORD GORING: Because it is found. In point of fact, I found it myself, and stupidly forgot to tell the butler anything about it as I was leaving. (*goes over to the writing-table and pulls out the drawers*) It is in this drawer. No, that one. This is the brooch, isn't it? (*holds up the brooch*)

MRS CHEVELEY: Yes. I am so glad to get it back. It was . . . a present.

LORD GORING: Won't you wear it?

MRS CHEVELEY: Certainly, if you pin it in. (LORD GORING *suddenly clasps it on her arm*) Why do you put it on as a bracelet? I never knew it could be worn as a bracelet.

LORD GORING: Really?

MRS CHEVELEY (*holding out her handsome arm*): No; but it looks very well on me as a bracelet, doesn't it?

LORD GORING: Yes; much better than when I saw it last.

MRS CHEVELEY: When did you see it last?

LORD GORING (*calmly*): Oh, ten years ago, on Lady Berkshire, from whom you stole it.

MRS CHEVELEY (*starting*): What do you mean?

LORD GORING: I mean that you stole that ornament from my cousin, Mary Berkshire, to whom I gave it when she was married. Suspicion fell on a wretched servant, who was sent away in disgrace. I recognised it last night. I determined to say nothing about it till I had found the thief. I have found the thief now, and I have heard her own confession.

MRS CHEVELEY (*tossing her head*): It is not true.

LORD GORING: You know it is true. Why, thief is written across your face at this moment.

MRS CHEVELEY: I will deny the whole affair from beginning to end. I will say that I have never seen this wretched thing, that it was never in my possession.

> MRS CHEVELEY *tries to get the bracelet off her arm, but fails.* LORD GORING *looks on amused. Her thin fingers tear at the jewel to no purpose. A curse breaks from her*

LORD GORING: The drawback of stealing a thing, Mrs Cheveley, is that one never knows how wonderful the thing that one steals is. You can't get that bracelet off, unless you know where the spring is. And I see you don't know where the spring is. It is rather difficult to find.

MRS CHEVELEY: You brute! You coward! (*she tries again to unclasp the bracelet, but fails*)

LORD GORING: Oh! don't use big words. They mean so little.

MRS CHEVELEY (*again tears at the bracelet in a paroxysm of rage, with inarticulate sounds. Then stops, and looks at* LORD GORING): What are you going to do?

LORD GORING: I am going to ring for my servant. He is an admirable servant. Always comes in the moment one rings for him. When he comes I will tell him to fetch the police.

MRS CHEVELEY (*trembling*): The police? What for?

LORD GORING: Tomorrow the Berkshires will prosecute you. That is what the police are for.

MRS CHEVELEY (*is now in an agony of physical terror. Her face is distorted. Her mouth awry. A mask has fallen from her. She is, for the moment, dreadful to look at*): Don't do that. I will do anything you want. Anything in the world you want.

LORD GORING: Give me Robert Chiltern's letter.

MRS CHEVELEY: Stop! Stop! Let me have time to think.

LORD GORING: Give me Robert Chiltern's letter.

MRS CHEVELEY: I have not got it with me. I will give it to you tomorrow.

LORD GORING: You know you are lying. Give it to me at once. (MRS CHEVELEY *pulls the letter out, and hands it to him. She is horribly pale*) This is it?

MRS CHEVELEY (*in a hoarse voice*): Yes.

LORD GORING (*takes the letter, examines it, sighs, and burns it over the lamp*): For so well-dressed a woman, Mrs Cheveley, you have moments of admirable common sense. I congratulate you.

MRS CHEVELEY (*catches sight of* LADY CHILTERN'S *letter, the cover of which is just showing from under the blotting-book*): Please get me a glass of water.

LORD GORING: Certainly. (*Goes to the corner of the room and pours out a glass of water. While his back is turned* MRS CHEVELEY *steals* LADY CHILTERN'S *letter.* When LORD GORING *returns with the glass she refuses it with a gesture*)

MRS CHEVELEY: Thank you. Will you help me on with my cloak?

LORD GORING: With pleasure. (*puts her cloak on*)

MRS CHEVELEY: Thanks. I am never going to try to harm Robert Chiltern again.

LORD GORING: Fortunately you have not the chance, Mrs Cheveley.

MRS CHEVELEY: Well, if even I had the chance, I wouldn't. On the contrary, I am going to render him a great service.

LORD GORING: I am charmed to hear it. It is a reformation.

MRS CHEVELEY: Yes. I can't bear so upright a gentleman, so honourable an English gentleman, being so shamefully deceived and so –

LORD GORING: Well?

MRS CHEVELEY: I find that somehow Gertrude Chiltern's dying speech and confession has strayed into my pocket.

LORD GORING: What do you mean?

MRS CHEVELEY (*with a bitter note of triumph in her voice*): I mean that I am going to send Robert Chiltern the love-letter his wife wrote to you tonight.

LORD GORING: Love-letter?

MRS CHEVELEY (*laughing*): 'I want you. I trust you. I am coming to you. Gertrude.'

> LORD GORING *rushes to the bureau and takes up the envelope, finds it empty, and turns round*

LORD GORING: You wretched woman, must you always be thieving? Give me back that letter. I'll take it from you by force. You shall not leave my room till I have got it.

> *He rushes towards her, but* MRS CHEVELEY *at once puts her hand on the electric bell that is on the table. The bell sounds with shrill reverberations, and* PHIPPS *enters*

MRS CHEVELEY (*after a pause*): Lord Goring merely rang that you should show me out. Good-night, Lord Goring!

> *Goes out followed by* PHIPPS. *Her face is illumined with evil triumph. There is joy in her eyes. Youth seems to come back to her. Her last glance is like a swift arrow.* LORD GORING *bites his lip, and lights a cigarette*

END OF ACT THREE

ACT FOUR

Same as Act Two. LORD GORING *is standing by the fireplace with his hands in his pockets. He is looking rather bored.*

LORD GORING (*pulls out his watch, inspects it, and rings the bell*): It is a great nuisance. I can't find anyone in this house to talk to. And I am full of interesting information. I feel like the latest edition of something or other.

Enter SERVANT

JAMES: Sir Robert is still at the Foreign Office, my lord.

LORD GORING: Lady Chiltern not down yet?

JAMES: Her ladyship has not yet left her room. Miss Chiltern has just come in from riding.

LORD GORING (*to himself*): Ah! that is something.

JAMES: Lord Caversham has been waiting some time in the library for Sir Robert. I told him your lordship was here.

LORD GORING: Thank you. Would you kindly tell him I've gone?

JAMES (*bowing*): I shall do so, my lord.

Exit SERVANT

LORD GORING: Really, I don't want to meet my father three days running. It is a great deal too much excitement for any son. I hope to goodness he won't come up. Fathers should be neither seen nor heard. That is the only proper basis for family life. Mothers are different. Mothers are darlings. (*throws himself down into a chair, picks up a paper and begins to read it*)

Enter LORD CAVERSHAM

LORD CAVERSHAM: Well, sir, what are you doing here? Wasting your time as usual, I suppose?

LORD GORING (*throws down paper and rises*): My dear father, when one pays a visit it is for the purpose of wasting other people's time, not one's own.

LORD CAVERSHAM: Have you been thinking over what I spoke to you about last night?

LORD GORING: I have been thinking about nothing else.

LORD CAVERSHAM: Engaged to be married yet?

LORD GORING (*genially*): Not yet; but I hope to be before lunchtime.

LORD CAVERSHAM (*caustically*): You can have till dinnertime if it would be of any convenience to you.

LORD GORING: Thanks awfully, but I think I'd sooner be engaged before lunch.

LORD CAVERSHAM: Humph! Never know when you are serious or not.

LORD GORING: Neither do I, father.

A pause

LORD CAVERSHAM: I suppose you have read *The Times* this morning?

LORD GORING (*airily*): *The Times?* Certainly not. I only read the *Morning Post.* All that one should know about modern life is where the duchesses are; anything else is quite demoralising.

LORD CAVERSHAM: Do you mean to say you have not read *The Times* leading article on Robert Chiltern's career?

LORD GORING: Good heavens! No. What does it say?

LORD CAVERSHAM: What should it say, sir? Everything complimentary, of course. Chiltern's speech last night on this Argentine Canal Scheme was one of the finest pieces of oratory ever delivered in the House since Canning.

LORD GORING: Ah! Never heard of Canning. Never wanted to. And did . . . did Chiltern uphold the scheme?

LORD CAVERSHAM: Uphold it, sir? How little you know him! Why, he denounced it roundly, and the whole system of modern political finance. This speech is the turning-point in his career, as *The Times* points out. You should read this article, sir. (*Opens* The Times) 'Sir Robert Chiltern . . . most rising of our young statesmen . . . Brilliant orator . . . Unblemished career . . . Well-known integrity of character . . . Represents what is best in English public life . . . Noble contrast to the lax morality so common among foreign politicians.' They will never say that of you, sir.

LORD GORING: I sincerely hope not, father. However, I am delighted at what you tell me about Robert, thoroughly delighted. It shows he has got pluck.

LORD CAVERSHAM: He has got more than pluck, sir, he has got genius.

LORD GORING: Ah! I prefer pluck. It is not so common, nowadays, as genius is.

LORD CAVERSHAM: I wish you would go into Parliament.

LORD GORING: My dear father, only people who look dull ever get into the House of Commons, and only people who are dull ever succeed there.

LORD CAVERSHAM: Why don't you try to do something useful in life?

LORD GORING: I am far too young.

LORD CAVERSHAM (*testily*): I hate this affectation of youth, sir. It is a great deal too prevalent nowadays.

LORD GORING: Youth isn't an affectation. Youth is an art.

LORD CAVERSHAM: Why don't you propose to that pretty Miss Chiltern?

LORD GORING: I am of a very nervous disposition, especially in the morning.

LORD CAVERSHAM: I don't suppose there is the smallest chance of her accepting you.

LORD GORING: I don't know how the betting stands today.

LORD CAVERSHAM: If she did accept you she would be the prettiest fool in England.

LORD GORING: That is just what I should like to marry. A thoroughly sensible wife would reduce me to a condition of absolute idiocy in less than six months.

LORD CAVERSHAM: You don't deserve her, sir.

LORD GORING: My dear father, if we men married the women we deserved, we should have a very bad time of it.

Enter MABEL CHILTERN

MABEL CHILTERN: Oh! . . . How do you do, Lord Caversham? I hope Lady Caversham is quite well?

LORD CAVERSHAM: Lady Caversham is as usual, as usual.

LORD GORING: Good-morning, Miss Mabel!

MABEL CHILTERN (*taking no notice at all of* LORD GORING, *and addressing herself exclusively to* LORD CAVERSHAM): And Lady Caversham's bonnets . . . are they at all better?

LORD CAVERSHAM: They have had a serious relapse, I am sorry to say.

LORD GORING: Good-morning, Miss Mabel.

MABEL CHILTERN (*to* LORD CAVERSHAM): I hope an operation will not be necessary.

LORD CAVERSHAM (*smiling at her pertness*): If it is, we shall have to give Lady Caversham a narcotic. Otherwise she would never consent to have a feather touched.

LORD GORING (*with increased emphasis*): Good-morning, Miss Mabel!

MABEL CHILTERN (*turning round with feigned surprise*): Oh, are you here? Of course you understand that after your breaking your appointment I am never going to speak to you again.

LORD GORING: Oh, please don't say such a thing. You are the one person in London I really like to have to listen to me.

MABEL CHILTERN: Lord Goring, I never believe a single word that either you or I say to each other.

LORD CAVERSHAM: You are quite right, my dear, quite right as far as he is concerned, I mean.

MABEL CHILTERN: Do you think you could possibly make your son behave a little better occasionally? Just as a change.

LORD CAVERSHAM: I regret to say, Miss Chiltern, that I have no influence at all over my son. I wish I had. If I had, I know what I would make him do.

MABEL CHILTERN: I am afraid that he has one of those terribly weak natures that are not susceptible to influence.

LORD CAVERSHAM: He is very heartless, very heartless.

LORD GORING: It seems to me that I am a little in the way here.

MABEL CHILTERN: It is very good for you to be in the way, and to know what people say of you behind your back.

LORD GORING: I don't at all like knowing what people say of me behind my back. It makes me far too conceited.

LORD CAVERSHAM: After that, my dear, I really must bid you good-morning.

MABEL CHILTERN: Oh! I hope you are not going to leave me all alone with Lord Goring? Especially at such an early hour in the day.

LORD CAVERSHAM: I am afraid I can't take him with me to Downing Street. It is not the Prime Minister's day for seeing the unemployed.

Shakes hands with MABEL CHILTERN, *takes up his hat and stick, and goes out, with a parting glare of indignation at* LORD GORING

MABEL CHILTERN (*takes up roses and begins to arrange them in a bowl on the table*): People who don't keep their appointments in the park are horrid.

LORD GORING: Detestable.

MABEL CHILTERN: I am glad you admit it. But I wish you wouldn't look so pleased about it.

LORD GORING: I can't help it. I always look pleased when I am with you.

MABEL CHILTERN (*sadly*): Then I suppose it is my duty to remain with you?

LORD GORING: Of course it is.

MABEL CHILTERN: Well, my duty is a thing I never do, on principle. It always depresses me. So I am afraid I must leave you.

LORD GORING: Please don't, Miss Mabel. I have something very particular to say to you.

MABEL CHILTERN (*rapturously*): Oh! is it a proposal?

LORD GORING (*somewhat taken aback*): Well, yes, it is – I am bound to say it is.

MABEL CHILTERN (*with a sigh of pleasure*): I am so glad. That makes the second today.

LORD GORING (*indignantly*): The second today? What conceited ass has been impertinent enough to dare to propose to you before I proposed to you?

MABEL CHILTERN: Tommy Trafford, of course. It is one of Tommy's days for proposing. He always proposes on Tuesdays and Thursdays, during the season.

LORD GORING: You didn't accept him, I hope?

MABEL CHILTERN: I make it a rule never to accept Tommy. That is why he goes on proposing. Of course, as you didn't turn up this morning, I very nearly said yes. It would have been an excellent lesson both for him and for you if I had. It would have taught you both better manners.

LORD GORING: Oh! bother Tommy Trafford. Tommy is a silly little ass. I love you.

MABEL CHILTERN: I know. And I think you might have mentioned it before. I am sure I have given you heaps of opportunities.

LORD GORING: Mabel, do be serious. Please be serious.

MABEL CHILTERN: Ah! that is the sort of thing a man always says to a girl before he has been married to her. He never says it afterwards.

LORD GORING (*taking hold of her hand*): Mabel, I have told you that I love you. Can't you love me a little in return?

MABEL CHILTERN: You silly Arthur! If you knew anything about . . . anything, which you don't, you would know that I adore you. Everyone in London knows it except you. It is a public scandal the way I adore you. I have been going about for the last six months telling the whole of society that I adore you. I wonder you consent to have anything to say to me. I have no character left at all. At least, I feel so happy that I am quite sure I have no character left at all.

LORD GORING (*catches her in his arms and kisses her. Then there is a pause of bliss*): Dear! Do you know I was awfully afraid of being refused!

MABEL CHILTERN (*looking up at him*): But you never have been refused yet by anybody, have you, Arthur? I can't imagine anyone refusing you.

LORD GORING (*after kissing her again*): Of course I'm not nearly good enough for you, Mabel.

MABEL CHILTERN (*nestling close to him*): I am so glad, darling. I was afraid you were.

LORD GORING (*after some hesitation*): And I'm . . . I'm a little over thirty.

MABEL CHILTERN: Dear, you look weeks younger than that.

LORD GORING (*enthusiastically*): How sweet of you to say so! . . . And it is only fair to tell you frankly that I am fearfully extravagant.

MABEL CHILTERN: But so am I, Arthur. So we're sure to agree. And now I must go and see Gertrude.

LORD GORING: Must you really? (*kisses her*)

MABEL CHILTERN: Yes.

LORD GORING: Then do tell her I want to talk to her particularly. I have been waiting here all the morning to see either her or Robert.

MABEL CHILTERN: Do you mean to say you didn't come here expressly to propose to me?

LORD GORING (*triumphantly*): No; that was a flash of genius.

MABEL CHILTERN: Your first.

LORD GORING (*with determination*): My last.

MABEL CHILTERN: I am delighted to hear it. Now don't stir. I'll be back in five minutes. And don't fall into any temptations while I am away.

LORD GORING: Dear Mabel, while you are away, there are none. It makes me horribly dependent on you.

Enter LADY CHILTERN

LADY CHILTERN: Good-morning, dear! How pretty you are looking!

MABEL CHILTERN: How pale you are looking, Gertrude! It is most becoming!

LADY CHILTERN: Good-morning, Lord Goring!

LORD GORING (*bowing*): Good-morning, Lady Chiltern!

MABEL CHILTERN (*aside to* LORD GORING): I shall be in the conservatory, under the second palm tree on the left.

LORD GORING: Second on the left?

MABEL CHILTERN (*with a look of mock surprise*): Yes; the usual palm tree.

Blows a kiss to him, unobserved by LADY CHILTERN, *and goes out*

LORD GORING: Lady Chiltern, I have a certain amount of very good news to tell you. Mrs Cheveley gave me up Robert's letter last night, and I burned it. Robert is safe.

LADY CHILTERN (*sinking on the sofa*): Safe! Oh! I am so glad of that. What a good friend you are to him – to us!

LORD GORING: There is only one person now that could be said to be in any danger.

LADY CHILTERN: Who is that?

LORD GORING (*sitting down beside her*): Yourself.

LADY CHILTERN: I! In danger? What do you mean?

LORD GORING: Danger is too great a word. It is a word I should not have used. But I admit I have something to tell you that may distress you, that terribly distresses me. Yesterday evening you wrote me a very beautiful, womanly letter, asking me for my help. You wrote to me as one of your oldest friends, one of your husband's oldest friends. Mrs Cheveley stole that letter from my rooms.

LADY CHILTERN: Well, what use is it to her? Why should she not have it?

LORD GORING (*rising*): Lady Chiltern, I will be quite frank with you. Mrs Cheveley puts a certain construction on that letter and proposes to send it to your husband.

LADY CHILTERN: But what construction could she put on it? . . . Oh! not that! not that! If I in – in trouble, and wanting your help, trusting you, propose to come to you . . . that you may advise me . . . assist me . . . Oh! are there women so horrible as that . . . ? And she proposes to send it to my husband? Tell me what happened. Tell me all that happened.

LORD GORING: Mrs Cheveley was concealed in a room adjoining my library, without my knowledge. I thought that the person who was waiting in that room to see me was yourself. Robert came in unexpectedly. A chair or something fell in the room. He forced his way in, and he discovered her. We had a terrible scene. I still thought it was you. He left me in anger. At the end of everything Mrs Cheveley got possession of your letter – she stole it, when or how, I don't know.

LADY CHILTERN: At what hour did this happen?

LORD GORING: At half-past ten. And now I propose that we tell Robert the whole thing at once.

LADY CHILTERN (*looking at him with amazement that is almost terror*): You want me to tell Robert that the woman you expected was not Mrs Cheveley, but myself? That it was I whom you thought was concealed in a room in your house, at half-past ten o'clock at night? You want me to tell him that?

LORD GORING: I think it is better that he should know the exact truth.

LADY CHILTERN (*rising*): Oh, I couldn't, I couldn't!

LORD GORING: May I do it?

LADY CHILTERN: No.

LORD GORING (*gravely*): You are wrong, Lady Chiltern.

LADY CHILTERN: No. The letter must be intercepted. That is all. But how can I do it? Letters arrive for him every moment of the day. His secretaries open them and hand them to him. I dare not ask the servants to bring me his letters. It would be impossible. Oh! why don't you tell me what to do?

LORD GORING: Pray be calm, Lady Chiltern, and answer the questions I am going to put to you. You said his secretaries open his letters.

LADY CHILTERN: Yes.

LORD GORING: Who is with him today? Mr Trafford, isn't it?

LADY CHILTERN: No. Mr Montford, I think.

LORD GORING: You can trust him?

LADY CHILTERN (*with a gesture of despair*): Oh! how do I know?

LORD GORING: He would do what you asked him, wouldn't he?

LADY CHILTERN: I think so.

LORD GORING: Your letter was on pink paper. He could recognise it without reading it, couldn't he? By the colour?

LADY CHILTERN: I suppose so.

LORD GORING: Is he in the house now?

LADY CHILTERN: Yes.

LORD GORING: Then I will go and see him myself, and tell him that a certain letter, written on pink paper, is to be forwarded to Robert today, and that at all costs it must not reach him. (*goes to the door, and opens it*) Oh! Robert is coming upstairs with the letter in his hand. It has reached him already.

LADY CHILTERN (*with a cry of pain*): Oh! you have saved his life; what have you done with mine?

Enter SIR ROBERT CHILTERN. *He has the letter in his hand, and is reading it. He comes towards his wife, not noticing* LORD GORING'S *presence*

SIR ROBERT CHILTERN: 'I want you. I trust you. I am coming to you. Gertrude.' Oh, my love! Is this true? Do you indeed trust me, and want me? If so, it was for me to come to you, not for you to write of coming to me. This letter of yours, Gertrude, makes me feel that nothing that the world may do can hurt me now. You want me, Gertrude.

LORD GORING, *unseen by* SIR ROBERT CHILTERN, *makes an imploring sign to* LADY CHILTERN to *accept the situation and* SIR ROBERT CHILTERN'S *error.*

LADY CHILTERN: Yes.

SIR ROBERT CHILTERN: You trust me, Gertrude?

LADY CHILTERN: Yes.

SIR ROBERT CHILTERN: Ah! why did you not add you loved me?

LADY CHILTERN (*taking his hand*): Because I loved you.

LORD GORING *passes into the conservatory*

SIR ROBERT CHILTERN (*kisses her*): Gertrude, you don't know what I feel. When Montford passed me your letter across the table – he had opened it by mistake, I suppose, without looking at the handwriting on the envelope – and I read it – oh! I did not care what disgrace or punishment was in store for me, I only thought you loved me still.

LADY CHILTERN: There is no disgrace in store for you, nor any public shame. Mrs Cheveley has handed over to Lord Goring the document that was in her possession, and he has destroyed it.

SIR ROBERT CHILTERN: Are you sure of this, Gertrude?

LADY CHILTERN: Yes; Lord Goring has just told me.

SIR ROBERT CHILTERN: Then I am safe! Oh! what a wonderful thing to be safe! For two days I have been in terror. I am safe now. How did Arthur destroy my letter? Tell me.

LADY CHILTERN: He burned it.

SIR ROBERT CHILTERN: I wish I had seen that one sin of my youth burning to ashes. How many men there are in modern life who would like to see their past burning to white ashes before them! Is Arthur still here?

LADY CHILTERN: Yes; he is in the conservatory.

SIR ROBERT CHILTERN: I am so glad now I made that speech last night in the House, so glad. I made it thinking that public disgrace might be the result. But it has not been so.

LADY CHILTERN: Public honour has been the result.

SIR ROBERT CHILTERN: I think so. I fear so, almost. For although I am safe from detection, although every proof against me is destroyed, I suppose, Gertrude . . . I suppose I should retire from public life? (*he looks anxiously at his wife*)

LADY CHILTERN (*eagerly*): Oh yes, Robert, you should do that. It is your duty to do that.

SIR ROBERT CHILTERN: It is much to surrender.

LADY CHILTERN: No; it will be much to gain.

SIR ROBERT CHILTERN *walks up and down the room with a troubled expression. Then comes over to his wife, and puts his hand on her shoulder*

SIR ROBERT CHILTERN: And you would be happy living somewhere alone with me, abroad perhaps, or in the country away from London, away from public life? You would have no regrets?

LADY CHILTERN: Oh! none, Robert.

SIR ROBERT CHILTERN (*sadly*): And your ambition for me? You used to be ambitious for me.

LADY CHILTERN: Oh, my ambition! I have none now, but that we two may love each other. It was your ambition that led you astray. Let us not talk about ambition.

LORD GORING *returns from the conservatory, looking very pleased with himself, and with an entirely new buttonhole that someone has made for him*

SIR ROBERT CHILTERN (*going towards him*): Arthur, I have to thank you for what you have done for me. I don't know how I can repay you. (*shakes hands with him*)

LORD GORING: My dear fellow, I'll tell you at once. At the present moment, under the usual palm tree . . . I mean in the conservatory . . .

Enter MASON

MASON: Lord Caversham.

LORD GORING: That admirable father of mine really makes a habit of turning up at the wrong moment. It is very heartless of him, very heartless indeed.

Enter LORD CAVERSHAM. MASON *goes out*

LORD CAVERSHAM: Good-morning, Lady Chiltern! Warmest congratulations to you, Chiltern, on your brilliant speech last night. I have just left the Prime Minister, and you are to have the vacant seat in the cabinet.

SIR ROBERT CHILTERN (*with a look of joy and triumph*): A seat in the cabinet?

LORD CAVERSHAM: Yes, here is the Prime Minister's letter. (*hands letter*)

SIR ROBERT CHILTERN (*takes letter and reads it*): A seat in the cabinet!

LORD CAVERSHAM: Certainly, and you well deserve it too. You have got what we want so much in political life nowadays – high character, high moral tone, high principles. (*To* LORD GORING):

Everything that you have not got, sir, and never will have.

LORD GORING: I don't like principles, father. I prefer prejudices.

> SIR ROBERT CHILTERN *is on the brink of accepting the Prime Minister's offer, when he sees his wife looking at him with her clear, candid eyes. He then realises that it is impossible*

SIR ROBERT CHILTERN: I cannot accept this offer, Lord Caversham. I have made up my mind to decline it.

LORD CAVERSHAM: Decline it, sir!

SIR ROBERT CHILTERN: My intention is to retire at once from public life.

LORD CAVERSHAM (*angrily*): Decline a seat in the cabinet, and retire from public life? Never heard such damned nonsense in the whole course of my existence. I beg your pardon, Lady Chiltern. Chiltern, I beg your pardon. (*To* LORD GORING): Don't grin like that, sir.

LORD GORING: No, father.

LORD CAVERSHAM: Lady Chiltern, you are a sensible woman, the most sensible woman in London, the most sensible woman I know. Will you kindly prevent your husband from making such a . . . from talking such . . . Will you kindly do that, Lady Chiltern?

LADY CHILTERN: I think my husband is right in his determination, Lord Caversham. I approve of it.

LORD CAVERSHAM: You approve of it? Good heavens!

LADY CHILTERN (*taking her husband's hand*): I admire him for it. I admire him immensely for it. I have never admired him so much before. He is finer than even I thought him. (*To* SIR ROBERT CHILTERN): You will go and write your letter to the Prime Minister now, won't you? Don't hesitate about it, Robert.

SIR ROBERT CHILTERN (*with a touch of bitterness*): I suppose I had better write it at once. Such offers are not repeated. I will ask you to excuse me for a moment, Lord Caversham.

LADY CHILTERN: I may come with you, Robert, may I not?

SIR ROBERT CHILTERN: Yes, Gertrude.

> LADY CHILTERN *goes with him*

LORD CAVERSHAM: What is the matter with this family? Something wrong here, eh? (*tapping his forehead*) Idiocy? Hereditary, I suppose. Both of them, too. Wife as well as husband. Very sad. Very sad indeed! And they are not an old family. Can't understand it.

LORD GORING: It is not idiocy, father, I assure you.

LORD CAVERSHAM: What is it then, sir?

LORD GORING (*after some hesitation*): Well, it is what is called nowadays a high moral tone, father. That is all.

LORD CAVERSHAM: Hate these new-fangled names. Same thing as we used to call idiocy fifty years ago. Shan't stay in this house any longer.

LORD GORING (*taking his arm*): Oh! just go in here for a moment, father. Third palm tree to the left, the usual palm tree.

LORD CAVERSHAM: What, sir?

LORD GORING: I beg your pardon, father, I forgot. The conservatory, father, the conservatory – there is someone there I want you to talk to.

LORD CAVERSHAM: What about, sir?

LORD GORING: About me, father.

LORD CAVERSHAM (*grimly*): Not a subject on which much eloquence is possible.

LORD GORING: No, father; but the lady is like me. She doesn't care much for eloquence in others. She thinks it a little loud.

LORD CAVERSHAM *goes into the conservatory.* LADY CHILTERN *enters*

LORD GORING: Lady Chiltern, why are you playing Mrs Cheveley's cards?

LADY CHILTERN (*startled*): I don't understand you.

LORD GORING: Mrs Cheveley made an attempt to ruin your husband. Either to drive him from public life, or to make him adopt a dishonourable position. From the latter tragedy you saved him. The former you are now thrusting on him. Why should you do him the wrong Mrs Cheveley tried to do and failed?

LADY CHILTERN: Lord Goring?

LORD GORING (*pulling himself together for a great effort, and showing the philosopher that underlies the dandy*): Lady Chiltern, allow me. You wrote me a letter last night in which you said you trusted me and wanted my help. Now is the moment when you really want my help, now is the time when you have got to trust me, to trust in my counsel and judgement. You love Robert. Do you want to kill his love for you? What sort of existence will he have if you rob him of the fruits of his ambition, if you take him from the splendour of a great political career, if you close the doors of public life against him, if you condemn him to sterile failure, he who was made for triumph and success? Women are not meant to judge us, but to forgive us when we need forgiveness. Pardon, not punishment, is their mission. Why should you scourge him with rods for a sin done in his youth, before he knew you, before he knew himself? A man's life is of more value than a woman's. It has larger issues, wider scope, greater ambitions. A woman's life revolves in curves of emotions. It is upon lines of intellect that a man's life progresses. Don't make any terrible mistake, Lady Chiltern. A woman who can keep a man's love, and love him in return, has done all the world wants of women, or should want of them.

LADY CHILTERN (*troubled and hesitating*): But it is my husband himself who wishes to retire from public life. He feels it is his duty. It was he who first said so.

LORD GORING: Rather than lose your love, Robert would do anything, wreck his whole career, as he is on the brink of doing now. He is making for you a terrible sacrifice. Take my advice, Lady Chiltern, and do not accept a sacrifice so great. If you do, you will live to repent it bitterly. We men and women are not made to accept such sacrifices from each other. We are not worthy of them. Besides, Robert has been punished enough.

LADY CHILTERN: We have both been punished. I set him up too high.

LORD GORING (*with deep feeling in his voice*): Do not for that reason set him down now too low. If he has fallen from his altar, do not thrust him into the mire. Failure to Robert would be the very mire of shame. Power is his passion. He would lose everything, even his power to feel love. Your husband's life is at this moment in your hands, your husband's love is in your hands. Don't mar both for him.

Enter SIR ROBERT CHILTERN

SIR ROBERT CHILTERN: Gertrude, here is the draft of my letter. Shall I read it to you?

LADY CHILTERN: Let me see it.

SIR ROBERT CHILTERN *hands her the letter. She reads it and then, with a gesture of passion, tears it up*

SIR ROBERT CHILTERN: What are you doing?

LADY CHILTERN: A man's life is of more value than a woman's.[3] It has larger issues, wider scope, greater ambitions. Our lives revolve in curves of emotions. It is upon lines of intellect that a man's life progresses. I have just learnt this, and much else with it, from Lord Goring. And I will not spoil your life for you, nor see you spoil it as a sacrifice to me, a useless sacrifice!

SIR ROBERT CHILTERN: Gertrude! Gertrude!

LADY CHILTERN: You can forget. Men easily forget. And I forgive. That is how women help the world. I see that now.

SIR ROBERT CHILTERN (*deeply overcome by emotion, embraces her*): My wife! my wife! (*To* LORD GORING): Arthur, it seems that I am always to be in your debt.

LORD GORING: Oh dear no, Robert. Your debt is to Lady Chiltern, not to me!

SIR ROBERT CHILTERN: I owe you much. And now tell me what you were going to ask me just now as Lord Caversham came in.

LORD GORING: Robert, you are your sister's guardian, and I want your consent to my marriage with her. That is all.

LADY CHILTERN: Oh, I am so glad! I am so glad! (*Shakes hands with* LORD GORING)

LORD GORING: Thank you, Lady Chiltern.

SIR ROBERT CHILTERN (*with a troubled look*): My sister to be your wife?

LORD GORING: Yes.

SIR ROBERT CHILTERN (*speaking with great firmness*): Arthur, I am very sorry, but the thing is quite out of the question. I have to think of Mabel's future happiness. And I don't think her happiness would be safe in your hands. And I cannot have her sacrificed!

LORD GORING: Sacrificed!

SIR ROBERT CHILTERN: Yes, utterly sacrificed. Loveless marriages are horrible. But there is one thing worse than an absolutely loveless marriage. A marriage in which there is love, but on one side only; faith, but on one side only; devotion, but on one side only, and in which of the two hearts one is sure to be broken.

LORD GORING: But I love Mabel. No other woman has any place in my life.

LADY CHILTERN: Robert, if they love each other, why should they not be married?

SIR ROBERT CHILTERN: Arthur cannot bring Mabel the love that she deserves.

LORD GORING: What reason have you for saying that?

SIR ROBERT CHILTERN (*after a pause*): Do you really require me to tell you?

LORD GORING: Certainly I do.

SIR ROBERT CHILTERN: As you choose. When I called on you yesterday evening I found Mrs Cheveley concealed in your rooms. It was between ten and eleven o'clock at night. I do not wish to say anything more. Your relations with Mrs Cheveley have, as I said to you last night, nothing whatsoever to do with me. I know you were engaged to be married to her once. The fascination she exercised over you then seems to have returned. You spoke to me last night of her as of a woman pure and stainless, a woman whom you respected and honoured. That may be so. But I cannot give my sister's life into your hands. It would be wrong of me. It would be unjust, infamously unjust to her.

LORD GORING: I have nothing more to say.

LADY CHILTERN: Robert, it was not Mrs Cheveley whom Lord Goring expected last night.

SIR ROBERT CHILTERN: Not Mrs Cheveley! Who was it then?

LORD GORING: Lady Chiltern.

LADY CHILTERN: It was your own wife. Robert, yesterday afternoon Lord Goring told me that if ever I was in trouble I could come to him for help, as he was our oldest and best friend. Later on, after that terrible scene in this room, I wrote to him telling him that I trusted him, that I had need of him, that I was coming to him for help and advice. (SIR ROBERT CHILTERN *takes the letter out of his pocket*) Yes, that letter. I didn't go to Lord Goring's, after all. I felt that it is from ourselves alone that help can come. Pride made me think that. Mrs Cheveley went. She stole my letter and sent it anonymously to you this morning, that you should think . . . Oh! Robert, I cannot tell you what she wished you to think . . .

SIR ROBERT CHILTERN: What! Had I fallen so low in your eyes that you thought that even for a moment I could have doubted your goodness? Gertrude, Gertrude, you are to me the white image of all good things, and sin can never touch you. Arthur, you can go to Mabel, and you have my best wishes! Oh! stop a moment. There is no name at the beginning of this letter. The brilliant Mrs Cheveley does not seem to have noticed that. There should be a name.

LADY CHILTERN: Let me write yours. It is you I trust and need. You and none else.

LORD GORING: Well, really, Lady Chiltern, I think I should have back my own letter.

LADY CHILTERN (*smiling*): No; you shall have Mabel. (*takes the letter and writes her husband's name on it*)

LORD GORING: Well, I hope she hasn't changed her mind. It's nearly twenty minutes since I saw her last.

Enter MABEL CHILTERN *and* LORD CAVERSHAM

MABEL CHILTERN: Lord Goring, I think your father's conversation much more improving than yours. I am only going to talk to

Lord Caversham in the future, and always under the usual palm tree.

LORD GORING: Darling! (*kisses her*)

LORD CAVERSHAM (*considerably taken aback*): What does this mean, sir? You don't mean to say that this charming, clever young lady has been so foolish as to accept you?

LORD GORING: Certainly, father! And Chiltern's been wise enough to accept the seat in the cabinet.

LORD CAVERSHAM: I am very glad to hear that, Chiltern . . . I congratulate you, sir. If the country doesn't go to the dogs or the Radicals, we shall have you prime minister, someday.

Enter MASON

MASON: Luncheon is on the table, my lady! (MASON *goes out*)

MABEL CHILTERN: You'll stop to luncheon, Lord Caversham, won't you?

LORD CAVERSHAM: With pleasure, and I'll drive you down to Downing Street afterwards, Chiltern. You have a great future before you, a great future. Wish I could say the same for you, sir. (*to* LORD GORING.) But your career will have to be entirely domestic.

LORD GORING: Yes, father, I prefer it domestic.

LORD CAVERSHAM: And if you don't make this young lady an ideal husband, I'll cut you off with a shilling.

MABEL CHILTERN: An ideal husband! Oh, I don't think I should like that. It sounds like something in the next world.

LORD CAVERSHAM: What do you want him to be then, my dear?

MABEL CHILTERN: He can be what he chooses. All I want is to be . . . to be . . . oh! a real wife to him.

LORD CAVERSHAM: Upon my word, there is a good deal of common sense in that, Lady Chiltern.

They all go out except SIR ROBERT CHILTERN. *He sinks into a chair, wrapped in thought. After a little time* LADY CHILTERN *returns to look for him*

LADY CHILTERN (*leaning over the back of the chair*): Aren't you coming in, Robert?

SIR ROBERT CHILTERN (*taking her hand*): Gertrude, is it love you feel for me, or is it pity merely?

LADY CHILTERN (*kisses him*): It is love, Robert. Love, and only love. For both of us a new life is beginning.

CURTAIN

THE IMPORTANCE OF BEING EARNEST

To
ROBERT BALDWIN ROSS
in appreciation, in affection

PERSONS IN THE PLAY

JOHN WORTHING JP

ALGERNON MONCRIEFF

REVEREND CANON CHASUBLE DD

MERRIMAN, *butler*

LANE, *manservant*

LADY BRACKNELL

THE HONOURABLE GWENDOLEN FAIRFAX

CECILY CARDEW

MISS PRISM, *governess*

THE SCENES OF THE PLAY

ACT ONE *Algernon Moncrieff's flat in Half-Moon Street, London*

ACT TWO *The garden at the Manor House, Woolton*

ACT THREE *The drawing-room at the Manor House, Woolton*

TIME: *The Present*

FIRST PERFORMANCE

St James's Theatre, London, on 14 February 1895

THE IMPORTANCE OF BEING EARNEST

ACT ONE

Morning-room in Algernon's flat in Half-Moon Street. The room is luxuriously and artistically furnished. The sound of a piano is heard in the adjoining room. LANE *is arranging afternoon tea on the table; after the music has ceased,* ALGERNON *enters.*

ALGERNON: Did you hear what I was playing, Lane?

LANE: I didn't think it polite to listen, sir.

ALGERNON: I'm sorry for that, for your sake. I don't play accurately – anyone can play accurately – but I play with wonderful expression. As far as the piano is concerned, sentiment is my forte. I keep science for life.

LANE: Yes, sir.

ALGERNON: And, speaking of the science of life, have you got the cucumber sandwiches cut for Lady Bracknell?

LANE: Yes, sir. (*hands them on a salver*)

ALGERNON (*inspects them, takes two, and sits down on the sofa*): Oh! . . . by the way, Lane, I see from your book that on Thursday night, when Lord Shoreman and Mr Worthing were dining with me, eight bottles of champagne are entered as having been consumed.

LANE: Yes, sir; eight bottles and a pint.

ALGERNON: Why is it that at a bachelor's establishment the servants invariably drink the champagne? I ask merely for information.

LANE: I attribute it to the superior quality of the wine, sir. I have often observed that in married households the champagne is rarely of a first-rate brand.

ALGERNON: Good heavens! Is marriage so demoralising as that?

LANE: I believe it *is* a very pleasant state, sir. I have had very little experience of it myself up to the present. I have only been married once. That was in consequence of a misunderstanding between myself and a young person.

ALGERNON (*languidly*): I don't know that I am much interested in your family life, Lane.

LANE: No, sir; it is not a very interesting subject. I never think of it myself.

ALGERNON: Very natural, I am sure. That will do, Lane, thank you.

LANE: Thank you, sir.

LANE *goes out*

ALGERNON: Lane's views on marriage seem somewhat lax. Really, if the lower orders don't set us a good example, what on earth is the use of them? They seem, as a class, to have absolutely no sense of moral responsibility.

Enter LANE

LANE: Mr Ernest Worthing.

Enter JACK. LANE *goes out*

ALGERNON: How are you, my dear Ernest? What brings you up to town?

JACK: Oh, pleasure, pleasure! What else should bring one anywhere? Eating as usual, I see, Algy!

ALGERNON (*stiffly*): I believe it is customary in good society to take some slight refreshment at five o'clock. Where have you been since last Thursday?

JACK (*smiling and sitting down on the sofa*): In the country.

ALGERNON: What on earth do you do there?

JACK (*pulling off his gloves*): When one is in town one amuses oneself. When one is in the country one amuses other people. It is excessively boring.

ALGERNON: And who are the people you amuse?

JACK (*airily*): Oh, neighbours, neighbours.

ALGERNON: Got nice neighbours in your part of Shropshire?

JACK: Perfectly horrid! Never speak to one of them.

ALGERNON: How immensely you must amuse them! (*goes over and takes sandwich*) By the way, Shropshire is your county, is it not?

JACK: Eh? Shropshire? Yes, of course. Hallo! Why all these cups? Why cucumber sandwiches? Why such reckless extravagance in one so young? Who is coming to tea?

ALGERNON: Oh! merely Aunt Augusta and Gwendolen.

JACK: How perfectly delightful!

ALGERNON: Yes, that is all very well; but I am afraid Aunt Augusta won't quite approve of your being here.

JACK: May I ask why?

ALGERNON: My dear fellow, the way you flirt with Gwendolen is perfectly disgraceful. It is almost as bad as the way Gwendolen flirts with you.

JACK: I am in love with Gwendolen. I have come up to town expressly to propose to her.

ALGERNON: I thought you had come up for pleasure? . . . I call that business.

JACK: How utterly unromantic you are!

ALGERNON: I really don't see anything romantic in proposing. It is very romantic to be in love. But there is nothing romantic about a definite proposal. Why, one may be accepted. One usually is, I believe. Then the excitement is all over. The very essence of romance is uncertainty. If ever I get married, I'll certainly try to forget the fact.

JACK: I have no doubt about that, dear Algy. The divorce court was specially invented for people whose memories are so curiously constituted.

ALGERNON: Oh! there is no use speculating on that subject. Divorces are made in heaven – (JACK *puts out his hand to take a sandwich.* ALGERNON *at once interferes*) Please don't touch the cucumber sandwiches. They are ordered specially for Aunt Augusta. (*takes one and eats it*)

JACK: Well, you have been eating them all the time.

ALGERNON: That is quite a different matter. She is my aunt. (*takes plate from below*) Have some bread and butter. The bread and butter is for Gwendolen. Gwendolen is devoted to bread and butter.

JACK (*advancing to table and helping himself*): And very good bread and butter it is too.

ALGERNON: Well, my dear fellow, you need not eat as if you were going to eat it all. You behave as if you were married to her already. You are not married to her already, and I don't think you ever will be.

JACK: Why on earth do you say that?

ALGERNON: Well, in the first place girls never marry the men they flirt with. Girls don't think it right.

JACK: Oh, that is nonsense!

ALGERNON: It isn't. It is a great truth. It accounts for the extraordinary number of bachelors that one sees all over the place. In the second place, I don't give my consent.

JACK: Your consent!

ALGERNON: My dear fellow, Gwendolen is my first cousin. And before I allow you to marry her, you will have to clear up the whole question of Cecily. (*rings bell*)

JACK: Cecily! What on earth do you mean? What do you mean, Algy, by Cecily! I don't know anyone of the name of Cecily.

Enter LANE

ALGERNON: Bring me that cigarette case Mr Worthing left in the smoking-room the last time he dined here.

LANE: Yes, sir.

LANE *goes out*

JACK: Do you mean to say you have had my cigarette case all this time? I wish to goodness you had let me know. I have been writing frantic letters to Scotland Yard about it. I was very nearly offering a large reward.

ALGERNON: Well, I wish you would offer one. I happen to be more than usually hard up.

JACK: There is no good offering a large reward now that the thing is found.

Enter LANE *with the cigarette case on a salver.* ALGERNON *takes it at once.* LANE *goes out*

ALGERNON: I think that is rather mean of you, Ernest, I must say. (*opens case and examines it*) However, it makes no matter, for, now that I look at the inscription inside, I find that the thing isn't yours after all.

JACK: Of course it's mine. (*moving to him*) You have seen me with it a hundred times, and you have no right whatsoever to read what is written inside. It is a very ungentlemanly thing to read a private cigarette case.

ALGERNON: Oh! it is absurd to have a hard and fast rule about what one should read and what one shouldn't. More than half of modern culture depends on what one shouldn't read.

JACK: I am quite aware of the fact, and I don't propose to discuss modern culture. It isn't the sort of thing one should talk of in private. I simply want my cigarette case back.

ALGERNON: Yes; but this isn't your cigarette case. This cigarette case is a present from someone of the name of Cecily, and you said you didn't know anyone of that name.

JACK: Well, if you want to know, Cecily happens to be my aunt.

ALGERNON: Your aunt!

JACK: Yes. Charming old lady she is, too. Lives at Tunbridge Wells. Just give it back to me, Algy.

ALGERNON (*retreating to back of sofa*): But why does she call herself little Cecily if she is your aunt and lives at Tunbridge Wells? (*Reading*) 'From little Cecily, with her fondest love.'

JACK (*moving to sofa and kneeling upon it*): My dear fellow what on earth is there in that? Some aunts are tall, some aunts are not tall. That is a matter that surely an aunt may be allowed to decide for herself. You seem to think that every aunt should be exactly like your aunt! That is absurd! For heaven's sake give me back my cigarette case. (*Follows* ALGERNON *round the room.*)

ALGERNON: Yes. But why does your aunt call you her uncle? 'From little Cecily, with her fondest love to her dear Uncle Jack.' There is no objection, I admit, to an aunt being a small aunt, but why an aunt, no matter what her size may be, should call her own nephew her uncle, I can't quite make out. Besides, your name isn't Jack at all; it is Ernest.

JACK: It isn't Ernest; it's Jack.

ALGERNON: You have always told me it was Ernest. I have introduced you to everyone as Ernest. You answer to the name of Ernest. You look as if your name was Ernest. You are the most earnest-looking person I ever saw in my life. It is perfectly absurd your saying that your name isn't Ernest. It's on your cards. Here is one of them. (*taking it from case*) 'Mr Ernest Worthing, B4, Albany'. I'll keep this as a proof that your name is Ernest if ever you attempt to deny it to me, or to Gwendolen, or to anyone else. (*puts the card in his pocket*)

JACK: Well, my name is Ernest in town and Jack in the country, and the cigarette case was given to me in the country.

ALGERNON: Yes, but that does not account for the fact that your small Aunt Cecily, who lives at Tunbridge Wells, calls you her dear uncle. Come, old boy, you had much better have the thing out at once.

JACK: My dear Algy, you talk exactly as if you were a dentist. It is very vulgar to talk like a dentist when one isn't a dentist. It produces a false impression.

ALGERNON: Well, that is exactly what dentists always do. Now, go on! Tell me the whole thing. I may mention that I have always suspected you of being a confirmed and secret Bunburyist;[4] and I am quite sure of it now.

JACK: Bunburyist? What on earth do you mean by a Bunburyist?

ALGERNON: I'll reveal to you the meaning of that incomparable expression as soon as you are kind enough to inform me why you are Ernest in town and Jack in the country.

JACK: Well, produce my cigarette case first.

ALGERNON: Here it is. (*hands cigarette case*) Now produce your explanation, and pray make it improbable. (*sits on sofa*)

JACK: My dear fellow, there is nothing improbable about my explanation at all. In fact, it's perfectly ordinary. Old Mr Thomas Cardew, who adopted me when I was a little boy, made me in his will guardian to his granddaughter, Miss Cecily Cardew. Cecily, who addresses me as her uncle from motives of respect that you could not possibly appreciate, lives at my place in the country under the charge of her admirable governess, Miss Prism.

ALGERNON: Where is that place in the country, by the way?

JACK: That is nothing to you, dear boy. You are not going to be invited . . . I may tell you candidly that the place is not in Shropshire.

ALGERNON: I suspected that, my dear fellow! I have Bunburyed all over Shropshire on two separate occasions. Now, go on. Why are you Ernest in town and Jack in the country?

JACK: My dear Algy, I don't know whether you will be able to understand my real motives. You are hardly serious enough. When one is placed in the position of guardian, one has to adopt a very high moral tone on all subjects. It's one's duty to do so. And as a high moral tone can hardly be said to conduce very much to either one's health or one's happiness, in order to get up to town I have always pretended to have a younger brother of the name of Ernest, who lives in the Albany, and gets into the most dreadful scrapes. That, my dear Algy, is the whole truth pure and simple.

ALGERNON: The truth is rarely pure and never simple. Modern life would be very tedious if it were either, and modern literature a complete impossibility!

JACK: That wouldn't be at all a bad thing.

ALGERNON: Literary criticism is not your forte, my dear fellow. Don't try it. You should leave that to people who haven't been at a university. They do it so well in the daily papers. What you really are is a Bunburyist. I was quite right in saying you were a Bunburyist. You are one of the most advanced Bunburyists I know.

JACK: What an earth do you mean?

ALGERNON: You have invented a very useful younger brother called Ernest, in order that you may be able to come up to town as often as you like. I have invented an invaluable permanent invalid called Bunbury, in order that I may be able to go down into the country whenever I choose. Bunbury is perfectly invaluable. If it wasn't for Bunbury's extraordinary bad health, for instance, I wouldn't be able to dine with you at Willis's tonight, for I have been really engaged to Aunt Augusta for more than a week.

JACK: I haven't asked you to dine with me anywhere tonight.

ALGERNON: I know. You are absurdly careless about sending out invitations. It is very foolish of you. Nothing annoys people so much as not receiving invitations.

JACK: You had much better dine with your Aunt Augusta.

ALGERNON: I haven't the smallest intention of doing anything of the kind. To begin with, I dined there on Monday, and once a week is quite enough to dine with one's own relations. In the second place, whenever I do dine there I am always treated as a member of the family, and sent down with either no woman at all, or two. In the third place, I know perfectly well whom she will place me next to, tonight. She will place me next Mary Farquhar, who always flirts with her own husband across the dinner-table. That is not very pleasant. Indeed, it is not even decent . . . and that sort of thing is enormously on the increase. The amount of women in London who flirt with their own husbands is perfectly scandalous. It looks so bad. It is simply washing one's clean linen in public. Besides, now that I know you to be a confirmed Bunburyist I naturally want to talk to you about Bunburying. I want to tell you the rules.

JACK: I'm not a Bunburyist at all. If Gwendolen accepts me, I am going to kill my brother, indeed I think I'll kill him in any case. Cecily is a little too much interested in him. It is rather a bore. So I am going to get rid of Ernest. And I strongly advise you to do the same with Mr . . . with your invalid friend who has the absurd name.

ALGERNON: Nothing will induce me to part with Bunbury, and if you ever get married, which seems to me extremely problematic, you will be very glad to know Bunbury. A man who marries without knowing Bunbury has a very tedious time of it.

JACK: That is nonsense. If I marry a charming girl like Gwendolen, and she is the only girl I ever saw in my life that I would marry, I certainly won't want to know Bunbury.

ALGERNON: Then your wife will. You don't seem to realise, that in married life three is company and two is none.

JACK (*sententiously*): That, my dear young friend, is the theory that the corrupt French drama has been propounding for the last fifty years.

ALGERNON: Yes; and that the happy English home has proved in half the time.

JACK: For heaven's sake, don't try to be cynical. It's perfectly easy to be cynical.

ALGERNON: My dear fellow, it isn't easy to be anything nowadays. There's such a lot of beastly competition about. (*The sound of an electric bell is heard*) Ah! that must be Aunt Augusta. Only relatives, or creditors, ever ring in that Wagnerian manner. Now, if I get her out of the way for ten minutes, so that you can have an opportunity for proposing to Gwendolen, may I dine with you tonight at Willis's?

JACK: I suppose so, if you want to.

ALGERNON: Yes, but you must be serious about it. I hate people who are not serious about meals. It is so shallow of them.

Enter LANE

LANE: Lady Bracknell[5] and Miss Fairfax.

ALGERNON *goes forward to meet them. Enter* LADY BRACKNELL *and* GWENDOLEN

LADY BRACKNELL: Good-afternoon, dear Algernon, I hope you are behaving very well.

ALGERNON: I'm feeling very well, Aunt Augusta.

LADY BRACKNELL: That's not quite the same thing. In fact the two things rarely go together. (*Sees* JACK *and bows to him with icy coldness*)

ALGERNON (*to* GWENDOLEN): Dear me, you are smart!

GWENDOLEN: I am always smart! Am I not, Mr Worthing?

JACK: You're quite perfect, Miss Fairfax.

GWENDOLEN: Oh! I hope I am not that. It would leave no room for developments, and I intend to develop in many directions. (GWENDOLEN *and* JACK *sit down together in the corner*)

LADY BRACKNELL: I'm sorry if we are a little late, Algernon, but I was obliged to call on dear Lady Harbury. I hadn't been there since her poor husband's death. I never saw a woman so altered; she looks quite twenty years younger. And now I'll have a cup of tea, and one of those nice cucumber sandwiches you promised me.

ALGERNON: Certainly, Aunt Augusta. (*goes over to tea-table*)

LADY BRACKNELL: Won't you come and sit here, Gwendolen?

GWENDOLEN: Thanks, mamma, I'm quite comfortable where I am.

ALGERNON (*picking up empty plate in horror*): Good heavens! Lane! Why are there no cucumber sandwiches? I ordered them specially.

LANE (*gravely*): There were no cucumbers in the market this morning, sir. I went down twice.

ALGERNON: No cucumbers!

LANE: No, sir. Not even for ready money.

ALGERNON: That will do, Lane, thank you.

LANE: Thank you, sir. (*goes out*)

ALGERNON: I am greatly distressed, Aunt Augusta, about there being no cucumbers, not even for ready money.

LADY BRACKNELL: It really makes no matter, Algernon. I had some crumpets with Lady Harbury, who seems to me to be living entirely for pleasure now.

ALGERNON: I hear her hair has turned quite gold from grief.

LADY BRACKNELL: It certainly has changed its colour. From what cause I, of course, cannot say. (ALGERNON *crosses and hands tea*) Thank you. I've quite a treat for you tonight, Algernon. I am going to send you down with Mary Farquhar. She is such a nice woman and so attentive to her husband. It's delightful to watch them.

ALGERNON: I am afraid, Aunt Augusta, I shall have to give up the pleasure of dining with you tonight after all.

LADY BRACKNELL (*frowning*): I hope not, Algernon. It would put my table completely out. Your uncle would have to dine upstairs. Fortunately he is accustomed to that.

ALGERNON: It is a great bore, and, I need hardly say, a terrible disappointment to me, but the fact is I have just had a telegram to say that my poor friend Bunbury is very ill again. (*exchanges glanccs with* JACK) They seem to think I should be with him.

LADY BRACKNELL: It is very strange. This Mr Bunbury seems to suffer from curiously bad health.

ALGERNON: Yes; poor Bunbury is a dreadful invalid.

LADY BRACKNELL: Well, I must say, Algernon, that I think it is high time that Mr Bunbury made up his mind whether he was going to live or to die. This shilly-shallying with the question is absurd. Nor do I in any way approve of the modern sympathy with invalids. I consider it morbid. Illness of any kind is hardly a thing to be encouraged in others. Health is the primary duty of life. I am always telling that to your poor uncle, but he never seems to take much notice . . . as far as any improvement in his ailment goes. I should be much obliged if you would ask Mr Bunbury, from me, to be kind enough not to have a relapse on Saturday, for I rely on you to arrange my music for me. It is my last reception, and one wants something that will encourage conversation, particularly at the end of the season when everyone has practically said whatever they had to say, which, in most cases, was probably not much.

ALGERNON: I'll speak to Bunbury, Aunt Augusta, if he is still conscious, and I think I can promise you he'll be all right by Saturday. Of course the music is a great difficulty. You see, if one plays good music, people don't listen, and if one plays bad music people don't talk. But I'll run over the programme I've drawn out, if you will kindly come into the next room for a moment.

LADY BRACKNELL: Thank you, Algernon. It is very thoughtful of you. (*rising, and following* ALGERNON) I'm sure the programme will be delightful, after a few expurgations. French songs I cannot possibly allow. People always seem to think that they are improper, and either look shocked, which is vulgar, or laugh, which is worse. But German sounds a thoroughly respectable language, and indeed, I believe is so. Gwendolen, you will accompany me.

GWENDOLEN: Certainly, mamma.

LADY BRACKNELL *and* ALGERNON *go into the music-room,* GWENDOLEN *remains behind*

JACK: Charming day it has been, Miss Fairfax.

GWENDOLEN: Pray don't talk to me about the weather, Mr Worthing. Whenever people talk to me about the weather, I always feel quite certain that they mean something else. And that makes me so nervous.

JACK: I do mean something else.

GWENDOLEN: I thought so. In fact, I am never wrong.

JACK: And I would like to be allowed to take advantage of Lady Bracknell's temporary absence . . .

GWENDOLEN: I would certainly advise you to do so. Mamma has a way of coming back suddenly into a room that I have often had to speak to her about.

JACK (*nervously*): Miss Fairfax, ever since I met you I have admired you more than any girl I have ever met since . . . I met you.

GWENDOLEN: Yes, I am quite well aware of the fact. And I often wish that in public, at any rate, you had been more demonstrative. For me you have always had an irresistible fascination. Even before I met you I was far from indifferent to you. (JACK *looks at her in amazement*) We live, as I hope you know, Mr Worthing, in an age of ideals. The fact is constantly mentioned in the more expensive monthly magazines, and has reached the provincial pulpits, I am told; and my ideal has always been to love someone of the name of Ernest. There is something in that name that inspires absolute confidence. The moment Algernon first mentioned to me that he had a friend called Ernest, I knew I was destined to love you.

JACK: You really love me, Gwendolen?

GWENDOLEN: Passionately!

JACK: Darling! You don't know how happy you've made me.

GWENDOLEN: My own Ernest!

JACK: But you don't really mean to say that you couldn't love me if my name wasn't Ernest?

GWENDOLEN: But your name is Ernest.

JACK: Yes, I know it is. But supposing it was something else? Do you mean to say you couldn't love me then?

GWENDOLEN (*glibly*): Ah! that is clearly a metaphysical speculation, and like most metaphysical speculations has very little reference at all to the actual facts of real life, as we know them.

JACK: Personally, darling, to speak quite candidly, I don't much care about the name of Ernest . . . I don't think the name suits me at all.

GWENDOLEN: It suits you perfectly. It is a divine name. It has a music of its own. It produces vibrations.

JACK: Well, really, Gwendolen, I must say that I think there are lots of other much nicer names. I think Jack, for instance, a charming name.

GWENDOLEN: Jack? . . . No, there is very little music in the name Jack, if any at all, indeed. It does not thrill. It produces absolutely no vibrations . . . I have known several Jacks, and they all, without exception, were more than usually plain. Besides, Jack is a notorious domesticity for John! And I pity any woman who is married to a man called John. She would probably never be allowed to know the entrancing pleasure of a single moment's solitude. The only really safe name is Ernest.

JACK: Gwendolen, I must get christened at once – I mean we must get married at once. There is no time to be lost.

GWENDOLEN: Married, Mr Worthing?

JACK (*astounded*): Well . . . surely. You know that I love you, and you led me to believe, Miss Fairfax, that you were not absolutely indifferent to me.

GWENDOLEN: I adore you. But you haven't proposed to me yet. Nothing has been said at all about marriage. The subject has not even been touched on.

JACK: Well . . . may I propose to you now?

GWENDOLEN: I think it would be an admirable opportunity. And to spare you any possible disappointment, Mr Worthing, I think it only fair to tell you quite frankly beforehand that I am fully determined to accept you.

JACK: Gwendolen!

GWENDOLEN: Yes, Mr Worthing, what have you got to say to me?

JACK: You know what I have got to say to you.

GWENDOLEN: Yes, but you don't say it.

JACK: Gwendolen, will you marry me? (*Goes on his knees.*)

GWENDOLEN: Of course I will, darling. How long you have been about it! I am afraid you have had very little experience in how to propose.

JACK: My own one, I have never loved anyone in the world but you.

GWENDOLEN: Yes, but men often propose for practice. I know my brother Gerald does. All my girl-friends tell me so. What wonderfully blue eyes you have, Ernest! They are quite, quite, blue. I hope you will always look at me just like that, especially when there are other people present.

Enter LADY BRACKNELL

LADY BRACKNELL: Mr Worthing! Rise, sir, from this semi-recumbent posture. It is most indecorous.

GWENDOLEN: Mamma! (*he tries to rise; she restrains him*) I must beg you to retire. This is no place for you. Besides Mr Worthing has not quite finished yet.

LADY BRACKNELL: Finished what, may I ask?

GWENDOLEN: I am engaged to Mr Worthing, mamma. (*they rise together*)

LADY BRACKNELL: Pardon me, you are not engaged to anyone. When you do become engaged to someone, I, or your father, should his health permit him, will inform you of the fact. An engagement should come on a young girl as a surprise, pleasant or unpleasant, as the case may be. It is hardly a matter that she could be allowed to arrange for herself . . . And now, I have a few questions to put to you, Mr Worthing. While I am making these enquiries, you, Gwendolen, will wait for me below in the carriage.

GWENDOLEN (*reproachfully*): Mamma!

LADY BRACKNELL: In the carriage, Gwendolen!

GWENDOLEN *goes to the door. She and* JACK *blow kisses to each other behind* LADY BRACKNELL'S *back.* LADY BRACKNELL *looks vaguely about as if she could not understand what the noise was. Finally turns round*

Gwendolen, the carriage!

GWENDOLEN: Yes, mamma. (*goes out, looking back at* JACK)

LADY BRACKNELL (*sitting down*): You can take a seat, Mr Worthing. (*looks in her pocket for note-book and pencil*)

JACK: Thank you, Lady Bracknell, I prefer standing.

LADY BRACKNELL (*pencil and note-book in hand*): I feel bound to tell you that you are not down on my list of eligible young men, although I have the same list as the dear Duchess of Bolton has. We work together, in fact. However, I am quite ready to enter your name, should your answers be what a really affectionate mother requires. Do you smoke?

JACK: Well, yes, I must admit I smoke.

LADY BRACKNELL: I'm glad to hear it. A man should always have an occupation of some kind. There are far too many idle men in London as it is. How old are you?

JACK: Twenty-nine.

LADY BRACKNELL: A very good age to be married at. I have always been of opinion that a man who desires to get married should know either everything or nothing. Which do you know?

JACK (*after some hesitation*): I know nothing, Lady Bracknell.

LADY BRACKNELL: I am pleased to hear it. I do not approve of anything that tampers with natural ignorance. Ignorance is like a delicate exotic fruit; touch it and the bloom is gone. The whole theory of modern education is radically unsound. Fortunately, in England, at any rate, education produces no effect whatsoever. If it did, it would prove a serious danger to the upper classes, and probably lead to acts of violence in Grosvenor Square. What is your income?

JACK: Between seven and eight thousand a year.

LADY BRACKNELL (*makes a note in her book*): In land, or in investments?

JACK: In investments, chiefly.

LADY BRACKNELL: That is satisfactory. What between the duties expected of one during one's lifetime, and the duties exacted from one after one's death, land has ceased to be either a profit or a pleasure. It gives one position, and prevents one from keeping it up. That's all that can be said about land.

JACK: I have a country house with some land, of course, attached to it – about fifteen hundred acres, I believe; but I don't depend on that for my real income. In fact, as far as I can make out, the poachers are the only people who make anything out of it.

LADY BRACKNELL: A country house! How many bedrooms? Well, that point can be cleared up afterwards. You have a town house,

I hope? A girl with a simple, unspoiled nature, like Gwendolen, could hardly be expected to reside in the country.

JACK: Well, I own a house in Belgrave Square, but it is let by the year to Lady Bloxham. Of course, I can get it back whenever I like, at six months' notice.

LADY BRACKNELL: Lady Bloxham? I don't know her.

JACK: Oh, she goes about very little. She is a lady considerably advanced in years.

LADY BRACKNELL: Ah, nowadays that is no guarantee of respectability of character. What number in Belgrave Square?

JACK: One hundrd and forty-nine.

LADY BRACKNELL (*shaking her head*): The unfashionable side. I thought there was something. However, that could easily be altered.

JACK: Do you mean the fashion, or the side?

LADY BRACKNELL (*sternly*): Both, if necessary, I presume. What are your politics?

JACK: Well, I am afraid I really have none. I am a Liberal Unionist.[6]

LADY BRACKNELL: Oh, they count as Tories. They dine with us. Or come in the evening, at any rate. Now to minor matters. Are your parents living?

JACK: I have lost both my parents.

LADY BRACKNELL: Both? . . . That seems like carelessness. Who was your father? He was evidently a man of some wealth. Was he born in what the Radical papers call the purple of commerce, or did he rise from the ranks of the aristocracy?

JACK: I am afraid I really don't know. The fact is, Lady Bracknell, I said I had lost my parents. It would be nearer the truth to say that my parents seem to have lost me . . . I don't actually know who I am by birth. I was . . . well, I was found.

LADY BRACKNELL: Found!

JACK: The late Mr Thomas Cardew, an old gentleman of a very charitable and kindly disposition, found me, and gave me the name of Worthing,[7] because he happened to have a first-class ticket for Worthing in his pocket at the time. Worthing is a place in Sussex. It is a seaside resort.

LADY BRACKNELL: Where did the charitable gentleman who had a first-class ticket for this seaside resort find you?

JACK (*gravely*): In a hand-bag.

LADY BRACKNELL: A hand-bag?

JACK (*very seriously*): Yes, Lady Bracknell. I was in a hand-bag – a somewhat large, black leather hand-bag, with handles to it – an ordinary hand-bag in fact.

LADY BRACKNELL: In what locality did this Mr James, or Thomas, Cardew come across this ordinary hand-bag?

JACK: In the cloakroom at Victoria Station. It was given to him in mistake for his own.

LADY BRACKNELL: The cloakroom at Victoria Station?

JACK: Yes. The Brighton line.

LADY BRACKNELL: The line is immaterial. Mr Worthing, I confess I feel somewhat bewildered by what you have just told me. To be born, or at any rate bred, in a hand-bag, whether it had handles or not, seems to me to display a contempt for the ordinary decencies of family life that reminds one of the worst excesses of the French Revolution. And I presume you know what that unfortunate movement led to? As for the particular locality in which the hand-bag was found, a cloakroom at a railway station might serve to conceal a social indiscretion – has probably, indeed, been used for that purpose before now – but it could hardly be regarded as an assured basis for a recognised position in good society.

JACK: May I ask you then what you would advise me to do? I need hardly say I would do anything in the world to ensure Gwendolen's happiness.

LADY BRACKNELL: I would strongly advise you, Mr Worthing, to try and acquire some relations as soon as possible, and to make a definite effort to produce at any rate one parent, of either sex, before the season is quite over.

JACK: Well, I don't see how I could possibly manage to do that. I can produce the hand-bag at any moment. It is in my dressing-room at home. I really think that should satisfy you, Lady Bracknell.

LADY BRACKNELL: Me, sir! What has it to do with me? You can hardly imagine that I and Lord Bracknell would dream of allowing our only daughter – a girl brought up with the utmost care – to marry into a cloakroom, and form an alliance with a parcel. Good-morning, Mr Worthing!

LADY BRACKNELL *sweeps out in majestic indignation.*

JACK: Good-morning! (ALGERNON, *from the other room, strikes up the Wedding March.* JACK *looks perfectly furious, and goes to the door*) For goodness' sake don't play that ghastly tune, Algy! How idiotic you are!

The music stops and ALGERNON *enters cheerily*

ALGERNON: Didn't it go off all right, old boy? You don't mean to say

Gwendolen refused you? I know it is a way she has. She is always refusing people. I think it is most ill-natured of her.

JACK: Oh, Gwendolen is as right as a trivet. As far as she is concerned, we are engaged. Her mother is perfectly unbearable. Never met such a Gorgon . . . I don't really know what a Gorgon is like, but I am quite sure that Lady Bracknell is one. In any case, she is a monster, without being a myth, which is rather unfair . . . I beg your pardon, Algy, I suppose I shouldn't talk about your own aunt in that way before you.

ALGERNON: My dear boy, I love hearing my relations abused. It is the only thing that makes me put up with them at all. Relations are simply a tedious pack of people, who haven't got the remotest knowledge of how to live, nor the smallest instinct about when to die.

JACK: Oh, that is nonsense!

ALGERNON: It isn't!

JACK: Well, I won't argue about the matter. You always want to argue about things.

ALGERNON: That is exactly what things were originally made for.

JACK: Upon my word, if I thought that, I'd shoot myself . . . (*a pause*) You don't think there is any chance of Gwendolen becoming like her mother in about a hundred and fifty years, do you, Algy?

ALGERNON: All women become like their mothers. That is their tragedy. No man does. That's his.

JACK: Is that clever?

ALGERNON: It is perfectly phrased. And quite as true as any observation in civilised life should be.

JACK: I am sick to death of cleverness. Everybody is clever nowadays. You can't go anywhere without meeting clever people. The thing has become an absolute public nuisance. I wish to goodness we had a few fools left.

ALGERNON: We have.

JACK: I should extremely like to meet them. What do they talk about?

ALGERNON: The fools? Oh! about the clever people of course.

JACK: What fools.

ALGERNON: By the way, did you tell Gwendolen the truth about your being Ernest in town, and Jack in the country?

JACK (*in a very patronising manner*): My dear fellow, the truth isn't quite the sort of thing one tells to a nice, sweet, refined girl. What extraordinary ideas you have about the way to behave to a woman!

ALGERNON: The only way to behave to a woman is to make love to her, if she is pretty, and to someone else, if she is plain.

JACK: Oh, that is nonsense.

ALGERNON: What about your brother? What about the profligate Ernest?

JACK: Oh, before the end of the week I shall have got rid of him. I'll say he died in Paris of apoplexy.[8] Lots of people die of apoplexy, quite suddenly, don't they?

ALGERNON: Yes but it's hereditary, my dear fellow. It's a sort of thing that runs in families. You had much better say a severe chill.

JACK: You are sure a severe chill isn't hereditary, or anything of that kind?

ALGERNON: Of course it isn't!

JACK: Very well, then. My poor brother Ernest is carried off suddenly, in Paris, by a severe chill. That gets rid of him.

ALGERNON: But I thought you said that . . . Miss Cardew was a little too much interested in your poor brother Ernest? Won't she feel his loss a good deal?

JACK: Oh, that is all right. Cecily is not a silly romantic girl, I am glad to say. She has got a capital appetite, goes for long walks, and pays no attention at all to her lessons.

ALGERNON: I would rather like to see Cecily.

JACK: I will take very good care you never do. She is excessively pretty, and she is only just eighteen.

ALGERNON: Have you told Gwendolen yet that you have an excessively pretty ward who is only just eighteen?

JACK: Oh! one doesn't blurt these things out to people. Cecily and Gwendolen are perfectly certain to be extremely great friends. I'll bet you anything you like that half an hour after they have met, they will be calling each other sister.

ALGERNON: Women only do that when they have called each other a lot of other things first. Now, my dear boy, if we want to get a good table at Willis's, we really must go and dress. Do you know it is nearly seven?

JACK (*irritably*): Oh! it always is nearly seven.

ALGERNON: Well, I'm hungry.

JACK: I never knew you when you weren't . . .

ALGERNON: What shall we do after dinner? Go to a theatre?

JACK: Oh no! I loathe listening.

ALGERNON: Well, let us go to the club?

JACK: Oh, no! I hate talking.

ALGERNON: Well, we might trot round to the Empire at ten?

JACK: Oh, no! I can't bear looking at things. It is so silly.

ALGERNON: Well, what shall we do?

JACK: Nothing!

ALGERNON: It is awfully hard work doing nothing. However, I don't mind hard work where there is no definite object of any kind.

Enter LANE

LANE: Miss Fairfax.

Enter GWENDOLEN. LANE *goes out*

ALGERNON: Gwendolen, upon my word!

GWENDOLEN: Algy, kindly turn your back. I have something very particular to say to Mr Worthing.

ALGERNON: Really, Gwendolen, I don't think I can allow this at all.

GWENDOLEN: Algy, you always adopt a strictly immoral attitude towards life. You are not quite old enough to do that. (ALGERNON *retires to the fireplace*)

JACK: My own darling!

GWENDOLEN: Ernest, we may never be married. From the expression on mamma's face I fear we never shall. Few parents nowadays pay any regard to what their children say to them. The old-fashioned respect for the young is fast dying out. Whatever influence I ever had over mamma, I lost at the age of three. But although she may prevent us from becoming man and wife, and I may marry someone else, and marry often, nothing that she can possibly do can alter my eternal devotion to you.

JACK: Dear Gwendolen!

GWENDOLEN: The story of your romantic origin, as related to me by mamma, with unpleasing comments, has naturally stirred the deeper fibres of my nature. Your Christian name has an irresistible fascination. The simplicity of your character makes you exquisitely incomprehensible to me. Your town address at the Albany I have. What is your address in the country?

JACK: The Manor House, Woolton, Hertfordshire.

ALGERNON, *who has been carefully listening, smiles to himself and writes the address on his shirt-cuff. Then picks up the* Railway Guide.

GWENDOLEN: There is a good postal service, I suppose? It may be necessary to do something desperate. That, of course, will require serious consideration. I will communicate with you daily.

JACK: My own one!

GWENDOLEN: How long do you remain in town?

JACK: Till Monday.

GWENDOLEN: Good! Algy, you may turn round now.

ALGERNON: Thanks, I've turned round already.

GWENDOLEN: You may also ring the bell.

JACK: You will let me see you to your carriage, my own darling?

GWENDOLEN: Certainly.

JACK (*To* LANE, *who now enters*): I will see Miss Fairfax out.

LANE: Yes, sir.

JACK *and* GWENDOLEN *go out*

LANE *presents several letters on a salver to* ALGERNON. *It is to be surmised that they are bills as* ALGERNON, *after looking at the envelopes, tears them up.*

ALGERNON: A glass of sherry, Lane.

LANE: Yes, sir.

ALGERNON: Tomorrow, Lane, I'm going Bunburying.

LANE: Yes, sir.

ALGERNON: I shall probably not be back till Monday. You can put up my dress clothes, my smoking jacket, and all the Bunbury suits . . .

LANE: Yes, sir. (*handing sherry*)

ALGERNON: I hope tomorrow will be a fine day, Lane.

LANE: It never is, sir.

ALGERNON: Lane, you're a perfect pessimist.

LANE: I do my best to give satisfaction, sir.

Enter JACK. LANE *goes off*

JACK: There's a sensible, intellectual girl! the only girl I ever cared for in my life. (ALGERNON *is laughing immoderately*) What on earth are you so amused at?

ALGERNON: Oh, I'm a little anxious about poor Bunbury, that is all.

JACK: If you don't take care, your friend Bunbury will get you into a serious scrape some day.

ALGERNON: I love scrapes. They are the only things that are never serious.

JACK: Oh, that's nonsense, Algy. You never talk anything but nonsense.

ALGERNON: Nobody ever does.

JACK *looks indignantly at him and leaves the room.* ALGERNON *lights a cigarette, reads his shirt-cuff and smiles*

END OF ACT ONE

ACT TWO

The garden at the Manor House. A flight of grey stone steps leads up to the house. The garden, an old-fashioned one full of roses. Time of year, July. Basket chairs, and a table covered with books, are set under a large yew tree. MISS PRISM *is discovered seated at the table.* CECILY *is at the back watering flowers.*

MISS PRISM (*calling*): Cecily, Cecily! Surely such a utilitarian occupation as the watering of flowers is rather Moulton's duty than yours? Especially at a moment when intellectual pleasures await you. Your German grammar is on the table. Pray open it at page fifteen. We will repeat yesterday's lesson.

CECILY (*coming over very slowly*): But I don't like German. It isn't at all a becoming language. I know perfectly well that I look quite plain after my German lesson.

MISS PRISM: Child, you know how anxious your guardian is that you should improve yourself in every way. He laid particular stress on your German, as he was leaving for town yesterday. Indeed, he always lays stress on your German when he is leaving for town.

CECILY: Dear Uncle Jack is so very serious! Sometimes he is so serious that I think he cannot be quite well.

MISS PRISM (*drawing herself up*): Your guardian enjoys the best of health, and his gravity of demeanour is especially to be commended in one so comparatively young as he is. I know no one who has a higher sense of duty and responsibility.

CECILY: I suppose that is why he often looks a little bored when we three are together.

MISS PRISM: Cecily! I'm surprised at you. Mr Worthing has many troubles in his life. Idle merriment and triviality would be out of place in his conversation. You must remember his constant anxiety about that unfortunate young man his brother.

CECILY: I wish Uncle Jack would allow that unfortunate young man, his brother, to come down here sometimes. We might have a good influence over him, Miss Prism. I am sure you certainly would. You know German, and geology, and things of that kind influence a man very much.

CECILY *begins to write in her diary*

MISS PRISM (*shaking her head*): I do not think that even I could produce any effect on a character that according to his own brother's admission is irretrievably weak and vacillating. Indeed I am not sure that I would desire to reclaim him. I am not in favour of this modern mania for turning bad people into good people at a moment's notice. As a man sows so let him reap. You must put away your diary, Cecily. I really don't see why you should keep a diary at all.

CECILY: I keep a diary in order to enter the wonderful secrets of my life. If I didn't write them down, I should probably forget all about them.

MISS PRISM: Memory, my dear Cecily, is the diary that we all carry about with us.

CECILY: Yes, but it usually chronicles the thing's that have never happened, and couldn't possibly have happened. I believe that memory is responsible for nearly all the three-volume novels that Mudie sends us.

MISS PRISM: Do not speak slightingly of the three-volume novel, Cecily. I wrote one myself in earlier days.

CECILY: Did you really, Miss Prism? How wonderfully clever you are! I hope it did not end happily? I don't like novels that end happily. They depress me so much.

MISS PRISM: The good ended happily, and the bad unhappily. That is what fiction means.

CECILY: I suppose so. But it seems very unfair. And was your novel ever published?

MISS PRISM: Alas! no. The manuscript unfortunately was abandoned. (CECILY *starts*) I use the word in the sense of lost or mislaid. To your work, child, these speculations are profitless.

CECILY (*smiling*): But I see dear Dr Chasuble coming up through the garden.

MISS PRISM (*rising and advancing*): Dr Chasuble! This is indeed a pleasure.

Enter CANON CHASUBLE

CHASUBLE: And how are we this morning? Miss Prism, you are, I trust, well?

CECILY: Miss Prism has just been complaining of a slight headache. I think it would do her so much good to have a short stroll with you in the park, Dr Chasuble.

MISS PRISM: Cecily, I have not mentioned anything about a headache.

CECILY: No, dear Miss Prism, I know that, but I felt instinctively that you had a headache. Indeed I was thinking about that, and not about my German lesson, when the rector came in.

CHASUBLE: I hope, Cecily, you are not inattentive.

CECILY: Oh, I am afraid I am.

CHASUBLE: That is strange. Were I fortunate enough to be Miss Prism's pupil, I would hang upon her lips. (MISS PRISM *glares*) I spoke metaphorically. My metaphor was drawn from bees. Ahem! Mr Worthing, I suppose, has not returned from town yet?

MISS PRISM: We do not expect him till Monday afternoon.

CHASUBLE: Ah yes, he usually likes to spend his Sunday in London. He is not one of those whose sole aim is enjoyment, as, by all accounts, that unfortunate young man his brother seems to be. But I must not disturb Aegeria and her pupil any longer.

MISS PRISM: Aegeria? My name is Laetitia, doctor.

CHASUBLE (*bowing*): A classical allusion merely, drawn from the pagan authors. I shall see you both no doubt at evensong?

MISS PRISM: I think, dear doctor, I will have a stroll with you. I find I have a headache after all, and a walk might do it good.

CHASUBLE: With pleasure, Miss Prism, with pleasure. We might go as far as the schools and back.

MISS PRISM: That would be delightful. Cecily, you will read your *Political Economy* in my absence. The chapter on the Fall of the Rupee you may omit. It is somewhat too sensational. Even these metallic problems have their melodramatic side.

Goes down the garden with DR CHASUBLE

CECILY (*picks up books and throws them back on table*): Horrid political economy! Horrid geography! Horrid, horrid German!

Enter MERRIMAN *with a card on a salver*

MERRIMAN: Mr Ernest Worthing has just driven over from the station. He has brought his luggage with him.

CECILY (*takes the card and reads it*): 'Mr Ernest Worthing, B4, Albany, W'. Uncle Jack's brother! Did you tell him Mr Worthing was in town?

MERRIMAN: Yes, miss. He seemed very much disappointed. I mentioned that you and Miss Prism were in the garden. He said he was anxious to speak to you privately for a moment.

CECILY: Ask Mr Ernest Worthing to come here. I suppose you had better talk to the housekeeper about a room for him.

MERRIMAN: Yes, miss.

MERRIMAN *goes out*

CECILY: I have never met any really wicked person before. I feel rather frightened. I am so afraid he will look just like everyone else.

Enter ALGERNON, *very gay and debonair*

He does!

ALGERNON (*raising his hat*): You are my little cousin Cecily, I'm sure.

CECILY: You are under some strange mistake. I am not little. In fact, I believe I am more than usually tall for my age. (ALGERNON *is rather taken aback*) But I am your cousin Cecily. You, I see from your card, are Uncle Jack's brother, my cousin Ernest, my wicked cousin Ernest.

ALGERNON: Oh! I am not really wicked at all, cousin Cecily. You mustn't think that I am wicked.

CECILY: If you are not, then you have certainly been deceiving us all in a very inexcusable manner. I hope you have not been leading a double life, pretending to be wicked and being really good all the time. That would be hyprocrisy.

ALGERNON (*looks at her in amazement*): Oh! Of course I have been rather reckless.

CECILY: I am glad to hear it.

ALGERNON: In fact, now you mention the subject, I have been very bad in my own small way.

CECILY: I don't think you should be so proud of that, though I am sure it must have been very pleasant.

ALGERNON: It is much pleasanter being here with you.

CECILY: I can't understand how you are here at all. Uncle Jack won't be back till Monday afternoon.

ALGERNON: That is a great disappointment. I am obliged to go up by the first train on Monday morning, I have a business appointment that I am anxious . . . to miss!

CECILY: Couldn't you miss it anywhere but in London?

ALGERNON: No; the appointment is in London.

CECILY: Well, I know, of course, how important it is not to keep a business engagement, if one wants to retain any sense of the beauty of life, but still I think you had better wait till Uncle Jack arrives. I know he wants to speak to you about your emigrating.

ALGERNON: About my what?

CECILY: Your emigrating. He has gone up to buy your outfit.

ALGERNON: I certainly wouldn't let Jack buy my outfit. He has no taste in neckties at all.

CECILY: I don't think you will require neckties. Uncle Jack is sending you to Australia.

ALGERNON: Australia! I'd sooner die.

CECILY: Well, he said at dinner on Wednesday night, that you would have to choose between this world, the next world, and Australia.

ALGERNON: Oh, well! The accounts I have received of Australia and the next world, are not particularly encouraging. This world is good enough for me, cousin Cecily.

CECILY: Yes, but are you good enough for it?

ALGERNON: I'm afraid I'm not that. That is why I want you to reform me. You might make that your mission, if you don't mind, cousin Cecily.

CECILY: I'm afraid I've no time, this afternoon.

ALGERNON: Well, would you mind my reforming myself this afternoon?

CECILY: It is rather Quixotic of you. But I think you should try.

ALGERNON: I will. I feel better already.

CECILY: You are looking a little worse.

ALGERNON: That is because I am hungry.

CECILY: How thoughtless of me. I should have remembered that when one is going to lead an entirely new life, one requires regular and wholesome meals. Won't you come in?

ALGERNON: Thank you. Might I have a buttonhole first? I never have any appetite unless I have a buttonhole first.

CECILY: A Maréchal Niel? (*picks up scissors*)

ALGERNON: No, I'd sooner have a pink rose.

CECILY: Why? (*cuts a flower*)

ALGERNON: Because you are like a pink rose, cousin Cecily.

CECILY: I don't think it can be right for you to talk to me like that. Miss Prism never says such things to me.

ALGERNON: Then Miss Prism is a short-sighted old lady. (CECILY *puts the rose in his buttonhole*) You are the prettiest girl I ever saw.

CECILY: Miss Prism says that all good looks are a snare.

ALGERNON: They are a snare that every sensible man would like to be caught in.

CECILY: Oh, I don't think I would care to catch a sensible man. I shouldn't know what to talk to him about.

They pass into the house. MISS PRISM *and* DR CHASUBLE *return*

MISS PRISM: You are too much alone, dear Dr Chasuble. You should get married. A misanthrope I can understand – a womanthrope, never!

CHASUBLE (*with a scholar's shudder*): Believe me, I do not deserve so neologistic a phrase. The precept as well as the practice of the primitive church was distinctly against matrimony.

MISS PRISM (*sententiously*): That is obviously the reason why the primitive church has not lasted up to the present day. And you do not seem to realise, dear doctor, that by persistently remaining single, a man converts himself into a permanent public temptation. Men should be more careful; this very celibacy leads weaker vessels astray.

CHASUBLE: But is a man not equally attractive when married?

MISS PRISM: No married man is ever attractive except to his wife.

CHASUBLE: And often, I've been told, not even to her.

MISS PRISM: That depends on the intellectual sympathies of the woman. Maturity can always be depended on. Ripeness can be trusted. Young women are green. (DR CHASUBLE *starts*) I spoke horticulturally. My metaphor was drawn from fruits. But where is Cecily?

CHASUBLE: Perhaps she followed us to the schools.

Enter JACK *slowly from the back of the garden. He is dressed in the deepest mourning, with crape hatband and black gloves*

MISS PRISM: Mr Worthing!

CHASUBLE: Mr Worthing?

MISS PRISM: This is indeed a surprise. We did not look for you till Monday afternoon.

JACK (*shakes* MISS PRISM'S *hand in a tragic manner*): I have returned sooner than I expected. Dr Chasuble, I hope you are well?

CHASUBLE: Dear Mr Worthing, I trust this garb of woe does not betoken some terrible calamity?

JACK: My brother.

MISS PRISM: More shameful debts and extravagance?

CHASUBLE: Still leading his life of pleasure?

JACK (*shaking his head*): Dead!

CHASUBLE: Your brother Ernest dead?

JACK: Quite dead.

MISS PRISM: What a lesson for him! I trust he will profit by it.

CHASUBLE: Mr Worthing, I offer you my sincere condolence. You have at least the consolation of knowing that you were always the most generous and forgiving of brothers.

JACK: Poor Ernest! He had many faults, but it is a sad, sad blow.

CHASUBLE: Very sad indeed. Were you with him at the end?

JACK: No. He died abroad; in Paris, in fact. I had a telegram last night from the manager of the Grand Hotel.

CHASUBLE: Was the cause of death mentioned?

JACK: A severe chill, it seems.

MISS PRISM: As a man sows, so shall he reap.

CHASUBLE (*raising his hand*): Charity, dear Miss Prism, charity! None of us are perfect. I myself am peculiarly susceptible to draughts. Will the interment take place here?

JACK: No. He seems to have expressed a desire to be buried in Paris.

CHASUBLE: In Paris! (*shakes his head*) I fear that hardly points to any very serious state of mind at the last. You would no doubt wish me to make some slight allusion to this tragic domestic affliction next Sunday. (JACK *presses his hand convulsively*) My sermon on the meaning of the manna in the wilderness can be adapted to almost any occasion, joyful, or, as in the present case, distressing. (*all sigh*) I have preached it at harvest celebrations, christenings, confirmations, on days of humiliation and festal days. The last time I delivered it was in the cathedral, as a charity sermon on behalf of the Society for the Prevention of Discontent among the Upper Orders. The bishop, who was present, was much struck by some of the analogies I drew.

JACK: Ah! that reminds me, you mentioned christenings, I think, Dr Chasuble? I suppose you know how to christen all right? (DR CHASUBLE *looks astounded*) I mean, of course, you are continually christening, aren't you?

MISS PRISM: It is, I regret to say, one of the rector's most constant duties in this parish. I have often spoken to the poorer classes on the subject. But they don't seem to know what thrift is.

CHASUBLE: But is there any particular infant in whom you are interested, Mr Worthing? Your brother was, I believe, unmarried, was he not?

JACK: Oh yes.

MISS PRISM (*bitterly*): People who live entirely for pleasure usually are.

JACK: But it is not for any child, dear doctor. I am very fond of children. No! the fact is, I would like to be christened myself, this afternoon, if you have nothing better to do.

CHASUBLE: But surely, Mr Worthing, you have been christened already?

JACK: I don't remember anything about it.

CHASUBLE: But have you any grave doubts on the subject?

JACK: I certainly intend to have. Of course I don't know if the thing would bother you in any way, or if you think I am a little too old now.

CHASUBLE: Not at all. The sprinkling, and, indeed, the immersion of adults is a perfectly canonical practice.

JACK: Immersion!

CHASUBLE: You need have no apprehensions. Sprinkling is all that is necessary, or indeed I think advisable. Our weather is so changeable. At what hour would you wish the ceremony performed?

JACK: Oh, I might trot round about five if that would suit you.

CHASUBLE: Perfectly, perfectly! In fact, I have two similar ceremonies to perform at that time. A case of twins that occurred recently in one of the outlying cottages on your own estate. Poor Jenkins the carter, a most hard-working man.

JACK: Oh! I don't see much fun in being christened along with other babies. It would be childish. Would half-past five do?

CHASUBLE: Admirably! Admirably! (*takes out watch*) And now, dear Mr Worthing, I will not intrude any longer into a house of sorrow. I would merely beg you not to be too much bowed down by grief. What seem to us bitter trials are often blessings in disguise.

MISS PRISM: This seems to me a blessing of an extremely obvious kind.

Enter CECILY *from the house*

CECILY: Uncle Jack! Oh, I am pleased to see you back. But what horrid clothes you have got on! Do go and change them.

MISS PRISM: Cecily!

CHASUBLE: My child! my child!

CECILY *goes towards* JACK; *he kisses her brow in a melancholy manner.*

CECILY: What is the matter, Uncle Jack? Do look happy! You look as if you had toothache, and I have got such a surprise for you. Who do you think is in the dining-room? Your brother!

JACK: Who?

CECILY: Your brother Ernest. He arrived about half an hour ago.

JACK: What nonsense! I haven't got a brother.

CECILY: Oh, don't say that. However badly he may have behaved to you in the past he is still your brother. You couldn't be so heartless as to disown him. I'll tell him to come out. And you will shake hands with him, won't you, Uncle Jack? (*runs back into the house*)

CHASUBLE: These are very joyful tidings.

MISS PRISM: After we had all been resigned to his loss, his sudden return seems to me peculiarly distressing.

JACK: My brother is in the dining-room? I don't know what it all means. I think it is perfectly absurd.

Enter ALGERNON *and* CECILY, *hand in hand. They come slowly up to* JACK

JACK: Good heavens! (*motions* ALGERNON *away*)

ALGERNON: Brother John, I have come down from town to tell you that I am very sorry for all the trouble I have given you, and that I intend to lead a better life in the future. (JACK *glares at him and does not take his hand*)

CECILY: Uncle Jack, you are not going to refuse your own brother's hand?

JACK: Nothing will induce me to take his hand. I think his coming down here disgraceful. He knows perfectly well why.

CECILY: Uncle Jack, do be nice. There is some good in everyone. Ernest has just been telling me about his poor invalid friend Mr Bunbury whom he goes to visit so often. And surely there must be much good in one who is kind to an invalid, and leaves the pleasures of London to sit by a bed of pain.

JACK: Oh! he has been talking about Bunbury, has he?

CECILY: Yes, he has told me all about poor Mr Bunbury, and his terrible state of health.

JACK: Bunbury! Well, I won't have him talk to you about Bunbury or about anything else. It is enough to drive one perfectly frantic.

ALGERNON: Of course I admit that the faults were all on my side. But I must say that I think that brother John's coldness to me is peculiarly painful. I expected a more enthusiastic welcome, especially considering it is the first time I have come here.

CECILY: Uncle Jack, if you don't shake hands with Ernest I will never forgive you.

JACK: Never forgive me?

CECILY: Never, never, never!

JACK: Well, this is the last time I shall ever do it. (*shakes hands with* ALGERNON *and glares*)

CHASUBLE: It's pleasant, is it not, to see so perfect a reconciliation? I think we might leave the two brothers together.

MISS PRISM: Cecily, you will come with us.

CECILY: Certainly, Miss Prism. My little task of reconciliation is over.

CHASUBLE: You have done a beautiful action today, dear child.

MISS PRISM: We must not be premature in our judgements.

CECILY: I feel very happy.

They all go out except JACK *and* ALGERNON

JACK: You young scoundrel, Algy, you must get out of this place as soon as possible. I don't allow any Bunburying here.

Enter MERRIMAN

MERRIMAN: I have put Mr Ernest's things in the room next to yours, sir. I suppose that is all right?

JACK: What?

MERRIMAN: Mr Ernest's luggage, sir. I have unpacked it and put it in the room next to your own.

JACK: His luggage?

MERRIMAN: Yes, sir. Three portmanteaus, a dressing case, two hat-boxes, and a large luncheon-basket.

ALGERNON: I am afraid I can't stay more than a week this time.

JACK: Merriman, order the dog-cart at once. Mr Ernest has been suddenly called back to town.

MERRIMAN: Yes, sir. (*goes back into the house*)

ALGERNON: What a fearful liar you are, Jack. I have not been called back to town at all.

JACK: Yes, you have.

ALGERNON: I haven't heard anyone call me.

JACK: Your duty as a gentleman calls you back.

ALGERNON: My duty as a gentleman has never interfered with my pleasures in the smallest degree.

JACK: I can quite understand that.

ALGERNON: Well, Cecily is a darling.

JACK: You are not to talk of Miss Cardew like that. I don't like it.

ALGERNON: Well, I don't like your clothes. You look perfectly ridiculous in them. Why on earth don't you go up and change? It is perfectly childish to be in deep mourning for a man who is actually staying for a whole week with you in your house as a guest. I call it grotesque.

JACK: You are certainly not staying with me for a whole week as a guest or anything else. You have got to leave . . . by the four-five train.

ALGERNON: I certainly won't leave you so long as you are in mourning. It would be most unfriendly. If I were in mourning you would stay with me, I suppose. I should think it very unkind if you didn't.

JACK: Well, will you go if I change my clothes?

ALGERNON: Yes, if you are not too long. I never saw anybody take so long to dress, and with such little result.

JACK: Well, at any rate, that is better than being always over-dressed as you are.

ALGERNON: If I am occasionally a little over-dressed, I make up for it by being always immensely over-educated.

JACK: Your vanity is ridiculous, your conduct an outrage, and your presence in my garden utterly absurd. However, you have got to catch the four-five, and I hope you will have a pleasant journey back to town. This Bunburying, as you call it, has not been a great success for you. (*goes into the house*)

ALGERNON: I think it has been a great success. I'm in love with Cecily, and that is everything.

Enter CECILY *at the back of the garden. She picks up the can and begins to water the flowers*

But I must see her before I go, and make arrangements for another Bunbury. Ah, there she is.

CECILY: Oh, I merely came back to water the roses. I thought you were with Uncle Jack.

ALGERNON: He's gone to order the dog-cart for me.

CECILY: Oh, is he going to take you for a nice drive?

ALGERNON: He's going to send me away.

CECILY: Then have we got to part?

ALGERNON: I am afraid so. It's a very painful parting.

CECILY: It is always painful to part from people whom one has known for a very brief space of time. The absence of old friends one can endure with equanimity. But even a momentary separation from anyone to whom one has just been introduced is almost unbearable.

ALGERNON: Thank you.

Enter MERRIMAN

MERRIMAN: The dog-cart is at the door, sir.

ALGERNON *looks appealingly at* CECILY

CECILY: It can wait, Merriman . . . for five . . . minutes.

MERRIMAN: Yes, miss.

Exit MERRIMAN

ALGERNON: I hope, Cecily, I shall not offend you if I state quite frankly and openly that you seem to me to be in every way the visible personification of absolute perfection.

CECILY: I think your frankness does you great credit, Ernest. If you will allow me, I will copy your remarks into my diary. (*goes over to table and begins writing in diary*)

ALGERNON: Do you really keep a diary? I'd give anything to look at it. May I?

CECILY: Oh no. (*puts her hand over it*) You see, it is simply a very young girl's record of her own thoughts and impressions, and consequently meant for publication. When it appears in volume form I hope you will order a copy. But pray, Ernest, don't stop. I delight in taking down from dictation. I have reached 'absolute perfection'. You can go on. I am quite ready for more.

ALGERNON (*somewhat taken aback*): Ahem! Ahem!

CECILY: Oh, don't cough, Ernest. When one is dictating one should speak fluently and not cough. Besides, I don't know how to spell a cough. (*writes as* ALGERNON *speaks*)

ALGERNON (*speaking very rapidly*): Cecily, ever since I first looked upon your wonderful and incomparable beauty, I have dared to love you wildly, passionately, devotedly, hopelessly.

CECILY: I don't think that you should tell me that you love me wildly, passionately, devotedly, hopelessly. Hopelessly doesn't seem to make much sense, does it?

ALGERNON: Cecily!

Enter MERRIMAN

MERRIMAN: The dog-cart is waiting, sir.

ALGERNON: Tell it to come round next week, at the same hour.

MERRIMAN (*looks at* CECILY, *who makes no sign*): Yes, sir.

MERRIMAN *retires*

CECILY: Uncle Jack would be very much annoyed if he knew you were staying on till next week, at the same hour.

ALGERNON: Oh, I don't care about Jack. I don't care for anybody in the whole world but you. I love you, Cecily. You will marry me, won't you?

CECILY: You silly boy! Of course. Why, we have been engaged for the last three months.

ALGERNON: For the last three months?

CECILY: Yes, it will be exactly three months on Thursday.

ALGERNON: But how did we become engaged?

CECILY: Well, ever since dear Uncle Jack first confessed to us that he had a younger brother who was very wicked and bad, you, of course, have formed the chief topic of conversation between myself and Miss Prism. And, of course, a man who is much talked about is always very attractive. One feels there must be something in him, after all. I dare say it was foolish of me, but I fell in love with you, Ernest.

ALGERNON: Darling. And when was the engagement actually settled?

CECILY: On the 14th of February last. Worn out by your entire ignorance of my existence, I determined to end the matter one way or the other, and after a long struggle with myself I accepted you under this dear old tree here. The next day I bought this little ring in your name, and this is the little bangle with the true lover's knot I promised you always to wear.

ALGERNON: Did I give you this? It's very pretty, isn't it?

CECILY: Yes, you've wonderfully good taste, Ernest. It's the excuse I've always given for your leading such a bad life. And this is the box in which I keep all your dear letters. (*kneels at table, opens box, and produces letters tied up with blue ribbon*)

ALGERNON: My letters! But, my own sweet Cecily, I have never written you any letters.

CECILY: You need hardly remind me of that, Ernest. I remember only too well that I was forced to write your letters for you. I wrote always three times a week, and sometimes oftener.

ALGERNON: Oh, do let me read them, Cecily?

CECILY: Oh, I couldn't possibly. They would make you far too conceited. (*replaces box*) The three you wrote me after I had broken off the engagement are so beautiful, and so badly spelled, that even now I can hardly read them without crying a little.

ALGERNON: But was our engagement ever broken off?

CECILY: Of course it was. On the 22nd of last March. You can see the entry if you like. (*shows diary*) 'Today I broke off my engagement with Ernest. I feel it is better to do so. The weather still continues charming.'

Algernon: But why on earth did you break it off? What had I done? I had done nothing at all. Cecily, I am very much hurt indeed to hear you broke it off. Particularly when the weather was so charming.

CECILY: It would hardly have been a really serious engagement if it hadn't been broken off at least once. But I forgave you before the week was out.

ALGERNON (*crossing to her and kneeling*): What a perfect angel you are, Cecily.

CECILY: You dear romantic boy. (*He kisses her, she puts her fingers through his hair*) I hope your hair curls naturally, does it?

ALGERNON: Yes, darling, with a little help from others.

CECILY: I am so glad.

ALGERNON: You'll never break off our engagement again, Cecily?

CECILY: I don't think I could break it off now that I have actually met you. Besides, of course, there is the question of your name.

ALGERNON: Yes, of course. (*Nervously.*)

CECILY: You must not laugh at me, darling, but it had always been a girlish dream of mine to love someone whose name was Ernest.

ALGERNON *rises*, CECILY *also*

There is something in that name that seems to inspire absolute confidence. I pity any poor married woman whose husband is not called Ernest.

ALGERNON: But, my dear child, do you mean to say you could not love me if I had some other name?

CECILY: But what name?

ALGERNON: Oh, any name you like – Algernon – for instance . . .

CECILY: But I don't like the name of Algernon.

ALGERNON: Well, my own dear, sweet, loving little darling, I really can't see why you should object to the name of Algernon. It is not at all a bad name. In fact, it is rather an aristocratic name. Half of the chaps who get into the bankruptcy court are called Algernon. But seriously, Cecily – (*moving to her*) – if my name was Algy, couldn't you love me?

CECILY (*rising*): I might respect you, Ernest, I might admire your character, but I fear that I should not be able to give you my undivided attention.

ALGERNON: Ahem! Cecily! (*picking up hat*) Your rector here is, I suppose, thoroughly experienced in the practice of all the rites and ceremonials of the church?

CECILY: Oh, yes. Dr Chasuble is a most learned man. He has never written a single book, so you can imagine how much he knows.

ALGERNON: I must see him at once on a most important christening – I mean on most important business.

CECILY: Oh!

ALGERNON: I shan't be away more than half an hour.

CECILY: Considering that we have been engaged since February the 14th, and that I only met you today for the first time, I think it is rather hard that you should leave me for so long a period as half an hour. Couldn't you make it twenty minutes?

ALGERNON: I'll be back in no time. (*kisses her and rushes down the garden*)

CECILY: What an impetuous boy he is! I like his hair so much. I must enter his proposal in my diary.

Enter MERRIMAN

MERRIMAN: A Miss Fairfax has just called to see Mr Worthing. On very important business, Miss Fairfax states.

CECILY: Isn't Mr Worthing in his library?

MERRIMAN: Mr Worthing went over in the direction of the rectory some time ago.

CECILY: Pray ask the lady to come out here; Mr Worthing is sure to be back soon. And you can bring tea.

MERRIMAN: Yes, miss. (*goes out*)

CECILY: Miss Fairfax! I suppose one of the many good elderly women who are associated with Uncle Jack in some of his philanthropic work in London. I don't quite like women who are interested in philanthropic work. I think it is so forward of them.

Enter MERRIMAN

MERRIMAN: Miss Fairfax.

Enter GWENDOLEN. *Exit* MERRIMAN

CECILY (*advancing to meet her*): Pray let me introduce myself to you. My name is Cecily Cardew.

GWENDOLEN: Cecily Cardew? (*moving to her and shaking hands*) What a very sweet name! Something tells me that we are going to be great friends. I like you already more than I can say. My first impressions of people are never wrong.

CECILY: How nice of you to like me so much after we have known each other such a comparatively short time. Pray sit down.

GWENDOLEN (*still standing up*): I may call you Cecily, may I not?

CECILY: With pleasure!

GWENDOLEN: And you will always call me Gwendolen, won't you?

CECILY: If you wish.

GWENDOLEN: Then that is all quite settled, is it not?

CECILY: I hope so.

A pause. They both sit down together

GWENDOLEN: Perhaps this might be a favourable opportunity for my mentioning who I am. My father is Lord Bracknell. You have never heard of papa, I suppose?

CECILY: I don't think so.

GWENDOLEN: Outside the family circle, papa, I am glad to say, is entirely unknown. I think that is quite as it should be. The home seems to me to be the proper sphere for the man. And certainly once a man begins to neglect his domestic duties he becomes painfully effeminate, does he not? And I don't like that. It makes men so very attractive. Cecily, mamma, whose views on education are remarkably strict, has brought me up to be extremely short-sighted; it is part of her system; so do you mind my looking at you through my glasses?

CECILY: Oh! not at all, Gwendolen. I am very fond of being looked at.

GWENDOLEN (*after examining* CECILY *carefully through a lorgnette*): You are here on a short visit, I suppose.

CECILY: Oh no! I live here.

GWENDOLEN (*severely*): Really? Your mother, no doubt, or some female relative of advanced years, resides here also?

CECILY: Oh no! I have no mother, nor, in fact, any relations.

GWENDOLEN: Indeed?

CECILY: My dear guardian, with the assistance of Miss Prism, has the arduous task of looking after me.

GWENDOLEN: Your guardian?

CECILY: Yes, I am Mr Worthing's ward.

GWENDOLEN: Oh! It is strange he never mentioned to me that he had a ward. How secretive of him! He grows more interesting hourly. I am not sure, however, that the news inspires me with feelings of unmixed delight. (*rising and going to her*) I am very fond of you, Cecily; I have liked you ever since I met you! But I am bound to state that now that I know that you are Mr Worthing's ward, I cannot help expressing a wish you were – well, just a little older than you seem to be – and not quite so very alluring in appearance. In fact, if I may speak candidly –

CECILY: Pray do! I think that whenever one has anything unpleasant to say, one should always be quite candid.

GWENDOLEN: Well, to speak with perfect candour, Cecily, I wish that you were fully forty-two, and more than usually plain for your age. Ernest has a strong upright nature. He is the very soul of truth and honour. Disloyalty would be as impossible to him as deception. But even men of the noblest possible moral character are extremely susceptible to the influence of the physical charms of others. Modern no less than ancient history supplies us with many most painful examples of what I refer to. If it were not so, indeed, history would be quite unreadable.

CECILY: I beg your pardon, Gwendolen, did you say Ernest?

GWENDOLEN: Yes.

CECILY: Oh, but it is not Mr Ernest Worthing who is my guardian. It is his brother – his elder brother.

GWENDOLEN (*sitting down again*): Ernest never mentioned to me that he had a brother.

CECILY: I am sorry to say they have not been on good terms for a long time.

GWENDOLEN: Ah! that accounts for it. And now that I think of it I have never heard any man mention his brother. The subject seems distasteful to most men. Cecily, you have lifted a load from my mind. I was growing almost anxious. It would have been terrible if any cloud had come across a friendship like ours would it not? Of course you are quite, quite sure that it is not Mr Ernest Worthing who is your guardian?

CECILY: Quite sure. (*a pause*) In fact, I am going to be his.

GWENDOLEN (*enquiringly*): I beg your pardon?

CECILY (*rather shy and confidingly*): Dearest Gwendolen, there is no reason why I should make a secret of it to you. Our little county newspaper is sure to chronicle the fact next week. Mr Ernest Worthing and I are engaged to be married.

GWENDOLEN (*quite politely, rising*): My darling Cecily, I think there must be some slight error. Mr Ernest Worthing is engaged to me. The announcement will appear in the *Morning Post* on Saturday at the latest.

CECILY (*very politely, rising*): I am afraid you must be under some misconception. Ernest proposed to me exactly ten minutes ago. (*shows diary*)

GWENDOLEN (*examines diary through her lorgnette carefully*): It is certainly very curious, for he asked me to be his wife yesterday afternoon at 5.30. If you would care to verify the incident, pray do so. (*produces diary of her own*) I never travel without my diary. One should always have something sensational to read in the train. I am so sorry, dear Cecily, if it is any disappointment to you, but I am afraid I have the prior claim.

CECILY: It would distress me more than I call tell you, dear Gwendolen, if it caused you any mental or physical anguish, but I feel bound to point out that since Ernest proposed to you he clearly has changed his mind.

GWENDOLEN (*meditatively*): If the poor fellow has been entrapped into any foolish promise I shall consider it my duty to rescue him at once, and with a firm hand.

CECILY (*thoughtfully and sadly*): Whatever unfortunate entanglement my dear boy may have got into, I will never reproach him with it after we are married.

GWENDOLEN: Do you allude to me, Miss Cardew, as an entanglement?

You are presumptuous. On an occasion of this kind it becomes more than a moral duty to speak one's mind. It becomes a pleasure.

CECILY: Do you suggest, Miss Fairfax, that I entrapped Ernest into an engagement? How dare you? This is no time for wearing the shallow mask of manners. When I see a spade I call it a spade.

GWENDOLEN (*satirically*): I am glad to say that I have never seen a spade. It is obvious that our social spheres have been widely different.

Enter MERRIMAN, *followed by the footman. He carries a salver, tablecloth and plate stand.* CECILY *is about to retort. The presence of the servants exercises a restraining influence, under which both girls chafe*

MERRIMAN: Shall I lay tea here as usual, miss?

CECILY (*sternly, in a calm voice*): Yes, as usual.

MERRIMAN *begins to clear table and lay cloth. A long pause.* CECILY *and* GWENDOLEN *glare at each other*

GWENDOLEN: Are there many interesting walks in the vicinity, Miss Cardew?

CECILY: Oh! yes! a great many. From the top of one of the hills quite close one can see five counties.

GWENDOLEN: Five counties! I don't think I should like that; I hate crowds.

CECILY (*sweetly*): I suppose that is why you live in town?

GWENDOLEN *bites her lip, and beats her foot nervously with her parasol*

GWENDOLEN (*looking round*): Quite a well-kept garden this is, Miss Cardew.

CECILY: So glad you like it, Miss Fairfax.

GWENDOLEN: I had no idea there were any flowers in the country.

CECILY: Oh, flowers are as common here, Miss Fairfax, as people are in London.

GWENDOLEN: Personally I cannot understand how anybody manages to exist in the country, if anybody who is anybody does. The country always bores me to death.

CECILY: Ah! This is what the newspapers call agricultural depression, is it not? I believe the aristocracy are suffering very much from it just at present. It is almost an epidemic amongst them, I have been told. May I offer you some tea, Miss Fairfax?

GWENDOLEN (*with elaborate politeness*): Thank you. (*Aside*) Detestable girl! But I require tea!

CECILY (*sweetly*): Sugar?

GWENDOLEN (*superciliously*): No, thank you. Sugar is not fashionable any more.

CECILY *looks angrily at her, takes up the tongs and puts four lumps of sugar into the cup.*

CECILY (*severely*): Cake or bread and butter?

GWENDOLEN (*in a bored manner*): Bread and butter, please. Cake is rarely seen at the best houses nowadays.

CECILY (*cuts a very large slice of cake and puts it on the tray*): Hand that to Miss Fairfax.

MERRIMAN *does so, and goes out with footman.* GWENDOLEN *drinks the tea and makes a grimace. Puts down cup at once, reaches out her hand to the bread and butter, looks at it, and finds it is cake. Rises in indignation*

GWENDOLEN: You have filled my tea with lumps of sugar, and though I asked most distinctly for bread and butter, you have given me cake. I am known for the gentleness of my disposition, and the extraordinary sweetness of my nature, but I warn you, Miss Cardew, you may go too far.

CECILY (*rising*): To save my poor, innocent, trusting boy from the machinations of any other girl there are no lengths to which I would not go.

GWENDOLEN: From the moment I saw you I distrusted you. I felt that you were false and deceitful. I am never deceived in such matters. My first impressions of people are invariably right.

CECILY: It seems to me, Miss Fairfax, that I am trespassing on your valuable time. No doubt you have many other calls of a similar character to make in the neighbourhood.

Enter JACK

GWENDOLEN (*catching sight of him*): Ernest! My own Ernest!

JACK: Gwendolen! Darling! (*offers to kiss her*)

GWENDOLEN (*drawing back*): A moment! May I ask if you are engaged to be married to this young lady? (*points to* CECILY)

JACK (*laughing*): To dear little Cecily! Of course not! What could have put such an idea into your pretty little head?

GWENDOLEN: Thank you. You may! (*offers her cheek*)

CECILY (*very sweetly*): I knew there must be some misunderstanding, Miss Fairfax. The gentleman whose arm is at present round your waist is my guardian, Mr John Worthing.

GWENDOLEN: I beg your pardon?

CECILY: This is Uncle Jack.

GWENDOLEN (*receding*): Jack! Oh!

Enter ALGERNON

CECILY: Here is Ernest.

ALGERNON (*goes straight over to* CECILY *without noticing anyone else*): My own love! (*offers to kiss her*)

CECILY (*drawing back*): A moment, Ernest! May I ask you – are you engaged to be married to this young lady?

ALGERNON (*looking round*): To what young lady? Good heavens! Gwendolen!

CECILY: Yes! to good heavens, Gwendolen, I mean to Gwendolen.

ALGERNON (*laughing*): Of course not! What could have put such an idea into your pretty little head?

CECILY: Thank you. (*presenting her cheek to be kissed*) You may. (ALGERNON *kisses her*)

GWENDOLEN: I felt there was some slight error, Miss Cardew. The gentleman who is now embracing you is my cousin, Mr Algernon Moncrieff.

CECILY (*breaking away from* ALGERNON): Algernon Moncrieff! Oh!

The two girls move towards each other and put their arms round each other's waists as if for protection

CECILY: Are you called Algernon?

ALGERNON: I cannot deny it.

CECILY: Oh!

GWENDOLEN: Is your name really John?

JACK (*standing rather proudly*): I could deny it if I liked. I could deny anything if I liked. But my name certainly is John. It has been John for years.

CECILY (*to* GWENDOLEN): A gross deception has been practised on both of us.

GWENDOLEN: My poor wounded Cecily!

CECILY: My sweet wronged Gwendolen!

GWENDOLEN (*slowly and seriously*): You will call me sister, will you not?

They embrace. JACK *and* ALGERNON *groan and walk up and down*

CECILY (*rather brightly*): There is just one question I would like to be allowed to ask my guardian.

GWENDOLEN: An admirable idea! Mr Worthing, there is just one question I would like to be permitted to put to you. Where is your brother Ernest? We are both engaged to be married to your brother Ernest, so it is a matter of some importance to us to know where your brother Ernest is at present.

JACK (*slowly and hesitatingly*): Gwendolen – Cecily – it is very painful for me to be forced to speak the truth. It is the first time in my life that I have ever been reduced to such a painful position, and I am really quite inexperienced in doing anything of the kind. However, I will tell you quite frankly that I have no brother Ernest. I have no brother at all. I never had a brother in my life, and I certainly have not the smallest intention of ever having one in the future.

CECILY (*surprised*): No brother at all?

JACK (*cheerily*): None!

GWENDOLEN (*severely*): Had you never a brother of any kind?

JACK (*pleasantly*): Never. Not even of any kind.

GWENDOLEN: I am afraid it is quite clear, Cecily, that neither of us is engaged to be married to anyone.

CECILY: It is not a very pleasant position for a young girl suddenly to find herself in. Is it?

GWENDOLEN: Let us go into the house. They will hardly venture to come after us there.

CECILY: No, men are so cowardly, aren't they?

They retire into the house with scornful looks

JACK: This ghastly state of things is what you call Bunburying, I suppose?

ALGERNON: Yes, and a perfectly wonderful Bunbury it is. The most wonderful Bunbury I have ever had in my life.

JACK: Well, you've no right whatsoever to Bunbury here.

ALGERNON: That is absurd. One has a right to Bunbury anywhere one chooses. Every serious Bunburyist knows that.

JACK: Serious Bunburyist! Good heavens!

ALGERNON: Well, one must be serious about something, if one wants to have any amusement in life. I happen to be serious about Bunburying. What on earth you are serious about I haven't got the remotest idea. About everything, I should fancy. You have such an absolutely trivial nature.

JACK: Well, the only small satisfaction I have in the whole of this wretched business is that your friend Bunbury is quite exploded. You won't be able to run down to the country quite so often as you used to do, dear Algy. And a very good thing too.

ALGERNON: Your brother is a little off colour, isn't he, dear Jack? You won't be able to disappear to London quite so frequently as your wicked custom was. And not a bad thing either.

JACK: As for your conduct towards Miss Cardew, I must say that your taking in a sweet, simple, innocent girl like that is quite inexcusable. To say nothing of the fact that she is my ward.

ALGERNON: I can see no possible defence at all for your deceiving a brilliant, clever, thoroughly experienced young lady like Miss Fairfax. To say nothing of the fact that she is my cousin.

JACK: I wanted to be engaged to Gwendolen, that is all. I love her.

ALGERNON: Well, I simply wanted to be engaged to Cecily. I adore her.

JACK: There is certainly no chance of your marrying Miss Cardew.

ALGERNON: I don't think there is much likelihood, Jack, of you and Miss Fairfax being united.

JACK: Well, that is no business of yours.

ALGERNON: If it was my business, I wouldn't talk about it. (*begins to eat muffins*) It is very vulgar to talk about one's business. Only people like stockbrokers do that, and then merely at dinner parties.

JACK: How can you sit there, calmly eating muffins when we are in this horrible trouble, I can't make out. You seem to me to be perfectly heartless.

ALGERNON: Well, I can't eat muffins in an agitated manner. The butter would probably get on my cuffs. One should always eat muffins quite calmly. It is the only way to eat them.

JACK: I say it's perfectly heartless your eating muffins at all, under the circumstances.

ALGERNON: When I am in trouble, eating is the only thing that consoles me. Indeed, when I am in really great trouble, as anyone who knows me intimately will tell you, I refuse everything except food and drink. At the present moment I am eating muffins because I am unhappy. Besides, I am particularly fond of muffins. (*rising*)

JACK (*rising*): Well, that is no reason why you should eat them all in that greedy way. (*takes muffins from* ALGERNON)

ALGERNON (*offering tea-cake*): I wish you would have tea-cake instead. I don't like tea-cake.

JACK: Good heavens! I suppose a man may eat his own muffins in his own garden.

ALGERNON: But you have just said it was perfectly heartless to eat muffins.

JACK: I said it was perfectly heartless of you, under the circumstances. That is a very different thing.

ALGERNON: That may be. But the muffins are the same. (*he seizes the muffin-dish from* JACK)

JACK: Algy, I wish to goodness you would go.

ALGERNON: You can't possibly ask me to go without having some dinner. It's absurd. I never go without my dinner. No one ever does, except vegetarians and people like that. Besides I have just made arrangements with Dr Chasuble to be christened at a quarter to six under the name of Ernest.

JACK: My dear fellow, the sooner you give up that nonsense the better. I made arrangements this morning with Dr Chasuble to be christened myself at 5.30, and I naturally will take the name of Ernest. Gwendolen would wish it. We can't both be christened Ernest. It's absurd. Besides, I have a perfect right to be christened if I like. There is no evidence at all that I have ever been christened by anybody. I should think it extremely probable I never was, and so does Dr Chasuble. It is entirely different in your case. You have been christened already.

ALGERNON: Yes, but I have not been christened for years.

JACK: Yes, but you have been christened. That is the important thing.

ALGERNON: Quite so. So I know my constitution can stand it. If you are not quite sure about your ever having been christened, I must say I think it rather dangerous your venturing on it now. It might make you very unwell. You can hardly have forgotten that someone very closely connected with you was very nearly carried off this week in Paris by a severe chill.

JACK: Yes, but you said yourself that a severe chill was not hereditary.

ALGERNON: It usen't to be, I know – but I dare say it is now. Science is always making wonderful improvements in things.

JACK (*picking up the muffin-dish*): Oh, that is nonsense; you are always talking nonsense.

ALGERNON: Jack, you are at the muffins again! I wish you wouldn't. There are only two left. (*takes them*) I told you I was particularly fond of muffins.

JACK: But I hate tea-cake.

ALGERNON: Why on earth then do you allow tea-cake to be served up for your guests? What ideas you have of hospitality!

JACK: Algernon! I have already told you to go. I don't want you here. Why don't you go!

ALGERNON: I haven't quite finished my tea yet! and there is still one muffin left.

JACK *groans, and sinks into a chair.* ALGERNON *still continues eating*

END OF ACT TWO

ACT THREE

The morning-room at the Manor House. GWENDOLEN *and* CECILY *are at the window looking out into the garden*

GWENDOLEN: The fact that they did not follow us at once into the house, as anyone else would have done, seems to me to show that they have some sense of shame left.

CECILY: They have been eating muffins. That looks like repentance.

GWENDOLEN (*after a pause*): They don't seem to notice us at all. Couldn't you cough?

CECILY: But I haven't got a cough.

GWENDOLEN: They're looking at us. What effrontery!

CECILY: They're approaching. That's very forward of them.

GWENDOLEN: Let us preserve a dignified silence.

CECILY: Certainly. It's the only thing to do now.

Enter JACK *followed by* ALGERNON. *They whistle some dreadful popular air from a British opera*

GWENDOLEN: This dignified silence seems to produce an unpleasant effect.

CECILY: A most distasteful one.

GWENDOLEN: But we will not be the first to speak.

CECILY: Certainly not.

GWENDOLEN: Mr Worthing, I have something very particular to ask you. Much depends on your reply.

CECILY: Gwendolen, your common sense is invaluable. Mr Moncrieff, kindly answer me the following question. Why did you pretend to be my guardian's brother?

ALGERNON: In order that I might have an opportunity of meeting you.

CECILY (*to* GWENDOLEN): That certainly seems a satisfactory explanation, does it not?

GWENDOLEN: Yes, dear, if you can believe him.

CECILY: I don't. But that does not affect the wonderful beauty of his answer.

GWENDOLEN: True. In matters of grave importance, style, not sincerity, is the vital thing. Mr Worthing, what explanation can you offer to me for pretending to have a brother? Was it in order that you might have an opportunity of coming up to town to see me as often as possible?

JACK: Can you doubt it, Miss Fairfax?

GWENDOLEN: I have the gravest doubts upon the subject. But I intend to crush them. This is not the moment for German scepticism. (*moving to* CECILY) Their explanations appear to be quite satisfactory, especially Mr Worthing's. That seems to me to have the stamp of truth upon it.

CECILY: I am more than content with what Mr Moncrieff said. His voice alone inspires one with absolute credulity.

GWENDOLEN: Then you think we should forgive them?

CECILY: Yes. I mean no.

GWENDOLEN: True! I had forgotten. There are principles at stake that one cannot surrender. Which of us should tell them? The task is not a pleasant one.

CECILY: Could we not both speak at the same time?

GWENDOLEN: An excellent idea! I always speak at the same time as other people. Will you take the time from me?

CECILY: Certainly.

GWENDOLEN *beats time with uplifted finger.*

GWENDOLEN *and* CECILY (*speaking together*): Your Christian names are still an insuperable barrier. That is all!

JACK *and* ALGERNON (*speaking together*): Our Christian names! Is that all? But we are going to be christened this afternoon.

GWENDOLEN (*to* JACK): For my sake you are prepared to do this terrible thing?

JACK: I am.

CECILY (*to* ALGERNON): To please me you are ready to face this fearful ordeal?

ALGERNON: I am!

GWENDOLEN: How absurd to talk of the equality of the sexes! Where questions of self-sacrifice are concerned, men are infinitely beyond us.

JACK: We are. (*clasps hands with* ALGERNON)

CECILY: They have moments of physical courage of which we women know absolutely nothing.

GWENDOLEN (*to* JACK): Darling.

ALGERNON (*to* CECILY): Darling!

They fall into each other's arms.

Enter MERRIMAN. *When he enters he coughs loudly, seeing the situation*

MERRIMAN: Ahem! Ahem! Lady Bracknell!

JACK: Good heavens!

Enter LADY BRACKNELL
The couples separate in alarm. Exit MERRIMAN

LADY BRACKNELL: Gwendolen! What does this mean?

GWENDOLEN: Merely that I am engaged to be married to Mr Worthing, mamma.

LADY BRACKNELL: Come here. Sit down. Sit down immediately. Hesitation of any kind is a sign of mental decay in the young, of physical weakness in the old. (*Turns to* JACK) Apprised, sir, of my daughter's sudden flight by her trusty maid, whose confidence I purchased by means of a small coin, I followed her at once by a luggage train. Her unhappy father is, I am glad to say, under the impression that she is attending a more than usually lengthy lecture by the University Extension Scheme on the Influence of a Permanent Income on Thought.[9] I do not propose to undeceive him. Indeed I have never undeceived him on any question. I would consider it wrong. But, of course you will clearly understand that all communication between yourself and my daughter must cease immediately from this moment. On this point, as indeed on all points, I am firm.

JACK: I am engaged to be married to Gwendolen, Lady Bracknell!

LADY BRACKNELL: You are nothing of the kind, sir. And now, as regards Algernon! . . . Algernon!

ALGERNON: Yes, Aunt Augusta.

LADY BRACKNELL: May I ask if it is in this house that your invalid friend Mr Bunbury resides?

ALGERNON (*stammering*): Oh! No! Bunbury doesn't live here. Bunbury is somewhere else at present. In fact, Bunbury is dead.

LADY BRACKNELL: Dead! When did Mr Bunbury die? His death must have been extremely sudden.

ALGERNON (*airily*): Oh! I killed Bunbury this afternoon. I mean poor Bunbury died this afternoon.

LADY BRACKNELL: What did he die of?

ALGERNON: Bunbury? Oh, he was quite exploded.

LADY BRACKNELL: Exploded! Was he the victim of a revolutionary outrage? I was not aware that Mr Bunbury was interested in social legislation. If so, he is well punished for his morbidity.

ALGERNON: My dear Aunt Augusta, I mean he was found out! The doctors found out that Bunbury could not live, that is what I mean – so Bunbury died.

LADY BRACKNELL: He seems to have had great confidence in the opinion of his physicians. I am glad, however, that he made up his mind at the last to some definite course of action, and acted under proper medical advice. And now that we have finally got rid of this Mr Bunbury, may I ask, Mr Worthing, who is that young person whose hand my nephew Algernon is now holding in what seems to me a peculiarly unnecessary manner?

JACK: That lady is Miss Cecily Cardew, my ward.

LADY BRACKNELL *bows coldly to* CECILY.

ALGERNON: I am engaged to be married to Cecily, Aunt Augusta.

LADY BRACKNELL: I beg your pardon?

CECILY: Mr Moncrieff and I are engaged to be married, Lady Bracknell.

LADY BRACKNELL (*with a shiver, crossing to the sofa and sitting down*): I do not know whether there is anything peculiarly exciting in the air of this particular part of Hertfordshire, but the number of engagements that go on seems to me considerably above the proper average that statistics have laid down for our guidance. I think some preliminary enquiry on my part would not be out of place. Mr Worthing, is Miss Cardew at all connected with any of the larger railway stations in London? I merely desire information. Until yesterday I had no idea that there were any families or persons whose origin was a Terminus.

JACK *looks perfectly furious, but restrains himself*

JACK (*in a clear, cold voice*): Miss Cardew is the granddaughter of the late Mr Thomas Cardew of 149 Belgrave Square, SW; Gervase Park, Dorking, Surrey; and The Sporran, Fifeshire, NB.

LADY BRACKNELL: That sounds not unsatisfactory. Three addresses always inspire confidence, even in tradesmen. But what proof have I of their authenticity?

JACK: I have carefully preserved the Court Guides of the period. They are open to your inspection, Lady Bracknell.

LADY BRACKNELL (*grimly*): I have known strange errors in that publication.

JACK: Miss Cardew's family solicitors are Messrs Markby, Markby and Markby.

LADY BRACKNELL: Markby, Markby and Markby? A firm of the very highest position in their profession. Indeed I am told that one of the Mr Markby's is occasionally to be seen at dinner parties. So far I am satisfied.

JACK (*very irritably*): How extremely kind of you, Lady Bracknell! I have also in my possession, you will be pleased to hear, certificates of Miss Cardew's birth, baptism, whooping cough, registration, vaccination, confirmation and the measles, both the German and the English variety.

LADY BRACKNELL: Ah! A life crowded with incident, I see; though perhaps somewhat too exciting for a young girl. I am not myself in favour of premature experiences. (*rises, looks at her watch*) Gwendolen! the time approaches for our departure. We have not a moment to lose. As a matter of form, Mr Worthing. I had better ask you if Miss Cardew has any little fortune?

JACK: Oh! about a hundred and thirty thousand pounds in the Funds. That is all. Goodbye, Lady Bracknell. So pleased to have seen you.

LADY BRACKNELL (*sitting down again*): A moment, Mr Worthing. A hundred and thirty thousand pounds! And in the Funds! Miss Cardew seems to me a most attractive young lady, now that I look at her. Few girls of the present day have any really solid qualities, any of the qualities that last, and improve with time. We live, I regret to say, in an age of surfaces. (*To* CECILY): Come over here, dear. (CECILY *goes across*) Pretty child! your dress is sadly simple, and your hair seems almost as nature might have left it. But we can soon alter all that. A thoroughly experienced French maid produces a really marvellous result in a very brief space of time. I remember recommending one to young Lady Lancing, and after three months her own husband did not know her.

JACK: And after six months nobody knew her.

LADY BRACKNELL (*glares at* JACK *for a few moments. Then bends, with a practised smile, to* CECILY): Kindly turn round, sweet child. (CECILY *turns completely round*) No, the side view is what I want. (CECILY *presents her profile*) Yes, quite as I expected. There are distinct social possibilities in your profile. The two weak points in our age are its want of principle and its want of profile. The chin a little higher, dear. Style largely depends on the way the chin is worn. They are worn very high, just at present. Algernon!

ALGERNON: Yes, Aunt Augusta!

LADY BRACKNELL: There are distinct social possibilities in Miss Cardew's profile.

ALGERNON: Cecily is the sweetest, dearest, prettiest girl in the whole world. And I don't care twopence about social possibilities.

LADY BRACKNELL: Never speak disrespectfully of society, Algernon. Only people who can't get into it do that. (*To* CECILY): Dear child, of course you know that Algernon has nothing but his debts to depend upon. But I do not approve of mercenary marriages. When I married Lord Bracknell I had no fortune of any kind. But I never dreamed for a moment of allowing that to stand in my way. Well, I suppose I must give my consent.

ALGERNON: Thank you, Aunt Augusta.

LADY BRACKNELL: Cecily, you may kiss me!

CECILY (*kisses her*): Thank you, Lady Bracknell.

LADY BRACKNELL: You may also address me as Aunt Augusta for the future.

CECILY: Thank you, Aunt Augusta.

LADY BRACKNELL: The marriage, I think, had better take place quite soon.

ALGERNON: Thank you, Aunt Augusta.

CECILY: Thank you, Aunt Augusta.

LADY BRACKNELL: To speak frankly, I am not in favour of long engagements. They give people the opportunity of finding out each other's character before marriage, which I think is never advisable.

JACK: I beg your pardon for interrupting you, Lady Bracknell, but this engagement is quite out of the question. I am Miss Cardew's guardian, and she cannot marry without my consent until she comes of age. That consent I absolutely decline to give.

LADY BRACKNELL: Upon what grounds may I ask? Algernon is an extremely, I may almost say an ostentatiously, eligible young man. He has nothing, but he looks everything. What more can one desire?

JACK: It pains me very much to have to speak frankly to you, Lady Bracknell, about your nephew, but the fact is that I do not approve at all of his moral character. I suspect him of being untruthful.

ALGERNON *and* CECILY *look at him in indignant amazement*

LADY BRACKNELL: Untruthful! My nephew Algernon? Impossible! He is an Oxonian.

JACK: I fear there can be no possible doubt about the matter. This afternoon during my temporary absence in London on an important question of romance, he obtained admission to my house by means of the false pretence of being my brother. Under an assumed name he drank, I've just been informed by my butler, an entire pint bottle of my Perrier-Jouët Brut '89; wine I was specially reserving for myself. Continuing his disgraceful deception, he succeeded in the course of the afternoon in alienating the affections of my only ward. He subsequently stayed to tea, and devoured every single muffin. And what makes his conduct all the more heartless is that he was perfectly well aware from the first that I have no brother, that I never had a brother, and that I don't intend to have a brother, not even of any kind. I distinctly told him so myself yesterday afternoon.

LADY BRACKNELL: Ahem! Mr Worthing, after careful consideration I have decided entirely to overlook my nephew's conduct to you.

JACK: That is very generous of you, Lady Bracknell. My own decision, however, is unalterable. I decline to give my consent.

LADY BRACKNELL (*to* CECILY): Come here, sweet child. (CECILY *goes over*) How old are you, dear?

CECILY: Well, I am really only eighteen, but I always admit to twenty when I go to evening parties.

LADY BRACKNELL: You are perfectly right in making some slight alteration. Indeed, no woman should ever be quite accurate about her age. It looks so calculating . . . (*In a meditative manner*) Eighteen, but admitting to twenty at evening parties. Well, it will not be very long before you are of age and free from the restraints of tutelage. So I don't think your guardian's consent is, after all, a matter of any importance.

JACK: Pray excuse me, Lady Bracknell, for interrupting you again, but it is only fair to tell you that, according to the terms of her grandfather's will, Miss Cardew does not come legally of age till she is thirty-five.

LADY BRACKNELL: That does not seem to me to be a grave objection. Thirty-five is a very attractive age. London society is full of women of the very highest birth who have, of their own free choice, remained thirty-five for years. Lady Dumbleton is an instance in point. To my own knowledge she has been thirty-five ever since she arrived at the age of forty, which was many years ago now. I see no reason why our dear Cecily should not be even still more attractive at the age you mention than she is at present. There will be a large accumulation of property.

CECILY: Algy, could you wait for me till I was thirty-five?

ALGERNON: Of course I could, Cecily. You know I could.

CECILY: Yes, I felt it instinctively, but I couldn't wait all that time. I hate waiting even five minutes for anybody. It always makes me rather cross. I am not punctual myself, I know, but I do like punctuality in others, and waiting, even to be married, is quite out of the question.

ALGERNON: Then what is to be done, Cecily?

CECILY: I don't know, Mr Moncrieff.

LADY BRACKNELL: My dear Mr Worthing, as Miss Cecily states positively that she cannot wait till she is thirty-five – a remark which I am bound to say seems to me to show a somewhat impatient nature – I would beg of you to reconsider your decision.

JACK: But my dear Lady Bracknell, the matter is entirely in your own hands. The moment you consent to my marriage with Gwendolen, I will most gladly allow your nephew to form an alliance with my ward.

LADY BRACKNELL (*rising and drawing herself up*): You must be quite aware that what you propose is out of the question.

JACK: Then a passionate celibacy is all that any of us can look forward to.

LADY BRACKNELL: That is not the destiny I propose for Gwendolen. Algernon, of course, can choose for himself. (*Pulls out her watch*) Come, dear – (GWENDOLEN *rises*) – we have already missed five, if not six, trains. To miss any more might expose us to comment on the platform.

Enter DR CHASUBLE

CHASUBLE: Everything is quite ready for the christenings.

LADY BRACKNELL: The christenings, sir! Is not that somewhat premature?

CHASUBLE (*looking rather puzzled, and pointing to* JACK *and* ALGERNON): Both these gentlemen have expressed a desire for immediate baptism.

LADY BRACKNELL: At their age? The idea is grotesque and irreligious! Algernon, I forbid you to be baptised. I will not hear of such excesses. Lord Bracknell would be highly displeased if he learned that that was the way in which you wasted your time and money.

CHASUBLE: Am I to understand then that there are to be no christenings at all this afternoon?

JACK: I don't think that, as things are now, it would be of much practical value to either of us, Dr Chasuble.

CHASUBLE: I am grieved to hear such sentiments from you, Mr Worthing. They savour of the heretical views of the Anabaptists, views that I have completely refuted in four of my unpublished sermons. However, as your present mood seems to be one peculiarly secular, I will return to the church at once. Indeed, I have just been informed by the pew-opener that for the last hour and a half Miss Prism has been waiting for me in the vestry.

LADY BRACKNELL (*starting*): Miss Prism! Did I hear you mention a Miss Prism?

CHASUBLE: Yes, Lady Bracknell. I am on my way to join her.

LADY BRACKNELL: Pray allow me to detain you for a moment. This matter may prove to be one of vital importance to Lord Bracknell and myself. Is this Miss Prism a female of repellent aspect, remotely connected with education?

CHASUBLE (*somewhat indignantly*): She is the most cultivated of ladies, and the very picture of respectability.

LADY BRACKNELL: It is obviously the same person. May I ask what position she holds in your household?

CHASUBLE (*severely*): I am a celibate, madam.

JACK (*interposing*): Miss Prism, Lady Bracknell, has been for the last three years Miss Cardew's esteemed governess and valued companion.

LADY BRACKNELL: In spite of what I hear of her, I must see her at once. Let her be sent for.

CHASUBLE (*looking off*): She approaches; she is nigh.

Enter MISS PRISM *hurriedly*

MISS PRISM: I was told you expected me in the vestry, dear canon. I have been waiting for you there for an hour and three-quarters. (*Catches sight of* LADY BRACKNELL, *who has fixed her with a stony glare.* MISS PRISM *grows pale and quails. She looks anxiously round as if desirious to escape*)

LADY BRACKNELL (*in a severe, judicial voice*): Prism! (MISS PRISM *bows her head in shame*) Come here, Prism! (MISS PRISM *approaches in a humble manner*) Prism! Where is that baby? (*General consternation. The* CANON *starts back in horror.* ALGERNON *and* JACK *pretend to be anxious to shield* CECILY *and* GWENDOLEN *from hearing the details of a terrible public scandal*) Twenty-eight years ago, Prism, you left Lord Bracknell's house, Number 104, Upper Grosvenor Street, in charge of a perambulator that contained a baby of the male sex. You never returned. A few weeks later, through the elaborate investigations of the Metropolitan Police, the perambulator was discovered at midnight standing by itself in a remote corner of Bayswater. It contained the manuscript of a three-volume novel of more than usually revolting sentimentality. (MISS PRISM *starts in involuntary indignation*) But the baby was not there. (*everyone looks at* MISS PRISM) Prism! Where is that baby? (*a pause*)

MISS PRISM: Lady Bracknell, I admit with shame that I do not know.

I only wish I did. The plain facts of the case are these. On the morning of the day you mention, a day that is for ever branded on my memory, I prepared as usual to take the baby out in its perambulator. I had also with me a somewhat old, capacious hand-bag, in which I had intended to place the manuscript of a work of fiction that I had written during my few unoccupied hours. In a moment of mental abstraction, for which I never can forgive myself, I deposited the manuscript in the basinette,[10] and placed the baby in the hand-bag.

JACK (*who has been listening attentively*): But where did you deposit the hand-bag?

MISS PRISM: Do not ask me, Mr Worthing.

JACK: Miss Prism, this is a matter of no small importance to me. I insist on knowing where you deposited the hand-bag that contained that infant.

MISS PRISM: I left it in the cloakroom of one of the larger railway stations in London.

JACK: What railway station?

MISS PRISM (*quite crushed*): Victoria. The Brighton line. (*sinks into a chair*)

JACK: I must retire to my room for a moment. Gwendolen, wait here for me.

GWENDOLEN: If you are not too long, I will wait here for you all my life.

Exit JACK *in great excitement*

CHASUBLE: What do you think this means, Lady Bracknell?

LADY BRACKNELL: I dare not even suspect, Dr Chasuble. I need hardly tell you that in families of high position strange coincidences are not supposed to occur. They are hardly considered the thing.

Noises heard overhead as if someone was throwing trunks about. Everyone looks up.

CECILY: Uncle Jack seems strangely agitated.

CHASUBLE: Your guardian has a very emotional nature.

LADY BRACKNELL: This noise is extremely unpleasant. It sounds as if he was having an argument. I dislike arguments of any kind. They are always vulgar, and often convincing.

CHASUBLE (*looking up*): It has stopped now. (*the noise is redoubled*)

LADY BRACKNELL: I wish he would arrive at some conclusion.

GWENDOLEN: This suspense is terrible. I hope it will last.

Enter JACK *with a hand-bag of black leather in his hand*

JACK (*rushing over to* MISS PRISM): Is this the hand-bag, Miss Prism? Examine it carefully before you speak. The happiness of more than one life depends on your answer.

MISS PRISM (*calmly*): It seems to be mine. Yes, here is the injury it received through the upsetting of a Gower Street omnibus in younger and happier days. Here is the stain on the lining caused by the explosion of a temperance beverage, an incident that occurred at Leamington. And here, on the lock, are my initials. I had forgotten that in an extravagant mood I had had them placed there. The bag is undoubtedly mine. I am delighted to have it so unexpectedly restored to me. It has been a great inconvenience being without it all these years.

JACK (*in a pathetic voice*): Miss Prism, more is restored to you than this hand-bag. I was the baby you placed in it.

MISS PRISM (*amazed*): You?

JACK (*embracing her*): Yes . . . mother!

MISS PRISM (*recoiling in indignant astonishment*): Mr Worthing, I am unmarried!

JACK: Unmarried! I do not deny that is a serious blow. But after all, who has the right to cast a stone against one who has suffered? Cannot repentance wipe out an act of folly? Why should there be one law for men, and another for women? Mother, I forgive you. (*tries to embrace her again*)

MISS PRISM (*still more indignant*): Mr Worthing, there is some error. (*pointing to* LADY BRACKNELL) There is the lady who can tell you who you really are.

JACK (*after a pause*): Lady Bracknell, I hate to seem inquisitive, but would you kindly inform me who I am?

LADY BRACKNELL: I am afraid that the news I have to give you will not altogether please you. You are the son of my poor sister, Mrs Moncrieff, and consequently Algernon's elder brother.

JACK: Algy's elder brother! Then I have a brother after all. I knew I had a brother! I always said I had a brother! Cecily – how could you have ever doubted that I had a brother! (*seizes hold of* ALGERNON) Dr Chasuble, my unfortunate brother. Miss Prism, my unfortunate brother. Gwendolen, my unfortunate brother. Algy, you young scoundrel, you will have to treat me with more respect in the future. You have never behaved to me like a brother in all your life.

ALGERNON: Well, not till today, old boy, I admit. I did my best, however, though I was out of practice. (*shakes hands*)

GWENDOLEN (*to* JACK): My own! But what own are you? What is your Christian name, now that you have become someone else?

JACK: Good heavens! . . . I had quite forgotten that point. Your decision on the subject of my name is irrevocable, I suppose?

GWENDOLEN: I never change, except in my affections.

CECILY: What a noble nature you have, Gwendolen!

JACK: Then the question had better be cleared up at once. Aunt Augusta, a moment. At the time when Miss Prism left me in the hand-bag, had I been christened already?

LADY BRACKNELL: Every luxury that money could buy, including christening, had been lavished on you by your fond and doting parents.

JACK: Then I was christened! That is settled. Now, what name was I given? Let me know the worst.

LADY BRACKNELL: Being the eldest son you were naturally christened after your father.

JACK (*irritably*): Yes, but what was my father's Christian name?

LADY BRACKNELL (*meditatively*): I cannot at the present moment recall what the general's Christian name was. But I have no doubt he had one. He was eccentric, I admit. But only in later years. And that was the result of the Indian climate, and marriage, and indigestion, and other things of that kind.

JACK: Algy! Can't you recollect what our father's Christian name was?

ALGERNON: My dear boy, we were never even on speaking terms. He died before I was a year old.

JACK: His name would appear in the Army Lists of the period, I suppose, Aunt Augusta?

LADY BRACKNELL: The general was essentially a man of peace, except in his domestic life. But I have no doubt his name would appear in any military directory.

JACK: The Army Lists of the last forty years are here. These delightful records should have been my constant study. (*rushes to bookcase and tears the books out*) M. Generals . . . Mallam, Maxbohm, Magley – what ghastly names they have – Markby, Migsby, Mobbs, Moncrieff! Lieutenant 1840, Captain, Lieutenant-Colonel, Colonel, General 1869. Christian names, Ernest John. (*puts book very quietly down and speaks quite calmly*) I always told you, Gwendolen, my name was Ernest, didn't I? Well, it is Ernest after all. I mean it naturally is Ernest.

LADY BRACKNELL: Yes, I remember now that the general was called Ernest. I knew I had some particular reason for disliking the name.

GWENDOLEN: Ernest! My own Ernest! I felt from the first that you could have no other name!

JACK: Gwendolen, it is a terrible thing for a man to find out suddenly that all his life he has been speaking nothing but the truth. Can you forgive me?

GWENDOLEN: I can. For I feel that you are sure to change.

JACK: My own one!

CHASUBLE (*to* MISS PRISM): Laetitia! (*embraces her*)

MISS PRISM (*enthusiastically*): Frederick! At last!

ALGERNON: Cecily! (*embraces her*) At last!

JACK: Gwendolen! (*embraces her*) At last!

LADY BRACKNELL: My nephew, you seem to be displaying signs of triviality.

JACK: On the contrary, Aunt Augusta, I've now realised for the first time in my life the vital importance of being earnest.

TABLEAU AND CURTAIN

LA SAINTE COURTISANE
or The Woman Covered in Jewels

LA SAINTE COURTISANE

or The Woman Covered in Jewels

The scene represents a corner of a valley in the Thebaid. On the right-hand side of the stage is a cavern. In front of the cavern stands a great crucifix. On the left, sand dunes. The sky is blue like the inside of a cup of lapis lazuli. The hills are of red sand. Here and there on the hills there are clumps of thorns.

FIRST MAN: Who is she? She makes me afraid. She has a purple cloak and her hair is like threads of gold. I think she must be the daughter of the Emperor. I have heard the boatmen say that the Emperor has a daughter who wears a cloak of purple.

SECOND MAN: She has birds' wings upon her sandals, and her tunic is the colour of green corn. It is like corn in spring when she stands still. It is like young corn troubled by the shadows of hawks when she moves. The pearls on her tunic are like many moons.

FIRST MAN: They are like the moons one sees in the water when the wind blows from the hills.

SECOND MAN: I think she is one of the gods. I think she comes from Nubia.

FIRST MAN: I am sure she is the daughter of the Emperor. Her nails are stained with henna. They are like the petals of a rose. She has come here to weep for Adonis.

SECOND MAN: She is one of the gods. I do not know why she has left her temple. The gods should not leave their temples. If she speaks to us let us not answer and she will pass by.

FIRST MAN: She will not speak to us. She is the daughter of the Emperor.

MYRRHINA: Dwells he not here, the beautiful young hermit, he who will not look on the face of woman?

FIRST MAN: Of a truth it is here the hermit dwells.

MYRRHINA: Why will he not look on the face of woman?

SECOND MAN: We do not know.

MYRRHINA: Why do ye yourselves not look at me?

FIRST MAN: You are covered with bright stones, and you dazzle our eyes.

SECOND MAN: He who looks at the sun becomes blind. You are too bright to look at. It is not wise to look at things that are very bright. Many of the priests in the temples are blind, and have slaves to lead them.

MYRRHINA: Where does he dwell, the beautiful young hermit who will not look on the face of woman? Has he a house of reeds or a house of burnt clay or does he lie on the hillside? Or does he make his bed in the rushes?

FIRST MAN: He dwells in that cavern yonder.

MYRRHINA: What a curious place to dwell in.

FIRST MAN: Of old a centaur lived there. When the hermit came the centaur gave a shrill cry, wept and lamented, and galloped away.

SECOND MAN: No. It was a white unicorn who lived in the cave. When it saw the hermit coming the unicorn knelt down and worshipped him. Many people saw it worshipping him.

FIRST MAN: I have talked with people who saw it.

[. . .]

SECOND MAN: Some say he was a hewer of wood and worked for hire. But that may not be true.

[. . .]

MYRRHINA: What gods then do ye worship? Or do ye worship any gods? There are those who have no gods to worship. The philosophers who wear long beards and brown cloaks have no gods to worship. They wrangle with each other in the porticoes. The [. . .] laugh at them.

FIRST MAN: We worship seven gods. We may not tell their names. It is a very dangerous thing to tell the names of the gods. No one should ever tell the name of his god. Even the priests who praise the gods all day long, and eat of their food with them, do not call them by their right names.

MYRRHINA: Where are these gods ye worship?

FIRST MAN: We hide them in the folds of our tunics. We do not show them to anyone. If we showed them to anyone they might leave us.

MYRRHINA: Where did ye meet with them?

FIRST MAN: They were given to us by an embalmer of the dead who had found them in a tomb. We served him for seven years.

MYRRHINA: The dead are terrible. I am afraid of Death.

FIRST MAN: Death is not a god. He is only the servant of the gods.

MYRRHINA: He is the only god I am afraid of. Ye have seen many of the gods?

FIRST MAN: We have seen many of them. One sees them chiefly at night time. They pass one by very swiftly. Once we saw some of the gods at daybreak. They were walking across a plain.

MYRRHINA: Once as I was passing through the market place I heard a sophist from Gilicia say that there is only one God. He said it before many people.

FIRST MAN: That cannot be true. We have ourselves seen many though we are but common men and of no account. When I saw them I hid myself in a bush. They did me no harm.

[. . .]

MYRRHINA: Tell me more about the beautiful young hermit. Talk to me about the beautiful young hermit who will not look on the face of woman. What is the story of his days? What mode of life has he?

FIRST MAN: We do not understand you.

MYRRHINA: What does he do, the beautiful young hermit? Does he sow or reap? Does he plant a garden or catch fish in a net? Does he weave linen on a loom? Does he set his hand to the wooden plough and walk behind the oxen?

SECOND MAN: He being a very holy man does nothing. We are common men and of no account. We toil all day long in the sun. Sometimes the ground is very hard.

MYRRHINA: Do the birds of the air feed him? Do the jackals share their booty with him?

FIRST MAN: Every evening we bring him food. We do not think that the birds of the air feed him.

MYRRHINA: Why do ye feed him? What profit have ye in so doing?

SECOND MAN: He is a very holy man. One of the gods whom he has offended has made him mad. We think he has offended the moon.

MYRRHINA: Go and tell him that one who has come from Alexandria desires to speak with him.

FIRST MAN: We dare not tell him. This hour he is praying to his god. We pray thee to pardon us for not doing thy bidding.

MYRRHINA: Are ye afraid of him?

FIRST MAN: We are afraid of him.

MYRRHINA: Why are ye afraid of him?

FIRST MAN: We do not know.

MYRRHINA: What is his name?

FIRST MAN: The voice that speaks to him at night time in the cavern calls to him by the name of Honorius. It was also by the name of Honorius that the three lepers who passed by once called to him. We think that his name is Honorius.

MYRRHINA: Why did the three lepers call to him?

FIRST MAN: That he might heal them.

MYRRHINA: Did he heal them?

SECOND MAN: No. They had committed some sin: it was for that reason they were lepers. Their hands and faces were like salt. One of them wore a mask of linen. He was a king's son.

MYRRHINA: What is the voice that speaks to him at night time in his cave?

FIRST MAN: We do not know whose voice it is. We think it is the voice of his god. For we have seen no man enter his cavern nor any come forth from it.

[...]

MYRRHINA: Honorius.

HONORIUS (*from within*): Who calls Honorius?

MYRRHINA: Come forth, Honorius.

My chamber is ceiled with cedar and odorous with myrrh. The pillars of my bed are of cedar and the hangings are of purple. My bed is strewn with purple and the steps are of silver. The hangings are sewn with silver pomegranates and the steps that are of silver are strewn with saffron and with myrrh. My lovers hang garlands round the pillars of my house. At night time they come with the flute players and the players of the harp. They woo me with apples and on the pavement of my courtyard they write my name in wine.

From the uttermost parts of the world my lovers come to me. The kings of the earth come to me and bring me presents.

When the Emperor of Byzantium heard of me he left his porphyry chamber and set sail in his galleys. His slaves bare no torches that none might know of his coming. When the King of Cyprus heard of me he sent me ambassadors. The two Kings of Libya who are brothers brought me gifts of amber.

I took the minion of Caesar from Caesar and made him my playfellow. He came to me at night in a litter. He was pale as a narcissus, and his body was like honey.

The son of the Prefect slew himself in my honour, and the Tetrarch of Cilicia scourged himself for my pleasure before my slaves.

The King of Hierapolis who is a priest and a robber set carpets for me to walk on.

Sometimes I sit in the circus and the gladiators fight beneath me. Once a Thracian who was my lover was caught in the net. I gave the signal for him to die and the whole theatre applauded. Sometimes I pass through the gymnasium and watch the young men wrestling or in the race. Their bodies are bright with oil and their brows are wreathed with willow sprays and with myrtle. They stamp their feet on the sand when they wrestle and when they run the sand follows them like a little cloud. He at whom I smile leaves his companions and follows me to my home. At other times I go down to the harbour and watch the merchants unloading their vessels. Those that come from Tyre have cloaks of silk and earrings of emerald. Those that come from Massilia have cloaks of fine wool and earrings of brass. When they see me coming they stand on the prows of their ships and call to me, but I do not answer them. I go to the little taverns where the sailors lie all day long drinking black wine and playing with dice and I sit down with them.

I made the Prince my slave, and his slave, who was a Tyrian, I made my lord for the space of a moon.

I put a figured ring on his finger and brought him to my house. I have wonderful things in my house.

The dust of the desert lies on your hair and your feet are scratched with thorns and your body is scorched by the sun. Come with me, Honorius, and I will clothe you in a tunic of silk. I will smear your body with myrrh and pour spikenard on your hair. I will clothe you in hyacinth and put honey in your mouth. Love –

HONORIUS: There is no love but the love of God.

MYRRHINA: Who is He whose love is greater than that of mortal men?

HONORIUS: It is He whom thou seest on the cross, Myrrhina. He is the Son of God and was born of a virgin. Three wise men who were kings brought Him offerings, and the shepherds who were lying on the hills were wakened by a great light.

The Sibyls knew of His coming. The groves and the oracles spake of Him. David and the prophets announced Him. There is no love like the love of God nor any love that can be compared to it.

The body is vile, Myrrhina. God will raise thee up with a new body which will not know corruption, and thou wilt dwell in the courts of the Lord and see Him whose hair is like fine wool and whose feet are of brass.

MYRRHINA: The beauty . . .

HONORIUS: The beauty of the soul increases till it can see God. Therefore, Myrrhina, repent of thy sins. The robber who was crucified beside Him He brought into Paradise. (*exit*)

MYRRHINA: How strangely he spake to me. And with what scorn he did regard me. I wonder why he spake to me so strangely.

[. . .]

HONORIUS: Myrrhina, the scales have fallen from my eyes and I see now clearly what I did not see before. Take me to Alexandria and let me taste of the seven sins.

MYRRHINA: Do not mock me, Honorius, nor speak to me with such bitter words. For I have repented of my sins and I am seeking a cavern in this desert where I too may dwell so that my soul may become worthy to see God.

HONORIUS: The sun is setting, Myrrhina. Come with me to Alexandria.

MYRRHINA: I will not go to Alexandria.

HONORIUS: Farewell, Myrrhina.

MYRRHINA: Honorius, farewell. No, no, do not go.

[. . .]

I have cursed my beauty for what it has done, and cursed the wonder of my body for the evil that it has brought upon you.

Lord, this man brought me to Thy feet. He told me of Thy coming upon earth, and of the wonder of Thy birth and the great wonder of Thy death also. By him, O Lord, Thou wast revealed to me.

HONORIUS: You talk as a child, Myrrhina, and without knowledge. Loosen your hands. Why didst thou come to this valley in thy beauty?

MYRRHINA: The God whom thou worshipped led me here that I might repent of my iniquities and know Him as the Lord.

HONORIUS: Why didst thou tempt me with words?

MYRRHINA: That thou shouldst see Sin in its painted mask and look on Death in its robe of Shame.

CURTAIN

A FLORENTINE TRAGEDY
(*a fragment*)

A FLORENTINE TRAGEDY
(a fragment)

Enter THE HUSBAND

SIMONE My good wife, you come slowly, were it not better
To run to meet your lord? Here, take my cloak.
Take this pack first. 'Tis heavy. I have sold nothing:
Save a furred robe unto the Cardinal's son,
Who hopes to wear it when his father dies,
And hopes that will be soon.
But who is this?
Why you have here some friend. Some
kinsman doubtless
Newly returned from foreign lands and fallen
Upon a house without a host to greet him?
I crave your pardon, kinsman. For a house
Lacking a host is but an empty thing
And void of honour; a cup without its wine,
A scabbard without steel to keep it straight,
A flowerless garden widowed of the sun.
Again I crave your pardon, my sweet cousin.

BIANCA This is no kinsman and no cousin neither.

SIMONE No kinsman, and no cousin! You amaze me.
Who is it then who with such courtly grace
Deigns to accept our hospitalities?

GUIDO My name is Guido Bardi.

SIMONE What! The son
Of that great Lord of Florence whose dim towers
Like shadows silvered by the wandering moon
I see from out my casement every night!
Sir Guido Bardi, you are welcome here,
Twice welcome. For I trust my honest wife,
Most honest if uncomely to the eye,
Hath not with foolish chatterings wearied you,
As is the wont of women.

GUIDO Your gracious lady,
Whose beauty is a lamp that pales the stars

And robs Diana's quiver of her beams,
Has welcomed me with such sweet courtesies
That if it be her pleasure, and your own,
I will come often to your simple house.
And when your business bids you walk abroad
I will sit here and charm her loneliness
Lest she might sorrow for you overmuch.
What say you, good Simone?

SIMONE My noble lord,
You bring me such high honour that my tongue
Like a slave's tongue is tied, and cannot say
The word it would. Yet not to give you thanks
Were to be too unmannerly. So, I thank you,
From my heart's core.
It is such things as these
That knit a state together, when a prince
So nobly born and of such fair address,
Forgetting unjust Fortune's differences,
Comes to an honest burgher's honest home
As a most honest friend.
And yet, my lord,
I fear I am too bold. Some other night
We trust that you will come here as a friend,
Tonight you come to buy my merchandise.
Is it not so? Silks, velvets, what you will,
I doubt not but I have some dainty wares
Will woo your fancy. True, the hour is late,
But we poor merchants toil both night and day
To make our scanty gains. The tolls are high,
And every city levies its own toll,
And 'prentices are unskilful, and wives even
Lack sense and cunning, though Bianca here
Has brought me a rich customer tonight.
Is it not so, Bianca? But I waste time.
Where is my pack? Where is my pack, I say?
Open it, my good wife. Unloose the cords.
Kneel down upon the floor. You are better so.
Nay not that one, the other. Despatch, despatch!
Buyers will grow impatient oftentimes.
We dare not keep them waiting. Ay! 'tis that,
Give it to me; with care. It is most costly.
Touch it with care. And now, my noble lord –

Nay, pardon, I have here a Lucca damask,
The very web of silver and the roses
So cunningly wrought that they lack perfume merely
To cheat the wanton sense. Touch it, my lord.
Is it not soft as water, strong as steel?
And then the roses! Are they not finely woven?
I think the hillsides that best love the rose,
At Bellosguardo or at Fiesole,
Throw no such blossoms on the lap of spring,
Or if they do their blossoms droop and die.
Such is the fate of all the dainty things
That dance in wind and water. Nature herself
Makes war on her own loveliness and slays
Her children like Medea. Nay, but, my lord,
Look closer still. Why in this damask here
It is summer always, and no winter's tooth
Will ever blight these blossoms. For every ell
I paid a piece of gold. Red gold, and good,
The fruit of careful thrift.

GUIDO Honest Simone,
Enough, I pray you. I am well content.
Tomorrow I will send my servant to you
Who will pay twice your price.

SIMONE My generous prince!
I kiss your hands. And now I do remember
Another treasure hidden in my house
Which you must see. It is a robe of state:
Woven by a Venetian; the stuff, cut-velvet:
The pattern, pomegranates: each separate seed
Wrought of a pearl: the collar all of pearls,
As thick as moths in summer streets at night,
And whiter than the moons that madmen see
Through prison bars at morning. A male ruby
Burns like a lighted coal within the clasp.
The Holy Father has not such a stone,
Nor could the Indies show a brother to it.
The brooch itself is of most curious art,
Cellini never made a fairer thing
To please the great Lorenzo. You must wear it.
There is none worthier in our city here,
And it will suit you well. Upon one side
A slim and horned satyr leaps in gold

To catch some nymph of silver. Upon the other
Stands Silence with a crystal in her hand,
No bigger than the smallest ear of corn,
That wavers at the passing of a bird,
And yet so cunningly wrought that one would say
It breathed, or held its breath.
Worthy Bianca
Would not this noble and most costly robe
Suit young Lord Guido well?
Nay, but entreat him;
He will refuse you nothing, though the price
Be as a prince's ransom. And your profit
Shall not be less than mine.

BIANCA Am I your 'prentice?
Why should I chaffer for your velvet robe?

GUIDO Nay, fair Bianca, I will buy your robe,
And all things that the honest merchant has
I will buy also. Princes must be ransomed
And fortunate are all high lords who fall
Into the white hands of so fair a foe.

SIMONE I stand rebuked. But you will buy my wares?
Will you not buy them? Fifty thousand crowns
Would scarce repay me. But you, my lord, shall
have them
For forty thousand. Is that price too high?
Name your own price. I have a curious fancy
To see you in this wonder of the loom
Amidst the noble ladies of the court,
A flower among flowers.
They say, my lord,
These highborn dames do so affect your grace
That where you go they throng like flies around you,
Each seeking for your favour.
I have heard also
Of husbands that wear horns, and wear them bravely,
A fashion most fantastical.

GUIDO Simone,
Your reckless tongue needs curbing; and besides,
You do forget this gracious lady here
Whose delicate ears are surely not attuned
To such coarse music.

SIMONE True: I had forgotten

Nor will offend again. Yet, my sweet lord,
You'll buy the robe of state. Will you not buy it?
But forty thousand crowns. 'Tis but a trifle,
To one who is Giovanni Bardi's heir.

GUIDO Settle this thing tomorrow with my steward
Antonio Costa. He will come to you.
And you will have a hundred thousand crowns
If that will serve your purpose.

SIMONE A hundred thousand!
Said you a hundred thousand? Oh! be sure
That will for all time, and in everything
Make me your debtor. Ay! from this time forth
My house, with everything my house contains
Is yours, and only yours.
A hundred thousand!
My brain is dazed. I will be richer far
Than all the other merchants. I will buy
Vineyards, and lands, and gardens. Every loom
From Milan down to Sicily shall be mine,
And mine the pearls that the Arabian seas
Store in their silent caverns.
Generous prince,
This night shall prove the herald of my love,
Which is so great that whatsoe'er you ask
It will not be denied you.

GUIDO What if I asked
For white Bianca here?

SIMONE You jest, my lord,
She is not worthy of so great a prince.
She is but made to keep the house and spin.
Is it not so, good wife? It is so. Look!
Your distaff waits for you. Sit down and spin.
Women should not be idle in their homes,
For idle fingers make a thoughtless heart.
Sit down, I say.

BIANCA What shall I spin?

SIMONE Oh! spin
Some robe which, dyed in purple, Sorrow might wear
For her own comforting: or some long-fringed cloth
In which a newborn and unwelcome babe
Might wail unheeded; or a dainty sheet
Which, delicately perfumed with sweet herbs,

Might serve to wrap a dead man. Spin what you will;
I care not, I.

BIANCA The brittle thread is broken,
The dull wheel wearies of its ceaseless round,
The duller distaff sickens of its load;
I will not spin tonight.

SIMONE It matters not.
Tomorrow you shall spin, and every day
Shall find you at your distaff. So, Lucretia
Was found by Tarquin. So, perchance, Lucretia
Waited for Tarquin. Who knows? I have heard
Strange things about men's wives. And now, my lord,
What news abroad? I heard today at Pisa
That certain of the English merchants there
Would sell their woollens at a lower rate
Than the just laws allow, and have entreated
The Signory to hear them.
Is this well?
Should merchant be to merchant as a wolf?
And should the stranger living in our land
Seek by enforced privilege or craft
To rob us of our profits?

GUIDO What should I do
With merchants or their profits? Shall I go
And wrangle with the Signory on your count?
And wear the gown in which you buy from fools,
Or sell to sillier bidders? Honest Simone,
Wool-selling or wool-gathering is for you.
My wits have other quarries.

BIANCA Noble lord,
I pray you pardon my good husband here,
His soul stands ever in the marketplace,
And his heart beats but at the price of wool.
Yet he is honest in his common way.
(*To* SIMONE) And you, have you no shame? A gracious prince
Comes to our house, and you must weary him
With most misplaced assurance. Ask his pardon.

SIMONE I ask it humbly. We will talk tonight
Of other things. I hear the Holy Father
Has sent a letter to the King of France
Bidding him cross that shield of snow, the Alps,

And make a peace in Italy, which will be
Worse than war of brothers, and more bloody
Than civil rapine or intestine feuds.

GUIDO Oh! we are weary of that King of France,
Who never comes, but ever talks of coming.
What are these things to me? There are other things
Closer, and of more import, good Simone.

BIANCA (*to* SIMONE) I think you tire our most gracious guest.
What is the King of France to us? As much
As are your English merchants with their wool.

[. . .]

SIMONE Is it so then? Is all this mighty world
Narrowed into the confines of this room
With but three souls for poor inhabitants? Ay!
There are times when the great universe
Like cloth in some unskilful dyer's vat
Shrivels into a hand's-breadth, and perchance
That time is now! Well! Let that time be now.
Let this mean room be as that mighty stage
Whereon kings die, and our ignoble lives
Become the stakes God plays for.
I do not know
Why I speak thus. My ride has wearied me.
And my horse stumbled thrice, which is an omen
That bodes not good to any.
Alas! my lord,
How poor a bargain is this life of man,
And in how mean a market are we sold!
When we are born our mothers weep, but when
We die there is none weep for us. No, not one.
(*passes to back of stage*)

BIANCA How like a common chapman does he speak!
I hate him, soul and body. Cowardice
Has set her pale seal on his brow. His hands
Whiter than poplar leaves in windy springs,
Shake with some palsy; and his stammering mouth
Blurts out a foolish froth of empty words
Like water from a conduit.

GUIDO Sweet Bianca,
He is not worthy of your thought or mine.
The man is but a very honest knave

Full of fine phrases for life's merchandise,
Selling most dear what he must hold most cheap,
A windy brawler in a world of words.
I never met so eloquent a fool.

BIANCA Oh, would that Death might take him where he stands!

SIMONE (*turning round*) Who spake of Death? Let no one
speak of Death.
What should Death do in such a merry house,
With but a wife, a husband, and a friend
To give it greeting? Let Death go to houses
Where there are vile, adulterous things, chaste wives
Who grow weary of their noble lords,
Draw back the curtains of their marriage beds,
And in polluted and dishonoured sheets
Feed some unlawful lust. Ay! 'tis so –
Strange, and yet so. *You* do not know the world.
You are too single and too honourable.
I know it well. And would it were not so,
But wisdom comes with winters. My hair grows grey,
And youth has left my body. Enough of that.
Tonight is ripe for pleasure, and indeed,
I would be merry, as beseems a host
Who finds a gracious and unlooked-for guest
Waiting to greet him. (*Takes up a lute*)
But what is this, my lord?
Why, you have brought a lute to play to us.
Oh! play, sweet prince. And, if I am bold,
Pardon, but play.

GUIDO I will not play tonight.
Some other night, Simone.
(*to Bianca*) You and I
Together, with no listeners but the stars,
Or the more jealous moon.

SIMONE Nay, but my lord!
Nay, but I do beseech you. For I have heard
That by the simple fingering of a string,
Or delicate breath breathed along hollowed reeds,
Or blown into cold mouths of cunning bronze,
Those who are curious in this art can draw
Poor souls from prison-houses. I have heard also
How such strange magic lurks within these shells
And Innocence puts vine-leaves in her hair,

And wantons like a maenad. Let that pass.
Your lute I know is chaste. And therefore play:
Ravish my ears with some sweet melody;
My soul is in a prison-house, and needs
Music to cure its madness. Good Bianca,
Entreat our guest to play.

BIANCA Be not afraid
Our well-loved guest will choose his place and moment:
That moment is not now. You weary him
With your uncouth insistence.

GUIDO Honest Simone,
Some other night. Tonight I am content
With the low music of Bianca's voice,
Who, when she speaks, charms the too amorous air
And makes the reeling earth stand still, or fix
His cycle round her beauty.

SIMONE You flatter her
She has her virtues as most women have,
But beauty is a gem she may not wear.
It is better so, perchance.
Well, my dear lord,
If you will not draw melodies from your lute
To charm my moody and o'er-troubled soul,
You'll drink with me at least? (*sees table*)
Your place is laid.
Fetch me a stool, Bianca. Close the shutters.
Set the great bar across. I would not have
The curious world with its small prying eyes
To peer upon our pleasure.
Now, my lord,
Give us a toast from a full brimming cup. (*starts back*)
What is this stain upon the cloth? It looks
As purple as a wound upon Christ's side.
Wine merely is it? I have heard it said
When wine is spilt blood is spilt also,
But that's a foolish tale.
My lord, I trust
My grape is to your liking? The wine of Naples
Is fiery like its mountains. Our Tuscan vineyards
Yield a more wholesome juice.

GUIDO I like it well,
Honest Simone; and, with your good leave,

Will toast the fair Bianca when her lips
Have like red rose-leaves floated on this cup
And left its vintage sweeter. Taste, Bianca.

(BIANCA *drinks*)

Oh, all the honey of Hyblean bees,
Matched with this draught were bitter!
Good Simone,
You do not share the feast.

SIMONE It is strange, my lord,
I cannot eat or drink with you tonight.
Some humour, or some fever in my blood,
At other seasons temperate, or some thought
That like an adder creeps from point to point,
That like a madman crawls from cell to cell,
Poisons my palate and makes appetite
A loathing, not a longing. (*goes aside*)

GUIDO Sweet Bianca,
This common chapman wearies me with words.
I must go hence. Tomorrow I will come.
Tell me the hour.

BIANCA Come with the youngest dawn!
Until I see you all my life is vain.

GUIDO Ah! loose the falling midnight of your hair,
And in those stars, your eyes, let me behold
Mine image, as in mirrors. Dear Bianca,
Though it be but a shadow, keep me there,
Nor gaze at anything that does not show
Some symbol of my semblance. I am jealous
Of what your vision feasts on.

BIANCA Oh! be sure
Your image will be with me always. Dear,
Love can translate the very meanest thing
Into a sign of sweet remembrances.
But come before the lark with its shrill song
Has waked a world of dreamers. I will stand
Upon the balcony.

GUIDO And by a ladder
Wrought out of scarlet silk and sewn with pearls
Will come to meet me. White foot after foot,
Like snow upon a rose-tree.

BIANCA As you will.
You know that I am yours for love or Death.

GUIDO Simone, I must go to mine house.

SIMONE So soon? Why should you? the great Duomo's bell
Has not yet tolled its midnight, and the watchmen,
Who with their hollow horns mock the pale moon,
Lie drowsy in their towers. Stay awhile.
I fear we may not see you here again,
And that fear saddens my too simple heart.

GUIDO Be not afraid, Simone. I will stand
Most constant in my friendship. But tonight
I go to mine own home, and that at once.
Tomorrow, sweet Bianca.

SIMONE Well, well, so be it.
I would have wished for fuller converse with you,
My new friend, my honourable guest,
But that it seems may not be.
And besides,
I do not doubt your father waits for you,
Wearying for voice or footstep. You, I think,
Are his one child? He has no other child.
You are the gracious pillar of his house,
The flower of a garden full of weeds.
Your father's nephews do not love him well.
So run folk's tongues in Florence. I meant but that;
Men say they envy your inheritance
And look upon your vineyard with fierce eyes
As Ahab looked on Naboth's goodly field.
But that is but the chatter of a town
Where women talk too much.
Good-night, my lord.
Fetch a pine torch, Bianca. The old staircase
Is full of pitfalls, and the churlish moon
Grows, like a miser, niggard of her beams,
And hides her face behind a muslin mask
As harlots do when they go forth to snare
Some wretched soul in sin. Now, I will get
Your cloak and sword. Nay, pardon, my good lord,
It is but meet that I should wait on you
Who have so honoured my poor burgher's house,
Drunk of my wine, and broken bread, and made
Yourself a sweet familiar. Oftentimes
My wife and I will talk of this fair night
And its great issues.

Why, what a sword is this!
Ferrara's temper, pliant as a snake,
And deadlier, I doubt not. With such steel
One need fear nothing in the moil of life.
I never touched so delicate a blade.
I have a sword too, somewhat rusted now.
We men of peace are taught humility,
And to bear many burdens on our backs,
And not to murmur at an unjust word,
And to endure unjust indignities.
We are taught that and, like the patient Jew,
Find profit in our pain.
Yet I remember
How once upon the road to Padua
A robber sought to take my packhorse from me;
I slit his throat and left him. I can bear
Dishonour, public insult, many shames,
Shrill scorn, and open contumely, but he
Who filches from me something that is mine,
Ay! though it be the meanest trencher-plate
From which I feed mine appetite – oh! he
Perils his soul and body in the theft
And dies for his small sin. From what strange clay
We men are moulded!

GUIDO Why do you speak like this?

SIMONE I wonder, my Lord Guido, if my sword
Is better tempered than this steel of yours?
Shall we make trial? Or is my state too low
For you to cross your rapier against mine,
In jest, or earnest?

GUIDO Naught would please me better
Than to stand fronting you with naked blade
In jest, or earnest. Give me mine own sword.
Fetch yours. Tonight will settle the great issue
Whether the prince's or the merchant's steel
Is better tempered. Was not that your word?
Fetch your own sword. Why do you tarry, sir?

SIMONE My lord, of all the gracious courtesies
That you have showered on my barren house
This is the highest.
Bianca, fetch my sword.
Thrust back that stool and table. We must have

An open circle for our match at arms,
And good Bianca here shall hold the torch
Lest what is but a jest grow serious.

BIANCA (*to* GUIDO) Oh! kill him, kill him!

SIMONE Hold the torch, Bianca.
(*They begin to fight*)
Have at you! Ah! Ha! would you? (*he is wounded by* GUIDO)
A scratch, no more. The torch was in mine eyes.
Do not look sad, Bianca. It is nothing.
Your husband bleeds, 'tis nothing. Take a cloth,
Bind it about mine arm. Nay, not so tight.
More softly, my good wife. And be not sad,
I pray you be not sad. No: take it off.
What matter if I bleed? (*tears bandage off*)
Again! again!
(SIMONE *disarms* GUIDO)
My gentle lord, you see that I was right.
My sword is better tempered, finer steel,
But let us match our daggers.

BIANCA (*to Guido*) Kill him! kill him!

SIMONE Put out the torch, Bianca. (*Bianca puts out torch*)
Now, my good lord,
Now to the death of one, or both of us,
Or all the three it may be. (*They fight*)
There and there.
Ah, devil! do I hold thee in my grip?

SIMONE *overpowers* GUIDO *and throws him down over table*

GUIDO Fool! take your strangling fingers from my throat.
I am my father's only son; the State
Has bout one heir, and that false enemy France
Waits for the ending of my father's line
To fall upon our city.

SIMONE Hush! your father
When he is childless will be happier.
As for the state, I think our state of Florence
Needs no adulterous pilot at its helm.
Your life would soil its lilies.

GUIDO Take off your hands.
Take off your damned hands. Loose me, I say!

SIMONE Nay, you are caught in such a cunning vice

That nothing will avail you, and your life
Narrowed into a single point of shame
Ends with that shame and ends most shamefully.

GUIDO Oh! let me have a priest before I die!

SIMONE What wouldst thou have a priest for? Tell thy sins
To God, whom thou shalt see this very night
And then no more for ever. Tell thy sins
To Him who is most just, being pitiless,
Most pitiful being just. As for myself . . .

GUIDO Oh! help me, sweet Bianca! help me, Bianca,
Thou knowest I am innocent of harm.

SIMONE What, is there life yet in those lying lips?
Die like a dog with lolling tongue! Die! Die!
And the dumb river shall receive your corse
And wash it all unheeded to the sea.

GUIDO Lord Christ receive my wretched soul tonight! (*he dies*)

SIMONE Amen to that. Now for the other.

SIMONE *rises and looks at* BIANCA. *She comes towards him as one dazed with wonder and with outstretched arms.*

BIANCA Why
Did you not tell me you were so strong?

SIMONE Why
Did you not tell me you were beautiful?
(*he kisses her on the mouth*)

CURTAIN

NOTES

A Woman of No Importance

1 (p. 226) *American girls* This and many of the following jokes about American women are derived from Wilde's newspaper article 'The American Invasion', in the *Court and Society Review*, 1887. He offered himself as a jesting authority on American women after his lecture tour of America in 1882.

2 (p. 236) *married women's property* a cynical reference to the Married Women's Property Act of 1882

An Ideal Husband

3 (p. 357) *A man's life is of more value than a woman's* In distinguishing the roles of men and women, Lord Goring is paraphrasing sentiments put forward by John Ruskin in 'Of Queen's Gardens', *Sesame and Lilies* (1865), Section 68:

> The man's power is active, progressive, defensive. He is eminently the doer, the creator, the discoverer, the defender ... But the woman's power is for rule, not for battle ... and her intellect is ... for ... sweet ordering, arrangement and decision ... Her great function is Praise ...

The Importance of Being Earnest

4 (p. 367) *Bunburyist* Wilde's coinage for one who leads a double life, possibly derived from the name of one of his Dublin friends, Henry S. Bunbury, who, like Wilde himself, moved to England

5 (p. 370) *Lady Bracknell* In October 1892, Wilde was invited by Lady Queensberry, mother of his new young lover Lord Alfred Douglas, to her home in Bracknell. She urged prudence and propriety in relation to Wilde's dealings with her son, just as Lady Bracknell cautions her daughter's suitor.

6 (p. 376) *Liberal Unionist* a Liberal who splintered from Gladstone's Party in 1886 in order to challenge his bill to introduce Home Rule for Ireland. The Liberal Unionists

voted with the Conservative opposition and helped to bring down Gladstone's government. Like Lady Bracknell, they resisted change. Wilde supported Home Rule policies.

7 (p. 376) *Worthing* Wilde was staying in Worthing when he wrote this play.

8 (p. 379) *died in Paris of apoplexy* a laughing reference to Ibsen's *Ghosts* (1881), in which Paris is presented as the capital of decadence and its diseases

9 (p. 406) *Influence of a Permanent Income on Thought* a jesting reference to a key aspect of feminist thinking during the era of the New Woman, addressed subsequently by Virginia Woolf in *A Room of One's Own* (1929)

10 (p. 414) *manuscript in the basinette* The confusion of baby with manuscript is a further example of Wilde's dialogue with Ibsen, and refers to Hedda Gabler who valued the manuscript of Lovborg's philosophical treatise more highly than her own unborn child.